The Collected Stories
of Elizabeth Bowen

The Books of Elizabeth Bowen

NOVELS

Eva Trout (1968)
The Little Girls (1964)
A World of Love (1955)
The Last September (1929, 1952)
The Heat of the Day (1949)
The Death of the Heart (1939)
The House in Paris (1936)
To the North (1933)

SHORT STORIES

Early Stories (1951)
Ivy Gripped the Steps (1946)
Look at All Those Roses (1941)

NON-FICTION

Seven Winters and Afterthoughts (1962)
A Time in Rome (1960)
The Shelbourne Hotel (1951)
Collected Impressions (1950)
Bowen's Court (1942, 1964)

POSTHUMOUS

Pictures and Conversations (1975)

JUVENILE

The Good Tiger (1965)

These are Borzoi Books,
published in New York by Alfred A. Knopf.

THE

COLLECTED

STORIES *of*

ELIZABETH

BOWEN

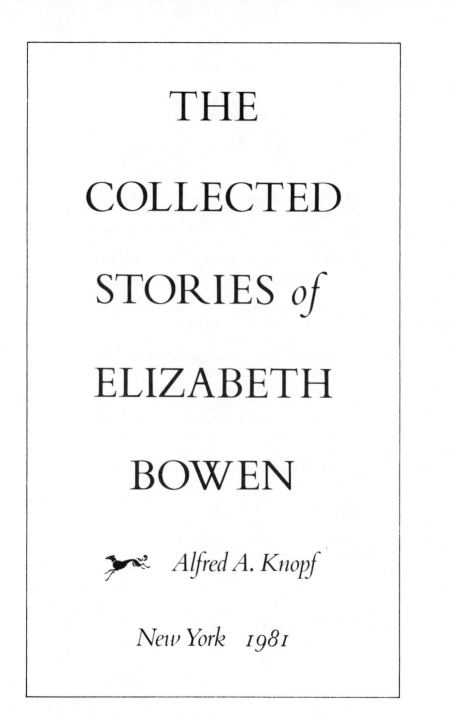 *Alfred A. Knopf*

New York 1981

THIS IS A BORZOI BOOK
PUBLISHED BY ALFRED A. KNOPF, INC.

Illustrations on pages 13, 101, 347, 571, and 749
are by Joan Hassall.

Library of Congress Cataloging in Publication Data.
Bowen, Elizabeth, 1899–1973.
The collected stories of Elizabeth Bowen.
Bibliography: p.
PR6003.06757A15   1981   823'.912   80-8729
ISBN 0-394-51666-4

Manufactured in the United States of America
First American Edition

Contents

The War Years

Post-War Stories

Introduction

When the history of English civilization is looked back upon as one of the strange and glorious manifestations of the human spirit – and may that day be rather more distant than it sometimes seems now – London in the blitz will have, I feel sure, its own very important place in the chronicle. More important than the war of which it was but a part, more important than all the passing social and political vagaries of the post-war years. It will be there with the trenches of the First World War as an extraordinary revelation of English behaviour and feeling. And there will be only two English writers who convey what life in blitzed London was like – Elizabeth Bowen and Henry Green. They were both very fine writers and it is to be hoped that this chance will make their names familiar enriching household words to our descendants curious about our ancient times – more familiar than seems conceivably possible at this time when, as too often happens, writers fall into neglect in the decades immediately following their deaths.

If this does happen – and I think it will – the readers of the twenty-first and -second centuries will have a treat in store for them. They will find in Elizabeth Bowen's novel *The Heat of the Day* and in some of her short stories – 'In the Square', 'The Demon Lover', 'Careless Talk', and, above all, 'Mysterious Kôr' – acute perceptions of the first impact of ever present danger and death upon a great city. Perceptions which range from marvellous realistic observation of daily life to the innermost recesses of the human soul, haunted by the transience of joy or guilt as the bombs fell. It is often as though Elizabeth Bowen's mastery of the shape and form and talk of the world around her combine with her miraculous psychological insight to give us moments of sudden vision just as the bombs themselves exploded London's surface beauty or squalor to reveal long-forgotten depths beneath. Indeed it is the way in which the form of these stories typifies the world and people they depict that is surely the clue to us, if we required one, that we are dealing with that rare phenomenon – a writer of instinctive formal vision.

I establish first Elizabeth Bowen's natural artistic power because she is so careful a craftswoman, so conscious, even at times arrogantly conscious, of the shapes, the inversions, the verbal exactitudes in which she clothes her vision, that it would be easy to ignore the instinctive literary creator that lies beneath – that must, I believe, lie beneath all good art, even that of Henry James, the influence of whose shapes sometimes seems superficially too apparent in her work. Anyone so elegant and civilized, so certain of values that to state them would seem to her inept and naïve, so concerned for lack of show – even the bravery that man needs so desperately in a precarious world must never assert itself too crudely, though bravado if worn with sophistication is an allowable foible – so absolutely resolute in acceptance of life, so uninterested in its passing political forms, so urbane even in the Irish countryside she loved and saw so clearly, so concerned that compassion should never show a sloppy side – any such person inevitably seems to fit very little with Rousseau's noble savage, yet the instinctive artist is there at the very heart of her work and gives a strength, a fierceness and a depth to her elaborations, her delight in words, her determination that life seen will only survive on the page when it has met the strictest demands of form and elegance.

This natural force, I think, is what distinguishes her from the many and very various writers to whom she has affinities – Henry James, Aldous Huxley, Saki, Ivy Compton Burnett, even Virginia Woolf. She is with them in the various degrees by which shapes and manners control emotions, but her control comes always from intelligence (the sort of intelligence which she saw as inseparable from civilized behaviour), it never comes from intellect or abstraction. Occasionally, as in 'Sunday Evening' or the farcical ghost story 'The Cat Jumps', she is dealing with the intelligentsia or stereotyped 'progressives', but she always sees them from outside, never from above, with that satirical view of intellectual superiority that Aldous Huxley found in his early novels. For all her years spent in Boar's Hill among Oxford academics she remained always an upper-class woman of hardy, firm intelligence, she was never the slave of the brilliant academic world as Virginia Woolf, a greater genius, too often was. She deals with coteries but far more with families and yet, here, unlike Ivy Compton Burnett, though her nails are ready to scratch, it is with heart that she responds to all the ecstasies and desperations, the frustrations, the deadened routines, and the sudden-awakened emotional currents of family life. She can be witty (though not, I think, very successfully funny) but not at the expense of her feeling. One has the sense that, for her, passion and love are so essentially moulded into life that she has no need for the desperate restraints of Mrs Woolf, the evasions of Ivy Compton Burnett, or the open romanticism, wonderfully civilized though it is, of Rosamund Lehmann.

She came of a tough, landowning family who had origins in Cromwell's puritan settlers yet, as her father's periodic mental disorders show, there was also the strain of hysteria so common in the puritan gentry. But in her it was surely taken up and satisfied not only by her creative art, but by her incorporation of love – both emotional and physical – into the essential shape of life, as part of the essence of orderly, well-bred manners. Of course, she accepted, as a worldly woman, the vagaries and aberrations and sophistications of the 1920s and 1930s, but there is none of the frenzy or the muddle so familiar to us now from the erotic memories of Bloomsbury or of the world of Lawrence. She was tolerant but she was certain. As she said to her own lover, love was an essential part of her religion, she could not imagine a God who would not accept love as the reason for human aberrance from any strictly laid down code. This is the foundation for the many wonderful stories in this collection which illumine moments in the lives of husbands and wives, or wives and lovers, or, simply, lovers. Passion is there, but it is worn always with poise, or, if it is not, there is an aura of absurdity or a ghostly haunting of regret or shame. Yet, for all the poise, the worldly elegance, the enlacing of passion with worldly routine – dressing for dinner, the country walk in the country weekend, the arrival at the West End restaurant for luncheon – love is still deeply romantic in Elizabeth Bowen's work, central and without the *froideur* that, in Virginia Woolf's novel, is destroying Clarissa Dalloway's life. Elizabeth Bowen has, of course, one of the principal features of the great romantics – a total connection with her own childhood, and, by an imaginative force, with many other kinds of children.

Some of the most totally satisfying stories in this collection are those that concern children. They are in many moods. An early story, 'Daffodils', gives us an immediate clue – the story of a schoolmistress who invites some of her pupils, seen through her window, to entertainment at her rather lonely lodgings. But they have other things to do, their own life – she is no more than a curiosity to them. We are established in the schoolgirls' own world. And in two stories, 'Charity' and 'The Jungle', she establishes what that world is – in the first what 'home life' means to a child, when one schoolgirl visits another in the holidays, in the second what 'school' is like. And it is not only with girls that she is at home. 'The Visitor' is a superb account of a boy being entertained and housed by friends while his mother is dying – the aloofness of a child in such circumstances, and his total lostness. It is a story to rank with the best pieces of Copperfield's boyhood.

But she does not see childhood as all pathos or polite noninvolvement with the adult world. In 'Maria' and 'The Little Girl's Room', we have a marvellous picture of the devilish games either imagined or played upon the adult world by children whose aloofness is tinged with diabolic contempt. Here we are in the world of Saki, but without his self-conscious malignity that borders on whimsy. And, at the last, Elizabeth Bowen shows us how all this passing childhood, concerned or unconcerned, angelic or devilish, does not always leave the human soul free in maturity. In 'The Apple Tree' a young woman is mentally imprisoned in the vision of a suicide she came upon at school, but she is freed by an understanding and sympathetic older woman. The hero of 'Ivy Gripped the Steps', arguably her finest story, is not so lucky – even in his return to the South Coast just freed from military control after D Day, he cannot free his timid, lonely soul from the boyhood trauma he knew when he found that a beautiful, rich woman's apparent love for him was no more than a bored exercise in charm.

This sense of childhood's pervasiveness and of passion as essential parts of a life lived elegantly and bravely was perhaps made possible for Elizabeth Bowen by her apparent total acceptance of ghosts, of the occult. In part, this also ties her to the 1920s and 1930s, to the late Kipling stories. But there is a difference – Kipling speculates sceptically, or where he accepts for the sake of the story, the ghostly has Poe-like overtones of horror or revenge. In only one or two Elizabeth Bowen stories is the ghost malign, vengeful: in 'The Demon Lover', where a woman's fickleness breeds its own horror, and, perhaps, in 'Green Holly', the funny-horrible story of Intelligence workers in the last war beset in their dreary isolation by untimely ghosts of murder. For the rest, ghosts are acceptable statements of the continuity of time and life; so much so that, in the fullest war-horror, the wife of 'The Happy Autumn Fields' may find relief from the sight of her bombed London house by living in a family of a hundred years earlier found in an old diary. Ghosts make sense of life not nonsense.

Nevertheless, they have a period flavour. And much more so, I think, for the modern reader, will be the murder in the background of so much of Elizabeth Bowen's fictional life. The characters, especially women, also turn out to have been associated with murder, or to be acquitted murderesses. This for someone of my age brings back the past. In all those pre-1939 decades of my childhood and adolescence, murder and above all murderesses held the headlines of the popular newspapers. It was both sensational and macabre – and I believe it to be one of the finest virtues of the abolition of capital punishment that it brought to an end this prurient interest in women who were to be hanged. It is one of the only passing journalistic aspects of Elizabeth Bowen's stories. As the war came on it gave way to the spies of her last novels and stories. The horrors in the cupboard became those that are still with us now.

Are there failures in her stories? 'Gone Away', I think, suggests that life as lived was enough for her, and speculation about the future of her society had no place in her scheme of things. Could she move outside her social world? In emotion and sympathy, I think, she could. After all, the girls and the young man in the wonderful 'Mysterious Kôr' are very middle-class; and she could visualize the problems of others, as in her story about the loneliness of new housing estates. Only her ear lets her down a little – she is over-anxious to establish the difference of what she hears, there are too many 'we really didn't ought to have's in the speech of those she heard from a distance. And the maid's dialogue about the bombed house, 'Oh, Madam', seems to be on the level of the H.M. Tennent matinée performance that it became.

But the failures are so very few, the triumphs so many, especially as time passes by, for, though the seeds of her mastery are in her early stories, the development in so craftful a writer is inevitably vast. Perhaps in the superb 'Sunday Afternoon' the bringing together of her two sides – the urban, the loyalist of London however horrible the blitz years, and the cultured gentry world of Ireland's countryside – shows her at her best. Here we are at once in a marvellously evoked moment of place and time and in the never changing conflict of youth's hopeful imagination and the regretful doubts of the ageing. But that is only one of many marvels these stories open to us.

June 1980   ANGUS WILSON

First Stories

Breakfast

'BEHOLD, I die daily,' thought Mr Rossiter, entering the breakfast-room. He saw the family in silhouette against the windows; the windows looked out into a garden closed darkly in upon by walls. There were so many of the family it seemed as though they must have multiplied during the night; their flesh gleamed pinkly in the cold northern light and they were always moving. Often, like the weary shepherd, he could have prayed them to keep still that he might count them.

They turned at his entrance profiles and three-quarter faces towards him. There was a silence of suspended munching and little bulges of food were thrust into their cheeks that they might wish him perfunctory good-mornings.

Miss Emily further inquired whether he had slept well, with a little vivacious uptilt of her chin. Her voice was muffled: he gathered that the contents of her mouth was bacon, because she was engaged in sopping up the liquid fat from her plate with little dice of bread, which she pushed around briskly with a circular movement of her fork. It was not worth sitting down till she had finished, because he would be expected to take her plate away. Why was the only empty chair always beside Miss Emily?

Last night in the lamplight he had almost begun to think he liked Miss Emily. She was the only lady present who had not beaten time with hand or foot or jerking head while they played 'Toreador Song' on the gramophone. But here, pressed in upon her by the thick fumes of coffee and bacon, the doggy-smelling carpet, the tight, glazed noses of the family ready to split loudly from their skins . . . There was contamination in the very warm edge of her plate, as he took it from her with averted head and clattered it down among the others on the sideboard.

'Bacon?' insinuated Mrs Russel. 'A *little* chilly, I'm afraid. I do hope there's plenty, but we early birds are sometimes inclined to be *rather* ravenous.'

She added: 'There's an egg,' but there was no invitation in her tone.

She could never leave a phrase unmodified. He could have

answered with facetious emphasis that he was *almost* inclined to believe he would *rather* have enjoyed that egg.

Dumbly, he took two rashers of the moist and mottled bacon.

'And then,' Hilary Bevel was recounting, 'it all changed, and we were moving very quickly through a kind of pinkish mist – running, it felt like, only all my legs and arms were somewhere else. That was the time when *you* came into it, Aunt Willoughby. You were winding up your sewing machine like a motor car, kneeling down, in a sort of bunching bathing dress . . . ' She dared indelicacy, reaching out for the marmalade with a little agitated rustle to break up the silence with which her night's amazing experiences had been received.

Miss Emily, always kindly, tittered into her cup. She kicked the leg of Rossiter's chair and apologized; and he watched her thin, sharp shoulders shining through her blouse.

Mrs Russel's eye travelled slowly round the table; there slowed and ceased the rotatory mastication of her jaws. Above her head was a square of white light reflected across from the window to the overmantel. He wished that the sheen of the tablecloth were snow, and that he could heap it over his head as that eye came round towards him.

'Now for it,' he braced himself, clenching his hands upon his knife and fork, and squaring his elbows till one touched Miss Emily, who quivered.

'I'm afraid you couldn't hardly have heard the gong this morning, Mr Rossiter. That new girl doesn't hardly know how to make it sound yet. She seems to me just to give it a sort of *rattle*.'

Damn her impudence. She censored him for being late.

'Oh, I – I heard it, thank you!'

They had all stopped talking, and ate quite quietly to hear him speak. Only Jervis Bevel drained his coffee-cup with a gulp and gurgle.

'The fact is, I was – er – looking for my collar-stud.'

'Ah, yes. I'm afraid you've sometimes been a little reckless about buying new ones before you were quite sure you'd lost the others, haven't you, Mr Rossiter? Only fancy,' – she looked round to collect the attention of the breakfasters; there was a sensation to follow – 'Annie found *three* good ones, really good ones, under the wardrobe, when she was turning out your room.'

'I can't think how they get there,' he protested, conscious of inanity.

'Perhaps they took little legs unto themselves and walked,' suggested Hilary Bevel.

'Perhaps the wardrobe got up in the night and sat on top of them,' bettered Miss Emily.

There was a rustle of laughter, and she cast down her eyes with a deprecatory titter.

The remark was a success. It was really funny. It was received by Mrs Russel with a warm benignity: 'Really, Emily, you do say silly things.' She laughed her gentle breathy laugh, gazing at Mr Rossiter, who wriggled.

'I say – er – Bevel, when you've finished with that newspaper — '

Jervis Bevel looked insolently at him over the top of the paper. 'Sorry, I've only just begun. I left it lying on your plate some time, then I didn't think you'd have much time to read it, being rather rushed.'

Rossiter hated Bevel, with his sleek head. He was not aware that he was rushed. What business had Bevel got to tell him so?

'Well, when you *have* finished — '

Hilary Bevel was staring at him across the table as though she had never seen him before. She had eyebrows like her brother's, owl's eyebrows, and long-lidded, slanting eyes; and affected a childish directness and ingenuousness of speech which she considered attractive. Her scarlet, loose-lipped mouth curled itself round her utterances, making them doubly distinct.

'Mr Rossiter's got another tie on, a *crimson* tie!' said Hilary Bevel.

Rossiter was instantly aware, not only of his tie but of his whole body visible above the table-edge. He felt his ears protruding fan-wise from his head, felt them redden, and the blush burn slowly across his cheekbones, down his pricking skin to the tip of his nose.

Mrs Russel's attention was temporarily directed from himself by a skirmish with Aunt Willoughby. The click of swords was audible to all.

'Oh, but you wouldn't, Aunt Willoughby. Not when they've got five or six rooms to settle up every day, you wouldn't. You see, with you, when poor uncle was alive, it was a different thing altogether. What I mean to say is, in proportion to the size of the family you had more of them, in a kind of way. It was a larger staff.'

'Ah then, Rosie, but what I always used to say, "You do what I expect of you and we won't expect any more than that. I'm reasonable," I used to say, "I won't expect any more than that." *Annie* could tell you that was what I used to say to her. As my dear husband used to say,' Aunt Willoughby raised her voice, antici-pating an interruption, 'there are those that can get good work out of their servants and those that can't. We mustn't be set up about it; it's just a gift, like other gifts, that many haven't got. I've had such a happy, *happy* home,' she sighed towards the attentive Miss Emily. 'Always so comfortable, it was.'

'Annie *is* a funny girl,' reflected Mrs Russel; 'she said to me – of course I never take the things those girls say seriously – "I wouldn't go back to Mrs Willoughby not for anything you might give me, I wouldn't." I said, "But she spoke so well of you, Annie," and she just wagged her head at me, sort of. She *is* a funny girl! Of course, I didn't ought to tell you, but it made me laugh at the time, it did really.'

'I came down on her rather *hard*,' admitted Aunt Willoughby swiftly. 'I was so particular, you see, and she *had* some dirty ways. Now I shouldn't wonder – when was it you lost those collar-studs, Mr Rossiter?'

'I don't exactly remember,' said Rossiter, basely. He felt Mrs Russel's approval warm upon him, but was sorry to have failed Aunt Willoughby, who, disconcerted, relapsed into irrelevancy.

Miss Emily harked back.

'Oh, Hilary, you are awful – why shouldn't he?'

'Well, I didn't say he shouldn't, I simply said it *was* one. They'll be jealous of you at the office, won't they, Mr Rossiter?'

Mr Rossiter, eyeing her contemplatively, supposed that Miss Bevel was a 'merry' girl.

'It may mean an *occasion* for Mr Rossiter,' said Mrs Russel from her Olympia behind the urn. 'You shouldn't draw attention to it, girls.'

The light glanced on Hilary's waved and burnished hair as she turned her head towards Aunt Willoughby.

'*Nobody* takes *any* notice of little me, when *I* go gadding, do they, Auntie! Why, it's all round the table in a minute if I come down with half an inch of new coloured cammie-ribbon sticking out above my jumper!'

'You wouldn't put it in at all if you didn't think it was going to notice,' remarked her brother, without raising his eyes from the *Daily Express*.

'I wouldn't put on anything at all if I was quite invisible, if that's what you mean!'

Miss Emily glanced apprehensively at the unshaken barricade of newspaper.

'Oh, Hilary, you are *awf* — '

Jervis had apparently not heard.

'Hilary!' said Mrs Russel, 'I'm afraid you're shocking Mr Rossiter!' She lingered on the name as though he were something delicious to eat.

'I believe,' thought Rossiter, 'they all want to marry me! Is this insight or delirium? P'raps not Aunt Willoughby, but — '

He appraised Jervis round the edge of the newspaper. Surely he was showier, more attractive? Why couldn't he divert some of their attentions; take on, say, Miss Emily and Mrs Russel? Mrs Russel was old enough to be the mother of either of them.

A hand shot out suddenly from behind the urn. Rossiter jumped.

' — had your second cup of coffee yet,' Mrs Russel was saying. 'You look quite poetic, Mr Rossiter' – she was referring to his abstracted glare – 'Aren't you going to pass along your cup?'

'Thank you – *half* a cup, if you please.'

'There's no *hurry*.' She glanced over her shoulder at the round relentless clock-face on the mantel. 'You see, you eat rather faster than the others, Mr Rossiter, though they have had a bit of a start this morning!'

Did he really bolt his food and make, perhaps, disgusting noises with his mouth?

'That's why I always say we'd rather breakfast early – all of us, even the ones who haven't necessarily got to rush. It's so much homier, one feels, than rough-and-tumble modern breakfast nowadays. Everybody sort of rushing in and scrambling and snatching and making *grabs* at things off a table at the side. There's nothing so homely,' said Mrs Russel with conscious brilliance, 'as a comfortable sit-down family to breakfast.'

'My God!' said Jervis irritably, 'there's going to be another strike on that damned railway – they're cutting down the trains again. Why *pretend* railways are a convenience – that's what I should like to know?'

No one could tell him.

He pushed his chair back from the table, impatiently, and crossed his legs.

'Pore old thing, then,' trilled Hilary. 'Diddums wazzums cwoss.'

'They're *not* taking off the eight-forty-seven, are they?'

'Not the eight-*forty-seven*?'

'They are. That means either the eight-twenty-seven or the eight-fifty-three. The *eight-fifty-three*!'

'The eight-twenty-seven,' they decided unanimously.

'Then that'll just have to mean breakfast earlier,' said Mrs Russel brightly; 'you won't mind, will you, girls?' Her appeal included Aunt Willoughby, who made no response. 'You see, we couldn't hardly rush them over their breakfasts, could we?'

This was 'home comforts.' This was one of the privileges for which Rossiter paid her twenty-four shillings a week. Being sat round and watched while you were eating. Not being *rushed*. He had a vision of a 'rushed breakfast,' of whirling endlessly through space while one snapped at a sausage with little furtive bites; of munching bread and marmalade with the wind of one's velocity whistling through one's teeth.

Would it be better? Could it be worse?

Not worse than his chair-edge creaking against Miss Emily's; the unceasing consciousness of her unceasing consciousness of him. Not worse than Hilary Bevel, *vis-à-vis*; with her complacent prettiness, her tinkling, laboured witticisms. Not worse than Aunt Willoughby's baffled, bearded morosity; than Jervis Bevel's sleek disdain.

He would escape from Mrs Russel, her advances, her criticisms, her fumbling arguments that crushed you down beneath their heavy gentleness until you felt you were being trampled to death by a cow. By a blind cow, that fumbled its way backwards and forwards across you . . .

The 'girls' delivered their ultimatum in chorus.

'England expects,' declaimed Hilary, turning her eyes towards the ceiling, 'effery woman to – er – do – er herr dew-ty.'

'It's *nice* to be down early,' said Miss Emily earnestly, 'with a nice long day stretching out in front of me.'

'Breakfast will be at quarter to eight sharp,' said Mrs Russel. 'Mr Rossiter, we really must *try* not to lose our collar-studs.'

All his days and nights were loops, curving out from breakfast time, curving back to it again. Inexorably the loops grew smaller, the breakfasts longer; looming more and more over his nights, eating more and more out of his days.

Jervis Bevel's eyes swerved over to the mantelpiece. He pushed his chair back farther over the bristling carpet pile.

'Well,' he said, 'I think it's almost time — '

The room broke up, the table grew smaller again as they all rose from their chairs. Mrs Russel and Aunt Willoughby gathered themselves together; Hilary seized Miss Emily by the back of the waist and punted her laughingly towards the door.

The coffee and the bacon and the hostility and the christian forbearance blew out before them into the chilly hall.

Daffodils

Miss Murcheson stopped at the corner of the High Street to buy a bunch of daffodils from the flower-man. She counted out her money very carefully, pouring a little stream of coppers from her purse into the palm of her hand.

' — ninepence – ten – eleven – pence   halfpenny – *a   shilling*! Thank you very much. Good afternoon.'

A gust of wind rushed up the street, whirling her skirts up round her like a ballet-dancer's, and rustling the Reckitts-blue paper round the daffodils. The slender gold trumpets tapped and quivered against her face as she held them up with one hand and pressed her skirts down hastily with the other. She felt as though she had been enticed into a harlequinade by a company of Columbines who were quivering with laughter at her discomfiture; and looked round to see if anyone had witnessed her display of chequered moirette petticoat and the inches of black stocking above her boots. But the world remained unembarrassed.

Today the houses seemed taller and farther apart; the street wider and full of a bright, clear light that cast no shadows and was never sunshine. Under archways and between the houses the distances had a curious transparency, as though they had been painted upon glass. Against the luminous and indeterminate sky the Abbey tower rose distinct and delicate.

Miss Murcheson, forgetting all confusion, was conscious of her wings. She paused again to hitch up the bundle of exercise books slithering down beneath her elbow, then took the dipping road as a bird swings down into the air. Her mouth was faintly acrid with spring dust and the scent of daffodils was in her nostrils. As she left the High Street farther behind her, the traffic sounded as a faint and murmurous hum, striking here and there a tinkling note like wind-bells.

Under her detachment she was conscious of the houses, the houses and the houses. They were square, flat-faced and plaster-fronted, painted creams and greys and buffs; one, a purplish-rose colour. Venetian shutters flat against the wall broadened the line of the windows, there were coloured fanlights over all the doors.

Spiked railings before them shut off their little squares of grass or gravel from the road, and between the railings branches swung out to brush against her dress and recall her to the wonder of their budding loveliness.

Miss Murcheson remembered that her mother would be out for tea, and quickened her steps in anticipation of that delightful solitude. The silver birch tree that distinguished their front garden slanted beckoning her across the pavement. She hesitated, as her gate swung open, and stood looking up and down the road. She was sorry to go in, but could not resist the invitation of the empty house. She wondered if tomorrow would fill her with so strange a stirring as today. Soon, in a few months, it would be summer and there would be nothing more to come. Summer would be beautiful, but this spring made promise of a greater beauty than summer could fulfil; hinted at a mystery which other summers had evaded rather than explained. She went slowly up the steps, fumbling for her latch-key.

The day's dinner still hung dank and heavy in the air of the little hall. She stood in the doorway, with that square of light and sound behind her, craving the protection and the comfort with which that dark entrance had so often received her. There was a sudden desolation in the emptiness of the house.

Quickly she entered the sitting-room and flung open the window, which set the muslin curtains swaying in the breeze and clanked the little pictures on the walls. The window embrasure was so deep that there was little light in the corners of the room; armchairs and cabinets were lurking in the dusk. The square of daylight by the window was blocked by a bamboo table groaning under an array of photographs. In her sweeping mood she deposed the photographs, thrust the table to one side, and pulled her chair up into the window. 'I can't correct my essays in the dark,' she asserted, though she had done so every evening of the year.

'How tight-laced you are, poor Columbines,' she said, throwing away the paper and seeing how the bass cut deep into the fleshy stems. 'You were brave above it all, but – there now!' She cut the bass and shook the flowers out into a vase. 'I can't correct,' she sighed, 'with you all watching me. You are so terribly flippant!'

But what a curious coincidence: she had set her class to write an essay upon Daffodils! 'You shall judge; I'll read them all out loud. They *will* amuse you.' She dipped her pen in the red-ink pot with an anticipatory titter.

With a creak of wheels a young woman went by slowly, wheeling a perambulator. She leant heavily on the handle-bar, tilting the perambulator on its two back wheels, and staring up, widemouthed, at the windows.

'How nice to be so much interested,' thought Miss Murcheson, pressing open the first exercise-book. 'But I'm sure it can't be a good thing for the baby.'

The essays lacked originality. Each paragraph sidled up self-consciously to openings for a suitable quotation, to rush each one through with a gasp of triumph.

> And then my heart with pleasure fills
> And dances with the daffodils.

> Fair daffodils, we weep to see
> You fade away so soon

She wondered if any of her class could weep for the departure of a daffodil. Mostly they had disclaimed responsibility for such weakness by the stern prefix, 'As the poet says – '. Flora Hopwood had, she remembered, introduced a 'Quotation Dictionary', which must have been round her circle.

'I must forbid it. Why can't they see things for themselves, think them out? I don't believe they ever really see anything, just accept things on the authority of other people. I could make them believe anything. What a responsibility teaching is — But is it? They'd believe me, but they wouldn't care. It wouldn't matter, really.

'They're so horribly used to things. Nothing ever comes new to them that they haven't grown up with. They get their very feelings out of books. Nothing ever surprises or impresses them. When spring comes they get preoccupied, stare dreamily out of the windows. They're thinking out their new hats. Oh, if only I didn't know them quite so well, or knew them a little better!

'If I had a school of my own,' she meditated, running her eyes down the pages and mechanically underlining spelling-mistakes, 'I would make them think. I'd horrify them, if nothing better. But here – how ever can one, teaching at a High School? Miss Peterson would —

'They *do* like me. At least, one set does, I know. I'm rather a cult, they appreciate my Titian hair. They'd like me more, though, if I knew how to do it better, and knew better how to use my eyes. Their sentimentality embarrasses me. In a way they're so horribly mature, I feel at a disadvantage with them. If only they'd be a little more spontaneous. But spontaneity is beyond them at present. They're simply calves, after all, rather sophisticated calves.'

She dreamed, and was awakened by familiar laughter. Nobody's laughter in particular, but surely it was the laughter of the High School? Three girls were passing with arms close linked, along the pavement underneath her window. She looked down on the expressive, tilted ovals of their sailor hats; then, on an impulse, smacked the window-sill to attract their attention. Instantly they turned up three pink faces of surprise, which broadened into smiles of recognition.

'Hullo, Miss Murcheson!'

'Hullo, children! Come in for a minute and talk to me. I'm all alone.'

Millicent, Rosemary and Doris hesitated, eyeing one another, poised for flight. 'Righto!' they agreed unanimously.

Miss Murcheson, all of a flutter, went round to open the front door. She looked back at the sitting-room as though she had never seen it before.

Why had she asked them in, those terrible girls whom she had scarcely spoken to? They would laugh at her, they would tell the others.

The room was full of them, of their curiosity and embarrassment and furtive laughter. She had never realized what large girls they were; how plump and well-developed. She felt them eyeing her stack of outraged relatives, the photographs she swept off on to a chair; their eyes flitted from the photographs to the daffodils, from the daffodils to the open, red-scored exercise books.

'Yes,' she said, 'your writings, I daresay. Do you recognize them? I was correcting "Daffodils" and they made me dreary – sit down, won't you? – *dreary*. I wonder if any of you have ever used your senses; smelt, or *seen* things — Oh, *do* sit down!

She seemed to be shouting into a forest of thick bodies. They seated themselves along the edge of an ottoman in a bewildered row; this travestied their position in the class-room and made her feel, facing them, terribly official and instructive. She tried to shake this off.

'It's cruel, isn't it, to lie in wait for you like this and pull you in and lecture you about what you don't feel about daffodils!'

Her nervous laughter tinkled out into silence.

'It was a beastly subject,' said someone, heavily.

'Beastly? Oh, Mill – Rosemary, have you never seen a daffodil?' They giggled.

'No, but looked at one?' Her earnestness swept aside her embarrassment. 'Not just heard about them – "Oh yes, daffodils: yellow flowers; spring, mother's vases, bulbs, borders, flashing past flower-shop windows" – but taken one up in your hands and felt it?'

How she was haranguing them!

'It's very difficult to be clever about things one's *used* to,' said Millicent. 'That's why history essays are so much easier. You tell us about things, and we just write them down.'

'That's why you're so lazy; you're using *my* brains; just giving me back what I gave you again, a little bit the worse for the wear.'

They looked hurt and uncomfortable.

Doris got up and walked over to the fireplace.

('Good,' thought Miss Murcheson, 'it will relieve the tension a bit if they will only begin to prowl.')

'What a pretty photograph, Miss Murcheson. Who is it? Not – not *you*?'

'*Me*?' said Miss Murcheson with amusement. 'Yes. Why not? Does it surprise you, then?'

'You've got such a *dinky* hat on!' cried the girl, with naïve astonishment.

The others crowded round her.

'You look so different,' said Doris, still scrutinizing the photograph. 'Awfully happy, and prosperous, and – cocksure.'

'Perhaps it was the hat!' suggested Millicent.

'Oh, *Millicent*! No, I'm sure Miss Murcheson was *thinking* about something else.'

'Or somebody.'

'Oh, Doris, you are awful!'

They all giggled, and glanced apprehensively across at her.

She wondered why she was not more offended by them.

'As a matter of fact,' she enlightened them, '*that* was because of daffodils. It just illustrates my point, curiously enough.'

They were still absorbed.

'Oh, Miss *Murcheson*!'

'*Miss* Murcheson!'

'When was it taken?'

'Last Easter holidays. Nearly a year ago. At Seabrooke. By a friend of mine.'

'*Do-oo* give me one!'

' — And me?'

'I'm afraid that's the only print I've got; and that's mother's.'

'Were there more?'

'Yes, various people took them. You see, I haven't faced a real camera for years, so when I got these snaps they were scrambled for by people who'd been asking me for photos.'

'People?' She was rising visibly in their estimation.

'Oh yes. Friends.'

'Why *daffodils*?' reverted Rosemary.

'Somebody had just given me a great big bunch.' She was impressed by their interest. 'I wonder if daffodils will ever make any of you look like that.'

'It all depends, you see,' said Millicent, astutely. 'Nobody has ever given us any. If they *did* perhaps — '

'*Really*?' said Miss Murcheson, with innocent concern. 'Take all those, if they would really inspire you! No, dears, I'd *like* you to.'

She gathered the daffodils together and lifted them, dripping, from the vase.

The girls retreated.

'Oh no, really, *not* your daffodils — '

'We don't mean — '

'Not *your* daffodils, Miss Murcheson. It wasn't *that* a bit.'

Evidently a false move on her part. She was bewildered by them; could not fathom the depths of their cinema-bred romanticism.

Doris had put away the photograph and stood with her back to the others, fingering the ornaments on the chimney-piece.

'There are lots of things,' she said rapidly, 'that you only feel because of people. That's the only reason things are there for, I *think*. You wouldn't notice them otherwise, or care about them. It's only sort of — ' she stopped. Her ears glowed crimson underneath her hat.

'Association,' they sighed, ponderously.

'That's exactly what's the matter,' cried Miss Murcheson. 'We've got all the nice, fresh, independent, outside things so smeared over with our sentimentalities and prejudices and – associations – that we can't see them anyhow but as part of ourselves. That's how you're – we're missing things and spoiling things for ourselves. You – we don't seem able to *discover*.'

'Life,' said Doris sententiously, 'is a very big adventure. Of course we all see *that*.'

The other two looked at her quickly. All three became suddenly hostile. She was encouraging them to outrage the decencies of conversation. It was bad form, this flagrant discussion of subjects only for their most secret and fervid whisperings.

To her, they were still unaccountable. She had not wished to probe.

'I don't think that's what I meant,' she said a little flatly. 'Of course your lives will be full of interesting things, and those will be your own affairs. Only, if I could be able, I'm always trying, to make you care about the little fine things you might pass over, that have such big roots underground.

'I should like you to be happy as I've been, and as I'm going to be,' she said impulsively. 'I should love to watch you after you've left my form, going up and up the school, and getting bigger, and then, when you've left, going straight and clearly to the essential things.'

The tassel of the blind cord tapped against the window-sill, through the rustling curtains they looked out on to the road.

They had awaited a disclosure intimate and personal. The donor of those last year's daffodils had taken form, portentous in their minds. But she had told them nothing, given them the stone of her abstract, colourless idealism while they sat there, open-mouthed for sentimental bread.

'Won't you stay to tea?' she asked. 'Oh, *do*. We'll picnic; boil the kettle on the gas-ring, and eat sticky buns – I've got a bag of sticky buns. We'll have a party in honour of the daffodils.'

The prospect allured her, it would be a fantastic interlude.

They all got up.

'Doris and Millicent are coming to tea with me, Miss Murcheson. Mother's expecting us, thanks most awfully. Else we should have loved to.'

'We should have loved to,' echoed the others. 'Thanks most awfully.'

She felt a poignant disappointment and relief, as standing with her eyes on the daffodils, she heard the children clattering down the steps.

Tomorrow they will be again impersonal; three pink moons in a firmament of faces.

The three, released, eyed one another with a common understanding.

'Miss Murcheson has never really *lived*,' said Doris.

They linked arms again and sauntered down the road.

The Return

MR and Mrs Tottenham had come home.

The moist brown gravel of the drive and sweep bore impress of their fly wheels. Lydia Broadbent listened from the doorstep to the receding gritty rumble of the empty fly, and the click and rattle as the gate swung to. Behind her, in the dusky hall, Mr Tottenham shouted directions for the disposal of the luggage, flustered servants bumped against each other and recoiled, and Porloch the gardener shouldered the heavy trunks with gasps and lurches, clutching at the banisters until they creaked.

Lydia heard Mrs Tottenham burst open the drawing-room door and cross the threshold with her little customary pounce, as though she hoped to catch somebody unawares. She pictured her looking resentfully round her, and knew that presently she would hear her tweaking at the curtains. During her six weeks of solitude the house had grown very human to Lydia. She felt now as if it were drawing itself together into a nervous rigor, as a man draws himself together in suffering irritation at the entrance of a fussy wife.

'Were these all the letters, Lydia? I hope none were forwarded to Wickly? Porloch, do be careful of the paint! The fly was very stuffy, Lydia. I wish you'd ordered one of Bicklesfield's. His are always clean.'

Mrs Tottenham had darted out of the drawing-room, swept up her letters from the table, and stood hesitating at the bottom of the stairs.

'You might order tea immediately. Yes, the drawing-room for today.' A red shimmer of firelight invited them through the open door. 'Herbert, *Her*-bert!'

Mr Tottenham was clattering in the smoking-room. His face peered crossly at them round the door.

'I wondered if you had gone upstairs. Porloch has been very careless of the paint. You might have watched him, Lydia!' She vanished slowly into the gloom above.

Lydia went into the drawing-room and stood warming her hands before the fire. A servant with a lighted taper passed from gas-bracket to gas-bracket and the greenish lights sprang upwards in her wake. Outside the brown gloom deepened over the November garden. The young distorted trees loomed dark and sullen, the air was thick with moisture, heavy with decay.

Today there had been no time to think. Lydia was aware but dimly of a sense of desolation and of loss. Something was shattered that had built itself around her during these coherent weeks, something violated which had been sacred unawares. Every fibre of her quivered with hostility to these invaders who were the owners of the house. She was at odds with herself again, at odds with her surroundings. She stared at her gaunt reflection in the fireplace and knew that her best companion had drawn back again, forbidding her. She would be baffled once again by the hostility of Lydia Broadbent, her derision, her unsparing scorn. 'I was such friends with myself when they left us together; we were so harmonious and at ease with each other, me and myself and the house. Now we are afraid and angry with each other again.'

Mr and Mrs Tottenham were impossible. They were childless, humourless and dyspeptic. They were not even funny. There was nothing bizarre about them, or tragic or violent or farcical. They neither loved nor hated each other, there was nothing they did not know about each other; no mystery or fear between them. In the early days of their marriage they had been actively and articulately unhappy. She had had a lover; he had left her for months together and lived in some drab wickedness elsewhere. Then her lover had deserted her, he had been left more money; they had drifted together again, bought 'The Laurels', spun the shams and miseries around them like a web and lurked within them. They visited, were reputable and entertained; and kept a home for Mr Tottenham's nephew, their expectant heir.

'Lydia?'

The thin voice fluted over the banisters. Lydia hurried upstairs, flicked at a panel of Mrs Tottenham's door and entered, her footsteps muffled among the woolliness of many rugs. There was a blot of yellow light from a candle on the writing-table. Mrs Tottenham stood beside the bed, staring at two sheets of close-written paper and an envelope, which she held out fan-wise between rigid fingers, as one holding a hand at cards.

'Did – has my husband taken his mail yet? Did he overlook the letters?'

'I think Mr Tottenham's post is still lying on the hall table. Is there anything you want to show him?' They had all their correspondence in common; it was quite impersonal.

'No, no, Lydia, shut the door, please. Is tea up? It *is* draughty: I should have liked a fire. You might get the things out of my dressing-bag – there, it's over on the sofa.'

This constant attendance was to begin again. Lydia was well schooled to it; why had she forgotten?

She unpacked the combs and brushes, and Mrs Tottenham fidgeted before the glass.

'Light the gas, please. I hate this half-light!' There was resentment in her glance towards the window, where the last daylight leaked in faintly through draperies of parchment-coloured lace. Why was Mrs Tottenham so agitated, tugging her hat off and patting at her crimped and faded hair?

She bent to a level with the mirror; haggard-eyed and grinning with anxiety, she searched her bleached and baggy face to find what prettiness was there. Lydia watched her with apathetic curiosity from where, on her knees beside the sofa, she unwrapped the shoes and bottles from their little holland bags.

'Have you seen the photo,' asked Mrs Tottenham suddenly, 'of me when I was twenty-five? On the chiffonier – the plush-framed one – you *must* know it!'

Lydia assented.

'It's a good one, isn't it? D'you think it's like me – now, I mean?'

'Quite a likeness, really, considering.'

'*Considering?*' (How sharp her voice was!)

'Oh, change of fashions makes a difference, doesn't it, and, well . . . time, of course.'

'Of course I know it wasn't taken yesterday, Lydia. *I* don't need telling. But I'm a lot younger than Mr Tottenham to look at. There was a gentleman at the Hydro took us for father and daughter, really he did!'

Her voice was by turns peremptory, confidential, almost appealing. It died out into silence.

The room was restive and disturbed. 'Oh, you unhappy house,' thought Lydia. 'They have broken into your silence and given you nothing in return.'

'Tea will be ready, I think,' she reminded. Mrs Tottenham turned sharply from the glass, and Lydia saw with amazement that she had reddened her lips. They shone with sticky brightness in her sallow face.

Mrs Tottenham was conscious of her glance. 'Shows rather, doesn't it?' she queried diffidently, and rubbed her mouth with the back of her hand till the red was smeared out over her cheeks.

'One looks so washy after a journey. Just a touch of colour – one wouldn't notice it, hardly, if it wasn't for the glare.' Her muttered extenuations were not addressed to Lydia.

They heard the tea-tray rattling through the hall. Lydia turned the light out, and they prepared to descend. Mrs Tottenham pawed her in the twilight. 'You needn't mention to Mr Tottenham I've opened any of my letters. I'll be showing him the rest. This one was rather particular – from a friend of mine, it was.' An appeal still quavered in her husky tones which her paid companion had never heard before.

From the drawing-room they saw Mr Tottenham scurrying across the grass, drawn teawards by the lighted window. There was something quick and furtive about him; Lydia had never been able to determine whether he dodged and darted as pursuer or pursued.

'Wretched evening, wretched.' He chattered his way across the crowded room. 'Been talking to Porloch – garden's in an awful way; shrubberies like a jungle. Did 'e sell the apples?'

He darted the inquiry at Lydia, turning his head sharply towards her, with his eyes averted as though he could not bear to look at her. At first she had imagined that her appearance repulsed him. She knew herself for a plain woman, but now she had learnt that he never looked at anybody if he could avoid it.

'Oh, he sold them well, I believe. I thought he wrote about them?'

'Oh yes, yes, sharp man, Porloch. Dickie been running round for his things?'

'Not often. He says he wants his letters forwarded to Elham till further notice.'

The reference to Elham tickled Dickie's uncle. He put his cup down, giggled, mopped at his mouth and darted a side glance at his wife.

Mrs Tottenham was not listening. She sat very stiff and upright, staring straight before her, crumbling at her cake.

'Hey, Mollie! Dickie's gone to Elham. Didgehear that? Pore old Dickie's gone to Elham again! Never wrote and told me, never told me anything. The young dog!'

The silence was once more outraged by his falsetto giggles.

He held his cup out for Lydia to refill, and she watched with fascination the convulsive movements his throat made while he drank.

'Hey, Mollie! Don't forget we're going to the Gunnings to-morrow. Write it down, my dear girl, write it down, and tell them about orderin' the cab.' He always referred to Lydia obliquely as 'they' or 'them'.

'Gunnin's a good fellow,' he informed the fireplace.

'This cake is uneatable, Lydia. Wherever did you buy it?' Her grumble lacked conviction; it was a perfunctory concession to her distrust of her companion's housekeeping.

'Birch's. I'm sorry, Mrs Tottenham. Aren't you ready for more tea? It's nice and hot for you, isn't it, after the journey?'

Lydia felt as though she had caught her own eye, and was embarrassed and discomfited. She listened with derision to her glib and sugary banalities of speech. 'The perfect companion!' taunted the hostile self. 'What about all those fine big truths and principles we reasoned out together? Yesterday we believed you were sincere. *"Nice and hot after the journey."* Bah!'

The mirror in the overmantel now fascinated Mrs Tottenham. She finished her tea mechanically, laid her cup down and stood before the fireplace, patting and tweaking at her hair. Her husband looked at her contemptuously. 'Pretty little daughter I've got!' he mumbled, with his mouth full of cake. It was a bitter comment on the mistake made by the gentleman at the Hydro.

Mrs Tottenham put her hands before her face and hurried from the room.

Lydia began to gather up the tea things, and a servant darkened the windows with a musty clatter of Venetian blinds. Mr Tottenham's chair creaked as he stretched his legs out to the fire. The room was hot with the smell of tea and tea-cakes, and the smell of upholstery and wilting ferns was drawn out by the heat.

The hall outside was cold and quiet. The sense of the afternoon's invasion had subsided from it like a storm. Through a strip of door the morning-room beckoned her with its associations of the last six weeks. She saw the tall uncurtained windows grey-white in the gloom.

Her book lay open on a table: she shut it with a sense of desolation. It would never be finished now, it was too good a thing to read while *they* were in the house; to be punctuated by *her* petulant insistent chatter, *his* little shuffling, furtive steps. If only this room were all her own: inviolable. She could leave the rest of the house to them, to mar and bully, if she had only a few feet of silence of her own, to exclude the world from, to build up in something of herself.

If she did not go upstairs now Mrs Tottenham would call her, and that, in this room, would be more than she could bear. Vaguely she pictured headlines: '"Laurels" Murder Mystery. Bodies in a Cistern. Disappearance of Companion.' The darkness was all lurid with her visionary crime.

Mrs Tottenham had not been round the house. She did not say the rooms smelt mouldy, and she left the curtain-draperies alone.

Lydia wondered deeply.

'Did you know Sevenoaks?'

The question abashed her. What had Mrs Tottenham to do with Sevenoaks?

'N – no. Scarcely. I've been over there sometimes for the day, from Orpington.'

'A friend of mine lives there – a Mr Merton. He wrote to me today. He's come back from the Colonies and bought a place there. It's funny to hear from an old friend, suddenly. It makes me feel quite funny, really.'

She did not sound funny. Her voice was high-pitched with agitation. Lydia had been told all about Mrs Tottenham's friends, and seldom listened. But she did not remember Mr Merton.

'He wants to come and see us. I really hardly like, you know, to suggest the idea to Mr Tottenham.'

'I thought you'd all your friends in common. How well these night-dresses have washed! They must have laundered nicely at the Hydro.'

'Ah, but this is different, you see.' She laughed a little conscious laugh. 'Mr Merton was a particular *friend* of mine. I – Mr Tottenham didn't used to know him.'

'I see,' said Lydia vaguely. 'A friend of yours before your marriage.'

'Well, no. You see, I was very young when I was married. Quite an inexperienced young girl – a child, you might almost say.'

Lydia supposed that Mrs Tottenham *had* been young. She strained her imagination to the effort.

'I did very well for myself when I married Mr Tottenham,' the wife said sharply. 'I must say I never was a fool. My mother'd never brought me up to go about, but we did a good deal of entertaining at one time, Mr Tottenham's friends and my own, and we always had things very nice and showy. But it was a lonely life.'

Mrs Tottenham's confidences were intolerable. Better a hundred times that she should nag.

'So you liked the Hydro – found it really comfortable?'

'Oh yes, But it's the coming back – to this . . . Lydia, you're a good sort of girl. I wonder if I ought to tell you.'

'Don't tell me anything you would regret,' said Lydia defensively, jerking at the drawer-handles.

'You see, Mr Merton was a good deal to me at one time; then we tore it, and he went off to Canada and married there. I heard he'd been unhappy, and that there was the rumour of a split. Of course he didn't write or anything; we had ab-so-lutely *torn* it; but I couldn't help hearing things, and she seems to have been a really bad sort of woman – there were children, too. He's bringing the children back with him to Sevenoaks.

'He wants to come and see me. He's been thinking about me a great deal, he says, and wondering if I've changed, and wishing – He always was a straight sort of man; it was only circumstances drove him crooked. I daresay I was a good bit to blame. I've kept his photograph, though I know I didn't ought, but I liked having it by me to look at.'

She had unlocked a drawer and held a stiff-backed photograph up beneath the light, scrutinizing it. Lydia listened to a distant surge of movement in the house beneath her; steps across the oil-cloth, windows shutting, voices cut off by the swinging of a door. She felt, revoltedly, as though Mrs Tottenham were stepping out of her clothes.

'He says he's hardly changed at all. Seventeen years – they go past you like a flash, he says, when you're working.'

'Seventeen years,' said Lydia deliberately, 'are bound to make a difference to a woman. Did you care for him?'

Mrs Tottenham made no answer; she was staring at the photograph. Her eyes dilated, and she licked her lips.

'I suppose you'll be glad to see him again?' suggested Lydia. She felt suddenly alert and interested, as though she were watching through the lens of a microscope some tortured insect twirling on a pin.

Mrs Tottenham sat down stiffly on the sofa, and laid the photo on her lap. Suddenly she clasped her hands and put them up before her eyes.

'I couldn't,' she gasped. 'Not after all these years I couldn't. Not like this. O Lord, I've got so ugly! I can't pretend – I haven't got the heart to risk it. It's been so real to me, I couldn't bear to lose him.

'It's all gone, it's all gone. I've been pretending. I used to be a fine figure of a woman. How can I have the heart to care when I couldn't keep him caring?'

'You broke it off. It was all over and done with, you told me so. It was wrong, besides. Why should either of you want to rake it up when it was all past and done with seventeen years ago?'

'Because it *was* wrong. It's this awful *rightness* that's killing me. My husband's been a bad man, too, but here we both are, smirking and grinning at each other, just to keep hold of something we neither of us want.'

Lydia was terrified by the dry, swift sobbing. She felt suddenly hard and priggish and immature. All her stresses, her fears and passions, were such twilight things.

Mrs Tottenham stood upright and held the photograph in the flame of the gas jet, watching the ends curl upwards. For all her frizzled hair and jingling ornaments and smudgy tentative cosmetics she was suddenly elemental and heroic.

It was over.

Lydia went quietly out of the room and shut the door behind her.

The place was vibrant with the humanity of Mrs Tottenham. It was as though a child had been born in the house.

The Confidante

'You are losing your imagination,' cried Maurice.

It was a bitter reproach. He stood over her, rumpling up his hair, and the wiry tufts sprang upright, quivering from his scalp.

Penelope gulped, then sat for a moment in a silence full of the consciousness of her brutality. She had never dreamed that her secret preoccupation would be so perceptible to Maurice. Unconsciously she had been drawing her imaginations in upon herself like the petals of a flower, and her emotions buzzed and throbbed within them like a pent-up bee.

The room was dark with rain, and they heard the drip and rustle of leaves in the drinking garden. Through the open window the warm, wet air blew in on them, and a shimmer of rain was visible against the trees beyond.

'I never meant — ' began Penelope.

'I beg your pardon,' said Maurice stiffly. 'I suppose I am becoming quite insufferable. I have been making perfectly unjustifiable demands on your sympathy and patience and – imagination. I am an egotistical brute, I daresay. Of course there is not the slightest reason why you — ' His indulgence intimated that there was, on the contrary, every reason why she should . . . 'I felt a bit *jarred* just now,' he excused himself, with simple pathos.

'I never meant , a bit — ' resumed Penelope.

'I know, I know,' said Maurice, all magnanimity. The sickly sweetness of this reconciliation overpowered her.

'What a pair of fools we are!' she cried hysterically. 'Maurice, dear, we're wearing this thing thin. I'm afraid I've been doing gallery to you and Veronica for the last six months, and you've both played up to me magnificently. But — '

'Veronica — ' protested Maurice.

'Oh, yes, Veronica comes here too. She comes and sits for hours over there, just where you are now. There's not an aspect of your emotional relationship that we've not discussed. Veronica's coming here this afternoon,' she said abruptly. 'She's a chilly person. I'd better light the fire.'

'God!' said Maurice.

Penelope was on her knees before the fireplace, her head almost inside the grate. Her voice came hollowly from the dark recess.

'I thought you'd be surprised,' she said. ('Damn, it will *not* light!')

'Surprised!' said Maurice. 'Penelope' – his tone had the deadly reasonableness of a driven man's – 'I think you hardly realize what you're doing. I know you meant well, my good girl, but really — It puts us in such an impossible position. Surely you must see.'

'I see quite well,' she assured him. 'You and she both breathe and have your being in an atmosphere of conspiracy; it's your natural element, of course. To force you into the straighter, broader courses of the uncomplex would be as cruel as to upset a bowl with goldfish in it and leave them gasping on the tablecloth. Ooh!' She sat back on her heels and ruefully beheld her grimy fingers.

Maurice tried his hardest to endure her. She heard him breathing heavily.

'It's really quite *unnecessary* to have a fire,' she soliloquized. 'But it makes a point in a room, I always think. Keeps one in countenance. Humanizes things a bit. Makes a centre point for — '

She became incoherent. Maurice's irritation audibly increased. They were both conscious of the oppression of the darkening, rain-loud room.

'You're forcing our hands rather,' said Maurice.

'Forcing you into the banality of meeting each other sanely and normally in my drawing-room, with no necessity to converse in allusions, insinuations, and *double entendres*? With me blessing you both and beaming sympathetically on you from afar? Bullying you into that? . . .

'I'm sorry!' she flashed round on him, impenitently.

'You don't understand,' he winced, and looked round him for his hat. 'I think it would be best for me to go.'

'I suppose I mustn't keep you,' she conceded with polite reluctance. 'But I think you really ought to see Veronica. She has – she will have something of particular importance to say to you. I shall go, of course.'

'Oh, don't!'

'But surely — ?'

'There's nothing we can keep from you. And it makes it easier for both of us – as things are.'

'But do you never want to be alone with her?'

Maurice considered.

'I don't believe,' said Penelope, swiftly, 'that you two have ever been alone together for a second since your – acquaintanceship – began.'

'No,' said Maurice, sombrely. 'There have always been out-siders.'

'Audiences,' murmured Penelope.

'I beg your pardon?'

'Oh, nothing. Well, you'll be alone this afternoon. I'm going out,' she said with firmness.

'But don't you *understand*?'

'Oh, I understand the strain will be colossal – would have been. But there've been developments – suddenly. Veronica'll have a great deal to tell you. Has it never occurred to you she might get free after all? There'll be heaps to say,' she said, significantly.

'For heaven's sake — !' He threw up his hands again and paced the room in agitation, stumbling over stools.

'That was why I pulled up just now,' she continued. 'Seemed hard, perhaps, apathetic and unsympathetic when you were talking all that about awfulness, refined irony, frustration, and things. I was thinking how soon you'd – if you only knew — And then you told me I was losing my imagination.'

'For which I have already begged your pardon,' said Maurice, patiently.

Penelope rose from the hearthrug and threw herself on to the Chesterfield. Maurice turned to her with a goaded expression, and she regarded him with shining eyes. Then the door opened with a jerk, and Veronica entered stiffly, with a rustle of agitation.

Maurice drew back into the shadow, and Veronica hesitated for a moment in the centre of the room, then groped out her hands towards Penelope, as though she could see little in this sudden gloom.

'Tell me,' she cried, without preliminaries, 'you, you heard from Victor?'

Penelope, who had risen, glanced across at Maurice. He took his cue.

'Veronica!' he quavered huskily.

Veronica's shoulders twitched. She turned on him in the dusk like a wild thing, with an expression that was almost baleful.

'You!' she said.

'Er – yes,' admitted Maurice. 'I'd simply no idea that I should . . . I just came in. By chance, you know.'

'It's just as well, isn't it?' interposed Penelope. 'We've – you've simply got to talk things out, Veronica; tell him. Show him Victor's letter.' She moved towards the door.

'Don't go!' shrieked Veronica. 'You've got to explain to him. I can't,' she said, with the finality of helplessness.

The rain had stopped, and through a sudden break in the clouds the watery sunshine streamed across the garden. Veronica sat down on an ottoman facing the window, and Penelope knelt beside her, looking at her pitifully.

The long, pale oval of her face was marred and puckered by emotion, fair hair lay in streaks across her forehead, her clothes were glistening from the rain. Many tears had worn their mournful rivulets through the lavish powder on her nose. Her gloved hands lay across her lap, in one was clutched a sheet of blue-grey notepaper. She would not look at Maurice, but turned pathetic eyes on Penelope and made appeal with soundless moving lips.

'Veronica has had a letter from Victor,' said Penelope, slowly and distinctly. 'He releases her from her engagement. He says . . . he explains . . . He is not so blind as you both seem to have thought, and he has seen for some time that Veronica was not happy. He has noticed that she has been listless and preoccupied, and has interpreted her unhappiness – rightly! He is convinced, he says, that Veronica has ceased to care for him, but that she is too scrupulous, or not quite brave enough perhaps, to speak out and make an end of things herself. He knows that her affections are elsewhere, and he believes that he is doing the best thing he can for her by setting her free.'

Veronica had turned a little, and sat facing Maurice. Penelope saw the gold flicker of her lashes; the blue letter fluttered to the ground from between her writhing fingers.

'The trousseau was all bought,' she faltered. 'The going-away dress came from Pam's this morning, just before I got that letter.'

Penelope could not speak; she felt utterly inadequate. Maurice shifted his position; and stood leaning up against the window-frame; with intensity of interest he turned his head and looked into the garden.

'It's stopped raining,' he observed. Veronica did not move; but Penelope saw her eyes slide sideways, following his movements under drooping lids.

'How do you know all this,' Maurice asked abruptly, 'what Victor says and that, when you've had no time to read his letter?'

'He wrote to me, too,' said Penelope. She heard her own voice, self-conscious and defiant.

'To *you*! Why you?'

'But we know each other – rather well. Since much longer than he's known Veronica. And, well, you see I'm her cousin. He thought I'd make things easier for her. Do the explaining as far as possible. Probably he thought I'd speak to you.'

She stealthily touched her pocket and smiled to feel the crisp thick letter-paper crackle beneath her hand. Then she wondered if the sound were audible to the others, and glanced guiltily from one to the other of them. But they sat there silent, embarrassed, heavily preoccupied, one on either side of her.

'So now — ,' she said with bright aggressiveness. She could have shaken them.

'I do not think,' said Veronica, in a small determined voice, 'that I am justified in accepting Victor's sacrifice.'

'He is extraordinarily generous,' said Maurice, without enthusiasm.

'The loneliness,' went on Veronica, gazing wide-eyed down some terrible vista. 'Picture it, Penelope, the disappointment and the blankness for him. I could never have loved him, but I would have been a good wife to him.' (Her voice rose in a crescendo of surprise. She thought 'How genuine I am!') 'We – we had made so many plans,' she faltered; fumbled, found no handkerchief, and spread her hands before her face.

Penelope gave a little gasp, half sympathetic. She was praying hard for tact.

'Veronica,' she said, 'I don't think you should let that stand between you and Maurice. You mustn't be too soft-hearted, dear. I don't think Victor's altogether unhappy. He's relieved, I know. You see, the last few weeks have been an awful strain for him, as well as – other people.'

'How do you know?'

'He told me.'

'You've been discussing me. Oh, Penelope, this is intolerable!'

'He had been talking to me; he had no one else. For a long time, I suppose, he put me in the position of a sister-in-law.'

'That was going too far!' cried Maurice. 'Had you neither of you the slightest idea of loyalty to Veronica?'

Penelope ignored him. She leant suddenly forward, crimson-cheeked, and kissed Veronica.

'Oh, my dear,' she said, 'did you think that because you couldn't care about Victor nobody else could? Do you expect him to go on giving you everything when you've got nothing to give him?'

They looked at her, dazzled by a flash of comprehension. When she rose from between them she left a gap, a gap she knew to be unbridgeable for both. They were face to face with the hideous simplicity of life. She had upset their bowl and left the two poor goldfish gasping in an inclement air.

'Now at last you two have got each other,' she cried, smiling at them from the threshold. 'Nothing more to bother or disturb you. Just be as happy and as thankful as you can!'

They sat in silence till the last ironical echo died away. Then '*Don't go!*' they cried in unison.

But she was gone.

Requiescat

MAJENDIE had bought the villa on his honeymoon, and in April, three months after his death, his widow went out there alone to spend the spring and early summer. Stuart, who had been in India at the time of Howard Majendie's death, wrote to Mrs Majendie before starting for home and her reply awaited him at his club; he re-read it several times, looking curiously at her writing, which he had never seen before. The name of the villa was familiar to him, Majendie had been speaking of it the last time they dined together; he said it had a garden full of lemon trees and big cypresses, and more fountains than you could imagine – it was these that Ellaline had loved. Stuart pictured Mrs Majendie walking about among the lemon trees in her widow's black.

In her letter she expressed a wish to see him – in a little while. 'I shall be returning to England at the end of June; there is a good deal of business to go through, and there are several things that Howard wished me to discuss with you. He said you would be willing to advise and help me. I do not feel that I can face England before then; I have seen nobody yet, and it is difficult to make a beginning. You understand that I feel differently about meeting you; Howard wished it, and I think that is enough for both of us. If you were to be in Italy I should ask you to come and see me here, but as I know that you will be going straight to Ireland I will keep the papers until June, all except the very important ones, which I must sign without quite understanding, I suppose.' In concluding, she touched on his friendship with Howard as for her alone it was permissible to touch. Stuart wired his apologies to Ireland and planned a visit to the Italian lakes.

Three weeks afterwards found him in the prow of a motor-boat, furrowing Lake Como as he sped towards the villa. The sky was cloudless, the hills to the right rose sheer above him, casting the lengthening shadows of the afternoon across the luminous and oily water; to the left were brilliant and rugged above the clustered villages. The boat shot closely under Cadenabbia and set the orange-hooded craft bobbing; the reflected houses rocked and quivered in her wake, colours flecked the broken water.

'Subito, subito!' said the boatman reassuringly and Stuart started; he did not know that his impatience was so evident. The man shut off his engines, let the boat slide further into the shore, and displacing Stuart from the prow, crouched forward with a ready boat-hook. They were approaching the water-stairway of the villa.

For a few moments after he had landed, while the motor-boat went chuffing out again into the sunshine, Stuart stood at the top of the stairway looking irresolutely through the iron gates. He was wondering why he had come to Italy, and whether he even cared at all for Mrs Majendie. He felt incapable of making his way towards her under the clustered branches of those trees. If there had been a little side-gate it would have been easier to go in; it would not have been so difficult, either, if he had ever been here with Howard Majendie. But this was *Her* place; she had loved it because of the fountains.

He pushed open the big gate, already cold in the shadow, and followed the upward curve of the avenue among the lemon trees. Beyond the villa disclosed itself, unlike all that he had expected; he was surprised at his own suprise and did not realize till then how clearly he must have visualized it. There was a wide loggia, a flight of steps, a terrace on a level with the loggia running along the side of the hill. Cypress trees rose everywhere, breaking up the view. He passed under the windows, climbed the steps and crossed the loggia, not looking to left or right for fear that he might see her suddenly, or even one of her books. The loggia had an air of occupation; it was probable that on any of those tables, or among the cushions, he might see her book, half open, or the long-handled lorgnettes that Majendie had given her in France.

The servant said that Mrs Majendie was in the garden. She showed Stuart into a tall, cool parlour and disappeared to find her mistress. Stuart, distracted by a scent of heliotrope, made an un-seeing circle of the room; he was standing before a Florentine chest when the girl came back with a message. Mrs Majendie would see him in the garden. It would have been easier to meet her here; he had pictured them sitting opposite to one another in these high-backed chairs. He followed the girl obediently out of the house, along the terrace, and down a long alley between hedges of yew. The white plume of a fountain quivered at the end, other fountains were audible in the garden below. He could hear footsteps, too; someone was approaching by another alley that converged with his beyond the fountain. Here they met.

She was less beautiful than he had remembered her, and very tall and thin in her black dress. Her composure did not astonish him; her smile, undimmed, and the sound of her voice recalled to him the poignancy of his feelings when he had first known her, his resentment and sense of defeat – she had possessed herself of Howard so entirely. She was shortsighted, there was always a look of uncertainty in her eyes until she came quite near one, her big pupils seemed to see too much at once and nothing very plainly.

'I never knew you were in Italy,' she said.

He realized that it would have been more considerate to have written to prepare her for his visit.

'I came out,' he said, 'quite suddenly. I had always wanted to see the Lakes. And I wanted to see you, but perhaps I should have written. I – I never thought . . . It would have been better.'

'It doesn't matter. It was very good of you to come. I am glad that you should see the villa. Are you staying near?'

'Over at Varenna. How beautiful this is!'

'The lake?'

'I meant your garden.' They turned and walked slowly back towards the house. 'I hope I didn't take you too much by surprise?'

'Oh no,' she said. It almost seemed as though she had expected him. 'Yes, it is beautiful, isn't it? I have done nothing to it, it is exactly as we found it.'

They sat down on a stone bench on the terrace, looking a little away from one another; their minds were full of the essential things impossible to be said. Sitting there with her face turned away from him, every inch of her had that similitude of repose which covers tension. His lowered eyes took in her hands and long, thin fingers lying against the blackness of her dress. He remembered Howard telling him (among those confidences which had later ceased) how though he had fallen in love with the whole of her it was her hands that he first noticed when details began to detach themselves. Now they looked bewildered, helpless hands.

'I took you at your word,' he said; 'I wanted to help; I hoped there might be something I could do, and in your letter — '

'I took you at your word in asking for help. There is a great deal I must do, and you could make things easier for me, if you will. I shall be very grateful for your help about some business; there are papers I must sign and I don't understand them quite. There were things that Howard had never explained.' She looked full at him for a moment and he knew that this was the first time she had uttered her husband's name. It would be easier now.

'He had told me everything,' he said quickly, as though to intercept the shutting of a door. 'I was always to be there if you should need me – I had promised him.' She must realize that she owed him nothing for the fulfilment of a duty. He thought she did, for she was silent, uttering no word of thanks.

'Why did you so seldom come and see us?' she asked suddenly. 'Howard had begun to notice lately, and he wondered.'

'I was in India.'

'Before you went to India.' A little inflection in her voice made him despise his evasion.

'There is a time for all things, and that was a time for keeping away.'

'Because he was married?'

Stuart did not answer.

'We wanted you,' she said, 'but you didn't understand, did you?'

She did not understand, how could she? She must have discussed it all, those evenings, with the Majendie that belonged to her; he had not understood either.

'I was mistaken, I suppose,' he said. 'I – I should have learnt later.'

There was a slight contraction of her fingers, and Stuart knew that he had hurt her. If he hurt her like this a little more, it would probably be possible to kill her; she was very defenceless here in the garden that Majendie had bought her, looking out at the unmeaning lake. He had crowded out all tenderness for her, and her loneliness was nothing but a fact to him.

'There were messages for you,' she said, turning her head again.

'Were there?'

'He said — ,' her lips moved, she glanced at him a little apprehensively and was silent. 'I have written down everything that he said for you. And I believe he left you a letter.'

'Can you remember the messages?' he asked curiously.

'I wrote them down; I have them in the house.' She looked at him again with that short-sighted intensity; she knew every word of the messages, and with an effort he could almost have read them from her eyes.

'Did he expect to see me?'

'Yes, once he knew that he was ill. He knew that you could not possibly leave India before April, but he kept on – expecting. I wanted to cable to you and he wouldn't let me. But I know he still believed, above all reason, that you'd come.'

'If I'd known, if — '

'You think I should have cabled without telling him?' She thought he blamed her and she evidently feared his anger. Curious . . . He had been so conscious of her indifference, before; he had been a person who did not matter, the nice friend, the family dog – relegated. It was that that had stung and stung. After all he need never have gone to India, it had been a resource of panic. It had saved him nothing, and there had been no question of saving *her*. He wondered why she had not cabled; it was nothing to her whether he went or came, and Howard's happiness was everything.

'Yes, I wonder you didn't cable.'

'I am sorry; I was incapable of anything. My resource was – sapped.'

He looked at her keenly; it was a doctor's look.

'What have you been doing since?' he asked (as the medical man, to whom no ground was sacred). 'What are you going to do?'

'I was writing letters, shutting up the house. And here I'm trying to realize that there's nothing more to do, that matters. And afterwards — '

'Well?'

'I don't know,' she said wearily; 'I'd rather not, please . . . Afterwards will come of itself.'

He smiled as now he took upon himself the brother-in-law, the nice, kind, doggy person. 'You should have somebody with you, Ellaline. You should, you owe it to yourself, you owe it to' – he realized there was no one else to whom she owed it – 'to yourself,' he repeated. 'You must think, you must be wise for yourself now.'

She looked, half-smiling, at him while he counselled. He had never achieved the fraternal so completely.

'It's not that I don't think,' she said. 'I think a great deal. And as for wisdom – there is not much more to learn once one has grown up. I am as wise as I need be – "for myself." '

'When are you going back to England?'

'If you would do one or two things for me I needn't go back until the autumn.'

'You can't stay here all the summer.'

'No,' she said, looking round at the cypresses – how pitiful she was, in Howard's garden. 'They say I couldn't, it would be too hot; I must go somewhere else. But if you could help me a little this autumn I could finish up the business then.'

'I may have to be in Ireland then.' He tore himself away from something brutally, and the brutality sounded in his voice.

She retreated.

'Of course,' she said, 'I know you ought to be there now – I was forgetting.'

Because he was a person who barely existed for her (probably) she had always been gentle with him, almost propitiatory. One must be gentle with the nice old dog. It was not in her nature to be always gentle, perhaps she had said bitter things to Howard who mattered to her; there was a hint of bitterness about her mouth. At himself she was always looking in that vague, half-startled way, as though she had forgotten who he was. Sometimes when he made a third he had found her very silent, still with boredom; once or twice he had felt with gratification that she almost disliked him. He wondered what she thought he thought of her.

Now it was the time of the Angelus, and bells answered one another from the campaniles of the clustered villages across the lake. A steamer, still gold in the sun, cleft a long bright furrow in the shadowy water. The scene had all the passionless clarity of a Victorian water-colour.

'It is very peaceful,' Stuart said appropriately.

'Peaceful?' she echoed with a start. 'Yes, it's very peaceful . . . David' (she had called him this), 'will you forgive me?'

'Forgive you?'

'I think you could understand me if you wished to. Forgive me the harm I've done you. Don't, don't hate me.'

How weak she was now, how she had come down! 'What harm have you done to me?' he asked, unmoved.

'You should know better than I do. I suppose I must have hurt you, and through you, Howard. An – an intrusion isn't a happy thing. You didn't give me a chance to make it happy. You came at first, but there was always a cloud. I didn't want to interfere, I tried to play the game. Now that we've both lost him, couldn't you forgive?'

'I'm sorry I should have given you the impression that I resented anything – that there was anything to resent. I didn't know that you were thinking that. Perhaps you rather ran away with a pre-conceived idea that because you married Howard I was bound to be unfriendly to you. If you did, you never showed it. I never imagined that I had disappointed you by anything I did or didn't do.'

'It was not what you didn't do, it was what you *weren't* that made me feel I was a failure.' (So *that* was the matter, he had hurt her vanity!)

'A failure,' he said, laughing a little; 'I thought you were making a success. If I didn't come oftener it was not because I did not think you wanted me.'

'But you said just now — '

'A third is never really wanted. I had set my heart on seeing Howard happy, and when I had, I went away to think about it.'

'Oh,' she said hopelessly. She had guessed that he was putting her off. 'Shall we walk a little down the terrace? There is a pergola above, too, that I should like you to see.' She was taking for granted that he would not come to the villa again.

They rose; she stood for a moment looking irresolutely up and down the terrace, then took a steeper path that mounted through the trees towards the pergola. Stuart followed her in silence, wondering. The world in her brain was a mystery to him, but evidently he had passed across it and cast some shadows. For a moment he almost dared to speak, and trouble the peace of the garden with what had been pent up in him so long; then he knew that he must leave her to live out her days in the immunity of finished grief. The silence of imperfect sympathy would still lie between them, as it had always lain; his harshness could no longer cast a shadow in her world, that was now as sunless as an evening garden. His lips were sealed still, and for ever, by fear of her and shame for his dead loyalty to Howard. The generosity of love had turned to bitterness within him, and he was silent from no fear to cause her pain.

'Beautiful,' he said, when they reached the pergola and could look down on lake and garden through the clustered roses.

'Will you be long at Varenna?'

'I don't expect so, no. Some friends want me to join them on Lake Maggiore, and I think of going on tomorrow afternoon.'

'That will be better,' she said slowly. 'It *is* lonely seeing places alone – they hardly seem worth while.'

'I'm used to it – I'm going back to India in six months,' he said abruptly.

'Oh, I didn't know.' Her voice faltered. He had not known himself till then. Her face was whiter than ever in the dusk of the pergola, and her hands were plucking, plucking at the creepers, shaking down from the roses above white petals which he kept brushing from his coat.

'I'm sorry you're going back,' she said. 'Everybody will be sorry.'

'I won't go until I have finished everything that I can do for you.'

An expression came into her eyes that he had never seen before. 'You have been a friend,' she said. 'Men make better things for themselves out of life than we do.'

'They don't last,' he said involuntarily.

'I should have said that so far as anything is immortal — ' He watched a little tightening of her lips.

'It takes less than you think to kill these things; friendship, loyalty — '

'Yours was unassailable, yours and his'; she spoke more to herself than to him. 'In those early days when we three went about together; that time in France, I realized that.'

'In France?' he said stupidly.

'Yes. Don't you remember?'

He remembered France; the days they had spent together, and the long evenings in starlight, and the evening he had strolled beside her on a terrace while Majendie tinkered with the car. It was a chilly evening, and she kept drawing her furs together and said very little. The night after, he had lain awake listening to her voice and Majendie's in the next room, and making up his mind to go to India.

'Yes,' he said. 'Now, will you let me have the papers and we could go through them now? I could take any that are urgent back to town with me; I shall be there in a week.'

She twisted her hands irresolutely. 'Could you come tomorrow, before you go? I would have them ready for you then, if you can spare the time. I'm tired this evening; I don't believe I would be able to understand them. Do you mind?'

'No, of course not. But may I come in the morning? I am going away early in the afternoon.'

She nodded slowly, looked away from him and did not speak. She was evidently very much tired.

'I think I ought to go,' he said after a pause.

'If you hurried you could catch that steamer down at Cadenabbia.'

'Then I'll hurry. Don't come down.'

'I won't come down,' she said, holding out her hand. 'Good-bye, and thank you.'

He hurried to the end of the pergola, hesitated, half turned his head, and stopped irresolutely. Surely she had called him? He listened, but there was no sound. She stood where he had left her, with her back towards him, leaning against a pillar and looking out across the lake.

Turning, he pushed his way between the branches, down the overgrown path. The leaves rustled, he listened again; somebody was trying to detain him. As the slope grew steeper he quickened his steps to a run, and, skirting the terrace, took a short cut on to the avenue. Soon the lake glittered through the iron gates.

She leant back against the pillar, gripping in handfuls the branches of the climbing rose. She heard his descending footsteps hesitate for a long second, gather speed, grow fainter, die away. The thorns ran deep into her hands and she was dimly conscious of the pain. Far below the gate clanged, down among the trees. The branches of the roses shook a little, and more white petals came fluttering down.

All Saints

THE Vicar moved about the chancel in his cassock, thoughtfully extinguishing the candles. Evensong was over, and the ladies who had composed the congregation pattered down the aisle and melted away into the November dusk. At the back of the church some-body was still kneeling; the Vicar knew that it was the emotional-looking lady in black waiting to speak to him as he came down to the vestry; he feared this might be a matter for the confessional and that she might weep. The church was growing very dark; her black draperies uncertainly detached themselves from the shadows under the gallery. As he came down towards her, her white face looked up at him, she made a rustling movement and half rose. A curious perfume diffused itself around her, through the chilly mustiness of the pew.

She murmured a request; the Vicar bowed his head. 'I will wait for you in the church porch,' she said in a clear voice with a suggestion of a tremolo. 'Perhaps we could walk across the church-yard?'

He hurried to the vestry with the sense of a reprieve.

She was waiting in the porch with her hands clasped, and smiled anxiously at the Vicar, who turned to lock the door behind him.

'Such a beautiful church!' she said as they walked on together.

'We consider it very beautiful.'

'How the people must love it.' Her manner was very childlike; she half turned to him, shyly, then turned away.

'Would you like another window?'

'A window?'

'A coloured window for the Lady Chapel. I would love to give you a window.' She made the offer so simply that the Vicar felt as though he was being offered a kitten.

'But my dear lady, windows like that are very expensive.'

'I know,' she said eagerly, 'but I would be quite able to afford one.'

'A – a memorial window?'

'Memorial?'

'Of some relation or dear friend who has passed over?'

'Oh no,' she said vaguely, 'I know so many people who have died, but I think none of them would care about a window.'

'Then you have no particular purpose?'

'I think coloured windows are so beautiful. They make one feel so religious and good.'

The Vicar was nonplussed; he wished to say a great deal to her but did not know how to begin. Her ingenuousness half touched and half offended him. She was not young, either; he could hardly explain her to himself as young. Yet standing up so straight among the slanting tombstones she had no congruity with the year's decline; the monotone of twilight, the sullen evening with its colourless falling leaves rejected her; she was not elderly, he thought. She was perennial, there was that about her that displeased the Vicar; she was theatrical. Having placed her, he felt more at ease.

He said: 'I will place your very kind offer before the Vestry,' and took a few steps in the direction of the lych-gate. She looked up at him with fine eyes that she had once learnt how to use; she was so little conscious of the Vicar's masculinity that he might have been one of the tombstones, but eyes that have learnt their lesson never forget.

'Must you go at once?' she said pathetically. 'I want to talk a little more about the window. I would like to go and look from outside at the place where it is going to be.'

They retraced their steps a little and took a path that skirted the north side of the church and passed underneath the two east windows.

'I know you are not a resident,' said the Vicar. Still a diffident man, he disliked these inquiries; however oblique, they savoured too strongly of parsonic officiousness. But still, one ought to know.

'Do you think of paying us a long visit? The country is hardly at its best just now. Do you like the village?'

'I think the village is sweet – it does appeal to me. So quaint and homely. I am staying here in lodgings; they are most uncomfortable, but I sleep well, and the eggs are fresh. And then I love the country. My real name is Mrs Barrows.'

'Do you intend a long stay?' repeated the Vicar trying not to feel that her last sentence was peculiar.

'I want to watch them putting up the window. After that, I don't know. I don't think I could bear to be long away from London. Perhaps I might buy a cottage here, if you would help me.'

Evidently she was a person of means.

'This is the Lady Chapel window,' said the Vicar suddenly.

'Oh,' she cried in consternation. 'I did not know it was so small. We must make it larger – I think this would never hold them.'

'Hold whom?'

'All Saints – I want it to be an All Saints window. I went to church last Thursday; I heard the bells ringing and went in to see. I thought perhaps it was a wedding. I found a service, so I stayed, and you were preaching an All Saints Day sermon. It was beautiful; it gave me the idea. You said "called to be saints" was meant for all of us; I'd never heard of that idea. I'd thought the saints were over long ago; I'd seen old pictures of them when I was a child. I thought yours was a beautiful idea. It helped me so.'

'It is not only an *idea*, it is quite true.'

'I know. But it was beautiful of you to think of it.'

'Oh dear, oh dear, oh dear,' said the Vicar, half aloud.

'But then, of course, I supposed there must still be saints. And I thought of two or three people, then of quite a number. Ladies I have met, who have affected me – most strongly – and one dear boy I know — '

'We have most of us been privileged — '

'Don't you think,' she said, with round eyes, 'that saints must often seem quite unconventional?'

'In so far as conventionality is error – yes.'

'There,' she cried, 'I knew you'd agree with me. Wouldn't you describe a saint as somebody who, going ahead by their own light — '

'By a light that is given them — '

'That's what I meant – doesn't care what anybody says and helps other people; really makes it possible for other people to go on living?'

'Well, yes.' The Vicar hesitated over this definition.

'Don't saints seem always very strong?'

'There is a great strength in them, but there is weakness too; they have a great deal in themselves to combat before — '

'Before they can fight other people's battles.'

'Nobody can fight another's battle! We have got to fight our battles for ourselves – against ourselves.'

'Oh,' she said a little flatly, 'now that wasn't my idea. When I'm in a difficulty, or even in the blues, I just go to one of these friends of mine and talk it out, and, well, it's quite extraordinary the difference I feel. I see light at once. It's as if they took a burden off my shoulders.'

'There is only One who can do that. Can't you try and get straight to the Divine?'

Her voice out of the darkness – it was now very dark – sounded lonely and bewildered.

'No, I don't seem to want to. You see, I'm not at all good.'

'All the more reason — '

She ignored the interruption. 'It's power; that's what some people have; they're what I call good people – saints. And you know, these friends I was talking about; they're not at all conventional and they never go to church, except, perhaps, to weddings. And one or two of them are – oh, *very* unconventional. You'd be surprised.'

They walked across the churchyard, just able to see the path by the reflected light on the wet flagstones. The Vicar tried to help her: 'And you find that contact with certain personalities brings with it healing and invigoration?'

She grasped eagerly at the phrase. 'Healing and invigoration, yes, that's what I mean. It isn't anything to do with love or friendship. When I was younger I thought that loving people was meant to help one; it led me – oh, so wrong. Loving is only giving, isn't it? Just a sort of luxury, like giving this window. It doesn't do you any good, or the person either. But people like — ' – she named a notorious lady – 'I can't tell you how she's helped me. She's so brave, nobody seems too bad for her. She never despises you. And I've another friend who is a spiritualist.'

'Error!'

'She told me all about myself; she was so wonderful, her eyes went through and through. She said, "You're going the wrong way," and then it all came to me. She helped me so. And another who was a missionary's wife — '

This seemed simpler, but he wondered what he could get at behind it all.

'She didn't live with him. She had met him first at a revivalist meeting; she said he was too wonderful, but he couldn't have been as wonderful as her. She used to come and see me in the mornings, when I was in bed; I was very lonely then, a dear friend and I had just parted. She never talked religion, but there was something wonderful about her face.'

'And all this has really helped you? Force of example — '

'I don't want to copy them: I only want to know they're there.'

'What holds you in them isn't of themselves.'

'Isn't it?'

'It's simply a manifestation.'

She failed to understand him.

'They are able to help you – that is their privilege and God's will. But they can't do everything.'

'They do, you see; they see I can't do anything to help myself, and I suppose there must be a great many other people like me. They get at something I can't reach and hand it down to me – I could put it like that, couldn't I? That's what saints have always done, it seems to me.'

'Nobody was ever meant to be a go-between,' he said with energy. 'You've simply no conception — '

'I get everything I want that way,' she said placidly. 'I'm a very weak sort of person, I only want to be helped. Saints are the sort of people who've been always helping people like me; I thought I'd like to put up a window as a sort of thank-offering to them. Crowds and crowds of people I wanted to put in, all with those yellow circles round their heads, dressed in blue and violet – I think violet's such a beautiful colour. And one big figure in the foreground, just to look like helpfulness, holding out both hands with the look I've sometimes seen on people's faces. When can I know for sure about the window? I mean, when will you tell me if they'll let me put it up?'

'I don't know,' said the Vicar, agitatedly, hurrying towards the lych-gate and holding it open for her to pass through. 'I'll come round and see you about it. Yes, I know the house.'

'Oh, would you?' she said, shyly. 'Well, that would be kind. You know, talking about helpfulness, you're one of that sort of people. You don't know what it's meant to me to hear you preaching. You'd hardly believe — '

'Good-night,' said the Vicar abruptly. He raised his hat, turned on his heel, and fled through the darkness . . .

The New House

COMING up the avenue in the February dusk he could see the flash and shimmer of firelight through the naked windows of the library. There was something unearthly in those squares of pulsing light that fretted the shadowy façade, and lent to the whole an air of pasteboard unreality.

The scrunch beneath his feet of the wet gravel brought his sister to the doorstep.

'*Herbert!*' she cried, 'oh, do come in and see it all. You've been such ages today – what *were* you doing?'

'Your messages,' he said; 'they delayed me. That stupid fellow at Billingham's had made a muddle over those window measurements for the blinds; I had to go over to the workshop and give the order personally.'

Standing in the hall, he was surprised to hear his voice ring out into spaciousness.

'I never realised how big it was,' he said with gratification. 'Why, Cicely, you're all in the dark. You might have lighted up and made the place look a bit more festive. It's all very well to *hear* how big one's house is, but I'd like to see it with my own eyes.'

'I'm sorry,' said Cicely; 'as a matter of fact I'd only just come in myself. I was out in the garden.'

'*Gardening?*'

'No. Just poking about. You never heard anything like the way the thrushes sing. I never knew before they could sing like that. Or perhaps I'd never had time to listen. And the snowdrops are coming out all along the kitchen garden border. Oh, Herbert — '

'I shouldn't have thought that a house-move was exactly the most leisurely time to listen to thrushes. But of course — !'

'But I *had* been working.'

His injured dignity was impenetrable, like a barrier of steel. She turned aside from it with a shrug.

'Come in and see what I have done. The library — *Janet!*' she called down a dark archway. 'Janet, *tea!* The master's in.'

Down the far end of the long room was an open fireplace. His chair was pushed up to the fire and an impromptu tea-table covered with newspaper had been set beside it. His books were stacked in piles against the walls, and their mustiness contested with the clean smell of scrubbed and naked boards.

'A nice room,' said Herbert. 'On Sunday I shall have a good long day at the picture-hanging. I can't have these windows, Cicely; they're quite indecent. Haven't you even got a dust sheet to pin up across them? Any tramp — '

'I'll see. There won't be much light, though, anyhow. The man was in today about the fittings, and he says they won't be able to turn the gas on at the main till tomorrow afternoon. We shall have to do our best by candlelight. I've got some ready.'

She folded paper into a spill and lighted a long row of candles, ranged in motley candlesticks along the chimney-piece.

'Tut-tut,' said Herbert. 'We shall find it very difficult to work. How tiresome these people are.'

'Yes,' said Cicely.

He resented her tone of detachment. She had blown out her spill and stood twisting the charred ends of paper between her fingers. Long streaks of hair had loosened themselves and hung across her forehead, her cheeks were smeared with dust, her tall thin figure drooped with weariness, but her eyes were shining in the firelight with a strange excitement.

She became conscious of his irritated scrutiny.

'I must be looking simply awful — '

'Yes,' said Herbert.

'I'd better try and tidy before tea.'

'Yes. If we *are* going to have tea. If it doesn't come at once I really can't be bothered. There's a great deal for me to do, and *I* can't afford to waste any time.'

He was a hungry man and peevish, having snatched a hasty and insufficient lunch. He thought that he detected a smile of indulgence as she raised her voice and shouted:

'Janet – *hurry!*'

They heard Janet stumbling up the three steps from the kitchen. She entered with the squat brown tea-pot, one hand splayed against her heart.

'Such a house!' she gasped. 'It's that unexpected, really it is!'

They ate in silence. All Herbert's old irritation with his sister surged up within him. She was such a vague, uncertain, feckless creature; the air of startled spirituality that had become her as a girl now sat grotesquely on her middle-aged uncomeliness. He contrasted her with the buxom Emily. Emily would have known how to make her brother comfortable. But, of course, Emily had married.

She spoke.

'I suppose I might take mother's furniture. It really is mine, isn't it? Just that little work-table, and the book-shelf, and the escritoire.'

'I don't see what you mean by "*take* it." It'll all be in the same rooms, in the same house as the rest. Of course, poor mother gave them to you. But I don't see how that makes any difference. I was thinking we might put that little escritoire in the drawing-room. It will look very well there.'

Cicely was silent.

Herbert brushed the crumbs out of the creases in his waistcoat.

'Poor mother,' he unctuously remarked.

'Come and see the house,' said Cicely – she was aware that her quick speech shattered what should have been a little silence sacred to the memory of the dead – 'come and see what you'd like to begin on, and what Janet and I had better do tomorrow. We got the bedrooms tidy, but your basin and jug are odd, I'm afraid. The cases of crockery haven't arrived yet —

'I haven't got a basin and jug at all,' she said defensively.

Every step of Herbert's through the disordered house was a step in a triumphal progress. Every echo from the tiles and naked boards derided and denied the memory of that small brick villa where he and Cicely had been born, where their mother's wedded life had begun and ended; that villa now empty and denuded, whose furniture looked so meagre in this spaciousness and height.

He carried a candlestick in either hand and raised them high above his head as he passed from room to room, peering round him into corners, looking up to moulded cornices and ceilings.

Standing in the big front bedroom he saw himself reflected in the mirrored doors of a vast portentous wardrobe, and beamed back at his beaming, curiously-shadowed face. Behind him he saw Cicely seat herself on the edge of the wire mattress, and place her candle carefully beside her on the floor. The mahogany bedroom suite loomed up round them out of the shadows. She sensed his radiant satisfaction with relief.

'It *is* a lovely house,' she said. 'Oh, Herbert, I do hope you're going to be happy!'

'I hope we both are,' he amended kindly. 'We must have some people staying, Cicely. The Jenkins, and that lot. Entertain a bit – after all, my dear girl, we can afford it now!'

He was glad when she did not seem to realize how their circumstances had bettered – it gave him the opportunity for emphatic reminders.

They passed out on to the landing, and stood looking down into the depths of the well-staircase.

'I'm sure mother did want us both to be happy,' said Cicely, peering over the banisters. Herbert felt eerily as though she were deferring to the opinion of some unseen presence below them in the darkness.

'Of course she wished us the best, poor mother,' He clattered a little ostentatiously past her down the stairs.

'She would have loved this house!' Her voice came softly after him, and he heard her limp hand slithering along the banister-rail.

'Damn the gas-man,' he muttered, feeling his way across the hall, where his candle-flames writhed and flickered in a draught. It was enough to give anyone the creeps, thus groping through an echoing, deserted house with a ghost-ridden, lackadaisical woman trailing at his heels. If only they'd had the gas on.

Cicely was a fool: he'd teach her!

At the root of his malaise was a suspicion that the house was sneering at him; that as he repudiated the small brick villa so the house repudiated him; that Cicely and the house had made a pact against him, shutting him out.

He was so bourgeois and no parvenu. He, Herbert Pilkington, was good enough for any house bought with his own well-earned money. He pushed savagely against the panels of the drawing-room door.

This was the largest room in the house. A pale light fell across the floor from the scoops of two great bow-windows, and there was a glimmer in the mirrors – fixtures – panelling the walls.

Herbert put down his candles and stood back in admiration.

'Next year,' he said, 'we will buy a grand piano; it would look well there, slanting out from that corner.

'The shutters – we ought to shut the shutters.' Fussily he wrestled with the catches. For all his middle-aged precision he was like a child delirious over some new toy.

'It needs children; it's a room for children,' said Cicely, when the clatter had subsided.

Something in her tone filled him with a sense of impropriety. She was gripping the edges of the chimney-piece and staring down into the grate. Her knuckles stood out white and strained.

'Herbert, Richard Evans wrote to me again yesterday. Today I answered him. I – I am going to be married.'

Sitting on the Chesterfield, Herbert scrutinized his boots. He heard his voice say:

'Who is going to see about the furniture?'

His mind grappled with something immeasurably far away.

Cicely repeated, 'I am going to be married.'

Suddenly it flashed across him: he was full of angry light.

'Married!' he shouted, '*Married – you!*'

'I thought it was too late,' she whispered, 'till quite lately. Then, when mother went, everything was broken up; this move came –

all my life I seem to have been tied up, fastened on to things and people. Why, even the way the furniture was arranged at No. 17 held me so that I couldn't get away. The way the chairs went in the sitting-room. And mother. Then, when I stayed behind to see the vans off; when I saw them taking down the overmantels, and your books went out, and the round table, and the sofa, I felt quite suddenly "I'm free." I said to myself, "If Richard asks me again — " But I thought he must be tired of asking me. I said, "If only he asks me again I can get away before this new house fastens on to me." '

With her stoop, her untidiness, her vagueness and confusion, her irritating streaks of mysticism, he wondered: Could any man find her desirable?

He remembered Richard Evans, thin and jerky and vaguely displeasing to his orderly mind; with his terrible spasms of eloquence and his straggly moustache. He had come in often when they were at No. 17 and sat for hours in the lamplight, with his shadow gesticulating behind him on the wall.

'Nobody needs me,' she was saying. 'Nobody wants me, really, except him. I see it now, and I've got to — '

'What about *me*? Don't *I* count? Don't *I* need you? What about all these years; the housekeeping?' His voice rose to a wail, 'and what the devil am I to do about the move?'

'Of course I'll see you through the move. Really, Herbert — '

'I've been a good brother to you. We've got along very well; we've had a happy little home together all these years, haven't we, and now poor mother's gone — '

His eloquence choked him. He was stabbed by the conviction that she should be saying all this to him. Instead she stood there, mulishly, hanging down her head.

'You're too old to marry,' he shouted; 'it's – it's *ridiculous!*'

'Richard doesn't think so.'

'You don't seem to realize you're leaving me alone with this great house on my hands, this great *barn* of a house; me a lonely man, with just that one silly old woman. I suppose Janet'll go off and get married next! Nobody's too old to marry nowadays, it seems.'

'No,' she said with placid conviction. 'You'll marry, of course.'

'*Marry – me?*'

She turned to look at him, pink, self-confident, idiotically pretty.

'But of course. That's what I've been feeling. While I was here — Men are so conservative! But this is no sort of life for you really, Herbert; you want a wife, a pretty, cheery wife. And children — '

'Children!'

'Oh, don't shout, Herbert. Yes, you don't want the family to die out, do you, after you've made such a name for it, done such fine big things?'

He felt that two springs were broken in the sofa, and pressed the cushions carefully with his hand to discover the extent of further damage.

'Damn it all,' he said querulously, 'I can't get used to another woman at my time of life!'

'Herbert, you've got no imagination.' Her tone was amused, dispassionate. She was suddenly superior, radiant and aloof; his no longer, another man's possession.

Her speech chimed in with his thoughts.

'Every man's got to have one woman!'

Taking one of the candles, she turned and left the room.

He sat there almost in the darkness; putting one hand up he fidgeted with his tie. Sleeking down his hair he smiled to find it crisp, unthinned and healthy.

Slowly and cumbrously the machinery of his imagination creaked into movement.

He saw the drawing-room suffused with rosy light. Chairs and sofas were bright with the sheen of flowered chintzes, hung about with crisp and fluted frills. Over by the fire was the dark triangle of a grand piano; the top was open and a woman, with bright crimpy hair, sat before it, playing and singing. 'A pretty, cheery wife.' There was a crimson carpet, soft like moss, and a tall palm shadowed up towards the ceiling. Muffled by the carpet he heard the patter of quick feet. The little girl wore a blue sash trailing down behind her, and there was a little boy in a black velvet suit. They could do very well without Cicely's escritoire.

Lunch

'AFTER all,' said Marcia, 'there are egoists and egoists. You are one sort of egoist, I am the other.'

A ladybird had dropped on to her plate from a cluster of leaves above, and she invited it on to her finger and transferred it very carefully to the rail of the verandah.

'Differentiate,' said the stranger, watching the progress of the ladybird.

They were lunching on the verandah, and the midday sun fell through a screen of leaves in quivering splashes on to the table-cloth, the elusive pattern of Marcia's dress, the crude enamelled brilliance of the salad in a willow-pattern bowl, the dinted plate and cutlery slanting together at angles of confusion. The water was spring water, so cold that a mist had formed on the sides of their tumblers and of the red glass water-jug. They considered helpings of cold lamb, and their heads and faces were in shadow.

Through the open window the interior of the coffee-room was murky and repellent; with its drab, dishevelled tables, and chairs so huddled *tête-à-tête* that they travestied intimacy. It was full of the musty reek of cruets and the wraiths of long-digested meals, and of a brooding reproach for their desertion whenever they turned their heads towards it. A mournful waitress, too, reproached them, flicking desultorily about among the crumbs.

From under the verandah the hotel garden slanted steeply down to the road; the burning dustiness beneath them was visible in glimpses between the branches of the lime trees. Cyclists flashed past, and an occasional motor whirled up clouds of dust to settle in the patient limes. Behind their screen of leaves they two sat sheltered and conversant, looking out to where, beyond the village, the country fell away into the hot blue distances of June, and cooled by a faint wind that crept towards them through a rustle and glitter of leaves from hay-fields and the heavy shade of elders.

The jewels flashed in Marcia's rings as she laid down knife and fork, and, drumming with her fingers on the table, proceeded to expatiate on egoists.

'Don't think I'm going to be clever,' she implored him, 'and talk like a woman in a Meredith book. Well, quite baldly to begin with, one acknowledges that one puts oneself first, doesn't one? There may be other people, but it's ourselves that matter.'

He had relaxed his face to a calm attentiveness, and, leaning limply back in his chair, looked at her with tired, kindly eyes, like the eyes of a monkey, between wrinkled lids.

'Granted, if you wish it for the sake of argument. But — '

'But you are protesting inwardly that the other people matter more? They do matter enormously. But the more they matter to you, still the more you're mattering to yourself; it merely raises your standard of values. Have you any children?'

'Six,' said the tired man.

'I have three,' said Marcia. 'And a husband. Quite enough, but I am very fond of them all. That is why I am always so glad to get away from them.'

He was cutting his lamb with quiet slashing strokes of his knife, and eating quickly and abstractedly, like a man whose habits of life have made food less an indulgence than a necessity. She believed that she was interesting him.

'My idea in life, my particular form of egoism, is a determination not to be swamped. I resent most fearfully, *not* the claims my family make on me, but the claims I make on my family. Theirs are a tribute to my indispensability, mine, a proof of my dependence. Therefore I am a perfectly charming woman, but quite extraordinarily selfish. That is how all my friends describe me. I admire their candour, but I never congratulate them on their perspicacity. My egoism is nothing if not blatant and unblushing.

'Now you go on!' she said encouragingly, helping herself to salad. 'Tell me about your selfishness, then I'll define how it's different from mine.'

He did not appear inspired.

'Yours is a much better kind,' she supplemented. 'Finer. You have given up everything but the thing that won't be given up. In fact, there's nothing wrong in your sort of egoism. It's only your self-consciousness that brings it to life at all. In the middle of your abject and terrible unselfishness you feel a tiny strain of resistance, and it worries you so much that it has rubbed it sore. It's mere morbidity on your part, that's what I condemn about it. Turn your family out into the street and carouse for a fortnight and you'll be a better man at the end of it. Mine is healthy animal spirits, mine is sheer exuberance; yours is a badgered, hectic, unavowed resistance to the people you love best in the world because, unknowingly, you still love yourself better.'

'You wouldn't know the meaning of healthy animal spirits with six children on my income. I suppose what you are trying to say about me, is . . . the turning of the worm?'

'No,' said Marcia, 'not exactly turning. I wonder if I am making a fool of myself? I don't believe you are an egoist at all. My ideas are beginning to desert me; I am really incapable of a sustained monologue on any subject under the sun. You see, generally I talk in circles; I mean, I say something cryptic, that sounds clever and stimulates the activities of other people's minds, and when the conversation has reached a climax of brilliancy I knock down my hammer, like an auctioneer, on somebody else's epigram, cap it with another, and smile round at them all with calm assurance and finality. By that time everybody is in a sort of glow, each believing that he or she has laid the largest and finest of the conversational eggs.

'Goodness, you've finished! Would you just call through the window and ask that woman if there's anything else to eat? She's been taking such an interest in our conversation and our profiles. Say strawberries if possible, because otherwise I have a premonition it will be blancmange.'

The stranger put his head and shoulders through the window. Marcia studied his narrow back in the shabby tweed jacket, his thinning hair and the frayed edges of his collar. One hand gripped the back of his chair; she thought, 'How terrible to see a man who isn't sunburnt.' She listened to his muffled conversation with the waitress, and pushed her plate away, deploring the oiliness of the salad.

With flushed face he reappeared, and two plump arms came through the window after him, removed their plates, and clattered on to the table a big bowl of strawberries and a small greyish blancmange in a thick glass dish.

'I wonder if I'm tiring you,' said Marcia remorsefully. 'I know you came out here to be quiet, and I've done nothing but sharpen my theories on you ever since we made common cause against the coffee-room – it *was* worth while, too, wasn't it? Never mind, I'll let you go directly after lunch, and you shall find the tranquillity you came to look for underneath a lime tree loud with bees. (I never take the slightest interest in Nature, but I always remember that touch about the bees. I came across it in a book.) I see a book in your pocket. If I wasn't here you'd be reading with it propped up against the water-jug, blissfully dipping your strawberries into the salt and wondering why they tasted so funny. But do let's eat them in our fingers, anyway. I never eat them with a spoon unless there's cream . . . My husband says he finds me too exhilarating for a prolonged *tête-à-tête*.'

He smiled at her with embarrassment, then leant his elbow on the warm rail of the verandah and looked down on to the road.

'It's so hot,' he said with sudden petulance, 'so beastly *hot*. I didn't realize how hot it was going to be or I wouldn't have bicycled out.'

'It's not very hot here, is it? Those leaves — '

'No, but I was thinking about the hotness everywhere else. This makes it worse.'

'Fancy *bicycling*. Do let me give you some blancmange; I think it is an heirloom. Did you come far?'

'From Lewisham.' He added, 'I work in a publisher's office.'

'A publisher – how interesting! I wonder if you could do anything to help a boy I know; such a charming boy! He has written a book, but — '

He flushed. 'I am not a – an influential member of the firm.'

'Oh, then, p'raps you couldn't. Tell me, why did you come here today? I mean why *here* specially?'

'Oh, for no reason. Just at random. Why did you?'

'To meet somebody who hasn't turned up. He was going to have brought a lunch-basket and we were to have picnicked down by the river. Oh, nobody I shouldn't meet. You haven't blundered into an elopement. I've got no brain for intrigue. After lunch we were going to have sketched – at least, he would have sketched and I should have talked. He's by way of teaching me. We were to have met at twelve, but I suppose he's forgotten or is doing something else. Probably he wired, but it hadn't come before I started.'

'Do you paint?'

'I've got a paint-box.' She indicated a diminutive Windsor and Newton and a large water-colour block lying at her feet.

'I'm sorry,' he said diffidently. 'I'm afraid this must be something of a disappointment.'

'Not a bit.' She clasped her hands on the table, leaning forward. 'I've really loved our lunch-party. You *listened*. I've met very few people who could really listen.'

'I've met very few people who were worth listening to.'

She raised her brows. Her shabby man was growing gallant.

'I am certain,' she smiled, 'that with your delicate perceptions of the romantic you would rather we remained incognito. Names and addresses are — '

'Banality.'

The leaves rustled and her muslins fluttered in a breath of warm wind. In silence they turned their faces out towards the distance.

'I love views,' she said, 'when there isn't anything to understand in them. There are no subtleties of emotion about June. She's so gloriously elemental. Not a month for self-justification, simply for self-abandonment.'

He turned towards her quickly, his whole face flushed and lighted up for speech.

With a grind and screech of brakes a big car drew up under the lime trees.

Marcia leaned over the verandah rail.

'*John*,' she cried. 'Oh, John!'

She reached out for her parasol and dived to gather up her sketching things.

'How late you are,' she called again, 'how *late* you are! Did you have a puncture, or what were you doing?'

She pushed back her chair with a grating sound along the tiled floor of the verandah, and stood looking down bright-eyed at his weary, passive, disillusioned face.

'I was right,' she said, 'there are two sorts of egoists, and I am both.'

The Lover

HERBERT PILKINGTON rang the electric bell and, taking a few steps back, looked up to contemplate the house-front. In the full glare of the westerly sun it all looked trim and orderly enough; Cicely had not done so badly for herself, after all, by marrying Richard Evans. Herbert congratulated himself on having foreseen the whole thing from the beginning and furthered it with tact and sympathy. Of course it had been difficult to get poor Cicely off . . . The hall-door was opened suddenly by Cicely's nervous little maid, who, flattening herself against the passage wall to allow of his entrance, contrived, by dodging suddenly under his arm, to reach the drawing-room door before him and fling it wide.

Richard and Cicely were discovered seated at opposite ends of the sofa and looking very conscious. Cicely wore a pink blouse; she looked prettier than Herbert could have imagined and curiously fluffy about the head. The white-walled drawing-room, dim in the ochreous twilight of drawn blinds, was hung with Richard's Italian water-colours and other pictorial mementos of the honeymoon; it smelt very strongly of varnish, and seemed to Herbert emptier than a drawing-room ought to be. The chairs and sofas had retreated into corners, they lacked frilliness; there was something just as startled and staccato about the room as there was about Cicely and Richard. Poor Mother and Dear Father eyed one another apprehensively from opposite walls; the very tick of the clock was hardly regular.

They always gave one a warm welcome; Cicely was quite effusive, and long Richard Evans got up and stood in front of the fireplace, delightedly kicking the fender.

'*Tea!*' commanded Cicely through the crack of the door; just as she had done at No. 17 and at the New House, during the few short months of her reign there.

'Hot day,' said Herbert, sitting down carefully.

'*Richard's* hot,' said Cicely proudly; 'he's been mowing the lawn.'

'Home early?'

'Well, yes. One must slack off a bit this weather.'

'Idle dog,' said Herbert archly.

'*Doesn't* being engaged agree with Herbert!' cried Cicely, slapping his knee. (She had never taken these liberties at No. 17.) 'Don't you feel wonderful, Herbert? Isn't it not like anything you ever felt before?'

Herbert ran one finger round the inside of his collar and smiled what Doris called his quizzical smile.

'Only three weeks more,' contributed Richard. 'And how's the trousseau getting on?'

'My trousseau?'

'Ha, ha! Hers, of course. My dear Herbert, those dressmaker women have got you in their fist. If they don't choose to let her have the clothes in time she'll put the whole thing off.'

Herbert was not to be alarmed. 'Oh, they'll hurry up,' he said easily. 'I'm making it worth their while. By Gad, Cicely, she does know how to dress.'

'They are most wonderful clothes – she is lucky, isn't she, Richard?'

Herbert beamed complacency. 'She deserves it all,' he said.

'I think she's getting handsomer every day.'

'Happiness does a good deal for us all,' said Herbert gallantly.

'By the way,' said Cicely, winking across at Richard (an accomplishment he must have taught her), 'look carefully round the room, Herbert, and see if you see anyone you know.'

Herbert, who had taken Richard's place on the sofa and was sitting with his hands in his pockets and his legs stretched out, turned his head as far as his collar would permit and made an elaborate inspection of the chimney-piece, the whatnot, the pianotop.

'Very well she looks up there, too,' he said, raising himself a little with arched back for a better view, then relapsing with a grunt of relief. He had seen what he expected, the portrait of his beloved looking out coyly at him from between two top-heavy vases. 'Where did you get that, Cicely?'

'She brought it round *herself*, the day before yesterday. She came in just before supper; I was out, but she stayed a long time talking to Richard. Oh, Richard, look at Herbert getting crimson with jealousy!' Herbert, who never changed colour except after meals or from violent exertion, beamed with gratification. 'Never mind, Herbert,' said Cicely, '*I'm* jealous, too, you see.'

Herbert was often irritated by the way that Richard and Cicely looked at one another across him. He did not enjoy the feeling of exclusion. But of course he and Doris would be able to look at each other across people just like that when *they* were married.

'Do bring it over here, Richard,' said Cicely, nodding at the portrait. 'I want to look at it again.' Tea was carried in, not noise-lessly, but quite unnoticed. The brother and sister were looking at the photograph. Herbert leant back, smiling at it with an absent and leisurely pride. Cicely bent forward in eager and short-sighted scrutiny. She seemed to be looking for something in it that she could not find.

A young lady with symmetrically puffed-out hair returned both regards from out of a silver frame with slightly bovine intensity. Her lips were bowed in an indulgent smile – perhaps the photo-grapher had been a funny man – a string of pearls closely encircled a long plump neck.

'She has framed it for you very handsomely,' said Herbert. 'I said to her when we were first engaged, "Never stint over a present when it is necessary" – I think that is so sound. "Of course I do not approve of giving indiscriminately," I said, "but when they must be given let them be handsome. It is agreeable to receive good presents, and to give them always makes a good impression."'

Cicely looked guilty; Richard had insisted on consigning the coal-scuttle that Herbert had given them to the darkest corner of the study.

'Doris always understands me perfectly,' continued Herbert, examining the frame to see if the price were still on the back. 'I think it will never be necessary for me to say anything to her twice. If I even express an opinion she always remembers. It's quite extra-ordinary.'

'Extraordinary,' echoed Richard. His voice had often an ironical note in it; this had prejudiced Herbert against him at first, he seemed rather a disagreeable fellow, but now Herbert knew that it did not mean anything at all. Richard, though not showy-looking, was really a good sort of chap.

Cicely, a little pink (or perhaps it was only the reflection from her blouse), drew up the tea-table and began pouring out. There was a short silence while Richard replaced the photograph; they heard two blue-bottles buzzing against the ceiling.

Richard hacked three-quarters of a new cake into slices, placed the plate invitingly at Herbert's elbow and sat down on a music-stool. Lifting his feet from the floor he rotated idly till Cicely passed him his cup, which he emptied in three or four gulps and put down, then sat gazing expectantly at his brother-in-law.

'Marriage is a wonderful thing,' said Herbert conversationally, recrossing his legs. 'Look at you two now, how comfortable you are. It's all been most successful.'

Cicely had never known till this moment whether Herbert really approved of them.

'The most surprising people,' he continued, 'make a success of matrimony. Of course, people have varying ideas of comfort; everybody does not understand this, therefore there have been, alas, unhappy marriages.'

'But the right people always find each other in the end,' said Cicely dreamily. 'You did sort of feel, didn't you, Herbert, when you first met Doris — '

'Women have these fancies' – Herbert was all indulgence for them – 'Doris has confessed to me that she was affected, quite extraordinarily affected, by our first meeting. It made little or no impression upon me. But Doris is a true woman.'

'What *is* a true woman?' asked Richard suddenly. Herbert thought it must be very uncomfortable to live with a person who asked these disconcerting, rather silly questions. He supposed Cicely was used to his ways. Cicely sat stirring her tea and smiling fatuously at her husband.

Herbert, after consideration, decided to turn the question lightly aside. 'I think we all know,' he said, '*when we find her*.' He wished Doris were sitting beside him instead of Cicely; he would have looked at her sideways and she would have been so much pleased. As it was, he looked across the table at the bread and butter, and Richard jumped up and offered him some more.

'Yes, but what does she *consist* of?' asked Richard excitedly, forgetting to put down the plate. Herbert was silent; he thought this sounded rather indelicate.

'*Sensibility*?' suggested Cicely.

'Infinite sensibility,' said Richard, 'and patience.'

'Contrariness,' added Cicely.

'Inconsistency,' amended Richard.

'Oh *no*. Contrariness, Richard, and weak will.'

Herbert looked from one to the other, supposing they were playing some sort of game.

'She is infinitely adaptable, too,' said Richard.

'She has to be, poor thing,' said Cicely (this did not come well from Cicely).

'Dear me, Cicely,' interposed Herbert, blinking; 'so you consider women are to be pitied, do you?'

Cicely opened her mouth and shut it again. She clasped her hands.

'This does not speak well for Richard,' said Herbert humorously. 'Doris would be much amused. Now I suppose *Doris* is to be pitied, isn't she?'

'Oh *no*, Herbert,' cried Cicely quickly.

'She doesn't seem unhappy. In fact, I believe there are very few young ladies Doris would change places with at present. And I think you are wrong, my dear Richard; I consider woman most consistent, if she is taught – and she can be easily taught. She is simpler and more child-like than we are, of course. Her way in life is simple; she is seldom placed in a position where it is necessary for her to think for herself. She need never dictate – except, of course, to servants, and there she's backed by her husband's authority. All women wish to marry.'

Richard and Cicely listened respectfully.

'A true woman,' continued Herbert, warming to his subject, 'loves to cling.'

'But she mustn't cling heavily, must she?' asked Cicely.

'She clings not only to her husband but in a lesser degree to her household and' – he coughed slightly – 'children. Her sphere — '

' – Is the home,' said Richard quickly. 'But suppose she hasn't got a home?'

'She may now hope till a quite advanced age to obtain a home by matrimony. If she cannot she must look for work. It is always possible for an unmarried woman to make herself useful if she is willing and' – he considered carefully – 'bright.'

'Do you like women to be bright?' asked Cicely eagerly.

'It depends,' said Herbert guardedly. He had hated Cicely when she was skittish; it had sat grotesquely upon her as a spinster, though now that she was married a little matronly playfulness did not ill become her. 'Doris is bright, bright and equable.'

Remembering with resentment how uncomfortable Cicely had sometimes made him, he raised his voice a little. 'She has no *moods*. She has simple tastes. She is always very bright and equable.'

'So you really suit each other very well,' summarized Richard, twirling on the music-stool. 'Appreciation is everything to a woman. I congratulate her.'

'Yes,' said Herbert simply. 'But you should congratulate *me* – it is more usual, I think. But we are past all that now; dear me, how many letters there were to answer! And now there are the presents to acknowledge. A very handsome inkstand and a pair of vases came this morning. And in another three weeks we shall be at Folkestone!' . . .

His sister and brother-in-law were so silent that he thought they must have gone to sleep. They were an erratic couple; matrimony seemed to have made them stupid. Richard sat biting his moustache and staring at Cicely, who, with bent head, absently smoothed out creases in the table cloth. One might almost have said they were waiting for him to go. It was curious how little of this he had suspected in Cicely, although she was his sister. In the evenings he knew that Richard and she read poetry together, and not improbably kissed; through the folding doors he could hear their cold supper being laid out in the dining-room. How could he have guessed that something inside her had been clamouring for these preposterous evenings all her life? She had seemed so contented, sewing by the lamp while he smoked and read the paper and Poor Mother dozed.

It was wasting pity to be sorry for them; he turned from his anaemic relations to review his long perspective of upholstered happiness with Doris. One might almost say that the upholstery *was* Doris. Herbert, feeling his heart grow great within him, could have written a testimonial to all the merchants of Romance. Having given love a trial he had found it excellent, and was prepared to recommend it personally, almost to offer a guarantee. Dear Doris would be waiting for him this evening; demure, responsive, decently elated; he was going to visit at her home. This intention he communicated to Richard and Cicely, who rose in vague and badly-feigned distress. Herbert had said nothing about *going*, as it happened, but since they had so understood him – well, they were scarcely entertaining; he had been there long enough.

They saw him to the gate and stood together under the laburnum tree, watching him down the road. Richard's arm crept round Cicely's shoulders. 'But this, ah God, is love!' he quoted.

And Herbert had forgotten them before he reached the corner.

Mrs Windermere

IN the doorway of Fullers', Regent Street, they came face to face. Mrs Windermere grasped both Esmée's wrists, drew them towards her bosom, and cried in her deep tremolo, '*My dear!*'

Esmée had not imagined Mrs Windermere out of Italy. She had never pictured that little pug-dog face without the background of flickering olives, or of velvety sun-gold walls, with cypresses dotted here and there like the exclamation-marks in the lady's conversation. Mrs Windermere now regarded her with intensity through the long fringes of her hat-brim. She said, 'The same Esmée!' and gently massaged the wrists with her thumbs.

'This is splendid,' said Esmée inadequately, conscious of a rising pinkness and of the long stream of outcoming ladies dammed by their encounter. 'What a funny coincidence!'

'God guided me, dearest!' Mrs Windermere always mentioned the Deity with confidential familiarity; one felt she had the entrée everywhere. 'I meant to have lunched at Stewart's.'

'I'm sorry you've *had* lunch.'

'I will have more,' said Mrs Windermere recklessly. They pushed their way upstairs and stood over a little table in the window while it was vacated. Esmée untwined the dangling parcels from her fingers and propped up her umbrella in a corner. Mrs Windermere scanned the menu with the detachment of the satiated, and Esmée confessed that she was hungry. 'Then it must be rissoles,' said her friend enticingly – 'little chicken rissoles. I will have a cup of chocolate and an *éclair*.' She gave the orders to the waitress and sat looking at Esmée and tapping a corner of the menu card against her mouth.

'But you don't live in town?'

'No,' said Esmée; 'I'm up for the day. You would have written, wouldn't you, if we hadn't met? I should have been so much disappointed if we'd never — '

'I hope to come and stay with you.'

'That will be lovely,' said Esmée, answering the smile. There was a moment's silence. 'Do you miss Italy?'

'Ye-es.' It was an absent answer; Mrs Windermere's thoughts

were concentrated elsewhere. 'There's something *strange* about you, child,' she said.

Esmée now remembered how her conversation had been always little rushing advances on the personal. She had a way of yawning reproachfully with a little click of the teeth and a 'Surely we two know each other too well to talk about the *weather*?' if one tried to give the conversation an outward twist. Esmée had found their first walks together very interesting, they had had the chilly, unusual, dream-familiar sense of walking in one's skin. 'There *is* something strange,' said Mrs Windermere.

'*You* look just the same as ever.'

'There's a stillness here,' said the other, slipping a hand beneath her fur. 'Like the stillness in the heart of the whirlwind. Get right into it, live in your most interior self, and you're unchangeable. You haven't found it yet; you're very young, you've never penetrated.'

'I don't think I have, perhaps,' said Esmée thoughtfully, under the returning influence of Italy. 'Perhaps I rather like *twirling*.'

'Ye-es,' said Mrs Windermere, leaning back in her chair. Her lustrous eyes looked out mournfully, contentedly, from under pouchy lids, through the long fringes of her hat; her *retroussé* nose was powdered delicately mauve, the very moist lips had a way of contracting quickly in the middle of a sentence in an un-puglike effort to retain the saliva. Curly bunches of grey hair lay against her cheeks, a string of Roman pearls was twisted several times round her plump throat; her furs were slung across her bosom and one shoulder; her every movement diffused an odour of Violet de Parme. She had not removed her gloves, and opulent rolls of white kid encircled wrist and forearm; her sleeves fell back from the elbow. She was an orthodox London edition of her Italian self.

'Twirling,' she repeated, narrowing her eyes. She looked round the mild, bright, crowded room, rustling with femininity, with its air of modest expensiveness. 'Simply twirling? How' – with an obvious connection of ideas – 'is your husband?'

'Very well indeed. He would like so much — ' Esmée could not picture Wilfred meeting Mrs Windermere. 'He would have liked to have come up with me today,' she concluded.

'Ye-es,' said the other, looking beyond at something. 'How did he ever come to let you go to Italy – alone?'

'I wasn't alone, though, was I? I was with Aunt Emma. Someone had to take her and I'd never travelled.'

'Spiritually, you *were* alone. You were alert, a-tiptoe, breathlessly expectant. *I* came – but it might not have been I! How did he come to let you go like that? Men of his type are not so generous.'

'But he isn't *that* type.'

The waitress brought the cup of chocolate, the *éclair* and the rissoles. Mrs Windermere stretched out across the dishes, gently disengaged the fork from Esmée's fingers, and turned her hand palm upwards on the table.

'That little hand told me everything,' she said. 'And do you know, child, you have his image at the back of your eyes. I *know* the type – little loyal person.'

'Wilfred likes me to travel,' said Esmée feebly. 'He finds me rather a tiresome companion when he wants to talk about places, and you see he never has time to take me abroad himself.'

'That was a very *young* marriage,' said Mrs Windermere, leaning forward suddenly.

'Oh. Do you think so?'

'But you're younger now, after four years of it. Warier, greedier, more *dynamic*. No children! – *never* to be any children?'

'I don't know.'

'So *wise* and yet *so* foolish.' She sipped delicately the hot chocolate, put the cup down, and once more slipped her hand under her fur. 'The Mother-heart,' she said, 'is here. It grows and grows – stretching hands out, seeking, *finding*.'

'I expect there are a great many outlets,' said Esmée, helping herself to another rissole, 'even if one never has any children of one's own. But I hope — '

'What you are seeking,' said Mrs Windermere firmly, 'is a *lover*.' She took her fork up, speared the *éclair*, and watched the cream ooze forth slowly with a smile of sensual contentment. She had been saying things like this repeatedly, all the time they were in Italy. But they didn't, somehow, sound quite nice in Fullers'. Esmée thought she saw a woman near them looking up.

'I don't think I *am*, you know,' she argued gently, wondering at what date Mrs Windermere had arranged to come and stay with them.

'Oh, child, *child* . . . You can't, you know, there's been too much between us. And the Mother-heart knows, you know; the yearning in it brings about a vision. I see you treading strange, dim places; stumbling, crying out, trying to turn back, but always following – the Light.' Mrs Windermere laid down her fork and licked the cream from her lips. 'And then,' she said slowly, 'I see the Light die out – extinguished.'

There was a pause. 'Thank you very much,' said Esmée earnestly; 'it – it saves a lot to know beforehand. I mean if the Light is going to go out there's something rather desperate about my following it, isn't there? Wouldn't it be — '

'The Light,' interrupted Mrs Windermere, 'is yours to guard.'

'But wouldn't it be — '

Mrs Windermere bowed her head and drew her furs together.

'Such a *child*,' she sighed.

'I think I'll have an *éclair* too,' said Esmée timidly. 'Won't you have another one to keep me company?'

'*I?*' started Mrs Windermere. 'I? *Éclair*? What? Oh well, if it's going to make you *shy*, my watching.'

Esmée ordered two more *éclairs*. 'What,' she inquired, 'are your plans? Did you think of going back to Italy?'

'With the swallows – not before the swallows. I must smother down the panting and the tugging, because my friends can't let me go. They just rise up and say I mustn't. Commands, of course, are nothing, but *entreaties*! Did I tell you in Italy what some people call me?' She laughed deprecatingly and watched the waitress threading her way between the tables with the *éclairs*. 'They call me "The Helper." It sounds like something in a mystery play, doesn't it?'

'Oh yes. It's – it's a beautiful name.'

'It does seem to be a sort of gift,' said Mrs Windermere, looking beyond her, 'something given one to *use*. You see, I do see things other people can't see, and tell them, and help them to straighten out. Well, take your case . . . And I've another friend in Italy, the one I was going to stay with after we parted – I don't know if I told you about her? Well, she left her husband. She *grew up*, and found she didn't need him any more. Well, I saw all that for her and was able to help her. I told the other man how things stood – such a manly fellow! He'd been hanging back, not understanding. Well, they went. I bought their tickets for them and saw them off to Italy. They've been having difficult times, but they'll straighten out – I'm still able to help them. I've been staying there a good deal. I *am* able to help them.'

'I suppose they did feel it was the right thing to do,' said Esmée.

'And you,' said Mrs Windermere, bringing her suddenly into focus. 'What *is* going to happen to *You*? I must come down and have a look at this husband of yours, this Wilfred. Let me see — '

She dived suddenly, her bag was on the floor. She reappeared with it, and its mauve satin maw gaped at Esmée while she fumbled in its depths. Out came a small suède notebook, and Mrs Windermere, feverishly nibbling the point of the pencil, ran her eye down the pages.

'The twentieth?' she said. 'I could come then if you could have me. If not, the fourteenth of the next, for the week-end – but if I came on the twentieth I could stay longer. Failing the fourteenth — '

Esmée pondered, lowering her lashes. 'I'm afraid, I'm *awfully* afraid it will have to be the fourteenth of next. All this month there'll be Wilfred's relations.'

'Little *caged* thing,' said Mrs Windermere tenderly. 'Very well, the fourteenth.' She jotted down something in her notebook, looked across at Esmée, smiled, and jotted down some more, still with her head on one side and the little secret smile. 'Ideas, ideas, coming and going . . . And now! You to your shoppingses and I – well, childie?'

'Please, the bill,' said Esmée to the waitress. 'You *must* let me, please,' she whispered to Mrs Windermere.

'No, I *don't* like — Oh well, well. I haven't got a Wilfred. Thanks, dear child!'

They pushed their chairs back and went downstairs together. At the door, Esmée drew a valedictory breath. 'It's been ever so nice,' she said. 'Lovely. Such a bit of luck! And now, I suppose — '

'Which way? Oh, Peter Robinson's? Well, I'll come with you. It doesn't matter about my little shoppingses.'

Firmly encircling Esmée's wrist with a thumb and forefinger she led her down Regent Street.

The Shadowy Third

HE was a pale little man, with big teeth and prominent eyes; sitting opposite to him in a bus one would have found it incredible that there could be a woman to love him. As a matter of fact there were two, one dead, not counting a mother whose inarticulate devotion he resented, and a pale sister, also dead.

The only woman of value to him came down every evening to meet the 5.20, and stood very near the edge of the platform with her eyes flickering along the moving carriages. She never knew from which end of the train he would alight, because, as he told her, it was only by the skin of his teeth that he caught it at all, and he often had to jump in at the nearest open door and stand the whole way down among other men's feet, with his hand against the rack to steady himself. He could have come down easily and luxuriously by the 6.5, in the corner of a smoking carriage, but he gave himself this trouble for the sake of three-quarters of an hour more with her. It was the consciousness of this, and of many other things, which made her so speechless when they met. Often they were through the barrier and half-way down the road before she found a word to say. She was young, with thin features and light hair and eyes, and they had been married less than a year.

When they turned from the road down the tree-shadowed lane he would shift his bag from one hand to the other and steal an arm round her shoulders. He loved her shy tremor, and the little embarrassed way she would lean down to make a snatch at his bag, which he would sometimes allow her to carry. Their house was among the first two or three on a new estate, and overlooked rolling country from the western windows, from the east the house-backs of new roads. It had been built for him at the time of his first marriage, four years ago, and still smelt a little of plaster, and was coldly distempered, which he hated, but they said it was not yet safe to paper the walls.

Today she said, 'Come down and have a look at the garden, Martin; I've been planting things.' So he put down his bag and they walked to the end of the garden, where a new flower-bed looked scratched-up and disordered, and was edged with little drooping plants.

'Very pretty,' he said, looking at her and absently prodding at the mould with his umbrella. 'I suppose they'll grow?'

'Oh yes, Martin, they're going to grow right up and hide the board-fence; it's so ugly.'

'If they're going to be so tall you should have planted them at the back and put the smaller things in front. As it is, everything else would be hidden.'

'Why, *yes*,' she cried, disheartened. 'I never thought of that – oh, *Martin*! It seemed such a pity to go walking over the new flower-bed, leaving footmarks; that's why I put them near the edge – and now I can't unplant them. What a lot there is to learn! Will you take me to the Gardening Exhibition next summer? I was reading about it – there are corners of gardens by all the famous people, and stone seats, and fountains – we might buy a sundial there, and there are lectures you can go to, and prize roses. We should learn a lot.'

'Next summer? Well, we'll see,' he said. 'Meanwhile don't over-do it – all this gardening.' They skirted the flower-bed and went to lean up against the fence, resting their elbows on the top. She was half an inch taller than he, and her high heels gave her a further advantage. A little wind blew in their faces as they looked out towards the fading distance. The fields were dotted here and there with clumps of elm; with here and there a farmhouse roof, the long roofs and gleaming windows of a factory.

'This open country stretches for such miles,' she said dreamily. 'Sometimes, on these quiet misty days, I begin to think the sea's over there, and that if the clouds along the distance lifted I should see it suddenly, shining. And, with this wind, I could be sure I smell and hear it.'

'Yes, I know. One often gets that feeling.'

'Do *you*?'

'Well, no,' he said confusedly, 'but I'm sure one does. I can imagine it.' Someone had said the same thing to him, just here, three or four years ago.

'You often understand before I say things, don't you, Martin? Isn't it curious? All sorts of woman's discoveries that I've made about this house were nothing new at all to you. Like my idea about a fitment cupboard for that corner of the landing. Fancy that having occurred to you!'

He did not answer. He had taken off his hat, and she watched the wind blowing through his fair hair, as soft and fine as a baby's. Little wrinkles were coming in the forehead that she thought so noble, and his face – well, one could not analyse it, but it was a lovely face. She pictured him swaying for forty minutes in the train, with his hand against the luggage-rack, in order to be with her now, and said, 'Oh, Martin, Martin!'

'Let's come into the house.'

'No, not into the house.'

'Why not? It's cold, you're cold, little woman.' He drew her arm through his and chafed her hand.

'Let's stay out,' she begged. 'It isn't time for supper. It isn't beginning to get dark yet. Do stay out – dear Martin!'

'Why,' he said, looking round at her, 'one would think you were afraid of the house.'

'Hoo!' she laughed, 'afraid of *our* house!'

But he was still dissatisfied. Something was making her restless; she was out in the garden too much. And when she was not in the garden she was always walking about the house. One or two days, when he had stayed at home to work, he had heard her on the stairs and up and down the passages; up and down, up and down. He knew that women in her state of health were abnormal, had strange fancies. Still —

Now she was talking about the new sundial; where they were going to put it. Nasturtiums were to be planted round the foot, she said, because nasturtiums grew so fast and made a show. Her mind had a curious way of edging away from the immediate future. Next summer! Why, she would have other things besides sundials to think of then. What a funny little woman she was!

'I wonder you never thought of having a sundial before,' she insisted. 'Did Anybody ever think of it?'

'Well, no,' he said, 'I don't think it ever occurred to me.'

'Or *Anybody*?'

'No, nor anybody.'

She looked up at the house, silhouetted against the evening sky. 'It's funny living in such a new house – I never had. I wonder who will come after us.'

'We're not likely to move for some time,' he said sharply.

'Oh no – only if we *did*. It seems so very much our house; I can't imagine anybody else at home here, we have made it so entirely – you and I. What was it like the first month or two?'

'Very damp,' he said, now wishing to return to the sundial.

'Did you have the drawing-room very pretty?'

'Oh yes, there were a great many curtains and things. I had to take down all the pictures, they were going mouldy on the walls. It was always a pretty room, even with nothing in it at all. But it's nothing without *you* in it, Pussy.'

'You didn't miss me for a long time,' she said, with her cheek against his.

'Always,' he said, 'always, always, always.'

'Oh no,' she said seriously, 'you know you couldn't have been lonely.'

'*Lonely* – I was wretched!'

'Oh, hush!' she cried with a start, putting her hand over his lips.

'Anyway' – he kissed her fingers – 'nobody is lonely now. Come into the house.'

She hung back on his arm a little but did not again protest; they went in by a glass door into the kitchen passage. As they passed through the archway into the hall he put out his hand to sweep something aside; then smiled shamefacedly. It was funny how he always expected that *portière*. *She* had declared that a draught came through from the kitchen, and insisted on putting it up. *She* had filled the house with draperies, and Pussy had taken them down. When the *portière* was there he had always been forgetting it, and darting through to change his boots in the evening would envelop his head and shoulders ridiculously in the musty velvet folds. Funny how he could never accustom himself to the changes; the house as it *had* been was always in his mind, more present than the house as it *was*. He could never get used to the silence half-way up the stairs, where the grandfather clock used to be. Often he found himself half-way across the hall to see what was the matter with it; it had been a tiresome clock, more trouble than it was worth, with a most reverberating tick. Pussy had put a bracket of china there in its place.

Because it was a chilly autumn evening they had lighted a fire in the drawing-room, the curtains were drawn; what an evening they would spend together after supper! An armchair had been pulled forward and a work-basket gaped beside it; he wondered what Pussy had been sewing. He stood in the hall, looking in through the open door, and remembered *Her* making baby-clothes by the fire and holding them up in her fingers for him to see. Sometimes he had barely raised his eyes from his book – she had never been able to understand his passion for self-education. As she finished the things she had taken them upstairs and locked them away, and sometimes she would put down her sewing and rattle her work-box maddeningly, and look at him across the fire and sigh . . . It would be wonderful to watch Pussy sewing. He could hear her moving about in the hall – such a Pussy! – hanging up his over-coat, then opening the oak chest and rattling things about in it for all the world as though she were after a mouse.

'I found some pictures,' she said, coming up behind him with a stack of something in her arms. 'Come into the drawing-room and we'll look.' The young fire gave out a fitful light, and they knelt down on the hearthrug and put their heads together over the pictures. 'Nursery pictures,' said Pussy – she must have been up in the attic, he wished he had cleared the contents of it out of his house. He stared at the smiling shepherdesses, farmer-boys and

woolly lambs. 'They *are* nursery pictures, aren't they, Martin? I
didn't know you'd actually bought the *pictures*. Had – had Anybody chosen the curtains, too? Did you get as far as that?'
'I don't know,' he said. 'I don't really, Pussy; I don't remember.'
'And did you take it all to pieces again? Did you alone, or did
Anybody help you? I wonder you didn't leave it, Martin; you
didn't want the room for anything else. But I suppose it would
have made you sad, or other people sad.'
'Have you done anything to the room yet, Pussy?'
'I just pulled the furniture about a little, then I went to look for a
fender in the attic and found these pictures. I don't know if there
were any curtains, Martin; shall I buy some more? I saw some
cretonnes specially for that kind of room, all over clowns and rabbits
and little scarlet moons.'
'I'll bring some patterns – or come up to town some day and
we'll choose them together.'
She did not answer, she was looking at the pictures.
'Martin, was that one going to have been called Martin too,
Martin Ralph?'
'I don't know, it hadn't been decided.'
'Didn't Anybody choose a name for him, although he didn't
live? He was a real person.'
'It had never been decided, Pussy. I'm going to get you a longer
sofa, so that you can put your feet up. We can choose it when we
choose the chintzes.'
'Oh, you mustn't. This one is very comfortable; I never sit in it,
but that's because I just don't take to it.'
'I hate the look of it.'
'Well, get rid of it,' she said, smiling, 'as neither of us wants a
sofa. Did Anybody ever sit on that one?'
As far as he remembered, it was the only thing in the room that
she had ever sat on. She had never looked comfortable on it. She
had a way of sitting with her head at the darkest end and straining
her eyes over her work, then blinking up at him when he spoke. Of
course she ought to have worn glasses; he hated women in glasses,
and she knew it, but her short-sightedness annoyed him and he had
frequently said so. *She* used to come and meet him at the station –
he came back by the 6.5 in those days, sometimes by the 6.43 –
and it had so greatly irritated him to watch her grimacing and
screwing up her eyes at the carriages that he had slipped through
the barrier behind her and pretended when she came home that he
had not known she was there. Perhaps the little chap would have
been short-sighted if he had lived . . .
The maid came in to say that supper was ready, and they went
into the dining-room. Here the curtains were undrawn and they

could see the lights twinkling out in the windows of the other houses. He often felt as though those windows were watching him; their gaze was hostile, full of comment and criticism. The sound of the wind among the bushes in the garden was like whispered comparisons. He said they saw a good deal too much of the neighbours, and Pussy said she liked the friendly lights. 'I wouldn't like to be shut in all round, but I couldn't live without *any* people. The next-doors have been so kind. She came in with some plants this morning, and stayed talking quite a long time, and said if there was ever anything she could do . . . She spoke so nicely of you, Martin. She's known you by sight ever since you were a little boy.'

'Oh, it's funny to have lived in the same place all one's life. All these people – well, they're sometimes rather tiresome.'

'Tiresome?'

'One gets tired of their being the same. Would you like to travel, Pussy?'

'Oh, *Martin*!' Her eyes grew wistful; the prospect seemed remote.

'Well, we will,' he said, with energy. 'We'll go to Switzerland – some summer.'

'I'd rather go to Italy – Venice.'

'Oh, not Venice. I don't think you'd care for Venice. It's nothing very much really.'

'Have *you* been there?'

'Yes, for a bit. I didn't care about it.'

'You never told me!' Her eyes that had been looking into his looked suddenly away, the colour surged up under his clear skin. She began to fidget with the spoons on the table.

'More, Martin?'

'Yes, please – I say, Pussy, you're not eating. You must eat, darling.'

'Oh, I *am*, don't bother. I want to talk.' She lifted her eyes again and glanced at him, the light glinting on her golden eyelashes and on her hair. 'I've been so lonely all day – well, not lonely, but the house was so quiet, I could hear myself think. I went into the east room and sat on the window-seat. It is a cold room; I don't know how we'll make it warm enough.'

'It has never been used, you see.'

'We must have fires there this winter. Has it *never* been used? Didn't Anybody ever sit there or go in and out? Oh, they must have, Martin. It's not an empty-feeling room, like the attic.'

'Did you stay there long?'

'No, I didn't, I was feeling restless. The white chest of drawers is locked; I wonder where the key is? We shall be wanting to use it.'

'The key's lost,' he said in sudden fear. 'I know it's lost. I'll go up there some day and force open the drawers myself – they're empty.'

'How funny to lock them if they're empty.'

'What did you imagine was inside?' he asked uneasily.

'Oh, nothing in particular . . . Martin, I think I will go up to town and buy those chintzes myself. And there are other things I want.'

He remembered how he had heard Her in the east room those last two months before she went, opening and shutting the drawers. It had disturbed him, working at his desk in the dining-room below, and he had come up angrily once or twice. He could hear Her scuffling to her feet at his approach, and when he entered She was always standing by the window, looking intently out. She used to say, 'Yes, all right. I won't, I'm sorry, Martin,' and come downstairs after him, humming. She had never seemed to have enough to do; before the child came she had been in an aimless bustle, but afterwards she did nothing, nothing at all, not even keep house for him decently. That was probably what had made her ill – that and the disappointment. All the time he had felt Her watching his face; always on the verge of saying something . . .

When they returned to the drawing-room the fire had burnt down a little. Martin piled on wood, then sat back in the shadow watching Pussy, who, with a reading lamp at her elbow, had begun to sew. He never read these evenings; a table of bric-à-brac had been pushed up against the doors of the bookcase with the gilt-bound classics and encyclopaedias which had beguiled his evenings other years. Books, after all, were musty things, and all the book-learning in the world didn't make him more valuable to Pussy, whose eyes wandered when he spoke to her of dynasties or carnivorous plants. He would pull her work-box towards him and amuse himself sorting its contents. One evening he came on a thimble-case which made him start. 'Where did you get that, Pussy?' he asked fiercely. It appeared that she had had it since she was a little girl. Strange that it should be the same as another, so familiar once! He confiscated it and brought her a morocco one next day, with a new thimble in it that did not fit.

This evening, watching her head and hands in the circle of light, he could hardly keep at the other side of the hearthrug from her. She was preoccupied, worked very slowly; at intervals she smoothed out her sewing on her knee, with her head on one side. Pussy was long-sighted, and always looked at things from as far away as possible. When he spoke, her intent eyes fixed themselves on him unseeingly.

'What are you thinking about, Pussy?'

She evidently did not wish to tell him. She smiled, looked round the room a little fearfully, smiled again and took up her work.

'*Pussy?*'

'Oh, I don't know; I'm so happy. I'm so glad to have you back. I wonder if anyone was ever so happy.'

'Then why do you look so sad?'

'I was thinking it would be so terrible not to be happy. I was trying to imagine what I'd feel like if you didn't care.'

'*Didn't care!*'

'I – I couldn't imagine it,' she admitted. He could no longer keep the length of the hearthrug between them when she smiled like that. She continued with his arm round her. 'You never let me know the feel of wanting. Just the littlest differences in you would make me eat my heart out. I should never be able to ask you for things. I should just look and look at you, trying to speak, and then you would grow to hate me.'

' – and then?'

' – Don't look at me like that, Martin – and then I should get ill, and if you didn't want me to come back I'd die . . . Silly, I was only imagining. You shouldn't have made me talk.'

'You shouldn't imagine things like that,' he said sombrely. 'What makes you do it? It's – it's morbid: you might do yourself a great deal of harm. And besides, it's – it's — '

'Do things like that happen? Could a person go on loving and loving and never be wanted?'

'How should *I* know?'

'I think,' she said, 'that not to want a person must be a sort, a sort of murder. I think a person who was done out of their life like that would be brought back by the injustice much more than anybody who was shot or stabbed.'

'Are these the sort of things you think about all day?'

She looked at his white face, and laid her head against his shoulder and began to whimper. 'Oh, Martin, don't be angry. I am so frightened, I am so frightened.'

'Hush!'

'We're not safe and I don't believe we're even good. It can't be right to be so happy when there isn't enough happiness in the world to go round. Suppose we had taken somebody else's happiness, somebody else's life . . . '

'Pussy, hush, be quiet. I forbid you. You've been dreaming. You've been silly, imagining these horrors. My darling, there's no sin in happiness. You shouldn't play with dreadful thoughts. Nothing can touch us.'

'I sometimes feel the very room hates us!'

'Nothing can touch us,' he reiterated, looking defiantly into the corners of the room.

The Evil that Men Do –

AT the corner by the fire-station, where Southampton Row is joined by Theobald's Road, a little man, hurrying back to his office after the lunch hour, was run over by a motor-lorry. He had been stepping backward to avoid a taxi when worse befell him. What was left of him was taken to hospital and remained for some days unidentified, as no papers of any sort were to be found in his pockets.

The morning after this occurrence a lady living on the outskirts of a country town received a letter in an unfamiliar writing. The appearance of the envelope startled her; it was so exactly what she had been expecting for the last four days. She turned it over, biting her lip. The dining-room was darker than usual, it was a dull, still morning, and she had risen and dressed with growing apprehension. Her husband was away, and the windows seemed farther than ever now that she occupied his place and breakfasted alone. She poured out a cup of tea and raised the plated cover of a dish. The sight of a lonely sausage decided her. She opened the letter.

Before she had read to the end she leant forward to think, with her knuckles doubled under her chin. Other people have that sinister advantage over one of being able to see the back of one's head. For the first time in her life she had the uncomfortable sense that somebody had done so, that somebody had not only glanced but was continuously staring. Her husband did not make her feel like this.

'Fancy,' she thought. 'Just an hour and ten minutes exactly. Just that little time, and all these years I never knew. Think of living among all these people and never knowing how I was different.'

She folded up the letter for a moment, and began betting against herself on his Christian name. 'Evelyn,' she thought, 'or possibly Arthur, or Philip.' As a matter of fact it was Charles.

'I know you so well,' the letter continued. 'Before you drew your gloves off I knew that you were married. You have been living on the defensive for years. I know the books you read, and what you see in the streets you walk in of that town with the terrible name. You live in a dark house looking over a highway.

Very often you stand in the light of the windows, leaning your head against the frame, and trees with dull leaves send the sunshine and shadow shivering over your face. Footsteps startle you, you start back into the crowded room. The morning you get this letter, go out bareheaded into your garden and let the wind blow the sunshine through your hair. I shall be thinking of you then.

'Your husband and your children have intruded on you. Even your children hurt you with their little soft hands, and yet you are as you always were, untouched and lonely. You came slowly out of yourself at that poetry-reading, like a nymph coming out of a wood. You came towards me like a white thing between trees, and I snatched at you as you turned to go back — '

Her cheeks burnt.

'My goodness,' she cried, biting her thumb-nail. 'Fancy anybody being able to write like that! Fancy living at 28 Abiram road, West Kensington. I wonder if he's got a wife, I do wonder.' Delicious warmth crept down her. 'Poetry! I thought he wrote poetry. Fancy him having guessed I read it!'

'I am going to send you my poetry. It is not published yet, but I am having it typewritten. When it is published there shall be just your one initial on the dedication page. I cannot bear the thought of your living alone among those strange people who hurt you – familiar, unfamiliar faces and cold eyes. I know it all; the numb mornings, the feverish afternoons; the intolerable lamplit evenings, night — '

'Now,' she thought, 'I'm sure he has a wife.'

' – and your wan, dazed face turning without hope to the first gleams at the window — '

Ah, guilty, guilty, that she slept so well!

The cook came in.

When the meals for the day were ordered and her breakfast half-surreptitiously eaten with the letter tucked inside the tea-cosy, she went upstairs to her room and tried on the hat she had worn in London, folding the side-flaps of the mirror round her so that she could see her profile. She leant forward gazing at a point in space represented by the prismatic stopper of a scent-bottle. With a long, slow breath she went slowly through the action of drawing off a glove.

'Living,' she said aloud, 'for years and years on the defensive.' She looked into the mirror at the neat quiet room behind her, with the reflected pinkness from curtains and carpet over its white wall, and the two mahogany bedsteads with their dappled eiderdowns. There were photographs of her aunts, her children and her brother-in-law's wife along the mantelpiece, a print of the Good Shepherd above the washstand, and 'Love among the Ruins' over the beds.

On a bracket were some pretty vases of French china Harold had given her at Dieppe, and a photogravure of the Luxemburg gardens she had given Harold. In a bookcase were several selections from the poets, beautifully bound in coloured suède, and another book, white with gold roses, called *The Joy of Living*. She got up and slipped a novel from the local library into the bottom of a drawer.

'What on earth would be the good,' she reasoned, 'of going out into the garden when there is no sun and no wind and practically no garden?' She considered her reflection.

'I don't feel I could go down the High Street in this hat. There must be something queer about it. Half-past nine: Harold will be back at half-past eleven. I wonder if he's bringing me anything from London.'

She put a good deal of powder on her face, changed her hat and earrings, selected a pair of half-soiled gloves from a drawer and went downstairs. Then she ran quickly up again and wiped off all the powder.

'Like a wood nymph,' she murmured, 'coming out of a wood.'

When she was half-way down the High Street she found that she had forgotten her shopping-basket and her purse.

Harold came home at half-past eleven and found his wife still out.

He whistled for some minutes in the hall, looked vainly into her bedroom, the kitchen and the nursery, then went round to the office to put in some work. Harold was a solicitor. Coming in again at lunch-time he met her crossing the hall. She looked at him vaguely.

'Why, you *are* back early!'

'I was back two hours ago,' said he.

'Did you have a nice time in London?'

He explained, with his usual patience, that one does not expect to have a nice time when one goes up to London on business.

'Of course,' he said, 'we're all out to get what we can out of London. We all, as you might say, "pick it over." Only what I'm out for isn't pleasure – I leave that to you, don't I? – I'm out for other pickings.'

'Yes, Harold.'

'This is very good beef.'

'Yes, isn't it?' she cried, much gratified. 'I got it at Hoskins' – Mrs Peck deals there, she told me about it. It is much cheaper than at Biddle's, tuppence less in the pound. I have to cross over to the other side of the street now when I pass Biddle's. I haven't been there for days, and he looks as though he were beginning to suspect — '

She sighed sharply; her interest flagged.

'Ah, yes?' said Harold encouragingly.

'I'm tired of buying beef,' she said resentfully.

'Oh, come, tired of going down the High Street! Why, what else would you — '

She felt that Harold was odious. He had not even brought her anything from London.

'All my day,' she cried, 'messed up with little things!'

Harold laid down his knife and fork.

'Oh, do please go on eating!'

'Yes,' said Harold. 'I was only looking for the mustard. What were you saying?'

'Got any plans this afternoon?' he said after luncheon, according to precedent.

'I'm going to write letters,' she said, pushing past him into the drawing-room.

She shut the door behind her, leaving Harold in the hall. There was something in doing that, 'living on the defensive.' But were there any corners, any moments of her life for the last eight years which Harold had not pervaded? And, horrible, she had not only lived with him but liked him. At what date, in fact, had she ceased liking Harold? *Had* she ever — ?

She put her fingers quickly in her ears as though somebody had uttered the guilty thing aloud.

Seating herself at the writing-table, she shut her eyes and thoughtfully stroked her eyebrows with the pink feather at the tip of a synthetic quill pen. She drew the feather slowly down the line of one cheek and tickled herself under the chin with it, a delightful sensation productive of shivers.

'Oh,' she sighed, with a shuddering breath, 'how beautiful, beautiful you are.'

The top of a bus, lurching and rattling through obscurer London, the cold air blowing on her throat, moments under lighted windows when the faces had been mutually discernible, the sudden apparition of the conductor which had made him withdraw his hands from her wrist, their conversation – which she had forgotten . . . 'Ride, ride together, for ever ride' . . . When the bus stopped they had got down and got on to another. She did not remember where they had said good-bye. Fancy, all that from going to a poetry-reading instead of a picture-house. Fancy! And she hadn't even understood the poetry.

She opened her eyes and the practical difficulties of correspondence presented themselves. One could not write that sort of letter on Azure Bond; the notepaper he had used had been so indefinably *right*, somehow. She did not know how to address him. He had not begun with a 'Dear' anything, but that did seem rather abrupt. One could not call him 'Dear Mr Simmonds' after an hour and ten minutes of such bus-riding; how could you call a person Mr Simmonds when he said you were a nymph? Yet she couldn't take to 'Charles.' Everything practical, she found, had been crowded into the postscript of his letter – people said that women did that. He said he thought it would be better if she were to write to him at his office in Southampton Row; it was an insurance office, which somehow gave her confidence. 'Dear Charles,' she began.

It was a stiff little letter.

'I know it is,' she sighed, distressfully re-reading it. 'It doesn't sound abandoned, but how can I sound abandoned in this drawing-room?' She stood up, self-consciously. 'The cage that is,' she said aloud, 'the intolerable *cage!*' and began to walk about among the furniture. ' – Those chintzes are pretty, I am glad I chose them. And those sweet ruched satin cushions . . . If he came to tea I would sit over here by the window, with the curtains drawn a little behind me – no, over here by the fireplace, it would be in winter and there would be nothing but firelight. But people of that sort never come to tea; he would come later on in the evening and the curtains would be drawn, and I should be wearing my – Oh, "Like a nymph." How trivial it all seems.'

And Harold had wondered what there would be left for her to do if she didn't go down the High Street. She would show him. But if she went through with this to the end Harold must never know, and what would be the good of anything without Harold for an audience?

She again re-read the letter she had written:

' – Of course my husband has never entered into my inner life — ' and underlined the 'of course' with short definite lines. It was quite true; she left books of poetry about and Harold never glanced at them; she sat for hours gazing at the fire or (as Charles said) out of the window and Harold never asked her what she was thinking about; when she was playing with the children she would break off suddenly and turn away her face and sigh, and Harold never asked her what was the matter. He would go away for days and leave her alone in the house with nobody to talk to but the children and the servants and the people next door. But of course solitude was her only escape and solace; she added this as a post-script.

Harold entered.

'I left this,' he said, 'down at the office this morning by mistake. I thought I had forgotten it in London – I should not like to have done so. I was very much worried. I did not mention the matter as I did not want you to be disappointed.' He extended a parcel. 'I don't know whether it is pretty, but I thought you might like it.'

It was the most beautiful handbag, silver-grey, with the delicate bloom on it of perfect suède – darker when one stroked it one way, lighter the other. The clasp was real gold and the straps by which one carried it of exactly the right length. Inside it had three divisions; drawing out the pads of tissue paper one revealed a lining of ivory moiré, down which the light shot into the shadows of the sumptuously scented interior in little trickles like water. Among the silk folds of the centre compartment were a purse with a gold clasp, a gold case that might be used for either cigarettes or visiting cards, and a darling little gold-backed mirror. There was a memorandum-tablet in an outer pocket, and a little book of *papier poudré.*

They sat down on the sofa to examine it, their heads close together.

'Oh,' she cried, 'you don't mind, Harold? *Papier poudré?*'

'Not,' said Harold, 'if you don't put on too much.'

'And look – the little wee mirror. Doesn't it make me have a little wee face?'

Harold breathed magnanimously over the mirror.

'Harold,' she said, 'you *are* wonderful. Just what I wanted . . . '

'You can take it out shopping tomorrow morning, down the High Street.'

She shut the bag with a click, brushed away the marks of her finger-tips, and swung it by the straps from her wrist, watching it through half-closed eyes.

'*Harold*,' she sighed ineffably.

They kissed.

'Shall I post your letters?' he inquired.

She glanced towards the writing-table. 'Would you wait a moment? Just a moment; there's an address I must write, and a postscript.'

'My little wee wife,' said Harold contentedly.

'P.P.S.,' she added. 'You must not think that I do not love my husband. There are moments when he touches very closely my *exterior life.*'

She and Harold and the handbag went as far as the post together, and she watched the letter swallowed up in the maw of the pillar-box.

'Another of your insurance policies?' asked Harold.

'Only just to know the general particulars,' she said.

She wondered for some time what Charles would think when he came to the last postscript, and never knew that Fate had spared him this.

Sunday Evening

IT was six o'clock, the dusky sky was streaked with gold behind the beech trees and the bells were already beginning; they had sat like this since tea. Mrs Roche had turned half-round to watch the sunset, her hands were clasped along the back of her chair and her chin rested on her interwoven fingers. She blinked a little in the level light, and all the little lines were visible about her eyes and round her puckered mouth. Laura May and Mrs McKenna sat on the low window seat, faintly aureoled, their empty cups beside them on the floor. Archie Manning was somewhere on the sofa, away among the shadows of the room, leaning back with his legs so twisted that his big feet stuck grotesquely out into the light. They had almost forgotten his existence, and his masculinity did not obtrude itself upon the conversation.

Cups and silver held the last of the sunlight, the tall room gradually obscured itself; here and there a frame or mirror gleamed on the shadowed walls.

They were talking about the First Woman; something had been said of her in the sermon that morning, and the thought had germinated in their minds all day.

Little Mrs McKenna had had, so far, most to say; now she paused to light another cigarette, and Mrs Roche turned her eyes in Laura's direction – she did not move her head.

'Laura has been nothing but a dusky profile. What is she thinking about that makes her so silent?'

'Laura is one of these primitive women,' said Mrs McKenna, inhaling smoke; 'she doesn't think, she communes.'

Laura was a big fair girl; her silences made other people talkative, her virginal starts and blushes stimulated Mrs McKenna. She sat twisting and untwisting a gold chain round her neck, and said:

'Oh, I don't know really. I am very unoriginal, you know.'

'But nobody is original,' said Mrs Roche, in her deep voice. 'It's no good, really; all the oldest ideas are the best. But I was thinking, children, looking at the sunset, of her despair, on that first night, watching the light go out of the world. Think how it must have felt.'

'I expect Adam was reassuring,' said Mrs McKenna; 'he'd seen it happen before.'

'No, he hadn't; they were born on the same day – that is, weren't they? Bother, look it up in Genesis.'

'Yes, they were,' said Laura conclusively. She was full of information.

'So Adam had no time to be lonely – that was a pity. It would have made him so much more grateful — '

' – Psychologically,' interrupted Mrs Roche, 'how interesting it all is, supposing it were true. Eve, of course, was at first no practical assistance to him. There were no chores, no mending. They didn't wear fig-leaves till after the Fall.'

'That must have been nice,' said Mrs McKenna – 'I mean the no fig-leaves. But inexpressive — '

' – Yes, inexpressive. I was going to say, rather impersonal.'

'Oh, come, Gilda, if one's own skin isn't personal, what is!'

'I don't know,' said Mrs Roche slowly. 'I don't think it's very personal. After all, it's only the husk of one – unavoidably there. But one's clothes are part of what one has got to say. Eve was much more herself when she began putting flowers in her hair than when she sat about in just – no fig-leaves. And she was much more herself than ever when she had got the fig-leaves on, and you and I are much more ourselves than she was.'

'Then do you think covering oneself up is being real?' asked Laura. She entered the conversation with heavy, serious grace, as she would have entered a room.

'I don't know,' said Gilda Roche. 'The less of me that's visible, the more I'm there.'

Laura, looking at Gilda's face so nearly on a level with her own, believed that it was one of the dearest on earth, with those satirical eyes. It was in this belief that she came to stay for long week-ends, and was hurt by Mrs Roche's other incomprehensible friends. 'That's your mind?' she said. 'You mean you feel a deeper sense of identity behind reserve?'

Mrs Roche looked at her for a moment, then out over her head at the sunset. Mrs McKenna fidgeted; she disliked this interchange of the personal note. 'I don't agree with you,' she said, raising her voice to drown the insistence of the bells. 'I'm for off with everything – clothes, pose, reserve.'

'Oh, now, Fanny, keep a little pose.'

'Perhaps,' she conceded unblushingly, 'a little. Just a flower in the hair. Then to walk about among things like Eve among the trees, and feel them brushing up against me.'

'But the world is so crowded, Fanny,' said Gilda, who seemed to be enjoying Mrs McKenna. 'Just think, wherever you went it would be like walking in the park.'

'I am rather mixed,' said Laura; 'are we speaking metaphorically, or not?'

'*Not*,' said Mrs McKenna, poking her. 'Oh, decidedly not.' She had been longing to poke Laura for some time, every line of the girl's anatomy annoyed her.

The bells came pealing chime after chime, their echoes pervaded the darkening room. Archie stirred on the sofa.

'Don't they make one feel holy?' he said.

Laura, who had blushed for Archie during the parts of Mrs McKenna's conversation – one never knew what that little woman was going to say, her mind flickered about like a lizard – thought that it might now be possible to turn the current. 'I like them,' she asserted.

'I hate them! I *hate* them!' cried Mrs McKenna, putting her hands up over her ears and stamping her foot.

'They've been ringing for the last half-hour and you didn't seem to mind,' said Gilda Roche, bending down to knock the ash off her cigarette into Laura's tea-cup.

'Yes, but they come in at the pauses so reprovingly; like Wilson putting his owl's face round the door. He longs to clear away the tea-things, but you give him no encouragement, and he is afraid of tumbling over Archie's feet. He's been in three times.'

'I know,' said Gilda penitently. 'But if he takes away the tea-things it will leave us all sitting round in an empty circle, with no particular *raison d'être*.'

'Archie is feeling holy,' said Mrs McKenna, looking across at the sofa not without respect. 'I wonder what it feels like. At present his mind is in the past. When this present is the past it will linger longest in *this* particular part of the past (how difficult that was to say). Seven or eight Sundays hence, Archie, when you are in Africa, very lonely and primaeval, leaning on your gun, you will think back to one Sunday evening in the country, in Gilda's drawing-room, and you'll try and hum the chimes (unconsciously you're learning them now). You'll shut your eyes and see the big windows and the beeches, and Laura and me, and think what sweet women we were.'

'Oh, shall I?' said Archie in a discouraging tone.

Fanny McKenna was coming a little too near the mark; she was a discordant person altogether, and would have been better away. He was very happy with his head in the dark, listening to Gilda and watching Laura listen – he had been curiously attracted lately by the movements of her big head and big, rather incapable-looking white hands.

'I should like a life in the wilds,' said Mrs McKenna thoughtfully. 'It's a pity I can't go with you.'

'Yes,' said Archie politely.

'But it wouldn't suit me; I should be terrible – luxuriate, over-develop.'

'I thought that was what you wanted, Fanny,' said Gilda unwisely. ' "Off with everything," you know.'

'Not when there was nobody about. What would it matter if everything was off or on? Nobody would be the better for it. What's the good of being sincere when there's nobody to be sincere at?'

'There'd be Archie.'

'Well, anyway, there's William,' said Mrs McKenna conclusively. 'And I can't go. I'm afraid I don't love Archie enough. But he will be very lonely – won't you, Archie?'

'Oh, I don't know,' said Archie evasively, rolling his head about among the cushions. 'I suppose so. I suppose one will live a good bit in the past and future if one has got too much time to think and not enough to do in the present.'

'What future, Archie?' said Mrs Roche with curiosity.

'Oh, I don't know. Coming back, I suppose. I ought to be back in four years. I wonder where everybody will be.'

'I shall be here, a little greyer-haired, perhaps, and stupid; several of my friends will have given up coming down to see me, including Fanny – who will be wherever William isn't. Laura will probably be married — '

'Oh?' said Laura consciously.

' – and you will come down once or twice, and be very retrospective and sweet, Archie, then drift away too. Perhaps you will bring the girl you are engaged to down to see me, and she will kiss you on the way home and say I am a dear old thing, and not be the least bit jealous any more . . . I know I shall be very stupid some day; I can feel it coming down on me, like mist from the top of a mountain.'

'Laura will often come and see you,' consoled Mrs McKenna, 'and bring all the babies — '

'We must all write to Archie,' interposed Gilda. 'He will never answer, but he will expect the most enormous posts. It's queer that we three who have been talking so much about primaeval simplicity should have nothing much in front of us but drawing-rooms and gardens for the next four years, while Archie, who never asks for anything better than a sofa – from all I've seen of him – should be actually going out into the wilds to do things.'

'Why, yes,' said Mrs McKenna, 'Archie is actually going to revert. Laura would do that easily too. Now for you and me, Gilda, life is much more perilous. Archie and Laura would camp out quite happily, compassed about by a perfect cloud of lions, and so long as they weren't eaten – well, they'd just go on living. But for us the next four years are going to be most terribly dangerous. I have been feeling so happy lately that I know I must be terribly insecure, right at the edge of something. The struggle for life – they'll never know the meaning of it, will they, Gilda? The feeling that if you stopped for a moment you'd go out.'

Gilda's eyes narrowed. 'Yes, it's desperate, Fanny, isn't it? You contesting every inch and I longing to grow old beautifully — '

'And murdering,' said Fanny intensely, 'smothering your youth!'

Gilda began to laugh. 'I don't think you're right in saying that Archie and Laura live – just negatively. They are a great deal more than not dead. And you're very sweeping, Fanny; nobody likes to be dismissed as incomplex. Archie is a man of action, strenuous in his mind, and Laura is reposeful – which needs energy. That is why we love her.'

'Yes, don't we?' said Fanny generously, 'but we can't think how it's done.'

'Oh, all big things are reposeful,' said Gilda; 'look at the beech trees.'

'I am a very wiry Scotch fir,' said Fanny with relish. 'I stand against the skyline and cry out for gales. When they come I ecstasize. Gilda, you are a larch tree planted in a windy place. You look down and think you long for a valley, but every inch of you undulates. In a calm you'd go quite limp. *You* in a calm — !'

'It's all I want,' said Gilda. She raised her chin from her hands and leant back to look round the shadows of the room, her hands still resting on the back of the chair. She had an eternal youthfulness in gesture and repose. Archie, watching her silhouette against the fading sky, thought she was like a girl of nineteen.

'Hurry, hurry, hurry, hurry!' intoned Fanny suddenly, echoing the church bell, which was now ringing for late comers with a little note of urgency. 'Don't you think we might take Archie to church? It would give him some more to remember. We might arrive before the second lesson, if we started now, and he could sit between Laura and you in rather a dark pew, and share a book, and sing "Lead, Kindly Light" — '

'Oh, don't, Fanny!'

Fanny had wondered how much of this they were going to stand. She loved to see Gilda defending her lambs. 'Oh, it's only that tiresome little Mrs McKenna,' she assured them. 'Terribly flippant, isn't she?' She sighed. 'I wonder if anyone will ever think of me on Sunday evenings?'

'Only if they want a fourth at bridge,' said Archie brutally. It was extraordinary how nice boys could hurt.

'I've never been to evening church. I know nothing about it; is it poignant?' asked Gilda. 'Laura, we will go next time you're here.'

'You might go about eight weeks hence,' suggested Archie dis-interestedly. 'When I shall be – *there*, you know. It would be rather amusing. And I say, suppose you always write on Sunday evenings – no, of course you couldn't; the house is always full of people. It's awfully funny to think of those bells going, and all these chairs and sofas here, and people in them, and not me. It's funny to think of everywhere going on without one, and still going on if one never came back.'

'I'll keep your corner of the sofa for you, Archie. No one else shall sit in it.'

'Yes, you might.' The room was getting so dark that it did not matter what one said. Laura leaned back with her head against the window frame and sighed. Fanny, with her arms folded, peered down at her own little feet. Archie began to whistle under his breath. ' "Turn down an empty glass," ' he said.

'Four years will fly,' said Laura.

'All depends,' said Fanny. 'Four years hence — ' She shivered.

'Funny if we all met here again,' said Archie.

'We won't,' said Fanny with conviction.

'Who knows, who knows?' said Gilda.

'Who *wants* to know? We'd never dare go on.'

'Oh, Fanny, *dare?* . . . We've got to.'

'We want to,' said Laura quietly.

'Yes, by Jove,' said Archie. 'It's all been jolly good so far; one feels They wouldn't let one down.'

'*They?*' cried Fanny impatiently. 'They *who?* How dependent, how pitiful, how childish!'

'Well, you don't believe we're in the dark for ever now the sun's gone down,' said Gilda uncertainly.

'We guess it may come up again. We chance it. We're such optimists, such cowards!'

'Well, what do you believe?'

'Believe? I wouldn't *sell* myself.'

'I think *that's* pitiful,' said Laura.

The door opened.

'Yes, Wilson,' said Gilda, 'I think you might come in and take away the tea.' They heard Wilson fumbling for a moment, then the room sprang into light. They blinked a little, suddenly aware of the furniture, each other's bodies, and a sense of betrayal. Mrs McKenna rose briskly.

'We might have had some bridge,' she said. 'What a pity some of us can't play.'

She looked down at Laura.

Coming Home

ALL the way home from school Rosalind's cheeks burnt, she felt
something throbbing in her ears. It was sometimes terrible to live
so far away. Before her body had turned the first corner her mind
had many times wrenched open their gate, many times rushed up
their path through the damp smells of the garden, waving the
essay-book, and seen Darlingest coming to the window. Nothing
like this had ever happened before to either her or Darlingest; it was
the supreme moment that all these years they had been approaching, of which those dim, improbable future years would be spent in
retrospect.

Rosalind's essay had been read aloud and everybody had praised
it. Everybody had been there, the big girls sitting along the sides of
the room had turned and looked at her, raising their eyebrows and
smiling. For an infinity of time the room had held nothing but the
rising and falling of Miss Wilfred's beautiful voice doing the service
of Rosalind's brain. When the voice dropped to silence and the
room was once more unbearably crowded, Rosalind had looked at
the clock and seen that her essay had taken four and a half minutes to
read. She found that her mouth was dry and her eyes ached
from staring at a small fixed spot in the heart of whirling circles,
and her knotted hands were damp and trembling. Somebody
behind her gently poked the small of her back. Everybody in the
room was thinking about Rosalind; she felt their admiration and
attention lapping up against her in small waves. A long way off
somebody spoke her name repeatedly, she stood up stupidly and
everybody laughed. Miss Wilfred was trying to pass her back the
red exercise book. Rosalind sat down thinking to herself how dazed
she was, dazed with glory. She was beginning already to feel about
for words for Darlingest.

She had understood some time ago that nothing became real for
her until she had had time to live it over again. An actual
occurrence was nothing but the blankness of a shock, then the
knowledge that something had happened; afterwards one could
creep back and look into one's mind and find new things in it, clear
and solid. It was like waiting outside the hen-house till the hen

came off the nest and then going in to look for the egg. She would not touch this egg until she was with Darlingest, then they would go and look for it together. Suddenly and vividly this afternoon would be real for her. 'I won't think about it yet,' she said, 'for fear I'd spoil it.'

The houses grew scarcer and the roads greener, and Rosalind relaxed a little; she was nearly home. She looked at the syringa bushes by the gate, and it was as if a cold wing had brushed against her. Supposing Darlingest were out . . . ?

She slowed down her running steps to a walk. From here she would be able to call to Darlingest. But if she didn't answer there would be still a tortuous hope; she might be at the back of the house. She decided to pretend it didn't matter, one way or the other; she had done this before, and it rather took the wind out of Somebody's sails, she felt. She hitched up her essay-book under her arm, approached the gate, turned carefully to shut it, and walked slowly up the path looking carefully down at her feet, not up at all at the drawing-room window. Darlingest would think she was playing a game. Why didn't she hear her tapping on the glass with her thimble?

As soon as she entered the hall she knew that the house was empty. Clocks ticked very loudly; upstairs and downstairs the doors were a little open, letting through pale strips of light. Only the kitchen door was shut, down the end of the passage, and she could hear Emma moving about behind it. There was a spectral shimmer of light in the white panelling. On the table was a bowl of primroses, Darlingest must have put them there that morning. The hall was chilly; she could not think why the primroses gave her such a feeling of horror, then she remembered the wreath of primroses, and the scent of it, lying on the raw new earth of that grave . . . The pair of grey gloves were gone from the bowl of visiting-cards. Darlingest had spent the morning doing those deathly primroses, and then taken up her grey gloves and gone out, at the end of the afternoon, just when she knew her little girl would be coming in. A quarter-past four. It was unforgivable of Darlingest: she had been a mother for more than twelve years, the mother exclusively of Rosalind, and still, it seemed, she knew no better than to do a thing like that. Other people's mothers had terrible little babies: they ran quickly in and out to go to them, or they had smoky husbands who came in and sat, with big feet. There was something distracted about other people's mothers. But Darlingest, so exclusively one's own . . .

Darlingest could never have really believed in her. She could never have really believed that Rosalind would do anything wonderful at school, or she would have been more careful to be in to hear about it. Rosalind flung herself into the drawing-room; it was honey-coloured and lovely in the pale spring light, another little clock was ticking in the corner, there were more bowls of primroses and black-eyed, lowering anemones. The tarnished mirror on the wall distorted and reproved her angry face in its mild mauveness. Tea was spread on the table by the window, tea for two that the two might never . . . Her work and an open book lay on the tumbled cushions of the window-seat. All the afternoon she had sat there waiting and working, and now – poor little Darlingest, perhaps she had gone out because she was lonely.

People who went out sometimes never came back again. Here she was, being angry with Darlingest, and all the time . . . Well, she had drawn on those grey gloves and gone out wandering along the roads, vague and beautiful, because she was lonely, and then?

Ask Emma? No, she wouldn't; fancy having to ask *her*!

'Yes, your mother'll be in soon, Miss Rosie. Now run and get your things off, there's a good girl — ' Oh no, intolerable.

The whole house was full of the scent and horror of the primroses. Rosalind dropped the exercise-book on the floor, looked at it, hesitated, and putting her hands over her mouth, went upstairs, choking back her sobs. She heard the handle of the kitchen door turn; Emma was coming out. O God! Now she was on the floor by Darlingest's bed, with the branches swaying and brushing outside the window, smothering her face in the eiderdown, smelling and tasting the wet satin. Down in the hall she heard Emma call her, mutter something, and slam back into the kitchen.

How could she ever have left Darlingest? She might have known, she might have known. The sense of insecurity had been growing on her year by year. A person might be part of you, almost part of your body, and yet once you went away from them they might utterly cease to be. That sea of horror ebbing and flowing round the edges of the world, whose tides were charted in the newspapers, might sweep out a long wave over them and they would be gone. There was no security. Safety and happiness were a game that grown-up people played with children to keep them from understanding, possibly to keep themselves from thinking. But they did think, that was what made grown-up people – queer. Anything might happen, there was no security. And now Darlingest —

This was her dressing-table, with the long beads straggling over it, the little coloured glass barrels and bottles had bright flames in the centre. In front of the looking-glass, filmed faintly over with a cloud of powder, Darlingest had put her hat on – for the last time. Supposing all that had ever been reflected in it were imprisoned somewhere in the back of a looking-glass. The blue hat with the drooping brim was hanging over the corner of a chair. Rosalind had never been kind about that blue hat, she didn't think it was becoming. And Darlingest had loved it so. She must have gone out wearing the brown one; Rosalind went over to the wardrobe and stood on tip-toe to look on the top shelf. Yes, the brown hat was gone. She would never see Darlingest again, in the brown hat, coming down the road to meet her and not seeing her because she was thinking about something else. Peau d'Espagne crept faintly from among the folds of the dresses; the blue, the gold, the soft furred edges of the tea-gown dripping out of the wardrobe. She heard herself making a high, whining noise at the back of her throat, like a puppy, felt her swollen face distorted by another paroxysm.

'I can't bear it, I can't bear it. What have I done? I did love her, I did so awfully love her.

'Perhaps she was all right when I came in; coming home smiling. Then I stopped loving her, I hated her and was angry. And it happened. She was crossing a road and something happened to her. I was angry and she died. I killed her.

'I don't know that she's dead. I'd better get used to believing it, it will hurt less afterwards. Supposing she does come back this time; it's only for a little. I shall never be able to keep her; now I've found out about this I shall never be happy. Life's nothing but waiting for awfulness to happen and trying to think about something else.

'If she could come back just this once – Darlingest.'

Emma came half-way upstairs; Rosalind flattened herself behind the door.

'Will you begin your tea, Miss Rosie?'

'No. Where's mother?'

'I didn't hear her go out. I have the kettle boiling – will I make your tea?'

'No. *No*.'

Rosalind slammed the door on the angry mutterings, and heard with a sense of desolation Emma go downstairs. The silver clock by Darlingest's bed ticked; it was five o'clock. They had tea at a quarter-past four; Darlingest was never, never late. When they came to tell her about *It*, men would come, and they would tell Emma, and Emma would come up with a frightened, triumphant face and tell her.

She saw the grey-gloved hands spread out in the dust.

A sound at the gate. 'I can't bear it, I can't bear it. Oh, save me, God!'

Steps on the gravel.

Darlingest.

She was at the window, pressing her speechless lips together.

Darlingest came slowly up the path with the long ends of her veil, untied, hanging over her shoulders. A paper parcel was pressed between her arm and her side. She paused, stood smiling down at the daffodils. Then she looked up with a start at the windows, as though she heard somebody calling. Rosalind drew back into the room.

She heard her mother's footsteps cross the stone floor of the hall, hesitate at the door of the drawing-room, and come over to the foot of the stairs. The voice was calling 'Lindie! Lindie, duckie!' She was coming upstairs.

Rosalind leaned the weight of her body against the dressing-table and dabbed her face with the big powder-puff; the powder clung in paste to her wet lashes and in patches over her nose and cheeks. She was not happy, she was not relieved, she felt no particular feeling about Darlingest, did not even want to see her. Something had slackened down inside her, leaving her a little sick.

'Oh, you're *there*,' said Darlingest from outside, hearing her movements. 'Where did, where were — ?'

She was standing in the doorway. Nothing had been for the last time, after all. She had come back. One could never explain to her how wrong she had been. She was holding out her arms; something drew one towards them.

'But, my little *Clown*,' said Darlingest, wiping off the powder. 'But, oh — ' She scanned the glazed, blurred face. 'Tell me why,' she said.

'You were late.'

'Yes, it was horrid of me; did you mind? . . . But that was silly, Rosalind; I can't be always in.'

'But you're my mother.'

Darlingest was amused; little trickles of laughter and gratification ran out of her. 'You weren't *frightened*, Silly Billy.' Her tone changed to distress. 'Oh, Rosalind, don't be cross.'

'I'm not,' said Rosalind coldly.

'Then come — '

'I was wanting my tea.'

'Rosalind, *don't* be — '

Rosalind walked past her to the door. She was hurting Darlingest, beautifully hurting her. She would never tell her about that essay. Everybody would be talking about it, and when Darlingest heard and asked her about it she would say: 'Oh, that? I didn't think you'd be interested.' That would hurt. She went down into the drawing-room, past the primroses. The grey gloves were back on the table. This was the mauve and golden room that Darlingest had come back to, from under the Shadow of Death, expecting to find her little daughter . . . They would have sat together on the window-seat while Rosalind read the essay aloud, leaning their heads closer together as the room grew darker.

That was all spoilt.

Poor Darlingest, up there alone in the bedroom, puzzled, hurt, disappointed, taking off her hat. She hadn't known she was going to be hurt like this when she stood out there on the gravel, smiling at the daffodils. The red essay-book lay spread open on the carpet. There was the paper bag she had been carrying, lying on a table by the door; macaroons, all squashy from being carried the wrong way, disgorging, through a tear in the paper, a little trickle of crumbs.

The pathos of the forgotten macaroons, the silent pain! Rosalind ran upstairs to the bedroom.

Darlingest did not hear her; she had forgotten. She was standing in the middle of the room with her face turned towards the window, looking at something a long way away, smiling and singing to herself and rolling up her veil.

The Twenties

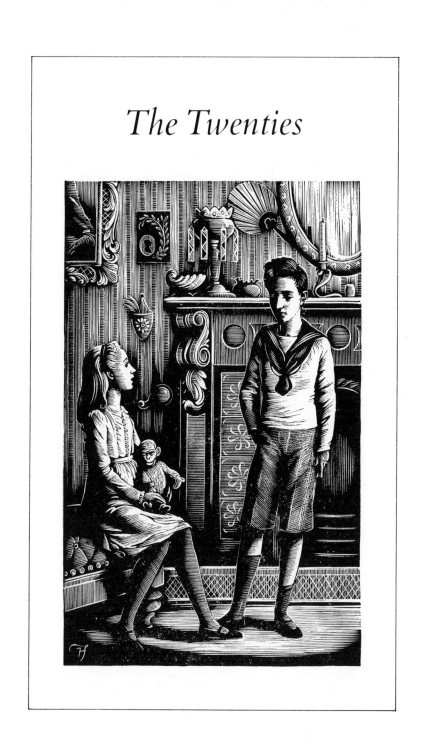

Ann Lee's

ANN LEE'S occupied a single frontage in one of the dimmer and more silent streets of south-west London. Grey-painted woodwork framed a window over which her legend was inscribed in far-apart black letters: 'ANN LEE – HATS.' In the window there were always just two hats; one on a stand, one lying on a cushion; and a black curtain with a violet border hung behind to make a background for the hats. In the two upper storeys, perhaps, Ann Lee lived mysteriously, but this no known customer had ever inquired, and the black gauze curtains were impenetrable from without.

Mrs Dick Logan and her friend Miss Ames approached the shop-front. Miss Ames had been here once before two years ago; the hat still existed and was frequently admired by her friends. It was she who was bringing Mrs Dick Logan; she hesitated beneath the names at the street corner, wrinkled up her brows, and said she hadn't remembered that Ann Lee's was so far from Sloane Square Station. They were young women with faces of a similar pinkness; they used the same swear-words and knew the same men. Mrs Dick Logan had decided to give up Clarice; her husband made such a ridiculous fuss about the bills and she had come to the conclusion, really, that considering what she had to put up with every quarter-day she might have something more to show for it in the way of hats. Miss Ames, who never dealt there, agreed that Clarice *was* expensive: now there was that shop she had been to once, Ann Lee's, not far from Sloane Street —

'Expensive?' Mrs Dick said warily.

'Oh well, not cheap. But most emphatically worth it. You know, I got that green there — '

'O-oh,' cried Mrs Dick Logan, 'that *expressive* green!'

So they went to find Ann Lee.

It was an afternoon in January, and their first sensation was of pleasure as they pushed open the curtained door and felt the warm air of the shop vibrate against their faces. An electric fire was reflected in a crimson patch upon the lustrous pile of the black carpet. There were two chairs, two mirrors, a divan and a curtain over an expectant archway. No hats were visible.

'Nice interior!' whispered Mrs Logan.

'Very much *her*,' returned Miss Ames. They loosened their furs luxuriously, and each one flashed sidelong at herself in a mirror an appraising glance. They had a sense of having been sent round on approval, and this deepened in the breast of Mrs Logan as their waiting in the empty shop was prolonged by minute after minute. Clarice came rushing at one rather: Mrs Logan was predisposed to like Ann Lee for her discreet indifference to custom. Letty Ames had said that she was practically a lady; a queer creature, Letty couldn't place her.

'I wonder if she realizes we're here,' whispered Letty, her brows again faintly wrinkled by proprietory concern. 'We might just cough – not an angry cough, quite natural. You'd better, Lulu, 'cause you've got one.'

Mrs Logan really had a slight catarrh, and the sound came out explosively. They heard a door softly open and shut, and the sound of feet descending two or three carpeted steps. There was another silence, then close behind the curtain one cardboard box was placed upon another, and there was a long, soft, continuous rustling of tissue paper. One might almost have believed Ann Lee to be emerging from a bandbox. Then the curtain twitched, quivered, and swung sideways, and some one gravely regarded them a moment from the archway. 'Good afternoon,' she said serenely, and 'Good afternoon.'

Her finger brushed a switch, and the shop became discreetly brilliant with long shafts of well-directed light.

'I've come back again,' Miss Ames brought out a shade dramatically, and Ann Lee nodded. 'Yes, so I see. I'm glad, Miss Ames. I had expected you.' She smiled, and Mrs Dick Logan felt chilly with exclusion. 'And I've brought my friend, Mrs Dick Logan.'

Ann Lee, with delicately arched-up eyebrows, turned to smile.

She was slight and very tall, and the complete sufficiency of her unnoticeable dress made Mrs Dick Logan feel gaudy. Her hands were long and fine, her outspread fingers shone against her dress – on a right-hand, non-committal finger she wore one slender ring. Her face was a serene one, the lips a shade austere, and her hair was closely swathed about her head in bright, sleek bands. There was something of the priestess about her, and she suffered their intrusion with a ceremonial grace. She was so unlike Clarice and all those other women, that Mrs Logan hardly knew how to begin, and was gratified, though half-conscious of a solecism, when Miss Ames said, 'My friend would like so much to see some hats. She's rather wanting two or three hats.'

Ann Lee's eyes dwelt dispassionately on Mrs Logan's face. She

looked questioningly at the eyebrows and searchingly at the
mouth, then said with an assumption that barely deferred to her
customer, 'Something quiet?'

Something quiet was the last thing Mrs Logan wanted. She
wanted something nice and bright to wear at Cannes, but she
hardly liked to say so. She put forward timidly, 'Well, not *too* quiet
– it's for the Riviera.'

'Really?' said Ann Lee regretfully – 'how delightful for you to be
going out. I don't know whether I have – no, wait; perhaps I have
some little model.'

'I rather thought a turban – gold, perhaps?'

'Oh, a *turban* – ? But surely you would be more likely to find
what you want out there? Surely Cannes — '

This made Mrs Logan feel peevish. Even if a person did look like
a Madonna or something, it was their business to sell a hat if they
kept a shop for that purpose. She hadn't followed Letty quite
endlessly through those miserable back streets to be sent away
disdainfully and told to buy her hats in France. She didn't care for
shopping on the Riviera, except with her Casino winnings; the
shops expected to be paid so soon, and Dickie made an even worse
fuss when he saw a bill in francs. She said querulously:

'Yes, but haven't you got anything of that sort? Any goldish,
sort of turbany thing?'

'I never have many hats,' said Ann Lee. 'I will show you
anything I have.'

Lulu glanced across at Letty, breathing more deeply with relief at
this concession, and Letty whispered, as Ann Lee vanished
momentarily behind the curtain: 'Oh, she's always like that; like
what I told you, queer. But the *hats*, my dear! You wait!'

When Ann Lee returned again carrying two hats, Mrs Logan
admitted that there had indeed been something to wait for. These
were the hats one dreamed about – no, even in a dream one had
never directly beheld them; they glimmered rather on the margin
of one's dreams. With trembling hands she reached out in Ann
Lee's direction to receive them. Ann Lee smiled deprecatingly upon
her and them, then went away to fetch some more.

Lulu Logan snatched off the hat she was wearing and let it slide
unnoticed from the brocaded seat of the chair where she had flung it
and bowl away across the floor. Letty snatched off hers too, out of
sympathy, and, each one occupying a mirror, they tried on every
single hat Ann Lee brought them; passing each one reverently and
regretfully across to one another, as though they had been crowns.
It was very solemn. Ann Lee stood against the curtain of the archway, looking at them gently and pitifully with her long pale eyes.
Her hands hung down by her sides; she was not the sort of person

who needs to finger the folds of a curtain, touch the back of a chair, or play with a necklace. If Mrs Logan and her friend Miss Ames had had either eyes, minds, or taste for the comparison, they might have said that she seemed to grow from the floor like a lily. Their faces flushed; soon they were flaming in the insidious warmth of the shop. 'Oh, *damn* my face!' groaned Miss Ames into the mirror, pressing her hands to her cheeks, looking out at herself crimsonly from beneath the trembling shadow of an osprey.

How could Lulu ever have imagined herself in a gold turban? In a gold turban, when there were hats like these? But she had never known that there were hats like these, though she had tried on hats in practically every shop in London that she considered fit to call a shop. Life was still to prove itself a thing of revelations, even for Mrs Dick Logan. In a trembling voice she said that she would certainly have *this* one, and she thought she simply must have *this*, and 'Give me back the blue one, darling!' she called across to Letty.

Then a sword of cold air stabbed into the shop, and Lulu and Letty jumped, exclaimed and shivered. The outer door was open and a man was standing on the threshold, blatant in the light against the foggy dusk behind him. Above the suave folds of his dazzling scarf his face was stung to scarlet by the cold; he stood there timid and aggressive; abject in his impulse to retreat, blustering in his determination to resist it. The two ladies stood at gaze in the classic pose of indignation of discovered nymphs. Then they both turned to Ann Lee, with a sense that something had been outraged that went deeper than chastity. The man was not a husband; he belonged to neither of them.

The intruder also looked towards Ann Lee; he dodged his head upwards and sideways in an effort to direct his line of vision past them. He opened his mouth as though he were going to shout; then they almost started at the small thin voice that crept from it to say 'Good evening.'

Ann Lee was balancing a toque upon the tips of her fingers, an imponderable thing of citron feathers, which even those light fingers hardly dared to touch. Not a feather quivered and not a shadow darkened her oval face as she replied, 'Good evening,' in a voice as equably unsmiling as her lips and eyes.

'I'm afraid I've come at a bad moment.'

'Yes,' she said serenely, 'I'm afraid you have. It's quite impossible for me to see you now; I'm sorry – I believe that hat is *you*, Mrs Logan. I'm sorry you don't care for black.'

'Oh, I do like black,' said Mrs Logan unhappily, feasting upon her own reflection. 'But I've got so many. Of course, they do set the face off, but I particularly wanted something rather sunny looking – now that little blue's perfect. How much did you . . . ?'

'Eight guineas,' said Ann Lee, looking at her dreamily.

Mrs Logan shivered and glanced vindictively towards the door. Ann Lee was bending to place the toque of citron feathers on the divan; she said mildly over her shoulder, with one slight upward movement of her lashes, 'We are a little cold in here, if you don't mind.'

'Sorry!' the man said, looking wildly into the shop. Then he came right in with one enormous step and pulled the door shut behind him. 'I'll wait then, if I may.' He looked too large, with his angular blue cloth overcoat double-buttoned across the chest, and as he stuffed his soft grey hat almost furtively under his arm they saw at once that there was something wrong about his hair. One supposed he couldn't help it waving like that, but he might have worn it shorter. The shoes on his big feet were very bright. Fancy a man like that . . . Lulu allowed a note of injury to creep into her voice as she said, 'I beg your pardon,' and reached past him to receive another hat from Letty. The shop was quite crowded, all of a sudden. And really, walking in like that . . . He didn't know what they mightn't have been trying on; so few shops nowadays were hats exclusively. He didn't see either herself or Letty; except as things to dodge his eyes past – obstacles. The way he was looking at Ann Lee was disgusting. A woman who asked eight guineas for a little simple hat like that blue one had got no right to expose her customers to this.

Letty, her hair all grotesquely ruffled up with trying-on, stood with a hat in either hand, her mouth half open, looking at the man not quite intelligently. One might almost have believed that she had met him. As a matter of fact, she was recognizing him; not as his particular self but as an Incident. He – It – crops up periodically in the path of any young woman who has had a bit of a career, but Ann Lee – really. Letty was vague in her ideas of Vestal Virgins, but dimly she connected them with Ann. Well, you never knew . . . Meanwhile this was a hat shop; the least fitting place on earth for the recurrence of an Incident. Perhaps it was the very priestliness of Ann which made them feel that there was something here to desecrate.

Ann Lee, holding the blue hat up before the eyes of Lulu, was the only one who did not see and tremble as the square man crossed the shop towards the fireplace and sat down on the divan beside the feather toque. He was very large. He drew his feet in with an obvious consciousness of offence and wrapped the skirts of his overcoat as uncontaminatingly as possible about his knees. His gaze crept about the figure of Ann. 'I'll wait, if you don't mind,' he repeated.

'I'm afraid it's no good,' she said abstractedly, looking past him

at the toque. 'I'm busy at present, as you can see, and afterwards
I've orders to attend to. I'm sorry. Hadn't you better — ?'

'It's four o'clock,' he said.

'*Four o'clock!*' shrieked Lulu. 'Good God, I'm due at the
Cottinghams!'

'Oh, don't go!' wailed Letty, whose afternoon was collapsing.
Ann Lee, smiling impartially, said she did think it was a pity not to
decide.

'Yes, but eight guineas.' It needed a certain time for decision.

'It's a lovely little hat,' pleaded Letty, stroking the brim
reverently.

'Yes, it's pretty,' conceded Ann Lee, looking down under her
lids at it with the faintest softening of the lips. They all drew
together, bound by something tense: the man before the fire was
forgotten.

'Oh, I don't know,' wailed the distracted Mrs Logan. 'I must
have that little black one, and I ought to get another dinner-hat –
You know how one needs them out there!' she demanded of Miss
Ames reproachfully. They both looked appealingly at Ann Lee.
She was not the sort of person, somehow, that one could ask to
reduce her things. There was a silence.

'It *is* four o'clock!' said the man in a bullying, nervous voice.
They jumped. 'You *did* say four o'clock,' he repeated.

Ann Lee quite frightened the two others; she was so very gentle
with him, and so scornfully unemphatic. 'I'm afraid you are
making a mistake. On Thursdays I am always busy. Good evening,
Mr Richardson; don't let us waste any more of your time. Now,
Mrs Logan, shall we say the blue? I feel that you would enjoy it,
though I still think the black is a degree more *you*. But I daresay
you would not care to take both.'

'I'll wait,' he said, in a queer voice. Unbuttoning his overcoat, he
flung it open with a big, defiant gesture as he leaned towards the
fire. 'Oh, the *toque!*' they screamed; and Ann Lee darted down and
forwards with a flashing movement to retrieve the frail thing from
beneath the iron folds of the overcoat. She carried it away again on
the tips of her fingers, peering down into the ruffled feathers; less
now of the priestess than of the mother – Niobe, Rachel. She
turned from the archway to say in a white voice, her face terrible
with gentleness, 'Then will you kindly wait outside?'

'It's cold,' he pleaded, stretching out his hands to the fire. It was a
gesture: he did not seem to feel the warmth.

'Then wouldn't it be better not to wait?' Ann Lee softly
suggested.

'I'll wait today,' he said, with bewildered and unshaken resolution. 'I'm not going away *today*.'

While she was away behind the curtain, rustling softly in that world of tissue paper, the man turned from the fire to look round at the contents of the shop. He looked about him with a kind of cringing triumph, as one who has entered desecratingly into some Holiest of Holies and is immediately to pay the penalty, might look about him under the very downsweep of the sacerdotal blade. He noted without comment or emotion the chairs, the lustrous carpet, Mrs Logan's hat, the ladies, and the mirrors opposite one another, which quadrupled the figure of each lady. One could only conclude that he considered Miss Ames and Mrs Logan as part of the fittings of the shop – 'customers' such as every shop kept two of among the mirrors and the chairs; disposed appropriately; symbolic, like the two dolls perpetually recumbent upon the drawing-room sofa of a doll's house. He stared thoughtfully at Miss Ames, not as she had ever before been stared at, but as though wondering why Ann Lee should have chosen to invest her shop with a customer of just *that* pattern. Miss Ames seemed for him to be the key to something; he puzzled up at her with knitted brows.

'Perhaps it would be better for us to be going?' said Miss Ames to Mrs Logan, her words making an icy transition above the top of his head. 'I'm afraid it's difficult for you to decide on anything with the place crowded and rather a lot of talking.'

Mrs Logan stood turning the blue hat round and round in her hands, looking down at it with tranced and avid eyes. 'Eight – sixteen – twenty-four,' she murmured. 'I do think she might reduce that little toque. If she'd let me have the three for twenty-two guineas.'

'Not she,' said Letty with conviction.

The man suddenly conceded their humanity. 'I suppose these are what you'd call expensive hats?' he said, looking up at Mrs Logan.

'Very,' said she.

'Several hundreds, I daresay, wouldn't buy up the contents of the shop, as it stands at present?'

'I suppose not,' agreed Mrs Logan, deeply bored – 'Letty, when *is* she coming back? Does she always walk out of the shop like this? Because I call it . . . I shall be so late at the Cottinghams, too. I'd be off this minute, but I just can't leave this little blue one. Where'll we get a taxi?'

'First corner,' said the man, rearing up his head eagerly. 'Round on your left.'

'Oh, thanks,' they said frigidly. He was encouraged by this to ask if they, too, didn't think it was very cold. Not, in fact, the sort of weather to turn a dog out. 'I'm sorry if I've inconvenienced you any way by coming in, but I've an appointment fixed with with Miss Lee for four o'clock, specially fixed, and you can imagine it was cold out there, waiting — ' The rustling of the paper ceased; they thought the curtain twitched. He turned and almost ate the archway with his awful eyes. Nothing happened; the sleek heavy folds still hung down unshaken to the carpet. 'I've an appointment,' he repeated, and listened to the echo with satisfaction and a growing confidence. 'But I don't mind waiting – I've done so much waiting.'

'Really?' said Miss Ames, in the high voice of indifference. Determined that she must buy nothing, she was putting her own hat on again resignedly. 'She's bound to be back in a jiff," she threw across reassuringly to Lulu, who sat bareheaded by a mirror, statuesquely meditative, her eyes small with the effort of calculation.

'I don't suppose either of you ladies,' said the man tremendously, 'have spent so much time in your whole lives trying on clothes in shops of this kind, as I've spent outside just this one shop, waiting. If any more ladies come in, they'll just have to take me naturally, for I'm going to sit on here where I am till closing time.'

Miss Ames, fluffing her side hair out in front of the mirror, repeated 'Really?' bland as a fish.

'I'm quite within my rights here,' said he, looking down now with approval at his feet so deeply implanted in the carpet, 'because you see, I've got an appointment.'

'There was no appointment, Mr Richardson,' said Ann Lee regretfully, standing in the archway.

Mrs Dick Logan, catching her breath, rose to her feet slowly, and said that she would have all three hats, and would Ann Lee send them along at once, please. It was an immense moment, and Miss Ames, who knew Dickie, thought as she heard Mrs Logan give her name and address in a clear unfaltering voice that there *was* something splendid about Lulu. The way she went through it, quarter-day after quarter-day . . . Miss Ames glowed for their common femininity as she watched her friend pick up yet another hat and try it on, exactly as if she could have had it too, if she had wished, and then another and another. Ann Lee, writing languidly in an order-book, bowed without comment to Mrs Logan's decision. And Letty Ames couldn't help feeling also that if Ann Lee had wished, Lulu would have had that other hat, and then another and another.

Mrs Logan stooped to recover her own hat from the floor. Ann Lee, looking down solicitously, but making no movement to assist her, meditated aloud that she was glad Mrs Logan was taking that little black. It was so much *her*, to have left it behind would have been a pity, Ann Lee couldn't help thinking.

As they gathered their furs about them, drew on their gloves, snapped their bags shut, and nestled down their chins into their furs, the two ladies glanced as though into an arena at the man sitting on the divan, who now leaned forwards to the fire again, his squared back towards them. And now? They longed suddenly, ah, how they longed, to linger in that shop.

'Good afternoon,' said Ann Lee. She said it with finality.

'Good afternoon,' they said, still arrested a second in the doorway. As they went out into the street reluctantly they saw Ann Lee, after a last dim bow towards them, pass back through the archway so gently that she scarcely stirred the curtains. The man beside the fire shot to his feet, crossed the shop darkly, and went through after her, his back broad with resolution.

There were no taxis where they had been promised to find them, and the two walked on in the direction of Sloane Street through the thickening fog. Mrs Dick Logan said that she didn't think she dared show her face at the Cottinghams now, but that really those hats were worth it. She walked fast and talked faster, and Miss Ames knew that she was determined not to think of Dickie.

When they came to the third corner they once more hesitated, and again lamented the non-appearance of a taxi. Down as much of the two streets as was visible, small shop-windows threw out squares of light on to the fog. Was there, behind all these windows, some one waiting, as indifferent as a magnet, for one to come in? 'What an extraordinary place it was,' said Mrs Logan for the third time, retrospectively. 'How she ever sells her things . . . '

'But she does sell them.'

'Yes.' She did sell them, Mrs Logan knew.

As they stood on the kerbstone, recoiling not without complaints from the unkindness of the weather, they heard rapid steps approaching them, metallic on the pavement, in little uneven spurts of speed. Somebody, half blinded by the fog, in flight from somebody else. They said nothing to each other, but held their breaths, mute with a common expectancy.

A square man, sunk deep into an overcoat, scudded across their patch of visibility. By putting out a hand they could have touched him. He went by them blindly; his breath sobbed and panted. It was by his breath that they knew how terrible it had been – terrible.

Passing them quite blindly, he stabbed his way on into the fog.

The Parrot

WHEN Mrs Willesden's parrot escaped, it rocketed in a pale-green streak across the sky and settled in the chestnut tree at the foot of the garden, where it became invisible among the branches. Invisible, that is to say, to Maud Pemberty and Eleanor Fitch, who stood staring up under their hands into the glare of the morning, until Maud located his head, a vermilion blot borne up and down like a buoy, slowly, by the undulations of a lower layer of the foliage. The chestnut tree blazed all over in the sunshine with candles of wax blossom. The scent of the pollen gave Eleanor Fitch shivers; about the end of May she would pass the tree on any pretext, sighing for something that she could not remember. Maud was in love, and chestnut flowers meant nothing to her; besides, as parlourmaid, she had more to do in the house than Miss Fitch, who was only a companion.

Now they both stood looking up at the parrot piteously, fearfully; Maud who had left the window open, and Eleanor who had been cleaning the cage. They advanced towards the tree unconsciously, step by lingering step, as though attracted; still with that mesmeric upward stare.

The parrot took no notice of them. It wobbled along the branch, peevishly disentangling its wing and tail feathers from the long-fingered leaves. Its tongue was in one corner of its beak; its head turned and its eyes rolled from side to side in a mixture of ecstasy and apprehension. Once or twice it lost its balance and tilted right forward with a muffled squawk until it was hanging nearly upside down. It would recover itself, look reproachfully down at its claws, and totter along further, till another clump of leaves swept down to assault it. It wore an air of silly bravado, and looked what it was, thoroughly idiotic.

Mrs Willesden had no brothers, cousins or lovers: none certainly who were sailors, and none of these, therefore, had brought the parrot home to her from Indian seas. Dark-faced men may have dazzled it, against the purple of the ocean, with the swinging gold of their earrings, and held it up to stroke the sleek vermilion of its head. This Eleanor would have wished to believe, and Mrs

Willesden even playfully asseverated; but the parrot had not, somehow, the aroma. It had no pedigree; Mrs Willesden had bought it at an auction at the other side of London: a very new-looking parrot, newer-looking even than the complete edition of Lord Lytton, or the mahogany chest of drawers. It was a guaranteed talker, but its conversation was neither entertaining, relevant, nor profane. It would mutter 'Poll, Po-oll, Pol-pol-pol' for hours, in an ecstasy of introspection, or say 'Lead, kindly Light' – just that, no more of the hymn. If one spoke to it, besought it, cursed it, wooed it, it would blink at one in a smoulder of malevolence, and say, 'Minnie? Minnie! Tom? Minnie!'

Mrs Willesden loved the parrot, and would sit beside it for hours in the afternoon. It was carried into the dining-room to meals, and its cage was placed beside her at the head of the table, on a butler's tray. Eleanor hated the parrot, and used to come down and clean its cage early in the morning before breakfast, so as to get that over. Thus it was that the parrot had escaped at a quarter past eight, before Mrs Willesden was awake, while yellow cotton blinds still unflickeringly sheathed her windows. Mrs Willesden slept late today; one did not care, one did not dare to wake her. Eleanor and Maud stood sodden-footed out in the dew, with now and then a backward glance up at Mrs Willesden's window, and their hands burnt and their fingers twitched with the desire to grab the parrot by its scaly legs and its wings and thrust it shrieking back into its cage.

Eleanor's mind went whirling round like a wheel on the hub of this moment. She knew that what had brought her here to be Mrs Willesden's companion had also brought about the escape of the parrot – her own immense ineffectuality. She knew that she was a clever girl, or she might possibly have loved Mrs Willesden; she knew that she was a wise girl, or she could not so continuously have tolerated her. She knew that she must be a nice-looking girl, or Mrs Willesden, whose sense of beauty had found its culminating expression in the parrot, would never have engaged her. She knew, however, that she could not be dangerously attractive, because although she was quite ready to marry anybody who seemed at all suitable, and thus escape from life with Mrs Willesden and the equally odious alternative of using her brains, nobody, even of the most unsuitable, had so far presented himself. She never thought about men, because she fully agreed with Mrs Willesden that this was not nice; she merely wondered sometimes when Mrs Willesden would have become a thing of the past. It was while thus wondering that she had turned away from the parrot's cage to look in a mirror, and, thus looking, had heard the unlatched door swing open and the silken sound of the flight. As things were now, Mrs

Willesden might very soon become a thing of the past; and a swift nostalgia for security made the sky blur and glitter, and the chestnut candles swim.

"Well, it's no good crying, Miss,' said Maud. 'It doesn't get us out of anything, what I mean.'

'I'm not,' said Eleanor quickly. 'Poll, pretty Polly-poll, come downsey!'

'Come downsey!' echoed Maud. ('Yah, get out of that, you dirty beast!) Well, he doesn't understand, Miss. He's just stupid.'

'Go into the house and get the cage, Maud. Stick a banana between the bars, so's he can only get at it from the inside, and put it down on the grass with the door open. Go quickly and – hush!'

Maud went, and Eleanor stood staring, still mesmerically, up at the parrot, while the imagined eyes of Mrs Willesden burnt into her back. She stared up at the parrot, but Polly was preoccupied with his feat of balance and was perpetually in profile. He was not to be mesmerised, and just as Maud emerged from the house with the cage held at arm's length and the door invitingly open, he toppled forward urgently, beat for a moment with his wings, then flopped into the air. He did not rise very high this time, but after describing one or two lopsided circles, as though with wings unevenly weighted, he skimmed the top of the garden wall, glittered for a second above it in poised uncertainty, and vanished.

'There!' said Maud, and Eleanor gathered her skirts together, gave one calculating glance, and was up and on to the top of the wall like a cat.

The parrot ambled slowly through the air, with, as it were, the jog of a fat pony translated into flight. It clumsily attempted a landing on some branches in the next garden and slid off again, its claws ripping the leaves. All along, in the pleasant irregular gardens of the road, glass-houses sparkled, flashing out rays, geraniums in the beds made neat little cubes of coral and scarlet, violas grew in great mauve cushions. A furtive young wind spilt the petals from the fruit trees on to the grass, stirred the pools they made, then crept away, frightened. Eleanor, equally furtive, knelt up on the wall, looked all round her, and tucked her skirts down. She calculated that the parrot must without fail come wheezily to earth at either the Cuthbertsons' or the Philpots'.

It could have a long wait to fly before it reached the poplars of the one garden which she could not possibly enter to retrieve it. The poplars tapered above all the trees of the gardens with a sort of elegant irresponsibility; they swayed towards one another and glittered with mirth. They rose from out of the four walls of the Lennicotts' garden, and within these walls no one in the road had set foot since the occupation of the Lennicotts.

Towards the poplars the parrot leisurely proceeded, as one in good time for an appointment, and somewhere down below them came to earth.

Mrs Willesden had told Eleanor that it was better not to ask about the Lennicotts, and that it was all very, very sad. Indeed, the less one knew the better, everybody felt, and ladies flinched as they told one another in low voices things about the Lennicotts which one did not care to say, but which demanded to be said. Mrs Willesden told Eleanor that sin was becoming, alas, very prevalent (though one did not care to talk to an unmarried girl about these things) and that she was thankful that her mother had not lived to see these days, and that her dear husband had also been spared. 'It is not even known,' she said, 'that they are the Lennicotts, but *he* is a Lennicott, and she is *called* Mrs. My library does not keep his novels, and that nice young man there looked very much surprised when I asked for them. Mrs Cuthbertson lent me a copy of one of them, but I found it very difficult to read, and so did she.'

'Was it improper?' asked Eleanor, in a low voice, winding wool quickly.

'One may be sure of that,' Mrs Willesden had replied, 'but as I tell you, I did not finish the book; it was so very dull. As far as I got, I did not see anything in it, and I glanced through to the end and did not see anything either. However, I should not have dreamed of keeping a book like that in the house with a young girl like you about – Eleanor, you had better rewind that wool, you are winding it too tightly . . .'

Even in London, it was said, many people would not know the Lennicotts, so they had come here, doubtless in the hopes of making nice friends. The road deplored the Lennicotts, and the neighbourhood envied the road. In the evenings, long shafts of blistering whiteness streamed out from the headlamps of cars and lent an unseemly publicity to the comings and goings of everybody's cats. These cars drew up perpetually outside the Lennicotts' with a long faint sound like a sniff. Though they entertained, the Lennicotts were not rowdy; one heard only, sometimes, low excited laughter of the kind that made one wish to stop and listen; and, very rarely, Mrs Lennicott's voice, which was very beautiful, came floating down among the trees of the road as she sang to her guests after dinner.

The parrot dropped down among the poplars, and Eleanor's heart dropped with it, like a stone. She heard a slight rattle at the upstairs window, and knew that Mrs Willesden's blind was up, and that soon everything would be over. She gathered herself together, her tongue curled back in her mouth with terror, and leapt from the top of the wall into the lane full of nettles that ran along the backs of the gardens, past the Willesdens', past No. 17's, 18's and 19's, till it broadened out under the Lennicotts' poplars into a small patch of common. As she turned the bend of the lane and heard the rustle of the poplars above her, she heard also, very distinctly and monotonously, the parrot saying 'Minnie? Minnie!' down in the garden inside the walls. Had it encountered anybody, or was it merely talking to itself?

Eleanor did not believe that early rising could possibly be compatible with moral obliquity. An outraged sense of fitness was therefore added to her astonishment when, having adjusted her pince-nez, she found herself looking down from the top of the Lennicotts' wall on to the unswerving centre-parting of Mrs Lennicott's marmalade-coloured hair. The parrot sat biting its nails on one end of a pergola, and Mrs Lennicott did not notice it because she was reading a book of poetry with large print and smoking a cigarette in a long holder. She sat in a deck-chair with her feet on a recumbent watering-can, and wore, as might have been expected, coloured leather shoes. When she heard the scratching sound of Eleanor's toes seeking purchase on the outer bricks, she looked up, smiled vaguely, with the sun on her gold lashes, and said, 'Good morning. Have you come to look for a tennis ball? Do come in!'

She had a long chin and a plump, oval, delicately coloured face. Her eyebrows arched very innocently, and she looked at Eleanor uncomprehendingly, but with an air of earnest effort, as though she were a verse of Georgian poetry that one could not possibly understand. 'Do come in!' she repeated.

'Thank you,' said Eleanor. 'I only wanted that parrot.' She pointed to the pergola, and Mrs Lennicott, laying her book face downwards on the grass, turned her head with interest in the same direction. Her hair was braided against her cheek. 'Really,' she said, 'is that your parrot? It is very beautiful. But do come in and take it away if you want it. I expect it is very valuable. It may have been here for some time, but I did not notice it because this garden is always full of birds, and I am very stupid about natural history.'

For the first time that morning the parrot looked straight at Eleanor; for the first time in their acquaintanceship it had a gleam of intelligence in its eye. 'Take me,' it seemed to say. 'I am an old sick bird, beaten out and weary. I have aspired and failed – it is finished. Take me.' A white sheath rolled up over its eyes; its feathers drooped.

Eleanor had an idea that if she did not breathe very deeply, if she walked lightly on the tips of her toes, taking as few steps as possible, and if she did not look quite straight at anything, especially Mrs Lennicott, she might, having entered the Lennicotts' garden, yet leave it uncontaminated. She therefore sprang from the wall, alighting on her hands and on the balls of her feet, as she had been taught at school, at the very brink of a flower-bed. As she stood upright she half saw, then turned irresistibly to watch, Mrs Lennicott rise with one ripple from the deck-chair and walk as though entranced towards the pergola, holding up her hands. Her dress hung ungirt from her bosom and swept the grass, so that its hem was dark with dew.

'Oh, how beautiful you are!' she sighed. 'How your head flashes! You must forgive me,' she said to Eleanor, 'but I have never looked very closely at a parrot before.'

Polly was obviously gratified. He ducked his head and fluttered his tail-feathers, and swayed a little from the claws. He conveyed by a multiplicity of innuendoes that Mrs Willesden and Eleanor were a pair of old frumps, and that even Minnie had left much to be desired, and that he knew a woman of distinction when he met one. Had Mrs Lennicott been allowed to engage him further in conversation, his capture from the rear might easily have been effected, but Eleanor was too precipitate. Her outstretched hands cast a shadow; Polly felt them coming and soared into the air with spread wings like a Phoenix. He squawked derision at Eleanor, and steered a zig-zag course to the verandah drain pipe, from the pipe to an upper window-sill, from the window-sill to a tank, from the tank to the ridge of the roof between two chimney pots.

'Oh, how terrible for you!' cried Mrs Lennicott, in real distress.

Eleanor's cheeks burnt; little wisps of hair came down and frisked in the light wind, tickling the back of her neck. The tides of her spirit were slow, drawn by the slow moon of her intelligence, but now anger stirred in her; she drew a gasp which shook her and locked her fingers together.

'I'm going to catch that parrot,' she said, turning to Mrs Lennicott. 'I'm going to catch it so's to wring its neck.'

'*Have* you ever wrung anything's neck?' asked Mrs Lennicott in an awed voice.

When Eleanor admitted that she hadn't, Mrs Lennicott, with obvious relief, invited her to come into the house and catch the parrot. 'It would be very easy,' she said, 'to get out on to the roof from the window of my husband's room. He has often talked of doing so when there was too much noise in the house, but the roof is not flat enough to hold a writing-table. I don't think he is awake, but if he were he would be delighted to help you.'

The shadow of the house fell cold on Eleanor as she left the wind and glitter and innocence of the morning behind and walked with Mrs Lennicott towards the steps of the verandah. Afterwards, there was so much lilac in the drawing-room and the place was so heavy with it that her other impressions were blurred, except that the room with its low and very many sofas lurked on sufferance round the great jutting triangle of the piano. She was still drawing shallow breaths and walking delicately, and had the sense of passing down a long low shining tunnel of wickedness, to where at the end she saw the parrot, a speck faintly visible against a familiar sky. Because it was on the west side of the house the room was in pale shadow, but beyond a great gold slab of sunshine lay across the pavement of the hall. Not thus fell the sunshine through the glass panels of a similar door on to Mrs Willesden's oil-cloth.

'You are one of the thin family, aren't you?' said Mrs Lennicott. 'There are girls on bicycles – so nice-looking – with rather a sharp-looking little dog that runs behind – though I am sure he is a dear little dog, and so faithful – no, the stairs are straight ahead, through that archway. Shall I go first?'

Eleanor said no, that she was not a Philpot.

'There are a great many people in this road, aren't there? I never knew there were so many people who didn't live in London. Of course, one sees the houses, but it is difficult to realise, isn't it, that they have insides and that they really mean anything!'

Mrs Lennicott preceded Eleanor with a displaced shimmer of the skirts, a fragrant swish. She was not the sort of woman who rustles. The stair carpet crunched under one's feet with a velvety resistiveness; it had, at the first contact, a sinister sleekness. There were prints on the staircase from which Eleanor turned away quickly, tingling. It was as though the earliest darts assailed her armour. She was here in those Lennicotts' very house; its shadows and scents were surcharged for her, every contact was intolerably significant.

Then a door opened above, and Mr Lennicott came out from his bedroom on to the landing.

Eleanor stopped dead and pressed back against the wall; her shoulder caught one of the picture-frames and made it swing wildly. She shut her eyes, and at the end of that shining and inexorable tunnel the parrot quivered and receded. She was menaced; the tunnel was narrowing down upon her; she wanted to go back.

'Who in God's name!' cried Mr Lennicott.

'It's a lady come to take away a parrot. darling.'

'Parrot?' said Mr Lennicott despairingly. 'When did we get a parrot? Why didn't you pay for it? Where's all that money I gave you? I told you this would happen again. You know they came and took away the sundial. Not that I care whether you had a sundial or parrots or an apiary, but the people who come to take them away are full of moral indignation – and you know — '

'It's *her* parrot,' said Mrs Lennicott, 'and it's on the roof. Do come up,' she added, turning back to Eleanor, 'and let me introduce my husband, Miss . . . oh, I am so stupid!'

'Fitch,' whispered Eleanor, and feeling her tongue curl back in her mouth again looked up slowly. First she saw Mr Lennicott's ankles, very thin with big bones and covered with black hairs. Then came yards, it seemed, of his dressing-gowned figure, a long thin strip, bent slightly and bulging where his hands went into his pockets; then his long chin with a blue bloom on it, then his quizzical Spanish face. 'If there's anything I can do — ?' said Mr Lennicott, and his teeth glimmered.

'*Is* there anything he can do?' asked Mrs Lennicott, sweeping round and leaning towards Eleanor, as she came up step by step, with such eager bright expansiveness that she almost embraced her. Her eyes were of that clear blueness which almost is not when they are empty of expression; they took colour like water. She was eager and impersonal.

The sun streamed in through the staircase window, and Mr Lennicott's dragons glowed; he might have stepped out of a cathedral window, and had indeed even that air of ornate asceticism.

'You could get out along my gutter,' he said, grasping the situation quickly, 'my room has an attic window, and from there to the ridge of the roof it's just a hoist.'

He wrapped his dressing-gown further round him with a big gesture, re-knotted the cord at the waist with an air of resolution, and, shuffling a little in his Turkish slippers, went back across the landing and held his door open for Eleanor.

'I expect the parrot isn't there any more,' said she. 'I – I expect it's gone . . . I won't mind about it today, thank you very much.'

'But it's such a *pity* to lose such a beautiful parrot!' wailed Mrs Lennicott.

'I think really I won't . . . '

'Oh, come on,' said Mr Lennicott's deep voice suddenly. 'A girl like you ought to be able to climb like a cat. No, look here, upon my word, you don't, though – I'll go up and collar the thing, and you lean out of the window and grab it.'

'You ought to put it *into* something,' said Mrs Lennicott. 'Just wait, I'll get a bandbox.' She brought a bandbox which was striped with many colours, and had a French name scrawled across the top. It was so big that Eleanor had to open her arms wide to embrace it, and tucked the lid, for better balance, under her chin. The wind was blowing in through Mr Lennicott's open window; his curtains rushed to meet them as Eleanor, contracted into an aching knot of terror, followed the be-dragoned back, leaving behind her Mrs Lennicott, the landing, and (save death) the only way of retreat. The room smelt of cigarettes and masculine unguents and had sloping ceilings. She remembered all those terrible books and pressed the bandbox closer to her chest, feeling morally as well as physically embuttressed by it.

Mr Lennicott, breathing through his teeth, grasped the window-sill and flung one leg over it on to the outside gutter. Eleanor wondered if she would have to appear at the inquest, and whether by that she would be compromised; she watched Mr Lennicott anxiously as, doubled like a brave on the warpath, he picked his way along the gutter, till he had passed the window and was out of sight.

Mrs Lennicott came in and sat on the bed, which made Eleanor feel better. She lit a cigarette and said that Trotsky never killed himself, and that it was a lovely day, and that Trotsky never took enough exercise, and that Eleanor mustn't worry. They heard a hoist and a scramble, and knew that Mr Lennicott must now be up on the roof.

'If you would hold the bandbox,' said Eleanor, 'I think I'll go too, as it's my parrot.' She didn't want the Lennicotts to think she was afraid of *that*.

'*Do*,' said Mrs Lennicott, and, with her cigarette holder cocked skywards from one corner of her mouth, relieved Eleanor of the bandbox. Eleanor, leaning towards the roof, followed Mr Lennicott along the gutter.

'Hallo-o!' hailed Mr Lennicott from above. 'That's sound. Come on, up here. Where's Piggy? Piggy coming too? It's – it's simply immense up here; you'd never believe. Come on – hoist!'

He gripped both her hands and hoisted. He was sitting astride of the roof, and Eleanor sat side-saddle, tucking down her skirts round her legs. White clouds had come up and bowled past before the wind like puff-balls; the poplars swayed confidentially towards one another, then swayed apart in mirth. One of the Philpot girls was mending a bicycle down in their garden, but she did not look up. Her bowed back looked narrow and virginal; Eleanor half-laughed elatedly, and smoothed her hair behind her ears.

'And the parrot?' she said, quickly recalling herself and looking from left to right.

The wind ruffled Mr Lennicott's hair, but he sat immobile, following the clouds with his eyes and smiling to himself. 'Parrot?' he echoed, starting violently. 'What parrot? Where? . . . Oh, by Jove, yes; where is it?'

'Here,' whispered Eleanor, for the parrot had come sidling down the roof towards them, and now sat down beside her. Its feathers were dishevelled, its eyes furtive, its head, dimmed seemingly in colour, drooped a little. It looked sadder, smaller, less of a buffoon. It pecked wearily and perfunctorily at Eleanor's fingers as they closed upon it, but said nothing as she tucked it under her arm.

'Poor beast,' said Mr Lennicott. 'I believe, you know, that the other birds have been nasty to it. They don't like anything a different colour from themselves; no one ever does, you know, it's damned funny.'

He mused upon this, while Eleanor thoughtfully regarded him.

'Did you *find* the parrot, Trotsky?' inquired Mrs Lennicott, putting her head out of the window beneath them.

'No – I mean, yes!' shouted back her husband. 'We've got the parrot here – not in at all good order, but giving no trouble at all. Where's the basket?'

Mrs Lennicott leaned out perilously far, encircling the bandbox with her long smooth arms. The lid was tilted a little sideways; she placed one finger upon it to keep it thus, and gurgled with pleasurable excitement as Mr Lennicott came sliding down the roof with the parrot under his arm, and crammed the bird into the box among the tissue paper. 'Clap down the lid!' shrieked Eleanor, scarlet with excitement. Mrs Lennicott, having obeyed her, withdrew slowly into the darkness of the room, pressing the bandbox closer to her bosom, and gazing at it awfully as it began to throb with the protests of the parrot.

So that was over, and Eleanor could take the parrot home and snap the door of its cage on it, and all that hour of the day would be gone; a nothing, an irrelevancy; a lost hour that had slipped through a crack in her life and vanished. She came down from the roof nothing but an empty stomach, with an empty head above it, through which desires vaguely hurried like the clouds. She sighed as she so often sighed beneath the chestnut tree, and did not want to leave the sunny landing where Mr Lennicott, behind her, slanted up against a door-post, and Mrs Lennicott, kneeling by the bandbox, tied the lid securely down with a length of yellow ribbon. The parrot was very quiet in there; perhaps it did not want to go home either.

'This seems quite safe, I think,' said Mrs Lennicott, handing her the bandbox, 'but don't carry it by the string. I hope this hasn't been very tiring for your parrot. I didn't think it looked very well.'

Eleanor repudiated the parrot – did she then so reek of what was Mrs Willesden's? 'It's not the sort of thing *I'd* ever keep,' she said vindictively, 'I'd like to have a greyhound, or a large mastiff. It belongs to a lady, otherwise it wouldn't have mattered at all. Now I must take it home . . . I – I really ought to take it home before it begins to make a noise again . . . No, really, thank you very much, I mustn't wait for anything to eat.'

'Not fruit?' marvelled Mrs Lennicott. It was like being held back by a thousand hands, they both so evidently wished to detain her.

Nobody had ever reached out for her like that so eagerly; she did not want to go back to that house of shut-out sunshine and great furniture, where the parrot was carried royally from room to room on trays, and she was nothing. But it was useless, not an inch of their way and hers lay parallel; to catch at them would mean, ultimately, only another of these wrenches. They had struck out across the open country, and it was so green there, Eleanor felt her feet aching from the high road.

All that they were suggesting, actually, was that she should go down with them to the dining-room and eat figs there, but it was not without remembrance of Proserpine, that she stood mulishly and shook her head. She had shared a roof and breasted the clouds with Mr Lennicott, and now she must be home in time to carry up the parrot and the breakfast tray into Mrs Willesden's room. How world lay overlapped with world; visible each from the other and yet never to be one! Along the wind, through the trees of the garden, came booming out the Philpots' breakfast gong.

No one spoke of meeting any more; had she, too, been a magical interlude for the Lennicotts, over which their lives would close? They went down to the garden, and the prints all down the staircase, flitting past her eyes regretfully, whispered, 'Stay, stay, stay!' And when they were out on the grass, and pointed out the path that ran to the gate standing wide to the road, fear returned to Eleanor. Should she come forth publicly out of those gates into the now awakened road, carrying this radiant bandbox?

'I think the back way would be really shorter,' murmured Eleanor.

'Back way?' said the Lennicotts.

'Over the wall . . . '

Mrs Willesden shut her windows on going to bed at nights, and it was Eleanor's duty to open them next morning, just a very little, when she brought in the parrot. Entering Mrs Willesden's bed-room for this purpose, it was difficult to believe that the winds and dews of May were a reality, or that there was running water anywhere and the shining bodies of bathers, or vigorous laughter, or open country – or roofs. The room was dim with seemly crimson curtains, and Mrs Willesden's wrappings lay ready to be put on, sheath by sheath.

'Polly's looking very well today,' said Mrs Willesden as usual, following the cage across the room with her eyes because she could not turn her head among the shawls. 'Pretty Polly, pretty little Poll-poll.'

'It got out,' said Eleanor abruptly. Mrs Willesden would have to know, lest otherwise she might find out; and she was, moreover, one contemptuously knew, a kind old lady.

'Dear me,' said Mrs Willesden, with placid admiration. 'The naughty pretty. Did he go flying far away?'

'I brought him back,' said Eleanor; 'he flew round and round the garden.'

'Looking for his banana tree and coral reefs, poor pretty boy,' sighed Mrs Willesden. 'And so you caught him, Eleanor? That was very smart of you, with nobody to help. No one knows where he mightn't have flown to: he might have met the most terrible people and never have come home again. And if strange people had caught him, even people quite respectable and honest, it would have put me in an embarrassing position – under compliment, I mean. I know it may be foolish and old-fashioned of me, but I do very much dislike being under compliment. So you caught him all alone?'

'Yes,' said Eleanor. 'He didn't give me much trouble. I – I caught him all alone.'

The parrot, rising on its perch, beat its wings and cried in a hoarse voice, 'Minnie, Minnie, *Minnie?*' It ended on a note of regret and bewilderment.

And Eleanor put down its cage quickly and walked over to the window. It was like the crowing of the cock.

The Visitor

ROGER was awakened early that morning by the unfamiliar sound of trees in the Miss Emerys' garden. It was these that had made the room so dark the previous evening, obscuring the familiar town lights that shone against the wall above his bed at home, making him feel distant and magnificently isolated in the Miss Emerys' spare-room. Now, as the sky grew pale with sunless morning, the ceiling was very faintly netted over with shadows, and when the sun washed momentarily over the garden these shadows became distinct and powerful, obstructive; and Roger felt as though he were a young calf being driven to market netted down in a cart. He rolled over on his back luxuriously, and lay imagining this.

But the imagination-game palled upon him earlier than usual, defeated by his returning consciousness of the room. Here was he alone, enisled with tragedy. The thing had crouched beside his bed all night; he had been conscious of it through the thin texture of his dreams. He reached out again now, timidly, irresistibly to touch it, and found that it had slipped away, withdrawn into ambush, leaving with him nothing of itself, scarcely even a memory.

He had never slept before in anybody's spare-room; theirs at home had been wonderful to him: a port, an archway, an impersonal room with no smell, nothing of its own but furniture; infinitely modifiable by the personality of brushes and sponge-bags, the attitude of shoe-trees, the gesture of a sprawling dress across a chair.

The Miss Emerys' spare-room had long serious curtains that hung down ungirt beside the window, fluted into shadows. One never touched the curtains; if one wanted to make the room dark, one drew a blind that had a lace edge and was stamped all over with a pattern of oak-leaves. Miss Emery, when she brought Roger up to bed last night, tried to do this, laid one hand on the acorn of the blind-cord, but Roger prayed her to desist and she desisted. She understood that no one liked to see the sky from bed. She was a sympathetic woman, and made Roger increasingly sorry for all the things he used to think about her blouses.

The furniture was all made of yellow wood, so shiny and one

knew so yielding, that one longed to stab and dint it. There were woollen mats that Miss Dora Emery had made – she had even promised to teach Roger. She had promised this last night, while Roger sat beside her in a drawing-room that positively rocked and shimmered in a blinding glare of gaslight. A half-finished rug lay across her knee and rolled and slid noiselessly on the floor when she moved; the woolly, half-animate thing filled Roger with a vague repulsion. 'I'm doing the black border now,' she had explained, tweaking the clipped strands through the canvas with a crotchet hook and knotting them with a flick of her wrist. 'Soon I'll be coming to the green part, the pattern, and I shall work in some touches of vermilion. You really must watch then, Roger, it will be so pretty, you'll really be amused.' Roger wondered if she would have come to the vermilion, even to the green, by the time his mother died. Miss Emery was not a quick worker. 'How much more black will there be before the pattern?' he inquired. 'Three inches,' said Miss Emery, and he measured out the distance with his finger.

There were paintings on the spare-room wall of moors with Scotch cattle, and over the chest of drawers there was a smaller picture in a green-and-gold frame called 'Enfin – Seuls.' French. It depicted a lady and gentleman holding each other close and kissing in a drawing-room full of palms; they seemed to be glad of something. The paper had a pattern on it, although Roger's father and mother had said that patterned wall-papers were atrocious. Roger looked at it, and jumped with his mind from clump to clump – they were like islands of daisies – pretending he was a frog who had been given a chance of just eight jumps to get away from a dragon.

A clock ticked out in the passage; it must be a very big one, perhaps a stationmaster's clock, given the Miss Emerys by a relation. It had no expression in its voice; it neither urged one on nor restrained one, simply commented quite impartially upon the flight of time. Sixty of these ticks went to make a minute, neither more nor less than sixty, and the hands of the clock would be pointing to an hour and a minute when they came to tell Roger what he was expecting to hear. Round and round they were moving, waiting for that hour to come. Roger was flooded by a desire to look at the face of the clock, and still hearing no one stirring in the house he crept across to the door, opened it a crack, quite noiselessly, and looking down the passage saw that the clock had exactly the same expression, or absence of expression, as he had imagined. Beyond the clock, a rich curtain of crimson velvet hung over the archway to the stairs, and a door painted pale blue stood open a little, showing the bathroom floor.

Roger had never believed that the Miss Emerys or any of the people he and his mother visited really went on existing after one had said good-bye to them and turned one's back. He had never expressed this disbelief to his mother, but he took it to be an understood thing, shared between them. He knew, of course, with his *brain*, that the Miss Emerys (as all the other people in the roads round them) went on like their clocks, round and round, talking and eating and washing and saying their prayers; but he didn't *believe* it. They were, rather, all rolled up swiftly and silently after one's departure and put away for another occasion, and if one could jump round suddenly, taking God by surprise, one would certainly find them gone. If one met a Miss Emery on one's walks, one assumed she must have sprung up somewhere just out of sight, like a mushroom, and that after one had passed her, nothingness would swing down to hide her like a curtain. Roger *knew* that all the doors round the Miss Emerys' landing opened on to rooms, or would do so if he walked through them when he was expected. But if he opened a door when he was not expected, would there be anything beyond it but the emptiness and lightness of the sky? Perhaps even the sky would not be there. He remembered the fairy tale of Curdie.

The spare-room opened off a very private little corridor that had no other door along it but the bathroom's. The Miss Emerys could not fully have realized the charm of this, or they would have taken the room for their own. Roger had an imaginary house that, when it was quite complete in his mind, he was some day going to live in: in this there were a hundred corridors raying off from a fountain in the centre; at the end of each there was a room looking out into a private garden. The walls of the gardens were so high and smooth that no one could climb over into anybody else's. When they wanted to meet, they would come and bathe together in the fountain. One of the rooms was for his mother, another for his friend Paul. There were ninety-seven still unappropriated, and now it seemed there would be ninety-eight.

Somebody in a room below pulled a blind up with a rush, and began to sweep a carpet. Day was beginning in a new house.

The Miss Emerys' breakfast-room was lovely. By the window, they had a canary in a cage, that sprang from perch to perch with a wiry, even sound. Outside, the little early-morning wind had died; the trees were silent, their leaves very still. Since there was no sun this morning, the breakfast table held without competition all the brightness, to radiate it out into the room. No sun could have been rounder or more luminous than the brass kettle genially ridiculous upon a tripod, a blue flame trembling beneath it. There were dahlias, pink and crimson, and marmalade in a glass pot shaped like a barrel cast a shadow of gold on the table-cloth. There was a monstrous tea-cosy, its frill peaked intelligently; and Miss Emery smiled at Roger over the top of it. There were parrots printed on the cosy – they battled with one another – so brilliant one could almost hear them screech. Could a world hold death that held that cosy? Miss Emery had pinned a plaid bow-tie into the front of her collar. Could she have done this if what Roger expected must soon happen to Roger? Must it happen, mightn't it be a dream?

'Come in, dear,' said Miss Emery, while he revolved this on the threshold, and Miss Dora Emery, who had not come to help him to dress (perhaps she was not allowed to), forced a lump of sugar quickly between the bars of the canary's cage, and came round the table to greet him. Roger eyed her cheek uncertainly; it was pink as a peach, and against the light its curve showed downy: he wondered what was expected of him. They eyed one another with a fleeting embarrassment, then Miss Dora jerked away a chair from the table, said 'And you sit there, in Claude's place,' and pushed back the chair with him on it, pausing over him for a second to straighten a knife beside his plate.

On the table, the hosts of breakfast were marshalled into two opposing forces, and a Miss Emery from either end commanded each. The toast, eggs, bacon, and marmalade had declared for Miss Dora; but the tea-pot and its vassals, the cruet and the honeycomb – beautifully bleeding in flowered dish – were for Miss Emery to a man. The loaf, sitting opposite to Roger, remained unabashedly neutral. Roger looked from one Miss Emery to the other.

'Plenty of milk? I expect so; Claude always liked plenty of milk in his tea. What I always say is – little boys like what's good for them, don't you worry, grown-ups!'

'Two pieces of bacon? Look, if this egg's too soft, mop it up with your bread; I should. They *say* it isn't polite, but — '

'Yes, please,' said Roger, and 'thank you very much, I will.' What jolly ladies the Miss Emerys were!

They were looking at him anxiously; were they afraid he was not quite pleased and comfortable? Perhaps they did not often have a visitor. They were aunts; they had once had a nephew called Claude, but he had grown up and gone to India, leaving only some fishing-tackle behind him and a book about trains which had been given to Roger. Were they looking piteously at him in the pangs of baffled aunthood? But were they perhaps wondering if he *knew*, how much he knew, and whether they ought to tell him? They were ladies with bright eyes that would fill up easily with emotion, white, quick hands and big bosoms. Roger could hear them saying, 'Little motherless boy, poor little motherless boy!' and they would snatch him and gather him in, and each successively would press his head deep into her bosom, so deep that perhaps it would never come out again.

Roger shrank into himself in fearful anticipation: he must escape, he must escape, he must escape . . . Yesterday had been one long intrigue for solitude, telling a fib and slipping away from his little sisters, telling a fib and slipping away from his father. Father didn't go to work now but walked about the house and garden, his pink face horribly crinkled up and foolish-looking, lighting cigarettes and throwing them away again. Sometimes he would search anxiously for the cigarette he had thrown away, and when he had picked it up would look at it and sigh desolately to find it had gone quite out. Father was an architect: he would go into this study, tweak a drawing out of a portfolio, run to his desk with it, pore over it, score it through; then start, look back at the door guiltily, return to stare and stare at the drawing, push it away, and go on walking about. Up and down the room he'd go, up and down the room, then dart sideways as though at a sudden loophole and disappear through the door into the garden. But he always came back again to where Roger was; he couldn't let one alone. His presence was a torment and an outrage. Roger disliked people who were ridiculous, and he had never cared to look long at his father. Father had dark-brown hair, all fluffy like a baby's, that stood out away from his head. His face was pink and always a little curly, his eyebrows thick and so far away from his eyes that when one came to them one had forgotten they ought to be there. Lois and Pamela loved him; they thought he was beautiful, so it was all quite fair; and Roger thought *she* was wonderful, the way she had always tolerated him and allowed him to kiss her. Always the best hour of the day for her and Roger had been when the little girls had gone to bed, and *he* had not yet come in. Now the pink face was curled up tight, and the eyes were scared and horrible, and the hands always reaching out to Roger to grab him with 'Come on, old man, let's talk. Let's talk for a bit.' And they had nothing to say, nothing. And at any moment this man who had no decency might begin talking about *her*.

Now, suppose the Miss Emerys were beginning to – no, the thing was unthinkable. And besides, perhaps they didn't even know.

'What's Roger going to do today?' Miss Emery asked her sister.

'We-ell,' said Miss Dora, considering. 'He could help you garden, couldn't he? you know you wanted somebody to help you sort the apples. You know you were saying only yesterday, "*If only*

I had somebody to help me sort the apples!" Now I wonder if Roger
likes sorting apples?'

'Well, I never have,' said Roger, 'but I expect it would be very
nice.'

'Yes, you'd love it,' said the Miss Emerys with enthusiasm.
'Claude loved it, didn't he, Doodsie?' added Miss Dora. 'Do you
remember how he used to follow you about at all times of the year,
even in March and April, saying, 'Aunt Doodsie, mightn't I help
you sort the apples?' How I did tease him: I used to say, 'Now then,
Mister, I know what you're after! Is it the sorting, or the apples?'
Claude was very fond of apples,' said Miss Dora, very earnest and
explanatory, 'he liked apples very much. I expect you do too?'

'Yes, very much, thank you.'

'Do you look forward to going back to school?' asked Miss
Emery, and her voice knew it was saying something dangerous.
Back to school . . . When Mother had died, Father would send
him away to school with all the other ugly little boys with round
caps. Father said it was the best time of one's life; Father had liked
school, he had been that kind of little boy. School *now* meant a
day-school, where one painted flowers and mothers came rustling
in and stood behind one and admired. They had a headmistress,
though they were more than half of them little boys, and there
were three older than Roger. Father said this wasn't the sort of
school for a grown man of nine. This was because Father didn't like
the headmistress; she despised him and he grew fidgety in her
presence.

'Which school?' said Roger disconcertingly, when he had
swallowed his mouthful of bread and honey.

'We-ell,' hesitated Miss Dora, 'the one you're at now, of course,'
she said, gathering speed. 'It seems to me a very nice school; I like
to see you going out to games; and that nice girl behind you with
the red hair.'

'Yes,' said Roger, 'that's Miss Williams.' He masticated silently,
reflecting. Then he said provocatively, 'I should like to stay there
always.'

'Oooh!' deprecated Miss Dora, 'but not with little girls. When
you're a bigger boy you'll think little girls are silly; you won't want
to play with little girls. Claude didn't like little girls.'

'How long *do* you think I'll stay?' asked Roger, and watched her
narrowly.

'As long as your father thinks well, I expect,' said Miss Dora,
brightly evasive – 'Doodsie, do call poor Bingo in – or shall I? –
and give him his brekky. I can hear him out in the hall.'

Roger ignored the liver-coloured spaniel that made a waddling
entrance and stood beside him, sniffing his bare knees.

'*Why* my father?' he pressed on, raising his eyebrows aggressively at Miss Dora.

' — Bingo-Bingo-Bingo-Bingo-*Bingo*!' cried Miss Dora suddenly, as in convulsive desperation, clapping her hands against her thighs. The spaniel took no notice of her; it twitched one ear, left Roger, and lumbered over to the fireplace, where it sat and yawned into the empty grate.

Roger spent the morning with Miss Emery, helping her sort the apples and range them round in rows along the shelves of the apple-room, their cheeks carefully just not touching. The apple-room was warm, umber and nutty-smelling; it had no window, so the door stood open to the orchard, and let in a white panel of daylight with an apple tree in it, a fork impaled in the earth, and a garden-hat of Miss Dora's hanging on the end of the fork, tilted coquettishly. The day was white, there were no shadows, there was no wind, never a sound. Miss Emery, her sleeves rolled up, came in and out with baskets of apples that were too heavy for a little boy to carry. Roger, squatting on the ground, looked them over for bruises – a bruised apple would go bad, she said, and must be eaten at once – and passed up to her those that were green and perfect, to take their place among the ranks along the shelves . . . 'That happy throng' . . . It *was* like the Day of Judgment, and the shelves were Heaven. Hell was the hamper in the musty-smelling corner full of bass matting, where Roger put the Goats. He put them there reluctantly, and saw himself a kind angel, with an imploring face turned back to the Implacable, driving reluctantly the piteous herd below.

The apples were chilly; they had a blue bloom on them, and were as smooth as ivory – like dead faces are, in books, when people bend to kiss them. 'They're cooking apples,' said Miss Emery, 'not sweet at all, so I won't offer you one to eat. When we've finished, you shall have a russet.'

'I'd rather, if I might,' said Roger, 'just bite one of these. Just bite it.'

'Well, bite then,' said Miss Emery. 'Only don't take a big one; that would be only waste, for you won't like it.'

Roger bit. The delicate bitter juice frothed out like milk; he pressed his teeth deep into the resisting whiteness till his jaws were stretched. Then in the attentive silence of the orchard he heard steps beginning, coming from the house. Not here, O God, not here! Not trapped in here among Miss Emery and the apples, when all he wanted when *that* came was to be alone with the clock. If it were here he would hate apples, and he would hate to have to hate them. He looked round despairingly at their green demi-lunes of faces peering at him over the edge of the shelves. His teeth met in his apple, and he bit away such a stupendous mouthful that he was sealed up terrifyingly. The fruit slipped from his fingers and bumped away across the floor. Not a bird or a tree spoke; Miss Emery, standing up behind him on a chair, was almost moveless – listening? The steps came slowly, weighted down with ruefulness. Something to hold on to, something to grip! . . . There was nothing, not even the apple. The door was darkened.

'The butcher *did* come, Miss. Are there any orders?' . . .

But that settled it – the apples were intolerable. Roger asked if he might go now and play in the garden. 'Tired?' said Miss Emery, disappointed. 'Why, you get tired sooner than Claude – he could go on at this all day. I'm afraid that apple disappointed you. Take a russet, dearie, look, off that corner shelf!'

She was kind; he had no heart to leave behind the russet. So he took it, and walked away among the trees of the orchard, underneath the browning leaves. One slid down through the air and clung against the wool of Roger's jersey; a bronze leaf with blue sheen on it, curled into a tired line. Autumn was the time of the death of the year, but he loved it, he loved the smell of autumn. He wondered if one died more easily then. He had often wondered about death; he had felt in *her* the same curiosity; they had peered down strangely together, as into a bear-pit, at something which could never touch them. She was older; she ought to have known, she ought to have known . . .

The grass was long and lustreless; it let his feet pass through reluctantly. Suppose it wove itself around them, grew into them and held them – Somebody's snare. He began the imagination game.

Miss Dora was leaning over the gate talking to some ladies; a mother and daughter, pink and yet somehow hungry-looking. They turned their heads at the sound of his footsteps in the grass; he dropped his eyes and pretended not to see them. They drank him in, their voices dropped, their heads went closer together. He walked past them through the trees, consciously visible, oh, every line of him conscious – this was how a little boy walked while his mother was dying . . . Yes, they had been great companions, always together. Yes, she was to die at any moment – poor little boy, wouldn't it be terrible for him! . . . He turned and walked directly away from them, towards the house. Their observation licked his back like flames.

Then he hated himself: he did like being looked at.

After lunch, Miss Dora took him down to the High Street with her to buy wool. His mouth was still sleek with apple-dumpling, his stomach heavy with it, though they had given him a magazine with horses in it, and sent him off for half an hour to digest. Now they walked by a back way; Miss Dora didn't want to meet people. Perhaps it was awkward for her being seen about with a little boy who half had a mother and half hadn't.

She walked and talked quickly, her hands in a muff; a feather nodded at him over the edge of her hat, the leaves rustled round her feet. He wasn't going to remember last autumn, the way the leaves had rustled . . . running races, catching each other up. He barred his mind against it, and bit his lip till he was quite sick. He wouldn't remember *coming in to tea* – not that.

'What's the matter, darling,' said Miss Dora, stopping short concernedly. 'Do you want to go somewhere? Have you got a pain?'

'No, oh no,' said Roger. 'I was just imagining those white mice. How awful losing them, how awful. Do go on about them, Miss Dora, go on about Claude.'

' — And when he was packing up to go back to school, *there* was the little nest, at the bottom of his play-box, and the little mother mouse, curled up, and Claude said . . . ' Miss Dora continued the Saga.

When they got to the town they saw far down at the other end of the High Street the two scarlet tam-o'-shanters of Lois and Pamela, bobbing along beside the lady who had taken *them*. Somebody had given Lois a new hoop; she was carrying it. Pamela was skipping on and off the kerb, in and out of the gutter. She didn't look as if she minded about Mother a bit. Pamela was so young; she was six. He wanted to go and tell Pamela that what she was doing was wrong and horrible, that people must be looking at her out of all the windows of the High Street, and wondering how she could.

'There are the little *sisters*, Roger – rrrrun!'

People would all say, 'There are those poor little children, meeting one another!' and tell each other in whispers, behind the windows of the High Street, what was going to happen. He didn't want to be seen talking to his sisters, a little pitiful group.

'Go – on, rrrrun!'

He hung back. He said he would go round and see them after tea, he thought. 'Shy of Mrs Biddle?' asked Miss Dora swiftly. He allowed her to assume it. 'Well, of course she *is* a little . . . I mean she isn't quite . . . ' said Miss Dora. 'But I expect the little girls like her. And I didn't think you were a shy little boy.'

Back at the Miss Emerys' by half-past three, Roger found that it was not tea-time, and that there was nothing to do, nothing to escape to. That walk with Miss Dora had shattered the imagination game; it wouldn't come back to him till tomorrow, not perhaps

for two days. He leaned against an apple tree, and tried sickly to
imagine Claude. A horrid little boy, a dreadful little boy; he would
have pulled Roger's hair and chaffed him about playing with his
mother. Mercifully, he had passed on irrecoverably into the middle
years; he was grown up now and would smile down on Roger
through the mists of Olympus. Roger didn't get on with other little
boys, he didn't like them; they seemed to him like his father, noisy
outside and frightened in. Bullies. The school he was going to
would be full of these little boys. He wondered how soon he would
go to school; perhaps his father was even now writing to the
schoolmaster – while Mother lay upstairs with her eyes shut, not
caring. Roger thought Father would find this difficult; he smiled at
the thought in leisurely appreciation. 'Dear Mr Somebody-or-
other, my wife is not dead yet, but she soon will be, and when she
is I should like to send my little boy to your school . . . If it is not
too expensive; I am not a rich man.' Roger's father often said, 'I am
not a rich man,' with an air of modest complacency.

Home was not so far away from Roger as he stood in the Miss
Emerys' garden. It was twenty minutes round by the road; from
the top of an apple tree one should be able to see the tall white
chimneys. There had been something wonderful – once – about
those chimneys, standing up against the distant beech trees,
dimming the beech trees, on a quiet evening, with their pale,
unstirring smoke. From up high, here, one would be able to see the
windows of the attics; see whether the windows were black and
open, or whether the white blinds were down. If he sat from now
on, high in an apple tree, he could watch those windows. Night
and day, nothing should escape him. When the blinds came down
gently and finally to cover them, Roger would know. There would
be no need to tell him, he would be armoured against that. Then he
could run upstairs to the Miss Emerys' landing, and be alone with
the clock. When they came up after him, puffed with a deep-drawn
breath to impart *that*, he could just turn round and say calmly,
rather tiredly, 'Oh, it's all right, thank you, I do know.' Then they
would look mortified and go away. Really-kind Miss Emery,
really-kind Father *would* look mortified; they wouldn't like having
the thing snatched away from them.

Roger gazed up into the apple tree. The branches were big and
far apart, the bark looked slippery. 'I'm afraid,' he thought, and
tried to drown it. He was a little boy, he was afraid of the pain of
death. 'I don't dare go up, and I don't dare go back to the house. I
must know, I can't let them tell me. Oh, help me, let them not have
to come and tell me! It would be as though they saw me see her
being killed. Let it not have to be!'

And now it would be and it must be, even while he deliberated and feared. Roger saw his father open the gate of the orchard and stand hesitatingly, looking round at the trees. He was hatless, his face was puckered up and scared – Oh, to run, to run quickly to somebody who would not know, who would think his mother was still alive, who need never know she was not! To be with somebody comfortable and ignorant, to grasp a cork handle through which this heat couldn't come blazing at him. Horrible footsteps, horrible grey figure coming forward again, and now pausing again desolately among the trees. 'Roger?' called the voice, 'Roger!'

Roger pressed back. He too was grey like the tree-trunks, and slimmer than they; he urged himself against one, hopelessly feigning invisibility, trying to melt. 'Roger!' came the voice continuously and wearily, 'Old man? Roger!'

Now he was coming straight towards one, he couldn't fail to see. He would drink one in and see one defenceless, and draw a big breath and say IT. No Miss Emery, no cook, no death, no refuge, and the tree shrinking away from before one.

'*Ah*, Roger!'

He thrust his fingers into his ears. 'I *know*, I *know*!' he screamed. 'Go away, I can't bear it. I know, I tell you.'

The pink face lengthened, the scared eyes of his father regarded him, as he stood there screaming like a maniac. A voice was raised, did battle with the din he made, and was defeated. Roger leaned with his arms flung round the girth of the apple tree, grinding his forehead into the bark, clamouring through the orchard. When his own voice dropped he heard how silent it was. So silent that he thought his father was dead too, lying in the long grass, till he turned and saw him beside him, holding something towards him, still standing.

He was holding out a picture-postcard; he meant Roger to take it. 'Steady, old man,' he was saying; 'steady, Roger, you're all jiggy: steady, old man!'

'What, what, what?' said Roger, staring wildly at the postcard. It was glazed and very blue; blue sea, infinitely smooth and distant, sky cloudless above it; white houses gathered joyously together by the shore, other white houses hurrying from the hills. Behind the land, behind everything, the clear fine line of a mountain went up into the sky. Something beckoned Roger; he stood looking through an archway.

'It came for you,' said Father, 'it's from Aunt Nellie; it's the Bay of Naples.'

Then he went away.

This was the blue empty place, Heaven, that one came out into at last, beyond everything. In the blue windlessness, the harmony of that timeless day, Roger went springing and singing up the mountain to look for his mother. He did not think again of that grey figure, frightened, foolish, desolate, that went back among the trees uncertainly, and stood a long time fumbling with the gate.

The Contessina

THE Contessina arrived at the hotel one Friday evening, with an aunt and uncle from Milan. It seemed so odd to everybody else to meet Italians staying on Lake Como; their arrival created quite a stir, and fanned many smouldering conversations into life again at tables where married couples and family parties sat. Even honeymoon couples were set gently bobbing as the ripples of interest widened and spread. The Contessina sat looking very demure, and ate her dinner like a little cat between the matt black mountain of her uncle and the glazed black mountain of her aunt.

There was general though unexpressed disappointment when the new arrivals, filing duck-like from the salle à manger, compressed themselves into the lift forthwith, and were shot bedwards without so much as a glance about the lounge.

Next morning the uncle and aunt made no appearance, but the Contessina sauntered through the lounge at about eleven o'clock carrying a cerise parasol; stood a moment hesitating in the doorway, then stepped across the road to the hotel terrace that overhung the lake. Here four young English ladies, all in white, were seated in a row along the parapet watching Mr Harrison and Mr Barlow going out for a row. Their backs were turned to the road, and they dangled eight beautifully shod white feet over the reflecting water that rose and fell in the shadow of the parapet as evenly and gently as a bosom.

The Contessina, leaning over, looked for some time thoughtfully at the row of feet, then down at her own, which were by three sizes smaller than any of them. The four young ladies, all unconscious, waved their hands and called out jolly things as the boat with the orange awning slid away across the water. Mr Harrison and Mr Barlow rowed beautifully; every second day they took a boat out, and the other mornings they played golf. They took each other on at tennis at five o'clock every evening on the hotel court, while people from the other hotels watched admiringly through the railings. The Contessina seated herself also on the parapet, shaking out her fluffy skirts round her; her parasol unfurled magically as though it had been wings. When Mr Barlow turned his head for the last time she was not even looking at the boat, but away beyond it to the opposite hills, cold purple in the shadow. Mr Barlow observed this with annoyance.

Two of the girls went off together, arm in arm, and the other two, producing their embroidery, moved back on to an iron seat under the shade of a chestnut tree. These trees, clipped low till they spread out into umbrellas, followed for some distance the line of the shore. The Contessina, now their *vis-à-vis*, eyed the couple unabashedly with the naked curiosity of childhood. She studied their dresses and their attitudes, and took in the embroidery they were doing stitch by stitch. Conversation between the two was desultory; they had known each other for three days, and were entering upon that interesting phase in a hotel acquaintanceship where small talk dies, commonplaces falter, and confidences begin. The Italian girl disturbed them; her very sitting there was calculated to disturb them, even had they been quite certain that she understood no language but her own.

In this they would have been mistaken. 'Good – *morning*,' said the Contessina.

'Oh? Good morning.'

'Ah speak English,' she continued, nodding encouragingly at them. Two dimples flickered, dints of rosy light in the warm twilight of her parasol. Her eyes, usually of amber, caught here and there a glint of red that danced between the disconcerting flickers of her lashes. A queer little face, so foreign.

'Really?' said Ursula; and Jenny, smiling, said, 'How nice!'

The Contessina once again nodded, gathering her forces. She was about sixteen evidently, and this was odd, because no English girls of sixteen had figures like that. She revealed herself against the sunny water, a thing of neat assured little curves. She had wrists and she had ankles, her waist had already decided itself, and it would have been evident to the discerning eye that there were many more dimples. Jenny and Ursula hated to seem rude and – well – *English*, but she really would be very difficult to talk to. Their next move should have been, traditionally, 'How do you like Italy?' But they could not ask her that.

'Have you been to England?' Ursula inquired.

'Oh, no-o!' tittered the Contessina, and tittered again in scorn. *England* – the very idea!

Jenny, who was very intellectual, suggested, 'Then you read English, I expect?'

'Oh, yes. Marie Corelli.'

'Oh, yes.'

'She is fa-ine.'

'Oh, yes. Do you play tennis?'

'Oh, no, I think it is terrible. Do you like Italian men?'

'I don't know any,' said Jenny, with indifference. After a moment's pause she smiled kindly at the Contessina, funny little thing. Ursula said that she had once had a most interesting friendship with an Italian lady; she had been really charming. The Contessina looked at her in wonder. 'But do you like ladies at *all*?' she asked.

They were spared further of this, for a voice behind them from the other side of the road shrilled out abruptly, '*Serafinetta, vien' qui!*' To the first call, and its repetition, the Contessina remained blandly deaf. As these persisted and were reinforced and bound together by a positive Niagara of sound, the Contessina at length responded, '*Vengo subito,*' and did not stir. '*Adesso,*' the voice implored, and the aunt, immensely canopied by a parasol of sombre lace, appeared in full sail from the hotel followed by the uncle. She did not look angry nor at all excited; foreigners simply could not help talking like that. The Contessina rose and shook her skirts out, smiled, sighed, shrugged, and nodding to her new acquaintances, went off to meet her aunt, her parasol tilted quite ineffably.

After lunch, the aunt, the uncle, and the Contessina got into the hotel boat, assisted by the concierge, and were rowed up and down for an hour by the two hotel boatmen, not far out and parallel with the shore. The Contessina could be seen leaning out from under the awning to trail her fingers in the water. At five o'clock, people began to gather round the tennis-court, and by the time Mr Harrison and Mr Barlow had at last appeared, the aunt, the uncle, and the Contessina were there too, sitting close together on a seat. The uncle had sunk deep down into his stomach, the aunt deep down into her bosom, and the Contessina's glances flitted about like butterflies, never pausing long. All three looked happy and contented, and the aunt was smiling with the most profound indulgence at the English ladies dressed for tennis with their large, flat feet. Mr Barlow, down the Contessina's end of the court, walked springily about on the balls of his feet, while his opponents took their places; hacking, slashing, and under-cutting with his racquet at the air with science and ferocity. He bit his lip, the air whistled through his teeth, his head, as he recovered from a lunge, jerked sideways and remained there, for he caught the eyes of the Contessina looking up at him. Her parasol was not up, for she was sitting in the shade, and her eyes, now merely amber, studied with a mild inquiry the foolishness of Mr Barlow.

He played quite brilliantly that evening; everybody sat alert to watch him, and the crowd beyond the railings thickened. His partner, a lady of a disenchanted spirit, reported afterwards that he was poaching more than ever, and had made three foot-faults. When the final set was over he pulled on his sweater over his shirt, buttoned his blazer over his sweater, and strolled, just casually, past the seat where the Italian family were sitting. They were still there; the aunt was slumbering like a lady of lineage, and the uncle had disappeared behind the *Popolo*. The Contessina was looking sideways at the view: the evening light upon the hills was indeed very beautiful, but perhaps she had not been looking at it long. Mr Barlow dropped his racquet – most annoying – at the Contessina's feet.

The Contessina looked down at the racquet in surprise, as though it had fallen from heaven. Mr Barlow's hand, arm, shoulder, and flushed bent neck came within her field of vision; she started violently. 'Thank you,' he said, rising, though she had done nothing to assist him. She bowed, and he beheld the dimples. 'Do you play tennis?' he asked softly.

'But no. But I do *wish*, I *wish*' . . . It was inexpressible; she caught a sharp breath. Her whipped-cream ruffles shifted, swelled, and sank.

'It's a good game,' murmured Mr Barlow, still more softly, glancing stealthily towards the aunt.

'It is like . . . you do resemble . . . gods!'

'Oh, *well*,' laughed he, and looked about him. Everybody hurried to escape the chill of dusk; the court was being rapidly deserted. 'Would you care to take a little stroll?' he suggested. She evidently failed to understand his idiomatic English. 'I mean, a walk.' She ducked to see if any wakefulness still gleamed beneath the eyelids of the aunt, while he, with arched eyebrows, peered over the *Popolo* to see what the uncle was doing. He nodded to reassure her, and she giggled. 'A *leetle* walk!' she stipulated. 'Oh, as little as anything,' agreed the delighted Mr Barlow. 'The sun's just setting; come as far as the edge of the lake.'

They watched the sunset together, standing on a little jetty. Beneath their feet the water lapped and gurgled. When they turned to go in Mr Barlow sighed. He did not take her back the shortest way.

That night his wife was more impossible than ever. He was as nice as anything to her, at the beginning, asked her twice if she had had a pleasant day, and said, 'Oh, come,' encouragingly, when she responded that she hadn't. Everything was always wrong with Mrs Barlow's days; she made a point of this, it was her little triumph. But she was such a tired woman now, these little triumphs made her feel no better. Tonight she would not talk and would not eat; the waiters, humane men, waxed openly solicitous, and this annoyed her husband. Their table was beside an open window;

beyond, the dark-blue velvet night hung like a curtain; one felt the sleeping presence of the lake, and on the water somebody with a guitar began to sing. It was a night of breathless heart-beats and of beating pulses, a night for love. A night to kiss a satin skin as warm as great grape-clusters hanging in the sun. No one round him, Mr Barlow knew, as much as glimpsed the possibilities of such a night. Married couples, family parties – even the honeymoon couples looked bloodless; besides, once the woman was one man's wife one ceased, as it were, to be a Gentleman and became a Player. The Contessina's table was in view, if one leant a little sideways to avoid a pillar, but the Contessina was making an excellent dinner, and had no time left to look about her. Scents crept in from the bushes in the garden, met the smell of dinner, did battle with it and retreated; but Mr Barlow had them, and his nostrils twitched. Now that the chill of dusk had passed, the night was very warm and grew to the accustomed eye still more astonishingly blue.

Mrs Barlow waved away the *Canneton sauté*, then recalled the waiter, and after much deliberation and hovering of the fork and spoon, selected half a dozen peas. These she floated in a pool of gravy and looked down upon despairingly, while her husband looked despairingly across at her. For the last half-hour they had hardly spoken, and the unmarried girls at the next table, a merry party, pressed each other's feet and discreetly giggled. They had all so often told each other marriage was like that. Mr Barlow was good-looking; the shape of his head was pleasant, and his sleeked-back hair defined it. His forehead, jaw, and ears were squared perfection, and his sulky mouth was beautifully cut. Mrs Barlow raised three peas to her lips, then recoiled from them.

'I shan't be able to digest *these*,' she said, and looked across at him with the solemn eyes of some one standing on the brink.

'Then why eat them?' said Mr Barlow. 'Oh, but I *must* eat,' said she; then her chest twitched with a miserable hiccup, as it came over her suddenly that any other woman's husband would have been saying this to *her*. 'Oh yes, of course,' agreed Mr Barlow, and he hummed very softly and tried to look away from her. The electric light poured down upon his wife; even her pink dress looked *triste* and faded, though it was new and expensive, and far too beautiful for the occasion. As for her fair hair – Mr Barlow always had preferred dark women, and he had realized long ago that it is never wise to make exceptions to one's rules of life.

After dinner the older people gathered on the verandah, while the girls went off together two by two. They would come up out of the dark like moths, glitter under the lights in their pale dresses, then vanish again. Harrison and a Mrs Pym announced that they were going to look for glow-worms, and a whole bevy of girls went after them. The Contessina sat with her relations in a little isolated group at the glassed-in end of the verandah. When Barlow, searching very diligently round them for a newspaper he had forgotten, jerked his head interrogatively towards the lake, she turned away and simply did not see. So he went down to the edge of the lake alone, swung his legs over the parapet, and sat listening to the water sucking at the stones beneath him. He lighted cigarette after cigarette, and allowed each to slip from between his relaxed fingers into the water. Each sizzled, then was silent. It was a pity one couldn't put oneself out like that. The Bellagio lights twinkled very near him, on a level with his eyes; the lake was, after all, so narrow. He longed to row somebody over in a boat, and climb with her into the inviolable dark beneath the trees of Serballoni Hill.

Harrison and Mrs Pym were coming up behind him; he could recognize their voices, talking very low.

'Lovely night,' he said, without turning. 'Oh, lovely,' said Harrison, with a jump. 'Lovely day tomorrow!' he continued. 'Look here'; he turned his head over the other shoulder, to where he knew Mrs Pym was standing. 'I want to take that little Italian kid out tomorrow over to San Giacomo. She's an awfully nice little kid; I promised and she's awfully keen. I said I'd take her over in a boat.'

'The little kid?' said Mrs Pym, grinning in the dark. 'They'd never allow her.'

'Yes, but look here, you work it. Oh, be a sport, woman! You talk their lingo, it'll be your show, you're taking her along, and Harrison and I just come along to row you.'

'Ah, yes,' said Mrs Pym evenly.

The Contessina's aunt found Mrs Pym quite charming. They discovered that they had several friends in common, in Milan and other parts of Italy. She said that it would be delightful for Serafinetta to go for an excursion with the English lady; she loved English ladies, and had had an American governess for three years. At four o'clock on Sunday afternoon, the Contessina was therefore delivered over by her aunt into the hands of Mrs Pym, who explained that English friends of her own had volunteered to row them. It was difficult to hire boatmen on a Sunday afternoon.

Mrs Pym was a fair, burnt-out young woman of twenty-five, who spoke in a deep hoarse drawl, wore pale-grey flannels for boating, and had beautiful feet. She never looked hot. Harrison faintly amused her – she had been Barlow's partner too often at tennis – though nobody, of course, was amusing beyond a certain point. She had reached this point earlier than usual with her husband. The Contessina was allowed to steer; she tugged the wrong rope systematically, looking about her, glinting all over with contentment and mirth. She was fascinated by the swing and dip of the sleek oars over the water. Around them, the blue sky and the blue water blazed; a quivering light struck up into their faces and beat against the underneath of the awning. Once a steamer passed them, slanting over to Bellagio; the boat was sucked into her wake and rocked madly, round her oily shadows slid and spread and darted. The Contessina clutched the sides of the boat and screamed with fear and joy.

The bay of San Giacomo was still golden in the late afternoon, as they grounded their boat on the little strip of beach under the tea-house. Above went up the great sheer sweep of the hill; tree-trunks crowded endlessly, impenetrably, up into the sky. Cars along the road to Milan shrieked like birds, high, high among those unseen branches. Stepping from the boat, the ladies stood looking up into the queer ribbed dusk of the tree-trunks, while the others carried up the oars to the tea-house and put them away for safety. The place was very still, the coast of the lake seemed for miles entirely deserted. Barlow returned and loomed above the Contessina speechlessly. She said, 'Let us go among the trees.'

The others fell away from them. Her ridiculous little feet were useless to her; the high heels flung her whole weight forward on to the blunt little toes, and these scrabbled unavailingly upon the baked, bald earth of the hill. Sometimes she missed her footing altogether, and her whole weight would swing from Barlow's arm. When he had dragged her up about ten feet, she said she would like to come down again, pulled him after her, and they slid the whole way. They skirted the hill and walked for some distance along the edge of the lake, in the opposite direction to that which the others had taken. When they came to a bank of cushiony grass she sat down, and he sat down beside her, tilting his panama over his eyes.

'This is very nice,' said Mr Barlow, looking at the Contessina. She had on a dress of heliotrope organdie, with a fichu folded across the bosom with that best discretion for the display of pretty curves. Her skin was very dark against the heliotrope, as fresh as a young petal, as brown as old, old ivory. Her white Tuscan hat enhanced this peculiar deliciousness, and the little loops of hair corrugated against the curves of her cheeks looked almost blue. Her puffed sleeves were very short, and there was a dimple on each elbow. 'This is very nice, you know,' repeated Mr Barlow, stooping to kiss one of the dimples.

'Oh, yes,' agreed the Contessina, looking down at the elbow.

'You know,' said Mr Barlow, 'you're just the sort of little girl I like; just the sort of little pal I've always wanted — '

'Leetle *what?*'

'Pal – little friend, you know. Amie.'

'Oh, yes. Do you like Italian girls?'

'Don't know about *girls*,' said Barlow, stressing the plural. She supposed, with a sigh, that like everybody else he preferred them married.

'No,' said Mr Barlow, looking at he tenderly, 'not married. No, not *married*, you know.'

'I think,' said she, 'that Englishmen are beautiful. They are like gods.'

'By Jove!' said the intoxicated Mr Barlow. Then he added, with a sigh: 'Some day, perhaps, you'll marry an Englishman.'

'Oh, no. I will marry an Italian gentleman, and then we will go and live in England.'

'But it would be too late then.'

'Oh, yes,' said the Contessina, looking thoughtfully at Mr Barlow. She smoothed the folds of her fichu, and spread the light flounces of her dress about her over the grass.

'Meanwhile,' said he, 'this is wonderful.'

'Oh, yes,' agreed the Contessina, 'it is like Heaven.'

They both paused and looked down at the lake. The Contessina was a little too much of the child that sits with its mouth open, confidently waiting for lollipops. Each lollipop being assimilated, she would thank him prettily, look up with candid greed, and wait for another. And this necessity for direct, unidiomatic English embarrassed Mr Barlow, master of innuendo and *double entendres*; this was more than throwing lollipops, it was spiking buns to an insatiable little eager bear at the end of a stick. But he couldn't resist her; he slid across the last intervening inches of grass and put his arm round the Contessina's waist. Anyone standing at an upper window of their hotel with a pair of field-glasses could have watched them from across the lake, but Mr Barlow decided to risk it. His arm tightened – 'Oh, please!' she said perfunctorily – and he kissed the Contessina a great many times. She turned her head from side to side, and once he caught her full on the mouth. 'Is that still like Heaven?' he whispered ardently, cupping her chin in his unoccupied hand. 'Oh, yes,' she said politely, just perceptibly wriggling her head.

There was another silence; this time he felt it wonderfully sympathetic. Then the Contessina, whose waist he still encircled, asked him how he liked his wife. Mr Barlow told her; he explained that life was sometimes very difficult.

'Oh, yes,' said the Contessina. 'I wonder how she does like you?'

'Oh, well . . .'

'How many children have you?'

'None,' said Mr Barlow indignantly.

'Oh, that is a pity,' she sighed, looking down into the lake.

'A pity?' said he, picking up a little hand whose fingers curled in his like a baby's. He looked down at it hungrily, while she too watched from under her lashes her hand and the approach of his lips; then he kissed it twice and crushed it up against him. 'It is a pity you have no son,' she sighed. 'He would be like a god.'

'Oh, he would, would he?' said Barlow, indisposed to abdicate.

'Yes,' she said regretfully. 'Who takes your wife in a boat? Does your wife like Italian men?'

'Really, I don't know. Wouldn't it be more interesting to talk about ourselves for a little? Do you know, if I had had a little girl like you to go through life with, I think everything would have been different. A dainty little thing, you know, a little, a little humming-bird.'

'But if I had gone through your life I should be fat,' said the Contessina.

She was adorable. 'You lovely little thing!' he cried, 'you *are* a lovely little thing!'

'You are very very kind,' she said, nestling against his arm like a kitten. 'When I came here I thought it would be so *triste* because there was nobody young but the ladies, but now I shall not have been dull.'

'You'll have something nice to remember. Now I'm going to give you some more to remember.' She uncoiled like a spring and was on to her feet in a flash. 'Oh, no,' she cried, jumping about with delight, and clapping her hands at him as though he were a puppy. 'That is enough to remember, that is enough!'

'Is it, indeed!' quoth Mr Barlow, turning pink with pleasurable excitement. He grabbed at her diaphanous skirts that swirled about her like a ballet dancer's. There was an angry sound of tearing muslin. 'Yah!' shrieked the Contessina, and Mr Barlow recoiled momentarily in dismay. He fell back from sitting posture on to his hands and crouched looking up at her; then, realizing the disadvantages of this position, drew in his long legs and sprang to his feet. The Contessina, breathless even beyond the point of shrieking, swept her mauve skirts round her and went tottering along the beach towards the promontory. She staggered with laughter, her whole body curved upon itself, bowed beneath her weight of mirth.

'Ha!' cried Mr Barlow, making after her with long strides. The air whistled between his teeth, he grinned; this was better than tennis. She was now within the compass of his extended arms, and he leaned forward to enclose her, a happy and confident gurgle rising in his throat. The Contessina ducked with a yelp of delight, sprang ahead surprisingly and missed her footing. She spun round, wavered, beat the air for a second, then came down, *smack*, on to her outstretched palms. Mr Barlow stopped short. 'God!' he whispered, and clapped his hand to his mouth.

The Contessina did not remain prone. Before her cavalier had recovered himself, she was sitting back on her heels to stare at her little bleeding and earthy palms that reared up into her gaze indignantly. Her pose might have been called 'Astonishment.' Then, while he yet beheld, the ivory of the face and neck now visible to him darkened, her open mouth, eclipsing her face, became a cavern into whose menacing profundity Mr Barlow's horrified eyes looked down. A shriek like a needle-point, rounding to a sustained boo-hoo, rent across the silence of San Giacomo. As in response, a stone from miles above dislodged itself and came hurtling down through the trees into the lake. This increased the panic of Mr Barlow, who made a frightened sound and looked about him furtively. She clamoured on without pause, shrieking and sobbing.

'Little darling — ' he tendered, dropping on his knees beside her.

'A-ah,' shrilled the Contessina. '*Va via*. I hate you. Go!'

'But look here, listen — '

'Aie, go; you are wicked. You have been wicked with me; it is not so you should behave with a young girl. A-ah!'

She was such a child. Mr Barlow, in a rush of paternal emotion, gathered her against him. '*There*,' he murmured, 'there – there – there!'

But the Contessina positively roared, and disengaging her fists assailed his breast and shoulders with a rain of blows. One of these caught him on the chin, and he released her sharply. Above the intimidating cavern of her mouth, between the smears and crumples of her face, two slits of eyes blazed out upon him icily. Those eyes were pale with contempt. Mr Barlow was appalled by them.

'Yah!' resumed the Contessina. 'Old stupid! Wicked old man!'

'You *are* a little devil,' said Mr Barlow wonderingly, getting up.

The Contessina rose also, with remarkable agility. The front of her dress was soiled irreparably cut right through at the knee and stained with blood. 'You have killed my dress,' she yammered, grimacing down at the torn flounces miserably. 'If it had been the most old and the most ugly I would not have spoilt it for *you*. You are not young, and you are not funny, and you have a hot face, and you do not behave well with a young girl. It is not right. There is no *young* man, an English or an Italian, who would behave so, it is *old* men who are stupid and devils. Let me go to the boat!'

'Oh, all right,' said he very coldly. 'Go on. *I* don't mind where you go. You are a silly little thing to spoil your dress like that, your aunt will be angry.' He wondered, as he spoke, whether she would involve him in a duel with the Italian uncle. With bowed head and heaving shoulders, she preceded him along the beach, sobbing and sniffing. 'Such a hullabaloo!' said Mr Barlow indignantly. 'I never take out a little girl if she doesn't know how to behave.' He followed at a distance.

Mrs Pym and Harrison appeared from round the opposite promontory. Mrs Pym looked vaguely at the Contessina. 'But dear *child* — ' she said, in faint expostulation, raising her eyebrows. 'Oh, I *say!*' said Harrison, 'Oh, I say, that's too bad. I say, *Barlow!*'

Barlow explained that she had slipped and fallen while engaged in throwing stones into the lake. Harrison did not hear; he was comforting the Contessina, murmuring things into her ear and patting her little heaving shoulders. The petal-curves of the big Tuscan hat drooped towards him.

'Oh, please,' she gasped, 'if you would be so kind . . . I would like to go back . . . Oh, please . . . Oh, please!'

Barlow, his neck burning scarlet, strode to the tea-house to reclaim the oars, and strode back in disdainful silence. The Contessina could no longer see him; it was as though he had slipped out of her vision down a crack, and the crack had closed above him for ever.

Going home, Harrison changed places with Barlow, and sat *vis-à-vis* to the Contessina. She blinked her tears away, the dimples came out tremulously, her lashes were still wet and the lower lashes clung to her cheek adorably. The sun was going down, the lake was of liquid flame with great cold blue shadows like swords stabbing across it. The hills were blue and sharp, the air crystal. The sleek oars swung and dipped to their reflections rhythmically, and Harrison's sleek head beneath the eyes of the Contessina bowed to the rhythm. The level sunshine crept along the air and brimmed with gold the little dints of mirth and pleasure in the Contessina's cheeks, and drew a curve of gold along the brim of her hat.

'You row like a god,' the Contessina said to Harrison. 'Do you like Italian girls?'

Human Habitation

FOR the twentieth time, as the wet dusk became impenetrably charged with darkness, Jefferies looked distrustfully up at Jameson and challenged him: 'I suppose you *are* sure we're going the right way?'

Jameson, the tall man, was carrying the map; he took one step to every one and a half of Jefferies, and thus their footsteps made an uneven, shuffling sound, unutterably wearisome, on the mud and shingle of the tow-path. For the last hour they had walked, save for Jefferies' interpolations, in complete silence. Now and then a pebble bounded slantwise from the impact of foot, cleared the sedgy brink of the canal, and spun with a *plonk*, vindictively, into the silent water. It was late September; not a breath of wind; the fine rain stung the air.

Jameson's thin profile had faded from against the darkening sky; his voice came from so uncannily high up that Jefferies started when it said, 'Well, my dear fellow, if you don't believe me, take the map yourself.'

'I've got no matches,' he remarked, craning up his head sullenly to give emphasis to his words. 'You said I couldn't possibly have finished my matches before we came to Middlehampton. Now I have finished them. I suppose you can lend me your matches when I want another pipe?'

Jameson stopped, stooped, fumbled, and tucking the map under his arm brought out his match-box and shook it anxiously. They both stood still to listen. 'There's not many more,' he said unnecessarily. It did not sound as though there were more than three in the box.

'We'd better not smoke for a bit,' he said aggrievedly; 'that is, if you want to see the map.'

'Oh, well, I suppose if you *know* we're making the right way. But what I can't understand is: why we don't see the lights of Middlehampton.'

'Well, the air's so dense with rain.'

'Can't be *so* dense. You said half an hour ago that Middlehampton must be three and a half miles off.'

They plodded on; collars up, caps down. 'Ow, *Lord!*' yelped little Jefferies, stumbling and skidding. 'Steady on – the canal.'

'Well, I ought to know the canal's there, oughtn't I? After walking beside it for four days.'

They had made friends towards the end of the London University session. They were reading Science. Jameson knew he liked walking tours, and Jefferies thought he very likely would. Jameson's bright bird-eyes, set so near together into his long thin nose, fascinated Jefferies. He was an awfully compelling sort of chap. The way he *talked* . . . So they went on a walking tour: it was to be at the end of the summer vacation, that they might return to College fearfully fit. They chose the canals of middle England; 'There's a regular network of 'em,' said Jameson, 'and you see some awfully jolly country. One reads a lot of poetry and stuff against the Midlands, but personally I think they're fine. And from our point of view, entirely undiscovered. Now if you go down West in summer, or even into the Home Counties – and of course Wales is hopeless, besides costing such a lot to get there – you find the whole place simply crammed with rich smart people swishing about in cars. You know, the real rotten sort. Even the smaller pubs are full of them. All the year's their holiday, and yet they come blocking up the place for Us Others *now*. Of course that's all going, but it makes me awfully sick. Girls, you know, absolute butterflies, and fellows who ought to be working.'

'Sick'ning,' had said Jefferies, who also disapproved of these things.

So they walked the Midlands, following the canals from village to village, making towards the town of Middlehampton, where there were some fine old churches and Jefferies had an aunt. They stayed the nights in public houses which were not comfortable, and in the evenings they used to sit downstairs and try to talk to people in the bar. Jameson said one should get to know the English Country as more than a poetic abstraction and its people as more than a political entity, and Jefferies agreed that this was very true. They did not find the people in the bars interesting, but Jameson said that that would come.

Then it had begun raining. It rained a little on the second day, nothing to speak of, and they laughed and turned their collars up. The third day was nearly all wet, though it cleared towards evening and a fine sunset crimsoned the canal. Today it had come on about lunch time, a different rain; finer, gentler, more inexorable, that made the air woolly, left a muddy taste in one's mouth and dulled everything. They trudged; the rain stung their faces to stiffness; their minds grew numb. Since four o'clock they had not passed a village; Jameson, glancing perpetually at the map, promised that there should be one, but that village hung ever back from them as they pressed on to meet it. Once, very far away, through a momentary lightening of the dimness, they had seen a church spire pricking through a blur of trees; and about four-thirty they had passed a row of brick cottages, standing uncompromisingly a little bit away from a bridge. Jefferies asked, 'Tea there?' and jerked his head interrogatively and wistfully towards them, but Jameson, after scanning the cottages for a moment of uncertainty, had said, 'Why, confound it all, man, we can't go bursting into English peoples' homes and ordering them to give us tea just because we're in a position to pay for it. Well, how'd you like . . . After all, it's not as though we were abroad.'

Jefferies had said, 'No; oh, no,' without conviction, and remembered that Jameson had eaten twice as much dinner as he had. So they went squelching on.

Since then, there had been nothing. Not even, recently, the looming blur of trees; never a house, never a light; there was not a sound to be heard of a voice calling, a dog barking, or the rattle of a cart. Only, ahead of them along the tow-path, they had the sense of just a possibility that something might approach them. Yes, once two barges had come up to meet them; the horse-hoofs being wrenched after every step from the sucking mud were louder than their impact. The water swished and gurgled under the prows; the smoke trickling from the chimneys of the cabins could not rise through the rain, but hung low and sullenly diffused itself. At the first prow a bargee was visible, dusky and inhuman; another man walked at the head of the first horse. Though it seemed as if for the whole afternoon they had been imminent, the dusk so suddenly disgorged them that Jameson and Jefferies had to spring into the hedge under the very nose of the horse with a violence that sent them sprawling among the prickly branches, to escape the tow-rope that would have mown them from their legs. The steaming flanks of the horses loomed beside them, and Jameson, recovering his balance, shouted from the hedge. 'This *is* the way to Middle-hampton?' For answer the man leading the horse hailed back to him tonelessly and went by, never turning his head again, as Jameson's clamoured reiteration was drowned by the clopping of the horses' hoofs, the squelching of the mud, the rushing of the water round the prows. The unlighted cavalcade faded slowly, and was swallowed up. Nothing else came to meet the two, and nothing else passed them.

As the walls of rain closed in about him and became impenetrably dark, Jefferies felt sundered by a world from the now almost invisible Jameson. There was nothing beside him but a living organism that breathed stertorously and struggled on, slanting forward a little into the rain. And beside that big, mindless body trudged another smaller body, shuffling, sometimes desperately changing step in an attempt to establish rhythm. On to these two bodies the dulling eyes of Jefferies' mind looked out. He thought dimly, 'If I lose consciousness of myself, shall I leave off being? I don't believe in Jameson, I don't believe he's even there; there's just something, if I put out my hand, to obstruct it; something against which I should fall if I fell towards the canal, sideways. Why should the fact that one of those men's legs ache bother me? I don't believe in either of them. Curse, how my legs ache! Curse my legs! There was once a man called Jameson, who asked a man called Jefferies to walk with him for years and years along a canal, and – they walked and walked till Jefferies forgot himself and forgot what he had ever been. What happened then? I can't remember . . . Curse, I'm potty. Oh, curse my legs, they're real anyhow. But are they? Perhaps somebody somewhere else feels a pain and thinks it is a pain in a man called Jefferies' legs, and so there seems to be a man called Jefferies with his legs aching, walking in the rain. But am I the person who is feeling the pain somewhere else, or am I what they imagine?' He was, he decided, something somebody else had thought; he felt utterly objective, walking, walking. Such a silence, it might have been a night in May . . . He put his hand out and brushed it along the hedge; the hedge was always there, and the rain soaked silently through it.

Jameson had stopped walking; Jefferies felt himself shoot suddenly ahead. He arrested himself and asked, 'Well?' numbly without turning round. Jameson didn't sound so sure of himself.

'Perhaps we might just look at the map again; it's reassuring – here, you're better with the matches; strike away, old man, and I'll be nippy with the map.' He rustlingly unfolded it. Jefferies took the matchbox, and before the third match, trembling out, had expired, Jameson, bending his long glistening nose over the map, had seen enough. The last glowing match-head spat as it struck the water, and Jefferies, sucking a burnt finger, looked towards Jameson with a mute and animal expectancy. The other said slowly:

'Well, I'm damned. Well, I *am* damned!'

'Why?' said Jefferies dully.

Jameson explained very quickly and with detachment that they had after all taken the wrong turning when they came to that fork. They *had* somehow; it was jolly queer. Jameson thought it really was most awfully queer. This arm of the canal only seemed to lead to a brickfield; it must be a jolly big brickfield, mustn't it, to have an arm of the canal all to itself. He laughed nervously, and they listened while his laughter died away. Jefferies was very quiet. He asked after some time, as though perfunctorily, what they were going to do.

'I saw there was a road marked from the brickfield, straight to Middlehampton. It goes without any turnings, a class B road, awfully good walking. We might pick up a bus. You see, all we shall have done is simply to have come two sides of a triangle. That is all we shall have done. It's bad luck, isn't it – we *have* had a run of bad luck.'

'Yes,' said Jefferies. 'Let's go on.' It tired him worse, just standing there. So they went on walking. They did not believe, perhaps, that they gained very much by walking; everything had slipped away from them. They just kept on for the sake of keeping on, and because they could not talk, they could not think. Jefferies felt as though an effort at coherent thought would bring about some rupture in his brain. He had begun to believe vaguely – the thing took form in his brain nebulously without any very definite mental process – that they had stepped unnoticingly over a threshold into some dead and empty hulk of a world drawn up alongside, at times dangerously accessible to the unwary. There was a canal there, but were there not canals in the moon – or was it Mars? The motionless water silently accompanied them, always just beyond Jameson, a half-tone paler than the sky – it was like a line ruled with a slate-pencil, meaninglessly, across some forgotten slate that has been put away.

'Look over there,' whispered Jameson. 'I'll swear I see lights.' He spoke so softly, as though he feared to scare the lights away, that it came into Jefferies' mind that he must mean people, carrying lanterns. 'Why,' he cried, looking with narrowed eyes through the rain, 'those are house-lights. Quite square, not moving – windows.'

'Then there must be a house,' deduced Jameson. 'There'll be people, you know, and they might let us come by the fire. They'd tell us the way, but I expect they'd ask us to stay for a bit. You know,' he said, as they approached, 'those are very dull lights – muffled. It looks to me as though they'd got the blinds down.'

'Yes, I expect they have; they wouldn't want everybody looking in. There are lights upstairs, too, d'you see? It must be quite a biggish house, if it's got two storeys. I expect the people are well-to-do, and live here because they like it. It would be rather a jolly place to live.' He saw a picture of the house in summer, white-faced and somehow Continental, blistering a little in the glare from the canal, with sun-blinds, and a garden with a white fence running down to the tow-path, and crimson hollyhocks slanting lazily against the fence. He thought there might be an elm or two, a bit to the side, to give shade to the house and garden: that would be very nice, Jefferies thought. 'I expect it must be awfully nice in

summer,' he said elatedly, turning to Jameson. 'Topping,' they
agreed. 'Why, if the weather cleared, I expect it would look
topping tomorrow.' It was extraordinary how happy they felt as
they approached the lights, and how benevolent.

There *was* a little garden, and the gate swung to behind them: the
latch clicked of its own accord. This brought some one to an upper
window before Jameson, standing at the door with raised hand a
shade portentously, had had time to knock. A blind swung
sideways, displaced by a body, the window was pushed up with a
rattle, and a woman's voice cried out in ecstasy and reproach, with
a note in it of immeasurable relief, '*Oh Willy!*'

So certain was she, that she momentarily unconvinced Jefferies
and Jameson of their own identities. They stepped back a pace or
two to see her better: she leaned against the window frame, keeping
the blind pushed sideways into folds with one elbow. They saw her
form against the dim, dark-yellow lamplight – Woman, all the
women of the world, hailing them home with relief and expectation. Something stirred warmly in both of them; it would be like
this to have a wife. She was up there with her child; they could hear
a burst of thin querulous wailing, at which she did not turn her
head, but only peered out more closely into the darkness. The rain
before the window shimmered in the outpoured lamplight.

'Well?' she cried. '*Come in.* You're late. Oh *Willy!*'

She was so blind to them down there that they were fain to stand
pretending; till Jefferies, wrenching himself free of something,
cried out ruefully, 'We're not.' He was so husky, it was doubtful
whether she could distinguish his words, but she started back and
stood rigid at the unfamiliar voice. Then she leaned forward to
thrust out her head at them.

'Get on with you,' she blustered. 'Get along, will you! This isn't
a public; the Green Man's beyond the brickyard. Don't come
bothering here, or I'll send my husband out to you, and if you
don't get along then he'll fetch his brother . . . ' She listened
a moment for the sound of their retreat, then added, '*and the
dog.*'

'But, Ma'am, I say!' expostulated Jameson in a cultured voice.
This was awkward: if she were going to take it like this, how could
they ask to come in to her fire? If only she could see them, if only it
were not so dark! She was a kind young woman; her arm, with
which she now impatiently held the blind back, was round against
the light – 'Just a minute, if you don't mind. We've missed our
way; would you be so kind as to direct us?'

They could feel her frown with the perplexity that was in her
voice as she asked: 'Who are you? What do you want?'

'We're students, walking; we've missed our way, and we've been walking hours without meeting a soul. Can we speak to your husband?'

'He's asleep,' she said quickly, 'and his brother and the dog are asleep, too, by the parlour fire. I don't want to wake them. If I stand here calling, the child won't sleep a wink all night. Will you promise you'll give no trouble? Straight? . . . Then I'll come down.'

She let the blind swing back, and they heard her footsteps recede towards the door. Then they waited, it seemed interminably. One window below, a bay on the ground floor, was lighted; the blinds were down here too, and were etched over with the symmetrical shadow of curtains. In this lighted, hidden room they heard a door open, and there was the sound of voices – statement, repetition, query, repetition, statement. Some one in there had been listening silently and noiselessly to all they said; now that some one was being deferred to and they knew that judgment on them trembled in the balance.

Though by now indifferent to rain, they had advanced in-stinctively into the shelter of the porch, and it was standing here that they heard the bolts creak back in their sockets and the rattle of a chain. Jameson had time to whisper, 'They're well enough barricaded!' before the woman's face looked round the door at them in a dim slit of light.

As Jameson had expected, and as Jefferies had been secretly convinced, it was not difficult to arrive at an understanding.

'You're what did you say? Students . . . oh, at college? Oh, then, you're quite young fellows.' She was easier with them now. 'Yes, you've taken the wrong turning miles away back. How did you come to? Very wet. It's a bad night; I'm sorry for any one that's out. Yes, you've still got a good bit before you. You must follow the track across the brickfield; that'll bring you out on to the Middlehampton road. Six miles, my husband reckons it, or six and a half. Yes, the buses do run on Wednesdays, but you'll have to wait now till the nine-thirty. It's about twenty minutes' walk from here to where the buses stop. No, there's no village or anything, just a cross-roads. We're in a lonely place.'

'Thanks,' said Jameson, reluctantly, 'then we'll be getting on. I dare say we shall find some shelter in the brickyard?'

She hesitated, playing with the bolt inside the door and peering urgently into their faces in the uncertain light.

'If you'd like to come in . . . ' she said at last slowly, 'I know I can trust you not to make a noise and disturb the child – and my husband and his brother. You can come into the living-room, there's only Aunt in *there*.'

They followed her in.

Revealed in what then seemed to them the dazzling glory of the lamplight, the young woman showed pleasant of feature, with shy, perturbed but not unfriendly eyes. Her back was still very straight; she was quite a girl, no older than they were. It seemed strange that it should have been her child that they had heard crying upstairs. She wore a pink blouse, a string of corals round her neck; and gave the impression of having recently adorned herself, but of being now so preoccupied that she was unaware of her finery. In her eyes there was a look of the anguished evasion of some dread; she seemed to the two young men to be feverishly aware of them yet not to care whether they were there or not. The lamp stood on the waxed covering of the table; beside the lamp, a little behind the girl, sat a very stout elderly woman immobile, her hands folded under her bosom, looking dispassionately across the pool of lamplight at the two young men. They stood caps in hand, their cheeks burning in the sudden warmth, their eyes blinking in the brightness, looking from the young woman to the older one, round at the pictures, furniture and ranged china of the room with an avidity perfunctorily concealed. Here was a Wife . . . an Aunt . . . a Living-room – *home*.

'I asked the gentlemen in, Auntie.'

'Ah,' said Auntie, of whom only the eyes were mobile, summing them up. 'Yes. They're very wet – did they come far?' Though she did not directly address him, she looked inquiringly at Jameson, who replied obliquely, addressing himself to the niece, that they had been walking since two o'clock, since leaving Pidsthorpe. 'Then they can't have had no tea,' deduced the old lady with obvious pleasure. Well no, they admitted that they hadn't.

Auntie was the soul of hospitality. She now released a smile which rippled out slowly, and embedded itself in her cheeks. She invited them to sit down, and asked them if they wouldn't like to take their coats off and hang them by the fire. When they had done this, had hung their coats up on two empty, two somehow significantly empty pegs, they seated themselves opposite her and smiled politely, and Jameson blinked his bird eyes and ruffled up his hair. The great plane of Auntie's bosom was heaved up and shifted by a sigh as she said, *she* wouldn't mind a cup of tea, if anybody else were having it, as they had had to wait already more than an hour for their suppers, and it was likely that they would have to wait some hours more – Lord only knew how long. She dwelt upon them with her eyes benevolently, and said she did like a bit of company. 'I really can't think,' she said, tilting her whole bulk confidentially towards them, 'I really can't think what's become of William. He's very regular, he's never missed his tea before. Oh, I do hope nothin' hasn't happened.'

The girl had slipped out of the circle of lamplight and was standing by the window, listening intently for something outside. She turned round slowly with her eyes dilated as her aunt reiterated: 'I *should* feel bad if anything had happened.'

'Oh, *Aunt*,' she deprecated, 'how you do go on! *Happened* – what should have happened? He's just been delayed.'

'Nothing hasn't ever delayed him before,' the other mused inexorably. 'I don't remember any other occasion when he's been delayed. *I'd* never believe he'd been going to the public, but *really* — '

'*Ooh*,' cried the girl, writhing her shoulders, as though intolerably stung.

'But I thought — ' objected Jameson eagerly, and broke off because Jefferies had kicked him under the table. They both remembered suddenly that they had seen only one window lighted on the downstairs floor. The realization that she had lied to them in fear made them both feel very large, forgiving, and protective. The old lady twinkled at them knowingly and hospitably, doing the honours of her niece's emotion as she did the honours of her niece's house. 'It's very anxious for her,' she said, inviting their appreciation with a gesture. She turned her eyes to the girl, after a few seconds' pregnant silence, and said, 'Well, Annie, let's have the supper on the table, and have a little tea and a little bit of something tasty, anyway. What I always say: expectin' and expectin' somebody and holdin' everything over for them's not the way to make 'em come. If he's coming, he come; and all the sooner for not being waited for.'

'*If he's coming!*' echoed the girl, turning round from the dresser where she was taking some plates down off a rack. '*If* he's coming to his own home! Any one would think you thought he'd fallen into the canal,' she cried excitedly, and then caught her breath, assailed with terror by her own words as though some one else had spoken them.

'Ah,' said Auntie, like the dropping of a stone.

The plates were of white earthenware with a gilt border and a gilt flower in the middle. Jefferies, bending to study them, thought they were significant and beautiful as, having lifted the lamp for a second to wipe over the table, she ranged them round mechanically, at regular intervals, as though she were dealing out the counters for a game. It did seem to Jefferies a game that they were all playing, a game that for her life's sake she must win; and every dish and bowl and knife that she put down to glitter under the lamp seemed a concession she was making to opponents, a handicap she was accepting. She passed to and fro between the table and the dresser mechanically, yet with a faint air of deliberation, and

sometimes she would pause and grope a little blindly along the
dresser with her fingers. The Aunt, looking into the lamp, tucked
in her lips, refolded her hands with precision, and settled down into
her bosom. A clock with a big round face ticked loudly on the
mantel; the dull scarlet fire rustled and twitched, and all at once the
kettle began singing, so loudly and so suddenly that Jefferies
started.

'Now you've only got to make the tea,' the Aunt prompted
inexorably, 'and take those kippers out of the oven. Oh, those *was*
good kippers; it'll be too bad if they're dried.'

Were Jefferies and Jameson to eat William's kippers? The girl
knelt down before the fire, opened the little oven and half took out
something the savouriness of which crept towards them. Then she
slid back the dish with a clatter, and softly, deprecatingly, but very
firmly shut the oven door. She remained kneeling on the hearthrug, her face to the fire, in an attitude of prayer; and said, without turning round, 'There's eggs, Auntie; I'll just do up a few
eggs.'

'And yet it does seem a pity not to eat the kippers!' said Auntie
thoughtfully.

This was horrible, something was being violated. 'It would be
very kind,' said Jefferies, 'if you'd let us have a cup of tea and a bit
of bread-and-butter. We oughtn't to have supper till we get to
where we're going to at Middlehampton; they'll be keeping supper
for us there.'

'Oh?' asked Jameson, looking at him dully.

'Yes,' said Jefferies with increased conviction. 'They'll be keeping supper for us there.'

So Auntie's kipper was brought to her on a plate, and the girl
came slowly to take her place at the table, carrying the enormous
teapot in both hands. As she bent to place it on its saucer, she
started violently, the saucer clattered, and she straightened herself,
and dammed with tense face and upraised hand the flow of Auntie's
conversation. Auntie had already told Jameson she had a nephew in
London, and now she was telling him how nice the nephew was.
They all started and hung poised: then they only heard the child
upstairs faintly and fitfully crying. 'Going up?'

'Oh no, it makes him worse, it makes him cry all night,' the
mother said listlessly.

The tea steamed in the cups and was fragrant. Jefferies, gazing
down into the brown translucency, watched the sugar he had
spooned in generously dissolve before he dimmed the clearness
with a cloud of milk. He laced his fingers round his cup, and their
tips, still numb, slowly thawed. The girl cut the loaf into slices very
methodically, and slid the butter-dish towards him from across the

table. He looked into her distraught eyes with nostalgia for something that they held.

Jameson, a creature of more easy expansions, had thawed visibly to his very depths. He beamed; his lips, slimy with excitement, glittered in the lamplight; he held the table. Aunt said 'Well, I never!' to him when she paused to take another slice of bread, or push her empty cup across to be refilled; the girl, while part of her mind (to Jefferies' understanding) still stood sentinel, leaned towards Jameson with startled eyebrows over the teapot. He painted that new Earth which was to be a new Heaven for them, which he, Jameson, and others were to be swift to bring about. He intimated that *they* even might participate in its creation. They gazed at it, and Jefferies gazed with them, but it was as though he had been suddenly stricken colour-blind. He could see nothing of the New Jerusalem, but the infinite criss-cross of brickwork and Jameson shouting at the corner of the empty streets. A sudden shifting of his values made him dizzy; he leaned back to think but could visualize nothing but the living-room: it expanded till its margin lay beyond the compass of his vision. After all, it all came back to this – individual outlook; the emotional factors of environment; houses that were homes; living-rooms; people going out and coming in again; people not coming in; other people waiting for them in rooms that were little guarded squares of light walled in carefully against the hungry darkness, the ultimately all-devouring darkness. After all, here was the stage of every drama. Only very faintly and thinly came the voice of Jameson crying in the wilderness.

Whatever you might deny your body, there must be always something, a somewhere, that the mind came back to.

Jameson did not refuse a third cup; he reached out across the table for it eagerly, still talking. 'Live?' he was saying: 'Why, we'll all live, live till we turn to the wall in a sleep of splendid exhaustion and never wake up again. You've seen a great perfect machine, how it roars round in an ecstasy? Well, that could be *us* – just realize it; there's nothing between our something and *that* something, cohesive, irresistible, majestic, but our *un-wills*, the feebleness of our desires. If every hand of the race were once, just once, outstretched unanimously, there would be nothing that those hands, that hand – I mean the *common* Hand – couldn't grasp; nothing too high, nothing too great. I – I always think that's an awfully solemn thought. Why, you know, there's a cry for life on the lips of every child, and we – you – people *stifle* it, because they're afraid of living. They think living's too *big* — Thanks, only half a slice, really.' He looked round vaguely for the butter-dish, and Jefferies thought that very much thus must have spoken Zarathustra.

'Well, you *do* talk!' said Aunt, with pacific enjoyment.

The girl had dropped away from Jameson; she leaned back once more, her folded hands lying listless and forgotten on the table before her, and looked up at the ring of lamplight on the ceiling. Her face was tilted back into the shadow; only her chin gleamed, and her thin throat. She didn't want what Jameson was offering her, she did not understand it. One could not feel she was a stupid girl; it was possible that she merely thought Jameson noisy. One felt that she had built up for herself an intricate and perhaps rather lonely life, monotone beneath the great shadow of William. Jameson was tapping out his points with his spoon against his cup and clamouring about cohesion, but he would be unable to understand the queer unity which had created and destroyed Annie. She might have been leaning now into the yellow circle, all one sparkle, laughing at them and flashing her eyes, a desirable and an acquirable thing.

'You know,' said Aunt archly to Jameson, 'that's Socialism you've been talking. Of course I wouldn't say I thought you meant anything of the sort by what you've been saying, but it might give some people considerable offence. It doesn't do sometimes to go talking Socialism, even for a bit of fun. But what I always say – boys will be boys, and young men too. I like a bit of fun.'

So Jameson began again: he was determined to do Auntie justice.

'Oh!' cried the girl unconsciously, beneath her breath. She turned her head and looked as though beseechingly at Jefferies, who stared back, and felt quite sick because he could do nothing for her. 'I've been listening all the time, too,' he whispered.

'Yes. You can hear steps for a long time, coming down the path.'

'Didn't you hear ours were double?'

'Yes, I did hear that. But I sort of didn't want to.'

'No. Would you like me to go out and meet him?'

'Oh no, you couldn't. He'd be angry I'd been letting on.'

'We'll have to be going now. Can't I do anything to help you?'

'Well, you can't, can you? I've just got to wait.'

'I wish I could make it be next morning,' he said violently, not quite knowing what he meant.

'What?' she asked dully. A tear trickled down her face.

'It's awful for you to be afraid.'

'Afraid? There's nothing to be afraid of; he's just – he's just late.'

'Yes, of course.' He felt there were things that could have been done to make it easier for her; he wanted to muffle Aunt's head up and wrench down the ticking clock. He could do neither of these things, so he said, 'Well, we must be getting on for that bus now,' in a loud voice, pushed back his chair and looked across at Jameson.

It was difficult to leave the living-room; they felt like candles wavering, soon to be extinguished. They hitched down their coats and struggled on with them, leaving the pegs by the fire empty and attentive for William's coat. Annie brushed her hand along Jameson's wet sleeve and sighed; then she preceded them to the door. Auntie sat amazed and plaintive at the disruption of the supper-table; after they had said good-bye she followed them with one long, hard, regretful stare, then let her eyes return to where they loved to rest. At their last glimpse of her she sat again immobile, her hands folded under her bosom, staring into the lamp.

Jefferies muttered, brushing against Annie in the doorway, 'If we pass him, is there . . . could we . . . ?'

'Oh no,' she said, with a desolate half-laugh, 'there's nothing you could say. If you pass him he'll be coming home.'

'Good-bye,' boomed Jameson abruptly holding out his big hand. 'You've been awfully good. Thank you ever so much for the tea and – and everything. You've been awfully good.'

'Oh no,' she said vaguely, and vaguely held out her hand to Jefferies. He started at the chilly contact, said 'Good-bye' gruffly, and dived past her into the cave of darkness beyond the threshold. Jameson stumbled after him and the door was abruptly shut. They heard the bolts creak forward and the chain rattle as they went, with hands before them, blindly down the path. They paused to let the fence and the canal take form again, which they did with an even greater dimness; then stepped down on to the tow-path, gently closing the gate. They went forward again, briskly, breathlessly, shuffle-shuffle; never quite in step. The air seemed colder, the rain heavier and finer. The tow-path still went on, it seemed so infinitely that, when hearing the sound of their footsteps suddenly constricted they found themselves approaching the looming masses of the brickfield, it was incredible that the path could have an end.

'Doesn't tea make one feel better?' said Jameson, speaking for the first time.

'Heaps . . . What a queer house!'

'I wonder when he'll be back?'

'Yes. We shall never know.'

They became aware half by instinct of a gap, a brief cessation in the hedge, and turned through it up a cart-track, splashing in the ruts, stumbling in the mud.

'She said the track was not long. We outstayed our time – think we'll get the bus, old fellow?'

'Don't know. Jameson, shan't we ever know if he came back?'

There was no answer.

They stumbled forward in the dark with tingling minds.

The Secession

A room at the Pension Hebe, falling vacant unexpectedly, was allotted to an English lady who had made a standing application for admittance earlier in the season. She arrived on foot one morning – the Signora only knew from what obscure hotel – her luggage wheeled behind her on a barrow. The Pension occupied the two top floors of a palazzo on a hill; from the Piazzi Berberini one ascended thither by a little steep street flanked by garden walls as high as battlements. Behind, one could hear fountains spattering among the leaves; and wistaria brimming over like froth down the sides of a mug reached its purple, pendulous fingers down to the pavement. Seen in any light, the English lady recorded in her diary, the Roman streets are very mysterious, and seen from above (her window commanded everything, and she paid a supplementary ten lire a day for the city's generosity) the roofs and gardens of Rome are scarcely less so. She had arrived at the blank hour of eleven, and she spent the remainder of her morning spread-eagled on her window-sill, looking out from a height which would have made another woman dizzy at a panorama which should have abashed her. At lunch-time she presentd herself a shade too punctually; she was already seated at her table against the wall when the other visitors, chiefly American, returned from sight-seeing.

She looked about her alertly, sifting everybody through as though expecting an acquaintance, and returning curious glances with dark, disconcerting penetration. She seemed more than thirty, with a long, fine nose that drooped a little over a short upper lip – a curious indentation sometimes flickered above her nostrils – and eyes set too close together beneath the slight, definite curves of her eyebrows: at some angles they had the appearance of a cast. She ate intelligently; her knife and fork poised and flitted, and she would pause to savour everything with a slight, critical compression of the lips. Once or twice she jerked her head up irrepressibly as though her thoughts had flamed into something precious, which she must tell at once to a *vis-à-vis*; then, disconcerted, she would question the blank air before her as though somebody had vanished. This was hardly marked enough to be noticeable; she seemed not an eccentric but a diffident, cultured person, with a thin back and shoulders, who would have visited Shelley's grave.

After a day or two, having had the good taste to make no advances, she began to know people in the Pension Hebe. She was asked to join one or two expeditions, and her tone, glance, and manner, rigid with expectation of the right reply, would ask, 'How much do you really want me?' She did not often accept. She was a very independent woman, sat a good deal in her own room, and must have known Rome very well, since one never met her in the accepted places. She dismissed acquaintances, but was 'out' for intimacies; she was as avid for them as she was for letters. The way she would pounce, drop hawk-like, on to her letters was remarkable; to read them publicly seemed scarcely delicate. For these, from the manner of her reading, were the kind of letters which should have been tucked away and taken to her room.

She did at length form an intimacy with a blonde, milk-white American lady, a Miss Phelps, whom one might say that she perpetually ambushed. Miss Phelps, first merely paralysed by her, warmed to gratification, then to reciprocal emotion; she was a person who came quickly and frothily to the boil, like milk. She told her travelling-companions, two other ladies from whom she never entirely detached herself, that Miss Selby was extremely cultivated, well-read, and very refined; and she would report the matter if not the detail of their conversations faithfully. With all that Miss Selby scarcely ever went out: wasn't it funny? She had not 'done' any of the places; she was '*keeping*' Rome. For when, for whom, was she keeping it? One didn't like to ask. That was Miss Selby's secret, which, like a soap-bubble at the end of a pipe, would bulge, subside, waver, wobble iridescently, and subside again. Later, among the trees of the Pincio it transpired that she was keeping Rome for Somebody. Ah, really? Miss Phelps found this beautiful. Miss Selby interrupted her sight to confess that she allowed herself daily small rations; she would stand looking, for instance, through the railings of the Forum without going in. Miss Phelps hoped aloud that the Somebody were imminent; she feared the strain of abstinence for one of Miss Selby's so strong intellectual appetites.

Next morning Miss Selby sought out her friend, half aghast; her morning's letter, thin sheets of fine scrawled writing, trembled in her hand. 'I am expecting my friend quite soon now,' she said. 'In a day or two' – she made a show of referring to the letter – 'the end of the week. He finds he has been detained unnecessarily. It was too bad, keeping him all this time.'

'Oh, a gentleman?' deprecated Miss Phelps, smiling gently. She had not failed, from the other's reticence, to assume this.

'A family friend, a Mr Humphrey Carr. He has lately retired. He asks – that is, I wanted to ask you . . . Of course, it would be unheard of, wouldn't it – that is, I suppose it would not be possible for – No, I *quite* see it wouldn't . . . But I just thought I'd ask you . . . ' She faltered. The question was finally referred to a committee of Miss Phelps's married friends, who delivered the ultimatum: if the Signora had a vacancy *in the other flat* for Mr Carr; if *he* sat in the salon after dinner in the evenings while *she* immediately retired, and if she joined their party at meals, leaving him to occupy the small single table, the situation of Miss Selby *vis-à-vis* to Mr Carr would be above reproach.

When Miss Selby began to wish that she had sent Humphrey to another hotel, to spend her days in his less distributed society, it is not known; but certainly she never betrayed herself. She would watch – perhaps with just the faintest compression of the lips as though some new strange dish had been placed before her – Humphrey dividing his attention scrupulously between the three American ladies, who as scrupulously passed him round. The dints above her nostrils would deepen and linger as she watched Miss Phelps's blue, calm, level-lidded eyes encounter briefly, but not too briefly, those of Mr Carr. Mildred Phelps seemed to her, she records, more than ever beautiful, with her wide calm gaze and classic breadth of brow. She was not young, the brows were sometimes wistful, and at dinner after a long exhausting day her face would often show drained-out and colourless beneath the glare of lights. She said, as they all said without reserve, that Mr Carr was so very nice, so cultured, so considerate. And what an archaeologist he was! She even added, he was charming.

Miss Selby having so long withheld herself now fell upon Rome in a kind of fury. She was tireless – she asserted this to Humphrey with a smile; he need not spare her. Sometimes she crept out alone, often they would join the others, but they two made at least one expedition a day by themselves. By these they both profited; he knew more, but she was quicker to apply her knowledge. Humphrey was a tall, pink, reserved man, a retired schoolmaster, who looked out at the world a shade distastefully through pince-nez. Always stooping, he would incline further to her deferentially as they went down the shady side of the streets together, or stood still in the dazzle of a piazza. She, quicker in motion, was quicker to arrest herself; she was eagerly sensitive – it was as though her every sense flung out unseen, quivering tentacles to draw in what they might. She would stop short, a hand on his arm, a finger to her lips as though they were to surprise something, with: 'Hark, Humphrey, listen to the fountain!' or, 'See, Humphrey, through that archway there – how blue!' He would say, 'Yes, oh, by Jove, yes!' a little uneasily. He felt her measure his appreciation; not the finest shade, the finest lack of a shade, could escape her.

Round her big straw hat she had knotted a Roman scarf; the ends, a striped cascade, hung down on one side of her face. Once, between these, he caught her watching with a bright, bird eye; though her head was scarcely turned in his direction. He was touched, he still remembers, by some quick emotion; behind the gaudy silk she was like some palpitating wild thing, a bird half-seen in a thicket. The emotion slipped away and left him numb; he was so much ashamed to have caught her unawares that he turned away his head and did not speak for two or three minutes: still he felt her eyes beseeching his return. He was numb; and worse, vacant and hollow. That, he supposed, was why he was so alive to other contacts, those American women . . . He echoed to their tapping like an empty jar. Ever since he had come to Rome he had been like this; something had died as he entered the salon of the Pension Hebe and she rose up to greet him from among her friends. He could not discharge himself of what he had come out to say: it was no longer there. It was horrible that this should be so, that nothing was to happen to her here, in Rome.

For himself, he felt bereaved; it was almost as though she were dead: his thoughts having lost their bourne of many years, wandered in confusion.

From that day on, the others, and Mildred Phelps in particular, more and more frequently accompanied them. Lena's suggestion, his consent, was not enough; she would reopen the question again and again insistently. 'You don't *mind*, do you, Humphrey? They have been so good.'

'Well, no-o, if you wish. Oh no,' he would concede, carefully reluctant.

'It does so please them.'

'As you wish, my dear.'

'Oh, I don't *wish* . . . but we don't mind, do we?' She would dwell a little on the pronoun, considering it. Then it would be always: 'You do like my friend, Mildred Phelps, don't you? I wanted you to meet each other. Don't you think she's sweet-looking, really rather beautiful?' If she asked this once, she asked a hundred times. And he, after a little surprised pause of self-interrogation, would repeat: 'Miss Phelps? Oh yes, very sweet-looking!'

Miss Selby sought out the earliest opportunity to make her friend aware of Mr Carr's admiration. One evening, when they had all returned from an expedition, she took Miss Phelps's arm, coming down the corridor, and drew her into her bedroom. 'We haven't seen each other for so long,' she said. 'Let's be together, shall we, until dinner? Watch my sunset!' She unlatched and pushed open the window, and, side by side, they leant out over Rome. The sun was melting down into a sea of yellow mist; soon the long blade of hills behind the Vatican would rise to cut away the brightness. Under the clear depths of yellow which dusk coming up from the gardens gradually infused and clouded, the grave polished faces of the buildings shone. Domes and campanili, the crest here and there of a hill or the tips of cypresses, had the air of floating buoys upon the ebbing tide of light. Miss Phelps and Miss Selby were pressed close together in the narrow frame of the window; their sides and elbows touched, they could have felt one another's hearts beating.

They were silent; Miss Selby's contemplation of that view compelled it. After some minutes of this her companion's placidity was troubled; she stirred with quickened breathing as though she felt the silence as a slip-noose being tightened about her. Miss Selby, turning from the city, focused her dark gaze myopically on the fair profile now brushed over as with pollen by the evening light. She asked if Mildred had enjoyed their day as much as she had. Mr Carr, she knew, had enjoyed it. Didn't Mildred find Mr Carr a pleasant person? Oh yes, Mildred said he was delightful. But seriously, putting aside all talk of superficial pleasantries, of companionableness, did Mildred *like* Mr Carr? Yes, Mildred did indeed.

Miss Selby let out a happy little sigh of relief. 'I'm so glad,' she said. 'He admires you so much.'

'Oh!' said Mildred, and her lashes fluttered. She could not blush.

'I knew he would. I felt that the moment I saw you. It's as though,' Miss Selby considered, 'very close friendship – sympathy – gave one the same eyes. I wanted you to meet him so much; I felt it would make something perfect. And it means a lot to me to know, now, that you like him, and that he likes you and admires, you, because . . . ' She paused, as to enjoy in secret the emotion distilling itself drop by drop from their silence. It was not with the sense of helping out confusion or diffidence that Mildred, playing a slow tune with the fingers of her right hand on the window-sill, said at last – 'Because? . . . Go on.'

'He has been for many years my friend,' said Miss Selby. 'He has asked me to marry him. I felt I should like you to share this . . . to know . . . '

'Oh,' said Mildred, staring before her, as though Rome showed itself new and strange to her in the light of the revelation. 'What a beautiful place for it to have happened in!' The close, dark eyes came closer to her cheek; their pressure side to side was increased. Keeping her face averted, she still felt herself transparent to this gaze and knew that her transparency must be darkened visibly by a hurrying shoal of thoughts. 'It's dear of you to share it,' she said quickly. 'When did – But that's impertinent: forgive me!'

Miss Selby, continuing to search her out, was again for a minute silent. Then she said: 'Some years ago Humphrey – spoke. He took me by surprise. I wasn't ready. I did not think, then, that I ever should be ready. I asked him to put that aside, for always. He was wiser than I; he said that some day he believed I would discover myself . . . *different*, and that until then he would be waiting. I never cared for – I feared, disliked – the idea of marriage; but do you know, Mildred, that knowledge was very precious to me. I had only to turn to him in the new way and he would be there. That readiness of his, hidden away from me, from everybody, became the centre of my life . . . Mildred, he *was* wise. He has a very deep insight. To acknowledge this to him made the moment more precious when I was able to write, "I am going to Rome. I want you to be there." And understanding everything, he came.'

'Yes,' said Mildred Phelps. 'When are you going to be married?'

'He hasn't spoken of that,' her friend said quickly. 'It's the coming nearer to that, every day, that makes these days so precious. It's the perfect understanding, the harmony, that makes your company, your friendship, dear, so beautiful to both of us, something that will be always interwoven with the deepest in our lives. I – I wanted you to understand.'

The sun had gone down, the night rose, the towers and domes still held the afterglow. Mildred said, 'You must be very happy,' and Miss Selby, shivering as though she had suddenly felt the air grow cold, drew in from the window and closed it, assenting, 'Yes, I am very happy,' in her gentle, cultivated voice. She was a little late for dinner that evening, having waited to enter something in her diary.

Humphrey Carr, those following days, came to be aware of curious implications in Miss Phelps's manner to himself. The whole party made an expedition to Hadrian's Villa across the Campagna, and when they had entered the garden he and she found themselves walking ahead of the others. As they passed from room to room with their skyey ceilings, over the broken pavements and among the broken shadows of the arches, it was as though some perverse and violent spirit entered into him; he tore aside something from between them and began to question her suddenly, almost to accuse her. Miss Phelps, perhaps less perfectly civilized than it would ever be possible for her to appear, stopped dead, spreading out one hand against the hot brick wall so solid yet with such silver-pink bloom of impermanence; and looked about her huntedly with a delightful tremor of panic. They were quite alone: the

archways were empty; the hill above swept up to the skyline
unpeopled, netted over with the shadows of olives. Mr Carr, her
Miss Selby's flushed friend, who had stumbled along beside her
with the hampered, peering diffidence of the myopic, now loomed
inexorable with his string of questions – he might even be cruel.
She felt that she was in the power of an emperor.

'Then what has happened?' he was repeating. 'Is it anything I
have done?'

'I don't know what you mean.'

'Won't you be frank – be true to your nature? If I have offended,
it would not be – *you* – to dismiss me unheard. And look back at
these days. They have been strange, haven't they, and precious for
some of us?'

She repeated dully: 'Yes, precious for some of us.' If there were
an implication there, he ignored it; he bent forward eagerly: 'Then
you've shared — '

'I think,' she interrupted, 'it is the *colouring*, the very air of Rome.
Even oneself feels intensified. The white houses and the dark skies,
the spurting-up lines of everything, the cypresses, the fountains.
You can't turn a corner without holding your breath. It's so
crowded . . . '

'Yes, yes,' he said, 'but you're quoting Lena Selby.' They still
stood by the wall, seeing nothing, facing one another.

'Did she say that to you, too?' she said, startled.

'Very likely; it explains nothing, it does not even make sense.'
The very thought of Lena darting about Rome and that crude scarf
with the trailing ends brought a note of injury and resentment into
his voice. '*You* are not so easily impinged upon. No, there is
something more. Miss Phelps – Mildred – I am intolerably situated.
We must understand one another, or there can be no way out.'

Her emotion seemed to her so powerful that she could hardly
contain it. She would not think, so she shut her eyes and pushed her
hand against the wall with all her might. This pressure upon herself
was wonderful; she had passed from friend to friend in vain,
hitherto – not one of them had known how to apply it. She had
heard a raw knife-edge of anger and eagerness in his scholarly
English voice, own brother to Miss Selby's. Between her lashes she
watched his throat contract as he waited for her to speak.

To her surprise she could not. She did not want him ever to go
away, and put her other hand out dumbly, blindly, in a gesture.

He seized at it, with, 'Oh, my dear!'

'But you belong; you, you . . . '

'There's nothing. There was never anything. Oh, believe me;
you have misunderstood. To be real, there must be two, you
know; and she was wiser than I, she would have none of it. I see

now how wise she was. I came out to tell her I was free, at last. I know she will be glad. She has such blessed insight. I have everything to thank her for.'

'Ah no! Because you came, you came . . .'

'It was an illusion!' he cried. 'We both saw. If she does not see now, she has deceived herself. I swear — ' He broke off, dropping her hand, which had lain inert in his, because he saw Miss Selby coming towards them through an archway. The other ladies followed her at a short distance; it was their voices which had attracted attention. Miss Phelps, startled, raised her eyes to follow the direction of his stare; for an instant they met Miss Selby's.

'If you have not discovered the Philosopher's Hall you must go there; it is beautiful and, I think, suggestive,' said Miss Selby, approaching. 'Also, there is a kind of underground arcade . . .'

The afternoon was hot; they flagged a little, returning; a film of vapour crept across the sky. The tram like a boat before the wind went rocking home across the empty Campagna. Mildred Phelps leant back, her hands before her face to shade it from the wide, bright glare; she said her head ached, she suffered terribly from headaches. Humphrey Carr read Mildred's Baedeker; his eyes were fastened to it in a kind of horror; all the interminable way he never once looked up, and never turned a page. Only Miss Selby, seated beside him, as eager, brilliant, indefatigable; she talked on, sketching out the skyline to her companions with a gesture, offering a thousand fugitive details of the wayside to their observation with a smile. Often the roar of the tram would rise to drown her voice, but they still saw her lips alive, her brain glowing through her features, while her dark glance flitted, stabbed and flitted from face to face. She made the gestures of gathering up some brightness and slowly for their approbation letting it trickle through her fingers. The American ladies, wound up in their veils, passively and smilingly marvelled at her. Afterwards, they said it had been a swan song.

That Miss Selby kept a diary (as a record, not as an outlet), entered her most trivial expenses in a notebook, and wore her keys round her neck, all proved that she was very methodical. From the account-book it was gathered that not a five-centesimi piece could have gone its way unconsidered; and from the diary that not a glance, a half-smile, an intonation, not the slightest interchange between any of them, had escaped her. She had charted the atmosphere of her company; she had been meticulously accurate.

Three days after the expedition to the Villa and the last appearance of Miss Selby, Humphrey Carr, alone in her disconcerted room, turned to see Mildred standing on the threshold looking at him like a stranger. Her eyes had purple circles round them; they looked past him to the ravished bureau, the wardrobe vomiting forth its dresses, the window open to the city and the sky.

'Will you come in?' he said courteously, in the tone of one already in possession; and she thought as she saw him standing among this litter of women's things that he might have been Miss Selby's husband.

'Oh no,' she whispered, frightened out of her resolve by the sense of intruding on a privacy – *theirs.*

'But I beg of you – ' he insisted, still in a sort of panic-stricken appeal to a stranger. A green Venetian necklace, straggling across the floor crunched beneath his clumsy forward step.

'Oh, oh!' she cried darting forward to tug at the end of the necklace. He tried to step clear of it, stood peering down through his glasses while she swept up the flakes of glass from about his feet. He brought waste and destruction with him everywhere. She got up and slipped the beads tenderly into a bureau drawer. Above, a photo of the tortured Laocöon had been slipped into the frame of the mirror. She asked, standing with her back to him, 'Have you, did you – find out anything yet? There's still nothing?'

'No, she left nothing to tell us.'

'Then she meant there should be nothing for us to know; and I think . . . '

'You think that wish is at *any price* to be respected? At the price, even, of a lost possibility of saving her?'

Her eyes wondered, quite intelligibly, 'What do you want to bring her back to?' Aloud, she only said meditatively, 'And she left everything. Her keys, her passport, all her money, her – her diary . . . ?'

'Yes. It will be *that* that will tell us. I do firmly believe now that we should be justified — '

She saw now plainly what had been there in her mind at the moment of her entrance, and knew that it was under Miss Selby's compulsion that she had come, tranced, quite unwillingly, to stand in the doorway of the room. The book lay by the dispatch-case, defenceless against outrage.

'*Me!*' she said, holding her hand out.

'No,' he said. 'There will be little there that *I* can't guess at, but something, perhaps, to offend *you.*'

Her face, still, mild and pale as milk, did not alter; she was holding her hand out mutely.

'Forgive me,' he continued, taking the book up, 'but I have been longest her friend – from her youth. It is surely for me?'

'Never,' she said, with an unperturbed reasonableness. 'You

were never that; you could never — ' She broke off, and then, with a violence that by contrast with her remote elegance seemed that of an apache, sprang forward and wrenched the book out of his grasp. She retreated to the doorway with it pressed against a bosom that could never have been so convulsed.

The two friends of the injured lady stared at one another over an abyss. At last Humphrey Carr shrugged his shoulders: an Englishman's inept and clumsy shrug. 'As you wish,' he said. 'If you're not frightened.'

'It's for me as a woman. Frightened? – what right have you to imply — ?' Again too much mistress of herself for speech, she subsided into a ruffling, preening, incoherent flutter, sat down on the edge of the bed with the open diary in her hands and began to read. He turned away and leant his elbows on the window-sill. After a few minutes of attentive silence he heard a quick movement behind him, the book sliding to the floor. He was startled to feel her shoulder brush his own as she leant out perilously far across the sill.

'Steady – steady,' he cried. 'It's a nasty height.'

'A nasty height,' she repeated, looking down as with desire at the lemon trees, the fountain so far below as to be inaudible. She looked for so long that he touched her shoulder to restrain her, and, shuddering, she followed him back into the room. She watched him pick up and begin to read the diary. He felt her eyes on him all the time, but she made no movement of protest. The book had lain open, face downwards, at the date of Miss Selby's conversation with Mildred, in the evening light, in that very window. Word for word, without comment, their conversation had been recorded, white-hot from the memory, in the fluent writing that did not seem to pause. The entry closed with this: '*I wonder, now that she has gone, why I have not pushed her through the window. It was so much in my mind to do this, and I see now it could have been done more easily than I thought.*'

Humphrey Carr raised his eyes slowly, but Mildred did not stay to meet them. With another of those wild movements so foreign to herself, she was gone; he heard the door swing to, and his isolation once more sifted down upon him.

He did not see Miss Phelps again; she left that evening with her friends – he was told, for Florence.

Making Arrangements

Six days after Margery's departure, a letter from her came for Hewson Blair. That surprised him; he had not expected her to write: surely the next move should be his? Assuming this, he had deliberated comfortably – there was time, it had appeared, for sustained deliberation – and now Margery had pounced back upon him suddenly. It was like being spoken to when he was settling down to a stiff book in the evening; Margery had often done this.

He remembered as he scrutinized the postmark that the last time she had written to him was from Switzerland, last Christmas. She always said she found him difficult to write to – why write now, then, when she might be better occupied? Hewson never sneered; his face lacked the finer mobility and his voice the finer inflections: he turned over the unopened letter, felt that it was compact and fat, and pinched the corners thoughtfully.

He found the name of a riverside hotel printed on the flap of the envelope, and re-read this several times with amazement, unable to conceive how a young woman who had gone away with somebody else to a riverside hotel – with white railings, Hewson imagined, and geraniums swinging in baskets, and a perpetual, even rushing past of the water – could spare some hours of her time there writing to her husband. Unless, of course, she simply wanted to tell him about Leslie.

Of course, she must have a considerable amount to say about Leslie after having lived with him under necessarily restricted conditions for the last six days. She had always told Hewson about her many friends, at great length, and as he was not interested in these people the information went in at one ear and out at the other. He imagined that Leslie was the one with the 'cello, though he might have been the one with the golf handicap – he could not say.

If she wanted to come back – he was slitting open the envelope carefully, and this made him pause a moment – if she wanted to come back he must write briefly and say he was sorry, he could not have her, he had made other arrangements. His sister was coming to keep house for him tomorrow, and the servants were even now getting ready the spare-room.

Hewson had just come in, having got away a little earlier than usual from the office, where people were beginning to know, and to speak to him awkwardly with scared faces. He had not, of course, been near the club. In stories, people who were treated as Margery had treated him threw up everything and went abroad; but Hewson did not care for travelling, and it would be difficult to leave his business just at present. He had never seen very much of Margery, his wheels went round without her; all this, if one could regard it rationally, came down to a few readjustments in one's menage and a slight social awkwardness which one would soon outgrow.

Parkins had just made up the library fire; she was drawing the curtains noiselessly across the windows. Hewson wondered what she had thought of Margery's letter as she enisled it, lonely, gleaming and defiant, on the silver salver on to which Margery had so often flung her gloves. Margery would fling her gloves on to the salver and her furs across the oak chest and swing humming into the library to read her letters by the fire. She would settle down over them like a cat over a saucer of milk, bend and smile and murmur over each, rustling the paper; and one by one drop them, crumpled, into the grate. Margery was a person who dealt summarily with her husks; bit through direct to the milky kernal of things and crunched delectably.

Tonight the grate was very tidy. Hewson watched Parkins' back and felt the room unbearably crowded.

'That's all right,' he said. 'That will do. Thank you, Parkins.'

He stood with his back to the fire, watching Parkins narrowly until she had left the room. Then he let Margery out of the envelope.

'It does seem funny to be writing to you again,' Margery wrote. 'I haven't for such ages – that note I left on the mantelpiece doesn't count, of course. Wasn't it dramatic, leaving a note like that! I couldn't help laughing; it just shows how true novels really are.

'Dear Hewson, there are several things, quite a lot, that I want sent after me at once. As I expect you saw, I didn't take more than my dressing-case. I know you will make all arrangements – you are so awfully good at that sort of thing. I suppose there are rather a lot of arrangements – I mean, like getting the divorce and sending my clothes on and writing to tell people; and I expect you would rather give away the dogs.

'We don't quite know how long a divorce takes or how one gets it, but as I told Leslie, who often gets rather depressed about all this fuss, you will be able to arrange it all beautifully. We are going abroad till it is all over; Leslie is so fearfully sensitive. We want to go quite soon, so I should be so much obliged if you could send those clothes off to me at once. I enclose a list.

'Leslie says he thinks I am perfectly wonderful, the way I think of everything, and I suppose it really is rather wonderful, isn't it, considering you always made all the arrangements. It just shows what one can do if one is put to it. Leslie would like to send a message; he feels he can't very well send his love, but he asks me to say how sorry he is for any inconvenience this will cause you, but that he is sure you cannot fail to feel, as we do, that it is all for the best. Leslie is fearfully considerate.

'Dear Hewson, I think you are too sweet, and you know I have always liked you. I feel quite homesick sometimes in this horrid hotel, but it's no good being sentimental, is it? We never suited each other a bit, and I never quite knew what you wanted me for. I expect you will be fearfully happy now and settle down again and marry some fearfully nice girl and get the rock-garden really nice without my horrid dogs to come and scratch it up. Now, about the clothes . . .'

Directions followed.

As Hewson read this letter he remembered Leslie (though he still could not say whether he was the one with the 'cello or the golf handicap), a young man with a very fair short moustache and flickering lashes, who liked his port. It seemed quite right that such a fair young man should admire Margery, who was dark. Many people had, indeed, admired Margery, which gratified Hewson who had married her. Many more people praised her clothes, which still further gratified Hewson who had paid for them. When he married Margery he stamped himself as a man of taste (and a man of charm, too, to have secured her), and he rose still higher in the estimation of his friends; while even men who had thought him a dull dog in the army or at Oxford began coming to the house again.

It was all very nice, and Hewson often found himself arrested in a trance of self-congratulation; when he came in in the evenings, for instance, and found firelight flooding and ebbing in the white-panelled hall and more cards on the table, and heard Parkins moving about in the dining-room, where through the slit of the door the glass and silver on the table sparkled under the low inverted corolla of the shade. Sometimes he would have to put his hand before his mouth, and pass for yawning, to conceal the slow smile that crept irresistibly across his face; as when he stood beside the really good gramophone and changed the records of thudding music for Margery and her friends to dance to. She danced beautifully with her slim, balanced partners; they moved like moths, almost soundlessly, their feet hiss-hissing faintly on the parquet. Hewson's hand brushed across the switchboard, lights would spring up dazzlingly against the ceiling and pour down opulently on to the amber floor to play and melt among the shadows of feet. This had all been very satisfactory.

Hewson never conceived or imagined, but he intended; and his home had been all that he had intended. He had a sense of fitness and never made an error in taste. He was not amusing, he did not intend to be an amusing man; but he had always intended to marry an amusing wife, a pretty little thing with charm. He considered that Margery was becoming to him, which indeed she was. He had a fine fair impassive face with the jaw in evidence and owl's eyebrows; he stood for dark oak and white panelling, good wine and billiard-tables. Margery stood for water-colours, gramophones, and rosy chintz. They had made a home together with all this; none of these elements was lacking, and thus their home had, rightly, the finality of completeness.

Tonight he dined early, and, though eating abstractedly, ate well. He knew the importance of this. They had taken out all the leaves, the table had shrunk to its smallest. Margery had often been away or out, and this evening was in no way different from many others. They brought his coffee to the table, and after coffee he went upstairs, slowly, turning out all but one of the hall lights behind him. He carried Margery's letter, and paused on the landing to look through the list again, because he had decided to get the things packed up tonight and sent off early tomorrow. As he did not wish to give Emily or Parkins Margery's letter (the list being punctuated by irrelevancies), he proposed to get the shoes and dresses out himself and leave them on the bed for Emily or Parkins to pack.

Yes, Margery was not unperceptive; he really did like making arrangements. The sense of efficiency intoxicated him, like dancing. He liked going for a thing methodically and getting it done; jotting down lists on pieces of paper and clipping the papers together and putting them away in the one inevitable drawer.

'You can't think what Hewson's like!' Margery would exult to their friends, waving a glass dessert-spoon at him from her end of the table. 'He does everything and finds everything and puts everything away and sends everything off. He's absolutely amazing!'

At this, all the way down the table the shirt-fronts and pink quarter-faces veered intently toward Margery would veer round, guffawing, toward Hewson, and become three-quarter faces, twinkling over with mirth, while the ladies, tittering deprecatingly, swayed toward Hewson, their mirth drawn out into a sigh. 'You must forgive us, Mr Blair,' they implied; 'but your wife is really *so* amusing!' And Hewson sat on solidly and kept the wine going.

Margery's room sprang into light nakedly; the servants had taken away the pink shades. The curtains were undrawn, and Emily, with a housemaid's one cannot say how conscious sense of the dramatic, had dropped a sheet over the mirror and swathed the dressing-table: bowls and bottles here and there projected, glacial, through the folds. The room was very cold and Hewson thought of ordering a fire, then recoiled in shyness from the imagined face of Emily or Parkins. He had not entered Margery's room since her departure – he preferred to think of it as a departure rather than a flight, an ignominious scurrying-forth unworthy of the home and husband that she left. He preferred to feel that if his wife sinned, she would sin like a lady.

Margery's directions were minute, though perhaps a trifle incoherent. Hewson sat down on the sofa along the end of the bed to study the list in the light of imminent activity. He must revise it systematically, making it out into headings: 'Contents of wardrobe, contents of chest by window, contents of dressing-table drawers.' Something caught his eye; he started. Margery's pink slippers, overlooked by Emily, peeped out at him from under the valance of the bed.

From the slippers, connections of ideas brought round his eyes to the fireplace again; he had never seen it black on a chilly evening; Margery had had everything, this was a really good room. She would never have a room like this again; Leslie would not be able to give it to her. What could have been the attraction? . . . Well, that was a blind alley; it was no good wandering down there.

She had written: 'I never quite know what you wanted me for.'

That statement amazed Hewson; it simply amazed him. He got up and walked round the room, staring at the shining furniture, challenging the pictures, thinking of the library fire, the dancing-floor under the downpour of light, the oval table in the dining-room compassed about for him always with an imaginary crowd of faces. Surely the sense of inclusion in all this should have justified Margery's existence to her. It was not as if he had ever bothered her to give him anything. He had assumed quite naturally that this sense of being cognate parts of a whole should suffice for both of them. He still could not understand where this had failed her.

He could not conceive what Leslie had held out to her, and what she had run to grasp.

Hewson advanced toward his reflection in the wardrobe mirror, and they stood eyeing one another sternly; then their faces softened. 'Lonely fellow,' Hewson condescended. The ghost of one of his old happy trances returned to his reflection; he saw the slow smile spread across its face, its fine face. That she should have fallen short of this . . .

He tugged at the handle of the wardrobe door, and his reflection swung toward him, flashed in the light and vanished. From the dusk within, cedar-scented and cavernous, Margery leaped out to him again as she had leaped up out of the envelope. There were so many Margerys in there, phalanx on phalanx, and the scent of her rushed out to fill this room, depose the bleak regency of Emily, and make the pictures, the chairs, the chintzes, the shadows in the alcove, suddenly significant. He drew out his fountain pen, detached a leaf from his notebook and headed it: 'Contents of Wardrobe.'

If he had been a different type of man Margery's chameleon quality would, he knew, have irritated him; the way she took colour from everything she put on, and not only took colour but became it, while shadowing behind all her changes an immutable, untouched, and careless self. Now the black dress – Hewson took it down and carried it over to the bed, and its long draperies swept the carpet, clinging to the pile, and seemed to follow him reluctantly – you would have said the black dress was the very essence, the expression of the innermost of her, till you met her in the flame-colour.

He took down the flame-colour next, and could hardly help caressing it as it lay across his arms, languishing and passive. The shimmer and rustle of it, the swinging of its pendent draperies round his feet, filled him with a sharp nostalgia, though they stood to him for nothing in particular – there had been that evening in the billiard-room. He laid the dress down reverently on the bed, like a corpse, and folded its gauzy sleeves across its bosom.

He was less tender with the one that followed, a creamy, slithery thing with a metallic brilliance that slipped down into his hands with a horrible wanton willingness. He had always felt an animosity towards it since they drove together to that dance. It slid and shone round Margery's limbs as though she were dressed in quicksilver; more beautiful than all the rest, more costly also, as Hewson knew. He let it drip down from his arms on to the bed and creep across the counterpane like a river.

He was summary, too, with the velvety things that followed, weighed down by their heavy fur hems. They were evenings at home to him, *tête-à-têtes* with their faint, discomfortable challenge; Margery tilting back her chin to yawn, or lolling sideways out of her chair to tickle her dog in the stomach, or shuffling illustrated papers. She would say: 'Talk to me, Hewson. Hewson, do talk . . . ' And later: 'Hewson, I suppose evenings at home are good for one. I'm so sleepy. That does show, doesn't it, how I need sleep?'

He worked more quickly after this, carrying the dresses one by one across the room, laying them on the bed, and pausing after each to compare his list with Margery's. Sometimes the name of a colour, the description of a stuff, would puzzle him, and he pored above the two lists with bent brows, unable to make them tally. Reluctantly he would inscribe a question mark. He heard ten strike, and began working even faster. He had still to make arrangements with the chauffeur: he liked to be in bed himself by half-past eleven, and he didn't approve of keeping the servants late.

Then, leaning deep into the cupboard, he saw the red dress, melting away into the shadows of the cedar-wood. It hung alone in one corner with an air of withdrawal. Hewson reached out, twitched it down; it hung limp from his hands, unrustling, exhaling its own perfume of chiffon. He stepped back; it resisted for an infinitesimal second, then, before he could release the tension on it, tore with a long soft sound.

It came out into the light of the room hanging jagged and lamentable, the long hem trailing. Hewson had torn it, torn the red dress; of all her dresses. He looked at it in fear and a kind of defiant anger. He assured himself the stuff was rotten; she had not worn it for so long. Had, indeed, Margery's avoidance of the red dress been deliberate?

With what motive, Hewson wondered, had this unique presentation of herself been so definitely eschewed? Did it make her shy – was she then conscious that it stood for something to be forgotten? He could never have believed this of Margery; he was startled to find that he himself should suspect it. Yet he returned to this: she had never worn the red dress since *that* occasion. He had watched for it speechlessly those ensuing weeks, evening after evening, but it had never appeared again. And here he had found it, hanging in the deepest shadow, trying to be forgotten.

Margery had put the red dress down on her list; she had underlined it. It was one of the dresses she wanted to take away to Leslie. Now it was torn, irreparably torn; she would never be able to wear it.

Hewson wondered whether Margery would be angry. He quailed a little, feeling the quick storm of her wrath about him; windy little buffets of derision and a fine sting of irony. She would certainly be angry when she knew, and go sobbing with rage to Leslie: Hewson wondered whether Leslie would be adequate. He debated whether he should pack the dress. Well, since it had admittedly stood for that to Margery as well as to himself, let her have it as it was! Hewson's wits stirred – this should be his comment. Why should he let her go to Leslie with that dress, the dress in which Hewson had most nearly won her? It had been pacific, their relationship; neither of them would have admitted a crescendo, a climax, a decrescendo; but there had been a climax, and the red dress shone in both their memories to mark it. He did not think he would let the Margery who lived for Leslie wear the red dress of his own irreclaimable Margery.

Smiling and frowning a little with concentration, he eyed the thing, then gripped the folds in both hands and tore the dress effortlessly from throat to hem, refolded it, and tore again. A fine dust of silk crimsoned the air for a moment, assailed his nostrils, made him sneeze. He laid the dead dress gently down among the other dresses and stood away, looking down at them all.

These were all his, his like the room and the house. Without these dresses the inner Margery, unfostered, would never have become perceptible to the world. She would have been like a page of music written never to be played. All her delightfulness to her friends had been in this expansion of herself into forms and colours. Hewson had fostered this expansion, as it now appeared, that Leslie might ultimately be delighted. From the hotel by the river the disembodied ghost of Margery was crying thinly to him for her body, her innumerable lovely bodies. Hewson expressed this to himself concisely and heavily, as a man should, as he stood looking down at the bed, half smiling, and said, 'She has committed suicide.'

From boyhood, Hewson had never cared for any thoughts of revenge. Revenge was a very wild kind of justice, and Hewson was a civilized man. He believed in the Good, in the balance of things, and in an eventual, tremendous pay-day. At once, the very evening Margery had left him, he had felt the matter to be out of his hands, and, wondering quite impartially how much she would be punished, had sat down almost at once to write and make arrangements with his sister. He had not, these last few days, felt sorrowful, venomous, or angry, because he had not felt at all; the making of these and other arrangements had too fully occupied him. He had always very lucidly and reasonably contended that the importance of mere feeling in determining a man's line of action is greatly overrated.

Now, looking down, he watched the dresses, tense with readiness to fall upon them if they stirred and pin them down and crush and crush and crush them. If he could unswervingly and unsparingly hold them in his eyes, he would be able to detect their movements, the irrepressible palpitation of that vitality she had infused into them. They lay there dormant; only the crimson dress was dead. He bent, and touched the creamy trickle of the ball-dress;

his finger dinted it and a metallic brightness spurted down the dint, filling it like a tide. He drew back his finger, cold yet curiously vibrant from the contact. The folds were cool; and yet he had expected, had expected . . . He brought down his outspread hands slowly; they paused, then closed on handfuls of the creamy stuff that trickled icily away between his fingers. The dress lay stretched out and provocative and did not resist him, and Hewson with dilated eyes stared down at it and did not dare to breathe.

He turned and crossed the room on tiptoe, peered out into the darkness of the trees, then drew the blinds down. He glanced round secretly and stealthily at the pictures; then he went over to the door and peered out, listening intently, on to the landing. Silence there and silence through the house. Shutting the door carefully behind him, he returned to the bedside.

It seemed to him, as he softly, inexorably approached them, that the swirls, rivers, and luxuriance of silk and silver, fur and lace and velvet, shuddered as he came. His shadow drained the colour from them as he bent over the bed.

Half an hour later, Hewson once more crossed the landing and went up to the box-room to look for Margery's trunk. He was intent and flushed, and paused for a moment under the light to brush some shreds of silver from his sleeve. He seemed unconscious that a wraith of flame-coloured chiffon drifted away from his shoulder as he walked, hung in the air, and settled on the carpet behind him. He came down again from the box-room breathing hard, bent beneath the trunk, and as he re-entered the bedroom something black and snake-like lying across the threshold wound round his feet and nearly entangled him. Approaching the bed, his steps were once more impeded; sometimes he was walking ankle-deep.

He pitched the trunk down in a clear space, propped it open and began to pack. Many of the fragments, torn too fine, were elusive; he stooped with the action of a gleaner to gather them in armfuls, then thrust them down into the trunk. The silks – they seemed still sentient – quivered under his touch; the velvets lay there sullenly, and sometimes, when he heaped them in, dripped out over the edge of the box again. Here and there an end of fur ruffled into deeper shadows under his excited breath. When he had amassed everything, Hewson beat with the flat of his hands upon the pile to make it level, spread tissue over it, and locked the trunk. Then he rang for Parkins and sat down to wait. He re-read Margery's list once again, folded it, and put it away in his pocket-book.

That night, Lippit the chauffeur received his instructions. He was to take Mrs Blair's box to the station at half-past eight the following morning, and despatch it to the given address per luggage in advance, having taken to the same station a ticket to be afterwards destroyed. This extravagance Hewson deplored, but the exigencies of the railway company demanded it. The trunk was strapped and corded and placed in the back hall in readiness for its early departure, and Hewson, seated comfortably at his table by the library fire, printed out two labels in neat black characters, then himself affixed them to the handles of the trunk.

'Would there be anything more, sir?' inquired Parkins, standing at attention.

'No, not tonight,' said Hewson courteously. 'I am sorry to have kept you late, Parkins: you had better go to bed.'

'Thank you, sir.'

'And oh, Parkins!'

'Sir?'

'You had better ask Emily to sweep out Mrs Blair's room again tonight. The carpet needs sweeping; she should pay particular attention to the carpet.'

Hearing the hall clock strike eleven, Hewson turned the lights out, quenched the astonished face of Parkins and went upstairs to bed.

The Storm

'DON'T come near me,' she said, turning sharply. 'I hate you! Why
do you keep on following me about?'

He said, 'Well, we've got to go down in the same tram.'

'I'll walk.'

'Not with those heels. You couldn't.'

'If you had any decency, you would.'

'I don't care for walking those long distances down hill. It shakes
me up. Besides, I feel another blister coming.'

He stooped to feel one foot, and the crimson of his face
deepened.

'O-oh!' she shuddered, pressing her handbag with both hands to
her bosom, and grimacing up at the sky.

He peered over the parapet. 'Hush,' he said, 'there are people on
the terrace just below us, listening.'

'Danish women,' she said scornfully, looking over at the three
flat hats, but she dropped into silence, shifting away from him as he
leant forward and spread his elbows out on the parapet with a
prolonged 'Phew!' They were high up on the terrace of a Villa;
dizzily high.

The air was warm and tense, stretched so taut that it quivered.
Breathing had become an affair of consciousness, and movement
they both felt to be impossible. Behind the terrace, the doorways of
the Villa grew solid with darkness, the high façade loomed. Colour
faded everywhere, the hills grew livid; forms assumed a menacing
distinctness, blade-like against the architecture of the clouds.

Immeasurably below them, the trees were clotted together in the
unnatural dusk. Steps from the terrace descended in a series of
inexorable zig-zags. If one went down the steps into the depths of
the garden, one might never come up again.

'I can't bear the noise of the fountains,' she said angrily. 'Why
doesn't somebody stop them? – they get louder and louder.'

He did not answer.

'What makes them like that, all of a sudden? Look at that pale
strip, along the horizon. That's the sun shining over Rome.' She

thought of the streets and the houses and the bright safe trams. 'Why didn't we stay in Rome – *Rupert?*'

His squared shoulders looked broader than ever, but did not inspire confidence.

'I don't know why we ever came up here,' she continued miserably.

'Well, you wanted to come . . .'

'Now you're going to be sulky. Oh, I can't think why we ever came to Italy at all!'

As he did not answer, she dragged herself a little further away from him down the terrace, trailing her gloved hand along the parapet. She could not bear to look down at the view any longer, nor dared she face the blind-eyed Villa behind her, so she stood with eyes shut, increasingly afraid. She knew that they were caught up here, impenetrably surrounded, on the nakedness of the heights. She was still at times, irrationally, afraid of God. Like other outlaws, it was probable that He had taken to the hills, and she had never cared to venture far into the country of outlaws. He had hung once about certain elemental passages in her life, and had been brought down upon her, sometimes, by Rupert. Here in Italy, in the churches or out in the sunshine, she had been feeling recently a complete security. And now here was Italy turning luridly upon her the whites of its eyes. She felt that she had been led up here and betrayed.

With a succession of uncertain impetuses she had reached the corner of the terrace, where the whole world fell away from under the Villa. The murmur of the Danish women's voices faded here, and she was less troubled by the insistence of the fountains. The darkening skies contracted and the balustrade and the wall of the house looked ash-pale, brittle, and impermanent. She longed to return to the village, and meditated how she would slip away through the chain of empty rooms, defying the echoes, across the courtyard and out into the street. From here, she could see the houses toppling up the hill, the awnings of the cafés colourless and undefined by shadow, the steep street empty in the dusk. Life, however dormant, lay accessible behind her. She reassured herself that she was on a peninsula rather than an island. She craved the comfortableness of strange voices, the impersonality of casual contacts, the touch of hands that would be nothing but human. She wanted an abstraction of humanity. The further proximity of Rupert had become intolerable; he was a bundle of potentialities and grievances; inextinguishably Rupert. She already fatigued herself sufficiently, and was fatigued by herself, without the super-imposition of Rupert.

Round the corner, she discovered that the terrace went no

further. It was swallowed up into the darkness of an archway, diminishing from sight in an ascent of steps. One could enter the house here, by a doorway to her left; the dark room within was attentive, the mustiness of it stole out on to the terrace and hung here, even on the edge of this illimitable space. Other smells crept up from below, and hung too, unable to disperse themselves, thickening the close air: sultriness from the blossoming trees below, a dank breath from water, and decay, faint and very sickly, from, perhaps, the small dead body of some animal under those impenetrable branches.

Here was a way of escape open to her: she could pass down the long chain of rooms, link on link of frescoed emptiness with garlands duskier in the dusk, with little bald, square windows, lashless eyes, staring out on to the darkening sky. She could regain the courtyard and the village without retracing her steps along the terrace, and bewilder Rupert, and defeat the beleaguering forces of God.

She could not do it; she was too much afraid of the dark rooms and the echoes. She put up her hands to her forehead because her head ached.

After the young woman in orange had passed her, she wondered dully where she had been going, whither she hurried so. Her urgency had cut like a knife through the opaque twilight, and her dress had been curiously brilliant in the drained-out colourlessness of the evening. The chief impression of her passing had been a rustling and a rushing sound, and though she had not passed in an imponderable moment there had been an effect of speed about her forehead and blown-back hair. She left a coolness of displaced air, like the single gesture of a fan. She had taken form out of the darkness of the stairway, simultaneously emerging and descending. At its foot there had been a sort of hesitancy – a gesture of return; then she had rushed forward with an impetus that made her almost luminous. She had vanished round the corner of the terrace, one could not say how long ago. Rupert would feel the wind of her movement, she might brush against him as she passed.

Rupert's wife went slowly to the corner of the terrace, leaned her hand against the blunted angle of the wall, and looking down the long perspective saw that it was empty. Rupert was gone and the other – she could not remember what other she had come to find.

Then she felt the wall of the Villa tilt for a moment over towards her as she cried, 'Oh, Rupert, Rupert, I have seen a ghost!'

Rupert had remained leaning forward on his elbows till the sound of her angry breathing from above him died away and the rustle of her dress diminished. The least sound twanged on the taut air. He turned his head with an imperceptible slowness to watch her down the terrace; she stooped badly and her head poked forward under that feathered hat. The contemptuous nonchalance of her trailed hand irritated him: she was not a person to have brought to Italy. Then the back of his eyes pricked as he remembered how ineffectual they both were, how they neither of them knew what they wanted, how suspiciously they watched one another, jealous of a gleam of certainty. Their journeyings were a forlorn hope, they never found what they had come to seek, nor even knew what they had come for. He bent down again to feel the blister on his foot, and when he raised his eyes she had turned the corner of the terrace. Round the corner, she would find nothing that interested her, and soon she would come slowly back again to tell him how there had been nothing, and to reproach him with Italy, and with the noise of the fountains. Although the whole afternoon he had been determined that she should not evade him, and had kept close on her heels, because she had been somehow eluding him in her displeasure, he now decided to evade *her*, to escape utterly, to walk through the village without her and be found sitting waiting for her in the tram. He would have liked, indeed, to follow the steep curves of that road down on to the Campagna, if it had not been for the blister on his foot.

Furtively with a quick resolution he darted away across the terrace into the Villa, through air that impeded his movements as in a dream. The sound of his footsteps, suddenly intensified by the constricting walls, rose up startlingly around him. Softly! – she might hear him, even from the end of the terrace! To his left and right, opposite one another, doorways showed him empty doorways in diminishing perspective, and the nakedness of floors. In the windless dusk the painted garlands swayed, it seemed, a little on the walls. From some pin's-head vanishing point, where beyond the long perspective the ultimate blank wall had faded into darkness, steps began. 'Hullo!' said Rupert nervously.

The shutter slammed. Black darkness drowned the room and the house shivered. 'Hell!' screamed Rupert. He did not know that there was a wind; indeed, it had been more than negative, that windlessness. He ran to the next room, and, pressing back the shutters against the embrasure of the window (they shook a little under his hands), saw the tops of the three cypresses that rose above the terrace making wild gestures against the sky.

The taut clouds, he knew, would never stand this buffeting. Why, the very slamming of that shutter must have ripped through them like a bullet. In flight before an imminent Something that he did not dare to imagine, he determined to go further into the Villa and find the passage and the steps up to the courtyard. He could not go on like this for ever, from one to another of these infinite rooms – they were too like one another. Each, too, might crash again at any moment into darkness, and Rupert did not like the dark. So he took the exit that a little door offered him, low in the centre wall, and found himelf in a half-familiar obscurity, like that of his own dining-room at home. It sounded small, and something facing him, as it were a side-board, he understood to be an altar. He guessed, too, rather than perceived, a tall cross up above it on the wall. This meant something, anyhow. 'This is the chapel,' said Rupert.

He enjoyed patronage, and had at all times adjusted to their (he believed) mutual satisfaction his relations with his Maker. An Agency had made arrangements for his passage across Life, at the price of moderate concessions on the part of Rupert, and to its divine supervision Rupert trustfully consigned himself. God was everywhere, making arrangements, even as a Cook's official met him on every platform when he travelled. Rupert remained sublimely passive; he was not a fussy man. So this was a chapel – he sat down in it to wait.

He did not realize whom he was disturbing till they slipped away behind some curtains into an opaquer darkness. Their rosaries tinkled swinging from their fingers as they passed him; their gowns, drawing together, relieved the floor of its blackness as they rose from their knees silently, even faintly revealing the pattern of the tiles. Six faces, incredibly long, turned towards him – no, not faces, wimples; they were nuns. 'Oh, pardon me,' said Rupert, as they passed out quietly.

Now that the shadows fell into order behind them, he found, his eyes growing accustomed, that the place was not after all impenetrably dusky. Three shafts lighted it, striking down from the level of the courtyard; under one of them, even, candlesticks faintly glimmered. In the front of the Villa, in those rooms he had come from, a shutter slammed again, then quickly another; there was a long rushing, scudding sound that died away round the corner in a whistle. Rupert felt that it was good for him to be here.

The Danish ladies were also alarmed. This was not Italy as they had been led to expect her, nor, indeed, as she had hitherto displayed herself to them. Deep within them, the Teutonic decencies were outraged by this exposure. They turned their eyes from the livid hills and gasped a little beneath the pressure of the sky. Above, the peevish Englishwoman had finished quarrelling with her husband; he leaned over the parapet, looking down on them, and they wondered if he were going to speak. They were tired of taking photographs of one another beside the fountains, and for this, also, it was now too dark. They wearied of poking their umbrellas up the mouths of the dolphins to intercept the spouting of the water. The exhalations and the darkness of the trees rose toward them like smoke. They wished to return to the village and buy postcards and drink chocolate in a café. 'Let us go up,' they said. And when they were not yet half-way to the first of the many angles of the ascending stairs the stoutest of them sat down suddenly and said, 'I cannot.' Later, the others succumbed and sat down also, mopping their faces; having taken off their hats that the perspiration might not injure the linings. The youngest, who, still consistent, felt justified in demanding a certain consistency of Nature, said that she did not see why it should be so hot and yet so black. 'Thunder,' said the stout one, and the others looked at her incredulously for a moment, then agreed. They all stared up at the sky, inquisitorially, and one of them, by twisting her neck for a moment, was able to observe that the Englishman had vanished from the upper terrace.

One does not speak much while contemplating a too great expanse of country under the imminence of a storm. They sat close together, so that their mackintoshes creaked in contact; each one enclosed within herself, aloof, chaste, inviolable to emotion. It was sitting thus that they heard the Englishwoman scream.

There was excitement in the scream, they thought pleasurable excitement. They turned their heads, and one of them conjectured that she had picked up a bracelet on the terrace. By the prolonged sustenance of her highest note, it might even have been a diamond bracelet.

'She is calling her husband.'

'The man Rupert.'

'He has gone in.'

They supposed that when she had finished screaming she would go in too, taking whatever she had found, and look for him in the Villa. But no, she came down the steps with her hands shaking; they heard the little loose coins jingling in her handbag. Her hat was pushed back from her forehead; she looked very white, not hot at all.

'I have seen a woman, a woman in yellow. She went round the corner and vanished. Did she come past you? She was a ghost.'

They listened very carefully, looked at one another, and assured her in their careful English that they had seen no woman. She herself was the only lady whom they had encountered in the gardens of the Villa.

'Not a lady,' she cried, pushing her hat back further from her forehead, 'a ghost, a ghost!'

They agreed that the gardens might be full of ghosts, and that many things were possible. Meanwhile, was Madame seeking her

husband? He had gone back into the Villa. Did not Madame feel
that it was likely to rain? While they hung expectantly upon the
silence of Madame the trees below them were sucked sideways
with a roar. Pale gashes curled forward, slit and dissipated themselves like waves where the wind flung forward whole branches.
Little eddies of sound sucked and whirled down in the shadows.
Above it all, there was a high whistling.

The pillar of a fountain, solid as marble, swerved, bent like a
bow, and flung a cloud of fine spray into their faces.

'The wind has come,' said the youngest lady, tucking away
strands of hair behind her ears and putting on her hat. The
Englishwoman stampeded like a horse: she cried, 'My husband!'
and went wildly up the steps again with an agility which surprised
them, her skirts shrieking in the wind.

The wind caught the Villa full in the face, one stinging challenge
like the slash of a gauntlet. Elegant, rococo, with an air of balance
delicately perilous, it yet struck down deep into the rock, deep as a
fortress. It braced itself, and now the assailing forces of the wind
came singing between the pillars of the parapet. Row on row, the
windows looked unflinchingly out into the sky, though here and
there the swinging-to of a shutter was like the nervous and
involuntary flicker of an eyelid. The attack begun, the clouds
brought up their artillery; lightning, splitting the sky, shimmered
across the flagstones of the terrace. The honey-coloured façade,
soaked and languorous with sunshine, stood up, naked, sensitive as
flesh, to the stinging onslaught of the rain that beat against the
windows with a faint, fine, infinitesimal clatter.

Deep in the heart of the house, the man Rupert was sitting in the
lower chapel. The light coming down from the shafts was
darkened, the candlesticks no longer gleamed. Little rapiers of
windy draught came whistling and stabbing at him, the curtains
twitched audibly, then faintly and more continuously rustled. The
chapel suffered Rupert, but did nothing to entice him. He
remembered with an immeasurable nostalgia their bedroom at the
hotel, warm, crude, actual; the patterned tapestry of the sofa, the
painted ceiling, his wife's garments, straggling, be-ribboned, the
thermos flask with the coffee that they had forgotten today. He
remembered the talk in the lounge. 'Going to the Forum?' 'No,
we've done the Forum . . . ,' 'they give good coffee and milk here,
but the butter is execrable . . . ,' 'a postcard of the Dying Gaul,'
'Gladiator,' 'We must do St Peter's – yes, yes, yes . . . '

Rupert watched the darkness where the curtains were, and
wondered if the nuns were coming back. Faintly envisaged, and
thus more faintly desirable, was his smoking-room at home, full of

the books he had never finished. Perhaps he had been sometimes too arbitrary in his refusals of hospitality – from books, places, people. He had been always hurrying on to a rendezvous, afraid lest he should miss God and the expedition thus proceed without him. He had hurried his wife along with him, reluctant and suspicious, looking back over his shoulder at the destruction of her cities, trailing after him with slack steps.

She had trailed away from him down the terrace, and he was surprised to find that now he was wanting her. This darkness, potentially, this frightening darkness, made him protective; something passive and weak was wanting, to come and cower against him. A dog, even, or one of the children that they might have had; but better than all, his wife. Failing this, he was at a loss – even, he admitted, frightened. The great thing, he knew, was to stop thinking about oneself. He veered full round towards his wife, mentally and emotionally. She was a listless creature, but now she would be tense, horribly at bay and afraid, propped against a doorpost, clutching at it. She was a coward, he knew; his heart swelled with delight and desire as he felt what a coward she was. She had never been on the side of the angels; he had never been able to explain to her about God. She could not understand that she was being catered for.

Rupert's wife, having taken shelter, stood in one of the front rooms by the window, breathing hard and flinching away from the lightning. She heard the Danes enter, and pressing herself back against the wall listened while they hesitated for a moment and turned, unconsciously, away from her; making their way through the chain of rooms in the direction of the village. Watching them, she observed something duck-like about their recessive backs. Rupert, she guessed, was somewhere near at hand, but might very possibly be inaccessible to her. She was now feeling very definitely in contest with an opposing will, and the storm slanting and flaring beyond the windows, darkness rolling up on darkness, set her tingling with the exultation of a definite encounter. The house enclosed her greedily; it impeded her, and yet it was an ally.

She also had it in her to project herself, to stamp on time her ineffaceable image. She had an urgency which made her timeless, like the woman on the terrace; which made her step clear of the dimensions. She had simply, as she now knew, beheld herself in a mirror as that other went past her; and stepped back, shaken, from her own reality. That was it: she was overcharged. She was too much for herself, and terribly in need of Rupert. He was a slight, dependent thing, and infinitely pitiable, trotting hard and a little hopelessly at the heel of his gigantic Somebody. She ached now

with the consciousness of her own sufficiency for him, her potency
to crowd out even God.

Crowd out? There was nobody there to oppose her. Up here in
the hills she had parleyed, and made an alliance. Rupert had been
sold to her; by a treachery of God, which would be inconceivable
to him, delivered up utterly into her hands. She sought for and
eventually found him, squatting on one of the stools by the altar,
low and toad-like, and her own shadow darkened his white face
upturned towards her as she stood in the square dull greyness of the
open door. They contemplated one another's outlines speechlessly;
self-sufficient, travelled, wary, and mutually pitiful.

Then: 'Rupert,' she cried, 'where were you? I've been looking
for you, looking for you everywhere!'

'I was waiting here. I knew if I went wandering about we would
miss each other. I thought it would be better to wait here till you
came to me – I didn't know where you had gone. This place, you
know, is part of a convent. It is full of nuns.'

'*Nuns?*' she said incredulously. She would not believe him, and
when, feeling his way over to the corner of their exit, he drew back
the curtain, he found that there was nothing behind it but stone: it
was a blocked-up archway.

'Well?' came her voice with a smile in it. It was beautiful to her
that Rupert had been making himself nuns.

'They *seemed* to me to be nuns,' he faltered, 'and they went away
here where the curtain is . . . A kind of archway . . . But they
may only have been shadows, black and white ones. You know,
the wind was so terrible that I couldn't hear anything, and I couldn't
see or think properly either. It was rather fine, I thought, to think
of good women still living in this house and coming here and
praying. It – it was a Testimony,' he concluded huskily. 'It seemed
to me extraordinarily fine.'

'Extraordinarily fine,' her voice echoed, soft and kindly. 'But,
Rupert, I was afraid and lonely. I wanted you. I was alone.'

'Afraid!' he cried gladly, clambering to his feet and making his
way toward her tall shadowiness. His hand stretched out and
touched hers and withdrew timidly: he did not often caress her. 'I
ought to have been with you . . . Darling . . . ' he said rustily.

'I'm all right now. But let's go, Rupert, let's go up to the village
together, and soon we can go down in the tram.' They heard
thunder, a dull sound, low and enveloping, and the room behind
her shimmered with two or three flashes. They thought the house
trembled.

'Not yet: stay here,' said Rupert.

'Does this make you feel religious?' she asked, shutting the door
behind her.

'Well, God's everywhere.'

They stood together by the musty canopy of the altar, shoulder to shoulder. His arm crept round her waist and lightly encircled her. 'Poor darling!' he whispered, 'poor dear!' She leaned toward him in the dark, her feathers brushed his cheek.

'You're very strong,' she said.

'I think when one believes in an ultimate Rightness . . . '

'Yes . . . '

She was beginning to understand, he thought. He was beginning to be able to win her over. God with him, she was learning to cling to him. And she ran her hands over his tweed shoulders, stroking them, sighing ineffably, knowing that he was delivered up utterly into her hands.

Charity

When Rachel had done showing Charity the garden, they both sat down in a wheelbarrow beside the flowering currant-bush, swung their legs exaggeratedly, and looked away from each other. There was still another hour before tea. The fact was, they were still rather strange to one another in the relation of guest and hostess. All the effects Rachel had planned for this afternoon had come off; yet somehow not quite come off, because there was an incalculable strangeness about Home today that had altogether surprised her. Nothing seemed as usual. By the time they were half-way round the house she was beginning to feel, each time she opened a door, 'Perhaps I am letting Charity in for more than I know?' When they looked into the bogey-hole under the stairs, and she told Charity by way of a joke that they kept the family ghost there, she felt horribly afraid. Even the currant-bush began to be affected; it smelt so hot and sharp that she felt she ought to explain it in some way. The zumming and bump of bees in and out of it filled up the silence embarrassingly. It seemed equally unlifelike to mention the bees and to ignore them, so she laughed aloud to herself unnaturally and kicked the wheel of the barrow.

Yet the strangeness perhaps lay in Charity. She wore a flowery hat from under which her nose came out at an unexpected angle, and when she took her hat off she patted her hair. When she talked to Father or Mother she had 'a manner.' She had got out of the train (backwards) in a bottle-green dress much longer than usual. Rachel had understood at once that there need be no fear of her not being a success at Home; on the other hand, she did not seem to be so much impressed by it all as one had expected. Her gaze ate things up and diminished them. Her own home and her unknown relations kept like a shadow behind her. She might almost have been one of the Little Daughters of Your Age that Mother invited to tea. Just now, as they slowly paraded the borders, Rachel had caught herself wishing that they were back in the garden at school. *There* it would have been thrilling to be walking about with Charity, arm in arm . . . She did not show her the Secret Place . . .

For this her heart smote her. 'Did you know,' she said, 'that I had rabbits of my own now?'

'Show!' said Charity.

With a lovely feeling of release they rushed off.

Rachel had been praying days ahead that Adela might be out for tea that first afternoon. Yet even when the gong sounded she could not be sure. She thought it better to prepare the ground, so said to Charity coming across the hall, 'You will laugh when you see my sister!'

'I thought she was grown up,' said Charity, looking down thoughtfully into a brass pot that held, besides a palm, several of Father's and Adela's cigarette-ends.

'Still, she's pretty mad,' said Rachel cautiously. She punched Charity in the small of the back to make her go first through the door, Charity punched her back, and they scuffled together on the threshold quite naturally, as at school. But Rachel was noticing how the dining-room and the round white table in the after-noon light looked less like themselves than like their own reflection in a looking-glass. Mother and Father made a smiling pattern one on each side of it. What a cheery pair of little girls!

They sat down: Mother and Father, not too apparently watching them, talked to each other. They broke off now and then to say encouraging things to the Little Friend, who sat with her chin tucked in, taking long drinks and smiling politely. Having dining-room tea in the holidays gave Rachel the unfamiliar and pleasant feeling of this houseful of grown-up people pivoting round on herself. Nobody else liked it; there were plain kinds of dripping-cake and gingerbread that nobody else cared for; Father would drink his two cups straight off and go away quickly; Adela would cry out, '*Must* we all watch this child eat?' cross her legs and jerk back her chair. Sitting thus, she would smoke and say, 'Oh lord! *Oh* lord!' and at last take Mother by the arm and march her out through the French window into the garden. Mother would go with her frowning and laughing, very much flattered, torn in herself and reluctant. Then it would be dreary sometimes, though not unprofitable, being left alone with the cakes.

Father was going over, for Charity's benefit, all his usual rather silly questions and jokes about school. 'Do they cane you?' he kept asking her. 'Do they make you talk Latin? Do you have dormitory feasts?' Charity gave little giggles. 'Ooh, Major Monstrevor, you *are* . . . !' She ate a refined tea, and did not want jam, she said, because it was sticky. Rachel was proud of her father's appearance, she thought he looked 'soldierly'; but she could not bear him to talk too much. In an access of nervousness and with some idea of causing a distraction, she leant over and said to her mother, 'Where's Adela? Isn't she in?'

Her heart went up into her throat at the question, and stayed there till Mother, absent-minded, brought herself to reply, 'Oh, Adela? Tennis.'

This was an answer to prayer, but it might be more awful than ever when Adela did come in. To hear her talk of her tennis made one hot all over: she might have been Suzanne at least: one did not know where to look.

Mother came out with the inevitable. Getting up, she beamed at them. 'And what are you going to do with yourselves?' said Mother.

There was an absolutely blank moment: everybody looked at Rachel. Rachel remembered that *this* was the afternoon she had been saving herself up for since the middle of term; she could have wept. If only she could be back at school again, telling Charity . . . But *this* was Charity, looking at her aloofly with critical little clear pale eyes. Charity waiting to be entertained. It was an absolutely blank moment. 'Oh, *I* dunno,' said Rachel. 'Just mouch round . . . '

Mother smiled helpfully; the smile stayed on a minute or two while her thoughts wandered.

'Rabbits?' said Father.

'She's seen the rabbits . . . '

So he took them into the study and showed Charity his butterfly collection. He took down cabinet after cabinet of the poor, brittle, bright-coloured creatures that one would rather die than touch. Rachel loathed the butterfiies and the way they would all quiver suddenly on their pins as though coming alive again; she was certain Charity loathed them too, but she felt grateful to Father. To make things go off well she exclaimed loudly at them as though she hadn't seen them before, and asked their names eagerly. She hoped Charity didn't remember what she had once said about Father's butterflies, on their way to gym. Charity, who didn't like her own father, had said that fathers were the limit. Rachel had agreed at once, though with a feeling of shock, and, seeking round for some shortcoming of her father's, thought of his collection. Wasn't it atrociously cruel, she had said, to stick a butterfly, still quite living, through with a pin! Anyhow, when she had said 'atrociously cruel!' she hadn't *meant* anything to do with Father.

He thought of something important, put away the butterfly-cabinets suddenly, and turned his back on the two of them, bored. So Rachel pushed Charity through the door (she seemed to have been pushing Charity through doors all day, but no solution yet offered itself), and they went back to the garden and played French-cricket there with a tennis-ball.

Charity played a brilliant game and couldn't be got out. Rather flushed, she began to enjoy herself, and soon with her eyes (apparently) quite tight shut she was scornfully knocking Rachel's bowling all over the place. At last she sent the tennis-ball in at the drawing-room window and knocked over a pot of azaleas.

'Crikey!' she said. 'Will They mind? Let's tell Them afterwards . . . I call this a silly old game!'

The rude way she said this made Rachel see light. It was this politeness that had been the matter all day. Inspired, she shouted, 'Silly fool yourself!' and came charging at Charity full tilt, in the rôle of Laughing Tomahawk. Charity, unprepared, lost her balance forthwith and rolled over. She lay kicking at Rachel with both feet for a moment or two, and it seemed as if things were going all right. Then she jumped up suddenly (that green frock!), stood dusting herself, and said in a cold voice, 'Shut up; I wish you wouldn't.' She was an absolute stranger; the green frock had pleats down the side and bobbly brass buttons. *What* one must have looked like, with one's scarlet yelling mouth, being Laughing Tomahawk! . . . Rachel was quenched.

'Shall we climb up,' she said, 'and sit on the roof of the bicycle shed?'

'I don't mind,' said Charity. 'Do you often?'

Rachel did. It was here that she read her books, designed cathedrals, made a new will every holidays, and kept the key to a terribly secret cipher under a flowerpot. It was here that she would lie pulling an elder-branch up and down above her head like a punkah, and dinting the roof with her heels while she thought about Charity. She felt embarrassed as she hoisted up Charity into this ring of terribly secret thoughts; she wished that she had gone up first to get the place into order. Sometimes the thoughts would simply be conversations, or sometimes the school was on fire, or there was nearly a bathing fatality. Sometimes there was a war on, and, as none of the men were brave enough, they were both going to fight.

'This must be awfully bad for the roof,' said Charity, jumping about. 'Just look at those dints. Do They mind?' But Rachel took out the cipher, and suddenly, effortlessly, unknowingly, like falling asleep at last when one has been trying and trying, they were together again. The evening went terribly fast.

Presently they heard a bicycle being rattled along and branches brushing against a bicycle wheel. Adela coming home. Adela's red felt hat was pulled right over her eyes like a sombrero; the top of her looked Spanish, and the rest, muffled up to the mouth, like an Antarctic explorer. She came back from tennis like this in the hottest weather because, one could only suppose, it looked rather professional. She managed to look languid and sinister, even pushing a bicycle down a narrow path through syringa bushes. 'Crikey!' said Charity audibly when she appeared.

Adela looked up at them darkly from under her hat, but kept her chin in her scarf and said nothing. They both rolled over on to their stomachs, and watched her over the edge of the roof while she put her bicycle away.

'You know that's bad for the roof,' said Adela in her dead-sounding voice as she came out again.

'(There!' said Charity to Rachel.)

'*Are* you,' said Adela, 'Faith, or Hope?' Charity giggled. She did not know that Adela had been talking about her, before she came, as the Charity Child, and asking Mother in Rachel's presence to have her thoroughly disinfected. 'You never know,' she had said, 'with Charity Children . . .'

Standing still in the path underneath them, like a pillar of salt in the six o'clock sunlight, Adela began to unwind (very guardedly, for fear of pneumonia) some of her wrappings. Her chin came out, chalky white like the tip of her nose, and her long thin jaw like rather a beautiful crocodile's. She grinned to herself; the joke was for neither of them, but she did not mind them seeing she was amused. 'I've heard the most *terrible* things about you,' she said, looking at Charity, and, shaking her head in a horrified way, walked away through the bushes. She left behind a fatal gash in the peace of the afternoon. When they kicked the roof it gave out a dungeony, clanking sound, and down in the shed underneath Adela's bicycle rattled.

Charity could not give her mind to the cipher again; she was very pink. 'What *have* you been telling her?' she asked in an agitated, pleased voice. Rachel said, 'Nothing'; she never told Adela anything. 'Well, I must say I didn't expect her like *that*,' said Charity sharply.

Adela did not seem to Rachel to have gone off so badly. This revived a particular hope that the awfulness of Adela might be simply her own delusion, and that she would seem just an Elder Sister to any one else. 'She isn't really so bad,' she said comfortably, deep in the cipher.

'Well, I must say . . . She isn't what I'd call very Good Style.'

Rachel was so angry, she did not know with whom, that she was hardly able to speak.

People were coming to dinner, so Rachel and Charity were to have 'a tray' in the spare-room. This felt very select, especially when one spread a lace handkerchief over the table in the window and imagined this was a restaurant; though there had been an uncomfortable moment when Rachel saw Charity unpack two beautiful evening dresses and hang them up in the wardrobe without saying a word. Was this, she wondered, the only house in the world where girls of twelve didn't come down to dinner? The spare-room was a magnificent room (like in somebody else's house), all mirrors; they danced a pyjama ballet surrounded by their reflections. The room got so dusky that when the tray with their poached eggs was brought in and put down they did not see it, and forgot that supper was there.

They sat in the window-sill, outside, told each other stories and listened to the rooks going to bed. There would be a sudden cry, a tree shaken, and the sky would be dark with them; then calling to one another again and again, they would drop back into the branches. Fewer rooks rose each time, and this gave one a feeling of great peacefulness, as though the whole earth were being hushed-up and reassured. These were the evenings that Rachel missed most when she went back to school.

The happiness that she had been waiting for all day seemed to have something to do with light behind the trees, the rooks, and the dry chintzy smell of the curtains when she leant back her head against them into the room. Also, there is something very heroic about dangling one's legs at a height.

Suddenly they remembered supper and dived into the darkness to look for the poached eggs. They lit one candle, and Charity, who could be very funny, sat languishing in the light of it, fluttered her lashes and ate off the tip of her fork. Rachel was a Guardsman, very adoring, and kept offering her champagne and cocktails. 'A *mushroom* cocktail,' she said coaxingly, and they both thought that sounded delicious. They imagined cocktails to be little red things like prawns, that sat at the bottom of glasses with their tails turned up.

Rachel, still in the character of Guardsman, jumped up, flung an arm round Charity's neck and kissed her violently. 'Oh, be *careful*, Captain de Vere,' squeaked Charity; 'you are dripping champagne from your moustache . . . *Oh*, my Reveille and Rossiter!' She mopped the champagne from Captain de Vere's moustache off the front of her pyjama-jacket, and wrung out her handkerchief into her plate.

Then she stiffened up and pushed Rachel away. The expression was wiped off her face suddenly, leaving it blank. 'Do *listen*,' she snapped out, listening herself all over. Rachel heard nothing at all for a moment; it was creepy, as though Charity were hearing a ghost. To encourage herself and hear better she lighted more candles, padding round the room in her bare feet and trying not to shake the matchbox. All she heard then was Adela moving about

next door, pulling drawers open and pushing them shut with a
rattle. For a moment she wondered what Adela could be doing at
midnight – she felt like midnight, miles from the ordinary,
delirious, rather guilty: then she remembered the gong hadn't gone
yet; it couldn't be more than eight. That could only be Adela
dressing for dinner.

When Charity heard this she got up and swaggered about the
room. It is wonderful what one can do on cocoa and a little
imagination. She made Rachel feel as a matter of course that
everybody else in the house was their enemy.

'Let's make a raid,' said she; 'let's tie up Her door handle!'

'Coo . . . ' wavered Rachel, greatly attracted.

'No, let's go in and pretend to be sick on Her bed.'

'But Mother'd — '

'Who cares for your mother?'

They took off the ropes from the waists of their dressing-gowns
and crept into the passage. Adela's door was ajar and her lights
lighted; she was humming, and seemed to be prowling about like a
panther. As though she had heard them, she pounced and appeared
in her doorway. She was tall, and every inch of her glared in the
gaslight. Rachel immediately curled up inside like a woodlouse,
because she felt Adela was going to 'rasp.' They stood there at bay
rather foolishly, the ropes of their dressing-gowns coiled up in their
hands like lassoes. But Adela's best 'Evening' manner had been
finally arranged and put on with her pearls and her earrings; she
wasn't going to take it off again, even for them.

'What the devil — ' she began pleasantly, as though to her own
friends.

Having nothing ready they stood curling up their bare toes, each
wondering what the other was going to do. Evening dress still
filled Adela's mind as she stood above them; frowning down as
though they were not there, she touched delicately, inquiringly,
one long earring after the other with the tip of a finger, and, with
head a little sideways, screwed one tighter. Having done this she
shook her head, at first very cautiously, but though the earrings
wagged violently they did not come off. Relief at this made Adela
still more pleasant. 'What *do* you want?' she said, and raising her
eyebrows smiled despairingly, as though she must be very kind to a
little idiot sister.

Charity moved. 'We came,' she said in an awed and breathy
voice, 'to ask if you would come in and say good-night to us?'

'Soppy,' said Adela, pleased. The gold fringe round her dress
swung as she stepped back into her room to close a cupboard door
and turn the light off. Saved, it seemed that they were.

'You have got a nerve!' said Rachel in a shaky whisper. But

Charity's features rolled up into an appalling 'face.' 'Come on; come now!' said Rachel, quite unnerved and tugging at the skirt of Charity's dressing-gown. '*Back* from the jaws of death, *Back* from the gates of Hell,' she was saying to herself, half aloud. She knew she must be what they all called 'very excited.' She was so excited that something throbbed in her ears, and she wanted to scream and rush back across the passage before a something that was worse than Adela put out a long arm and grabbed her into the dark room. She wanted to slam the spare-room door in the Enemy's face and barricade it, perhaps with the wardrobe. 'You won't get us,' she was prepared to call out, 'not if you burn the house down.' She felt like staying up all night. She tugged with all her might at Charity's dressing-gown.

'Leave go!' An unknown, scornful person flashed round suddenly. A dressing-gown was wrenched from her. 'Let *go*, you fool!' Full of wild suspicion and enmity, lost to one another, they scuffled, skidding on the oilcloth. Rachel cried, half sobbing from breathlessness, 'No, listen, Charity . . . Charity, don't be a beast.' Charity grew a year older each moment, her protests grew shriller and more reasonable . . . 'No, seriously, *listen*, Charity . . . '

'It's you that are the beast,' said Charity in a remote voice, as Adela showed up again in the dark doorway. With a wave, as though they had been sparrows quarrelling, Adela dispersed them. She put an arm round Charity's shoulders, and they walked off into the spare-room. 'My friend and I,' their two back views, short and tall, said of each other.

'*You* must go to bed,' said Adela, looking back. '*You're* excited.'

Rachel sat on her bed in the dark and thought over her day. Her door was ajar, and she heard a continuous murmur and mumble and laugh coming out of the spare-room. Then Adela came out, keeping on the same smile with which she had said good-night to Charity, to do for the visitors down in the drawing-room. She paused at the top of the stairs, touched her earrings again, and shook out the fringe of her dress. Then she turned the gas low and went down. "Well, I just hope,' thought Rachel, 'she *likes* being tucked up by Adela. I've never known any one tuck up so rottenly.' She felt contemptuous and, in a queer sort of way, happier than she had been all day. She knew Charity would be expecting her back, and presently, sure enough, she heard 'Coo-ee?'

'Coo-ee, Coo-ee,' Charity kept repeating, every few seconds. Rachel lay with her eyes shut, taking no notice, and then there began later a puzzled and angry silence. 'I shall go to sleep,' thought Rachel, beginning to count sheep. Then she began to believe she heard Charity sobbing. She lay listening for the irregular vague sounds, watching the circle of light from the gas-bracket wobble and fade on the ceiling over the spare-room door. When she was nearly asleep, Charity, hugging her elbows, crept out and stood on the landing.

'Oh, I can't sleep,' moaned Charity. 'Oh, I'm so homesick. Oh, I'm so lonely in there. Oh, what a *horrible* way to behave to a visitor . . . '

'Homesick?'

'Of course,' said Charity, shivering in a dignified way. 'Wouldn't you be homesick, away from your father and mother?'

Uninvited, she groped through the dark room and got into Rachel's bed, sobbing and shivering.

'Well, I must say, Charity,' said Rachel, making room for her, 'I don't understand you at all.'

The Back Drawing-Room

MRS HENNEKER having taken her place among them, inevitably they had begun to discuss the larger abstractions. They did not even hesitate to challenge the mortality of the soul, and Miss Eve, the violinist, said with that slight vibration her voice had caught from her fiddle-strings that she believed one was born doubting everything, and that *she* even doubted sometimes whether death meant extinction at all. Survival —

'Survival,' said Bellingham, the man in the low chair beside Lois, who had up to now been talking about Greece, 'simply isn't a matter of fitness, I consider; it's a matter of tenacity.'

Lois, who was getting sleepy, nodded at the fire like a mandarin, and after a pause said weightily, 'I should think that is very true'; but the young man with the horn-rimmed glasses challenged this remark of Bellingham's, sitting bolt upright and staring inexorably at him like an owl. He said in a deep drawl: 'Surely the two are synonymous?'

Bellingham was less well in hand than the rest of Mrs Henneker's pack; he did not want to discuss the larger abstractions, he wanted to talk about Greece, which he had lately visited, and Greece itself, in its actuality, not, as Mrs Henneker would have directed, Hellenism. Now he saw her leaning back and drawing herself up and narrowing her eyes for utterance, and he realized that if he took any notice of that young man they two would be left skirmishing in a back alley while the talk swept by without them. However brilliant his repartee, however remarkable his agility, it would be unnoticed by Lois, who even now hung passionately on the lips of Mrs Henneker.

So he repeated generally, with an inclusive glance challenging the semi-circle, that survival was a matter of tenacity. Now in Greece —

'Tenacity to what?' Lois asked the fire.

'*Ah* . . .' said somebody. 'Yes — '

'Well,' he hesitated, 'it depends what plane we're on. On the purely physical — '

The word attracted two young women in the corner, who leant

forward, suddenly illuminated, thinking he was going to talk about sex. Of course, the word had not always this connotation, but having read widely they knew it to be a word of possibilities.

' – On the purely physical alone,' said Mrs Henneker, 'there's always, isn't there, a slackening of the grip?' She illustrated this with her hands. 'Fitness and unfitness is such a purely objective way of pigeon-holing. Besides, all that is *circular*, isn't it? Fitness for what? To survive. But to survive what? What is one fit for?'

They all wondered. She swept a glance round them smilingly, to glean up any wandering attention. The little fair, plump man did not even look up at her; he did not seem to realize who she was. He sat with his legs crossed, his hands clasped on his knee, looking around him modestly and unintelligently, with an air of not having realized anybody. Somebody who came in late had brought him, with an apology, and had whispered an explanation into somebody else's ear. They had seated him, and he sat, looking propped-up and a little dejected, like an umbrella that an absent-minded caller has brought into the drawing-room. Once or twice, when the conversation prior to the entrance of Mrs Henneker had veered dangerously near the comprehensible, he had volunteered remarks – oh, quite intelligent – quoting a friend, a banker who sometimes wrote to him from Modern Athens. He obviously belonged to one type of club, read the confessions of eminent diplomats' wives, and lunched with friends who considered him an entertaining fellow. Now he submitted, looking up at Mrs Henneker with his little, perplexed blue eyes: 'It's extraordinary, isn't it, what one does survive . . . '

'After death,' said Mrs Henneker, hanging poised for a moment, then sweeping forward over him, 'the only criteria of our reality for those who have not passed over are the senses – *their* senses, or perhaps what I always think of as that finer internal fabric of the senses: I mean the soul.'

'But surely,' said the young man with the horn rims, deferentially, but as one having authority, 'the soul doesn't exist.'

'That's just the point of it,' said Lois, a little too bluntly; '*does* it?'

'Exist *when*?' said Bellingham crossly. 'Now, or when we're dead? I don't quite see what we're getting at.'

Mrs Henneker looked at him sideways like a wounded dove. 'The survival of the soul after death,' she said gently, 'the survival of the *us* – oh, surely, Mr Bellingham, of the *you* and of the *me*, is a matter, it always seems to me, that we are unable to consider, to weigh up for ourselves clearly, because in considering it we can only represent the thing to ourselves in terms of the *physical*. We stand aloof from the after life of the spirits of our friends, from that persisting essence of them which we call the spirit, in *giant ignorance*.

It is like shutting out, if such a thing were possible to imagine, the sensuous appeal of music because we have not the score under our eyes to analyse — '

'Analysis?' said the young man with the horn rims, holding her up politely: 'ah, there you interest me very much, Mrs Henneker. Now, you contend that there does exist in us a consciousness, an apprehension of the – er – people in the after state which will permit of quite definite analysis, like our power of apprehending music, or our sense of smell? A consciousness quite apart from the sensory manifestations of the spiritualist – table-rapping, gramophone-horns, planchette?'

'Oh, Spiritualism!' said Mrs Henneker, shrinking into herself. 'Oh, that's horrible, I think, that is so horrible! No, Mr Mennister, that way of approach, if it could or did ever mean anything, is vulgarized. Besides, have we need of verbal communication? No, I think we attain our consciousness of *them* as one attains that finer intercourse, if you like, *telepathic*, of two people, any two of us here, maybe, who are closely knit together, emotionally, or by unity of interest.'

'Ah,' said several people, rustling; 'yes . . . ' Lois leant sideways and fingered a fold of Mrs Henneker's dress.

'By a prolongation,' she continued, 'by an ever-increasing frequency of this intercourse, in presence and in absence, we possess within us and have access to a more and more complete personality, grafted on to our own. When that personality has emerged wholly from the muddle of our unperceptiveness, like Galatea out of the marble, a given relationship is complete.'

Her voice dropped beautifully from sentence to sentence, lingered over the peroration and was still.

'I don't quite see,' said Bellingham, and the young man with the horn rims looked at him in despair. Lois let a sharp little sigh escape her, and the little man beyond the fire brightened visibly.

Mrs Henneker was infinitely patient. 'I mean,' she said, speaking very slowly, 'that such a complete cognizance of one being by another must give the one *known* a second distinct vitality apart from that either of the known or of the knower. You know how during those rather terrible séances a face or body sometime takes form out of the psychic fluid generated by the medium. This face or body may become detached from her, liberated, and has then its own vitality and is definitely *objective* . . . ' She leant forward, spreading out her hands.

'Objective,' said Mennister. 'Ye-es. You contend that imagination, memory, cognizance, have the power of carrying themselves over from the *sub*jective into the *ob*jective?'

'Because you remember a thing,' said Lois diffidently, 'or even imagine it, or from loving it very much really know it, it *exists* apart from itself and from you, even though you don't remember it, imagine it, or know it any more?'

'Yes,' said Mrs Henneker simply, 'that is what I meant. I grope. I don't express myself very clearly, I'm afraid.'

They dissented murmuringly.

'That,' Mennister informed them, leaning back and putting the tips of his fingers together, 'is very interesting. Though we're not, of course, covering new ground. What it all comes down to ultimately is: a question of the visibility or – er – perceptibility of thought-forms. What Mrs Henneker contends for is: their indefinite or their even infinite survival. Mr Bellingham finds that survival is a matter of tenacity – though he hasn't yet distinguished tenacity, in this particular sense, from fitness, or given us any reason why we should oppose them. If we are to go all the way with Mrs Henneker' – he pulled out a stop in his voice and it became richly humorous – 'we accept that we may only hope for immortality in so far as we have attracted favourable attention, and become somebody else's thought-form. We then survive, not by our own tenacity, but by somebody else's. We — '

'In so much of Hardy's poetry — '

'Quite,' said Mr Mennister, suppressing the young woman who had contributed this remark. 'The idea is not a new one; it becomes increasingly popular, doesn't it? In fiction — '

'Popular fiction is not my line, of course,' said Bellingham swiftly. 'I know very little about it, but' – Mennister's glasses blazed at him, he looked up blandly at the ceiling – 'but, getting down to the ghost story, the ghost story pure and simple: well, I remember saying to a man only a few weeks ago, as we walked in the streets of Athens — '

Something stirred beyond the fire; the little man came alive from his torpor, uncrossed his legs and sat up, clearing his throat. 'Ah,' he said, 'ghosts! Yes. What a fascinating theme for speculation!'

Everybody turned to look at him; it was as though the umbrella had spoken.

'Very,' said Mennister dryly.

Mrs Henneker turned her mournful eyes full upon him and inquired, 'It *does* interest you?'

'Oh, Mrs Henneker!' said one of the young women, sobbing with laughter.

'One cannot fail to be interested,' said the little man earnestly, looking from Mrs Henneker to Lois, as though they were of equal importance, and even including Miss Eve and the two young women in the opposite corner – 'one cannot fail to be interested if one has *experienced* . . .'

He was getting out of hand, quite suddenly. Mennister hummed softly and raised his eyebrows, and Lois slid to the floor from her chair and sat at Mrs Henneker's feet, leaning up against her friend's knee protectively. Only Bellingham secretly and cynically grinned.

'Because I *have* had experience,' said the little man, looking at them in surprise. 'I can't, I really cannot account . . . '

Lois said 'Hell!' under her breath. 'Bring in the Yule log, this is a Dickens Christmas. We're going to tell ghost stories.' Mrs Henneker laid a hand on her shoulder and said, 'Hush, Lois!' and Miss Eve, who had been waiting for some time to catch Bellingham's eye, smiled at him with an air of secret understanding. Back and behind the artist, the woman in her was enchanting: this was what Miss Eve liked to convey.

There was something very guileless about the little man; he thought they were all so clever. 'I expect some of *you*'d make it fit in at once,' he said trustfully. 'I think it would fit in with some of that you've just been saying: about memory, or perhaps about love. May I tell you what occurred? It was very curious.

'A cousin of mine has property in Ireland. He is a sporting man; we have little in common, though I think all the world of him, he is a very nice fellow; and I have the greatest admiration for his wife – she is one of the few people I know who really makes her poultry pay, or she did so, at least, until these civic disturbances began. I have seen very little of them lately; they were worried about the place, and had several times been raided. Lately, since things in their part of the country began to improve, my cousin began writing again to say, 'Do come over.' My previous (and only other) visit there had been very pleasant; there was a good deal of croquet in the neighbourhood, and I am an enthusiastic player. I bicycle a good deal, too, and when my cousin wrote to say the roads, those pretty roads round there, were really safe again (not *good*, they are never good), I was greatly tempted to accept his invitation, and at length did so – that was last year. So I went over to Ireland.'

'Ireland,' said Mrs Henneker, 'unforgettably and almost terribly afflicted me. The contact was so intimate as to be almost intolerable. Those gulls about the piers of Kingstown, crying, crying: they are an overture to Ireland. One lives in a dream there, a dream oppressed and shifting, such as one dreams in a house with trees about it, on a sultry night.'

'Now *that*,' said Bellingham, 'just illustrates what I said about tenacity. Compared with Greece — '

'Quite,' said Mennister. 'A beastly country, I thought. Of course, their plays — '

The little man, having looked wistfully from one to another of them, at last raised his voice and continued:

'I went to Ireland, and found my cousins much as ever, and the place looking very well. Several dozen of her chickens had been stolen, but it turned out to be a case of an ill wind – she had since introduced a new strain of Leghorns, which were doing very well indeed. My cousin was as busy as usual, but he had arranged for me to borrow a bicycle belonging to the cook's brother: a new bicycle, which was supposed to be very good.

'The first day after my arrival I went out for a ride. We had not had time to talk very much the night before, but they had told me a certain amount of what had happened in the neighbourhood, and warned me that I should find the country around them dilapidated and rather depressing. And it did look indeed very sad. Sad, I should say, when one passed ruined cottages along the roadside, and a poor police-barrack like a box with its lid off, with the sky staring through the windows. When I got clear of these, however, my depression forsook me. I am always sensitive, I believe, to the beauty of landscape, and the country did that day look very beautiful in a pale-coloured, early-autumn way which is, I think, peculiar to Ireland. It was a very smooth, clear day, quite windless; with a pale grey sky, and no lights or shadows anywhere. The only accents in the landscape were the mountains; these were dark and grew darker – a bad sign, almost invariably portending rain. My bicycle went well for some hours, and I went easily along, free-wheeling a good deal, and perhaps a trifle absent-minded. I must have been absent-minded, for I rode right over a patch of sharp stones which had been put down (but not rolled) to mend the road. I am seldom so careless, and I acknowledged myself punished for it as with sinking heart I felt my back tyre go completely flat.'

'Quite,' said Mennister. 'You should write your cycling experiences – er, er – 'Potters on a Push-bike.' It is not impossible that they might be published, even read.' The others acknowledged by involuntary glances that Mennister had spoken with unnecessary sharpness; but the little man took correction with humility.

'I do perhaps linger,' he admitted, 'over the not quite necessary preface to my story. I will now proceed to the point of it, which is very curious. Well, my tyre, you must understand, went really flat, and after having tried to ride, and descended to re-pump it every two or three minutes, I began to feel that my plight was a miserable one. I am not a good walker, and I was a very considerable distance from my cousin's house. Though I could have retraced my way, I had no idea of my whereabouts; I was in strange country where I had never been before. To increase my embarrassment, the sky was growing perceptibly darker, and I had that uncomfortable feeling of being overtaken and closed in upon, which I – and I find several of my friends also – often experience in open country when heavy rain is imminent. I was greatly cheered, therefore, to gather from certain indications – hewn-stone walls along the roadside, good though dilapidated iron gates into the fields, and two avenue-like rows of beech trees making a tunnel over the road – that I was skirting the boundary of a gentleman's demesne, and that it was not impossible that I should pass the gate. I walked quickly, wheeling my bicycle, and heard now and then a big drop of rain fall – plop – into the leaves above my head. Soon, sure enough, I did come to the gates: they stood wide open with an expression of real Irish hospitality – it is whimsical of me, but I do always feel that people's gates and doorposts have expressions – and I walked in, after a glance at the lodge: there was a trickle of smoke coming out of the chimneys, but the door was barred across and the windows shuttered. I remember thinking this curious.

'Along the avenue the trees were planted closer together, and it was as dusky as evening. It was overgrown with moss, too, so that I could scarcely hear my own footsteps, only the rattle-rattle of my bicycle. Judging from the width of the avenue, it must be a big place I was coming to; and how I did hope somebody in it would understand repairs, or perhaps lend me a bicycle, or even offer to drive me home in a trap or a motor! In England, of course, one would not think of this, but the Irish, I find, are always unconventionality itself.'

'Quite,' said Mennister.

'*I* entirely agree,' said Bellingham.

'From now on,' said the little man, looking at Bellingham, Lois, and Mrs Henneker, 'I would like you to believe that all my impressions were distinct, quite distinct, but perhaps a little isolated from one another. In the intervals of these distinct impressions my mind was a little blurred; things slipped past it rather; as they do when one is tired, worried, or put out. I felt — '

'Oh, forgive me,' Miss Eve vibrated, releasing Bellingham momentarily from her eyes, 'but I *do* know how you felt, I *can* imagine! You felt an extraordinary sense of foreboding as you came up to that house with its great dark windows. You longed to fly, and something held you, gripped you, drew you in. You looked along the front of the house, expecting, expecting . . . '

'You had a sense of immanence,' said Mrs Henneker authoritatively. 'Something was overtaking you, challenging you, embracing yet repelling you. Something was coming up from the earth, down from the skies, in from the mountains, that was stranger than the gathered rain. Deep from out of the depths of those dark windows, something beckoned.'

'Like in that poem of De la Mare's — '

'Exactly,' said Mennister, again suppressing the young woman

who had spoken. 'It has been often described. Let Mr – Mr . . . er
. . . proceed to the point of his story.' His voice regretted that there
was one.

'Well, no, do you know,' said the little man politely, with the
reluctance of a Washington, 'I cannot say that I experienced, that I
remember to have experienced, what you have described, though
of course I possibly may have. I walked very quickly down the
avenue and across the gravel sweep to the steps of the house, and I
remember thinking humorously, as I hunted for the bell, that if the
bell *were* out of order (as bells in Irish houses often are – the Irish
don't mind, they are the soul of unconventionality) – that the
noise my poor bicycle made coming across the gravel would quite
sufficiently advertise our arrival.'

'And what was the house like?' asked Lois. 'Was it very
obviously haunted? *Weren't* there any dark windows?'

'I don't quite understand you. Dark windows? I cannot remember that the windows looked any darker than windows seen from
the outside, in daylight, usually do. I did not look in, of course.
The house seemed very large and high. I heard a dog running on a
polished floor and skidding, the way dogs do. The hall door was
open, and I could swear I did hear the bell tinkle, somewhere down
below, but still nobody came. I felt no more raindrops; the rain
held off, but the air was cold and heavy with it, and the trees were
very quiet. The place was completely and very closely encircled
with trees, and it was all so quiet I could hear myself breathe. Only,
now and then I heard the ping-pong of tennis-balls, somewhere
beyond the trees, and people calling to one another in the game.
Sometimes this sounded very clearly, sometimes as though a long
way away. I guessed that they must be having a tennis-party, and I
felt a little shy of presenting myself – unconventional as I knew
they would all be – all dusty and in my cycling knickerbockers. So
I propped my bicycle up at the foot of the steps, and presently, as
no one came, I walked into the house. I had never walked into
anybody's house like this before.'

'And the hall?' they cried.

'Hall?' he repeated, looking at them mystified. 'It was a very
ordinary hall, like in other country houses. There was a window on
the staircase, which sent down a little light; otherwise the place was
dark.'

'And the *smell*?'

'And the *sound*? Didn't you hear an echo. Hadn't you a queer
foreboding? Didn't you want to go but yet have to go on?'

'Well, no,' he hesitated, carefully considering. 'I do remember
that I felt a little awkward, coming in like that – well, even in
Ireland people might have wondered. And the misapprehensions

. . . these bad times, you know. Why, anybody seeing me suddenly might have shot me, in their impulsive, simple way. I was really worried, and I'm afraid I don't remember that I noticed anything particular. Well, the smell, yes. People evidently hung their mackintoshes there, and there were dogs in the house. I imagine, too, that they didn't throw away their old tennis-balls, but kept them somewhere on a tray, possibly for the dogs. I stood in the hall and coughed a little and rapped with my foot – like in a village shop, you know, when it is empty. I was very much ashamed of myself and felt very nervous, but I was really desperately worried about my poor bicycle and how I was going to get home. So I stood there, tapping with my foot.'

'Yes,' said Mennister, 'exactly. But, my dear fellow, you're an expert in the finer forms of torture. Don't you see, we're . . . ? tell us about the ghost. Something gripped you, rattled at you, made itself unpleasantly visible. For one who does not profess the modern manner – well, *mes compliments* – you've hit something quite distinctive for your *décor*. But all ghost stories have one of three possible climaxes, A, B, or C, and every climax has its complementary explanation. Get on to the climax, and I'll guarantee you the explanation pat — '

'Or is it possible he might care to finish his own story for himself?' suggested Bellingham, with detachment. 'One never knows.'

'Quite.'

'Oh, *hush*, appealed Mrs Henneker. 'Won't both of you hush? We are so *intrigued*. And then?'

'Well, I just stood there, tapping with my foot. No one came. Then a door at the back of the hall opened, somebody looked out. It was a lady's figure, standing right against the light, so that I could only see her outline, which was tall and pretty. I said something, began an explanation, but without speaking she turned and went in again, leaving the door open. I – I don't know what came over me. I – I followed her in.'

'Ah,' said Bellingham, with appreciation. 'Yes?'

'I followed her into a drawing-room, a back drawing-room, with an arch with a curtain over it, and a window looking out into some trees. It was nicely furnished, I thought, but a little sombre, because of the trees outside the window.'

'And smells? And sounds?' cried Lois and Miss Eve, while the others peered curiously, as though through bars, at the little man who sat perplexed and baffled, knowing nothing of atmosphere.

He said at length: 'It smelt chiefly of geraniums. I remember then, some fine tall plants in pots, standing on a table by the window. And the wallpaper smelt a little musty; I remember thinking as I stood there (among many other things) what an improvement central heating would have been. I looked round and could see nobody; then I heard sobbing, really a pitiful sound. Well, you may imagine – here was I, unintroduced, in a back drawing-room, really quite an intimate room, where I believe only favoured visitors are usually admitted, with a lady sobbing on the sofa. I saw her head move where I thought there was just a pile of cushions; it made me jump. The room received less and less light from the windows, probably because of the rain, which was now coming down heavily, and partly because of the thick lace curtains – really thicker than one cares for nowadays. I do not know for how long I listened; then I said (I remember saying it), 'My dear lady,' I said; 'really, my dear lady!' I felt so terribly sorry for her, do you know, I couldn't go away, though I had no right to be there, of course. I may say that I am not an impulsive person even for an Englishman, and that I am as a rule quite singularly loth to intrude. When she looked up I was quite startled — '

' – As though you had not known she had a face — '

'Why, ye-es, as though I had not known she had a face. She looked up at me, and her expression was – was like . . . '

'Drowning?'

'Drowning,' he accepted, with a grateful side-glance. 'Drowning, and I could do nothing for her. Do you know, it quite appalled me. I don't know whether drowning people are frightened: I submit that they are – I know I should be. I don't think that if my life did pass before me then, I should glance at it. I should be too much afraid, looking forward to all that was going to happen to me.'

'No, to the world,' amended Mrs Henneker, 'to the whole of a world, your world. Because it is the quenching of a world in horror and destruction that happens with a violent death; just as one knows a whole world is darkened when one sees a child crying its heart out. Even a good death means a world quenched, but beautifully, like a sunset. So she looked at you like that – with fear?'

'Yes, fear. It was terrible. She had not a young face; the way she was crying was not young either. I am not a *nervous* man; I tell you that up to now I felt nothing but embarrassment. But I could not look away from her eyes. I did not wonder what she thought of me; it did not seem as though there were room for her to think. And she was looking at where I was, not at me.'

'She was menaced . . . '

'Yes. It was terrible, more than distressing. It would have been no more than that if I had remained outside it, but I didn't. I make no bones about it – I was terrified. She made me feel the end of the world was coming, and I felt myself beginning to perspire all over, as I had not done the whole summer. I couldn't speak to her again; she – she . . . '

'Beat it back.'

'Beat it back. I stood there, and she put down her face again, all wet, among the cushions that were crumpled and faded and smelt musty from even where I stood. So I went back into the hall, thinking only of one thing, to get away quickly before something had actually happened. Every step seemed dangerous — '

' – Like the House of Usher — '

' – Terribly dangerous. The hall was as empty-sounding as ever, and I rushed down the steps, seized my bicycle, and wheeled it as fast as ever I could down the avenue again, simply not caring if they did think I was a burglar or a Republican, and fired at me from the bushes. Once I paused for just a second to listen, and the tennis-balls had stopped, and the voices too. There was nothing to say where they had all gone. It was quite quiet.'

'Except for the rain?'

'Yes, I heard the rain in the trees. The lodge was still shut up when I passed it; I was relieved at that – didn't want them to see me. Well, I just turned up my collar and trudged it. Nothing passed me, no conveyance, scarcely even a soul, except an old woman driving two cows – she looked at me queerly. Not a walk I should care to do again, wheeling a bicycle. Mercifully, the days were still longish; I got back to my cousin's before it was quite dark, and even so they were worried – I met them walking about on the avenue. They said (I remember), 'Well, you have been keeping up a pace, anyway!' and I was surprised to find myself panting, till I found I had done that big distance in under the two hours.

'I had a hot whisky at dinner, and told them where I'd been. I told them exactly, and my cousin seemed puzzled, kept on contradicting. "No, no, you couldn't have been *there*. No houses along that road." That irritated me; I made him get his motor map, and I traced where I'd been, every turn. Just where I expected there was a place marked Kilbarran, and I put my thumb on it at once and said, "That's the house!" He laughed and said, "That's impossible, there isn't a house there." I said, "Why?" and he said there hadn't been one for two years. "Oh, there *was* one," he said, "and this marks it; this is an old map." I can't tell you how angry I felt – for no reason. He said. "There was a place, you see, until two years ago – very fine it was; then they came one night and burnt it, the winter before last. We had expected it would have gone sooner, and the Barrans – the people themselves – did too, though they never said a word. Those women went about looking green."

'Well, he didn't say much more, and of course I didn't; but his wife sighed, then started off talking. She started talking about the people at Kilbarran – an old gentleman with two daughters, not young, and a gay, pretty niece who had been often there. She spoke as though they were dead; I rather assumed it, but asked. She said, "Oh no; they're in Dublin, I think, or England." I couldn't help saying she seemed to have rather lost interest in her old friends, and she looked at me (quite strangely, for such a practical woman) and said, "Well, how can one feel they're alive? How can they be, any more than plants one's pulled up? They've nothing to grow in, or hold on to." I said, "Yes, like plants," and she nodded. Then it was time for her to go and shut up the chickens.'

'That illustrates exactly — '

'Quite.'

But Mrs Henneker was silent, staring at the fire. She did not raise her lids when Lois rose, and only held her hand out, offering it vaguely in perfunctory valediction as others rose to go. Some one collected the little man and took him away quietly – in the confusion he protested, but was overruled. He lingered, looking round the room, and even escaped once and got half-way back to Mrs Henneker, his lips wide for further speech. But she was petulantly blind to him, and he was led away. When the rustle of departure had subsided and the street door down below had faintly slammed, the broken semi-circle drew closer together, intimately. They asked each other with raised eyebrows, 'Whose importation?' And this remained unanswered; no one knew.

'Dunno,' said Lois to the last inquirer. They all looked up expectantly at Mrs Henneker, but Mrs Henneker was silent. And the silence lasted, because Mennister was gone.

Recent Photograph

A Mr and Mrs Brindley lived for some years quietly and unknown to history in one of the more rural of London's outlying suburbs. One spring evening Mr Brindley, returning from business, cut his wife's throat with a razor, and afterwards turned in for the night with his head inside the gas oven, having mitigated the inside's iron inclemency with two frilly cushions. Towards evening of the following day their privacy was broken in upon, a paragraph announced them in a morning paper, and the villa, the avenue, and the entire neighbourhood arose and shone. The News Editor of the *Evening Crier* was on to the thing like a hawk; it was decided that the man they wanted on the job was young Lukin. So they sent down Lukin into Hertfordshire.

Mr Bertram Lukin had joined the staff of the *Evening Crier* some months before, having presented himself at a moment of crisis with a letter of recommendation from a provincial editor of standing. He was young and immeasurably keen, and he directed himself to the essentials of journalism with an intensity which kept him always strung to the tautness of a slight vibration, so that his pince-nez, fugitively poised, were always just perceptibly a-shimmer. He read a good deal of American literature, said 'Git!' and advised people to 'hustle.' He was getting on very well with the *Evening Crier*, the News Editor had his eye on him; but it had been a slack time lately, older men had unavoidably taken precedence of him with the only two murders, and nothing bigger had so far fallen to the share of Bertram Lukin than a city fire, extinguished with deplorable rapidity, in which no lives had been lost. Now, the very second the News Editor unleashed him, he was downstairs in one streak and into a taxi. 'Git like hell!' he told the driver feverishly, bouncing on the shiny cushions.

The streets were silver in the sunshine; London in the April morning glowed like a pearl. It was a morning for children to come to birth, and poems to be written, and the creative soul of Lukin stretched its wings out and leant breast-forward to the wind in an ecstasy of liberation. The back of the taxi was open, and he nodded sideways with a blind benevolence to the roofs of London fleeing behind him. He clasped across his knees the morning paper rolled into a baton, nothing but a symbol, for the paragraph was burningly engraved into his brain. 'A Mr Joseph Wellington Brindley, resident at Moyallo, Homewood Avenue, Elms' Hopley, Herts . . . discovered . . . is believed to have . . . the head being partially severed from the body . . . in comfortable circumstances, and had been married some years.' It was copy, Bertram Lukin's copy. God was in his heaven and all was right with the world. The taxi took the corners of the still empty residential streets abruptly, and Lukin's little exultant and forgotten body bounced and swayed.

The brickwork and the stucco faltered, the streets broadened out and lay open to the sun, and fields and allotments interspersed themselves among the houses. Clumps of trees stretched up their branches all fretted over with green; here and there a field was ridiculous with lambs, and above them larks surcharged with song went wobbling up into the blue. The world became too small for Bertram Lukin, who felt himself expanding infinitely; nowhere could contain him for self-sufficiency and happiness. He did not think the man was pressing hard enough on the speed-limit; and, glancing down continually at his watch, he began to beat upon the glass behind the driver's head, and make forward gestures at him, indicative of urgency.

Elms' Hopley was the sort of place where murders usually do occur; that is to say, the last place on earth that seems appropriate to such occurrences. The enterprise of the Metropolitan had already embraced it: the interior of the big blue-and-white station yawned at them as the driver drew up by the kerb to ask the way to Homewood Avenue. The sunshine had brought out all the awnings over the shops; trees were planted along the pavements and many bicycles were propped against the trees. In groups about the doors of shops people stood talking, while rival terriers, affecting ignorance of one another, sniffed sedulously along the gutters. A lady buying geraniums off a barrow sighted a friend, signalled wildly, waved away the vendor and darted across the street under the very bonnet of Lukin's taxi, her eyes dilated and lips wide for speech. The whole place was vital to Lukin, everybody was significant; a light burnt through it, making every detail poignant. It was like arriving at a house where there is a party going on.

He had his notebook out, and his neat writing sprawled and staggered a little as, the taxi making full speed to its bourne, he recorded here and there an observation. Homewood Avenue was the kind of road where many people love to live; it was flanked by innumerable little gates, and laburnum boughs dripped languorously over the pavement, slanting from among the sprightlier grace of Japanese plum. Lukin, one hand on the door, crouched against the side of the taxi: his eyes ate up the numbers on the gates. His heart leapt up as he saw, before one house, two or three people loitering. At the gate a very big policeman stood, impassible and blue. The police were in possession.

Lukin stopped the taxi at a short distance from this little group, told the man to wait at the end of the road, and descended with an air of unconsciousness. He glanced at the loiterers with a sort of unconvinced contempt, and drew in upon himself; an iota of his light was quenched. Then he turned his head resolutely down the road, and tried to look like a young man who happens to be visiting an aunt. His eyes went down to the faintly stirring shadows of the branches on the pavement, then stole gradually, cautiously, paving-stone by paving-stone, toward the feet of the policeman, very large and planted very square. He felt confident that he could be pleasant enough with anybody; he had a 'good manner,' and he wished the police-constable to know it, but he could not remember, somehow, how one should begin on a policeman. And this was so very important, Lukin knew. Then he saw another pair of feet, too familiar, in orange-leather American shoes, advancing cautiously, diagonally, towards the constable. The *Evening Query* man was down here too. He spoke American even better than Lukin, had been three years on his paper and written up all their murders; and he had the sort of eye one could not possibly like. Lukin, quite dispassionately, did not think that the fellow had at all a good manner. By the unusual hesitancy of his movements it was possible that the constable had already rebuffed him. Lukin stepped back, crossed the road, and, sauntering as though casually along the opposite pavement, cast up a rapid and devouring glance toward the windows of Moyallo, naked of muslin and unmasked by trees. Sinister blue curtains, a little arty, framed them all, and in a bay window of an upstairs room one saw the back of a mirror, an oval mirror. They had been that kind of people. Sheltering his notebook from observation he jotted down 'artistic,' faintly, with a query mark. Then he walked on very slowly, further down the road. The *Evening Query* man sighted him and hailed. Confound the fellow, he was coming across.

'You won't do much *here*,' he remarked, with malicious complacency. 'Sick'ning having that long run down, and in a taxi and all.'

'Oh no,' drawled Lukin, with the polite indifference of one already informed.

'I s'pose you didn't expect much,' said the other odiously. 'Well, I daresay it was a nice run down. I must be off now and write my stuff up.' He was evidently on to something; he was licking his chops. He was a spotty man, the spottiest man Lukin had ever met; it must be very distressing for him.

'Well, s'long,' said Lukin, very preoccupied, turning on his heel.

'*So* long,' said the *Evening Query* man, who could make anything he said sound unpleasantly significant. He patted his breast pocket with complacency and swaggered off in the direction of the High Street. He was a very spotty man. Lukin wondered what he really had got in that notebook. He sauntered on again in the opposite direction, down the road.

A large lady in an emerald-green jersey was leaning over a gate, her arms along the top bar folded comfortably beneath the abundance of her bosom. Her hair, with which the breeze dared take no liberties, was piled high above her forehead *à la* Pompadour. Her eyes dwelt amicably upon Lukin and caught his own as he advanced towards her; he felt himself grow great again with resolution. The one thing now was to get somehow, anyhow, into conversation with some one, any one. He would talk to this lady. The lady was willing to be talked to. A fringe of laburnum dipped and danced above her head; she was like somebody at a party, happy and very much entertained.

'Too *dreadful*, isn't it?' she said brightly, nodding across the road towards Moyallo. That was the hub and centre of the entertainment, and the host and hostess were behind those windows with the blue curtains, barred away by the policeman, very indifferent and cold.

'Dreadful!' he said eagerly, coming to a stop before her, and gleaming incredulously at her through his glasses. This was just the sort of lady to get into conversation with – he knew all about her; this sudden manifestation of her was too good to be true. 'A very great shock for you all, I'm afraid?' he hazarded.

'Oh dear, oh dear!' she sighed luxuriously. '*Shock*! – I should think it was. I really thought I should have fainted when my maid came in and told me. "What nonsense!" I said to her; "don't talk such absolute nonsense. I know her quite well; I was talking to her only yesterday." It was quite a time before I could believe the girl. Oh, I was upset!'

'Terrible,' he murmured, covertly unscrewing the top of his pen. 'Most painful, if you knew the unhappy couple well.'

'Oh yes, I did know them. Not very well, of course: one hardly likes to say it now, but I did not care much about her. I couldn't take to her, though she seemed very bright. As for *him* – well, as I was saying just now to another lady, we really ought to have known.'

'Ah!' he said profoundly. 'Drink? . . . '

'Nothing like that. Nothing you could put your finger on. But

we all said at once: that was just what we might have expected.
Now my little girl was in there quite a lot at one time; she had quite
an infatutation for Mrs Brindley this last year, the way girls do. She
had seen her just the other day, and been talking to her about a
blouse pattern. My little girl is very much upset. I hardly knew
how to tell her; I knew she'd be upset. And she was, *very* much
upset.'

'Too bad. And your daughter *knew* Mrs Brindley intimately?' He
now made no further effort to conceal his notebook, and she
glanced at it with interest.

'You're the Press, aren't you? I *thought* you'd all be coming
down. And this road used to be so quiet; I don't think we've ever
had any trouble of any sort, not even a burglary. What a *sad* life for
a young man, going from tragedy to tragedy! . . . ' She paused,
absorbed momentarily in an attempt to read what he had written.
'You know, I simply couldn't stand it. Of course, I am tender-
hearted, even for a woman. I can't stand horrors and tragedies. My
little girl quite laughs at me. I can't bear to squash a beetle.'

'One gets used to it,' he said, shaking his pen. 'A profession's a
profession, after all.'

'I suppose it *is*,' she sighingly conceded. 'And I know it doesn't do
to be too tender-hearted. So many sad things happen, don't they?'

'Yes, indeed. Now, I wonder if you'd be so kind . . . ' They
both felt happy and important; he was the Press and she was being
interviewed. They smiled at one another across the gate. She told
him a great deal, and the leaves of his notebook, black with
information, were flicked over one after another. She caught herself
up and paused once to sigh and say that her maid was the most
fearful gossip. She deprecated this, and complained that in vain had
she set her face against it. There was nothing those girls did not
know, she said, and nothing that they had not got the face to come
and tell one.

He glanced through his notes. She had told him everything there
was to tell about the Brindleys, every fact. He wanted something
now that wasn't fact, he wanted a bit of colour. The personal
touch. Recollecting his good manner, he expressed aloud a hope
that he was not taking up too much of her time, and regretted
inwardly that she had taken up so much of his. He had got to get
his copy written up and in by midday. It was now half-past ten.

'I'm very much obliged to you indeed,' he said again. 'You've
been most kind . . . There was one thing – let me see: you said
they had been married quite a short time? Mrs Brindley was quite
young, I gather?'

'Well, they'd been married four years, really. She was not so
very young: thirty-two.'

He considered that this was quite young enough to justify his headline. Nothing went so well in a headline as a Young Wife – except, of course, a Bride or a Girl Mother.

'I wish my little girl was in,' the lady sighed. 'Of course, it's all been very painful for her, and I hardly think she'd care to talk about it, but if she *could* bring herself to talk about it I expect she'd tell you things that would be very valuable. You know – quite an inside personal impression.'

'Very painful for a child,' he said politely, anticipating further incoherencies.

'Ah, well,' said the mother tenderly, 'she isn't what you'd call a child, you know; she's only that to me. To me she'll be always just my little Totsie; it is so difficult to realize how they grow. But the young fellows don't seem to consider her a baby. She's had quite a number of admirers since she was fourteen. She's just put her hair up. She's gone out this morning to her music; nothing would prevent her, though it seemed to me dreadful somehow, though of course there's nothing one can do. She's very musical, she loves her music. She really might be home at any moment now.'

Even as she spoke, the mother's eyes, looking vaguely up the road beyond his shoulder, focussed themselves and brightened. A young girl came walking briskly toward them, like a picture of the Primavera, but preoccupied; with a tight little mouth. She edged scornfully past the now augmented group about the gate of Moyallo, and advanced indifferently, swinging a portfolio. She was fair and plump and dapper, and walked as though she had no opinion of the pavement. She eyed Lukin comprehensively, dwelt a moment on his notebook, then glanced from him to her mother. 'Well?' she said.

'This is my little girl,' said the lady in the green jersey. 'Verbena, this gentleman is the Press.'

'So I see,' remarked Verbena, acknowledging the introduction with a nod. 'Please!' she said imperiously, as neither of the two made way for her. '*I* must be getting in, mother. I should have thought *you*'d have been busy this hour of the morning, too.'

The mother relieved the gate of her bulk, and stood aside dubiously, and Lukin receded unwillingly as Verbena swept between them. Pausing to hiss something into the ear of her mother, the friend of the late Mrs Brindley turned to Lukin a demilune of furiously crimson cheek. She disappeared into the house indignantly; her rigid back implying that though she did not think that this was much of a house, it was at least a sanctuary from outrage. Verbena, her mother deprecatingly admitted, did not think that a so public intimacy with the Press was, under the circumstances of her bereavement, altogether nice. Verbena preferred that they should go into the house. Would Lukin . . . ?

Lukin, replete with information, did not really want to, but he was sucked irresistibly forward in Verbena's wake. It seemed impossible that she could be so ever verdantly a little Totsie, even to a mother, as she now leant nonchalantly against the dining-room piano, sprawling her elbows across the top and turning over leaves of music. As they came in she knitted her eyebrows and began absorbedly to hum. She said that she supposed Mr Lukin would like some information, and looked coldly at him out of china eyes that were set in level with her face.

'It has all been very painful for Verbena,' said her mother, sitting down expectantly in an armchair.

'Your mother has already been most kind,' said Lukin, temporising wildly, looking at the clock on the mantelpiece.

'Ho, well,' she laughed, on a high single note of scorn. 'If you want to publish a whole pack of servants' gossip — '

'Oh, darling!'

' – Of course I know some papers wouldn't mind.'

'Your mother has been most good,' repeated Lukin with finality, even preparing to put away his notebook. He didn't want two stories, after all, and he knew perfectly well that Verbena was only going to contradict her mother's. He had the stuff half-written in his mind already; it was beginning to rise in his brain like a cake in an oven. The whole truth was, for the purposes of his profession, a thing of too various dimensions to be easily encompassed.

'Oh, well,' she murmured. 'I should have been sorry to part with it. I only *thought* — '

'What's that?'

She patted her back hair complacently, while her mother started, looking round at Lukin. The young man was like a bandit, suddenly, holding her daughter up. There was an impersonality about him one could hardly like. 'Just a little photograph I have,' said Verbena dreamily. 'A snap I took. *Of them.*'

To Lukin's vision the whole room shifted and lightened; he heard the clock stop ticking, and the silence bulged, swelled like a bubble from the bowl of a pipe, and burst in a flash of sound. The clock started ticking again wildly in his very brain. 'Yes?' he whispered.

'Yes,' said Verbena, and, licked about with silver light, like a nymph, divinely, she crossed the room and vanished through the door. The clock ticked on interminably, registering the flight of hours.

They were sitting on the sofa together, and Verbena, her brief little skirt strained tight across her plump little knees, had the photo lying on her lap. His eager hand stretched out for it, but with a quick movement she fended the hand away. So he just gazed down over the barrier of her arm so burningly at the photograph that the glazed print might almost have curled up beneath his eyes and shrivelled away to ashes. The tartan pattern of Verbena's skirt danced and shifted kaleidoscopically around it. A couple stood with arms entwined, their faces black with sunshine, in a garden, among spikes of leafage. The male figure had a faintly perceptible outward slant.

'I remember very well the day I took that snap,' Verbena said.

'Indeed?' said Lukin, with a look that yearned to violate her memory. She had a fat little white throat, and she bent back her head and shut her eyes in an ecstasy of reconstruction. Laughter, laughter had been the motive of that day, it seemed. She and Mrs Brindley had laughed as they pursued Mr Brindley round and round the garden. He never smiled, so he did not smile then, though he was a kind man, Verbena knew, but ambled uncomplainingly and unamusedly round and round the little zigzag gravel paths like an old billy-goat, with Verbena in pursuit with the camera, and Mrs Brindley endeavouring to head him off. It had been a Sunday morning. He was a near-sighted man, and his glasses had leaped from his nose and swung at the end of their chain wildly. So blinded, he had headed straight into an apple tree and cut his lip, and Mrs Brindley, who couldn't stick the sight of blood, had turned momentarily a queer pale green. Verbena had gone into the house with Mr Brindley and stuck a strip of plaster on his lip. She pointed out to Lukin, now, the strip of plaster in the photograph. He had sat grey and passive beneath her ministrations, stretching up his queer long neck. As they were going back to the garden he had turned and said to Verbena. 'No one else but me would do a thing like that, would they? Have you ever run straight into a tree?' and Verbena had laughed and said, No, she hadn't, and that she didn't suppose anybody but Mr Brindley ever would. She had learnt from his wife that that was the way Mr Brindley should be treated, just chaffed and laughed at, else he got so morbid. He was a clumsy man; he never laid hands on anything but it broke, or at any rate tumbled over, and then his wife would laugh. She was ever so good-tempered with him, Verbena said; she would only shout, 'You are an old duffer!' and sometimes she could hardly speak for laughing. This infected Verbena, and they had had some very cheerful times together. Mr Brindley never said anything; he would just stand there, looking shyly at his wife out of the corner of his eye. Once they had found him burying some broken china in the garden.

'She was ever so cheerful,' repeated Verbena, staring with her round eyes out of the window. Her mother's armchair creaked in a great pang as the lady shuddered irrepressibly. 'If people only knew . . .'

So they had caught Mr Brindley that morning, Verbena continued. Look, you could see in the photograph how he was tugging away. Stupidly – it showed, didn't it? – like an animal.

'What a long face!' said Lukin, peering down. Yes, a long face, and it was never different. He was very humble, and when he had knocked over anything or broken china he would go for a long walk alone and not come in till his wife was asleep. 'Joseph never does anything right,' she used to say, as cheerfully as anything; and among her friends it had been quite a byword. Verbena had never seen her out of temper; look, in the photograph you could see her smiling – there, that white bit; she had rather big, white teeth. Once when she and Verbena had been coming home from the cinema they had seen Mr Brindley, back from work, walking with his bag in his hand up and down in front of his own house, and sometimes stopping to stare up at the windows. You would have thought it was a strange house that he was afraid to go into.

Verbena's mother here interposed that she, too, had on several occasions noticed this. It gave her the creeps, somehow; it didn't seem right. She had felt inclined to put her head out of the window and shout at him.

'Gee!' said Lukin meditatively, biting his upper lip. 'Nothing else? Nobody? Then why did he, and why particularly then — ?'

'Oh, but of course – didn't mother tell you? He had lost his job a week before. His wife rang him up at the office *that* afternoon and discovered it. He had been going out every day just the same, goodness knows where to, and coming in later and later.'

'But they were in comfortable circumstances,' said the mother wonderingly. 'They had Incomes. *His* work was not worth very much; she told me so in front of him. They wouldn't have been seriously reduced. *I* can't see that that was a reason.'

'*I* can't see that it was a reason, either,' said Verbena; 'when he came home, she wouldn't have said very much to him. She would only have laughed.'

Verbena made Lukin a present of the photograph, and he received it reverently, and tucked it away in his notebook. He was burning now to be back at the *Evening Crier* offices, burning to be there; his impatient mind tugged at its moorings to his less mobile body. He discovered that he and she were sitting very close together, and he looked down, as though through a mile of ether, at the two blunt, smartly-shod little feet that she stuck straight out in front of her.

Wife's Discovery Precipitates Tragedy of Disappointed Man. That was the vital stuff the *Evening Crier* wanted. And he had

Recent Photograph, showing plaster over the scar that the Coroner might still discover on Mr Brindley's lip. It was patently Recent. He caught the eye of the clock, and was reminded that, though all this was excellent, he should have been by now half-way to town. 'I'm ever so obliged to you,' he said, rising. 'You've been just fine. You can rely on my discretion – absolutely.'

The face of the mother, upturned to him benevolently, was faintly clouded, as she realized what his absolute discretion meant. It had been, however, a delightful morning, and she held out her hand to him amicably at parting. She invited Lukin to pay them a call some Sunday afternoon, and said that they were always in for tea. 'You *are* always in for tea on Sundays, aren't you, darling?'

'Oh, occasionally,' said Verbena, very much detached, and tapping the barometer. The green lady, standing at the door, called out after him that their name was Thomas, and their house The Glen, as Lukin scuttled wildly down the steps.

He fled blithely up the road to find his taxi, without so much as a side-glance over to Moyallo. His heart was like a singing bird.

Joining Charles

EVERYBODY in the White House was awake early that morning, even the cat. At an unprecedented hour in the thick grey dusk Polyphemus slipped upstairs and began to yowl at young Mrs Charles's door, under which came out a pale yellow line of candle-light. On an ordinary morning he could not have escaped from the kitchen so easily, but last night the basement door had been left unbolted; all the doors were open downstairs, for the household had gone to bed at a crisis of preparation for the morrow. Sleep was to be no more than an interim, and came to most of them thinly and interruptedly. The rooms were littered with objects that had an air of having been put down momentarily, corded boxes were stacked up in the hall, and a spectral breakfast-table waiting all night in the parlour reappeared slowly as dawn came in through the curtains.

Young Mrs Charles came across to the door on her bare feet, and, shivering, let in Polyphemus. She was still in pyjamas, but her two suitcases were packed to the brim, with tissue paper smoothed on the tops of them: she must have been moving about for hours. She was always, superstitiously, a little afraid of Polyphemus and made efforts to propitiate him on all occasions; his expression of omniscience had imposed upon her thoroughly. His coming in now made her a little conscious; she stood still, one hand on the knob of the dressing-table drawer, and put the other hand to her forehead – what must she do? Between the curtains, drawn a little apart, light kept coming in slowly, solidifying the objects round her, which till now had been uncertain, wavering silhouettes in candlelight. So night fears gave place to the realities of daytime.

Polyphemus continued to melt round the room, staring malignly at nothing. Presently Agatha tapped and came in in her dressing-gown; her plaits hung down each side of her long, kind face, and she carried a cup of tea.

'Better drink this,' said Agatha. 'What can I do?' She drew back the curtains a little more in her comfortable, common-sense way to encourage the daylight. Leaning for a moment out of the window she breathed in critically the morning air; the bare upland country was sheathed but not hidden by mist. 'You're going to have a beautiful day,' said Agatha.

Mrs Charles shivered, then began tugging a comb through her short hair. She had been awake a long time and felt differently from Agatha about the day; she looked at her sister-in-law haggardly. 'I dreamed and dreamed,' said Mrs Charles. 'I kept missing my boat, saw it sliding away from the quay; and when I turned to come back to you all England was sliding away too, in the other direction, and I don't know where I was left – and I dreamed, too, of course, about losing my passport.'

'One would think you had never travelled before,' said Agatha tranquilly. She sat down on the end of the narrow bed where Mrs Charles had slept for the last time, and shaking out Mrs Charles's garments, passed them to her one by one, watching her dress as though she had been a child. Mrs Charles felt herself being marvelled at; her own smallness and youth had become objective to her at the White House; a thing, all she had, to offer them over again every day to be softened and pleased by.

As she pulled on the clothes she was to wear for so long she began to feel formal and wary, the wife of a competent banker going to join him at Lyons. The expression of her feet in those new brogues was quite unfamiliar: the feet of a 'nice little woman'. Her hair, infected by this feeling of strangeness that flowed to her very extremities, lay in a different line against her head. For a moment the face of a ghost from the future stared at her out of the looking-glass. She turned quickly to Agatha, but her sister-in-law had left her while she was buttoning her jumper at the neck and had gone downstairs to print some more labels. It had occurred to Agatha that there would be less chance of losing the luggage (a contingency by which this untravelled family seemed to be haunted) if Louise were to tie on new labels, with more explicit directions, at Paris, where she would have to re-register. Agatha was gone, and the cup of tea, untasted, grew cold on the dressing-table.

The room looked bare without her possessions and withdrawn, as though it had already forgotten her. At this naked hour of parting she had forgotten it also; she supposed it would come back in retrospect so distinctly as to be a kind of torment. It was a smallish room with sloping ceilings, and a faded paper rambled over roses. It had white curtains and was never entirely dark; it had so palpably a life of its own that she had been able to love it with intimacy and a sense of return, as one could never have loved an inanimate thing. Lying in bed one could see from the one window nothing but sky or sometimes a veil of rain; when one got up and looked out there were fields, wild and bare, and an unbroken skyline to emphasize the security of the house.

The room was up on the top floor, in one of the gables; a big household cannot afford a spare bedroom of any pretensions. To go downstairs one had to unlatch the nursery gate at the head of the top flight. Last time Charles was home it had been very unfortunate; he had barked his shins on the gate and shouted angrily to his mother to know what the thing was *still* there for. Louise fully realized that it was being kept for Charles's children.

During that first visit with Charles she had hardly been up to the second floor, where the younger girls slept in the old nursery. There had been no confidences; she and Charles occupied very connubially a room Mrs Ray gave up to them that had been hers since her marriage. It was not till Louise came back here alone that the White House opened its arms to her and she began to be carried away by this fullness, this intimacy and queer seclusion of family life. She and the girls were in and out of each other's rooms; Doris told sagas of high school, Maisie was always just on the verge of a love-affair, and large grave Agatha began to drop the formality with which she had greeted a married woman and sister-in-law. She thought Agatha would soon have forgotten she was anything but her own child if it had ever been possible for Agatha to forget Charles.

It would have been terrible if Louise had forgotten, as she so nearly had, to pack Charles's photograph. There it had stood these three months, propped up on the mantelpiece, a handsome convention in sepia, becomingly framed, from which the young wife, falling asleep or waking, had turned away her face instinctively. She folded back a layer of tissue paper before shutting her suitcase and poked down a finger to feel the edge of the frame and reassure herself. There it was, lying face down, wrapped up in her dressing-gown, and she would have seen Charles before she looked again at his photograph. The son and brother dominating the White House would be waiting on Lyons platform to enfold her materially.

Mrs Charles glanced round the room once more, then went downstairs slowly. Through the house she could hear doors opening and shutting and people running about because of her. She felt ashamed that her packing was finished and there was nothing for her to do. Whenever she had pictured herself leaving the White House it had been in the evening, with curtains drawn, and they had all just come out to the door for a minue to say goodbye to her, then gone back to the fire. It had been more painful but somehow easier. Now she felt lonely; they had all gone away from her, there was nobody there.

She went shyly into the morning-room as though for the first time and knelt down on the rug in front of a young fire. There was a sharp smell of wood-smoke; thin little flames twisted and spat through the kindling. A big looking-glass, down to the ground, reflected her kneeling there; small and childish among the solemn mahogany furniture; more like somebody sent back to school than someone rejoining a virile and generous husband who loved her. Her cropped fair hair turned under against her cheek and was cut in a straight line over the eyebrows. She had never had a home before, and had been able to boast till quite lately that she had never been homesick. After she married there had been houses in which she lived with Charles, but still she had not known what it meant to be homesick.

She hoped that, after all, nobody would come in for a moment or two; she had turned her head and was looking out at the lawn with its fringe of trees not yet free from the mist, and at the three blackbirds hopping about on it. The blackbirds made her know all at once what it meant to be going away; she felt as though someone had stabbed her a long time ago but she were only just feeling the knife. She could not take her eyes from the blackbirds, till one with a wild flutey note skimmed off into the trees and the other two followed it. Polyphemus had come in after her and was looking out at them, pressing himself against the window-pane.

'Polyphemus,' said Mrs Charles in her oddly unchildish voice, 'have you any illusions?' Polyphemus lashed his tail.

By midday (when she would be nearly at Dover) the fire would be streaming up briskly, but by that time the sun would be pouring in at the windows and no one would need a fire at all. The mornings were not cold yet, the girls were active, and it was only because of her going away that the fire had been lighted. Perhaps Agatha, who never hurt anything's feelings, would come in and sit not too far away from it with her basket of mending, making believe to be glad of the heat. 'I don't suppose there'll be fires at Lyons,' thought Mrs Charles. Somewhere, in some foreign room tomorrow evening when the endearments were over or there was a pause in them, Charles would lean back in his chair with a gusty sigh, arch his chest up, stretch out his legs and say: 'Well, come on. Tell me about the family.'

Then she would have to tell him about the White House. Her cheeks burnt as she thought how it would all come out. There seemed no chance yet of Agatha or Maisie getting married. That was what Charles would want to know chiefly about his sisters. He had a wholesome contempt for virginity. He would want to know how Doris, whom he rather admired, was 'coming along.' Those sisters of Charles's always sounded rather dreadful young women, not the sort that Agatha, Maisie or Doris would care to know. It seemed to Charles funny – he often referred to it – that Agatha wanted babies so badly and went all tender and conscious when babies were mentioned.

'She'll make no end of a fuss over our kids,' Charles would say. The White House seemed to Charles, all the same, very proper as an institution; it was equally proper that he should have a contempt for it. He helped to support the girls and his mother, for one thing, and that did place them all at a disadvantage. But they were dear, good souls – Mrs Charles knelt with her hands on her knees and the hands clenched slowly from anger and helplessness.

Mrs Ray, the mother of Charles, suddenly knelt down by his wife and put an arm round her shoulders without saying a word. She did these impulsive things gracefully. Mrs Charles relaxed and leant sideways a little against the kind shoulder. She had nothing to say, so they watched the fire struggle and heard the hall clock counting away the seconds.

'Have you got enough clothes on?' said Mother after a minute. 'It's cold in trains. I never do think you wear enough clothes.'

Mrs Charles, nodding, unbuttoned her coat and showed a ribbed-sweater pulled on over her jumper. 'Sensible of me!' she proudly remarked.

'You're learning to be quite a sensible little thing,' Mother said lightly. 'I expect Charles will notice a difference. Tell Charles not to let you go out in the damp in your evening shoes. But I expect he knows how to take care of you.'

'Indeed, yes,' said Mrs Charles, nodding.

'You're precious, you see.' Mother smoothed back the hair from against Mrs Charles's cheek to look at her thoughtfully, like a gentle sceptic at some kind of miracle. 'Remember to write me about the flat: I want to know everything: wallpapers, views from the windows, sizes of rooms — We'll be thinking about you both tomorrow.'

'I'll be thinking of you.'

'Oh, no, you won't,' said Mother, with perfect finality.

'Perhaps not,' Mrs Charles quickly amended.

Mother's son Charles was generous, sensitive, gallant and shrewd. The things he said, the things he had made, his imprint, were all over the White House. Sometimes he looked out at Louise with bright eyes from the family talk, so striking, so unfamiliar that she fell in love with the stranger for moments together as a married woman should not. He was quiet and never said very much, but he *noticed*; he had an infallible understanding and entered deeply, it seemed, into the sisters' lives. He was so good; he was so keen for them all to be happy. He had the strangest way of anticipating one's wishes. He was master of an inimitable drollery – to hear him chaff Agatha! Altogether he was a knightly person, transcending modern convention. His little wife had come to them all in a glow from her wonderful lover. No wonder she was so quiet; they used to try and read him from her secret, sensitive face.

A thought of their Charles without his Louise troubled them all with a pang when Louise was her dearest. Charles in Lyons uncomplaining, lonely, tramping the town after business to look for a flat. The return of Louise to him, to the home he had found for her, her room upstairs already aghast and vacant, the emptiness that hung over them, gave them the sense of pouring out an oblation. The girls were heavy, with the faces of Flemish Madonnas; Doris achieved some resemblance to Charles, but without being handsome. They had cheerful dispositions, but were humble when they considered themselves; they thought Louise must have a great deal of love in her to give them so much when there was a Charles in her life.

Mrs Ray, with a groan at her 'old stiff bones', got up from the hearthrug and sat on a chair. She thought of something to say, but was not quite ready to say it till she had taken up her knitting. She had hoped to have finished this pair of socks in time to send out by Louise with his others: she hadn't been able to – Mrs Ray sighed. 'You're making my boy very happy,' she said, with signs in her manner of the difficulty one has in expressing these things.

Louise thought: 'Oh, I love you!' There was something about the hands, the hair, the expression, the general being of Mother that possessed her entirely, that she did not think she could live without. She knelt staring at Mother, all in a tumult. Why be so lonely, why never escape? She was too lonely, it couldn't be borne; not even for the sake of the White House. Not this morning, so early, with the buffeting strangeness of travel before her, with her wrists so chilly and the anticipation of sea-sickness making her stomach ache. The incommunicableness of even these things, these little ills of the body, bore Mrs Charles down. She was tired of being brave alone, she was going to give it up.

It is with mothers that understanding and comfort are found. She wanted to put down her head on a bosom, this bosom, and say: 'I'm unhappy. Oh, help me! I can't go on. I don't love my husband. It's death to be with him. He's grand, but he's rotten all through — ' She needed to be fortified.

'Mother — ' said Louise.

'Mm-mm?'

'If things were not a success out there — If one weren't a good wife always — ' Mother smoothed her knitting out and began to laugh; an impassable, resolute chuckle.

'What a *thing* — ' she said. 'What an idea!'

Louise heard steps in the hall and began kneading her hands together, pulling the fingers helplessly. '*Mother*,' she said, 'I feel — '

Mother looked at her; out of the eyes looked Charles. The steady, gentle look, their interchange, lasted moments. Steps came hurrying over the flags of the hall.

'I can't go — '

Doris came in with the teapot. She wasn't grown up, her movements were clumsy and powerful, more like a boy's. She should have been Charles. Her heavy plait came tumbling over her shoulder as she bent to put down the teapot – round and brown with a bluish glaze on it. Sleep and tears in the dark had puffed up her eyelids, which seemed to open with difficulty: her small eyes dwindled into her face. '*Breakfast*,' she said plaintively.

Rose, the servant, brought in a plate of boiled eggs – nice and light for the journey – and put them down compassionately.

'Even Rose,' thought Mrs Charles, getting up and coming to the table obediently because they all expected her to, 'even Rose — ' She looked at the breakfast-cups with poppies scattered across them as though she had not seen them before or were learning an inventory. Doris had begun to eat as though nothing else mattered. She took no notice of Louise, pretending, perhaps, to make things easier for herself, that Louise were already gone.

'Oh, Doris, not the *tussore* tie with the *red* shirt.' Whatever White House might teach Mrs Charles about common sense, it was her mission to teach them about clothes. 'Not,' said Mrs Charles, with bravado rising to an exaggeration of pathos, 'not on my last day!'

'I dressed in the dark; I couldn't see properly,' said Doris.

'You won't get eggs for breakfast in France,' said Maisie with a certain amount of triumph as she came in and sat down.

'I wonder what the flat'll be like?' said Maisie. 'Do write and tell us about the flat – describe the wallpapers and everything.'

'Just think,' said Doris, 'of Charles buying the furniture! "*Donnez-moi une chaise!*" "*Bien, Monsieur.*" "*Non. Ce n'est pas assez comfortable pour ma femme.*"'

'Fancy!' said Maisie, laughing very much. 'And fancy if the flat's high up.'

'There'll be central-heating and stoves. Beautiful fug. She actually won't be chilly.' Mrs Charles was always chilly: this was a household joke.

'Central heating is stuffy — '

Doris broke away suddenly from the conversation. 'Oh!' she said violently, 'Oh, Louise, you are *lucky!*'

A glow on streets and on the pale, tall houses: Louise walking with Charles. Frenchmen running in blousey overalls (Doris saw), French poodles, French girls in plaid skirts putting the shutters back, French ladies on iron balconies, leaning over, watching Charles go up the street with Louise and help Louise over the crossings; Charles and Louise together. A door, a lift, a flat, a room, a kiss! 'Charles, Charles, you are so splendid! Mother loves you and the girls love you and I love you — ' 'Little woman!' A French curtain fluttering in the high, fresh wind, the city under the roofs – forgotten. All this Doris watched: Louise watched Doris.

'Yes,' smiled Louise. 'I *am* lucky.'

'Even to be going to France,' said Doris, and stared with her dog's eyes.

Louise wanted to take France in her two hands and make her a present of it. 'You'll be coming out soon, Doris, some day.' (It was not likely that Charles would have her – and did one, anyhow, dare let the White House into the flat?)

'Do you really think so?'

'Why not, if Mother can spare you?'

'*Louise!*' cried Maisie reproachfully – she had been sitting watching – 'you aren't eating!'

Agatha, sitting next her, covered up her confusion with gentle, comforting noises, cut the top off an egg and advanced it coaxingly. That was the way one made a child eat; she was waiting to do the same for Charles's and Louise's baby when it was old enough. Louise now almost saw the baby sitting up between them, but it was nothing to do with her.

'You'll be home in *less* than the two years, I shouldn't be surprised,' said Mother startlingly. It was strange, now one came to think of it, that any question of coming back to the White House had not been brought up before. They might know Mrs Charles would be coming back, but they did not (she felt) believe it. So she smiled at Mother as though they were playing a game.

'Well, two years at the very least,' Mother said with energy.

They all cast their minds forward. Louise saw herself in the strong pale light of the future walking up to the White House and (for some reason) ringing the bell like a stranger. She stood ringing and ringing and nobody answered or even looked out of a window. She began to feel that she had failed them somehow, that something was missing. Of course it was. When Louise came back next time she must bring them a baby. Directly she saw herself coming up the steps with a child in her arms she knew at once what was wanted. Wouldn't Agatha be delighted? Wouldn't Maisie 'run on'? Wouldn't Doris hang awkwardly round and make jokes, poking her big finger now and then between the baby's curling pink ones? As for Mother – at the supreme moment of handing the baby to Mother, Louise had a spasm of horror and nearly dropped it. For the first time she looked at the baby's face and saw it was Charles's.

'It would do no *good*,' thought Mrs Charles, cold all of a sudden and hardened against them all, 'to have a baby of Charles's.'

They all sat looking not quite at each other, not quite at her. Maisie said (thinking perhaps of the love-affair that never completely materialized): 'A great deal can happen in two years,' and began to laugh confusedly in an emotional kind of way. Mother and Agatha looked across at each other. 'Louise, don't forget to send us a wire,' said Mother, as though she had been wondering all this time she had sat so quiet behind the teapot whether Louise would remember to do this.

'Or Charles might send the wire.'

'Yes,' said Louise, 'that would be better.'

Polyphemus, knowing his moment, sprang up on to Mrs Charles's knee. His black tail, stretched out over the tablecloth, lashed sideways, knocking the knives and forks crooked. His one green eye sardonically penetrated her. *He* knew. He had been given to Charles as a dear little kitten. He pressed against her, treading her lap methodically and mewing soundlessly, showing the purple roof of his mouth. 'Ask Charles,' suggested Polyphemus, 'what became of my other eye.' 'I know,' returned Mrs Charles silently. '*They* don't, they haven't been told; you've a voice, I haven't – what about it?' 'Satan!' breathed Mrs Charles, and caressed fascinatedly the fur just over his nose.

'Funny,' mused Agatha, watching, 'you never have cared for Polyphemus, and yet he likes you. He's a very transparent cat; he is wonderfully honest.'

'He connects her with Charles,' said Maisie, also enjoying this interchange between the wife and the cat. 'He's sending some kind of a message – he's awfully clever.'

'Too clever for me,' said Mrs Charles, and swept Polyphemus off her knee with finality. Agatha was going as far as the station; she went upstairs for her hat and coat. Mrs Charles rose also, picked up her soft felt hat from a chair and pulled it on numbly, in front of the long glass, arranging two little bits of hair at the sides against her cheeks. 'Either I am dreaming,' she thought, 'or someone is dreaming me.'

Doris roamed round the room and came up to her. 'A book left behind, Louise; *Framley Parsonage*, one of your books.'

'Keep it for me.'

'For two years – all that time?'

'Yes, I'd like you to.'

Doris sat down on the floor and began to read *Framley Parsonage*. She went into it deeply – she had to go somewhere; there was nothing to say; she was suddenly shy of Louise again as she had been at first, as though they had never known each other – perhaps they never had.

'Haven't you read it before?'

'No, never, I'll write and tell you, shall I, what I think of it?'

'I've quite forgotten what *I* think of it,' said Louise, standing above her, laughing and pulling on her gloves. She laughed as though she were at a party, moving easily now under the smooth compulsion of Somebody's dreaming mind. Agatha had come in quietly. 'Hush!' she said in a strained way to both of them, standing beside the window in hat and coat as though *she* were the traveller. 'Hush!' She was listening for the taxi. Mother and Maisie had gone.

Wouldn't the taxi come, perhaps? What if it never came? An intolerable jar for Louise, to be deprived of going; a tear in the mesh of the dream that she could not endure. 'Make the taxi come soon!' she thought, praying now for departure. 'Make it come soon!'

Being listened for with such concentration must have frightened the taxi, for it didn't declare itself; there was not a sound to be heard on the road. If it were not for the hospitality of *Framley Parsonage* where, at this moment, would Doris have been? She bent to the pages absorbedly and did not look up; the leaves of the book were thin and turned over noisily. Louise fled from the morning-room into the hall.

Out in the dark hall Mother was bending over the pile of boxes, reading and re-reading the labels upside down and from all aspects. She often said that labels could not be printed clearly enough. As Louise hurried past she stood up, reached out an arm and caught hold of her. Only a little light came down from the staircase window; they could hardly see each other. They stood like two figures in a picture, without understanding, created to face one another.

'Louise,' whispered Mother, 'if things should be difficult — Marriage isn't easy. If you should be disappointed – I know, I feel – you do understand? If Charles — '

'Charles?'

'I do love you, I do. You would tell me?'

But Louise, kissing her coldly and gently, said: 'Yes, I know. But there isn't really, Mother, anything to tell.'

The Jungle

TOWARDS the end of a summer term Rachel discovered the Jungle. You got over the wall at the bottom of the kitchen garden, where it began to be out of bounds, and waded through knee-high sorrel, nettles and dock, along the boundary hedge of Mr Morden's property until you came to a gap in the roots of the hedge, very low down, where it was possible to crawl under. Then you doubled across his paddock (this was the most exciting part), round the pond and climbed a high board gate it was impossible to see through into a deep lane. You got out of the lane farther down by a bank with a hedge at the top (a very 'mangy' thin hedge), and along the back of this hedge, able to be entered at several points, was the Jungle. It was full of secret dog-paths threading between enormous tussocks of bramble, underneath the brambles there were hollow places like caves; there were hawthorns one could climb for a survey and, about the middle, a clump of elders gave out a stuffy sweetish smell. It was an absolutely neglected and wild place; nobody seemed to own it, nobody came there but tramps. Tramps, whose clothes seem to tear so much more easily than one's own, had left little fluttering tags on the bushes, some brownish newspaper one kicked away under the brambles, a decayed old boot like a fungus and tins scarlet with rust that tilted in every direction holding rain-water. Two or three of these tins, in some fit of terrible rage, had been bashed right in.

The first time Rachel came here, alone, she squeezed along the dog-paths with her heart in her mouth and a cold and horrible feeling she was going to find a dead cat. She knew cats crept away to die, and there was a sinister probability about these bushes. It was a silent July evening, an hour before supper. Rachel had brought a book, but she did not read; she sat down under the elders and clasped her hands round her knees. She had felt a funny lurch in her imagination as she entered the Jungle, everything in it tumbled together, then shook apart again, a little altered in their relations to each other, a little changed.

At this time Rachel was fourteen; she had no best friend at the moment, there was an interim. She suffered sometimes from a constrained, bursting feeling at having to keep things so much to herself, yet when she compared critically the girls who had been her great friends with the girls who might be her great friends she couldn't help seeing that they were very much alike. None of them any more than the others would be likely to understand . . . The Jungle gave her a strong feeling that here might have been the Perfect Person, and yet the Perfect Person would spoil it. She wanted it to be a thing in itself: she sat quite still and stared at the impenetrable bramble-humps.

On the last day of term Rachel travelled up in the train with a girl in a lower form called Elise Lamartine, who was going to spend the holidays riding in the New Forest. Elise had her hair cut short like a boy's and was supposed to be fearfully good at French but otherwise stupid. She had a definite quick way of doing things and a thoughtful slow way of looking at you when they were done. Rachel found herself wishing it weren't the holidays. She said, off-hand, as she scrambled down from the carriage into a crowd of mothers: 'Let's write to each other, shall we?' and Elise, beautifully unembarrassed, said, 'Right-o, let's!'

During the holidays Rachel became fifteen. Her mother let down her skirts two inches, said she really wasn't a little girl any more now and asked her to think about her career. She was asked out to tennis parties where strange young men had a hesitation about calling her anything and finally called her Miss Ritchie. Her married sister Adela promised that next summer holidays she'd have her to stay and take her to 'boy and girl dances'. 'Aren't I a girl now?' asked Rachel diffidently. 'You oughtn't to be a girl in that way till you're sixteen,' said Adela firmly.

Rachel had one terrible dream about the Jungle and woke up shivering. It was something to do with a dead body, a girl's arm coming out from under the bushes. She tried to put the Jungle out of her mind; she never thought of it, but a few nights afterwards she was back there again, this time with some shadowy person always a little behind her who turned out to be Elise. When they came to the bush which in the first dream had covered the arm she was trying to tell Elise about it, to make sure it *had* been a dream, then stopped, because she knew she had committed that murder herself. She wanted to run away, but Elise came up beside her and took her arm with a great deal of affection. Rachel woke up in a gush of feeling, one of those obstinate dream-taps that won't be turned off, that swamp one's whole morning, some-times one's day. She found a letter from Elise on the breakfast-table.

Elise wrote a terrible letter, full of horses and brothers. So much that might have been felt about the New Forest did not seem to have occurred to her. Rachel was more than discouraged, she felt blank about next term. It was impossible to have a feeling for anyone who did so much and thought nothing. She slipped the letter under her plate and didn't intend to answer it, but later on she went upstairs and wrote Elise a letter about tennis parties. 'There has been talk,' she wrote, 'of my going to boy and girl dances, but I do not feel keen on them yet.'

'Who is your great friend now?' asked Mother, who had come in and found her writing. She put on an anxious expression whenever she spoke like this, because Rachel was a Growing Daughter.

'Oh, no one,' said Rachel. 'I'm just dashing off something to one of the girls.'

'There was Charity. What about Charity? Don't you ever write to her now?'

'Oh, I like her all right,' said Rachel, who had a strong sense of propriety in these matters. 'I just think she's a bit affected.' While she spoke she was wondering whether Elise would get her remove or not. Rachel was going up into IVA. It would be impossible to know anybody two forms below.

Next term, when they all came back, she found Elise had arrived in IVB (one supposed on the strength of her French), but she was being tried for the Gym Eight and spent most of her spare time practising for it. Rachel looked in at the Gym door once or twice and saw her doing things on the apparatus. When she wasn't doing things on the apparatus Elise went about with the same rather dull girl, Joyce Fellows, she'd been going about with last term. They sat together and walked together and wrestled in the boot-room on Saturday afternoons. Whenever Rachel saw Elise looking at her or coming towards her she would look in the other direction or walk away. She realized how the holidays had been drained away by imagination, she had scarcely lived them; they had been wasted. She had a useless, hopeless dull feeling and believed herself to be homesick. By the end of the first fortnight of term she and Elise had scarcely spoken. She had not been back again to the Jungle, of whose very existence she somehow felt ashamed.

One Sunday, between breakfast and chapel, they brushed against each other going out through a door.

'Hullo!' said Elise.

'Oh – hullo!'

'Coming out?'

'Oh – right-o,' said Rachel, indifferent.

'Anywhere special? I know of a tree with three apples they've forgotten to pick. We might go round that way and just see — '

'Yes, we might,' agreed Rachel. They went arm in arm.

It was early October, the day smelt of potting-sheds and scaly wet tree-trunks. They had woken to find a mist like a sea round the house; now that was being drawn up and the sun came wavering through it. The white garden-gate was pale gold and the leaves of the hedges twinkled. The mist was still clinging in sticky shreds, cobwebs, to the box-hedges, the yellow leaves on the espaliers, the lolling staggering clumps of Michaelmas daisies; like shreds of rag, Rachel thought, clinging to brambles.

Elise's apple tree was half way down the kitchen-garden. They looked up: one of the apples was missing. Either it had fallen or some interfering idiot had succeeded in getting it down with a stone. The two others, beautifully bronze, nestled snugly into a clump of leaves about eight feet up. The girls looked round; the kitchen-garden was empty.

'One could chuck things at them,' said Rachel, 'if one didn't make too much row.'

'I bet I could swing myself up,' said Elise confidently. She stepped back, took a short run; jumped and gripped a branch overhead. She began to swing with her legs together, kicking the air with her toes. Every times she went higher; soon she would get her legs over that other branch, sit there, scramble up into standing position and be able to reach the apples.

'How gymnastic we are!' said Rachel with the sarcastic admiration which was *de rigueur*. Elise half-laughed, she hadn't a breath to spare. She stuck out her underlip, measured the branch with her eye. Her Sunday frock flew back in a wisp from her waist; she wore tight black stockinette bloomers.

' – *Elise*' shrieked a voice from the gate. 'Rachel *Ritchie*! Leave that tree alone – what are you doing?'

'Nothing, Miss Smyke,' shouted Rachel, aggrieved.

'Well, don't,' said the voice, mollified. 'And don't potter! Chapel's in forty minutes – don't get your feet wet.'

Elise had stopped swinging, she hung rigid a moment, then dropped with bent knees apart. 'Damn!' she said naturally. Rachel said 'dash' herself, sometimes 'confound'. She knew people who said 'confound' quite often, but she had never had a friend of her own who said 'Damn' before. 'Don't be profane,' she said, laughing excitedly.

Elise stood ruefully brushing the moss from her hands 'Damn's not profane,' she said. 'I mean, it's nothing to do with God.' She took Rachel's arm again, they strolled towards the end of the kitchen-garden. 'Are you getting confirmed next term?'

'I think I am. Are you?'

'I suppose I am. Religion's very much *in* our family, you see. We were Huguenots.'

'Oh, I always wondered. Is that why you're called — '

' – Elise? Yes, it's in our family. Don't you like it?'

'Oh, I *like* it . . . But I don't think it suits you. It's such a silky delicate kind of a girlish name. You, you're too — ' She broke off; there were people you couldn't talk to about themselves without a confused, excited, rather flustered feeling. Some personalities felt so much more personal. 'You ought to have some rather quick hard name. Jean or Pamela . . . or perhaps Margaret – *not* Marguerite.'

Elise was not listening. 'I ought to have been a boy,' she said in a matter-of-fact, convinced voice. She rolled a sleeve back. 'Feel my muscle! Watch it – look!'

'I say, Elise. I know of a rather queer place. It's near here, I discovered it. I call it the Jungle, just to distinguish it from other places. I don't mean it's a bit exciting or anything,' she said rapidly, 'it's probably rather dirty; tramps come there. But it is rather what I used to call "secret".' She was kicking a potato down the path before her, and she laughed as she spoke. Lately she had avoided the word 'secret'. Once, at the end of a visit, she had shown a friend called Charity a 'secret place' in their garden at home, and Charity had laughed to the others about it when they were all back at school.

'Which way?'

'Over the wall – you don't mind getting your legs stung?'

The nettles and docks were rank-smelling and heavy with dew. One was hampered by Sunday clothes; they tucked their skirts inside their bloomers and waded through. 'It's a good thing,' said Rachel, 'we've got black stockings that don't show the wet. Brown are the limit, people can see a high-water mark.' The wet grass in Mr Morden's paddock squashed and twanged, it clung like wet snakes as they ran, cutting their ankles. She pulled up panting in the lane below. 'Sure you're keen?' said Rachel. 'There may be blackberries.'

When they came to the Jungle she pushed in ahead of Elise, parting the brambles recklessly. She didn't mind now if she *did* find a dead cat: it would be almost a relief. She didn't look round to see what Elise was doing or seemed to be thinking. They were down in a hollow, it was mistier here and an early morning silence remained. A robin darted out of a bush ahead of her. It was an even better place than she had remembered; she wished she had come here alone. It was silly to mix up people and thoughts. Here was the place where the dead girl's arm, blue-white, had come out from under the bushes. Here was the place where Elise, in the later dream, had come up and touched her so queerly. Here were the rags of her first visit still clinging, blacker and limper . . . the same boot —

'Like a nice boot?' she said facetiously.

Elise came up behind her, noisily kicking at one of the tins. 'This is an awfully good place,' she said. 'Wish *I'd* found it.'

'It isn't half bad,' said Rachel, looking about her casually.

'Do you like this sort of thing – coming here?'

'I bring a book,' said Rachel defensively.

'Oh, that would spoil it. I should come here and make camp fires. I should like to come here and go to sleep. Let's come here together one Saturday and do both.'

'I think sleeping's dull,' said Rachel surprised.

'I love it,' exclaimed Elise, hugging herself luxuriously. 'I can go to sleep like a dog. If wet wouldn't show too much on the back of my dress I'd lie down and go to sleep here now.'

'My dear – how *extraordinary*!'

'Is it?' said Elise, indifferent. 'Then I suppose I'm an extra-ordinary person.' She had stopped in front of a bush; there were a few blackberries, not very good ones; just like a compact, thick boy in her black tights she was sprawling over the great pouffe of brambles, standing on one foot, balancing herself with the other, reaching out in all directions. But for that way she had of sometimes looking towards one, blank with an inside thoughtful-ness, one couldn't believe she had a life of her own apart from her arms and legs. Rachel angrily doubted it; she crouched beside the bush and began eating ripe and unripe blackberries indiscriminately and quickly. 'I am a very ordinary person,' she said aggressively, to see what would come of it. She wondered if Elise had a notion what she was really like.

'No, you're not,' said Elise, 'you're probably clever. How old are you?'

'I was fifteen in August. How old — '

'I shall be fifteen in March. Still, it's awful to think you're a whole form cleverer than I am.'

'I'm not clever,' said Rachel quickly.

Elise laughed. 'One queer thing,' she said, 'about being clever is that clever people are ashamed of it . . . Look what worms some of these brains here are – I say, if I eat any more of them I shall be sick. They're not a bit nice really, they're all seed, but I never can help eating things, can you?'

'Never,' said Rachel. 'At home I often used to eat three helpings – I mean of things like *éclairs* or pheasant or treacle tart – our cook makes it awfully well. I don't now that I have started staying up to late dinner. That makes an awful difference to what one eats in a day, helpings apart.'

'I'd never eat three helpings because of my muscles. I mean to keep awfully strong, not get flabby like women do. I know all the things men don't eat when they're in training. Do you?'

'No. Do you stay up to late dinner?'

'We don't have late dinner,' said Elise scornfully. 'We have supper and I've stayed up to that ever since I was eight.'

Elise's people must be very eccentric.

They were seen coming breathless across the garden twenty minutes late for chapel and found Miss Smyke at the door with a flaming sword. 'What did I say?' asked Miss Smyke, rhetorical. 'What did I *tell* you? It's no use going into chapel now,' she said spitefully (as though they would want to). 'They're at the Te Deum. Go up and change your stockings and stay in your dormitories till you're sent for.' She turned and went back into chapel, looking satisfied and religious.

Being punished together was intimate; they felt welded. They were punished more severely than usual because of Elise, who had a certain way with her under-lip . . . She had a way with her head, too, that reminded Rachel of a defiant heroic person about to be shot. It didn't come out, mercifully, that they had broken bounds; the Jungle remained unmenaced. They were ordered apart for the rest of the day (which sealed them as 'great friends') and Rachel, usually humiliated by punishment, went about feeling clever and daring. On Monday evening she kept a place beside her for Elise at supper, but after some time saw Elise come in arm in arm with Joyce Fellows and sit down at another table. She looked away. After supper Elise said, 'I say, why didn't you come? Joyce and I were keeping a place for you.'

Term went on, and it was all rather difficult and interesting. Rachel was a snob; she liked her friends to be rather distinguished, she didn't like being 'ordered about' by a girl in a lower form. That was what it amounted to; Elise never took much trouble about one, her down-right manner was peremptory: when she said, 'Let's — ' it meant (and sounded like), 'You can if you like: *I'm* going to.' Whenever they did things together it ended in trouble; Rachel began to wish Elise wouldn't stick out her lip at people like Casabianca and look down her nose. Mistresses spoke scornfully about 'Going about with the younger ones'. They never asked her to 'influence' Elise, which showed that they knew. IVB seemed a long way down the school, yet Elise would swagger ahead of one along passages and throw back, without even looking: 'Buck up: do come on!' Then there was Joyce Fellows; a silly, blank-faced, rather unhappy 'entourage'.

One evening in prep Charity did a drawing on a page of her notebook, tore it out and passed it across to Rachel. It was called 'Jacob (Rachel's Rajah)', and was a picture of Elise in trousers hanging upside down from a beam in the gym roof and saying, in a balloon from her mouth, 'Buck up, come here, I'm waiting.' Rachel couldn't climb ropes and hadn't a good head when she did get to the top of things, so this was unkind. The name was stupid but the drawing was rather clever. Rachel showed it to Elise at supper and Elise turned scarlet and said, 'What a darned silly fool!' She hadn't much sense of humour about herself.

The next evening there was a drawing of a figure like two tennis balls lying on Charity's desk. (Charity's figure was beginning to develop feminine curves at an alarming rate.) Charity looked, laughed and picked the drawing up with the very tips of her finger and thumb. 'Of course I don't *mind* this,' she said, 'but I suppose you know your beastly little common friend has no business in our form-room?'

Rachel's cheeks burnt. It wouldn't have mattered a bit if the drawing had been clever, but Elise couldn't draw for toffee: it was just silly and vulgar. 'I don't know why you should think it was you,' she said, 'but if the cap fits — '

Later she rounded on Elise. 'If you did want to score off Charity you might have invented a cleverer way.'

'*I* don't pretend to be clever,' said Elise.

'I'd never have shown you the Jacob one if I'd thought you were going to be such a silly serious ass,' stormed Rachel.

Elise stared with her wide-open pale grey eyes that had, this moment, something alert behind them that wasn't her brain. 'You knew that wouldn't be my idea of a funny joke,' she said, 'didn't you?'

Rachel hesitated. Elise, with tight lips, made a scornful little laughing sound in her nose.

'As a matter of fact,' said Rachel, 'I didn't think it mattered showing you what all my friends in my form think. You know you have got into a fearfully bossy way with everybody.'

'I don't know what you're talking about,' said Elise. 'I don't s'pose you do either. What do you mean by "everybody"? I never take any notice of anybody unless I happen to like them, and if they think I'm bossy I can't help it. It's not me who's bossy, but other people who are sloppy?'

'Do you think I'm sloppy?'

'Yes, you are rather sloppy sometimes.'

It was at supper, a dreadful place to begin a conversation of this sort. Rachel and Elise had to remain side by side, staring at the plates of the girls opposite, biting off and slowly masticating large mouthfuls of bread-and-jam. Then Rachel half-choked over a mouthful, turned away quickly and flung herself into the conversation of two girls on the other side. They all three talked 'shop' about algebra prep. Elise just sat on there, perfectly natural and disconcertingly close. When Rachel peeped round she did not notice. She sat badly, as always, her head hunched forward between her shoulders, and Rachel knew her lip was out and had a feeling that she was smiling. When grace was over they pushed back their chairs and bolted out in different directions. Out in the hall everybody was crowding up to the noticeboard. Rachel turned away and went into the classroom and sat at her desk. When the others had gone she came out and looked at the notice-board. The lists for the next match were up and Elise was in the Lacrosse Eleven.

The last Sunday but one, in the afternoon, Rachel went back to the Jungle. It was December, goldenly fine; the trees were pink in the afternoon light, rooks circled, grass was crisp in the shadows from last night's frost. She had started out in an overcoat with a muffler up to her nose and rabbit-skin gloves, but soon she untwisted the muffler and stuffed the gloves into her pocket. The lovely thin air seemed to have turned warmer; her breath went lightly and clearly away through it. The wall, the hedge, the gate of the paddock gave her a bruised feeling.

She stumbled across the paddock, tripping up on the long ends of her muffler, with her unbuttoned overcoat flapping against her legs. 'It will be a good end to this kind of a term,' she thought. 'If Mr Morden catches me.'

It really hadn't been much of a term. She hadn't worked, she hadn't been a success at anything, she hadn't made anyone like her. The others in IVA had been nice to her since she 'came back', but they forgot her unintentionally; they had got into the way of doing things together in twos and threes since the beginning of term and she got left out – naturally. She felt lonely, aimless, absolutely inferior; she tried a lot of new ways of doing her hair, designed a black velvet dress for herself and looked forward to going home. She brought names, Charity's and the other girls', rather un-naturally into her letters so that Mother shouldn't suspect she was being a failure. She felt so sick for Elise that she prayed to be hit by a ball on the head every time she went out to Lacrosse.

Elise had the most wonderfully natural way of not seeing one. She said 'Sorry' when she bumped into one in the passage, shared a hymn-book in chapel when they found themselves side by side, and when she caught up and passed one going out to the playing-field side-glanced indifferently as though one were one of the seniors. She had got her colours after her third match; no one under fifteen had ever got their colours before. All the important people were taking her up and talking about her. IVA agreed that they would not have minded, they'd have been glad, if she'd only been humble and nice to begin with and not such an absolutely complacent pig. They never talked about her in front of Rachel and Rachel never mentioned her.

Down in the lane there were deep ruts; she walked between them on crumbling ridges. A dog was barking somewhere at Mr Morden's, snapping bits out of the silence, then letting it heal again. The bank to the Jungle was worn slippery; Rachel pulled herself up it from root to root. The Jungle was in shadow; the grass had fallen like uncombed hair into tufts and was lightly frosted. 'It's nice to come back,' said Rachel. 'I never was really *here* that last time, it's awfully nice to come back.' She bent down, parting the brambles; the leaves were purple and blackish; some rotting brown leaves drifted off at her touch.

Coming out from the brambles, an arm was stretched over the path. 'Not, O God, in this lonely place,' said Rachel – 'let there not be a body!'

She was shaken by something regularly, put up a hand to her heart with the conscious theatrical movement of extreme fear and found it thumping. The hand lay a yard ahead of her – she could have taken three steps forward and stepped on it – the thumb bent, the red, square-tipped fingers curling on to the palm.

'Elise, is this you?' whispered Rachel. She waited, plucking leaves from the bramble, hearing the dog bark, then went round to where Elise was lying in a valley between the brambles.

Elise lay half on her side, leaning towards the arm that was flung out. Her knees were drawn up, her other arm flung back under her head which rested, cheek down, on a pile of dead leaves as on a pillow and was wrapped up in a muffler. The muffler was slipping away from her face like a cowl. Down in the sheltered air between the bushes she was flushed by sleep and by the warmth of the muffler. She was Elise, but quenched, wiped-away, different; her mouth – generally pressed out straight in a grudging smile – slackened into a pout; thick short lashes Rachel had never noticed spread out on her cheeks. Rachel had never looked full at her without having to pass like a guard her direct look; her face now seemed defenceless. Rachel stood looking down – the only beautiful thing about Elise was the cleft in her chin. She stood till her legs ached, then shifted her balance. A twig cracked; Elise opened her eyes and looked up.

'I told you I'd come here and sleep,' she said.

'Yes – isn't it fearfully cold?'

Elise poked up her head, looked round and lay back again, stretching luxuriously. 'No,' she said, 'I feel stuffyish. Have you just come?'

'Yes. I'm going away again.'

'Don't go.' Elise curled up her legs to make room in the valley. 'Sit down.'

Rachel sat down.

'Funny thing your just coming here. Have you come much?'

'No,' said Rachel, staring into the brambles intently as though she were watching something that had a lair inside them moving about.

'I brought Joyce Fellows once; we came in here to smoke cigars. I hate smoking – Joyce was as sick as a cat.'

'How *beastly!*'

'Oh, I don't suppose there's anything left now, we covered it up. Anyhow, I shall never smoke much. It's so bad for the wind.'

'Oh, by the way,' said Rachel, 'congratulations about your colours.'

Elise, her hands clasped under her head, had been lying looking at the sky. 'Thanks so much,' she said, now looking at Rachel.

'Aren't we mad,' said Rachel uneasily, 'doing this in December?'

'Why shouldn't we if we're warm enough? Rachel, why shouldn't we? – Answer.'

'It'll be dark soon.'

'Oh, dark in your eye!' said Elise, 'there's plenty of time . . . I say, Rachel, I tell you a thing we might do — '

Rachel wound herself up in her muffler by way of a protest. She had a funny feeling, a dancing-about of the thoughts; she would do anything, anything. ''Pends what,' she said guardedly.

'You could turn round and round till you're really comfy, then I could turn round and put my head on your knee, then I could go to sleep again . . . '

The round cropped head like a boy's was resting on Rachel's knees. She felt all constrained and queer; comfort was out of the question. Elise laughed once or twice, drew her knees up higher, slipped a hand under her cheek where the frieze of the overcoat tickled it.

'All right?' said Rachel, leaning over her.

'Mm – *mmm.*'

The dog had stopped barking, the Jungle, settling down into silence, contracted a little round them, then stretched to a great deep ring of unreality and loneliness. It was as if they were alone on a ship, drifting out . . .

'Elise,' whispered Rachel, 'do you think we — '

But the head on her knees had grown heavy. Elise was asleep.

Shoes:
An International Episode

THEIR room was in morning disorder. To keep the french window open at its widest an armchair smothered in clothes had been pushed up, a curtain tied back with one of Mrs Aherne's stockings. She had stripped the beds – one could never be certain hotel femmes-de-chambre did this thoroughly – and two great scrolls of bedclothes toppled over the room like baroque waves. The two had breakfasted; the coffee-tray, lodged on a table-edge among brushes, collars and maps, was littered with cigarette-ends, stained beet sugar and crumbs of roll. Mr Aherne did not care for the crumby part and had an untidy habit of scooping this out with his thumb.

Outside, the pale glare of morning, unreal like mid-summer sunshine remembered at Christmas, painted garden tree-tops, blonde tiled roofs, and polished some green glass balls cemented on to a wall till one wanted to reach out and touch them.

Mrs Aherne, feeling French and sophisticated, wandered round in her dressing-gown smoking a cigarette. Her husband bowing forward into the looking-glass carefully parted his hair. It was exquisite to be leisurely. Her chemise, back from a French laundress, was delicate on her skin.

'All the same,' she said, 'I wish you would hurry up with that glass. What about *my* hair?'

'You look lovely the way you are,' said Mr Aherne, studying himself sympathetically.

She felt she did. She really was a pretty thing; blonde, brown, vigorous. She said:

'I should hate them to think all Englishwomen were frumpy.'

'You may be certain they don't. I saw two of them turn and have a good look at you going out of the dining-room — '

'Really? . . . Oh, don't be so silly!'

Mr Aherne, in shirt-sleeves, looking like one of those nice advertisements of shaving-soap, dived out into the passage to bring in the shoes. He reappeared, put them down and looked at them with a smile. These two pairs of shoes, waiting outside for him every morning, still seemed a formal advertisement to the world of their married state. 'Nice little couple,' said Edward Aherne.

Dillie didn't notice the shoes at once; she, in possession of the looking-glass, was powdering over the sunburn at the base of her throat. But when she turned round she said sharply:

'Edward, what are *these* doing in here? They're not mine!'

The female shoes, uncertainly balanced because of their high heels, listed towards the strong shoes of Edward timidly and lackadaisically. They were fawn kid, very clean inside (so probably new), low at the insteps, with slim red heels and a pattern in scarlet leather across the strap and over the toe-cap. They were tiny (size three or three-and-a-half) and looked capable solely of an in-effectual, somehow alluring totter.

'These are *not* my shoes,' repeated Mrs Aherne ominously.

Edward, incredulous, came to look at the shoes. His face went into stiff lines, conscious of being searched.

'*I* never — '

'I didn't suppose you did . . . ' She flashed with anger. 'Oh, but what little horrors! How *could* they think — !'

'They didn't think; they got muddled up about rooms.'

'There was no mistake about *your* shoes.'

'I wonder,' said Edward archly, 'who yours have been spending the night with!'

Not feeling French any longer, she wasn't amused. She threw her cigarette out of the window – to smoke more than one after breakfast made her feel stuffy, anyhow.

Dillie was an advanced, intelligent girl who had married Edward two years ago. Since then they had travelled a good deal. She had been constant to the good resolutions made on her honeymoon: not to be insular, not to behave like a 'dear little thing'. She never grumbled at rich cooking, at having no egg for breakfast and no pudding; when Latins ogled she frowned in the other direction but did not complain to Edward. She tried to share Edward's elation when café waiters brought her *La Vie Parisienne*. 'They wouldn't bring *that* to most Englishwomen!' Edward used to exclaim: she wondered why they didn't bring it to Frenchwomen either. She walked about France in good brogues and didn't mind if her feet looked a shade powerful. She took six-and-a-halfs for ordinary wear and, when she wanted to be really comfortable, sevens.

To be annoyed by the simpering shoes was unworthy; she said reasonably: 'Well, find mine, and put those wherever mine were.'

'Everyone else's have been taken in, I noticed; ours were the last.'

He was *too* helpless; she snorted. 'Then give them to me!'

The passage outside was stuffy and panelled with doors. Dillie paced up and down, swinging the shoes by their straps, raging.

Those doors were cynical. She looked at the numbers each side of their own; No. 19 clicked open and a man with no collar looked out at her ardently, but with a shake of the head shut the door again in discouragement. Dille bristled. She was now quite certain the horrors belonged to his wife, or at any rate (one couldn't blink at these things) to the lady in there with him. If he hadn't put the matters on such a basis she would have knocked and presented them. She jumped as door No. 11 opened behind her and a lady in red crêpe-de-chine came out on a gust of geranium powder.

'*Ceux sont à vous, peut-etre?*' said Dillie, advancing the shoes nervously and forgetting '*Madame*'. The lady said '*Merci*', and went by in repudiation, chillingly. The shoes were in no worse taste than her own and, at least, cleaner. Dillie, now on the defensive, returned to her room. 'Better ring, I suppose,' she said stormily.

The worst, at any crisis, of these jolly little hotels is that the *sommelier* is the waiter and disappears between ten and eleven, delegating upstairs business to the femme-de-chambre who is sympathetic but irrational. The femme-de-chambre, on appearance, was desolated for Madame but knew nothing. She dangled the horrors temptingly; they were '*des jolies chaussures . . . mignonnes*'.

'*Je ne pourrais pas même les porter. Aussi, je les deteste. Enlevez-les.*'

The femme-de-chambre languished at Edward.

'*Enlevez-les*,' Edward said sternly. '*Et allez demander. Les chaussures de Madame . . .* '

'*C'est ça!*' agreed the femme-de-chambre, inspired. She vanished and did not return.

Meanwhile it was half-past ten. 'We meant to have done that *jubé* before lunch and if we do it now we won't get back till one. By that time the *hors-d'oeuvres* will have been picked over and we shall get nothing but those beastly little bits of sausage. How greedy the French are. And I always did think this hotel was sinister. I told you so at the time, Edward.'

'Oh, my darling . . . '

'Well, not last night, but I had that cherry brandy and there was the moon.'

They went out, finally, into the hardening brilliance. Dillie, unwillingly elegant in snakeskins she'd been keeping for the Americans in Carcassonne, tottered over the *pavé*. Edward turned down his panama over his eyes and assumed with his chin a subdued expression. It really *was* annoying for Dillie. They went unseeingly through the market: he offered Dillie peaches. 'How,' she said scornfully, 'can we possibly eat peaches in a cathedral?'

'Oh . . . we *are* going there?' said Edward deferentially.

'Well, we don't want to waste a morning absolutely, I suppose. We will at least,' she said vindictively '*begin* the *jubé*.'

As they turned down the Rue des Deux Croix towards the cathedral bold in sunshine, somebody swept off a hat ineffably. It was the collarless man with the expression, now in a very low, tight collar over which his neck hung out voluptuously. Dillie wore one of the local hats of thin, limp, peach-coloured straw; Edward side-glanced vainly under the drooping brim. She did not speak; he said nothing.

The cathedral mounted over them, they blinked, incredulous, up at the façade. Lost to one other, they went silently into the pointed, chilly darkness.

After half an hour the back of Edward's neck was aching from much admiration; he said he would like a drink. Dillie, who had pinned back the flap of her hat, looked through him ethereally. She supposed men were like that. '*I'll* just sit here,' she said. 'Edward . . . ?'

'Dearest?'

'Has one got a terribly little soul? How could one have felt shoes mattered!'

He couldn't imagine, either. 'But you're sure,' he said respectfully, 'you wouldn't care for a *little* drink?'

She couldn't even bring the idea into focus, so he went out alone to the café. He thought how much more spiritual women were. But before his drink arrived she came limping across the square. She thought perhaps she had better have something to pick her up. 'You see, my feet are rather hurting. I can't – absorb. It's these high heels on the *pavé*.'

He ordered another mixed vermouth, and a syphon. 'Just think how you'd feel if you were wearing things like those . . . like the horrors.'

'Just think of wearing them always. Oh, Edward, what a conception of women!'

'What a conception!' echoed Edward with vehemence, looking round for the waiter. He laid a hand for a moment on the hand of his wife and companion, but she, relentlessly intelligent, slipped hers away. She was waiting for something, she had planned a discussion. The vermouths arrived; Edward looked at his wisely. 'Queer thing, life,' he said, marking time.

'Queer,' accepted Dillie. 'Of course they *were* pretty,' she said, and looked at him sideways.

'*I* thought so — ' said Edward rashly.

'I knew you did! Why couldn't you say so? Oh, Edward, do I deserve that kind of thing? Can't you be frank? I could see that at once by the way you looked at them. You are so transparent. Why *can't* you be frank?'

'It seems rather a waste to be frank if I'm transparent.'

'I suppose no men really want to respect women. Frenchmen are franker, that's all. What men really want — '

'My darling, I do wish you wouldn't generalize about "men".' She was ignoring her vermouth; he felt constrained to put down his glass.

'I do sometimes wonder how really modern you are.'

'Darling — '

'Don't keep on calling me "darling"; it's like being patted. Would I have come out all this way with you and be staying in this stuffy embarrassing dishonest hotel eating unwholesome food, miles from all my friends, if I were simply a little wifie?'

'I knew you really wanted to go to the seaside with the Phippses.'

This was too much. 'If I had wanted to go to the seaside with the Phippses I'd have gone. You know we believe in freedom.'

'Of course I know. I think we do nearly always mean the same thing, only sometimes one of us expresses it unhappily. I *did* think you liked the food here; you agreed that half the fun of a morning abroad was wondering what there would be for lunch.'

'There are no vitamines. The salads are so oily. However,' said Dillie, 'we needn't go on like this, need we, just outside the cathedral?' She had a nice sense of locality and was most particular as to where they quarrelled and where they made love. Smiling at him with a calculated amiability, she began sipping her vermouth.

At lunch, when they had finished with the *hors d'oeuvres*, Edward asked the waiter, who seemed to be influential, about Dillie's shoes. The waiter, surprised and interested, admitted someone must have deceived himself. It was curious.

'*C'est ennuyant pour Madame*,' Edward said accusingly.

Dillie said in an undertone: 'Can't you possibly think of anything stronger?' Edward frowned at her. '*Très ennuyant*,' he said with a Gallic gesticulation: Dillie guarded the wine-bottle. The waiter watched in surprise, as though it occurred to him that foreigners gesticulated a good deal. He would make inquiries; without doubt some lady had also deceived herself. Reassuringly, he swept away the *hors-d'oeuvres*.

'*Quelque dame* couldn't possibly have *se trompèed*,' said Dillie, furious. 'Somebody in this hotel is definitely dishonest.'

'As a matter of fact,' Edward said, 'this *is* rather interesting. I had heard the best type of French were becoming increasingly Anglophile. Someone will send your brogues along certainly; they're probably back by now, but meanwhile, someone will have been taking note of them, to copy.' Any sign of a theory justifying itself gave Edward a happy, fulfilled feeling. He smiled. 'She will certainly get them copied.'

'Oh, do you really think so? Do you think p'raps it was one of those women who turned last night when I went out of the dining-room?'

Edward said he should not be at all surprised.

'O-oh . . . Then I do hope we haven't seemed unpleasant. I shouldn't like them to think one at all grudging. It *is* remarkable, isn't it, how we seem to be setting the tone. You know, I'm quite sure if brogue shoes came to be worn over here generally, there'd be quite a change in the Latin attitude towards women – I do wish you'd *listen*, Edward, and not keep looking furtively at the menu. If you want to read it, read it; I don't mind you being greedy so long as you're sincere about it.'

'I only wanted to see what was coming next – My darling, you know your husband lives to be sincere with you! – As a matter of fact, it's *vol-au-vent*: you like that, don't you? Now *do* go on about the Latin attitude . . . '

They were lunching half out of doors, under a roof that covered part of the garden. Now and then, lizards flickered over the tiles at their feet. Just beyond, shadow came to an end with an edge like metal; there was a glare of gravel, palm trees leaned languid together, creeper poured flaming over a wall, and a row of young orange trees in bright glazed vases swaggered along a balustrade. Balanced in the hot stillness, the green glass balls on the wall-top snatched one's attention with their look of precariousness. At the garden's end, impermanent yellow buildings, fit to go down at a puff; intense and feverish, like a memory of Van Gogh's. A long cat, slipping from vase to vase, fawned on its reflection in an unnatural ecstasy.

Dillie looked at all this, sideways. 'You do like this?' said Edward, anxious.

'If only it weren't so hot; I hate being hot after lunch. And the glare is so awful. Everything one looks at has – has an echo.'

'That's rather clever. I do wish you'd write, Dillie.'

Dillie liked being told she ought to write; she replied with complacency that she lacked the creative imagination. 'I'm afraid I'm too critical. I do wish one could be more imposed upon.'

'Yes, I do wish one could!'

'Oh, but *you* are,' said Dillie firmly. That disposed of Edward; she brushed some crumbs from under her elbows and settled down to explain why. They had coffee brought out, and liqueurs, and remained talking after the last of the other guests had stared and gone. They both felt they *analysed* better in France; and of course wine did intensify the personality. They discussed Edward and Dillie, Dillie in relation to Edward, Edward to Dillie, Edward and Dillie to Dillie's shoes, and Dillie's shoes to the Latin attitude. They discussed sex. They vaguely glowed at each other with admiration.

The waiter hung round, flicking at empty tables; they saw him as a tree, dimly; they had no idea how aggravating they were. Clasped hands supporting their flushed faces, they looked mistily past the waiter.

When he broke into their circle of consciousness they were surprised. The shoes, he was more than delighted to say, had been traced. A lady had found them outside her door and taken them into her room in mistake for her own. She had returned them to No. 20; they awaited Madame above. Dillie said 'There!' in triumph, got up and went out carefully between the tables. She had a pleasant feeling of extension, as though she were everywhere, on the table-tops, in the wine-bottles, in the waiter; wise with all of them. Every experience meant something; each had its place. She groped down the corridor, blind in the sudden darkness, singing.

Their room was still darker; the shutters were latched. Dillie kicked the snakeskin shoes off her aching feet, then let daylight in with a bang and a blast of hot air. She turned•to look for her brogues.

Reflected, swan-like, into the waxy floor, the Horrors awaited her. Heel to heel, they radiated sex-consciousness; dangling their little scarlet straps. '*Les chaussures de Madame*' – shoes attributed to Dillie Aherne, the frank and equal companion of Edward. 'You *damned*!' said Dillie. 'You absolutely *damned* damned!' Then she picked them up (she could never explain what came to her) and threw them one by one out of the window, aiming very carefully at a particular point in the sky. One struck the dining-room roof and ricocheted off it. The other spun on the sky with a flash of bright heel and dropped into a palm tree. Dillie grinned fearfully after them; then, shocked unutterably, buried her face in the curtain. Tears came on; she was caught in them, helpless, as in a thunder-shower.

Edward and she were both interested in her temper and in a kind of way proud of it. It was an anachronism but rather distinctive. But it sometimes came on her unprepared and so frightened and really hurt her. 'Oh!' she cried, trembling, 'Oh oh *oh*!' The curtain tore.

At the sound of the shoe on the roof Edward ran out, looked down at the shoe and up at the window. He saw his Dillie back in the darkness, hiding her face in the curtain.

'A shoe's just come down . . . Oh?'

Dillie wound herself up in the curtain.

Edward swallowed. 'Shall – shall I come up?' he said loyally.

Dillie unwound, and leant out to give emphasis. 'You can tell them the other's up in a palm tree – it has as much business there as in my room. Tell them they're vilely cynical and that we shall be leaving tonight.' She slammed the shutter.

'Scene in the best French manner,' Edward admitted. Several

other shutters opened an inch or two; he felt people looking out at him sympathetically. He hurried across to the foot of a likely palm: up there, sure enough, was the little siren, lodged at the base of two fronds. It looked as though a shake of the tree should bring it down easily: he tried two or three and they didn't. He walked round the tree, looking up; he bombarded the shoe with pebbles; it faintly wobbled. He eyed it, without prejudice . . . it *was* rather a nice little shoe. Perhaps it belonged to the girl in pleated green organdie, with the gazelle eyes . . . (An ultra-feminine type, Dillie and he had agreed.) It would look rather jolly with pleated green organdie . . . The scarlet straps would compete with the scarlet hat – under which the gazelle eyes looked out deprecatingly, mysteriously. He wondered what she would think of him, trying to rout her shoe out of a palm with a piece of bamboo – the bamboo was too short. He might have swarmed up the trunk, but that would look silly and ruin his trousers. When she appeared, he would say to that girl . . .

He hoped Dillie wouldn't summon him. Her tempers, once over the crying stage, were very explicit. Hypnotically, the sky glittered through the fronds; caressing one shoe, gazing up at the other, Edward remained in a dream.

Dillie sat on her bed in the smothering darkness, wondering what to do now. She thought that, to keep her word at its present high value with Edward, she should pull the suitcases out and begin packing. She sighed; she did hope Edward would rush in and overpersuade her before she had put in the first layer. 'It's nothing personal,' she repeated, 'it's just that I cannot tolerate cynical inefficiency. I'm sorry, Edward; I just happen to be made like that.' She felt that if she could not say this to somebody soon it would lose its first edge of conviction; she peeped through the shutters, but Edward was standing stupidly under a palm tree and *she* wasn't going to call him. Reluctantly, she rolled up two jumpers. It really was queer how men failed one; one looked to them at a crisis, and they just walked away and stood under a tree with their legs apart. She tossed some paper out of a suitcase, trying to think of the French for 'inefficiency'.

Somebody knocked. Dillie stood still a moment; her lips moved. She powdered her nose which, still flushed with anger, felt larger than usual, then opened the door fiercely. An arch little boy in a blouse, called Anatole, stood outside with her brogues. '*V'la les chaussures de Monsieur*,' said Anatole, putting them down briskly. And he had been sent, he said, to look for the shoes that Madame had taken this morning, that did not belong to Madame at all, that belonged to another lady who now searched for them everywhere. He looked at Dillie, severely.

Dillie faltered, '*Comment?*'

Anatole very politely shrugged. '*Mais voila les chaussures de Monsieur,*' he repeated, and held out her brogues encouragingly.

' – *de Monsieur.*' It was the moment, certainly, for Dillie to make a demonstration. *Now* she could show them. '*Ceux ne sont pas —* ' began Dillie. But she went scarlet and stopped. *Was* Anatole worth it – so small, so sleek, already so irreclaimable? She looked down; her good brogues sat there stodgily, square on the parquet. There was no nonsense about them. '*Les chaussures de Monsieur . . .* '

'*Allez-vous-en!*' snapped Dillie, and slammed the door.

Ten minutes later, felt hat pulled on jauntily, she clattered happily to and fro on the parquet, brogued once more to resume the day. She was loth to waste an hour. She must make Edward feel how he was forgiven. She parted the shutters and looked out; a curious group intrigued her.

Edward, crossing the garden, was followed by the waiter at one end of a ladder and Anatole at the other. A girl in green ruffles was supported in indignation by two men, one in a Homburg, one in a flat cap. She was just the sort of girl for the shoes, Dillie observed with triumph. Edward was pink; it was trying for him, but one must not be sentimental. The waiter propped the ladder against the palm and after some discussion began to go up it; Anatole held the bottom and Edward directed.

'*Je ne sais pas comment c'est arrivé,*' Edward kept explaining. '*À gauche, un peu plus à gauche! Là – secouez-le . . . Je ne sais pas comment c'est arrivé. Ça a l'air, n'est-ce pas, d'être tombé! Oui, c'est tombé, sans doute.*'

It was painful, in fact, to listen to the lying of Edward. Dillie, hot to the very back-bone, turned from the window; she even shut the shutters defensively. She kept moving about the room, jerked her hat off and came to a full-stop in front of the glass. Her eyes in the half-dark were haggard and rather profound; she looked startled. She tried to see Edward's Dillie: her thoughts raced round and round till one half suspected, inside this whirlwind of thought, there was nothing at all! She remembered the two Ahernes, vis-à-vis, at happy lunchtime, analysing each other; she envied them now like strangers. Such assurance, such a *right* kind of self-sufficiency . . . Goaded, Dillie pulled her hat on again, seized her stick and made for the door – then, in a queer kind of panic, returned and stood waiting for something, someone. The travelling clock loudly, officiously ticked.

Edward at last came up. He rippled a tap and entered, ruefully smiling. He was still rather warm.

'Well!' said Dillie.

'Squared 'em all. Wasn't it like a French farce though – not the improper kind. See us?'

'Partly. That terrible girl with the hips. Aren't French women *hard*, Edward!'

'Oh no, she was wonderfully sporting. Once she got her shoe back, she seemed rather amused. After all, Dillie, allowing for tastes, one does value one's shoes. I liked the two men she was with, too; of course they began by being rather aggressive – the French have a strong sense of property – but they finished up quite sympathetic and nice. You know, I always think — '

' – Did they *guess*?'

They looked at each other a moment in naked discomfort. Edward blinked. '*I* don't know: didn't ask them. Of course, the shoes had been traced to our room . . . '

'I dare say,' Dillie said, unconcerned, 'she thought you looked like the Prince of Wales. You do, in that suit.'

'Do I? Good!'

Dillie steeled herself. Edward *was* rather pathetic. If one had been a 'wee wifey' sort of person one would have clung to his chest, stroked the back of his nice neck and dithered: 'Oh, Edward, I've been such a beast, such a fool!' Dillie was glad she wasn't going to do this: it would have lowered her in Edward's eyes. It would have been shocking to drop the thing to the emotional plane and let it remain there, unanalysed, undiscussed.

'Queer,' she said bravely, 'what one gains with these people by an apparent access of uncontrol . . . They'd admire hysterics – Don't you agree?' she said sharply.

Edward went to the basin and made a loud noise with the tap. He rubbed water up his face. He gurgled into the water.

'What *do* you think – really, Edward?'

'Can't think now – I'm too hot.'

'Edward, you *don't* think I — ? Surely, Edward — '

'Coming out?' said Edward, looking round for his hat.

Dillie felt quite hollow. What was Edward thinking? How dare he! . . . 'Edward, kiss me . . . You *do* believe in me? *Edward!* Kiss me!'

But Edward still seemed bothered about his hat. She supposed this might well be the end of their marriage.

Then a kiss from Edward, uncertainly placed, began to be prolonged with some ardour in the dark room.

'You poor little angel!'

'You know, I did throw them out of the window.'

'You take things too hard, darling.'

'You do see I was right?' she said anxiously. She heard Edward breathe hard, considering.

'Under these particular circumstances – yes, I'm sure you were.'

'You weren't ashamed of me?' She couldn't let go of his coat-sleeve till he had answered.

'It was awful for you.'

'It was just,' she said, 'that I *cannot* tolerate cynical inefficiency.'

'You were quite right . . . Shall we go out now and have a rather long, cool drink before we look at any more of the cathedral? Bière blonde or something . . . Coming?'

'Yes,' she said, 'if you really must.' With infinite patronage, infinite affection, she took his arm.

Mr and Mrs Aherne, free, frank on terms of perfect equality, clattered down the corridor, disturbing some dozen siestas. Talking loudly together about the Latin mentality, they passed with a blink and a gasp into the reeling glare of the afternoon.

The Dancing-Mistress

ABOUT half-past three at the end of November a sea-fog came up over the edge of the cliff and, mounting the plate-glass windows, filled the Metropole ballroom with premature twilight. The fantastic trees in the garden sank in like a painting on blotting-paper; the red roofs of surrounding houses persisted an hour in ever-ghostlier violet and faded at last. Below the gold ceiling the three chandeliers draped in crystal flowered reluctantly into a thin batch of lights: the empty floor of the ballroom was pointed with yellow reflections.

The door of the ladies' cloak-room kept creaking and swinging, gusts of chatter came out from the little girls being unpeeled from their wraps. Inside was a shuffle of feet on the muffling carpet, water gushing in basins, a clatter of ivory brush-backs on marble slabs. The mothers and governesses wanted elbow-room for their business with combs, for the re-tying of sashes and tugging of woolly gaiters from silk-clad legs. With their charges, they over-flowed into the corridor. Here, all along, it was chilly and rustling with muslins; Shetlands and cardigans were flung over the radiators; little girls sat in rows on the floor to put on their dancing-sandals. Miss James, the dancing-mistress, hurrying past in her fur coat with her dispatch-case, with her frail forward slant like a reed in the current, was obliged to pick her way over their legs. This she did with stereotyped little weary amused exclamations: her pianist followed in silence, a sharper, more saturnine profile against the brocaded wallpaper.

Miss James and the pianist went into the ballroom, where they opened their dispatch-cases behind the piano and, holding the mirror for one another, dusted over their faces with large soft puffs. The pianist moistened the tips of her fingers to flatten her hair back; it was polished against her skull like a man's. Miss James took the mirror and, biting her lip, glanced once more at herself in the oval with a slanting, fleeting, troubled kind of reproach.

The pianist looked up at the chandeliers, then scornfully out at the mist. 'I'm so glad we've got back to artificial – it seems much more natural, I think. – I say *sure* you don't feel too rotten?'

'Not as rotten as all that, I suppose,' said Miss James, indifferent. She had taken two classes already today; before the second she had declared a headache.

Miss Joyce James had begun as a pupil of Madame Majowski's; she worked for her now. Six days a week she went all over the country giving lessons; in the mornings she got up early to perfect her dancing at Mme Majowski's studio. She had eight dancing dresses like clouds, in gradations of beauty, a black satin tunic for studio practice, and besides these and the fur coat to cover them nothing at all but a cloth coat-and-skirt that looked wrong in the country and shabby in town. She was twenty-one, pretty but brittle and wax-like from steam-heated air. All day long she was just an appearance, a rhythm; in studio or ballroom she expanded into delicate shapes like a Japanese 'mystery' flower dropped into water. Late at night, she stopped '*seeming*' too tired to '*be*'; too tired to eat or to speak; she would finish long journeys asleep with her head on the pianist's shoulder: her sister received her with Bovril and put her to bed. Her eyebrows tilted outwards like wings; over her delicate cheekbones looked out, slightly tilted, her dreamy and cold eyes in which personality never awakened.

Miss James and Miss Peel the pianist sat for some minutes more in the window-embrasure behind the piano, side to side in jaded intimacy like a couple of monkeys. There was a radiator beside them. Miss Peel, having shivered out of her coat, kept spreading out her hands to the radiator, chafing them gently together, then spreading them out again, drawing in a reserve of warmth through the hands for her whole body. Her thin shoulder-blades rippled the silk of her dress as she bent forward. Miss James kept her eyes on the door, watching the children in, vacantly counting. As each came in its name jumped back to her memory as though a ticket had clicked up over its head. Though her mind was blank of this party of children from Wednesday to Wednesday, she never hesitated or was confused between the Joans and Jeans, the Margerys or the Mollies.

The little girls swung themselves in through the glass doors in twos and threes and skidded over the floor. The mothers and governesses sat down in groups round the walls with a resigned look of un-expectation. Their murmuring made a fringe round the silence, they nodded across at each other. The ballroom was gaunt in the vague smoky daylight, like a large church.

Three minutes before the class was due to begin, the hotel secretary appeared in the doorway, looking towards the piano. Miss Peel was sorting her music; she paused for a moment. 'There's Lulu,' she murmured.

'I know,' said Miss James.

Lulu, Romano-Swiss, fervent and graceful, looked away from them guiltily, looked round the room officially, switched on a dozen more lights. Miss James picked up a valse and frowned at it. She sighed, she was so tired. Two more little girls squeezed in past the secretary's elbow. The door swung to with a sigh.

'He's gone,' said Miss Peel and went back to her music.

'I know,' said Miss James.

A quarter to four. They both glanced at their wristwatches, sighed and admitted the hour. The dancing-mistress came round the piano, the pianist sat down in front of 'Marche Militaire', shook back a slave-bangle up either arm, and waited, her eyes on Miss James who stood at the top of the room and looked down steadily into a looking-glass at the bottom.

'Good afternoon!' she said, silvery. The little girls ran forward, shaking out their dresses. 'Fall in for the March! Grizelda leading . . . Skirts out, right foot pointed . . . GO! . . . *Right*, left – right – right – right — Heads *well* up – *that's* right! . . . Skirt, Phyllis . . . Toes, Jean! . . . Oh, *toes*, Margery – Margery, what *are* you doing . . . *to-o-o-es!*'

Miss Peel spanked out the 'Marche Militaire'. Grizelda, impeccable, head erect, face blank, toes pointed quiveringly, led the twenty-five twice round the room and up the centre. Then they divided, ones right, twos left, met again, came up in twos, in fours, and then spaced out for the exercises. That was that.

The five positions: they performed like compasses. First . . . second . . . third . . . fourth . . . fifth! For each a chord, a shock of sound tingling out into silence. The dancing-mistress kept them in the fifth position and melted down between the lines to look.

Margery Mannering never did anything right. Her week was darkened by these Wednesdays. She was perfectly certain Miss James hated her – Miss James did. She was an overdressed little girl who belonged to a grandmother. She had red sausage-curls tied up with lop-eared white bows and spectacles that misted over, blinding her, when she got hot. She stood crooked forward anxiously. A coldness fingered its way down her spine as Miss James came softly to her down the room in her blue dress that fell into points like a hyacinth-bell and fluted out.

'Now, Margery . . . Margery Mannering. What are you doing *now?*'

They looked hard at each other; all the rest waited. Margery thought, 'She'd like to kill me.' Miss James thought, 'I would like to kill her – just once.' Her face had a hard wistfulness. 'Just *think*,' she gently invited. The girls in front turned round. Margery looked at her feet. Just feet, they were, like other people's; boat-like in dancing-sandals. Oh, she had taken the *third* position!

'Yes,' said Miss James and nodded. 'Now do you see? . . . Now you can take those positions again by yourself. – Music, please – Go!' The chords clanged vindictively, like choppers falling. '*Now* do you see?'

Margery had pretty-child affectations that sat forlornly upon her. Now she flung back her hard curls; they bounced on her back. She peered up through misted spectacles like a plump small animal in the bite of a trap – like a rat, perhaps, that no one decently pities.

'Yes, Miss James.'

'Then please remember,' said Miss James, and walked away. The unrealized self in her made itself felt, disturbing her calm with a little shudder of pleasure. A delicate pink touched her cheekbones, she thought of Lulu, she was almost a woman.

Next the springing exercises, so graceful, from which the few little boys were excluded. Rows and rows of little girls kicking the air pointedly, showing the frills on their underclothes, waving their bent arms and fluttering fingers apart and together, tossing their heads. There were gleaning movements, throwing and catching movements, movements that should have scattered roses about the room. Miss Peel played 'Oh where, and oh where, has my little dog gone!' with a kind of saturnine prance.

Grizelda and Lois and Cynthia, Jean Jones and Doris excelled at varying movements; they were set to dance by themselves, to show the others. When someone was dancing alone as a glory the music was different, Margery Mannering thought; the choppers became curling feathers, fluttering in towards one and waving out.

The skipping began and finished; they passed the exercises with ribbons and Indian clubs. The fancy dances began. Little Cynthia was Spain itself in the Spanish dance; the grown-ups sighed at her, she was so sweet. Miss James told her that *next* Wednesday she could come, if she liked, with some castanets. Grizelda and Doris were best in the Irish Jig; so saucy, quite Irishly saucy. The Gavotte made two more couples illustrious; they were given the floor to themselves. 'If one could only teach you to curtsey,' Miss James sighed. If she could only, only teach them to curtsey. They went down on themselves all skewered; feet got lost behind them; knees stuck out in front.

'Just *look*, children: watch me' . . . But they all stood round sceptical; they knew they would never be able to curtsey like that. She sank with bowed head; with arms curved before her she melted into the floor. She flowed down into it and, flowing up again, stood. 'If I had a dress like that . . . ' Doris thought. 'She's not like a person at all,' thought Jean Jones.

The hotel secretary stood looking in through the glass door. His eyes came a little nearer together, his face was intent. Miss Peel played a slow ripple; in her mind Miss James was curtseying.

After the fancy dancing there was an interval. The little girls flocked and slid to the chairs round the wall. Margery Mannering went back and sat by her grandmother's maid, who was knitting a bedsock. 'Got into trouble again, I see,' said the grandmother's maid and wetted her thin lips. 'You did ought to have practised that Spanish dance.' 'You mind your own business,' said Margery, who was rude to servants. She slid along three empty chairs and sat by herself. She watched Miss James go round the room, congratulating the mothers of little girls who had been dancing nicely. Governesses she did not congratulate; she was too tired.

Cynthia sat with her mother just beyond Margery Mannering; they were holding each other's hands excitedly and talking about castanets. Cynthia never seemed bare of being loved, it was round her at school, everywhere, like a sheath. Miss James came round to them, smiling. Margery watched, her head well back on her thick neck, playing with one of her ringlets, and Miss James felt something catch at her, going by. She had again that shudder of life in her; a quick light came into her eyes. 'Don't kick that chair,' she said, put on her smile again and went on.

Miss Peel was back at the radiator. 'How d'you feel?' she said. 'Must you go round all those hags? Are you bad?'

'I suppose I'll get through . . . Did you hear me killing that Mannering child?'

'Which one?'

'Oh, you *know*. The red one.' She laughed a little and sat stroking one of her arms. 'She makes me feel awful . . . I – I don't know how it is.'

'Has she got anyone with her?'

'Only a maid.'

'Perhaps she'll die,' said Miss Peel brightly, and ran her eye over a fox-trot.

'Oh, she couldn't,' said Miss James, startled. She couldn't do without Margery Mannering; she wanted to kill her. She got up and said: 'Now all take your partners for the waltz.'

'Lulu's been back,' said Miss Peel hurriedly. 'When are you going to see him?' Miss James shrugged her shoulders and walked off. The music began.

By this time the fog had been stained to solid darkness; the windows were slabs of night. The chandeliers were in full flower. Children went round and round, smoothly spinning; the tall looking-glass at the end of the room doubled them into a crowd; they were doubled again on the outside darkness. She could not think why nobody came to draw the curtains. When she felt him again at the door, looking in at her with that straight level look of desire, she went towards him, pulled open the door, and said, 'Do please draw the curtains. The room looks so ugly; the mothers don't like it. People can see in.'

'You will give up your train, just once, just tonight?' he said. 'Yes?'

'No, I can't, I'm tired; I've got a headache. Besides, you know Peelie's here; she wouldn't go home alone.'

He skirted the floor and went round to the three windows, touching a cord somewhere so that the curtains trembling with movement slid over them noiselessly. Returning, he brushed Miss Peel's back as she played. 'I want her tonight,' he said over her shoulder. 'We all three have supper together – Yes? I put you both into the 8.40. Yes? Dear Peelie, yes?'

She nodded, in time with the music.

'Dear Peelie – *good*!'

She wriggled her shoulders, he hurried away.

'All arranged,' he said joyously. 'I get a taxi immediately. We all three had supper together down by the Pier.'

'Go away,' Joyce James whispered. 'You're dreadful; you'll ruin me – *One* two three, *one* two three. *Time*, Jean and Betty, time, time! What are you doing! – Mollie, don't talk while you're dancing! Margery Bates, remember you're a gentleman; what does a gentleman do with his hands? . . . *Toes*, Margery Mannering: *why* don't you *dance* on your *toes*?'

Lulu saw something wrong at the end of the room; the chairs were pushed crooked; he went to arrange them. Again he brushed past her. 'Till then, I keep watching. You are so beautiful. I would give my soul, my body, all that I have . . . '

She walked away, clapping her hands together – '*One* two three, *one* two three,' watching the couples go round. Then she suddenly cried to the music, to all the children: 'STOP!'

Of course it was Margery Mannering. She did not know how to waltz; she went bumping and hopping round on the flat of her feet, with her partner all limp. Miss James went over in silence and took her partner away.

'I shall have to take you myself. – All you others sit down for a moment. – We shall go on till I've taught you. And will you please *try*, Margery. You see you are wasting everyone else's time – Music, please!'

All alone on the empty floor, Miss James waltzed with Margery Mannering. They did not speak; they heard one another's breathing; the girl's light, the child's loud and painful. The thump of Margery's heart was like the swelling and bursting of great black bubbles inside her: now the bubbles were in her throat. Her hot body sagged on Miss James's cold bare arm. Her eyes, stretched with physical fear like a rabbit's, stared through the clouding spectacles at the mild white hollow of Miss James's throat. From her spectacles, light flashed up sharply into her partner's face as they circled under the chandeliers. Miss James's hand like a cold shell gripped the hot hand tighter.

'She really is patient and good,' said the mothers, nodding. 'She's so thorough.' They congratulated themselves. 'Look at the pains she takes with that poor little stupid. Wonderful; she keeps smiling.'

And indeed, she was smiling. Lulu watched through the door; his eyes got larger and darker and closer together, his face came closer up to the glass. Miss Peel played on mechanically; she watched him watching.

'I'm giddy,' said Margery suddenly.

'It's no good. I shall keep you on till you've learnt.'

In the taxi, the girls leant back silently. Lulu, his back to the driver, sat watching the town lights flash over their faces. The fog was lifting, but the taxi went slowly through spectral streets like a blind snorting animal. Sometimes the driver pulled up with a jar; the girls nodded forward, the window-frames rattled. Joyce's close-fitting hat was pulled over her eyebrows; her half-hidden face was impassive. Peelie sat with her hat on her knees, she looked over Lulu's head, sombrely humming. Joyce rolled her head with a sigh and an impatient movement; Peelie and Lulu both reached for the window-strap; Lulu was first there and let down the window. Mist came curling in, the air freshened; the taxi had turned down through the old town and the lonely crying of sirens came from the harbour. 'They're awful,' Joyce shuddered.

'She *is* tired,' said Peelie to Lulu across her.

'She will be better after supper.'

'She won't eat,' said Peelie, discouraging.

'Won't you eat dinner?' said Lulu, imploring. He touched Joyce's knee, left a hand there. Peelie eyed the hand sharply. Joyce took no notice. Peelie's foot felt a gentle pressure. 'That's *my* foot.' 'Oh, so sorry, Peelie.' The taxi crawled past a terrace of balconied houses and sharply drew up.

The 'Star' Private Hotel was modest and friendly. It was six o'clock; they went in and sat in the lounge. Peelie was pleased at Lulu's discretion; *here* they would meet no one who'd recognize Lulu and Joyce and go away talking to make scandal about the Metropole dancing class. It did not do for Lulu, who showed ladies into their bedrooms, or Joyce who spent hours in clumsy men's arms, to be patently man and woman; their public must deprecate any attraction. Poor Lulu was also distressingly beautiful; the shabby other visitors kept turning round to look – at the grace of his height, his dark-ivory forehead (foreign men do so much more with a forehead), the ripple-back of his hair, his gaze of shy ardency Joyceward, narrowed by low straight lids. He went off to order the supper – just supper, they said, fish or something, with coffee to follow. Peelie shook Joyce's arm suddenly.

'Do wake up,' she said. 'Can't you really love anyone?'

'I didn't want to – you brought me . . . Well then, give me my powder-puff.'

'You've got heaps on – it's colour you want. Haven't you got — '

'No, you know I don't have any; Majowski hates it.'

'You may be thankful Lulu's Swiss. He wouldn't let you just sit there yawning if he were an Italian.'

'No. He's going to keep an hotel – isn't it awful. With two private funiculars. On the top of a glacier or something. Oh well, *he* won't melt any glaciers!' Joyce changed a yawn to a laugh; she laughed weakly, ruefully, almost in spite of herself, biting in her mouth at one corner and shrugging her slight shoulders.

'What are you laughing for?' said Lulu, coming back. They did not answer; he showed them into the dining-room. The room was empty, not a waitress there. He guided them to their table with an arm lightly round Joyce's waist; as he pulled her chair out she had to step back closer against him. Peelie's hard unabashed eyes contemplated them curiously. Each conscious of the two others they waited, then something in Peelie's eyes made it impossible, shameful for him not to press Joyce closer and kiss her twice on the cheek, high up, where the patch of colour sometimes appeared. Peelie laughed, Joyce laughed uncertainly, Lulu uneasily smiled: they sat down. Joyce unfastened her coat and let it slide down her shoulders, showing her neck and the soft rucked top of the hyacinth dress. Her eyes glittered under the hanging lights with their cold white shades.

'Did you see me killing that child?' she asked Lulu, eagerly turning. 'You were there at the door, you must have seen. Wasn't I dreadful – Peelie thinks I was dreadful.'

'Which child?' he said, while his eyes asked doubtfully, 'Who's there? What's there? *Are* you, at all? I want you.'

'Tell him, Peelie.'

'That fat Mannering child with red hair, she means. I only said: "Don't hate her so's the others can notice."'

'But I do hate her, don't I? Isn't it awful of me. I made her waltz till she cried. But I did teach her'.

Peelie eyed her exaltedness. 'She's quite awake now,' she said, congratulatory, to Lulu. 'I daresay she's quite hungry.' But soon the film crept back, Joyce faded like the roofs into this afternoon's mist; she let her hand lie coldly in Lulu's under the table. As Jean Jones had thought, she was not like a person at all.

When supper was finished they strolled back towards the harbour to look for a taxi. The salt air was milder, lamps made pale stains on the mist. It was high tide; under the mist, to their left, the dark, polished water sucked hard-lipped at the embankment. The edge of the road was protected by chains slung from posts; Peelie went to look over, stood idly clanking and swinging the chain with her knee.

'I wonder what you two would do next if I fell in and never bobbed up again.'

'Oh, *Peelie!*'

'Well, I won't – not *this* woman. All the same, I do wonder . . . '

Her meditation, tinged with contempt for them, broke up sharply when, hearing no more behind her, she turned to see where they were. Lulu had caught Joyce out of the lamplight . . . He was not so unlike an Italian. They stood as one figure till with a gasp he stepped back from her. Joyce stood vaguely, huddling up her coat-collar and looking round for Peelie. They started towards each other under the lamp. Peelie thought: 'Now what's coming?' but all Joyce said was: 'We must get that taxi. I can't go any further. Oh, Peelie, I'm *dead!*'

It was a long drive from the harbour up to the Central Station. No one spoke. Lulu's hands hung between his parted knees; he kept wringing and chafing his hands together. Joyce slipped deeper, deeper into her great fur collar, a swerve of the taxi flung her on Peelie's shoulder; she did not stir, she leaned there inert, asleep. Peelie slipped an arm along the back of the seat; supporting her; this was how they were going to travel home. Light from a picture-palace blared in, disturbing them like a trumpet-blast, on to the small set face of the sleeper, her hat pushed down unevenly over one eye. Lulu, startled, cried out: 'It's not fair!'

'Hush! . . . Nothing's fair.'

'In six weeks I go back to Switzerland. What does she care? – Nothing. And still you are having her day after day.'

'You and I, you and she, she and I, we'll forget each other anyhow – that's nature.'

'Don't you care?'

'Not so much.'

'Peelie . . . '

'Um?'

'*Peelie* . . . I . . . let me just . . . '

She beckoned. Two or three minutes were taken up by a cautious shuffling, balancing, edging; they rose and changed places like people passing each other in a boat. She sustained Joyce's weight till his arm touched her own, supplanting it, under Joyce's shoulders. Joyce never stirred, never woke; she lay quiet under their movements, their whispers and anxious breathing.

'Don't touch her head, you'll wake her – *don't*, Lulu; just let it roll – I do – it finds its own place. Just keep your arm – so – loosely; keep your hand on her other side so's she won't flop back . . . You'll be as stiff as hell in a few minutes – I am, always. Don't try moving, that's worse; just relax . . . '

Joyce sighed; her sleeping body crept closer against him, her head rolled into the hollow of his shoulder – 'found it's own place'. She sighed again with her cheek on his breast; she was comfortable here. Lulu's face came down, scarcely breathing; his chin was just over her little black hat.

Joyce smiled. A new life, the self's, moulded her lips in a soft line. Her face was all broken up, vivid in sleep . . . She was dancing with Margery Mannering. 'I'll kill you, I'll kill you,' she said like a knife. Something burst behind Margery's stretched eyes; she fainted . . . Joyce smiled in her sleep.

Aunt Tatty

THE train stopped every ten minutes after it left the junction: each time Pellew jumped up to clutch his hat and stick in a spasm of nervousness. The screech of brakes, the jolt that passed down the coaches repeated themselves in his vitals. Each time the white station palings, the lamp and the porter slid into view again he would gulp, put a hand to his tie and experience once more that sense of fatality. At the back of the station for Eleanor's home there was a group of beeches; their beautiful bare green trunks like limbs stood boldly out in the February sunshine. He stepped from the train and stood staring: they were so beautiful they were a kind of escape, yet they brought round again his yearly chagrin, his suspicion of being cheated. Then he remembered Eleanor – if he could be said to have forgotten her – and turning, saw her a few feet away, blinking, a thin colour creeping up her face.

'Hullo – Paul.'

'Eleanor . . . splendid!'

'Splendid!' They shook hands. He couldn't remember when they had last shaken hands; he supposed when they had been introduced. He looked down, sideways, at the little fiery crocuses spurting against the fence.

'I've never seen crocuses in a station before,' he said hurriedly. 'Wallflowers, of course, and stocks. I . . . some railways offer prizes . . .'

'I saw you looking at the beech trees, too,' said Eleanor, with a triumphant, informed little air, as though she had stolen a march on him. They walked down the platform together towards the barrier. They each told themselves that they must avoid any show of emotion with people, Eleanor's neighbours, about – but *wasn't* Spring . . . As Paul tasted the air and coming out on to the road saw the pale fields washed over with sunshine, with knolls of trees rising here and there like islands, he tingled. He hated constraint – this business, this effort ahead. He wished he could have come down and spent the day here alone. Eleanor wore – as a kind of symbol – a straw hat, new-looking, pulled down over her eyes, but her shoes were wintry, heavily covered in mud; she had splashed mud over her ankles up to the edge of her skirt. In spite of being so thin she looked womanly and capable, a regular country girl, and he couldn't believe he had held her crushed in his arms, helpless. London altered her, he could only suppose.

She walked fast, swinging along with a stick. She was embarrassed and silent. More tentatively than by an inspiration he wheedled her into a copse by the side of the road, put his stick down and threw his arms round her. A blackbird fluted, all round little crumpled primrose-leaves were pushing up through the beech mould. She strained her face away, showing the fine line of her jaw; he felt her go rigid against him under her bulky tweed coat. 'Not here,' she cried, 'not here, don't; it's like the village people. Don't, Paul!'

It was in the country, Paul knew, that his shortcomings began to appear. He wasn't a gentleman. He wore a grey suit, but it did not look right somehow. His technique was all wrong; he should not go further than Chiswick or Richmond – unless to the Continent. He reached for his stick philosophically. 'As a matter of fact, my dear,' he said, startled to frankness, 'there seemed nothing to say.'

She emerged from the copse ahead of him, cautiously, and went on rapidly down the road.

Down the avenue Eleanor's mother came strolling to meet them. Paul braced himself. His position was perfectly simple, he was Mr Pellew, a friend of the Jennings' (Eleanor's friends in town). He had met Eleanor with them. He just happened to be in this part of the world, seeing churches. He had suggested himself to luncheon and they had sent him a friendly reply.

'Seeing churches' – Eleanor's mother beamed on his cultivation. Diffuse yet stately, she had Eleanor's fine hardness with an alloy, melted over the edge of the mould, running into a form of its own, a privileged kind of formlessness. Little girls – they resolved themselves into three – came running out of the bushes and slung themselves on to Eleanor's arms. Young sisters.

They brought with them out of the bushes some kind of a gummy smell; twigs and little pieces of young leaf clung to their reefer coats and their pigtails. 'Scaramouches!' said their mother, contented. They stared at Paul politely but indifferently, as though he did not come into their world at all. Paul thought: he would show them. He wondered whether it would be big-boyish and popular – brotherly – if he were to tweak their pig-tails but he dared not; these were not town little girls; one never quite knew.

Eleanor seemed pervaded all at once with an anxious vexation. She kept glancing sideways – across him – at her mother's profile. She pulled little bunches of grey buds off the flowering currant trees and crumbled them between her fingers.

'You live in London,' said Eleanor's mother positively.

'I suppose in a kind of way I do.'

'So much going on there,' sighed Eleanor's mother with a polite affectation of chagrin. 'One's terribly out of it . . . Patsey, run on and look for Aunt Tatty. I can't think where she's gone to' – A child sped away – 'Mr Pellew will be hungry. Do you write about churches?'

'Mr Pellew doesn't write at all,' said Eleanor sharply.

'So many people nowadays do.' The mother wrinkled her brows up; she had got him all wrong, he wasn't an author at all; now there would be all this fearful business of readjustment. She turned to Paul with a gesture and laughed despairingly, confidentially, lovably. He laughed back, the remaining little girls tittered. Still laughing, they passed round the bend of the avenue into sight of the house.

The sun struck full on the square façade and in at the windows, which with their blinds half down had an appearance of blinking. Tufts of winter jasmine grew at the foot of the steps that went steeply and massively up to the open hall-door. Two puppies asleep at the top twitched, yawned, stretched and came bounding down curved like bows. They made straight for Paul and jumped up; they remained on their hind legs, propping their rigid fore-paws against his knees, grinning ineffably. 'Nice fellows then, nice boys,' said Paul, brushing them off politely.

'Don't they give you a welcome – dogs do *know*,' said Eleanor's mother.

'I should be sorry to think they did,' said Paul genially. He looked sideways at Eleanor, who stiffened. She said with just old stimulating perversity, that inflection . . . 'As a matter of fact, Mr Pellew doesn't care for animals.'

'Fancy!' said Eleanor's mother.

She wandered about the drawing-room, from table to table, showing him bowl after bowl of spiky leaves. He wandered after her. 'Hyacinths?'

'Oh no; I hate the waxy smell. They're unhealthy, I always think. These are tulips – muscari – daffs. They'll be out in a week. I had early tulips by Christmas.'

'Had you really? Eleanor, you are terribly un-exotic.'

Eleanor had taken her hat off; she showed her crisp, light-brown hair brushed sideways across her forehead, her thin face with the jaw a shade prominent, the nose so adorably crooked, her dark, rather deep-set eyes; her whole expression eager, serious, immature. Her smile, which came doubtfully, was also a little crooked; this crookedness lent it the air of a greater complexity than her nature possessed, of ruefulness, of subtle uncertainty, of the constant re-weighing of values. She was slender and strong-looking; she stooped.

She smiled when he said she was un-exotic. 'Nobody said I was.'

'That's what's so — '

' – Oh, please hush! I don't think the door's shut.' He shut it; the feeling of being shut in together evidently frightened her. 'Do remember,' she said, 'you're just someone who's come to lunch. Do be natural – like anyone of that sort would be. And don't – don't *look* at me, Paul. You make me so ashamed and uncomfortable.'

'Ashamed?'

'Oh, it's not that mother would notice, but it seems all wrong here. You see this is my home, Paul, and it's me too, what I've always been . . . Do open the door again. It's so . . . well, you know. Shutting ourselves in. I'm only supposed to be showing you the bulbs and the Bartolozzi.'

'Ah yes,' he said, 'and I haven't seen the Bartolozzi, have I?' He made no attempt to open the door again, so she opened it herself, doggedly.

'Then I can't really see,' he said in a low voice, 'why I've come down at all. You won't hear of my having it out with them all; you won't let me touch you — '

She winced. 'You don't understand,' she said. 'It was different in London. But here – I do hate feeling . . . common.'

'I'm sorry,' he said, 'I'm a man, you're a woman. Love is rather common, I dare say.'

'Don't be so intellectual!' she said bitterly. 'Do be more human – and give us all time. Can't you do what you promised? Make friends with them all. Be something more than just a man. Make mother feel you're real. Be jolly with the children, like the other men who come here.' ('Evidently,' thought Paul, 'I *ought* to have tweaked their pig-tails.') 'Then tell mother yourself about us – when she's had time to see for herself.'

'Everything?'

'Of course not – it would sound terrible put into words. I think mother would die. Just say you began to like me when I was in London.' She stood with her face turned away from him, listening distractedly all the time for a possible step in the hall, speaking confusedly.

'So you're ashamed, on the whole, of what happened in London?'

'It seems so unreal. It's got no background. It isn't what one could possibly build up one's life on.'

They heard steps at last, coming downstairs and beginning to cross the flagstones. Eleanor brought out a bundle of knitting from behind a cushion and sat down, swinging her legs, on the end of the sofa, with her shoulders clad in a fluffy blue jumper hunched forward a little. She frowned at her work like a schoolgirl, chaste and negative. Paul wheeled round to study the Bartolozzi engravings which, more than a dozen, hung in a pattern all over one wall. Chintz-covered chairs were drawn up to the fireplace in a semi-circle; the women of the family would sit thus, looking up at the mantelpiece where the men, the brothers killed in the war, the dead father, the brother in India, stood lined up in their silver frames, staring out at nothing frankly and fearlessly. The family jaw repeated itself. The pendulum of the Dresden clock swung lazily, the fire rustled, Eleanor's needles clicked.

'"One's life",' he impatiently thought. 'This is living, O Daughter of the House, this is how time passes, this is how you approach death!'

A lady with white hair piled up on her forehead came in, preceded by one dog and followed by another. She glanced at Pellew a moment, penetratingly over her rimless glasses. 'Eleanor,' she said in a deep voice, 'you haven't introduced this Mr Pellew to your Aunt Tatty.'

Eleanor hated, evidently, this failure in social alertness. Aggrieved, she performed the introduction. 'Mr Pellew,' she added, 'is a friend of the Jennings'.'

'I know, I know,' said Aunt Tatty; 'you told me that twice. I'm not such an old lady.' She ran her eyes over him candidly, so intelligently that he shifted his attitude. He felt for the first time that morning in touch with a fellow-being, at once on guard and at ease. 'I hear,' said she, 'that all you friends of the Jennings', their what they call "set", are remarkably clever and modern. Splendid for Eleanor – I should be quite out of touch. Do you care for the country?'

Paul looked out of the window for reference. 'Depends,' he said guardedly.

'I daresay,' said Aunt Tatty, and glanced at his knees. 'Too bad, the dogs have been jumping up. You should control your dogs, Eleanor, they are impossible. We shall never have modern visitors . . . Dogs,' she added, in explanatory aside, 'are a habit, I think.'

Lunch went through with strands of talk spun out fine till they dwindled to thin little patches of silence. Pellew, his back to the fire, sat between two young sisters and Eleanor watched him. 'Have you got a pony?' 'Oh no, we ride horses . . . ' 'Isn't that pretty!' (pointing to a coloured prism falling from the water-jug).

'What, that? Haven't you seen one before?' 'The colours . . . ' 'I
don't care for violet,' said the younger sister, wrinkling up her
nose. 'Do you keep rabbits?' 'We did, but they died. Do you?' 'I
used, but they died too.' 'Oh! I didn't know men kept rabbits.'
'That was when I was a little boy.' 'Oh.' They were here to eat not
to talk and they turned from him politely and finally. 'All their
lives,' thought Paul, 'they'll go on eating slabs and slabs and slabs
of roast mutton . . . '

Eleanor's mother came in to lunch with a pile of literature which
she placed on the table beside her. She kept fingering leaflets. She
was longing to talk to Aunt Tatty about the Women's Institute.
Every now and then she would draw a long breath and lean over
vaguely towards her sister-in-law. He could see thought struggling
up from the depths of her mild eyes. Then she would recollect him.
She kept 'bringing him in'. 'It is a great movement,' she told him,
'a great movement. Here, we have taken up basket-work. We are
so keen. But I don't suppose,' she faltered, her eyebrows knitted
again in despair at herself, 'that you'd know very much about
basket-work! One gets so absorbed – terrible. It isn't like architecture. Do talk to me about churches. It would be lovely to
know . . . '

Aunt Tatty listened impartially. She sat with her shoulders a little
shrugged, the weight of her body tilted; when she was not eating it
seemed that, below the edge of the table, her hands were clasped on
her knees and she were leaning upon them. She looked round at her
relations as though she had not yet wholly identified herself with
them, still had the faculty of seeing them. Yet she had an air of
being permanently among them; she didn't exert herself. Whenever
Paul looked at her she always seemed to be looking at Eleanor. She
was a stoutish, aristocratic old lady in a 'good' black. During a
longer pause than usual, while the mother fingered her leaflets and
Eleanor stared at her plate, she said to Pellew:

'Do tell us about the Jennings.'

Ursula Jennings (Maltby before her marriage) had been a school
friend of Eleanor's. He thought of her as a dark young woman, at her
ease everywhere, emphasizing without declaring herself, reserved,
daring, patronizing, subtle, discreet. Indescribable. He didn't, as a
matter of fact, care for Ursula Jennings. He had 'owed her one' for
her manner ever since that first evening, with Eleanor. He didn't
believe she cared for Eleanor really. He had always known William
and couldn't at the moment, from sheer nervousness, visualize
him. Fattish . . . sceptical? Good on Venetians – seventeenth
century? That wouldn't say anything *here*. He put himself into the
Jennings' drawing-room, determined to build them both up from
the outside, detail by detail, but all he saw was Eleanor getting up

from a gold chair under the red lacquer lamp, uncertainly, with her curiously square, pale face; thin, awkward, serious, eager, to hold out her hand to him. He felt startled, a little angry as though someone had touched him, and said in an abrupt voice:

'I haven't seen anything of them lately.'

Eleanor's mother put down a brochure on rabbit-keeping. 'But surely . . . ' she objected, 'Eleanor said you'd been there so much.'

'I mean, not since then.'

'That was only three weeks ago,' said Eleanor's mother, gently informative, smiling.

'In London, I expect,' said Aunt Tatty, 'people who are all friends, who are "a set", see each other almost every day.' She twinkled her spectacles at Pellew and smiled knowingly.

Pellew, standing in the open door at the top of the steps, waved an arm at some trees and exclaimed, 'Those are – splendid!' They did not, it is true, burn in like the station trees – he was tired now and could not receive impressions so sharply. These were not bare beech, stretching up full in sunshine, but elms with the sun behind them. A slight wind, imperceptible in the shelter of the house, tossed their branches so that the sky behind them twinkled. It was towards the end of the afternoon; the wheels went round more easily but he drooped, he could feel them all drooping, with social fatigue. They had paraded the garden and the paddocks; feeling high-pitched, he kept pulling them up to indicate and exclaim at what nobody else saw.

'Yes, that's our barn roof – that's moss makes it so green. Yes, isn't it green. What were you going to say?'

'Nothing. Only it's *so* green. With that light on it.'

'Yes, it is green . . . ' After a little glance across at each other, a slight pause, they would pass on.

Embarrassment kept prevailing. Pellew felt an awful bounder. He wasn't used to being entertained, he kept initiating, he couldn't go properly passive. He tried to make his mind slack as an empty sack to be trailed along, but he couldn't; there was something in it that kept catching on things, bumping. He walked between Eleanor and her mother (Aunt Tatty had stayed in the house to write letters). They hesitated along the garden borders, stopping, lifting here and there a leaf with the point of a walking-stick and bending down to peer under it. Meanwhile he stood behind them and yawned, stretching his whole being. He looked along the espaliers, up at the brick walls, down at the turned soil and blunt-tipped enamelled noses of young plants poking up through it, and yawned again. 'Life,' he thought, 'life!' Gravely Eleanor picked him a crocus which he gravely put in his button-hole. She walked bare-headed with her bare hands deep in her coat-pockets; keeping close beside her he slipped his fingers into a pocket and touched her wrist. Feeling the muscles contract in a shiver he thought with surprise: 'So she loves me!'

Now they were back on the steps again; her mother had gone in murmuring something, sighing. 'Those trees . . . ' he repeated, pensively, with a kind of inspiration to the inept.

Eleanor said at last, 'I suppose we *feel* the country; we don't — '

'Aestheticize about it?'

'You do rather, don't you.' Absently and kindly, like a sister, she put a hand on his shoulder and leant a little upon it. 'I do care for you,' she said frowning at the elm trees. 'It's so difficult, isn't it? Don't be discouraged.'

'I thought *you* were. I should have liked so much to have kissed you – just once.'

'Do I seem awfully different?' she asked wistfully.

He looked back over his shoulder into the hall. All round the doors stood ajar letting in panels of afternoon light; in the drawing-room window, Aunt Tatty was at a writing-table, silhouetted against a strip of sunny lawn. Loyal to Eleanor's privacy, it was for him to say rapidly, 'Hush!' She drew into herself, the hand slipped from his shoulder, there flitted across her face an expression of disappointment. He had rebuffed her.

'If you'd care,' she said with an effort, 'I'll show you the church. You may as well see *one* church, I suppose,' she added, smiling unhappily. 'Do you know, Paul, till your letter came I hadn't had to tell a lie for three years. I remember the last quite distinctly; it was something to do with Aunt Tatty's coffee, when we were abroad. I hate lying – I wish I were not such a coward . . . Would you dare, do you think, after all, speak to mother tonight?'

She was taking him to the church by a way of her own; down an overgrown track through a thicket. He went ahead, parting the interlaced branches of hazel and willow and holding them back for her. They walked unsteadily over tussocks of pale, wintry grass and desiccated bracken. 'I'm afraid,' he objected, 'we've made that rather difficult, now. Are you so certain, then, that they like me?'

She didn't answer, only stared at him.

'You see,' he said gently, 'I'm not at all their sort. I'm not your sort, really. I'm afraid you'll have to get used to the idea of their not liking it.'

'It's hard at present, naturally. We're not in the way of new people.'

'I'm too new. There's nothing to go on. I'm all in a void. I'm a phenomenon for them.'

'Paul — '

He strode on a few feet ahead of her, speaking over his shoulder, pressing his way through the branches. She cried his name again, and as he gave no sign of hearing came hurrying after him. 'I do care, I do!' she exclaimed with a catch in her voice; 'I feel in a thicket everyway. Yet I have been happy; I came back from town feeling dazed. I prayed you might write, though I'd made you swear you wouldn't. Paul, I'm yours, honestly – look at me.'

He stepped back and put his arms round her, not ardently as he had done in the morning but with a queer mixture of diffidence and desperation. He caught one passionate and frightened look from her eyes before she closed them. 'Now we're alone,' he said, 'listen to me, Eleanor. How do you feel . . . Wouldn't you come back to town with me now, come abroad, and we'd write to them from there? Married – I meant married. It's nothing desperate we both want to do, after all; I wouldn't be spoiling your life – a life's what I want to give you. I've made myself some sort of a place in the world, I've a good deal of money. They'd get used to me afterwards. Wouldn't you come?'

'Why like that, why — '

'It's the only chance. Oh, I'm not so uncivilized really. I'd wait any time, please anyone, if I were sure of you at the end. But I couldn't be, all this is sapping us. At the end of some more of these days there wouldn't be anything of us left. We have been real people – we *are* real people, at the back of us – somewhere. And you're great; it's that that I've felt in you. Don't make life an affair of behaviour – you try but it isn't.'

'What is it then?'

'I don't know – why make it anything? – let it make you something. Will you come back with me?'

'Why must I come?' she cried miserably. 'It's not fair to make me decide. I don't know what's real; all today I've been absolutely bewildered. It's so difficult. I can't even imagine mother – afterwards. It might kill her, or she might hardly be worried a bit — '

' – All tomorrow,' he said, 'they'll be pulling me to pieces gently. They won't even know they're doing it, but there will be nothing left of me – and nothing in you could survive it. They couldn't tell you a thing about me I haven't told you myself, but to hear them say it would absolutely finish me for you. We wouldn't see each other again. You must decide. I felt today: this is going to be the crisis, I felt it as soon as I saw you there on the platform, more when we met your mother, most of all when we came into the house. "Think what your brothers would have thought" – that would be your mother's last shot. I shouldn't have got on well with your brothers, Eleanor.'

'I do like you for saying that – but I think you're wrong.' She added in a matter-of-fact voice, as though the ideas had followed each other in natural sequence: I'm coming with you – only look, Paul, what shall I do? – I haven't a hat.'

He was so much startled, he laughed aloud. She smiled, and they stood staring at one another, transformed by this one wild moment. The afternoon light came slanting on to them through the branches, they were trellised over with thin definite shadows which moved to and fro, to and fro as the branches tossed. The thicket closing round them with its damp, mossy smell, its tunnels of blue shadow, might have been a forest through which they were roving unhampered. He cried 'Beautiful!' and they kissed spontaneously and eagerly, as though meeting again. With her hands on his shoulders she looked about her triumphantly, at her lover, at the trees, as though she were having her own way at last, as though this idea had been hers and only the opposition had come from him. 'I can't go back to the house,' she said; 'I must buy a hat on the way. I'll wait here and you walk down to the village, to the Green Man, and hire a car. There are new people there who won't know me. Then we can drive to the junction. We can't go up by the slow train, feeling like this, and it wouldn't do to wait about at our station. Don't let's lose time, Paul. Come quickly.'

'Where does this path lead? Where are we going?'

It was a short cut that bisected the avenue some yards ahead. She slipped an arm through his own and was hurrying him along; she no longer smiled; she looked very serious and exalted. Her profile, the hair blown back from her forehead, made him feel he was running away with a Joan of Arc. They stumbled over the tussocks; in his hurry he stepped on the first primrose he'd seen that year, deep down in its leaves in the middle of the path. He did not realize how close they were to the avenue till Eleanor, without caution, had hurried him half way across it. Then he glanced to his left, stopped dead and said softly, 'Done in.'

Aunt Tatty, strolling from the direction of the house, had hailed them and was cheerfully waving.

'Having a look round the place?' called Aunt Tatty.

Eleanor, also turning, took her hand from Paul's arm and vaguely stared at her approaching aunt. She seemed less confused than utterly taken aback. Aunt Tatty advanced without embarrassment; possibly she had seen nothing. She wore an astrakhan coat and a decided-looking felt hat; grey Shetland muffled the amplitude of her chin.

'Don't you feel cold, Eleanor, wandering about without a hat? Seems to me it's turned chilly. I'm just taking your mother's letters and mine to post, for the sake of the walk – Will you come with me?' she turned to Pellew. 'I could show you the post-office.

Pretty, but not much in the way of architecture – Eleanor, your mother's been looking for you.'

While Paul watched, something in Eleanor faded. As though at the suggestion from Aunt Tatty she shivered faintly and turned up her coat-collar. 'Don't go!' he said sharply and clumsily. 'You promised,' he insisted, holding her eyes, 'to show me the church.'

She looked blank. 'I think, Mr Pellew,' interposed Aunt Tatty, 'that while Eleanor's mother is looking for her we mustn't detain Eleanor.'

'In half an hour I'll be at the church,' said Eleanor, and, without looking again at her aunt or her lover, walked away in the direction from which Aunt Tatty had come.

Pellew wondered if just such blind black moments as this preceded murder. He found himself moving forward numbly, sucked in the wake of the stout lady. She was in full sail again, with the invulnerable complacency of a man-of-war. Yet at the very crisis of his sickness and anger there was something grateful in this contact after the aloofness and erratic fires of Eleanor.

'Fancy not having looked at the church yet,' Aunt Tatty was observing; 'wasn't that what you came for? But of course,' she went on, 'one could see that it wasn't that. You two are in love with each other, aren't you?'

Pellew began laughing awkwardly, with self-derision. 'Were we so unnatural?'

'I could guess beforehand – Eleanor is quite transparent. It occurred at once to her mother, even, although she, as I dare say you noticed, is a good deal vaguer than I am. Churches,' sniffed Aunt Tatty – 'of all the childish inventions – *Churches!*'

'I'm an architect by profession, you know,' said Pellew stiffly.

'Oh, I dare say you may be,' said Aunt Tatty, and looked at him keenly. 'But that doesn't explain, you know, why you couldn't be more direct with us. Why you couldn't have declared yourself frankly, or have let Eleanor confide in her mother – You *do*, I suppose, mean to marry her?' she sharply added.

'Of course,' said Pellew, surprised by her manner, by her queer alternations of irony and bustle. 'But I do, of course, anticipate trouble. Well, as you noticed at once, I'm not Eleanor's sort. Not any of your sort. I feel up against so much in her here that I never suspected. If I'd guessed what it was going to be like here, I wouldn't only have *funked* coming down, I wouldn't have come at all — '

'Wisest not, perhaps — ' said Aunt Tatty.

'All my feeling is for her as a woman. Socially, I find her difficult. Socially, she seems to find me impossible.'

'Really – is that really so, now?' Aunt Tatty said eagerly.

Suddenly flushed, she seemed annoyed all at once by the warmth of her muffler, which she loosened with quick little tugs, poking out her pink chin impatiently over the folds.

'Not an easy basis for marriage,' she said dogmatically, with a queer note of triumph. '*I* didn't marry on that,' she informed him, '*I* wouldn't. And I might have at one time, there were a good many reasons . . . besides some affection on both sides. But I didn't. Later on, I married much better. Of course I had plenty of opportunities. Which is more,' said the Aunt complacently, 'than Eleanor may have.'

'That does make a difference.'

His irony was lost upon her preoccupation. 'I have sometimes wondered — ' she began, then suddenly broke off.

'Really?'

'I was rather wild at one time,' admitted Aunt Tatty. 'Intellectually, I mean,' she qualified hastily, touching the brim of her hard hat. 'I hesitated; I suppose I was quite unhappy. He was nothing socially; quite young, but there was promise – brilliancy. But the promise,' cried Aunt Tatty triumphantly, 'didn't fulfil itself. I'd been right all along. He went downhill in every way – rapidly.'

'Disappointed, perhaps?'

'Faugh!' said Aunt Tatty. 'One disappointment! . . . So you see I've had nothing to regret. There's no protection in life like a lack of courage. I've been a happy woman, Mr Pellew.'

Something unreal in her tone, some lack of simplicity, made him say with a touch of impertinence, 'You are to be congratulated.' They were approaching the lodge gates. 'Come out into the open,' she said, sardonic and genial, 'take your chances.'

'Which, quite frankly,' he said, 'you think are the worst in the world?'

'In so far as Eleanor is my niece, they'll be as bad as I know how to make them. In so far as you're a clever modern young man whom I quite like – well, I couldn't wish you anything better than to be clear of the lot of us. In so far,' she concluded, wistfully genuine, 'as my own curiosity is concerned (for I tell you, I *have* sometimes wondered –) I shall be sorry to see the end of this so soon. I should like to see what became of you both – though I'm perfectly certain, of course, how it must end, your marriage.'

'So you'll fight me over it?'

'Certainly.'

'By conviction?'

'By conviction,' she assented, loudly and definitely; a sharp sigh heaved up the lapels of astrakhan coat.

'Fairly?'

Silently, she handed him her letters. He took them and pushing through the lodge gates crossed the road and slipped them into the postbox. He stood a moment more with his back to her, mustering his forces, before he dared to turn round. She had remained leaning back on her walking-stick, watching his every movement, taking him in, measuring him with intensity. 'Fairly?' he asked again, coming back, raising his voice to be heard above a sudden clamour of rooks. He stared straight with some kind of a pang, a sharp conflict of confidence and antagonism, into her hard vivid face. She had touched the man in him.

'Yes,' said Aunt Tatty with a little laugh and braced herself, 'Fairly.'

'Then come back to the house,' he said. 'There is something I must say, at once, to Eleanor's mother.'

Dead Mabelle

THE sudden and horrible end of Mabelle Pacey gave her a publicity
with the European press worth millions to J. and Z. Gohigh of
Gohigh Films Inc., Cal., U.S.A. Her personality flashed like a
fused wire. Three-year-old films of Mabelle – with scimitar-curves
of hair waxed forward against the cheeks, in the quaint creations of
1924 – were recalled by the lesser London and greater provincial
cinemas. *The Merry Magdalene* – Mabelle with no hair to speak of,
in a dinner jacket – was retained for weeks by the 'Acropolis' and
the 'Albany', wide-porticoed palaces of the West End; managers of
the next order negotiated for it recklessly and thousands had to be
turned away during its briefer appearances in Edinburgh, Dublin
and Manchester. The release of her last, *Purblind*, was awaited
breathlessly. Her last, when brimming with delighted horror,
horrified delight, with a sense of foreknowledge as though time
were being unwound from the reel backwards, one would see all
Mabelle's unconsciousness under the descending claw of horror.
Nothing she had ever mimicked could approach the end that had
overtaken her. It was to be, this film, a feast for the epicure in
sensation; one would watch the lips smile, the gestures ripple out
from brain to finger-tips. It was on her return from the studio at the
end of the making of this very picture that she had perished so
appallingly.

The management of the Bijou Picturedrome at Pamsleigh considered themselves fortunate in having secured *The White Rider*, a
1923 production. Since dusk, on a framework erected above the
façade of the Picturedrome, green electricity scrawled 'Mabelle' in
the rainy sky. She was with them for three nights only; the habitués
streamed in; uncertain patrons, pausing under her superscription,
thumbed the edge of a florin, looked up and down the street, and
when the metal ticket finally clicked out, dived still two-thirds
reluctant into the stifling tunnel of tobacco fumes and plush. From
half-past five, for half an hour before the first showing, the
entrance curtain never settled down into stillness; at half-past eight
another rush began.

William Stickford's afternoon at the Bank went by distractedly.

He was intelligent, solitary, self-educated, self-suspicious; he had read, without system, enough to trouble him endlessly; text-books picked up at random, popular translations, fortnightly publications (scientific and so on) complete in so many parts, potted history and philosophy – philosophy all the time. On walks alone or lying awake in the dark he would speculate as to the nature of reality. 'What am I – but *am* I? If I am, what else is? If I'm not, is anything else? *Is* anything . . . ' He would start awake, sweating, from a nightmare of something that felt like an empty barrel rolling over the ups and downs in his brain and bumping into craters that were the craters of the moon, or of going round to the house where he lived to pay a surprise call on himself and being sent away with a head-shake, told point-blank he had never been heard of here. Sometimes – an idle but anguishing sport of the mind – he told himself he was the victim of some practical joke on the scale of the universe of which everybody and everything, from the stars and the Manager to the pipe-cleaners, tooth-soap and bootlaces fringing his existence, were linked in furtive enjoyment.

He never 'went with a girl'; his landlady deplored this; to do so, she said, would make him more natural-like. She liked a young fellow to *be* a young fellow, and William apparently wasn't. His Manager, a kind unperceptive old man who believed in the personal touch, asked him up for a musical evening to meet his nieces, but William achieved being shy and aggressive, looked askance round the side of his glasses, snubbed the nieces and couldn't relax with the Manager. The girls discouraged their uncle from asking him home again. A fellow at the Bank called Jim Bartlett succeeded in knowing him up to a point; *he* couldn't get Jim quite into focus but he supposed he liked him all right. Jim would force his way in of an evening, paw his books with a snigger of admiration and sit with his feet on the fender and the soles of his boots steaming till twelve o'clock, till one's brain went stiff and dry Theoretically, William needn't have listened, but he did listen; other existences tugged at him with their awful never-dismissable, never-disposable of possibility, probability even. Sometimes Jim forced him out. William was cinema-shy, he resisted the cinema till a man with important-looking initials mentioned it in a weekly review as an 'art-form'; then he went there with Jim and saw Mabelle. 'I can't think,' Jim had said, that first evening, impatiently gathering up his change at the box-office, 'how a lot of this girl's stuff ever gets past the censor.' William expected Mabelle's appeal to be erotic and went in armoured with intellectuality, but it was not erotic – that *he* could see.

The film had begun; with a startled feeling he had walked down the tilted gangway towards Mabelle's face and the dark-and-light glittering leaves behind. A caption: 'Can't you believe me?' then a close-up: Mabelle's face jumped forward at him, he stepped back on to Jim's toe and stared at a moon-shaped white light in an eye, expecting to see himself reflected. He stood for a moment, feeling embraced in her vision. 'Confound you!' said Jim and pushed him sharp to the left. They waded through to their places; William sat down, shaken, and put up a hand to his eyes. 'It's beastly jumpy,' he said, 'I always heard they were jumpy.'

'You get used to them – Gosh, what a lovely girl, isn't she? – Look at that, old man, look at that for a figure!'

It had been all very abstract, he recognized in it some hinterland of his brain. He understood that passion and purity, courage, deception and lust were being depicted and sat there without curiosity, watching Mabelle. That was some five months ago, before her death; she had long been known to the connoisseur, but her real vogue was only then beginning. She had an unusual way with her, qualities overlapped strangely; in that black-and-white world of abstractions she alone moved in a blur. Each movement, in unexpected relation to movements preceding it, outraged a pre-conception. William sat with an angry, disordered feeling as though she were a rising flood and his mind bulrushes. She had a slow, almost diffident precision of movement; she got up, sat down, put out a hand, smiled, with a sparklingly mournful air of finality, as though she were committing herself, and every time William wanted to rise in his seat and say 'Don't, don't – not before all these people!' Her under lids were straight, she would lean back her head and look over them. Her upper lids arched to a point, she had three-cornered eyes; when her face went into repose the lids came down slowly, hiding her eyes for moments together. When she looked up again that dark, dancing, direct look came out as it were from hiding, taking one unawares. It was as though she leaned forward and touched one.

William, who suffered throughout from a feeling of being detained where he had no business, was glad when the film was over. He said on the way home, 'She's awfully different from what I expected, I must say.' Jim Bartlett responded 'Aha?' He kept saying 'Aha!' with an infinite archness and refusing to volunteer much about Mabelle himself. 'She's got temperament,' was the most William got out of him. 'You know what I *mean*; temperament. Jolly rare thing. She ought to play Irish Storm in *The Green Hat*.' That night it was William who wanted to bring Jim in and keep him talking. Not that Jim's ineptitudes were any more tolerable, but he had a feeling of someone at home in him, in possession, very assured in the darkness, mutely and sardonically waiting till he was alone.

A week or so later he saw in the local paper that *The Fall*, featuring Mabelle, was showing at Belton, ten miles off. Eluding Jim, he bicycled that same evening over to Belton. He pedalled furiously, mounting the steep sleek high-road over the ridge, his brain a cold clamour of self-curiosity. Enlightened shamefully, burning, he bicycled home in the teeth of an icy wind. Next morning, cornered by Jim's too pressing inquiries, he lied as to where he had been. It had been Jim's fault, he shouldn't have asked him.

Thought, as he understood thought, became pale and meaning-less, reading scarcely more than a titillation of the eye-balls. Lapses appeared in his work. He was submerged by uneasiness, alter-nately, as it were, straining after a foot-fall and slamming a door.

There was this thing about Mabelle: the way she made love. She was tired, oh fearfully tired. Her forehead dropped down on the man's shoulder, her body went slack; there seemed no more hope for her than for a tree in a hurricane. When her head fell back in despair, while the man devoured her face horribly, one watched her forgotten arm hang down over his shoulder: the tips of the fingers twitched. What was she thinking about, what did women think about – *then*?

One night Jim Bartlett, routing about among William's posses-sions, pulled out the *Picturegoer* from between some books and the wall. On the cover Mabelle, full length, stood looking sideways, surprised and ironical, elegantly choked by a hunting-stock, hair ruffled up as though she had just pulled a hat off, hand holding bunched-up gauntlets propped on a hip. Jim, shocked into im-passivity, stared at the photograph. His pipe sticking out at an angle from his expressionless face reminded William of a pipe stuck into a snowman.

'Pretty photograph, isn't it?' said William aggressively, to shatter the bulging silence.

Jim removed his pipe thoughtfully. 'Upon my word,' he began, 'upon my *word*! You really *are* you know. I mean really, old man — '

'I got it for you, as a matter of fact. If you hadn't gone messing about I'd have — '

'Oo-hoo,' said Jim, 'we don't think. No, *don't* think — '

'Then don't think. And damn you, get out!'

They were always very polite to each other at the Bank; there was little coarse talk or swearing. Jim Bartlett was very much shocked and went home. Next morning William apologized. 'Say nothing more about it, old man,' said Jim nicely. 'I quite under-stand. Beg yours, I'm sure. If I'd had any idea you were going to take it like that — ' Good-feeling made him perfectly goggle-eyed.

He came round punctually that same evening to hear all about it. William was out; he remained out till half-past eleven. He did this three evenings successively, avoiding Jim at the Bank, and after that Jim didn't come any more.

If William had been open and manly about the business, as pal to pal, Jim Bartlett would have been discretion itself. As it was, in the course of events, he told all the other fellows. They told the Manager's nieces, who told the Manager: the Manager soon had occasion to speak to William seriously about work and excessive cinema-going. This concentration of interest upon him, of derision, hardened him outwardly, heightened his sensibility. He avoided the 'Bijou' at Pamsleigh, the 'Electra' at Belton, but took excursion tickets to London and saw Mabelle there. Expeditions to the remoter suburbs were often necessary, he would sup or take tea dazedly in gas-lit pastry-cooks' and wander between showings of the film through anonymous vacant streets. Life all these months rushed by him while he stood still.

William never looked at his newspaper before lunchtime; others did. One morning, coming to the Bank he was aware of a tension, of a scared shy greediness in the others' faces, of being glanced at and glanced across. Jim Bartlett came up once or twice, looked strangely, flinched off, cleared his throat and kept on beginning – 'I say . . .'

'What's up?' snapped out William, exasperated by what seemed a new form of persecution.

'Nothing much – seen the paper?'

'No.'

Jim Bartlett, driven and urgent, fidgeted round in a semi-circle under the blank and intense glare of William's glasses. 'There's something – look, come home to dinner.'

'Oh, thanks, I don't think so,' said William in the consequential sleek little voice he'd assumed. Jim tugged at the lobe of a crimson ear helplessly, shrugged a 'So be it, then', and went off.

In his sitting-room, the *Daily Mail* was propped against William's water-jug. Mabelle's name blazed out over the centre column, with 'Fearful Death'. With a sudden stillness, with a feeling of awful, extended leisure, William put out his hand for the paper. While he read he kept putting his hand up and touching his throat. Each time he did this he started as thought he had touched someone else, or someone else had touched him. He read carefully down to the end of the column, looked over the top of the paper and saw his chop slowly congealing behind it. He ran from the room and was violently sick. When this was over he took up the paper again, but he couldn't read well, the lines bulged and dipped. He waited a little to see if he was going to be sick any more, then went out and bought all the other papers. Coming out of the newsagent's he met the wind tearing down the street. He stood on the kerbstone, not knowing which way to go; the wind got into the papers and rattled and sang in them; they gave out an inconceivable volume of sound to which he believed the whole town must turn round and listen. He looked this way and that, then pressing the papers against him ran across the street and went into the church. Here he read all the other versions. Physical detail abounded. He sat for a long time crushed up to a wall in the gloom of a pew, then went back to the Bank.

Five weeks later, *The White Rider* featuring Mabelle Pacey came to Pamsleigh. 'Going?' said Jim to William, who seemed to have 'got over things' wonderfully well. 'Oh, I dunno,' said William, 'I've some work on at home' (he was doing one of those correspondence courses), 'I don't know that I've got time.'

On Monday and Tuesday he did not go to the Picturedrome; he disappeared utterly, no one knew where he had gone. The last day of Mabelle was Wednesday; Wednesday came.

The afternoon at the Bank went by, then, distractedly. Rain fell past the tall windows blurring the outlook, the trickle and stutter of drops racked the nerves. With dread, William looked up at the clock again and again, uneager as never before for release, half hoping by some resolution, some obduracy, to staunch the bleeding-away of the minutes. The door to the back passage was open for some minutes; William kept looking away from it, and while he was looking away Mabelle stood there, leaning a shoulder against the lintel, smiling and swinging a gauntlet. She was confident he would be there tonight. He faced round to the empty doorway. Mightn't she as well be *there* who wasn't anywhere? Who was not. She was incapable now of confidence, of a smile, of pressure against a lintel. He had faced for these last weeks her absolute dissolution. At that reiteration, in his mind and the doorway, of emptiness, he must have made some movement or sound, for the others looked up from their ledgers. William coughed and showed himself as in some agony of calculation; the faces dropped. The afternoon dwindled out, the office shrank in the dusk and began to be crowded with shadows. Somebody climbed on a chair with a taper; the gas coughed alight and the rain sliding and streaming down the window-panes scintillated against the thickening night. Woven securely into the room's industrious pattern William rested, but now the pattern was torn up violently into shreds of clamour and movement. They all went home. William lingered over his ledger a long time, but was finally drawn out after them.

At ten past eight he was pushing against the 'Bijou's' interior curtain. Its voluminousness, a world of plush, for some moments quenched and smothered him; a prickly contact to hands and face, exhaling a warm dankness. The attendant fought him out of it, taking away his ticket. 'Standing room only! — ' he grudged her her little triumph, he had been told that outside. He chose a place along the transverse gangway and gripped with hands still pricking from the plush a cold brass rail behind the expensive seats.

He looked down a long perspective, a flickering arcade of shadow. For twenty seconds or so there was no one – the trees' fretful movements, the dazzlingly white breaking-through of the sky. The orchestra wound off their tune with a flourish and sharply, more noticeably, were silent down in their red-lighted pit. The flutter and click of machinery streamed out across the theatre, like the terrified wings of a bird imprisoned between two window-panes – it gave him the same stretched sensation of horror and helplessness. A foreign whiteness, a figure, more than a figure, appeared; a white-coated girl on a white horse drawn sideways across the distant end of the drive. She listened, all tense, to that same urgent flutter and clicking, then wheeled the horse round and dashed forward into the audience, shadows streaming over her. William recoiled from the horse's great hammer-head, the hoofs dangerous as bells, the flick of the eyeballs. He looked up with a wrench at his being; advancing enormously, grinning a little at the moment's intensity, Mabelle looked down. They encountered. Visibly thundering, horse and rider darkened the screen.

Gripping the bar tight, William leaned back to look up at the bright, broadening shaft from the engine-room directed forward above him. Along this, fluid with her personality, Mabelle (who was now nothing) streamed out from reel to screen, thence rebounded to his perception. It was all, her intense aliveness, some quivering motes which a hand put out with intention would be able to intercept. The picture changed focus, receded; Mabelle, in better perspective, slipped from her horse and stood panting and listen-ing; the horse turned its head, listened too. Their sympathy, their physical fineness, sent a quiver across the audience. In protest, a burst of assertion, the music began again. '*Tum* – tirumti *tum* – turum ti *too*, rum ti *too* — ' Mabelle tied her horse to a tree and turned off cautiously into the forest.

The man was there, in a glade, that man she generally acted with, whom one had a dozen times watched her make herself over to, her recurring lover. He stood with his back to a tree, with a grin as of certainty, waiting for her. However much he might repel at the outset, however craven, false or overtly lustful he might show himself, he had her ultimately, he had to have her, every film. She liked her men fallible (evidently); unsympathetic to audiences, subject to untimely spasms of passion. It brought out all her coolness, her lovely desperation, her debonair fatedness. Her producer kept this well in mind. With unavailing wariness she now came stepping with her white-breeched legs, the light glancing off her riding-boots, high over the fallen trees, low under the over-hanging branches. Shadow struck off her head again and again. The man smiled, threw his cigarette away, stepped round his tree and closed with her . . . A poignant leap-back, one was shown the white horse standing, tormented by intuition, tossing its head uneasily, twitching its ears.

William had come late, the end was sooner than he expected. Mabelle in a black straight dress, in meekness and solitude, stood by a high stone mantel looking into a fire. The preceding caption was red, the light now tinged with a realistic redness. Flames, in leisurely anticipation of their triumph, spurted and leapt at her feet; the firelight fingered its way up her, crept round her arms' fine moulding, her throat, her chin, with curbed greed, assurance, affection almost. She stood there – to the eyes of that four-years later audience – dedicated. It was as though the fire knew . . . A log crashed in, she started, looked with appalled eyes away from the fire. She was waiting.

Oh, *Mabelle* . . . She was too real, standing there, while more and more of her came travelling down the air. She seemed perpetual, untouchable. You couldn't break that stillness by the fire; it could shatter time. You might destroy the film, destroy the screen, destroy her body; this endured. She was beyond the compass of one's mind; one's being seemed a fragment and a shadow. Perished, dissolved in an agony too fearful to contemplate (yet he had contemplated it, sucked meaning out till fact had nothing more to give), she returned to this, to this imperishable quietness. Oh, *Mabelle* . . .

Somewhere a door opening, light that lanced the darkness. Movement went through her like the swerve of a flame. She held her arms out, the illusion shattered, she was subject once again to destiny. William sharply turned with tight-shut eyes. He groped his way along the guiding bar, was at fault a moment, collided with the attendant looping back the curtain for the exodus. He went out slowly, into the glaring vestibule, down the three steps into the lit-up, falling rain. Rain brushed his face, drops here and there came through to the roots of his hair. He put his hat on; heard the drops, defeated, pattering on the brim.

The street, unreal as that projected scene, was wide; he hesitated half way across it, then slowly turned to the left. Behind, inside the open doors, he heard as it were a wave break, a crash of freed movement, a rasping sigh. The band played the National Anthem. Feasted with her they all came streaming out, and she, released from their attention, dismissed, dispelled now – where was she?

His way home was at an angle from the High Street, up a by-path. Water in the steep gutters hissed and gurgled. There were spaces of inky darkness, here and there some lamplight dimly caught a patch of humid wall. He looked back, once, towards the town and the Picturedrome. One moment 'Mabelle' was blazing emerald over the white façade; the next the lights were out, 'Mabelle', the doors beneath, had disappeared. So she went. In another month or so, when her horror faded and her vogue had died, her films would be recalled – boiled down, they said. He had heard old films were used for patent leather; that which was Mabelle would be a shoe, a bag, a belt round some woman's middle. These sloughed off, what of her? 'You're here,' he said, and put out a hand in the darkness. '*You* know *I* know you're here, you proud thing! Standing and looking. Do you see me? . . . You're more here than I . . . '

Going blindly, he passed within inches of a pair of lovers, plastered together speechlessly under the wall. A too urgent pressure had betrayed them by the creak of a mackintosh. Love! His exaltation shuddered at the thought of such a contact. Then for a moment under the blight of that dismal embrace, he had lost her. Mabelle . . . *Mabelle?* Ah, here . . .

Here, by him, burning into him with her actuality all the time. Burdening him with her realness. He paused again where a bicycle with lighted lamp had been leant up against some palings. The murky dark-yellow light streamed across the rain; some ghostly chrysanthemums drained of their pinks and yellows raised up their heads in a clump in it, petals dishevelled and sodden. As he watched, one stem with its burden detached itself and swayed forward, dipped through the lamplight and vanished. He listened and heard the stem snap. How – why – while the other stems stood up erect and unmoving, sustaining their burden? *Who* had — ?

Oh no, not that! He began to be terrified. 'Don't press me too hard, I can't stand it. I love you too much. Mabelle, look here – don't!' He looked beyond the chrysanthemums, left and right, everywhere. She was there, left, right, everywhere, printed on darkness.

William, at home in his sitting-room, walked about in a state of suspension, looking, without connection of thought, at his books and pictures. A clock struck twelve, it was already tomorrow. *This* morning he'd be at the Bank, back again in the everyday, no one the wiser. Now he could sleep a short time, then life, that abstraction behind the business of living, was due to begin again. *He* was alive, enclosed in a body, in the needs of the body; tethered to functions. In the gaslight it looked rather shabby, this business of living. Greasy stains on the tablecloth where he'd slopped his dinner over the edge of his plate, greasy rim round the inside of his hat where he'd sweated. This was how one impressed oneself on the material. And on the immaterial? – Nothing. Comfortless, perilous, more perishable than the brains in his skull even, showed his structure of thought. He had no power of being.

Of feeling? Only that life was worth nothing because of Mabelle who was dead. And by death, had he hope that he wouldn't quench himself utterly while Mabelle, who impinged herself everywhere, brightly burned on?

The right-hand top drawer of his bureau was empty of what such a drawer should contain: the means to the only fit gesture that he could have offered her. He had jerked the drawer open with an unconscious parade of decision, an imitation, more piteously faithful than he was aware, of something which, witnessed again and again under the spell of that constant effusion from Mabelle, had seemed conclusively splendid. The hand slipped, unfaltering into the back of the drawer, the gesture of pistol to temple, the trail of smoke fugitive over an empty screen . . .

He was denied this exit. Under the stare, vaguely mocking, of three-cornered eyes he bent down to study the note-books, the bitten pencil-stump, match-ends, attempt at a sonnet, a tie, crumpled up and forgotten, that littered the drawer.

The Working Party

COMBE FARM commanded the valley; it had a road of its own, gated across to keep the cattle from straying, that ran down past the mill and parallel with the river till it came to a full stop at the barn doors. The house was three-storied, old and solid, with an irregular line of roofs; it stood out remarkably with its group of poplars over the flat fields of the shallow and empty valley. A line of willows followed the meandering of the river.

Mrs Fisk, up at her bedroom window, could see down the road for a long way. When by twos and threes, at first very indistinctly and slowly, the Working Party came into sight her heart leapt to her mouth and she could hardly contain herself for apprehension and pleasure.

The road looked white and staring under the bright March sky; the women in their brown, black and navy afternoon dresses walked in the middle sedately. The thin unending dark line of them dotted itself away down the valley. Presently their voices began to be heard; one could see that they were carrying work-baskets. Now they began to be as conscious of Combe Farm as Mrs Fisk was of them; their eyes no longer wandered, they stopped talking and each put on a remote expression as though she were walking at large in a desert. Mrs Whales, Mrs Tuppett and Mrs Miller headed the procession; at the dim end one could recognize Miss Vincent, wobbling along on a bicycle between the cart-ruts.

The Working Party had met throughout the winter at the homes of members, turn by turn. The Lodge, the Vicarage, over the International Stores . . . Tea was provided. So far, it had not come to Combe Farm because that poor little thing Mrs Fisk had been really too recently married. Also (ostensibly) because the walk down the valley was too long for short afternoons. So she had eaten tea in all manner of parlours and had taken particular note of the way it was served. She had noted the china, the teaspoons, the doylies and saved herself up to outdo them. Then she invited the Members to meet at Combe Farm.

When at last she heard the latch of the gate click Mrs Fisk, who was twenty-one, went down on one knee for a moment by the

large mahogany bedstead and prayed that all might go off well –
nay, showily. Her husband was out with the men in some distant
fields, the farm-yard and house were quite quiet; she and the
Working Party were to be absolutely alone. She listened a moment
over the banisters, preening out the frills of her blouse, then went
downstairs jauntily.

Since before dinner she had been in a turmoil: ever so busy. For
two days she had kept the parlour fire burning to expel that uneasy
chilliness wont to settle upon the room. The parlour faced south-
east, the sun went off it early, which made it beautifully cool in
summer but in the afternoons at other times of the year a little sad.
It was a room in which she never felt comfortable but always
entirely ladylike. She picked double daffodils that had come out
under the south wall and settled them along the mantelpiece in the
ruby Bohemian goblets given her by her grandmother. The
daffodils lolling forward looked at her frowsily; she did not feel
pleased with them and wondered why she had been such a silly girl
and not gone for sprigs of flowering currant instead. It would be
just like her to do something stupid and ruin the Working Party. In
an earlier fit of self-distrust she had decided against making the
cakes herself, she had gone into town on the bus and bought
dainty-looking sugary ones with crystallized flowers – *gâteaux*. She
had been to a new shop where she paid sixpence each more for
them than anywhere else where they called them cakes. She turned
the cat off the fur rug, then coaxed it back because she remembered
that someone once said cats looked cosy. The cat came nimbling
back on the tips of its paws and looked at her scornfully. She
climbed on a step-ladder to loop back the curtains at the top and let
in more light, then she felt dizzy up there and screamed. Her
husband, who happened to be passing across the kitchen, had to come
in and help her down again. He kissed her – they had been married
so recently – but she struggled from his arms in a preoccupied
way, like a cat, and hurried away to blow dust off a fern.

He was a busy man and a farmer, his mind always wrinkled up
tight and knotted with other concerns. He went away from her
without even a sigh, he never so much as wondered . . . By
midday, when she should have been feeding the chickens, she was
still walking about the parlour, biting the tip of her tongue. She
couldn't make up her mind what to do with the table-cloth. She
knew perfectly well that the Working Party needed a bare table to
cut out on and scatter their pins over, but she couldn't bear to take off
her chenille tablecloth. It was the loveliest green with a bobbly
fringe, with a pile on it like an Axminster carpet and a sheen like
corn; when one stroked it against the light its colour deepened. She
decided to leave it there till they were all gathered round and had

had a good look at it, then whisk it off with an exclamation as though she had forgotten it. She moved a photograph of her own wedding group further forward so that they should all see her standing there with her 'sheaf' in her beautiful lace dress. She couldn't feel now, however, that her wedding-day *had* been so very important.

Phyllis the maid was down in the kitchen cutting platefuls and platefuls of bread-and-butter and sandwiches. She had never managed to cut them so thin before; she came up very much flushed to open the door for the Working Party, blowing back wisps of hair from her face and brushing the crumbs from her hands. She was stout and pink and her apron was most gratifyingly clean – Mrs Fisk stood watching her critically through the crack of the parlour door. Abruptly, with a swing of both arms, Phyllis headed the Working Party into the parlour.

All in a dream Mrs Fisk shook hands with them couple by couple and invited them to sit down. She still had a feeling that several of them must have got into the room somehow and be walking about *without* having been shaken hands with. None of them would remain sitting, more and more came in and the room became crowded and dark like a wood from the numbers of women standing up in it. The cat got up and walked away from under their feet; it would not stay still and look cosy. Mrs Fisk poked the fire, then all at once the room seemed too hot and she felt a sudden and violent need to open a window. The Vicar's wife sat down at last and this seemed a signal; in a moment or two only Mrs Fisk was left standing, her clasped hands pressed to her chin in anxiety, very conspicuous over the sea of hats like Combe Farm over the valley. They settled down with a creak and a slippery sound on the leather chairs, opened their work-baskets and stared at each other doubtfully.

'We can't get very far with the tablecloth on, Mrs Fisk,' Mrs Tuppett said warningly. She drew her long upper lip down and blinked over the top of her steel-rimmed glasses as though she had known from the first there was bound to be a hitch somewhere.

'Tck – tck – tck — ,' Mrs Skinner said patiently, looking round the room to see how different it was now and taking particular notice of the Bohemian goblets.

Mrs Fisk stood with her hands to her chin, all in a daze struggling to come out with her exclamation.

'There now!' she whispered at last with an effort. She couldn't get near the table because of the women sitting round it so closely. 'Such a *pretty* cloth,' said Miss Vincent, and, running her finger along it, admired the sheen. She said with a sigh. 'It's as soft as pussy-willows.' The clumps of pussy-willows along the valley were golden at present, yet Mrs Fisk felt somehow insulted. Miss Vincent and the Vicar's wife folded the tablecloth corner to corner and hung it over the back of a chair. 'There now!' said Mrs Fisk, again, watching them. Under the cloth the table, polished this morning, had been awaiting its moment; now it reflected the hands and faces moving above it, the square of the window, the wicker sides of the work-baskets. The basket-lids lolled from their hinges, turning up their tight plump satin-upholstered bosoms, scarlet and olive-green, bristling with pins and needles and splitting across in lines from very exuberance. The work was unfolded, scissors clattered about on the table, and now and then a reel of cotton escaped from its mistress and bowled away happily. Now that the Working Party was actually working, Mrs Fisk could not believe her eyes.

Mrs Fisk, alert as a fawn in a thicket, took up her work and began to herring-bone. Her stitches were large and eccentric, but she did not feel responsible for them. Every time she looked at her work she seemed to be missing something, yet whenever she paused with her needle up in the air and looked round her she seemed to be the only one idle. They were all very satisfied-looking and serious. She was the youngest there except for Euphemia Wolley. Euphemia sat by the fire sewing with a short thread and looking down her nose at her needle; her eyelids never so much as trembled whatever anyone said and her pale-blue felt hat was pushed to the back of her head at the most superior, I-don't-care-about-*you* kind of angle. Her needle, slanting one way with precision, zip – zip – zipped along the hem of a bed-jacket. Mrs Fisk and she had taught at the same Sunday school, and now for very spite she wouldn't so much as look round the parlour or take the least notice of anything. A flush spread slowly over her face from the tip of her nose and she seemed to despise everything that had not to do with bed-jackets. Mrs Hawke from the Lodge had the whitest neck in the world with a seed-pearl necklace nestling into a crease of it. She was so sympathetic and friendly that her face looked quite anxious and was never entirely vacant of one of its little smiles: before the last faded someone else would have said something and, though it might not be addressed to herself, Mrs Hawke never let anything pass without her own little pat at it, an understanding and tender smile. She was so nice to oneself that one was outraged at seeing her being equally nice to everyone else. She seemed to have perfect confidence in her fair waved hair which crimped out in little curtains under the sides of her hat, for she never once put up a hand to it. Mrs Fisk was determined to ask her to stay behind when the others had gone, to look round the garden – perhaps, one never knew, they might have a real talk. She only wished there were anything in the garden to offer Mrs Hawke or, for the matter of that, anything special for her to look at.

Mrs Whales was speaking; the lapels of her afternoon blouse were drawn together across her full bosom with a cameo brooch. 'I didn't think I'd be able to come today,' she told them. 'I'd been that put about over Marion. The spring brings her out in a rash all over and it makes her fretful. But I didn't like to miss a meeting, even though it *was* difficult. I haven't missed one meeting, you see.'

'Neither haven't Mrs Tuppett nor I,' said Mrs Miller.

'You *have* been splendid,' interposed Mrs Hawke. 'I only wish I had been more regular.'

'Ah well,' said the Vicar's wife indulgently.

'Well, one likes to do what one can, what I mean,' said Mrs Miller, and shook out a bed-jacket.

'I must say,' said Mrs Vincent, 'I shall be *sorry* when the meetings are over. Though I must confess,' she added mysteriously, 'that this afternoon, I very nearly turned back. Can you guess why?'

'Ah! Cows?'

Miss Vincent nodded. 'I don't seem able to get over it. Awkward, isn't it? Of course a bicycle helps; I always feel I could run round to the other side. But I've been like that ever since I was quite a tiny. I must confess, I've never been up the valley before. One would be so much alone if anything were to happen.'

'Our cows wouldn't look at you,' said Mrs Fisk scornfully. She had no use at all for Miss Vincent. 'I like them myself, they're company.' She thought, 'How like an old maid!'

Miss Vincent said eagerly, 'Oh, I dare say it is a bit lonesome for you. It's very pretty down here, but it does seem a long way from everywhere.' The others assented; they glanced nervously at the window as though they expected the solitude outside to come walking in.

Mrs Skinner gathered up her work on her knees and sat with her mouth open a moment in reminiscent silence. 'Poor Mrs Fisk that *was*,' she brought out. 'Mrs Fisk senior, couldn't keep a girl here anyhow. She often complained to me: "It's the place", she used to say. I was most intimate with your poor mother-in-law, you know, Mrs Fisk.She said to me shortly before she died, "I can't keep a girl anyhow". Of course she did the greater part of the work herself, but she needed help with the fowls. Oh, she was very much troubled latterly, poor soul. Nothing seemed to go right with her. I often said, "I do pity you, with all my heart I do". She was such a good soul – it seemed quite a happy release.'

'*I've* had no difficulties,' said Mrs Fisk and tossed her chin. The idea! She was wearing an emerald, crêpe-de-chine blouse with frills and a gold wrist-watch and must look, she knew, quite a different kind of a Mrs Fisk to William's poor mother who had petered out while *she* was still at school. Everybody looked twice at this Mrs Fisk, who was tipped with pink like a daisy on cheeks, nose and chin. A Working Party at Combe Farm in those days would have been a very different affair. 'No difficulties,' Mrs Fisk repeated firmly, and Euphemia Wolley bit off her thread with a twang.

The Vicar's wife standing up to cut out some more sleeves paused a moment to gaze at Mrs Fisk. She had yearning watery eyes, no children, and a flat, disappointed-looking figure. She had taken off her coat and stood leaning forward, in her plain shirt draped across with a watch-chain, one hand on the small of her back where the pain was, the other pulling her scissors open and shut, open and shut, like a hungry beak. She was spiritual-looking and might have been the patron saint of all the Euphemias. 'Very lucky, my dear,' said the Vicar's wife, and her tone said: 'That is not the lot of the human soul . . . that is not the lot of woman.' Then she cut out three pairs of sleeves and some pockets while the others drew in their work-baskets to give her more room on the table. Mrs Fisk, a shade chilled, felt once more like a confirmation candidate and wriggled her feet together. The clock ticked the first hour away, then broached the second. Now and then a clamour of starlings arose in the garden; later the cat caused a diversion by reappearing suddenly and getting on to Mrs Hawke's lap.

Tea was timed for four-thirty. Mrs Fisk, face to face with the clock, watched the hands jealously lest time should escape her. She once more divided the number of people into the number of cakes. She pictured the tea-tray as it ought to appear, in the doorway, being carried in. She did wonder if Phyllis would remember the silver strainer. She had never used a strainer – she and Phyllis enjoyed telling each other's fortunes from the tea leaves round the insides of their cups. She did wonder whether, after all, paper lace doylies might not look daintier under the *gâteaux* than crochet ones.

She wondered – Unable to bear separation from Phyllis at this crisis she got up with a murmur, squeezed round carefully past the back of the workers' chairs and crept from the room. She listened a moment, outside, to the imperturbable, strenuous buzzing; then, with a tremendous feeling of ownership, closed the door on her bees.

The kitchen was sunk a little into the foundations of the house at the back, half its depth below the front rooms. Eight steps went twisting down to it, at an angle, from the back of the hall. When the kitchen door at the foot was shut the steps were pitchy, it was like running down into a well. A half-moon of ground glass, very high up, strained a little light through, but this faded away in a patch on the opposite wall. Half way down Mrs Fisk, going precipitately, clutched at a banister and pulled up short so that she swung forward a little. There was (as she felt in that half moment that she should have expected) Somebody there.

A man sat on the steps below her, crumpled against the banisters. His back curled forward in a horrible way, one shoulder dropping to meet a knee that was clumsily doubled up. While she watched (perhaps because of the tug she had given the banisters) he fell together; a booted foot slid forward over the edge of a step and went clattering down the two next. The other shoulder, wedged in tightly between the banister-rails, kept the rest of his body from toppling after the foot.

'Dead,' thought Mrs Fisk, with the same sense of disgust and irritation with which she would stoop in the rainy dusk to pick up the sodden corpse of a chicken. Gathering in her skirts she crept downstairs past him, shoulder against the wall. At the bottom she pushed open the kitchen door to let in more light and looked up with peremptory anger, as though she expected the thing to account for itself. 'Dead!' she said angrily. 'There now!' It was Cottesby the cow-herd, and she saw the whole thing very lucidly. Cottesby the cow-herd, a greyish-faced man, had 'a heart'. For years he had threatened this; the idea of his end had seemed to be a companion to him. He had never liked her; he looked at her from under his cold shadow sanctimoniously and coldly. She noticed that in a last spasm he had ground his face into the banisters. His neck was twisted, his nose poked slyly out between two of the rails and the same two rails indented his forehead. 'At any moment,' thought Mrs Fisk, 'he'll come tumbling on top of me.' She stepped back into the kitchen.

Phyllis sat with her apron over her head, her fists blindly drumming on the edge of the kitchen table. There was little that Mrs Fisk did not know about hysterics; she directed herself with cold violence against the quivering bulk beneath the apron. The attack had, she realized, its justification. Phyllis had found herself cut off from the approach to the parlour by the appalling presence of Cottesby. It must have been Cottesby's intention, feeling death upon him, to seek out the Working Party for succour. He had come in by the back door and crossed the kitchen; at the foot of the stairs he had been overtaken. Mrs Fisk gave thanks to Heaven for so merciful an intervention. She snatched a water-jug, she slapped at the clawing, pink hands and heaving shoulders. Phyllis let out staccato noises like a steam-engine; she was being a thousand times more troublesome than Cottesby and it seemed a pity she had not died also. 'Shut up, you great gawky!' her mistress cried. 'Do remember the ladies!' She splashed another handful of water in Phyllis's face. 'Stay quiet, will you!' she thundered.

'I will, m'm,' said Phyllis, and hiccoughed. She was better already.

The kettle-lid leapt suddenly, a jet of white steam spouted across the kitchen. Mrs Fisk, still red with anger, recollected herself mechanically. Her silver urn and teapot stood with their lids back, open-mouthed. 'What of it?' asked Mrs Fisk, cold with defiance, and made the tea. Phyllis had finished cutting the bread and butter; the trays were ready; the *gâteaux*, violet, pink and orange, sat consciously upon their crochet mats. They looked very well. Mrs Fisk stared hard at them; she felt them communicate their composure. Nothing should wreck her.

She went to the foot of the stairs again and looked up. There was no doubt about Cottesby. His nose stuck out further than ever and a half-shut eye looked past it out of the shadows. '*You* won't run away,' said Mrs Fisk grimly, and indeed he could very well wait. Death, physically familiar enough to her, appeared at this moment supremely improper. She thought of Euphemia Wolley and set her teeth. Nothing should wreck her. She was a lucky one . . . She had told them all she was a lucky one. '*I've* had no difficulties,' she had said, and tossed her chin.

She measured out the distance between the wall and Cottesby. He had left her room to walk up past him, carrying the trays.

As the clock's hands crept down to half-past four the Working Party began to relax. The needles dawdled; many were unthreaded frankly and stuck into bosoms or work-basket lids. Garments were passed to and fro for admiration and comment; conversation languished. A dazed look came into the workers' faces, as though the afternoon were a dream; they shifted on their chairs and one or two yawned.

'Time flies, doesn't it,' said Mrs Skinner in an aggrieved voice because she wished it were more than twenty-past four. Mrs Fisk's absence seemed to her natural and encouraging; she was sitting close to the door, she listened, they all listened. Mrs Hawke, still sewing, looked up and smiled sympathetically though nobody had spoken. 'Well I must say,' confessed Mrs Whales, surprised at herself, 'I for one shall be glad of my tea.'

They heard the tea-tray, the light elegant tinkle of silver on china, cup slipping on saucer, that is like no other sound in the world. Mrs Fisk came in, arms wide, chin high over the urn. She was flushed, it was a great moment; even Euphemia looked at her. She was out of breath, her green jabot shifted as her chest went up and down, but she was perfectly calm. She explained that her Phyllis had been called away on a message. She did not seem to think that

it mattered. Everybody had seen her Phyllis, everybody knew she
had a Phyllis, nobody minded. They helped her replace the green
tablecloth.

Her teacloth had a lovely gloss on it and a six-inch border of
pillow lace; she shook it out of its folds with a gesture and laid it on
diamond-wise. She was very much at ease with them all – one
might say, patronizing. She shook back her frilly cuff to glance at
her wristwatch: half-past four to the minute. She shut the door
carefully after her when she went out for the second tray – funny,
when that gave her all the trouble of pushing it open again! When
she came back she was red and white in sudden patches, as though
her face had been painted.

'I declare,' she said ('Laughing' they remembered afterwards
'ever so'), 'I nearly tripped up on the stairs. I'm so unaccustomed to
carrying trays . . . Milk *and* cream, Mrs Hawke? . . . Mrs Rudd,
sugar?'

Once a lump slipped from the poised sugar-tongs into the
milk-jug, splashing her blouse. It was her sole misadventure. She
sat at the head of the table, under her own wedding-group. She
thought privately that *gâteaux* were the sandiest things she had ever
eaten: nothing but sponge inside with a thin acid layer of cream.
However, they were diminishing rapidly. Mrs Hawke appreciated
the yellow plum jam and might be persuaded to take a pot back
with her. Wondering whether Phyllis would break out again (she
had locked the back door and brought the key up with her so's
Phyllis couldn't escape *that* way) – wondering whether she and
William would be suspected, arrested, she kept offering everybody
more tea. Her tea-tray looked lovely, Mrs Hawke's own couldn't
beat it. Nobody else had such an artistic tea-service with garlands
of mauve wistaria. At a moment when everybody was talking she
thought she heard sounds in the back of the house. This might be
Cottesby, coming unstuck from the banisters, rolling down into a
heap by the kitchen door. She clattered the lid of the urn. Euphemia
Wolley, biting a slice of mauve *gâteau*, was staring across at her.
How Euphemia would turn up her eyes if they came in and took
one away. 'I hope that violet *gâteau* is to your taste, Euphemia?'

The Vicar's wife didn't eat cake in Lent; she had finished her tea
and she sat listening for something far off with the saddest
expression. 'I *do* so well remember dear Mrs Fisk senior,' she said in
an interval. 'I had tea with her here when I very first came, as a
bride. She had made everything on the table herself, I remember;
the bread, the butter . . . I did think her wonderful. Afterwards
she took me into her kitchen and showed me her beautiful copper
pans. Have you still got those beautiful copper pans?'

'Oh indeed yes,' said Mrs Fisk, 'Mr Fisk has had several offers for them, they are very much sought after. But Mr Fisk won't hear of parting from them, for the sake of association.'

'Association!' tittered Mrs Whales. 'Aren't they still used for preserving?'

'Very occasionally,' said Mrs Fisk with reserve, and turned her eyes down. She had an uneasy feeling as though the Vicar's wife were walking about the house in her sad way, opening and shutting doors.

'Yes, we saw a great deal of Mrs Fisk *senior*,' said the Vicar's wife. 'The Vicar was with her up to the End, you know.' The End had been in young Mrs Fisk's bed and she didn't care to dwell on it. To see the Vicar's wife sit staring and dreaming there made her feel cold all over, as though the walls were glass. Mrs Fisk saw a picture of the Vicar's wife and Euphemia composing Cottesby, laying him out on the kitchen table, gently and firmly closing that watchful eye. 'If she did lay out a corpse on my kitchen table,' thought Mrs Fisk wrathfully, 'she'd never let me forget it. She'd come in when I was rolling the pastry on it and look round in her watery way and say "Here's where we laid out dear Cottesby" . . . Her and her Mrs Fisk senior!' Two more cups came up to be refilled; she lifted the teapot and found it disconcertingly light. She tilted the urn and found it was empty.

Here was a breakdown. Half way through tea Phyllis was to have come in for the urn and refilled it from a second kettle brought to the boil meanwhile on the kitchen fire. She stared into the urn, her jaw dropping; she went numb for a moment, then she was filled all over with a horror of death. 'There's a man dead on the stairs,' she kept thinking and 'They'll each want a third cup. I've no more tea for my visitors.' Her mind ran to and fro between these two facts like a mouse between the sides of a trap. Euphemia Wolley seemed to divine the crisis; she drained her cup hastily and handed it to her next door neighbour. '*If* you please,' said Euphemia. Here was Mrs Hawke's, too, coming round. 'I never do drink more than two, but it's *so* good,' Mrs Hawke smiled, sure of conferring a pleasure.

Mrs Fisk felt sick. The whole tableful of cups seemed to take life and swim towards her, empty. 'A moment . . . ' she said indistinctly. She got up, clutching the urn by each handle and walked from the room not too steadily.

Out in the hall she groped round for a chair and in quickly gathering darkness sat down with the urn on her knees. She was struggling, she never *had* fainted. She was in terror of dropping the urn yet dared not stoop to put it down. When the blackness cleared and she saw straight again she went, shaking all over, and stood at the top of the steps. The steps turned a corner, Cottesby sat just round that corner and couldn't be seen. She listened and there, just below her, dead silent, Cottesby seemed to be listening too. She could smell his clothes, earthy and sour. She thought of his greyish nose sticking slyly out through the banisters and that eye she had seen, filled with darkness.

All at once, finally, absolutely, she was afraid to go down. The hall clock, 'Mother's clock' – 'Mrs Fisk' senior's – tick-tocked above her head, nagging at time. Behind the parlour door the voices petered out into silence; the Working Party was waiting for her, wondering what had become of her, anxiously listening.

Leaving the hall door ajar she fled, close in under the walls of the house. The first thin film of evening covered the sky; in the rickyard the pigeons fluttered and flopped: she fled through them, half mad from the outdoor silence, raising a cloud of dust and chaff. She rattled the gate, it was locked; she bundled her skirt up and climbed it. Stumbling, tottering on her high heels she fled up the valley; the cows looked after her placidly; further on, lambs fled to their mothers. Gates, wire, hedges themselves were no obstacle. The grey-green fields were uncomforting, the very colour of silence; the sky hung over the valley, from hill to hill, like a slack white sheet. The river slipped between reddening willows, sighing and shining. With the dread of her home behind her she fled up the empty valley. When she came in sight of the fields a mile from the house where her husband was working and saw men's figures dotted along the skyline, her voice, her wits, her sense of herself came back to her. Long before he could possibly hear she was calling out . . .

'*William*! Oh, come down to me, William! There's a man on the stairs – he's sick - he's *dead* – I daren't go past him! William! I'm frightened – frightened – I don't dare stay in the house – all alone with him – all alone – *William*!'

She had forgotten the Working Party.

Foothold

'MORNING!' exclaimed Gerard, standing before the sideboard, napkin under his arm. 'Sleep well? There are kidneys here, haddock; if you prefer it, ham and boiled eggs – I don't *see* any boiled eggs but I suppose they are coming in – did you see Clara?'

Thomas came rather dazedly round the breakfast table.

'He's hardly awake,' said Janet. 'Don't shout at him, Gerard – Good morning, Thomas – let him sit down and think.'

'*Are* the boiled eggs — ?' cried Gerard.

'Yes, of course they are. Can you possibly bear to wait?' she added, turning to Thomas. 'We are very virile at breakfast.'

Thomas smiled. He took out his horn-rimmed glasses, polished them, looked round the dining-room. Janet did things imaginatively; a subdued, not too buoyant prettiness had been superimposed on last night's sombre effect; a honey-coloured Italian table-cloth on the mahogany, vase of brown marigolds, breakfast-china about the age of the house with a red rim and scattered gold pimpernels. The firelight pleasantly jiggled, catching the glaze of dishes and coffee-pot, the copper feet of the 'sluggards' joy'. The square high room had, like Janet, a certain grace of proportion.

'I'm glad you don't have blue at breakfast,' said Thomas, unfolding his napkin. 'I do hate blue.'

'Did he see Clara?' asked Gerard, clattering the dish-lids. 'Do find out if he saw Clara!'

Janet was looking through a pile of letters. She took up each envelope, slit it open, glanced at the contents and slipped them inside again unread. This did not suggest indifference; the more she seemed to like the look of a letter the more quickly she put it away. She had put on shell-rimmed spectacles for reading, which completed a curious similarity between her face and Thomas's; both sensitive and untroubled, with the soft lines of easy living covering over the harder young lines of eagerness, self-distrust and a capacity for pain. When Gerard clamoured she raised her shoulders gently. 'Well, did you?' she said at last, without looking up from her letters.

'I'm afraid Clara's been encouraged away,' said Thomas. 'I specially left out some things I thought might intrigue her; a letter from Antonia, a daguerreotype of my grandmother I brought down to show you, rather a good new shirt – lavender-coloured. Then I lay awake some time waiting for her, but your beds are too comfortable. I had – disappointingly – the perfect night! Yet all through it I never quite forgot; it was like expecting a telephone call.'

'If you'd been half a man,' said Gerard, 'and Clara'd been half a ghost, you'd have come down this morning shaking all over with hair bright white, demanding to be sent to the first train.'

Janet, sitting tall and reposeful, swept her letters together with a movement and seemed faintly clouded. 'Well, I'm very glad Thomas isn't trying to go – tell me, why should Antonia's letters intrigue her? You complained they were rather dull. *I* find them dull, but then she isn't a woman's woman.'

'I just thought the signature ought to suggest an affinity. Names, you know. Meredith . . . Don't be discouraged, Gerard; I'm no sort of a test. I've slept in all sorts of places. There seems to be some sort of extra thick coating between me and anything other than fleshly.'

'*I've* never met her,' said Gerard, 'but then I'm a coarse man and Clara's essentially feminine. Perhaps something may happen this evening. Try going to bed earlier – it was half-past one when we were putting the lights out. Clara keeps early hours.'

'Have you noticed,' Janet said composedly, 'that one may discuss ghosts quite intelligently, but never any particular ghost without being facetious?'

' – Forgive my being so purely carnal,' exclaimed Thomas suddenly, 'but this is the most excellent marmalade. Not gelatinous, not slimy. I never get quite the right kind. Does your cook make it?'

He had noticed that here was 'a sensitiveness'. Thomas proceeded conversationally like the impeccable dentist with an infinitesimally fine instrument, choosing his area, tapping within it nearer and nearer, withdrawing at a suggestion before there had been time for a wince. He specialized in a particular kind of friendship with that eight-limbed, inscrutable, treacherous creature, the happily-married couple; adapting himself closely and lightly to the composite personality. An indifference to, an apparent unconsciousness of, life in some aspects armoured him against embarrassments. As Janet said, he would follow one into one's bedroom without noticing. Yet the too obvious 'tact', she said, *was* the literal word for his quality. Thomas was all finger-tips.

Janet slid her chair back noiselessly on the carpet and turned half round to face the fire. 'You're so nice and greedy,' she said, 'I do love having our food appreciated.'

'*I* appreciate it,' said Gerard. 'You know how I always hate staying away with people. I suppose I am absolutely smug. Now that we've come to this house I hate more than ever going up to the office.' He got up and stood, tall and broad, looking out of the window. Beyond, between the heavy fall of the curtains, showed the cold garden; the clipped shrubs like patterns in metal, the path going off in a formal perspective to the ascent of some balustraded steps. Beyond the terrace, a parade of trees on a not very remote skyline, the still, cold, evenly-clouded sky.

A few minutes afterwards he reluctantly left them. Janet and Thomas stood at the door and, as the car disappeared at the turn of the drive, Gerard waved goodbye with a backward scoop of the hand. Then they came in again to the fire and Thomas finished his coffee. He observed, 'The room seems a good deal smaller. Do you notice that rooms are adaptable?'

'I do feel the house has grown since we've been in it. The rooms seem to take so much longer to get across. I'd no idea we were buying such a large one. I wanted it because it was white, and late Georgian houses are unexigeant, but I promised myself – and everyone else – it was small.'

'Had you been counting on Clara, or didn't you know?'

'I was rather surprised. I met her coming out of your room about four o'clock one afternoon in November. Like an idiot I went downstairs and told Gerard.'

'Oh – why like an idiot?'

'He came dashing up, very excited – I suppose it was rather exciting – and I came after him. We went into all the rooms, flinging the doors open as quietly and suddenly as we could; we even looked into the cupboards, though she is the last person one could imagine walking into a cupboard. The stupid thing was that I hadn't looked round to see which way she had gone. Gerard was perfectly certain there must be some catch about that chain of doors going through from my room to his and from his down the steps to the landing where there is a bathroom. He kept saying, "You go round one way and I'll go the other." While we'd been simply playing the fool I didn't mind, but when he began to be rational I began to be angry and – well, ashamed. I said: "If she's . . . not like us . . . you know perfectly well we can't corner her, and if she should be, we're being simply eccentric and rude." He said "Yes, that's all very well, but I'm not going to have that damned woman going in and out of my dressing-room," and I (thinking "Supposing she really is a damned woman?") said "Don't be so silly, she wouldn't be bothered – why should she?" Then the wind went out of our sails altogether. Gerard went downstairs whistling; we had tea rather irritably – didn't say very much and didn't look at each other. We didn't mention Clara again.'

'*Is* she often about?'

'Yes – no – I don't know . . . I really *don't* know, Thomas. I am wishing so much, you see, that I'd never begun her – let her in. Gerard takes things up so fearfully. I know last night when he took that second whisky and put more logs on we would be coming to Clara.'

'Ah,' said Thomas. 'Really. *That* was what you were waiting for . . .'

' – The sun's trying to come out!' exclaimed Janet. She got up and pushed the curtains further apart. 'In an hour or so when I've finished my house things we'll go round the garden. I do like having a garden you haven't seen. We're making two herbaceous borders down to the beech hedge away from the library window. I do think one needs perspective from a library window; it carries on the lines of the shelves.'

'Precious, I think,' said Thomas, 'distinctly precious.'

'Yes, I've always wanted to be . . . The papers are in the library.'

Thomas gathered from headlines and a half-column here and there that things were going on very much as he had expected. He felt remote from all this business of living; he was recently back from Spain. He took down Mabbe's *Celestina* and presently pottered out into the hall with his thumb in the book, to wait for Janet. In the hall, he looked at his own reflection in two or three pieces of walnut and noticed a Famille Rose bowl, certainly new, that they must have forgotten last night when they were showing him those other acquisitions. He decided, treading a zig-pattern across them carefully, that the grey and white marble squares of the floor were *good*; he would have bought the house on the strength of them alone. He liked also – Janet was doubtful about it – Gerard's treatment of the square-panelled doors, leaf-green in their moulded white frames in the smooth white wall. The stairs, through a double-doorway, had light coming down them from some landing window like the cold interior light in a Flemish picture. Janet, pausing half way down to say something to someone above, stood there as if painted, distinct and unreal.

Janet had brought awareness of her surroundings to such a degree that she could seem unconscious up to the very last fraction of time before seeing one, then give the effect with a look that said 'Still there?' of having had one a long time 'placed' in her mind. He could not imagine her startled, or even looking at anything for the first time. Thinking of Clara's rare vantage point, in November, up by his bedroom door, he said to himself, 'I'd give a good deal to have been Clara, that afternoon.'

'If you don't really mind coming out,' said Janet, 'I should put on an overcoat.' As he still stood there vaguely she took the book gently away from him and put it down on a table.

'If *I* had a ghost,' said Thomas as she helped him into an overcoat, 'she should be called "Celestina". I like that better than Clara.'

'If I have another daughter,' said Janet agreeably, 'she shall be called Celestina.'

They walked briskly through the garden in thin sunshine. Thomas, who knew a good deal about gardens, became more direct, clipped in his speech and technical. They walked several times up and down the new borders, then away through an arch in the hedge and up some steps to the terrace for a general survey. 'Of course,' she said, 'one works here within limitations. There's a character to be kept – you feel that? One would have had greater scope with an older house or a newer house. All the time there's a point of view to be respected. One can't cut clear away on lines of one's own like at Three Beeches; one more or less modifies. But it contents me absolutely.'

'You ought to regret that other garden?'

'I don't, somehow. Of course, the place was quite perfect; it had that kind of limitation – it was too much our own. We felt "through with it". I had some qualms about leaving, beforehand; I suppose chiefly moral – you know, we do spoil ourselves! – but afterwards, as far as regret was concerned, never a pang. Also, practically speaking, of course the house *was* getting too small for us. Children at school get into a larger way of living; when they come home for the holidays — '

'I suppose,' said Thomas distastefully, 'they do take up rather a lot of room.'

She looked at him, laughing. 'Hard and unsympathetic!'

'Hard and unsympathetic,' accepted Thomas complacently. 'I don't see where they come in. I don't see the point of them; I think they spoil things. Frankly, Janet, I don't understand about people's children and frankly I'd rather not . . . You and Gerard seem to slough your two off in a wonderful way. Do you miss them at all?'

'I suppose we — '

'*You*, in the singular, thou?'

'I suppose,' said Janet, 'one lives two lives, two states of life. In terms of time, one may live them alternately, but really the rough ends of one phase of one life (always broken off with a certain amount of disturbance) seem to dovetail into the beginning of the next phase of that same life, perhaps months afterwards, so that there never seems to have been a gap. And the same with the other life, waiting the whole time. I suppose the two run parallel.'

'Never meeting,' said Thomas comfortably. 'You see I'm on one and your children are on the other and I want to be quite sure. Promise me: *never* meeting?'

'I don't think ever. But you may be wise, all the same, not to come in the holidays.'

They hesitated a moment or two longer on the terrace as though there were more to be said and the place had in some way connected itself with the subject, then came down by the other steps and walked towards the dining-room windows, rather consciously, as though someone were looking out. She wore a leather coat, unbuttoned, falling away from her full straight graceful figure, and a lemon-and-apricot scarf flung round twice so that its fringes hung down on her breast and its folds were dinted in by the soft, still youthful line of her jaw. Academically, Thomas thought her the most attractive woman of his acquaintance: her bodily attraction was modified and her charm increased by the domination of her clear fastidious aloof mind over her body.

He saw her looking up at the house. 'I do certainly like your house,' he said. 'You've inhabited it to a degree I wouldn't have thought possible.'

'Thank you so much.'

'You're not – seriously, Janet – going to be worried by Clara?'

'My dear, no! She does at least help fill the place.'

'You're not finding it empty?'

'Not the house, exactly. It's not . . . ' They were walking up and down under the windows. Some unusual difficulty in her thoughts wrinkled her forehead and hardened her face. 'You know what I was saying after breakfast about the house having grown since we came in, the rooms stretching? Well, it's not that, but my life – *this* life – seems to have stretched somehow; there's more room in it. Yet it isn't that I've more time – that would be perfectly simple, I'd do more things. You know how rather odious I've always been about *désœuvrées* women; I've never been able to see how one's day could fail to be full up, it fills itself. There's been the house, the garden, friends, books, music, letters, the car, golf, when one felt like it, going up to town rather a lot. Well, I still have all these and there isn't a moment between them. Yet there's more and more room every day. I suppose it must be underneath.'

Thomas licked his upper lip thoughtfully. He suggested, 'Something spiritual, perhaps?' with detachment, diffidence and a certain respect.

'That's what anybody would say,' she agreed with equal detachment. 'It's just that I'm not comfortable; I always have been comfortable, so I don't like it.'

'It must be beastly,' said Thomas, concerned. 'You don't think it may just be perhaps a matter of not quite having settled down here?'

'Oh, I've settled down. Settled, I shouldn't be surprised to hear, for life. After all, Thomas, in eight years or so the children will, even from your point of view, really matter. They'll have all sorts of ideas and feelings; they'll be what's called "adult". There'll have to be a shifting of accents in this family.'

'When they come home for the holidays, what shall you do about Clara?'

'Nothing. Why should I? She won't matter. Not,' said Janet quickly, looking along the windows, 'that she matters particularly now.'

Thomas went up to his room about half-past three and, leaving the door open, changed his shoes thoughtfully after a walk. 'I cannot think,' he said to himself, 'why they keep dogs of that kind when exercising them ceases to be a matter of temperament and becomes a duty.' It was the only reflection possible upon the manner of living of Gerard and Janet. His nose and ears, nipped by the wind, thawed painfully in the even warmth of the house. Still with one shoe off he crossed the room on an impulse of sudden interest to study a print (some ruins in the heroic manner) and remained leaning before it in an attitude of reflection, his arms folded under him on the bow-fronted chest-of-drawers. The afternoon light came in through the big window, flooding him with security; he thought from the dogs to Gerard, from Gerard to Janet, whom he could hear moving about in her room with the door open, sliding a drawer softly open and shut. A pause in her movements – while she watched herself in the glass, perhaps, or simply stood looking critically about the room as he'd seen her do when she believed a room to be empty – then she came out, crossed her landing, came down the three steps to his passage and passed his door.

'Hullo, Janet,' he said, half turning round; she hesitated a moment, then went on down the passage. At the end there was a hanging-closet (he had blundered into it in mistake for the bathroom); he heard her click the door open and rustle about among the dresses. Still listening, he pulled open a small drawer under his elbow and searched at the back of it, under his ties, for the daguerreotype of his grandmother. Somehow he failed to hear her; she passed the door again silently; still with a hand at the back of the drawer he called out: 'Come in a moment, Janet, I've something to show you,' and turned full round quickly, but she had gone.

Sighing, he sat down and put on the other shoe. He washed his hands, flattened his hair with a brush, shook a clean handkerchief out of its folds with a movement of irritation and, taking up the daguerreotype, went out after her. 'Janet!' he said aggrievedly.

'Thomas?' said Janet's voice from the hall below.

'*Hul-lo!*'

'I've been shutting the dogs up – poor dears. We'll have tea in the library.' She came upstairs to meet him, drawing her gloves off and smiling.

'But you were in – I thought you – oh well, never mind . . . ' He glanced involuntarily towards the door of her room; she looked after him.

'Yes, never mind,' she said. They smiled at each other queerly. She put her hand on his arm for a moment urgently, then with a little laugh went on upstairs past him and into her room. He had an instinct to follow her, a quick apprehension, but stood there rooted.

'Right-o; all clear,' she called after a second.

'Oh, right-o,' he answered, and went downstairs.

'By the way,' asked Thomas casually, stirring his tea, 'does one tell Gerard?'

'As you like, my dear. Don't you think, though, we might talk about *you* this evening? Yesterday we kept drawing on you for admiration and sympathy; you were too wonderful. We never asked you a thing, but what we should love really, what we are burning to do, is to hear about you in Spain.'

'I should love to talk about Spain after dinner. Before dinner I'm always a little doubtful about my experiences; they never seem quite so real as other people's; they're either un-solid or dingy. I don't get carried away by them myself, which is so essential . . . Just one thing: why is she so like you?'

'Oh! . . . did that strike *you*?'

'I never saw her properly, but it was the way you hold yourself. And her step – well, I've never been mistaken about a step before. And she looked in as she went by, over her shoulder, like you would.'

'Funny . . . So that was Clara. Nothing's ever like what one expected, is it?'

'No . . . ' said Thomas, following a train of thought. 'She did perhaps seem eagerer and thinner. If I'd thought at all at the time (which I didn't) I'd have thought – "Something has occurred to Janet: what?" As it was, after she'd been by the second time I was cross because I thought you shouldn't be too busy to see me. What do you know about her – facts, I mean?'

'Very little. Her name occurs in some title-deeds. She was a Clara Skepworth. She married a Mr Horace Algernon May and her father seems to have bought her the house as a wedding present.

She had four children – they all survived her but none of them seems to have left descendants – and died a natural death, middle-aged, about 1850. There seems no reason to think she was not happy; she was not interesting. Contented women aren't.'

This Thomas deprecated. 'Isn't that arbitrary?'

'Perhaps,' agreed Janet, holding out a hand to the fire. 'You can defend Clara, I shan't . . . Why should I?'

'How do you know this Clara Skepworth – or May – is your Clara?'

'I just know,' said Janet, gently and a little wearily conclusive – a manner she must often have used with her children.

Thomas peppered a quarter of muffin with an air of giving it all his attention. He masked a keen intuition by not looking at Janet, who sat with her air of composed unconsciousness, perhaps a shade conscious of being considered. He had the sense here of a definite exclusion; something was changing her. He had an intuition of some well he had half-divined in her having been tapped, of some reserve (which had given her that solidity) being drained away, of a certain sheathed and, till now, hypothetical faculty being used to exhaustion. He had guessed her capable of an intimacy, something disruptive, something to be driven up like a wedge, first blade-fine, between the controlled mind and the tempered, vivid emotions. It would not be a matter of friendship (the perfectness of his own with her proved it), she was civilized too deep down, the responses she made were too conscious; nor of love; she was perfectly mated (yet he believed her feeling for Gerard – so near to the casual eye, to the springs of her being – to be largely maternal and sensual).

In revulsion from the trend of his thoughts, he glanced at her: her comfortable beautiful body made the thing ludicrous. 'A peevish dead woman where we've failed,' he thought, 'it's absurd.' Gerard and he – he thought how much less humiliating for them both it would have been if she'd taken a lover.

'Gerard ought to be coming in soon.' Uneasy, like a watch-dog waking up at the end of a burglary, he glanced at the clock.

'Shall I put the muffins down by the fire again?'

'Why? Oh, no. He doesn't eat tea now, he thinks he is getting fat.'

'He's up to time usually, isn't he?'

'Yes – he's sure to be early this evening. I thought I heard the car then, but it was only the wind. It's coming up, isn't it?'

'Yes, lovely of it. Let it howl. (I like the third person imperative.)' He shrugged his folded arms up his chest luxuriously and slid down further into his chair. 'I like it after tea, it's so physical.'

'Isn't it?'

They listened, not for long in vain, for the sound of the car on the drive.

The drawing-room was in dark-yellow shadow with pools of light; Gerard and Janet were standing in front of the fire. Falling from Janet's arms above the elbows, transparent draperies hung down against the firelight. Her head was bent, with a line of light round the hair from a clump of electric candles on the wall above; she was looking into the fire, her arms stretched out, resting her finger-tips on the mantelpiece between the delicate china. Gerard, his fine back square and black to the room, bent with a creak of the shirt-front to kiss the inside of an elbow. Janet's fingers spread out, arching themselves on the mantelpiece as though she had found the chord she wanted on an invisible keyboard and were holding it down.

Thomas saw this from across the hall, through an open door, and came on in naturally. His sympathy was so perfect that they might have kissed in his presence; they both turned, smiling, and made room for him in front of the fire.

'Saturday tomorrow,' said Gerard, who smelt of verbena soap, 'then Sunday. Two days for me here. You've been here all day, Thomas. It doesn't seem fair.'

'I helped take the dogs for a walk,' said Thomas. 'It was muddy, we slid about and got ice-cold and couldn't talk at all because we kept whistling and whistling to the dogs till our mouths got too stiff. What a lot of virtue one acquires in the country by doing unnecessary things. Being arduous, while there are six or eight people working full time to keep one alive in luxury.'

'Sorry,' said Janet. 'I didn't know you hated it. But I'm sure it was good for you.'

'I wish you wouldn't both imply,' said Thomas, 'that I don't know the meaning of work. On Monday, when I get back to town, I'm going to begin my book on monasteries.'

'What became of that poem about the Apocalypse?'

'I'm re-writing it,' said Thomas with dignity.

'You are the perfect mixture,' said Janet, 'of Francis Thompson and H. G. Wells.'

'There's a dark room in my flat where a man once did photography. In a year, when I'm thirty-five, I shall retire into it and be Proust, and then you will both be sorry.'

The butler appeared in the doorway.

'Dinner . . .' said Gerard.

When Janet left them, Gerard and Thomas looked at each other vaguely and wisely between four candles over a pile of fruit. The port completed its second circle. Thomas sipped, remained with lips compressed and, with an expression of inwardness, swallowed.

'Very ni-ice,' he said. '*Very* nice.'

'That's the one I was telling you – light of course.'

'I don't do with that heavy stuff.'

'No, you never could, could you . . . I'm putting on weight – notice?'

'Yes,' said Thomas placidly. 'Oh, well, it's time we began to. One can't fairly expect, my dear Gerard, to *look* ascetic.'

'Oh, look here, speak for yourself, you Londoner. I live pretty hard here – take a good deal of exercise. It would be beastly for Janet if one got to look too utterly gross.'

'Ever feel it?'

'M-m-m-m – no.'

Thomas sketched with his eyebrows an appeal for closer sincerity.

'Well, scarcely ever. Never more than is suitable.' He sent round the port. 'Had a good day barring the dogs? I daresay you talked a good deal; you made Janet talk well. She is, isn't she – dispassionately – what you'd call rather intelligent?'

'Yes – you proprietary vulgarian.'

'Thanks,' said Gerard. He cracked two walnuts between his palms and let the shells fall on to his plate with a clatter. 'I suppose she showed you everything out of doors? I shall show it you again tomorrow. Her ideas are quite different from mine, I mean about what we're going to do here. I shall have my innings tomorrow. She's keeping the men at those borders when I want them to get started on levelling the two new courts. We've only one now – I suppose she showed it you – which is ridiculous with Michael and Gill growing up. Well, I mean, it *is* ridiculous, isn't it?'

'Entirely,' said Thomas. 'Don't cramp the children's development; let them have five or six.'

'How you do hate our children,' said Gerard comfortably.

There ensued a mellowed silence of comprehension. Gerard, his elbows spread wide on the arms of his chair, stretched his legs further under the table and looked at the fire. Thomas pushed his chair sideways and crossed his legs still more comfortably. A log on the fire collapsed and went up in a gush of pale flame.

Thomas was startled to find Gerard's eyes fixed sharply upon him as though in surprise. He half thought that he must have spoken, then that Gerard had spoken. 'Yes?' he said.

'Nothing,' said Gerard, 'I didn't say anything, did I? As a matter of fact I was thinking – *did* you see anything of Clara?'

'If I were you I should drop Clara: I mean as a joke.'

There was nothing about Gerard's manner of one who has joked. He smiled grudgingly. 'I do work my jokes rather hard. I'm getting to see when their days are numbered by Janet's expression.

As a matter of fact, I think *that*'s one form of nerves with me; I feel it annoys Janet and I don't seem able to leave it alone . . . *You* don't think, seriously, there's anything in this thing?'

'I told you this morning I wasn't a test.'

'But aren't you?' insisted Gerard, with penetration. 'How about since this morning? How do you feel things are – generally?'

'She's an idea of Janet's.'

'Half your philosophers would tell me I was an idea of Janet's. I don't care what she is; the thing is, is she getting on Janet's nerves? You know Janet awfully well: do be honest.'

'It needs some thinking about. I'd never thought of Janet as a person who *had* nerves.'

'I'd like to know one way or the other,' said Gerard, 'before I start work on those courts.'

'My dear fellow – *leave here*?' Such an abysm of simplicity startled Thomas, who thought of his friends for convenience in terms of himself. *He* wouldn't leave here, once established, for anything short of a concrete discomfort, not for the menacing of all the Janets by all the Claras. 'I've never seen Janet better,' he quickly objected, 'looking nicer, more full of things generally. You can't say the place doesn't suit her.'

'Oh yes, it suits her all right, I suppose. She's full of – something. I suppose I'm conservative – inside, which is so much worse – I didn't mind moving house, I was keener than she was on coming here. I wanted this place frightfully and I'm absolutely content now we've got it. I've never regretted Three Beeches. But I didn't reckon on one sort of change, and that seems to have happened. I don't even know if it's something minus or something plus. I think where I'm concerned, minus. It's like losing a book in the move, knowing one can't really have lost it, that it must have got into the shelves somewhere, but not being able to trace it.'

'Beastly feeling,' said Thomas idly, 'till one remembers having lent it to some devil who hasn't given it back.'

Gerard looked at him sharply, a look like a gasp. Then his eyes dropped, his face relaxed from haggardness into a set, heavy expression that held a mixture of pride and resentment at his own impenetrability, his toughness. Thomas knew the expression of old; when it appeared in the course of an argument he was accustomed to drop the argument with an, 'Oh well, I don't know. I daresay you are right.' Gerard now raised his glass, frowned expressively at it and put it down again. He said: 'I must be fearfully fatuous; I always feel things are so permanent.'

Thomas didn't know what to say; he liked Gerard chiefly because he *was* fatuous.

'She's seeing too much of this ghost,' continued Gerard. 'She

wouldn't if things were all right with her. I can't talk about
delusions and doctors and things because she's as healthy as I am,
obviously, and rather saner. I daresay this thing's *here* all right;
from the way you don't answer my question I gather you've been
seeing it too.'

'To be exact,' said Thomas, 'somebody walked past my door
this afternoon who turned out not to be Janet, though I'd have
sworn at the time it was.'

'Tell Janet?'

'Yes.'

Gerard looked up for a moment and searched his face. 'Didn't
you wonder,' he said, 'why she couldn't be natural about it? I
remember she and you and I talking rot about ghosts at Three
Beeches, and she said she'd love to induct one here. The first time
she came down and told me about Clara I thought she thought it
was fun. I suppose I was rather a hearty idiot; I rushed upstairs and
started a kind of rat-hunt. I thought it amused her; when I found it
didn't I had rather a shock . . . Things must be changing, or how
can this Clara business have got a foothold? It *has* got a foothold – I
worry a good bit when we're alone but we never discuss it, then
directly somebody's here something tweaks me on to it and every
time I try and be funny something gets worse . . . Oh, I don't
know – I daresay I'm wrong.' Gerard dived for his napkin; he
reappeared shame-faced. 'Wash this out,' he said, 'I've been talking
through my hat. That's the effect of you, Thomas. It's not that
you're so damned sympathetic, but you're so damned *un*sympathetic in such a provocative way.' He got up. 'Come on,' he said,
'let's come on out of here.'

Thomas got up unwillingly; he longed to define all this. Risking
a failure in tact he put forward, 'What you're getting at is: all this is
a matter of foothold?'

'Oh, I suppose so,' Gerard agreed non-committally. 'Let's wash
that out, anyway. Do let's come on out of here.'

Thomas talked about Spain. 'I can't think why we don't go there,'
cried Janet. 'We never seem to go anywhere; we don't travel
enough. You seem so much completer and riper, Thomas, since
you've seen Granada. Do go on.'

'Quite sure I don't bore you?' said Thomas, elated.

'Get on,' said Gerard impatiently. 'Don't stop and preen yourself. And, Janet, don't you keep on interrupting him. Let him get
on.'

Thomas got on. He did require (as he'd told Janet) to gather
momentum. Without, he was apt to be hampered by the intense,
complacent modesty of the oversubjective; at the beginning, Spain

refused to be detached from himself; he seemed to have made it. *Now* Spain imposed a control on him, selecting his language; words came less from him than through him, he heard them go by in a flow of ingenuous rapture.

Gerard and Janet were under the same domination. The three produced in each other, in talking, a curious sense of equality, of being equally related. Thomas concentrated a sporadic but powerful feeling for 'home' into these triangular contacts. He was an infrequent visitor, here as with other friends, but could produce when present a feeling of continuity, of uninterruptedness . . . It was here as though there had always been Thomas. The quiet room round them, secure from the whining wind, with its shadowy lacquer, its shades like great parchment cups pouring down light, the straight, almost palpable fall of heavy gold curtains to carpet, 'came together' in this peculiar intimacy as though it had lived a long time warm in their common memory. While he talked, it remained in suspension.

'O-oh,' sighed Janet and looked round, when he had finished, as though they had all come back from a journey.

'I suppose,' said Gerard, 'we are unenterprising. Are we?'

'A little,' conceded Thomas, still rather exalted, nursing one foot on a knee.

'Let's go abroad tomorrow!'

'You know,' exclaimed Janet, 'you know, Gerard, you'd simply hate it!' She made a gesture of limitation. 'We're rooted here.'

'Of course, there's one thing: if you hadn't both got this faculty for being rooted it wouldn't be the same thing to come and see you. I do hate "service-flat people"; I never know any.'

They all sighed, shifted their attitudes; sinking a little deeper into the big chairs. Thomas, aware almost with ecstasy of their three comfortable bodies, exclaimed: 'Would we ever really have known each other before there was this kind of chair? I've a theory that absolute comfort runs round the circle to the same point as asceticism. It wears the material veil pretty thin.'

Janet raised her arms, looked at them idly and dropped them again. 'What material veil?' she said foolishly.

Nobody answered.

'Janet's sleepy,' said Gerard, 'she can't keep awake unless she does all the talking herself. She's not one of your women who listen.'

'I wasn't sleepy till now. I think it's the wind. Listen to it.'

'Tomorrow, Janet, I'm going to show Thomas where those courts are to be. He says you didn't.'

'Thomas has no opinion about tennis courts; he'd agree with anyone. He really was intelligent about my borders.'

'Yes, I really was. You see, Gerard, tennis doesn't really affect me much. Pat-ball's my game.' Thomas lay back, looking through half-shut eyes at the wavering streaming flames. 'Clara's a dream,' he thought. 'Janet and I played at her. Gerard's a sick man.' He wanted to stretch sideways, touch Janet's bare arm and say to them both: 'There's just *this*, just this: weren't we all overwrought?'

Gerard, tenacity showing itself in his attitude, was sticking to something. He turned from one to the other eagerly. 'All the same,' he said, 'tennis courts or no tennis courts, why shouldn't we both, quite soon, go abroad?'

'Exactly,' said Thomas, encouraging.

'Because I don't want to,' said Janet. 'Just like that.'

'Oh . . . Tired?'

'Yes, tired-ish – with no disrespect to Thomas. I've had a wonderful day, but I *am* tired. Suppose it's the wind.'

'You said that before.'

She got up out of the depths of her chair, gathering up her draperies that slipped and clung to the cushions like cobwebs with perverse independence. 'Oh!' she cried. '*Sleepy!*' and flung her arms over her head.

'But you shatter our evening,' cried Thomas, looking up at her brilliance, then rising incredulous.

'Then you won't be too late,' she said heartlessly. 'Don't be too late!' She went across to the door like a sleepy cat. 'Good night, my dear Thomas.' After she closed the door they stood listening, though there was nothing to hear.

Their evening was not shattered, but it was cracked finely and irreparably. There was a false ring to it, never loud but an undertone. Gerard was uneasy; he got up after a minute or two and opened the door again. 'Don't you feel the room a bit hot?' he said. 'I'd open a window but the wind fidgets the curtains so. That's the only thing that gets on what nerves I have got, the sound of a curtain fidgeting; in and out, in and out, like somebody puffing and blowing.'

'Beastly,' said Thomas. 'I never open a window.' If he had been host he'd have invited Gerard to stop prowling and sit down, but one couldn't ask a man – even Gerard – to stop prowling about his own drawing-room when the prowling had just *that* 'tone'. So Thomas leant back rather exaggeratedly and sent up pacific smoke-wreaths.

'You look sleepy too,' said Gerard with some irritation. 'Shall we all go to bed?'

'Oh, just as you like, my dear fellow. I'll take up a book with me — '

' – No, don't let's,' said Gerard, and sat down abruptly.

The wind subsided during the next half-hour and silences, a kind of surprised stillness, spaced out their talk. Gerard fidgeted with the decanters; half way through a glass of whisky he got up again and stood undecided. 'Look here,' he said, 'there's something I forgot to ask Janet. Somebody's sent her a message and I must get the answer telephoned through tomorrow, first thing. I'll go up for a moment before she's asleep.'

'Do,' agreed Thomas, taking up *Vogue.*

Gerard, going out, hesitated rather portentously about shutting the drawing-room door and finally shut it. Thomas twitched an eyebrow but didn't look up from *Vogue,* which he went through intelligently from cover to cover. He remained looking for some time at a coloured advertisement of complexion soap at the end, then, as Gerard hadn't come back, got up to look for *Celestina,* where Janet had left it out in the hall. He crossed the hall soundlessly, avoiding the marble, stepping from rug to rug; with a hand put out for the *Celestina* he halted and stood still.

Gerard stood at the foot of the stairs, through the double doors, looking up, holding on to the banisters. Thomas looked at him, then in some confusion stepped back into the drawing-room. He had a shock; he wished he hadn't seen Gerard's face. 'What on earth was he listening for? . . . Why didn't he hear me? . . . I don't believe he's been up at all.' He took some more whisky and stood by the fire, waiting, his glass in his hand.

Quickly and noisily Gerard came in. 'She's asleep; it was no good.'

'Pity,' said Thomas, 'you ought to have gone up sooner.' They did not look at each other.

Thomas waited about – a social gesture purely, for he had the strongest possible feeling of not being wanted – while Gerard put out the downstair lights. Gerard wandered from one switch to another indeterminately, fumbling with wrong ones as though the whole lighting system were unfamiliar. Thomas couldn't make out if he were unwilling that either of them should go up, or whether he wanted Thomas to go up without him. 'I'll be going on up,' he said finally.

'Oh! Right you are.'

'I'll try not to wake Janet.'

'Oh, nothing wakes Janet – make as much noise as you like.'

He went up, his feet made a baffled, unreal sound on the smoothly carpeted stairs. The landing was – by some oversight – all in darkness. Away down the passage, firelight through his bedroom door came out across the carpet and up the wall. He watched – for Clara was somewhere, certainly – to see if anyone would step out across the bar of firelight. Nobody came. 'She may be in there,' he thought. Lovely to find her in there by the fire, like Janet.

Gerard turned out the last light in the hall and came groping up after him. 'Sorry!' he said. 'You'll find the switch of the landing outside Janet's door.' Thomas groped along the wall till he touched the door-panels. Left or right? – he didn't know, his fingers pattered over them softly.

'Oh, Clara,' came Janet's quiet voice from inside . . . 'I can't bear it. How could you bear it? The sickening loneliness . . . Listen, Clara . . . '

He heard Gerard's breathing; Gerard there three steps below him, listening also.

'Damn you, Gerard,' said Thomas sharply and noisily. '*I* can't find this thing. I'm lost entirely. Why did you put those lights out?'

The Cassowary

CRECY LODGE had stood empty for years; remote from the village it seemed to have been forgotten. The house hung doubtfully back from a by-road, obscured and almost smothered by limes; stucco gate-posts reared their depleted lions against a ground of evergreens. For Christmases, Crecy holly-branches had decorated the church; the theft was hallowed, yet those darkly cavernous or lividly-shuttered windows searching through the December garden still afforded spoilers an agreeable tremor. The chocolate gates were streaked a bright green from neglect and opened reluctantly, leaving green dust on the hands. In autumn when the new tenants arrived the drive was matted over with lime leaves that sent up a sodden odour, deadening the footsteps.

The house was under no discredit from any hint of the supernatural. It was over-large, and made no provision for modern living. Stuccoed and, but for the addition of a minaret on the east side, in the Gothic style, it was painted a pinkish grey and had a steep roof and pointed windows with low sills. It presented its worst aspect, the north, to an approach from the avenue, yet had a vulgar dignity, breadth and squareness sustaining its overdecoration with effect. From the west side ran out a long room with a rounded end and coloured windows that looked like an orangery but had been designed for a ballroom.

It did not seem likely that Mrs Lampeter would give a ball for her daughters. The girls were elderly as girls, though young as spinsters; speaking socially, they were awkwardly placed in years. They were tall, 'rousses', each with a high-up stare (from the remarkable length of their fine necks) through pince-nez high on the chiselled noses. To this diffusion of their glances, the brilliantly blank look it gave them, turning to the light, they owed a slight air of vacuity, 'artistic', sometimes fumbling, generally elegant. In resemblance they varied between a Burne Jones and one of those Gallic drawings of English tourists. Their way of speaking – rapid, slurred, imperious, was such that one had always difficulty in understanding them and some diffidence in asking them to repeat what they had said. Their mother seemed attentive to them and was a little bowed.

The Vicar's wife was their first visitor; they were discovered by her reading and sewing, grouped, and received her cordially in a drawing-room blackly dominated by a mantelpiece like a cenotaph. This so put the room out of tone that the water-colours faded into the wall, the chrysanthemums were extinguished, and the chandelier catching up in some few drops all of the rainy light was alone vivid.

Mrs Lampeter was supported in conversation by her elder daughter; they seemed travelled and interesting, subscribed to some weekly reviews and had lived near London. Mrs Bonner, predisposed to enthusiasm, rapidly 'took to them'. The younger Miss Lampeter sat sideways with a polite appearance of attention; she leaned forward absently now and then to pick from the carpet some shreds of lime-leaf that had come in on Mrs Bonner's heels. She was left-handed; Mrs Bonner noticed upon the hand that advanced a black ring of enamel, discreet with pearls. She *did* look 'engaged'; rather distant.

'I understand,' Mrs Lampeter said, 'there are not many young people about here?'

'Such a pity,' the caller nodded, resigned.

'Oh well,' cried the elder daughter surprisingly, 'we're accustomed to that!' The engaged Miss Lampeter, having come to an end of the lime leaves, resumed her embroidery with detachment.

'There are my two,' put out Mrs Bonner, becomingly nonchalant, 'Robert and Margery . . . '

A pale interest lit up the Lampeters. 'Couldn't they come to tea? Are they *quite* young?' exclaimed Miss Lampeter and, with eagerness, turned on the mother twin ovals of light from her pince-nez.

'They're away just at present. Margery's nineteen. Robert . . . ' (she made a particular effort to sound matter-of-fact when she talked about Robert) 'he's seventeen.'

Miss Lampeter considered a moment or two. 'I expect we could play ping-pong . . . Can they play ping-pong?' she asked Mrs Bonner.

Robert and Margery Bonner found themselves due for tea at the Lampeter's the first day of the holidays. Robert said blackly that this was the limit, and brooded. Margery wanted to know what they looked like and if they were rich. 'Are they pretty?' she asked. 'Who's she engaged to? Why doesn't she marry? I hate long engagements, they're governessy. And *what* made them come to that shattering house: are they under a cloud?'

'You'd better find out,' said Mrs Bonner, who also genuinely wanted to know these things.

'Extraordinary to be that age. What can they think about?'

'Do be nice,' Mrs Bonner said anxiously, seeing them off; she was never quite sure of her children. 'And remember to ask them about the holly for church.'

'I'll warn them that if they don't send some we'll steal it. We always have,' said the Vicar's daughter. To Robert she added, 'Hadn't Duckie better bring cricket-pads? They may be tigers at ping-pong.'

'*Funny!*' said Robert bitterly. He had been ravished from his laboratory, hands covered with chemical stains and smelling, he hoped, awful.

At tea in the dining-room Margery followed Phyllis's hand with her eyes; she guessed it pink-white, with dimples for knuckles and faintly freckled, but it fled everywhere with an independent shyness, passing dishes, gesturing, fluttering in a queer light way that seemed to be characteristic over hair around the exalted forehead. 'Wild as a deer,' thought Margery of the hand, which seemed apart from the rest of Phyllis's personality. 'If I'd a ring *there* I'd show it.' The Lampeter laughter, high in the roof of the mouth, was spontaneous and indefeasible. They emitted a ghostly childishness and seemed to be seated at table among a romping and laughter to which neither themselves nor their visitors contributed visibly. Their visitors stared like fishes, failing to understand them.

Robert's company manners were nice though sardonic. A clumsily built boy with an appearance of being continually bothered, he had a fixed interior-looking eye and hair that grew stiffly forward into a tuft when it should have grown back. His smile was so grudging that it became a compliment, suggesting to every comer her irresistibility, suggesting Robert was being amused in spite of himself. 'What a school-treat!' he would remark at intervals, looking critically up and down the laden table and helping himself to another slice of the Christmas cake that decorated the centre. He answered Mrs and Miss Lampeter in a deep indulgent voice and was very much liked by them.

In a pause of her restless hospitality Phyllis Lampeter, sitting by Margery, looked at her vaguely as though she realized her guest had other needs than the purely material but could not think what to say to her. Across a gulf of ten years they stared at each other doubtingly. Margery envied other people's experience but felt a contempt for what they had probably made of it. She concealed her uncertainty how to behave in a grown up world behind the directness of a successful woman of forty or a baby of four.

'Ripping ring!' she said clearly and suddenly, and pouncing on Phyllis's hand dragged it into the lamplight. 'Lucky . . .' she added, having assured herself as to the finger thus ornamented.

Phyllis laughed sharply. She glanced across at her sister in what might have been either elation or dread apprehension of having been watched. Only Nathalie's rather flat quarter-face was, however, towards them; she was talking to Robert.

'Who are you going to marry?' said Margery.

Phyllis touched her pince-nez; they wobbled so she readjusted them, higher up on her nose. Nothing but flashes of light from them, shielding the look behind, came to Margery. 'I don't know whether he's alive,' said Phyllis and, mastering an impulse to turn away, looked at her visitor anxiously.

'Awful for you,' said Margery.

'It is, rather,' said Phyllis and half-laughed deprecatingly. A hand slid forward in sisterly pressure on Phyllis's shoulder; above the top of her head Miss Lampeter's pre-Raphaelite oval appeared and, high up, another intelligent glimmer.

'Don't,' said Miss Lampeter, softly, and to Margery's embarrassment the sisters' hands touched.

'I wonder if this is how everyone behaved ten years ago,' thought Margery. She got up with alacrity at a suggestion from Miss Lampeter and they all went into the ballroom to play ping-pong.

'What a wonderful house this is!' said Margery, sitting down breathlessly on a sofa against the wall. The ball-room was lit by hanging lamps; it echoed disconcertingly and had a forgotten smell. To and fro on the panelled walls whisked the shadows of Phyllis Lampeter and Robert, still running round the ping-pong table. Mrs Lampeter had gone away to sit by the drawing-room fire, leaving what she evidently considered to be her party of young people to play by themselves. Nathalie Lampeter sat upright on the sofa, turning her long neck. 'We like it,' she said simply.

Her tall repose frightened Margery, who came out with – 'I *have* been a clumsy idiot. I shan't be asked here again.'

'Why not?' asked Miss Lampeter, with an obvious resolution to understand her little visitor's point of view. 'I suppose it was a perfectly natural question.'

'Seeing the ring . . . '

'Oh, quite. You couldn't be expected to guess that there might be anything painful.'

'Awful of me,' said Margery, longing to know more. It came.

'My sister is engaged,' said Miss Lampeter, 'to a Mr Melland, Paul Melland. He is a medical missionary and she saw him off to Central Africa two years ago. He used to write very regularly, but since a letter a year ago, a letter very much the same as usual saying that he was well, happy and interested in his work, nothing more has been heard of him. We have set inquiries on foot, even official inquiries, but he cannot be traced. Even his friends out there, his fellow-workers, know nothing of him. He left the station on an expedition up-country and cannot be traced.'

'It *sounds* like . . . ' said Margery, shaking her head lugubriously.

'You would think so, wouldn't you?'

'Awfully sad for you all.'

'Awfully sad,' agreed Miss Lampeter, with a certain amount of detachment.

'Did *you* know him well?'

Miss Lampeter, leaning forward, was watching the couple at the ping-pong table intently. Her head turned to and fro. 'Know him? Very well, yes; intimately . . . We thought,' she said, 'that a change of interests for Phyllis . . . country life . . . young society . . . '

'But he might come back?'

'Oh yes. I don't, personally, for a single moment cease to believe it.' Personally, Miss Lampeter seemed to believe a great deal. Behind this thin little trickle of information there was something stored up. 'Either she wants to make me feel there's something more up than appears to the eye,' thought Margery, 'or she thinks I'm a child or an idiot.' After another long, intense, yet blank look from Miss Lampeter's glasses she began to incline more and more to the former alternative. Nathalie ceased the tortoise movements of her head and, reflective, looking straight before her, sat like a statue. 'Paul was more to me than a brother,' she remarked in an aggrieved voice, and Margery believed that even this antique kind of bad form must have reached its limit.

'I am to regard this as confidential?'

'No,' said Miss Lampeter after a moment's consideration. 'No. Why? I believe it should save Phyllis pain and embarrassment if it were known generally . . . '

Margery made the first of a series of efforts to 'save' Phyllis by telling Robert as soon as the door of Crecy Lodge, where the sisters had lingered politely, was shut behind them. Their path of lamplight cut off, they groped in total blackness down the slippery drive. Margery's narrative came in jerks and Robert received it flippantly.

' "I wish I were a cassowary",' he said promptly,

> ' "On the plains of Timbuctoo,
> *I* should eat a Missionary,
> Coat and hat and hymn-book too."

I don't blame the cassowary.' He was in high spirits but soon, his mind returning ahead of him to the laboratory, became abstracted.

'What a brute you are,' said Margery. 'That's a real tragedy. I
don't call it funny at all.' She tripped over a root, clutched at Robert
and began laughing, and she was still laughing, and breathless
from impatience to be home and tell somebody else, when they
overtook Mrs Bonner in Vicarage Lane.

'But there's *nothing* funny about a missionary,' said Mrs Bonner
pained. 'He is very brave and splendid. It is *silly* of you, Robert.
You *are* silly . . . ' She laughed despairingly and wiped her eyes
. . . there was something irresistibly witty and winning in Robert's
poem about the cassowary. '*Preparatory* school humour!' said Mrs
Bonner scornfully, squeezing Robert's arm. 'Those unfortunate
women! I wonder whether there is anything one could do . . . '

There seemed nothing, except to surround the Miss Lampeters
with an atmosphere of solicitude, which must be very bright, and
to encourage forgetfulness. People in a nervous over-anxiety to do
this often complained that whenever a Lampeter entered a room
some outside power would twist round the most ordinary conversation in the direction of Central Africa, disappearances, or
sudden and fearful death. In spite of this Phyllis Lampeter became
in demand, flourished visibly and began to take on a satisfied
matronly little air of having made her market. Mr Melland, taboo
but intensely vital, accompanied her everywhere; it was like
meeting a married couple to whom the sister, her office of
protector and showman declining, became an awkward and often
superfluous third. The more Phyllis came in evidence with her Pot
of Basil the more the '*doutre-Manche*' in Nathalie's gait and attitudes
became accentuated.

Margery, however, did not care for widows; full of a spirit of
opposition she began a cult of Nathalie, who helped her with the
Girl Guides. Miss Lampeter was learning to moderate her first
estranging effusiveness and to alternate less clumsily between
rigidity and unreserve. She could not, however, cure herself of a
frequent use of the diminutive, and a 'little Margery', winsome,
bright, spontaneous and unknown at the Vicarage, became *persona
grata* at Crecy Lodge. The uneasy house grew familiar to Margery,
the loud shutting of the heavily-moulded doors, the cold limey
breath from the passages, the sheen along empty rooms where one
wandered of paint and marble in the immoderate glare from the
windows, and, most of all in the rooms they inhabited, a suggestion about the general arrangements of being provisional; a kind
of encamped and temporary expression about the furniture, the fall
of the draperies, the pictures and ornaments, choice but too thinly
disposed. By an almost over-discretion in the arrangement of the
drawing-room each member of the family seemed to have striven
and failed to impose on the others a feeling of permanence she

herself did not possess. The harmony of those evenings Margery passed with the Lampeters seemed to her, looking back afterwards, to have been upheld intact, like a ball of glass upon a fountain, by a perpetual jet of effort. Evening on evening spent in Crecy lamp and fire-light could never assure her that at any time, twelve hours after, they might not have stolen away, and that only vast unlit chandelier would be left there dripping iridescently over an empty floor.

Margery, upon whom country evenings, mud, seclusion and Robert's absence soon began to pall, left home about the middle of February on a round of visits to her school-friends. She remained some weeks in London, went to theatres, shingled her hair and received a proposal of marriage. She was surprised and a good deal sobered by her inability to accept the young man, a friend's brother, who appeared to her in all ways suitable. She forgot the Lampeters, first deliberately and then with such ease and natural-ness that when she did endeavour to remember them they returned reluctantly, very pale and almost indistinguishable. When she came home again, older, tenderer and more conscious, she avoided Crecy Lodge from some kind of shame.

In March, on a pale gusty day, she once more pushed open the chocolate gate reluctantly and, letting it swing behind her, listened to the wind that tore the lime trees and reflected on life's desolating continuity. Following the bend of the avenue she became exposed to the black stare of the windows, and in spite of another twinge of distaste and nervousness had to go forward. Having tugged the bell perfunctorily she walked unannounced, as she was privi-leged to do, into the arched hall and shouted for Nathalie and Phyllis. All round the doors were a little ajar, but nobody moved or answered. In pauses of the wind she should have been able to hear a fire rustle, the leaves of a book turn over or Nathalie's work-box creak, but it seemed for once as though the restless house were asleep.

'It's happened!' she thought in a flash, and, repeating this to herself without knowing at all what she meant, pushed through a swing door and went hurriedly down the passage into the ball-room. 'If they're not here,' she thought, 'they will really be gone.' But Miss Lampeter *was* there, in hat and furs, standing in the harlequin light of a window-embrasure and looking out steadfastly through a pane of blue glass. She knew Margery's step, and quickly, without turning, exclaimed: 'Paul's come back!'

Margery shut the door after her cautiously. 'Goodness!' she whispered.

'I hope,' said Miss Lampeter, 'I didn't startle you?'

'*You* must be startled.'

'N-no,' said Miss Lampeter slowly, with a kind of luxurious hesitation. 'Not startled . . . He's in London.'

'When, when . . . ?'

'We heard last night. Not a word before, not a rumour. Letters miscarried — '

'Phyllis – '

'We've had a terrible time with Phyllis; she wants to go up to London!'

'Naturally!'

'She can't,' said Miss Lampeter sharply. 'It would be hard on Paul, he's been ill. It wouldn't *do* . . . '

'But he'll want her,' said Margery angrily.

Miss Lampeter shook her head violently, flashing her glasses. 'It wouldn't do,' she repeated; 'you don't understand. We've had a most terrible time with her. I have to think for both of them. Mother is upset.'

'Altogether a very nice home-coming – Nathalie, don't be an ass!' Margery, coming up awkwardly, put an arm round her friend, who trembled all over as though she were going to cry.

'It's so difficult, it's too difficult. Nobody understands. I'm distracted, you see,' said Nathalie, and looked at Margery reproachfully. 'You see,' she added, '*I* must go to London . . . '

'I don't see . . . '

'I can't explain. Yet I shall have to explain . . . I could almost wish sometimes he hadn't come home.'

'Must anyone go to London? Can't he come — '

'*I* must see Paul.'

A swirl round the house, a door swinging, the rattle of windows along the north side of the room made Margery feel that someone else must be coming distractedly down the passage. She looked about in alarm with some idea of getting out through a window and a horrible sense of complicity.

'Anyone would say,' said Miss Lampeter, 'that I'd broken Phyllis's heart. But I can't let there be a mistake, can I? I've got to see Paul. And they none of them want me to.' She stood knitting her ringless fingers together, looking down at them in despair.

'You see, things are so difficult – life in a family. We've never spoken of this among ourselves. None of us liked to begin. Phyllis is everything to me – everything *else*. Love's so embarrassing, isn't it? I'm sure we've all felt, this last year, it was the only solution, his not coming back . . . Scenes are so dreadful; we've never had scenes in our family.'

'When's your train?'

'The twelve nine. Now let me go!' said Miss Lampeter sharply, freeing herself with a movement from some imaginary constraint. Margery, ashamed of this tempest and of something unknown in herself that was answering it, stood away from her, looking up at the coloured squares of sky.

'There's Phyllis,' said Margery suddenly. '*Now* what shall you do?'

Nathalie made a sudden assault on the latch, the french windows were snatched by a gust and flung violently back against the wall of the house. She stumbled out into the wind and went slanting against it, her skirts whipped round her legs, across the garden to the avenue trees. Margery ran out after her with her umbrella and purse. 'Tell Phyllis!' Miss Lampeter threw back over her shoulder.

Phyllis, looking across the garden, had appeared in the window. 'Gone, I suppose?' said Phyllis, vague, weary, a shade depressed.

'Do you mind?'

Phyllis took no notice; she said, 'I suppose I had better tell Mother.' She blinked, having appeared for the first time without her glasses; her eyes, large, bright, timid and inexpressive, were ringed with gold lashes. 'She isn't half dressed,' said Phyllis plaintively. 'She's taken the wrong umbrella. I don't know what Paul will think. I've had the most terrible time with her, she's so excited.'

Phyllis shut and latched the ballroom window and took Margery's arm: they went up the passage together into the drawing-room. Here, asking Margery to poke the fire for her, she sat down in her usual chair and took up her work. She sucked in her underlip, her chin was drawn plaintively back like a child's. Her attitude drooped.

'What a wind,' said Margery, listening nervously.

'I don't suppose,' said Phyllis, watching her needle, 'you know what to make of us all. I'm afraid all this is rather embarrassing. As a matter of fact it is embarrassing for all of us. In a kind of way, of course, we've been unsettled for years, but we were getting used to that and now all this has come and upset us completely. Of course, one is *deeply* thankful, but one can't help feeling that it would have been simpler if he hadn't come back. Of course I need not tell you, Margery that all this is strictly confidential. We have never spoken of this among ourselves. You see, we all mean so much to each other, Mother and Nathalie and I, that discussion is quite impossible. We should never have felt the same.'

'Nathalie's cared for Paul ever since we knew him. Her feelings are very strong. I never knew why they didn't marry: I don't really know Paul well enough in a way to ask. Anyhow, then I grew up and I suppose' – said Phyllis indifferently, looking round for the scissors – 'I was the more attractive. Paul asked me and Nathalie was so sweet about our engagement, but of course she knew I knew about *her* and it was most embarrassing. It must have been difficult for her, for the engagement has lasted for years; Paul couldn't afford to marry and it seemed almost a good thing when he went out to Central Africa. We corresponded quite regularly till one day I got a letter saying he was in love with Nathalie and asking me to release him. I was very much upset, naturally, and didn't know what to say, for I always felt Paul doesn't know his own mind very distinctly, and I didn't see really why he shouldn't marry me when he'd had the best years of my life and we'd been engaged so long. While I was still wondering what to do, his letters stopped, and later on we heard bad news from the Mission station. Then there didn't seem then any harm in my going on as I'd been before. You can't release a dead person, and I was so much accustomed to being engaged, you see. Nathalie was sweet to me and always talked of Paul as mine and let me be a kind of widow, but I always felt she meant to have him if he ever came back, and of course I fully intended, if that *should* happen, to give him up. Mother knew of it all, of course, and it was most distressing for her: she never speaks of it.'

Phyllis sighing, smoothed out her embroidery and remained looking pensively down at her ring. 'I must say,' she said plaintively, 'I don't think she's treated me fairly, do you, Margery? *I* ought to have gone up to London. After all, I am still engaged to Paul. I'm accustomed to being engaged.'

'She was in a hurry – naturally.'

'I don't think it's at all natural,' said Phyllis, working herself up. 'I call it highly unnatural. She's my own sister. And she has nothing to say to Paul that she can at all properly say.'

'Wouldn't you put that right?'

'No, I won't,' said Phyllis, high-pitched. 'I don't see why I should. I won't go back to nothing at all after being a kind of widow. It's preposterous.'

Rigid with indignation she blinked her gold lashes. 'Nathalie's accustomed to home life,' she said, and looked indignantly round the drawing-room.

Some memory in the room compelled her and she resumed her remote expression, the air, which had become part of herself, of pleasurable uncertainty, as of one expecting momentarily to be called away. That she was to be denuded of this, that her encampment in the bare house was to become a permanency, appalled Margery, who said violently:

'He should never have come back!'

'Oh, *Margery*,' smiled the engaged girl – the ringed hand

fluttered the hair round what seemed now a beaming, a bridal forehead – 'what a *ridiculous* thing to say!'

But Nathalie, having got her telegram off, now sat washed smooth by the speed of that friendly and eager train. It was an hour afterwards, Margery learnt, that in the crowd on Paddington platform Paul and Nathalie kissed – decorously, like husband and wife for a week parted.

'And I left my umbrella in the train!' she exclaimed afterwards.
' – Oh, Paul, Phyllis's umbrella!'

'That is too bad,' said Paul, perfunctory.

Telling

Terry looked up; Josephine lay still. He felt shy, embarrassed all at once at the idea of anyone coming here. His brain was ticking like a watch: he looked up warily.

But there was nobody. Outside the high cold walls, beyond the ragged arch of the chapel, delphiniums crowded in sunshine – straining with brightness, burning each other up – bars of colour that, while one watched them, seemed to turn round slowly. But there was nobody there.

The chapel was a ruin, roofed by daylight, floored with lawn. In a corner, the gardener had tipped out a heap of cut grass from the lawn-mower. The daisy-heads wilted, the cut grass smelt stuffy and sweet. Everywhere, cigarette-ends, scattered last night by the couples who'd come here to kiss. First the dance, thought Terry, then this: the servants will never get straight. The cigarette-ends would lie here for days, till after the rain, and go brown and rotten.

Then he noticed a charred cigarette stump in Josephine's hair. The short wavy ends of her hair fell back – still in lines of perfection – from temples and ears; by her left ear the charred stump showed through. For that, he thought, she would never forgive him; fastidiousness was her sensibility, always tormented. ('If you must know,' she had said, 'well, you've got dirty nails, haven't you? Look.') He bent down and picked the cigarette-end out of her hair; the fine ends fluttered under his breath. As he threw it away, he noticed his nails were still dirty. His hands were stained now – naturally – but his nails must have been dirty before. Had she noticed again?

But had she, perhaps, for a moment been proud of him? Had she had just a glimpse of the something he'd told her about? He wanted to ask her: 'What do you feel now? Do you believe in me?' He felt sure of himself, certain, justified. For nobody else would have done this to Josephine.

Himself they had all – always – deprecated. He felt a shrug in this attitude, a thinly disguised kind of hopelessness. 'Oh, Terry . . . ' they'd say, and break off. He was no good: he couldn't even put up a tennis-net. He never could see properly (whisky helped that at first, then it didn't), his hands wouldn't serve him, things he wanted them to hold slipped away from them. He was no good; the younger ones laughed at him till they, like their brothers and sisters, grew up and were schooled into bitter kindliness. Again and again he'd been sent back to them all (and repetition never blunted the bleak edge of these home-comings) from school, from Cambridge, now – a month ago – from Ceylon. 'The bad penny!' he would remark, very jocular. 'If I could just think things out,' he had tried to explain to his father, 'I know I could do *something.*' And once he had said to Josephine: 'I know there is Something I could do.'

'And they will know now,' he said, looking round (for the strange new pleasure of clearly and sharply seeing) from Josephine's face to her stained breast (her heavy blue beads slipped sideways over her shoulder and coiled on the grass – touched, surrounded now by the unhesitant trickle); from her breast up the walls to their top, the top crumbling, the tufts of valerian trembling against the sky. It was as though the dark-paned window through which he had so long looked out swung open suddenly. He saw (clear as the walls and the sky) Right and Wrong, the old childish fixities. I have done right, he thought (but his brain was still ticking). *She ought not to live* with this flaw in her. Josephine ought not to live, she had to die.

All night he had thought this out, walking alone in the shrubberies, helped by the dance-music, dodging the others. His mind had been kindled, like a dull coal suddenly blazing. He was not angry; he kept saying: 'I must not be angry, I must be just.' He was in a blaze (it seemed to himself) of justice. The couples who came face to face with him down the paths started away. Someone spoke of a minor prophet, someone breathed 'Caliban' . . . He kept saying: 'That flaw right through her. She damages truth. She kills souls; she's killed mine.' So he had come to see, before morning, his purpose as God's purpose.

She had laughed, you see. She had been pretending. There was a tender and lovely thing he kept hidden, a spark in him; she had touched it and made it the whole of him, made him a man. She had said: 'Yes, I believe, Terry. I understand.' That had been every-thing. He had thrown off the old dull armour . . . Then she had laughed.

Then he had understood what other men meant when they spoke of her. He had seen at once what he was meant to do. 'This is for me,' he said. 'No one but I can do it.'

All night he walked alone in the garden. Then he watched the french windows and when they were open again stepped in quickly and took down the African knife from the dining-room wall. He had always wanted that African knife. Then he had gone upstairs (remembering, on the way, all those meetings with Josephine, shaving, tying of ties), shaved, changed into flannels, put the knife into his blazer pocket (it was too long, more than an inch of the blade came out through the inside lining) and sat on his window-sill, watching sunlight brighten and broaden from a yellow agitation behind the trees into swathes of colour across the lawn. He did not think; his mind was like somebody singing, somebody able to sing.

And, later, it had all been arranged for him. He fell into, had his part in, some kind of design. Josephine had come down in her pleated white dress (when she turned the pleats whirled). He had said, 'Come out!' and she gave that light distant look, still with a laugh at the back of it, and said, 'Oh – right-o, little Terry.' And she had walked down the garden ahead of him, past the delphin-iums into the chapel. Here, to make justice perfect, he had asked once more: '*Do* you believe in me?' She had laughed again.

She lay now with her feet and body in sunshine (the sun was just high enough), her arms flung out wide at him, desperately, generously: her head rolling sideways in shadow on the enclosed, silky grass. On her face was a dazzled look (eyes half closed, lips drawn back), an expression almost of diffidence. Her blood quietly soaked through the grass, sinking through to the roots of it.

He crouched a moment and, touching her eyelids – still warm – tried to shut her eyes. But he didn't know how. Then he got up and wiped the blade of the African knife with a handful of grass, then scattered the handful away. All the time he was listening; he felt shy, embarrassed at the thought of anyone finding him there. And his brain, like a watch, was still ticking.

On his way to the house he stooped down and dipped his hands in the garden tank. Someone might scream; he felt embarrassed at the thought of somebody screaming. The red curled away through the water and melted.

He stepped in at the morning-room window. The blinds were half down – he stooped his head to avoid them – and the room was in dark-yellow shadow. (He had waited here for them all to come in, that afternoon he arrived back from Ceylon.) The smell of pinks came in, and two or three blue-bottles bumbled and bounced on the ceiling. His sister Catherine sat with her back to him, playing the piano. (He had heard her as he came up the path.) He looked at her pink pointed elbows – she was playing a waltz and the music ran through them in jerky ripples.

'Hullo, Catherine,' he said, and listened in admiration. So his new voice sounded like this!

'Hullo, Terry.' She went on playing, worrying at the waltz. She had an anxious, methodical mind, but loved gossip. He thought: Here is a bit of gossip for you – Josephine's down in the chapel, covered with blood. Her dress is spoilt, but I think her blue beads are all right. I should go and see.

'I say, Catherine — '

'Oh, Terry, they're putting the furniture back in the drawing-room. I wish you'd go and help. It's getting those big sofas through the door . . . and the cabinets.' She laughed: 'I'm just putting the music away,' and went on playing.

He thought: I don't suppose she'll be able to marry now. No one will marry her. He said: 'Do you know where Josephine is?'

'No, I haven't' – rum-tum-tum, rum-tum-*tum* – 'the slightest idea. Go on, Terry.'

He thought: She never liked Josephine. He went away.

He stood in the door of the drawing-room. His brothers and Beatrice were punting the big armchairs, chintz-skirted, over the waxy floor. They all felt him there: for as long as possible didn't notice him. Charles – fifteen, with his pink scrubbed ears – considered a moment, shoving against the cabinet, thought it was rather a shame, turned with an honest, kindly look of distaste, said, 'Come on, Terry.' He can't go back to school now, thought Terry, can't go anywhere, really: wonder what they'll do with him – send him out to the Colonies? Charles had perfect manners: square, bluff, perfect. He never thought about anybody, never felt anybody – just classified them. Josephine was 'a girl staying in the house', 'a friend of my sisters'. He would think at once (in a moment when Terry had told him), 'A girl staying in the house . . . it's . . . well, I mean, if it hadn't been *a girl staying in the house . . .* '

Terry went over to him; they pushed the cabinet. But Terry pushed too hard, crooked; the further corner grated against the wall. 'Oh, I say, we've scratched the paint,' said Charles. And indeed they had; on the wall was a grey scar. Charles went scarlet: he hated things to be done badly. It was nice of him to say: '*We've* scratched the paint.' Would he say later: 'We've killed Josephine?'

'I think perhaps you'd better help with the sofas,' said Charles civilly.

'You should have seen the blood on my hands just now,' said Terry.

'Bad luck!' Charles said quickly and went away.

Beatrice, Josephine's friend, stood with her elbows on the mantelpiece looking at herself in the glass above. Last night a man had kissed her down in the chapel (Terry had watched them). This must seem to Beatrice to be written all over her face – what else could she be looking at? Her eyes in the looking-glass were dark, beseeching. As she saw Terry come up behind her she frowned angrily and turned away.

'I say, Beatrice, do you know what happened down in the chapel?'

'Does it interest you?' She stooped quickly and pulled down the sofa loose-cover where it had 'runkled' up, as though the sofa legs were indecent.

'Beatrice, what would you do if I'd killed somebody?'

'Laugh,' said she, wearily.

'If I'd killed a woman?'

'Laugh harder. Do you know any women?'

She was a lovely thing, really: he'd ruined her, he supposed. He was all in a panic. 'Beatrice, swear you won't go down to the chapel.' Because she might, well – of course she'd go down: as soon as she was alone and they didn't notice she'd go creeping down to the chapel. It had been *that* kind of kiss.

'Oh, be quiet about that old chapel!' Already he'd spoilt last night for her. How she hated him! He looked round for John. John had gone away.

On the hall table were two letters, come by the second post, waiting for Josephine. No one, he thought, ought to read them – he must protect Josephine; he took them up and slipped them into his pocket.

'I say,' called John from the stairs, 'what are you doing with those letters?' John didn't meant to be sharp but they had taken each other unawares. They none of them wanted Terry to *feel* how his movements were sneaking movements; when they met him creeping about by himself they would either ignore him or say: 'Where are *you* off to?' jocosely and loudly, to hide the fact of their knowing he didn't know. John was Terry's elder brother, but hated to sound like one. But he couldn't help knowing those letters were for Josephine, and Josephine was 'staying in the house'.

'I'm taking them for Josephine.'

'Know where she is?'

'Yes, in the chapel . . . I killed her there.'

But John – hating this business with Terry – had turned away. Terry followed him upstairs, repeating: 'I killed her there, John . . . John, I've killed Josephine in the chapel.' John hurried ahead, not listening, not turning round. 'Oh, yes,' he called over his shoulder. 'Right you are, take them along.' He disappeared into the smoking-room banging the door. It had been John's idea that, from the day after Terry's return from Ceylon, the sideboard cupboard in the dining-room should be kept locked up. But he'd never said anything; oh no. What interest could the sideboard cupboard have for a brother of his? he pretended to think.

Oh yes, thought Terry, you're a fine man with a muscular back, but you couldn't have done what I've done. There had, after all, been Something in Terry. He *was* abler than John (they'd soon know). John had never kissed Josephine.

Terry sat down on the stairs saying: 'Josephine, Josephine!' He sat there gripping a baluster, shaking with exaltation.

The study door-panels had always looked solemn; they bulged with solemnity. Terry had to get past to his father; he chose the top left-hand panel to tap on. The patient voice said: 'Come in!'

Here and now, thought Terry. He had a great audience; he looked at the books round the dark walls and thought of all those thinkers. His father jerked up a contracted, strained look at him. Terry felt that hacking with his news into this silence was like hacking into a great, grave chest. The desk was a havoc of papers.

'What exactly do you want?' said his father, rubbing the edge of the desk.

Terry stood there silently: everything ebbed. 'I want,' he said at last, 'to talk about my future.'

His father sighed and slid a hand forward, rumpling the papers. 'I suppose, Terry,' he said as gently as possible, 'you really *have* got a future?' Then he reproached himself. 'Well, sit down a minute . . . I'll just . . . '

Terry sat down. The clock on the mantelpiece echoed the ticking in his brain. He waited.

'Yes?' said his father.

'Well, there must be some kind of future for me, mustn't there?'

'Oh, certainly . . . '

'Look here, father, I have something to show you. That African knife — '

'What about it?'

'That African knife. It's here. I've got it to show you.'

'What about it?'

'Just wait a minute.' He put a hand into either pocket: his father waited.

'It *was* here – I did have it. I brought it to show you. I must have it somewhere – that African knife.'

But it wasn't there, he hadn't got it; he had lost it; left it, dropped it – on the grass, by the tank, anywhere. He remembered wiping it . . . Then?

Now his support was all gone; he was terrified now; he wept.

'I've lost it,' he quavered, 'I've lost it.'

'What do you mean?' said his father, sitting blankly there like a tombstone, with his white, square face.

'What are you trying to tell me?'

'Nothing,' said Terry, weeping and shaking. 'Nothing, nothing, nothing.'

Mrs Moysey

MRS MOYSEY's nephew came home from Japan, suddenly, and paid her a long visit. She was very much touched by his liking to be with her, though flustered, because Mr Moysey had now been dead some time and her household had got out of a gentleman's ways. Leslie, however, was accommodating and kind and made every allowance; she implored him not to be shy about mentioning things and he very soon wasn't. He didn't want to be entertained, he sat most of the day in the dining-room bow-window, leaning back smoking and watching the people go up and down High Street. Sometimes he would ring the bell for the parlourmaid, or call to his aunt, to ask who somebody was. They were delighted to tell him. The people who interested Leslie most were ladies, young-middle-aged married ladies with nice figures.

Also, Mrs Moysey had been flustered by Leslie's arrival because she (and the household) had got into little ways of her own which seemed silly at once when one thought of anyone watching them. She went out either early, before everyone else was about, or late when most people were in again, coming home always with such an armful of parcels that she had to steady the top with her chin while she got out her latchkey. Then she would push the door gingerly back and slip in round it. Someone wittily said she looked like Christmas Eve every day. She spent most of the day in her bedroom; a room, very cosily furnished, overlooking the gardens behind the street. If anyone knocked she'd say 'Who's there?' in a muffled and rather fierce voice. She never said 'Come in', because she did not mean come in. If one persisted, after a minute or two she'd come out herself, rather flushed. Leslie, having experienced this, gave up knocking. He was full of delicacy. When his aunt came down for the evening, with her pale fluffy hair whipped up beautifully on the top of her head like confectioner's cream, an écru lace blouse and a string of green shells brought round twice and knotted over the bosom, he'd cry 'Auntie!' languidly rapturous, swing his feet off the rung of a chair and get up. He got up just slowly enough for her to feel every time how polished it was of Leslie to get up at all. In the evenings they were companionable, very cosy together, in spite of a habit of Mrs Moysey's of not sitting anywhere long or of fully relaxing, as though she were trying a new kind of stays that were not a success. At ten o'clock the parlourmaid brought in the decanters, Mrs Moysey would say, 'Well nightie-night I suppose,' and get finally up, between regret and alacrity.

Everybody in town knew Mrs Moysey and liked her, in spite of what was called 'the little failing'. Nobody specified what the little failing was; there existed an understanding. Yet it did seem curious that the parcels one saw her slip home with in the cold morning or in the evening dusk might be round, square or diamond-shaped, hard or bulgy, but were never cylindrical. And no one had ever seen her go into or come out of a – well, one wouldn't like to say what. But so flushed, so abrupt, so secretive – there wasn't a doubt.

Her friends, when first Leslie, exotic and waxlike, began to be displayed in the bow-window, were sympathetic and interested. There would be fewer temptations for poor Mrs Moysey now she was having young people about the house. Not long afterwards she gave a party and asked all the ladies Leslie admired most. They came, the drawing-room was unaccustomedly brilliant, they tinkled like lustres. But Leslie liked the ladies' conversation less than their figures. Perhaps he could have dealt with them better singly, at all events he went into a kind of stupor, blinked, and from looking at each of them not at all nicely passed to not looking at any of them at all. Before the end of tea he got up and went out; they could hear him moving glasses about in the dining-room and doing things with a syphon. They agreed on the way home that he was very Oriental-looking, that the failing evidently ran through their family and that it was disgusting of him to be living on his aunt.

Leslie did seem to have passed the fine line between staying and living. Mrs Moysey was gratified, but she began to be anxious on his behalf. How would Japan be getting on? Oughtn't he to be going back there? She didn't like to ask him. The servants were becoming a little unsettled, the housemaid developed weeping-fits and had to be sent away. The cook took to burning the dinner, was severe when Mrs Moysey mentioned it and talked about goings-on. Mrs Moysey never ate much dinner, she was not interested in meals, but when she saw Leslie turn his food over and over with his fork, frown, push his plate away, she flushed pinker than ever, her eyes pricked with shame and vexation and in trembling tones she begged him to overlook it. The parlourmaid was present, she was what is called 'faithful', but the starch all over her person seemed to have entered into her soul. She whisked Leslie's plate away, as much as to say. 'Well, don't then!'

In spite of bad cooking and lack of social amenities Leslie, full of solicitude for his aunt's feelings, did seem inclined to stay on. His temper was very equable; if it couldn't be called sunny it was not at any rate bad. Mrs Moysey was on this account all the more stupefied, shattered even, when creeping across the hall one morning on her way out to the shops she had a glimpse through the dining-room doorway, of Leslie distinctly 'put out'. Leslie, stiffly and whitely grinning, his teeth pressing away all the blood from his lip, was tearing a letter up into crumbs that fluttered slowly down on the light like a stage snowstorm. ' – — her!' said Leslie softly, almost tenderly, 'The — ! The – little — !'

'N-not bad news, Les, I hope?' said Mrs Moysey.

Leslie borrowed ten pounds from his aunt and went up to London. He said goodbye – not, he hoped, for more than a day or two; he smiled more than usual, masked little smiles; a lingering terrible tenderness tinted his manner. She hoped, listening with locked hands pressed under her bosom to the slam of the door, that he'd taken enough money, had nice friends in town and hadn't (oh, why should she think so?) gone up to commit a murder? He hadn't left an address. Mrs Moysey kept missing him terribly. She didn't come down that evening, she couldn't bear the look of the house. They brought her dinner up on a tray, and until nearly midnight the servants heard her playing the gramophone. Passers-by saw that the dining-room window was empty, or rather, that a table of plants, long displaced, had returned to it. Some waxy-leaved ferns and a dish of thick-fingered cacti, palpably crawling, carried on Leslie's tradition.

Three days later a young woman with hands in her mackintosh pockets stood looking up at the windows, made some irresolute movements and finally knocked. She and the parlourmaid stared at each other. Something in common between them, perhaps some potential resistance to Leslie the servant divined in her, travelled along the interchange. Resolutely anonymous, persisting that her name could mean nothing, she was admitted. Mrs Moysey, informed through her door, replied in a voice more stopped-up, and husky than usual, she wouldn't see anyone. The parlourmaid coughed. 'No, ma'am. I quite undersand, ma'am.' Five seconds later, she was tapping again. 'The young lady did say it was urgent.'

'Nothing's as urgent as all that. I'm not dressed, I tell you. I can't see her now.'

'She said she could wait, ma'am.'

'What *does* she want?'

'You don't think it could be something about Mr Leslie?'

'Don't be silly — ' But soon Mrs Moysey trailed over the

drawing-room carpet her long purple skirts. The young woman, not having seen her before, did not perceive a new flame, a new dignity: Aunthood. She saw a pink lady, expansive, with a curious toppling expression from the Pompadour-curves of her coiffure and round, apprehensive eyes.

'Yes?' said Mrs Moysey, without the formalities.

'Only, I came about your nephew — '

'Leslie – why, what's the matter?'

'Only that he's my husband. I . . . '

They looked at each other in fearful dismay.

'I don't think, you know, that you ought to come here saying things like this. I don't know you.'

'I didn't suppose you would,' said the young woman, sarcastic but quavering. 'My husband's not here, I suppose?'

'My nephew's not here.'

'No, he wouldn't be. I was a fool to write.' She wriggled her shoulders angrily, so that the mackintosh rustled. 'My name's Emerald. Emerald Voles. Yes, it *is*. I've got two babies – I could show you. They're at the Station Hotel.'

'*Young* babies?' said Mrs Moysey, crimson at this impropriety.

'Three and two – Aunt Moysey.'

Emerald had not a kind face. It was pinched, hard and aggressive; she spoke as though to call one Aunt were an insult. She might at least, Mrs Moysey thought plaintively, try and be winning. Perhaps she was hungry. Perhaps, thought Mrs Moysey, studying the concavities of the mackintosh, she hadn't much on underneath. She was not at all the type of girl one expected Leslie to fancy. Mrs Moysey was on the point of saying, with perfect conclusiveness, 'You must be wrong about this. Leslie would never have had a wife without curves.'

It was funny of her to be wearing a mackintosh. Mrs Moysey knew plenty of ladies who were not well off, but they didn't wear a mackintosh all day long. Perhaps she wanted to *look* deserted. It might be 'the confidence trick' – she had often been warned of it.

'Won't you take off your mackintosh?'

'Not till I've got something else to put on.'

'Oh, how dreadful! . . . Have you come from Japan?'

'Two years ago; just before Baby was born. I sold up most of my things to pay the passage. I had to get back to my mother – I needn't have hurried, it turned out; Mother died just after I started. Leslie was supposed to be coming back three months after; he didn't, of course, and I never got any money. I've never heard anything more of him. I wrote to the Consul where we'd been and to one or two other people, but that didn't come to anything; I suppose Leslie'd got in with some story first. So I just kept on living somehow and waited. Then the other day I got in touch with a lady I'd known out there. She was stiffish (showed what Leslie'd been saying), but she did let out that Leslie'd been sacked from his job and come home. She got me his address down here through the London branch of the firm – they'd been having some correspondence – I guessed he'd be with his Aunt Moysey,' Emerald added. With a (to Mrs Moysey) ghastly kind of complacency she looked round the room and sat down.

Mrs Moysey, surprised, as though struck by the aptness of the suggestion, sat down also. She hitched the top of herself further over her stays, adjusted the stays as inconspicuously as possible, released a long sigh from her body's constriction and said reflectively, 'Well, it's all been very unfortunate — '

'Very,' said Emerald pressingly.

'But I'm afraid I don't quite see how I — '

'If you'll wait for ten minutes I'll bring round the children at once. You might hesitate a minute or two over Daph, unless you'd seen her asleep or sulking, but there'll be no doubt at all about little Bobby.'

'But I'm not arranged for children,' wailed Mrs Moysey. Emerald (who, of course, could not help this) had left the room.

Ten minutes later, punctually, Emerald reappeared (Mrs Moysey watched through the curtains) more wolfish than ever, nose to the wind up the street, pushing a folding go-cart. Little Bobby in a blue woolly cap walloped forward over the strap of the go-cart, and Daph, with little flax curls like bobbins at the back of a tilted bonnet, swung from her mother's left hand, tripping alongside. Before the go-cart had begun to bump up to the front door steps Mrs Moysey, hot and cold from a sense of fatality, had acknowledged herself a great-aunt. The entrance clinched it. Daph, flattened against the maternal mackintosh, presented a coal-scuttle profile, but there was no doubt (as the snub-featured small dark face appeared round the mackintosh, was thrust forward – with cap snatched off from above and a dab at the curls – and presented itself square to the Aunt's gaze, embedded in jersey-collar and still swaying slightly from the arrested totter) about little Bobby.

'*There*! . . . ' whispered Mrs Moysey, appalled by what Leslie had done.

'Little duckie,' she said later, tremulous. She sat well back in the big chair with knees jutting forward, disposed in this attitude almost in spite of herself, presenting a capable, destined and so far unoccupied lap. Daph, let out of her reefer, vivified by the removal of the bonnet, sheered round her in a constellation of pink bows, clambered up suddenly, nestled. A roll of the head, a listening pressure, the head heavy and warm and wonderfully round

through the silver-fine hair . . . 'Little *duckie!*' . . . Bobby remained at a distance, he clutched and unclutched the arm of a chair
with an air of having secured property. He lifted and lowered his
eyelids, considering his great-aunt and sister sideways with a covert
intentness. His father's look.

As Emerald had decreed, the children remained at Mrs Moysey's
(where they should do very well) while Emerald took back to
London her persistent, charmless and unrelenting wifeliness to
continue the search. She kept repeating, 'Oh, *I* haven't come down
for anything. It's only the kiddies — ' but finally accepted a five-
pound note and a Shetland coatee to wear under her mackintosh.
She kissed the children in a queer, darting way, got away from them
into the hall, but broke out into one husky noise like a bark when,
there in the half-dark, she stumbled over the go-cart. 'It is *hard*,' she
said, 'isn't it?' and dabbed at her eyes and the tip of her nose with
savage efficiency.

'Dreadful,' agreed Mrs Moysey, yet looked at the hat-rack where
Leslie's check cap was still hanging with an irresponsible spasm of
pity for Emerald's quarry.

'I said I'd be a good wife to my man when I took him,' said
Emerald, 'and I've been a good wife to my man. Oh, I don't want
anyone's pity. But I must say it does seem hard. And having to part
from the kiddies — '

'Look, take my umbrella,' said Mrs Moysey. 'I don't often use it.
And if you want more money, write. And I'll write every day
about Billy and Daph, I do promise. And if Leslie comes back — '

'Wire at once and keep him here!' shouted back Emerald, now
half-way down the steps.

'And I'll be sure and remember the name of those rusks,' panted
Mrs Moysey. 'And I'll teach them to pray for you every night — '

'They don't pray,' shouted Emerald. '*I* never got any good out
of it.' She collided with someone, recoiled with a fierce exclamation and fled down the street.

The household, which had got so slowly and painfully into a
gentleman's ways, must have gained thereby in elasticity, for it
adapted itself without effort to Daph's and Bobby's. It absorbed the
children. A bubble or two, some ripples that widened and vanished,
then once more, above them, its unruffled surface of tranquil
secretiveness. From the street, little repaid one's eager and close
observation. They never came out. Now and then, their faces
bobbed up over a window-sill, a fat hand was star-fished against a
pane. Bars were screwed crosswise before an upstairs window,
behind which, as autumn drew in, a light would appear about five
o'clock. But no sooner was the light lit and the room with its
bustling occupants tantalizingly vivid than the whole would be

masked, triumphantly, by a crimson curtain. Neighbours looking out at the back could watch the couple, like young chickens, bowling about the garden under no visible supervision. Now and then the cook would come out and clap her hands at them; Mrs Moysey's window creaked up for an admonition, then closed again. Her periodic sallies to the shops became more frequent, flurried, more awkwardly timed than ever; her load of parcels increased – she almost staggered. She offered no explanations, her house was not open to visitors. From the grim maids, less than ever communicative, nothing could be elicited.

Curiosity, starved by this silence, became suspicion. The children were there, unannounced, unapologized for; young children, still fresh from the impropriety of birth. The social circumstances that could have mitigated this impropriety remained unpublished, without doubt non-existent. Covertly someone had 'had' them. But who? It was not, physiologically alone, to be believed of Mrs Moysey.

And further, discounting all this, was poor Mrs Moysey a proper companion or guardian for children at all? She'd been odder than ever just recently; her actions, her inaction, were capable only of the most sinister interpretation. When she did not appear for a day or two that meant 'a bout', and when she came out two or three days in succession this was a sign that 'the failing', increasing its hold on her, demanded further and further supplies. Ladies with children shuddered to think what those poor little tots were exposed to; ladies without children, eager for social activity, demanded some interference: 'a rescue' it came to be called. Leslie was cited; even he, though a thoroughly nasty young fellow, had felt there were limits, had been crowded unwillingly out by the life in that house . . . *Poor* Mrs Moysey, who might have been really so nice.

Poor Mrs Moysey was indeed not herself at all. She lived in a long agitation, a flutter of happiness. Every morning a sense of the present, more poignant than sense of the future in youth or the past in age, shot through her waking bemusedness like a pang. She wrote every day to Emerald, the letters got shorter and shorter, so little of this was articulate, less still was proper for Emerald to know. Daph and Bobby were good as gold, as angels, their appetites were unexceptional, their insides like faultless clockwork. It had been all right giving them pheasant, hadn't it, thoroughly minced? They did seem to fancy it so – Daph was learning a little poem to say to her Mummy. They asked every day for their Mummy (she closed every letter with this convention), wasn't it sweet? The sweetness of Daph and Bobby to Mummy-wards had, as a matter of fact, to be sounded for more and more urgently.

Mummy was less than a name to them; she was forgotten. The more Mrs Moysey perceived this with exultation and horror, the more conscientiously was Mummy evoked. But perhaps Leslie's children partook of his feeling for softness, for the curvilinear, for unrestraint. Mrs Moysey with scruples, with anguishing happiness, came to know that Emerald was supplanted.

Daph and Bobby had not their father's delicacy and were not to be impressed by the household with any respect for Mrs Moysey's door as a door. Having discovered these panels concealed their Aunt Moysey, they drummed on them ceaselessly. At first Mrs Moysey, after a scuffle of preparation would come out like a flannel and marabout cloud and envelop them; beneath her vast impetus, trailing boas and shawls, they would be borne along to the nursery, where she would endlessly play with them. Then one day unexpectedly (to the breathless housemaid, incredibly) the door was held open a crack and Daph and her brother oozed round it. This privileged oozing-round became on wet mornings and all afternoons a precedent. They were engulfed in the innermost secrecy of that secret house. The housemaid coming up with the coal, the parlourmaid with the tea-tray, came as before to the door and no further, heard conversation within, sometimes revelry, sometimes a sociable silence. Implacably, still no one else was admitted after the morning's dusting and sweeping, the attention that grate and washstand required, were finished. At six o'clock punctually Mrs Moysey's bell rang; the children, bewildered as from Arabian enchantment, would be discovered outside on the mat.

About this time it was noticeable that their complexions, manners, tempers were beginning to deteriorate. In a week the deterioration had become more rapid and their appetites began to be affected. The maids, in consultation, hit on 'bowels', but laxatives did little for their complexions and only temporarily improved their moral tone. Daph turned from dinner after dinner, so did Bobby; 'lovely mince' and 'num-num bread and mink' appalled those children once so hungry and grateful; they fought and bit each other, and often before five o'clock had to be carried up, screaming, to bed. They became, it seemed incurably, yellow, spotty and demented. Their darlingness was in prolonged eclipse. Mrs Moysey observed their condition anxiously, but when this was brought to her attention by the servants denied it with asperity.

'They're *little* children,' she explained to the cook. 'You're not used to little children. They have their little ups and downs – we all have. Try . . . try a little medicine.'

'I shouldn't care to give them any more medicine than what I have been giving them,' said the cook darkly. She looked hard at

Mrs Moysey. 'One would have thought,' she said, 'that they'd been having more than they should of what they shouldn't have to eat or drink. But of course that couldn't be . . . I sees to everything they eats and drinks myself. Everything.'

'Of course, of course,' agreed Mrs Moysey, more than usually flustered.

'A good slapping's what I'd be disposed to try,' the cook said, dispassionate as a goddess; 'they're getting spoilt, they are.'

'Never! I forbid you,' blazed out Mrs Moysey, then subsided into wateriness. 'Do promise me you'll never think of that.'

'It's for you to say, ma'am,' said the cook formally.

Mrs Moysey's visitors seemed fated to decline in popularity. For a long time cook talked of goings-on. Meanwhile, as day after day the screams of Daph and Bobby echoed down the High Street, the rescue party mobilized itself and sent a deputation to the Vicar.

Emerald traced Leslie to a residential hotel in West Kensington where, as he pointed out to her, he had been living perfectly quietly, not doing anyone any harm. 'Then *you* come along,' he kept saying in a white heat of indignation which outblazed her own. He might have been a St Anthony: she, from the air of spiritualized repudiation with which he viewed her untempting-ness, the most persistent of temptations. He was proof, in speech and spirit, against everything but forgivingness; in the tentacles of this icy and arid forgivingness, which began to hover about him from the time of her entry, she did have him ultimately. She placed her submission before him, wherever he turned, like a plate of unfinished cold mutton before a refractory child; he was dogged by her constancy as his children were, elsewhere, being dogged by the cook with their platefuls of lovely mince. She unceasingly talked of the kiddies. 'It does seem hard they shouldn't have a Daddy. Bobby's beginning to talk now; 'Dad-dad' he keeps saying. He can't understand, you see. Of course I've never told them anything, Leslie; I'd hate them to know — ' That plate of cold mutton was planked down before him again.

Leslie had not been alone in the hotel in West Kensington; he was there with a nice Mrs Moss he had met coming home from Japan. His delicacy, his consequent eagerness to avoid an encounter between Emerald and Mrs Moss – who might come in at any moment – played into Emerald's hands. Her entente with his Aunt Moysey clinched matters. His aunt must have 'taken things' wonderfully well or she'd never have taken the children. There would be needed, to re-win her entirely, nothing but a flourish of conjugality which he was resigned to perform. 'If you've squared things,' he questioned cautiously, 'if you're quite *certain* you've squared things?' Where the Voles as a *ménage* were concerned, Emerald had certainly; for himself, she said, he must look to his charms. 'Oh then, that's all right, sighed out Leslie, lay down like a sacrifice on the bed and let Emerald pack. She packed up his bag for him, summoned a taxi, settled his bill (wouldn't poor Mrs Moss be surprised when she had to settle her own!) and removed him forthwith. It wasn't half bad, Leslie thought, leaning back with closed eyes in the taxi while Emerald totted up her accounts in a notebook and counted her change, to be going about with a wife of one's own once again. One did need looking after. Mrs Moss, for instance, never did anything for him; she expected, in fact, the contrary: she was one of those clinging things.

In the train, however, Leslie began to feel indignant again with Emerald for her lack of motherly feeling. Having revolved the matter, uncertain if it were worth the effort of speech, he said dreamily, 'You know best, of course, but I must say I should never have dreamed of leaving young children where you've left yours.'

'It seemed to me proper,' said Emerald snappily.

'Oh well, if you've no prejudice,' Leslie said, raising his eyebrows. 'You know about Auntie, of course?'

'More than she knew about you.'

'Her habits?'

'Her *habits*?'

Leslie raised an elbow and dropped his head back in an expressive gesture. 'Tipples like hell', he said mournfully. Poor old dear!' He had made more friends locally than Mrs Moysey supposed.

'You don't *mean* that? Oh, Leslie . . . the horrid old creature! She looked so respectable – how could I know?'

'Dreadful, isn't it?' agreed Leslie. 'I must say, she keeps up appearances wonderfully. Never touches a drop at table. I daresay the kids will be all right. Bit scared, probably. Makes an impression on young children, that kind of thing. Still, I daresay they'll be all right.'

'I shall go mad,' said Emerald, looking grim and determined. After all this . . . her kiddies . . . But Leslie had gone to sleep.

Emerald shot past the parlourmaid into the hall; Leslie came in after her. He was much relieved at finding his good check cap still on the hat-rack; he took it down, looked at the lining and hung it up again. 'Home again, Phyllis,' he said to the parlourmaid affably. But Phyllis headed him into the impersonal dusky drawing-room as though he had been a caller. She jerked up the blinds and knelt down with a creak at the knee-joints to put a match to the fire. 'I'll tell the mistress,' said Phyllis, and looked round the room rather insultingly, as though taking an inventory of everything in there. But Emerald barred her exit. 'Where are the children?' 'I can't say, I'm sure, ma'am. Probably up in the mistress's room.'

As bad as that! If Emerald lacked the allurements, she was complete with every instinct proper to her sex. She charged upstairs and though on the first floor, still strange to her, might well have been at a loss, was attracted unerringly to those varnished panels, the impassable shining discretion of Mrs Moysey's door. Justified by maternity, she put an ear to the keyhole. She heard the double voice of her children upraised querulously, a silence, a short groan of acquiescence, the squeak of released chair springs, then Mrs Moysey moving immensely about in reluctance, distraction, uncertainty – or was it sheer lack of control? For some moments of keenest anxiety Emerald listened, then rap-a-tapped. '*Who's* there?' said the choked voice. Rap-a-tap-tap, insisted Emerald, 'Well, what *do* you want?' Rap-tap-tap.

Mrs Moysey came to the other side of the door, breathing urgently. With a gurgle she caught her breath back; she and Emerald listened intently for one another. Then encouraged by some misinterpreted quality in Emerald's silence she stealthily slid back the bolt. Emerald's fingers had crept to the door knob, she wrenched this round smartly, flung her weight on to the door and burst in, rebounding sideways from against Mrs Moysey and knocking over a screen which had concealed the room.

Emerald's children looked up at her out of a coloured earthquake-city. Unnerved by her manner they turned to retreat; gilt, flowered and brightly pictorial boxes scrunched with the unresistance of cardboard under their wildly-placed feet. They evacuated, with shaken majesty, an empire of chocolate boxes. A kind of road system of ribbons twisted over the carpet; a round lid with a pussy cat's head looking out of a horse-shoe bowled away from them, spun like a platter at Emerald's feet and was still. The boxes were very artistic and striking. Flower-sprays or Zoo scenes, dragons in synthetic embroidery, 'The Angelus', 'Lady Hamilton', girls' heads in the popular manner, the Tower of London by moonlight, hunting scenes, the Prince of Wales, 'The Monarch of the Glen', and more lids with an opulent restraint in their lettering were, with the boxes they covered, built up into towers and bridges or arranged in patterns. Others, rejected or not yet made use of, were scattered profusely.

'Oh, it's you, is it, Emerald?' said Mrs Moysey at last. 'Are you in such a hurry?'

Emerald was as nearly as possible shattered. The brave little woman felt deprived and beaten as never before. She couldn't collect herself and felt she could never forgive Mrs Moysey for having betrayed her.

'I came up to tell you,' she said in a voice dank with injury, 'I found Leslie this morning. I felt it was right you should know.'

'Indeed! Well, I'm glad,' Mrs Moysey said distantly. 'As a matter of fact,' she continued, surprised at herself for feeling resentful and still more surprised at feeling resentment gain ground in her, 'you've given me quite a shock. I'm not strong; I should have thought that you'd know that: you've frightened the children, too . . . There, hush, little darlings . . . There, Daffles, hush . . . Isn't that a funny Mummy? That was Mummy's surprise, wasn't it? Mummy came in and said "Peep-bo", didn't she? "Peep-bo", she said.'

The great-aunt went down on her knees with surprising agility and held her arms out over the littered floor. The children fled into them, buried their faces like ostriches, shaking with sobs. The blonde and the dark head pressed deeper into the crimson capaciousness; Mrs Moysey, closing her arms with protective finality, gently and gingerly rocked from the knees. 'There – there, Daph.' Daph peeped up across the protective shoulder, saw Emerald put out a hand, ducked her face down again and redoubled her screams.

'I'm afraid you'll have to keep back for a minute or two,' said Mrs Moysey. 'They're still rather frightened. I'm used to their ways, you see.'

'What a *thing* to say to a mother!' Emerald marvelled.

Mrs Moysey, looking down, was immersed in a business of stroking, murmuring, dabbing with her handkerchief, kissing, dabbing again.

'Something's very much wrong with their tempers,' continued Emerald, 'they never did this with me!' She sat down at a distance, repudiating the relatives huddled like Christians in the arena, and began to count the chocolate boxes. When she had come to fifty-eight she noticed that the doors of a wardrobe were open and that a far greater number of boxes were stacked up inside. She gave up in despair. It was all very cosy in here, one big chair – not more, for one sat at ease here in uncorseted freedom and wasn't driven to roam, constricted uneasily, questing for comfort – a table spead with manuscript books, a white bearskin tinged with firelight, a drum-shaped stool at the edge of the rug. On the stool, one more box with the lid off – not empty. The box was about the size of a dinner-plate and so far only a dozen chocolates were missing; the rest were arranged in a lovely design like a rose. They looked to Emerald the sort that would only be given to very immoral ladies by very rich men. They were now being eaten, there wouldn't be any more left. Emerald went back through her thoughts, testing every connection, her eye travelled back to the wardrobe, the town on the floor.

'Have you eaten all these, Aunt Moysey?' she asked, with the simplicity of a Riding Hood.

Aunt Moysey looked up at her over the children's heads. 'Well yes, I suppose I must have. One time and another . . . ' She looked round at her boxes, between wonder and a genuine gratification.

Emerald's rigid attention made further demands.

'They do rather mount up, I suppose. The fact is,' she went on, gathering speed and a certain recklessness, 'I don't throw my boxes away . . . They are so artistic, I think – well, look at that sunset, for instance; you couldn't buy a picture like that for quite a large sum if you asked for it in a gallery. I've made quite a little collection, haven't I, all these years? As a matter of fact, I look at them quite a lot.'

'Did you ever show them to Leslie?'

'Oh no. I mean, he'd have thought me so silly, you know. Gentlemen never seem to me to have quite the same feeling for beautiful things. Do you think so?'

'I can't say; I've never had any – beautiful things, I mean.'

'I know, I *know*,' said Mrs Moysey, 'that's what makes it so terrible of me, gratifying my fancies. That's why I'm so ashamed. Think of the little children now, starving all over the world! When I think of them I hardly know what to do.'

Her children had stopped crying and were struggling and pushing against her breast. She opened her arms and relinquished them, looking after them for a moment or two. Then she looked at their mother with a startlingly personal brightness, a flash of the self through her fumbling secretiveness like the flash of a rare shy bird through an overgrown thicket. The look glanced off from the obdurate face of Emerald, cold with thought. But she was tasting, perhaps for the first time, the sweetness of self-betrayal.

'So few people would understand,' she continued. 'It does sound terrible, doesn't it? I'd hate people – Leslie or you or the neighbours – to think ill of me. I've always been most careful. That's what's wonderful about children, isn't it; they understand. Bobby and Daph enter into everything – why, I'm even reading them my book.'

'Oh, I'm afraid you couldn't expect them to understand *that*. Are you writing a book?'

Mrs Moysey looked at Emerald sideways. It was as though the bird poised in the thicket, then with queer cry darted into the open. 'Oh yes, I wrote a good deal – a life of myself. Well, not my life strictly, that wouldn't be interesting to me; I do touch things up

here and there. There are so many points in a life when things so
nearly . . . I don't see any harm myself in putting those sorts of
things in – well, what is just one's life in *itself*, if you come to think
of it? Then there are some things, of course, I leave out. Well, you
wouldn't expect to find in a book about anyone's indigestion . . .
Daph and Bob are loving the story, they listen entranced — '

Here Mrs Moysey had to break off, for Emerald's failure to listen
had become as positive as an interruption. The eyes of the mother,
devoid of illusion, sharp with practical understanding, had meanwhile been ferreting out the handkerchief which, lately employed
in the aunt's ministrations, was now concealed in the fold of Mrs
Moysey's lap. The handkerchief, crumpled and clammy, was
blotched a dissolute pinky-brown. Mrs Moysey, attention arrested,
also looked down at the handkerchief. Emerald's gaze wheeled
sideways. Her children, puffy from crying, were reassembling
their city. Daph placed the Prince of Wales on The Angelus, Bobby
knocked him off again. They snarled at each other. Thick brown
stains, dispersed from their mouths by the dabbing of Mrs Moysey,
echoed over their faces. A thin brown dribble of chocolate ran
down Daph's frock.

'What have they had?' exclaimed Emerald. *'How much of that have
they eaten?'* There ensued an appalled silence, the hollow tumbling of
boxes. The children looked up at each other, then at their aunt. The
three were banded together by this interchange, which excluded
Emerald finally like the slam of a door. Emerald quivered all over.
Her thin hands quivered, locked in her lap, the movement ran up to
her shoulders, so piteously set in a decent woman's bravado. She
jerked her chin backwards with a convulsive movement, as though
lassoed from behind.

'They're never allowed any! They *know* they're never allowed
any! *You* know they're never allowed any. No wonder they're sick
and poisoned and don't know their own mother. Sold!' said
Emerald slowly, 'that's what I've been!'

There did indeed seem nobody she could trust.

'Hush!' cried out Mrs Moysey, then put her two hands to her
mouth for very horror.

'Stolen!' said Emerald. 'That's what they've been . . . my own
children.'

She said no more, for her virtue, her indignation more awful
than eloquence mounted into a wave that, dwarfing her, even,
toppled over the room. As though the weight of that wave were
to crash down both women put their arms for the menaced
children.

Bobs and Daffie, tottering to their feet in alarm, looked this and
that way, then with one movement flung themselves both, face

down, into Mrs Moysey's lap and clutched and clung there, you would have said in desperation.

'There . . . ' said Emerald, almost gently, and began the clik-cluk-cluk of a dry sobbing.

You would have said there was no place, no home in the world for decent women.

And Mrs Moysey – most unwilling victor – half clutching the children to her because Mother was so frightening, half pushing them from her because Mother was so lonely, poor Mrs Moysey – most unconvinced voluptuary – did not know where to look . . .

The Thirties

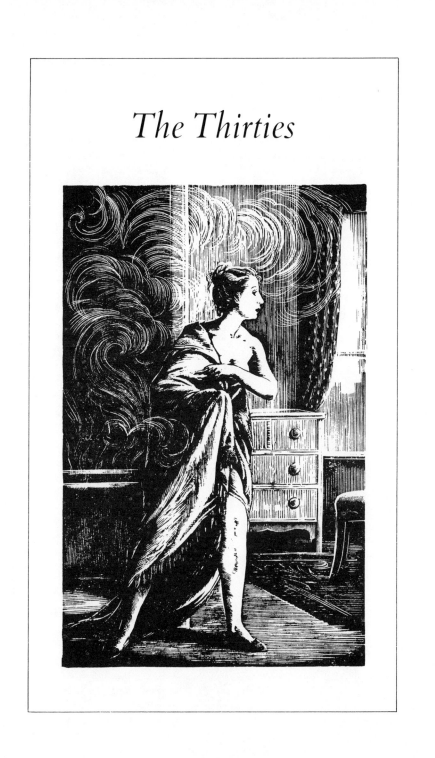

The Tommy Crans

HERBERT'S feet, from dangling so long in the tram, had died of cold in his boots; he stamped the couple of coffins on blue-and-buff mosaic. In the Tommy Crans' cloak-room the pegs were too high – Uncle Archer cocked H.M.S. *Terrible* for him over a checked ulster. Tommy Cran – aslant meanwhile, in the doorway – was an enormous presence. 'Come on, now, come!' he exclaimed, and roared with impatience. You would have said he was also arriving at the Tommy Crans' Christmas party, of which one could not bear to miss a moment.

Now into the hall Mrs Tommy Cran came swimming from elsewhere, dividing with curved little strokes the festive air – hyacinths and gunpowder. Her sleeves, in a thousand ruffles, fled from her elbows. She gained Uncle Archer's lapels and, bobbing, floated from this attachment. Uncle Archer, verifying the mistletoe, loudly kissed her face of a delicate pink sugar. 'Ha!' yelled Tommy, drawing an unseen dagger. Herbert laughed with embarrassment.

'Only think, Nancy let off all the crackers before tea! She's quite wild, but there are more behind the piano. Ah, is this little Herbert? Herbert . . .'

'Very well, thank you,' said Herbert, and shook hands defensively. This was his first Christmas Day without any father; the news went before him. He had seen his mother off, very brave with the holly wreath, in the cemetery tram. She and father were spending Christmas afternoon together.

Mrs Tommy Cran stooped to him, bright with a tear-glitter, then with a strong upward sweep, like an angel's, bore him to gaiety. '*Fancy* Nancy!' He fancied Nancy. So by now they would all be wearing the paper caps. Flinging back a white door, she raced Herbert elsewhere.

The room where they all sat seemed to be made of glass, it collected the whole daylight; the candles were still waiting. Over the garden, day still hung like a pink flag; over the trees like frozen feathers, the enchanted icy lake, the lawn. The table was in the window. As Herbert was brought in a clock struck four; the laughing heads all turned in a silence brief as a breath's intake. The great many gentlemen and the rejoicing ladies leaned apart; he and Nancy looked at each other gravely.

He saw Nancy, crowned and serious because she was a queen. Advanced by some urgent pushing, he made his way round the table and sat down beside her, podgily.

She said: 'How d'you do? Did you see our lake? It is all frozen. Did you ever see our lake before?'

'I never came here.'

'Did you see our two swans?'

She was so beautiful, rolling her ringlets, round with light, on her lacy shoulders, that he said rather shortly: 'I shouldn't have thought your lake was large enough for two swans.'

'It is, indeed,' said Nancy; 'it goes round the island. It's large enough for a boat.'

They were waiting, around the Christmas cake, for tea to be brought in. Mrs Tommy Cran shook out the ribbons of her guitar and began to sing again. Very quietly, for a secret, he and Nancy crept to the window; she showed how the lake wound; he could guess how, in summer, her boat would go pushing among the lily leaves. She showed him their boat-house, rusty-red from a lamp inside, solid. 'We had a lamp put there for the poor cold swans.' (And the swans were asleep beside it.) 'How old are you, Herbert?'

'Eight.'

'Oh, I'm nine. Do you play brigands?'

'I could,' said Herbert.

'Oh, I don't; I'd hate to. But I know some boys who do. Did you have many presents? Uncle Ponto brought me a train; it's more suitable for a boy, really. I could give it to you, perhaps.'

'How many uncles — ?' began Herbert.

'Ten pretence and none really. I'm adopted, because mummy and daddy have no children. I think that's better fun, don't you?'

'Yes,' replied Herbert, after consideration; 'anybody could be born'.

All the time, Nancy had not ceased to look at him seriously and impersonally. They were both tired already by this afternoon of boisterous grown-up society; they would have liked to be quiet, and though she was loved by ten magic uncles and wore a pearl locket, and he was fat, with spectacles, and felt deformed a little from everybody's knowing about his father, they felt at ease in each other's company.

'Nancy, cut the cake!' exclaimed Mrs Tommy, and they all clapped their hands for Nancy's attention. So the coloured candles were lit, the garden went dark with loneliness and was immediately curtained out. Two of the uncles put rugs on and bounded about the room like bears and lions; the other faces drew out a crimson band round the silver teapot. Mrs Tommy could not bear to put down the guitar, so the teapot fell into the hands of a fuzzy lady with several husbands who cried 'Ah, don't, now!' and had to keep brushing gentlemen's hands from her waist. And all the others leaned on each other's shoulders and laughed with gladness because they had been asked to the Tommy Crans'; a dozen times everyone died of laughter and rose again, redder ghosts. Teacups whizzed down a chain of hands. Now Nancy, standing up very straight to cut the cake, was like a doll stitched upright into its box, apt, if you should cut the string at the back, to pitch right forward and break its delicate fingers.

'Oh dear,' she sighed, as the knife skidded over the icing. But nobody heard but Herbert. For someone, seeing her white frock over that palace of cake, proposed 'The health of the bride'. And an Uncle Joseph, tipping the tea about in his cup, stared and stared with juicy eyes. But nobody saw but Herbert.

'After tea,' she whispered, 'we'll go and stand on the lake.' And after tea they did, while the others played hide and seek. Herbert, once looking back through a window, saw uncles chasing the laughing aunts. It was not cold on the lake. Nancy said: 'I never believed in fairies – did you either?' She told him she had been given a white muff and was going to be an organist, with an organ of her own. She was going up to Belfast next month to dance for charity. She said she would not give him the train after all; she would give him something really her own, a pink glass greyhound that was an ornament.

When Uncle Archer and Herbert left to walk to the tram terminus, the party was at its brightest. They were singing 'Hark the herald' around the drawing-room piano: Nancy sat on her Uncle Joseph's knee, more than politely.

Uncle Archer did not want to go home either. 'That was a nice little girl,' he said. 'Eh?'

Herbert nodded. His uncle, glad that the little chap hadn't had, after all, such a dismal Christmas, pursued heartily: 'Kiss her?' Herbert looked quite blank. To tell the truth, this had never occurred to him.

He kissed Nancy later; his death, even, was indirectly caused by his loss of her; but their interchanges were never passionate, and he never knew her better than when they had been standing out on the lake, beyond the cheerful windows. Herbert's mother did not know Uncle Archer's merry friends: she had always loved to live quietly, and, as her need for comfort decreased, she and Herbert saw less, or at least as little as ever of Uncle Archer. So that for years Herbert was not taken again across Dublin to the house with the lake. Once he saw Nancy carry her white muff into a shop, but he stood rooted and did not run after her. Once he saw Mrs Tommy Cran out in Stephen's Green throwing lollipops to the ducks: but he did not approach; there was nothing to say. He was sent to school, where he painfully learnt to be natural with boys: his sight got no better; they said he must wear glasses all his life. Years later, however, when Herbert was thirteen, the Crans gave a dancing-party and did not forget him. He danced once with Nancy; she was silenter now, but she said: 'Why did you never come back again?' He could not explain; he trod on her toes and danced heavily on. A Chinese lantern blazed up, and in the confusion he lost her. That evening he saw Mrs Tommy in tears in the conservatory. Nancy clung, pressing her head, with its drooping pink ribbons, to Mrs Cran's shoulder; pressing, perhaps, the shoulder against the head. Soon it was all right again and Mrs Tommy led off in 'Sir Roger', but Nancy was like a ghost who presently vanished. A week afterwards he had a letter:

Please meet me to tea at Mitchell's; I want your advice specially.

She was distracted: she had come in to Dublin to sell her gold wrist-watch. The Tommy Crans had lost all their money – it wasn't fair to expect them to keep it; they were generous and gay. Nancy had to think hard what must they all do. Herbert went round with her from jeweller to jeweller: these all laughed and paid her nothing but compliments. Her face, with those delicate lovely eyebrows, grew tragic under the fur cap; it rained continuously; she and Herbert looked with incredulity into the grown-up faces: they wondered how one could penetrate far into life without despair. At last a man on the quays gave her eight-and-six for the watch. Herbert, meanwhile, had spent eight shillings of his pocket-money on their cab – and, even so, her darling feet were sodden. They were surprised to see, from the window, Tommy Cran jump from an outside car and run joyfully into the Shelbourne. It turned out he had raised some more money from somewhere – as he deserved.

So he sold the house with the lake and moved to an ornamental castle by Dublin Bay. In spite of the grey scene, the transitory light from the sea, the terrace here was gay with urns of geraniums, magnificent with a descent of steps – scrolls and whorls of balustrade, all the grandeur of stucco. Here the band played for their afternoon parties, and here, when they were twenty and twenty-one, Herbert asked Nancy to marry him.

A pug harnessed with bells ran jingling about the terrace. 'Oh, I don't know, Herbert; I don't know.'

'Do you think you don't love me?'

'I don't know whom I love. Everything would have to be different. Herbert, I don't see how we are ever to live; we seem to know everything. Surely there should be something for us we don't know?' She shut her eyes; they kissed seriously and searchingly. In his arms her body felt soft and voluminous; he could not touch her because of a great fur coat. The coat had been a surprise from Tommy Cran, who loved to give presents on delightful occasions – for now they were off to the Riviera. They were sailing in four days; Nancy and Mrs Tommy had still all their shopping to do, all his money to spend – he loved them both to be elegant. There was that last party to give before leaving home. Mrs Tommy could hardly leave the telephone; crossing London, they were to give yet another party, at the Euston Hotel.

'And how could I leave them?' she asked. 'They're my business.'

'Because they are not quite your parents?'

'Oh, no,' she said, eyes reproachful for the misunderstanding he had put up, she knew, only from bitterness. 'They would be my affair whoever I was. Don't you see, they're like that.'

The Tommy Crans returned from the Riviera subdued, and gave no more parties than they could avoid. They hung sun-yellow curtains, in imitation of the Midi, in all the castle windows, and fortified themselves against despair. They warned their friends they were ruined; they honestly were – and there were heartfelt evenings of consolation. After such evenings Mrs Tommy, awaking heavily, whimpered in Nancy's arms, and Tommy approached silence. They had the highest opinion of Nancy, and were restored by her confidence. She knew they would be all right; she assured them they were the best, the happiest people: they were popular – look how Life came back again and again to beg their pardon. And, just to show them, she accepted Jeremy Neath and his thousands. So the world could see she was lucky; the world saw the Tommy Crans and their daughter had all the luck. To Herbert she explained nothing. She expected everything of him, on behalf of the Tommy Crans.

The two Crans were distracted by her apotheosis from the incident of their ruin. They had seen her queen of a perpetual Christmas party for six months before they themselves came down magnificently, like an empire. Then Nancy came to fetch them over to England, where her husband had found a small appointment for Tommy, excuse for a pension. But Tommy would not want that long; he had a scheme already, a stunner, a certainty; you just wrote to a hundred people and put in half a crown. That last night he ran about with the leaflets, up and down the uncarpeted castle stairs that were his no longer. He offered to let Herbert in on it; he would yet see Herbert a rich man.

Herbert and Nancy walked after dark on the terrace: she looked ill, tired; she was going to have a baby.

'When I asked you to marry me,' he said, 'you never answered. You've never answered yet.'

She said: 'There was no answer. We could never have loved each other and we shall always love each other. We are related.'

Herbert, a heavy un-young young man, walked, past desperation, beside her. He did not want peace, but a sword. He returned again and again to the unique moment of her strangeness to him before, as a child, she had spoken. Before, bewildered by all the laughter, he had realized she also was silent.

'You never played games,' he said, 'or believed in fairies, or anything. I'd have played any game your way; I'd have been good at them. You let them pull all the crackers before tea: now I'd have loved those crackers. That day we met at Mitchell's to sell your watch, you wouldn't have sugar cakes, though I wanted to comfort you. You never asked me out to go round the island in your boat; I'd have died to do that. I never even saw your swans awake. You hold back everything from me and expect me to understand. Why should I understand? In the name of God, what game are we playing?'

'But you do understand?'

'Oh, God,' he cried in revulsion. 'I don't want to! And now you're going to have a stranger child.'

Her sad voice in the dark said: 'You said then, "Anybody could be born!" Herbert, you and I have nothing to do with children – this must be a child like them.'

As they turned back to face the window, her smile and voice were tender, but not for him. In the brightly lit stripped room the Tommy Crans walked about together, like lovers in their freedom from one another. They talked of the fortune to be made, the child to be born. Tommy flung his chest out and moved his arms freely in air he did not possess; here and there, pink leaflets fluttered into the dark. The Tommy Crans would go on for ever and be continued; their seed should never fail.

The Good Girl

'. . . AND restored my faith in life,' concluded Captain Monteparnesi. He straightened out his gloves to the last finger, laid them down on the table, and gazed at Monica.

She could only gaze at the Alps. It was solemn, wonderfully like church. She was twenty-two: this, her third proposal, seemed a distinct echo. The Alps, so distantly, brightly painted over the bright lake, offered no inspiration, though from this very terrace they must often have been consulted. *His* passion, however, was of the purest; he was a Milanese of good family . . . He was still waiting; she did not know what to say.

The evening of her arrival, in April half-light, they had discovered themselves advancing towards each other down an immense corridor. They trod a magenta carpet fresh as the spring season; to this, in passing, he had lowered his eyes delicately. They passed: for both the perspective became forlorn. Those were seconds charged with fatality. At dinner, he, from his distant table, gave their party his courteously veiled attention. Naturally it had been Dagmar who, ashblonde, made play with her dark eyelids. Yet Monica had what her French friend, the Baronne de Besserat, called a '*je ne sais quoi*'. That night, this had been in evidence, had been remarkable even to Uncle Porgie – and heaven knew he was preoccupied! Uncle Porgie, lifting his glass to twinkle in the pink lamplight, paid Monica tribute: 'She's a dam' pretty girl, and a good girl, too!' Yet, all the time, under the table, he had been pursuing Dagmar's foot. When hers withdrew, his gave chase with audible pounces over the parquet: the pursuit gained in speed and compass, until there seemed to be no place under their table for the feet of a good girl.

Uncle Porgie was not anyone's uncle. That was his disappointment, he said; he had no niece. He had invited Monica to call him uncle also, since she was Dagmar's cousin, and when he invited her to accompany them to Italy, Dagmar declared she must. So Monica gently bounced across Italy in the back seat of the Rolls, beside the valet . . .

Captain Monteparnesi now tenderly coughed.

'Life,' replied Monica, 'is so difficult.'

'I place my life in your hands,' he said helpfully.

'Oh, thank you . . . Thank you, Captain Monteparnesi.'

So she got up carefully, as though balancing his life. She needed time to think – he understood perfectly. He kissed her right, then her left hand, then returned both regretfully. She walked away between the attendant tulips.

Captain Monteparnesi brought out his pocket-book from against his heart and made some calculations. He sighed; he was not a rich man. Then he went round to the garage for another look at the Rolls-Royce.

The Angelus came sweetly across the lake, but Dagmar, sitting out on her loggia, frowned at a tulip tree in extravagant blossom. She was beautiful (arms, neck, of supple ivory; her pale hair, brushed, you would think, with a gold-powdered brush, petal-curled at the nape), but that does not keep a girl going for ever. And nothing could have been more provoking than Uncle Porgie, who was kissing his way up her arm.

'Mind,' she said, and pushed at his head crossly as Monica stepped through the window. Their gold wicker chairs creaked.

'Darlin', where *have* you been? I've been so lonely. We've been talking about Rome.'

Uncle Porgie, straightening his tie, smiled at Monica in the friendliest way possible. Might not Rome be jolly? He knew of a thundering good hotel.

'But it's so far,' said Monica, and had, with surprise, a small pang. The heart, then, was not intact.

'No, no; surely it's all in Italy?'

The Rolls-Royce did, it is true, make short work of Italy, which is a country smaller than you would think. The Rolls had eaten up the Milan-Varese *auto strada* at what Uncle Porgie called a smooth eighty. He had often heard of this *auto strada*, on which there is no speed limit, and now he only regretted that the antiquities of this remarkable country could not be ranged for inspection along its smooth white kerbs. At Varese the *auto strada* had come to an end unaccountably, so here they all were; it seemed nice. You sat on the terrace, where tulips lifted gay little cups of light. In immediate response to the suggestion, electric bells depending from plane trees connected the terrace with the bar. Judas and almond trees frivolled among the austere cedars; cypresses marched to the lake from terrace to terrace, and wax-yellow freesias sweetened the April twilight. Placards forbidding children to play on the terrace discouraged Italian family life; English and Americans, fervently elsewhere, overlooked Varese. Antiquities did not impend; the view, though tasteful, was unexigent. The inhabitants of Varese were occupied in the manufacture of stockings; it seemed delightful that they should be so busy. Work, Uncle Porgie believed, kept men happy – that and the society of beautiful women. He sighed often, looking at the lake; he was a bit of an idealist. Visitors, arriving in pairs down the *auto strada* in a succession of whirring flashes, were expected to provide their own entertainment; in prolonged seclusion they fulfilled the expectations of the management. Cherry-clad little boys shot up in the lifts with bottles of champagne in buckets.

All this seemed strange to Monica. She had finished reading her book about Leonardo da Vinci, then, the afternoon after her arrival, had taken a walking-stick and the hotel dog and walked by high-walled alleys down to the lake. Here she found mud-flats, washing, stark damp reeds, no one about. The lake was intended for distant scenery. She spoke Italian to a child who ran away, then she walked up again. On the terrace she had come upon Captain Monteparnesi, engaged in sadness. He patted the dog. 'I love dogs,' he said, 'it is almost a madness with me.' In the course of their conversation he had forthwith explained: he was a solitary man, a widower. It was fortunate that he loved nature. 'But in the heart,' he said, 'of so much beauty, one feels oneself alone.'

In fact, he spoke English remarkably well. Sport, he had said, was also a madness to him. It was to be seen that Monica was a sports-girl. That was on Monday. Since, it had all blossomed . . . Today, Thursday, they talked of going away to Rome.

'I'm sorry you don't like Rome,' Dagmar said, discouraged. 'It sounds to me so historic. Uncle Porgie, if you are going down to the bar, let Alessandro know that I'd like a side-car. He'll send it up.'

Uncle Porgie, blowing out his cheeks (like a *putto* attending Aurora in one of those rather confused processions), patted Dagmar's knee, then trotted down to the bar. He was most suggestible.

'Mmwaow,' yawned Dagmar. She threw her arms over her head, and kicked one of her gilt-heeled slippers across the loggia.

Monica blushed with honesty. 'Dagmar . . . I do think we ought to be clear, you know, about Uncle Porgie. I had no idea when we left England that he was so much . . . *not* an uncle as all that.'

'Oh, dear,' Dagmar said, resigned. 'I am so stupid. I never know what anybody is talking about.'

'I do sometimes wonder if we ought not to go home.'

'Oh, I'm not going back by train; I can tell you that definitely. Darlin', you wouldn't be mean and leave me? After all, Monica, men aren't everything; I've never allowed them to count in my life.'

She should know. Men had not been nice to her. She had had to break off several engagements and leave a husband. Uncle Porgie called her his brave little woman . . . 'Darlin', let Alessandro in; he's got my side-car.' Alessandro was knocking portentously, like a postman – the hotel service was most discreet.

Monica put out Dagmar's evening things for her, untangled the long pearl rope, and opened some new powder. It made Dagmar tired to watch her; she sighed and went through to the bath. Soon she said plaintively, through the open door, 'Talk to me; tell me things. I get so bored, all alone here in my bath.' Steam, curling through the ivory bedroom, clouded the mirrors; Monica, relieved of her own pink reflection, was able to bring out: 'As a matter of fact, Captain Monteparnesi wants me to marry him.'

'Wants you to what?'

'Marry him.'

'Who does?'

'Captain Monteparnesi.'

'Oh, him.' There were some seconds of splashing and slow reflection. 'It's a pity his legs are like that.'

'He was a cavalry officer.'

'He must have held on to the horse very tight with his legs. Even so, they are short.'

'I do like him best sitting down. But he seems very idealistic and fond of the open air.'

'Italians are fearfully passionate,' said Dagmar gloomily. 'I know a girl who got bitten by an Italian. But, as I said, that is just their way. Does he make love in English?'

(Dagmar did not quite understand.) Monica said: 'He tells me about his life.'

'Oh, that kind! Monica, come and wrap little Dagmar up in a big bath towel. Really, I don't know what you will do in Rome with all those Italians. I think you're marvellous. Look, you must introduce him to us after dinner; after all, I am your chaperon, and Uncle Porgie is practically your guardian. I really think, Monica, you should have done that before, when you felt all this coming on.'

'But I can never find you.'

'Oh, nonsense, darlin'; we are always about.'

The introduction was not a success. Uncle Porgie could not, somehow, stomach a dago, but did his best. Monica, in pale pink, found herself sitting closer to Captain Monteparnesi than she had expected. Captain Monteparnesi attentively looked at Dagmar, who wore her air of floating lily-wise on the social current. Her smiles went hesitatingly to all of them, tender as young butterflies;

sometimes her smiles for Captain Monteparnesi were frequent and flashing.

They sat grouped by an indoor fountain. 'They are nervous,' said Captain Monteparnesi, pointing to the goldfish. 'Goldfish are highly nervous, impossible to tame.'

'I hear you are fond of animals?'

'I had a horse once that was shot under me.'

'Oh, dear, whatever did you do then?'

But something swelled in Monica's throat at the thought of the horse; she wanted to drop her head and weep where there had been an epaulette.

'Horses,' said Uncle Porgie, 'are like women, temperamental, fickle. Never know where you have 'em.' And – Oh, horror! – his foot went creeping towards Dagmar's.

'It would make any goldfish nervous,' exclaimed Monica quickly, 'living under a fountain.'

Her friend replied, 'One accustoms oneself to everything.' He behaved, in fact, with infinite sensibility. But afterwards, out on the terrace, he confessed he did not care for her aunt's lover; he did not find him an English type. 'But you,' he added, 'are my flower.'

She had not the heart to disagree with him. 'Pure!' he exclaimed, and kissed her shoulder. Behind them, the band thrilled in the empty ballroom. Tulips, gold ghosts, crowded up to the windows; cypresses gathered unseen, tense. She felt quite his own. But she also felt bound to explain: 'She is not my aunt, and he is her uncle.' He exclaimed: 'My flower!' (ravished by her remark), kissing her as low on the chest as her *décolletage* permitted. 'Oh, I don't think — ' But, murmuring indistinctly, he had begun to be rather Italian. She had never produced this effect before. '*Tiens!*' she could have exclaimed. Because really — But then she thought of her mother at Chislehurst, and of her old school, of which she hoped never to be unworthy. And from the night air, or because heaven had intervened, she sneezed, loudly and uncontrollably.

Stepping back from the portico as she went in, he accepted her good night. He blew his nose; you would think he had never panted with great emotion; it became once more evident that his passion was of the purest. How much relieved she was.

But the lounge was staring and still; a great many mirrors reflected its emptiness. Everybody was elsewhere; no one else in the hotel tried to be good. The lift sighed up with Monica. Dagmar's room was empty; an outraged little clock ticked angrily in the darkness; below, the band still throbbed on. The band had been hours silent before Dagmar came up.

In the course of the next day Monica found herself becoming by

imperceptible degrees engaged to Captain Monteparnesi. He constituted public opinion, for she saw no one else. Dagmar and Uncle
Porgie were busy always; round corners she heard chairs creak as
they bent over maps of Rome. That night she received, with
surprise but gratification, what appeared to be the betrothal kiss; he
left a rose in her place at dinner; afterwards they danced a waltz, a
foxtrot and then a one-step together in the empty ballroom. The
lonely band appeared very much encouraged. Couples looked
languidly in at the windows, then went away. Then he had a bottle
of champagne brought out to the terrace; they drank and, feeling
very much moved by the solemnity of the occasion, she talked to
him of her mother, then he spoke of his mother.

Then a terrible thing happened. They had walked down the
terraces, and, among the lemons and cypresses, had a conversation
about infinity, touching also upon ideals. The conversation, with
some caresses in character with its subject, naturally prolonged
itself. When they returned the hotel was shut up; not a light
shining; a clock behind in the town did indeed strike two. In this
leafy lakeside retreat one retired early; their behaviour had been
without precedent. Such a thing as this had never happened to
Monica; she reproached her Guglielmo with some sharpness. She
leaned on the door and sniffed with so much despair that he was
provoked to ask her point-blank if she were really an heiress. She
sobbed *indeed* not; he comforted her politely. He said, 'You have
always your charm.' It was a long time before anybody came. Then
the night-porter was horrified.

Dagmar was worse than horrified. She was surprised. She
pointed out, this was not what one had expected. Next morning,
curled up in bed, curtains drawn across the insistent daylight, she
said it seemed obvious they must now go at once to Rome. She
doubted if the hotel would keep them, now this had happened. The
night-porter had told the waiters, the waiters had told all the
chambermaids; she said Uncle Porgie was really very much
shocked. He was particular who Dagmar went about with; he had
always said she could not be too careful. Till now, he had thought
of Monica as a nice friend.

'Well, really . . . ' said Monica.

'I tell you how it will be, Monica; you will end by having a baby.
A girl cannot be too careful.'

'Well, really . . . '

'And an Italian and everything.'

'Whatever . . . '

'Darlin', Dagmar's being very, very loyal — '

Trembling with indignation, Monica sped down to the terrace,
for Guglielmo. But, courteously, he declined to her through a

crowd: this way, that way – right and left of a lady's head. The terrace was dark with Italian ladies who sat about him.

This morning, as a surprise, his relatives had all come out by train from Milan: his aunt, his mother, his widowed sister with her children, his sister who had still to marry and wore a dark moustache. He was pleased; he had missed them; he was accustomed to family life. They sat in black, with black furs, in the ardent sunshine, complimenting him upon the lake, while the Alps appeared to draw nearer in fascination. They sipped *aranciata*, but did not remove their gloves. In so large a family, necessarily, there has always been a bereavement.

Dagmar, looking down from her loggia, knew that her cousin could not have sinned with a man with so large and black a family, and once more it seemed unlikely to her that Monica ever would sin (in recognition of this, passing later through Milan, she made Uncle Porgie buy Monica a pair of coral drop ear-rings: for some people life held nothing). For Monica it was simpler; as he stood up to bow she really noticed his legs for the first time: she had never loved him. Naturally, however, she was still very much upset. She snipped the head off a tulip and walked away; it was her only gesture.

His family, evidently, were great with some information: they exchanged glances, and soon it transpired they brought good news. His unmarried cousin Liliana, who had so tenderly asked for him since their childhood, had become, last Friday, through the suicide of an uncle, direct heiress to the Piselli millions; so it became his duty to leave the divine panorama and hurry back to Milan. Young men might already be on her doorstep. Now his cousin Liliana, though no sports-girl, did not keep him up past midnight discussing infinity. He was seriously tired this morning, and had a slight chill on the liver. Not without emotion, he shortly afterwards wrote his farewell to Monica. 'You restored my faith in life,' he wrote; 'you could not have done more. But there are sterner calls.' Meanwhile his mother, a woman of tact, quietly packed for him. Then the family left the hotel together, quickly and quietly. It was not till months afterwards that she heard how nearly he had been entangled with an English girl of doubtful reputation.

Twenty minutes later the Rolls-Royce, bonnet turned towards Rome, passed the little party on its way to the station. Dagmar remarked: 'How is it that good Italian women are always dusty?' Uncle Porgie had no idea. Monica, eyes shut, hoped this might be the last she would hear of virtue.

But she was not to be so fortunate.

The Cat Jumps

AFTER the Bentley murder, Rose Hill stood empty two years.
Lawns mounted to meadows; white paint peeled from the
balconies; the sun, looking more constantly, less fearfully in than
sightseer's eyes through the naked windows, bleached the floral
wallpapers. The week after the execution Harold Bentley's legatees
had placed the house on the books of the principal agents, London
and local. But though sunny, up to date, and convenient, though so
delightfully situated over the Thames valley (above flood level),
within easy reach of a golfcourse, Rose Hill, while frequently
viewed, remained unpurchased. Dreadful associations apart, the
privacy of the place had been violated; with its terraced garden,
lily-pond and pergola cheerfully rose-encrusted, the public had
been made too familiar. On the domestic scene too many eyes had
burnt the impress of their horror. Moreover, that pearly bathroom,
that bedroom with wide outlook over a loop of the Thames . . .
'*The Rose Hill Horror*': headlines flashed up at the very sound of the
name. 'Oh, *no*, dear!' many wives had exclaimed, drawing their
husbands hurriedly from the gate. 'Come away!' they had urged
crumpling the agent's order to view as though the house were
advancing upon them. And husbands came away – with a backward glance at the garage. Funny to think a chap who was hanged
had kept his car there.

The Harold Wrights, however, were not deterred. They had light,
bright, shadowless, thoroughly disinfected minds. They believed
that they disbelieved in most things but were unprejudiced; they
enjoyed frank discussions. They dreaded nothing but inhibitions;
they had no inhibitions. They were pious agnostics, earnest for
social reform; they explained everything to their children, and were
annoyed to find their children could not sleep at nights because they
thought there was a complex under the bed. They knew all crime
to be pathological, and read their murders only in scientific books.
They had vita glass put into all their windows. No family, in fact,
could have been more unlike the mistaken Harold Bentleys.

Rose Hill, from the first glance, suited the Wrights admirably.
They were in search of a cheerful week-end house with a nice

atmosphere, where their friends could join them for frank discussions, and their own and their friends' children 'run wild' during
the summer months. Harold Wright, who had a good head, got the
agent to knock six hundred off the quoted price of the house. 'That
unfortunate affair,' he murmured. Jocelyn commended his inspiration. Otherwise, they did not give the Bentleys another thought.

The Wrights had the floral wallpapers all stripped off and the
walls cream-washed; they removed some disagreeably thick pink
shades from the electricity and had the paint renewed inside and
out. (The front of the house was bracketed over with balconies, like
an overmantel.) Their bedroom mantelpiece, stained by the late
Mrs Bentley's cosmetics, had to be scrubbed with chemicals. Also,
they had removed from the rock-garden Mrs Bentley's little dog's
memorial tablet, with a quotation on it from *Indian Love Lyrics*.
Jocelyn Wright, looking into the unfortunate bath – *the* bath, so
square and opulent, with its surround of nacreous tiles – said,
laughing lightly, she supposed anyone *else* would have had that
bath changed. 'Not that that would be possible,' she added; 'the
bath's built in . . . I've always wanted a built-in bath.'

Harold and Jocelyn turned from the bath to look down at the
cheerful river shimmering under a spring haze. All the way down
the slope cherry trees were in blossom. Life should be simplified
for the Wrights; they were fortunate in their mentality.

After an experimental week-end, without guests or children,
only one thing troubled them: a resolute stuffiness, upstairs and
down – due presumably, to the house's having been so long shut
up – a smell of unsavoury habitation, of rich cigarette-smoke stale
in the folds of unaired curtains, of scent spilled on unbrushed
carpets, an alcoholic smell – persistent in their perhaps too sensitive
nostrils after days of airing, doors and windows open, in rooms
drenched thoroughly with sun and wind. They told each other it
came from the parquet; they didn't like it, somehow. They had the
parquet taken up – at great expense – and put down plain oak
floors.

In their practical way, the Wrights now set out to expel, live out,
live down, almost (had the word had place in their vocabulary) to
'lay' the Bentley's. Deferred by trouble over the parquet, their
occupation of Rose Hill, which should have dated from mid-April,
did not begin till the end of May. Throughout a week, Jocelyn had
motored from town daily, so that the final installation of themselves and the children was able to coincide with their first
week-end party – they asked down five of their friends to warm
the house.

That first Friday, everything was auspicious; afternoon sky blue
as the garden irises; later, a full moon pendent over the river; a

night so warm that, after midnight, their enlightened friends, in pyjamas, could run on the blanched lawns in a state of high though rational excitement. Jane, Jacob and Janet, their admirably spaced-out children, kept awake by the moonlight, hailed their elders out of the nursery skylight. Jocelyn waved to them: they never had been repressed.

The girl Muriel Barker was found looking up the terraces at the house a shade doubtfully. 'You know,' she said, 'I do rather wonder they don't feel . . . *sometimes* . . . you know what I mean?'

'No,' replied her companion, a young scientist.

Muriel sighed. 'No one would mind if it had been just a short sharp shooting. But it was so . . . prolonged. It went on all over the house. Do you remember?' she said timidly.

'No,' replied Mr Cartaret. 'It didn't interest me.'

'Oh, nor me either!' agreed Muriel quickly, but added: 'How he must have hated her . . . '

The scientist, sleepy, yawned frankly and referred her to Krafft-Ebing. But Muriel went to bed with *Alice in Wonderland*; she went to sleep with the lights on. She was not, as Jocelyn realized later, the sort of girl to have asked at all.

Next morning was overcast; in the afternoon it rained, suddenly and heavily – interrupting, for some, tennis, for others, a pleasant discussion, in a punt, on marriage under the Soviet. Defeated, they all rushed in. Jocelyn went round from room to room, shutting tightly the rain-lashed casements along the front of the house. These continued to rattle; the balconies creaked. An early dusk set in; an oppressive, almost visible moisture, up from the darkening river, pressed on the panes like a presence and slid through the house. The party gathered in the library, round an expansive but thinly burning fire. Harold circulated photographs of modern architecture; they discussed these tendencies. Then Mrs Monkhouse, sniffing, exclaimed: 'Who uses "Trèfle Incarnat"?'

'Now, *who* ever would — ' her hostess began scornfully. Then from the hall came a howl, scuffle, a thin shriek. They sat too still; in the dusky library Mr Cartaret laughed out loud. Harold Wright, indignantly throwing open the door, revealed Jane and Jacob rolling at the foot of the stairs, biting each other, their faces dark with uninhibited passion. Bumping alternate heads against the foot of the banisters, they shrieked in concert.

'Extraordinary,' said Harold; 'they've never done that before. They have always understood each other so well.'

'I wouldn't do that,' advised Jocelyn, raising her voice slightly; 'you'll hurt your teeth. Other teeth won't grow at once, you know.'

'You should let them find that out for themselves,' disapproved

Edward Cartaret, taking up the *New Statesman*. Harold, in perplexity, shut the door on his children, who soon stunned each other
to silence.

Meanwhile, Sara and Talbot Monkhouse, Muriel Barker and
Theodora Smith, had drawn together over the fire in a tight
little knot. Their voices twanged with excitement. By that shock,
just now, something seemed to have been released. Even Cartaret
gave them half his attention. They were discussing *crime passionnel*.

'Of course, if that's what they really *want* to discuss . . . '
thought Jocelyn. But it did seem unfortunate. Partly from an
innocent desire to annoy her visitors, partly because the room felt
awful – you would have thought fifty people had been there for a
week – she went across and opened one of the windows, admitting
a pounce of damp wind. They all turned, startled, to hear rain crash
on the lead of an upstairs balcony. Muriel's voice was left in forlorn
solo: 'Dragged herself . . . whining "Harold" . . . '

Harold Wright looked remarkably conscious. Jocelyn said
brightly, 'Whatever *are* you talking about?' But, unfortunately,
Harold, on almost the same breath, suggested: 'Let's leave that
family alone, shall we?' Their friends all felt they might not be
asked again. Though they did feel, plaintively, that they had been
being natural. However, they disowned Muriel, who, getting up
abruptly, said she thought she'd like to go for a walk in the rain
before dinner. Nobody accompanied her.

Later, overtaking Mrs Monkhouse on the stairs, Muriel confided: absolutely, she could not stand Edward Cartaret. She could
hardly bear to be in the room with him. He seemed so . . . cruel.
Cold-blooded? No, she meant cruel. Sara Monkhouse, going into
Jocelyn's room for a chat (at her entrance Jocelyn started violently),
told Jocelyn that Muriel could not stand Edward, could hardly bear
to be in a room with him. 'Pity,' said Jocelyn. 'I had thought they
might do for each other.' Jocelyn and Sara agreed that Muriel was
unrealized: what she ought to have was a baby. But when Sara,
dressing, told Talbot Monkhouse that Muriel could not stand
Edward, and Talbot said Muriel was unrealized, Sara was furious.
The Monkhouses, who never did quarrel, quarrelled bitterly, and
were late for dinner. They would have been later if the meal itself
had not been delayed by an outburst of sex-antagonism between
the nice Jacksons, a couple imported from London to run the
house. Mrs Jackson, putting everything in the oven, had locked
herself into her room.

'Curious,' said Harold; 'the Jacksons' relations to each other
always seemed so modern. They have the most intelligent discussions.'

Theodora said she had been re-reading Shakespeare – this

brought them point-blank up against *Othello*. Harold, with Titanic force, wrenched round the conversation to relativity: about this no one seemed to have anything to say but Edward Cartaret. And Muriel, who by some mischance had again been placed beside him, sat deathly, turning down her dark-rimmed eyes. In fact, on the intelligent sharp-featured faces all round the table something – perhaps simply a clearness – seemed to be lacking, as though these were wax faces for one fatal instant exposed to a furnace. Voices came out from some dark interiority; in each conversational interchange a mutual vote of no confidence was implicit. You would have said that each personality had been attacked by some kind of decomposition.

'No moon tonight,' complained Sara Monkhouse. Never mind, they would have a cosy evening; they would play paper games, Jocelyn promised.

'If you can see,' said Harold. 'Something seems to be going wrong with the light.'

Did Harold think so? They had all noticed the light seemed to be losing quality, as though a film, smoke-like, were creeping over the bulbs. The light, thinning, darkening, seemed to contract round each lamp into a blurred aura. They had noticed, but, each with a proper dread of his own subjectivity, had not spoken.

'Funny stuff, electricity,' Harold said.

Mr Cartaret could not agree with him.

Though it was late, though they yawned and would not play paper games, they were reluctant to go to bed. You would have supposed a delightful evening. Jocelyn was not gratified.

The library stools, rugs and divans were strewn with Krafft-Ebing, Freud, Forel, Weiniger and the heterosexual volume of Havelock Ellis. (Harold had thought it right to install his reference library; his friends hated to discuss without basis.) The volumes were pressed open with paper-knives and small pieces of modern statuary; stooping from one to another, purposeful as a bee, Edward Cartaret read extracts aloud to Harold, to Talbot Monkhouse, and to Theodora Smith, who stitched *gros point* with resolution. At the far end of the library under a sallow drip from a group of electric candles, Mrs Monkhouse and Miss Barker shared an ottoman, spines pressed rigid against the wall. Tensely one spoke, one listened.

'And these,' thought Jocelyn, leaning back with her eyes shut between the two groups, 'are the friends I liked to have in my life. Pellucid, sane . . .'

It was remarkable how much Muriel knew. Sara, very much shocked, edged up till their thighs touched. You would have thought the Harold Bentleys had been Muriel's relatives. Surely, Sara attempted, in one's large, bright world one did not think of these things? Practically, they did not exist! Surely Muriel should not . . . But Muriel looked at her strangely.

'Did you know,' she said, 'that one of Mrs Bentley's hands was found in the library?'

Sara, smiling a little awkwardly, licked her lip. 'Oh,' she said.

'But the fingers were in the dining-room. He began there.'

'Why isn't he in Broadmoor?'

'That defence failed. He didn't really subscribe to it. He said having done what he wanted was worth anything.'

'Oh!'

'Yes, he was nearly lynched . . . She dragged herself upstairs. She couldn't lock any doors – naturally. One maid – her maid – got shut into the house with them: he'd sent all the others away. For a long time everything seemed so quiet: the maid crept out and saw Harold Bentley sitting half-way upstairs, finishing a cigarette. All the lights were full on. He nodded to her and dropped the cigarette through the banisters. Then she saw the . . . the state of the hall. He went upstairs after Mrs Bentley, saying: 'Lucinda!' He looked into room after room, whistling; then he said '*Here we are,*' and shut a door after him.

'The maid fainted. When she came to, it was still going on, upstairs . . . Harold Bentley had locked all the garden doors; there were locks even on the french windows. The maid couldn't get out. Everything she touched was . . . sticky. At last she broke a pane and got through. As she ran down the garden – the lights were on all over the house – she saw Harold Bentley moving about in the bathroom. She fell right over the edge of a terrace and one of the tradesmen picked her up next day.

'Doesn't it seem odd, Sara, to think of Jocelyn in that bath?'

Finishing her recital, Muriel turned on Sara an ecstatic and brooding look that made her almost beautiful. Sara fumbled with a cigarette; match after match failed her. 'Muriel, *you* ought to see a specialist.'

Muriel held out her hand for a cigarette. 'He put her heart in her hat-box. He said it belonged in there.'

'You had no right to come here. It was most unfair on Jocelyn. Most . . . indelicate.'

Muriel, to whom the word was, properly, unfamiliar, eyed incredulously Sara's lips.

'How dared you come?'

'I thought I might like it. I thought I ought to fulfil myself. I'd never had any experience of these things.'

'*Muriel . . .*'

'Besides, I wanted to meet Edward Cartaret. Several people said we were made for each other. Now, of course, I shall never marry. Look what comes of it . . . I must say, Sara, I wouldn't be you or Jocelyn. Shut up all night with a man all alone – I don't know how you dare sleep. I've arranged to sleep with Theodora, and we shall barricade the door. I noticed something about Edward Cartaret the moment I arrived: a kind of insane glitter. He is utterly patho-logical. He's got instruments in his room, in that black bag. Yes, I looked. Did you notice the way he went on and on about cutting up that cat, and the way Talbot and Harold listened?'

Sara, looking furtively round the room, saw Mr Cartaret making passes over the head of Theodora Smith with a paper-knife. Both appeared to laugh heartily, but in silence.

'Here we are,' said Harold, showing his teeth, smiling.

He stood over Muriel with a siphon in one hand, glass in the other.

At this point Jocelyn, rising, said she, for one, intended to go to bed.

Jocelyn's bedroom curtains swelled a little over the noisy window. The room was stuffy and – insupportable, so that she did not know where to turn. The house, fingered outwardly by the wind that dragged unceasingly past the walls, was, within, a solid silence: silence heavy as flesh. Jocelyn dropped her wrap to the floor, then watched how its feathered edges crept a little. A draught came in, under her bathroom door.

Jocelyn turned away in despair and hostility from the strained, pale woman looking at her from her oblong glass. She said aloud, 'There *is* not fear'; then, within herself, heard this taken up: 'But the death fear, that one is not there to relate! If the spirit, dismembered in agony, dies before the body! If the spirit, in the whole knowledge of its dissolution, drags from chamber to chamber, drops from plane to plane of awareness (as from knife to knife down an oubliette), shedding, receiving agony! Till, long afterwards, death, with its little pain, is established in the indifferent body.' There was no comfort: death (now at every turn and instant claiming her) was, in its every possible manifestation, violent death: ultimately, she was to be given up to terror.

Undressing, shocked by the iteration of her reflected move-ments, she flung a towel over the glass. With what desperate eyes of appeal, at Sara's door, she and Sara had looked at each other, clung with their looks – and parted. She could have sworn she heard Sara's bolt slide softly to. But what then, subsequently, of Talbot? And what – she eyed her own bolt, so bright (and, for the late Mrs Bentley, so ineffective) – what of Harold?

'It's atavistic!' she said aloud, in the dark-lit room, and, kicking her slippers away, got into bed. She took *Erewhon* from the rack, but lay rigid, listening. As though snatched by a movement, the towel slipped from the mirror beyond her bed-end. She faced the two eyes of an animal in extremity, eyes black, mindless. The clock struck two: she had been waiting an hour.

On the floor, her feathered wrap shivered again all over. She heard the other door of the bathroom very stealthily open, then shut. Harold moved in softly, heavily knocked against the side of the bath, and stood still. He was quietly whistling.

'Why didn't I understand? He must always have hated me. It's tonight he's been waiting for . . . *He wanted this house.* His look, as we went upstairs . . . '

She shrieked: 'Harold!'

Harold, so softly whistling, remained behind the imperturbable door, remained quite still . . . 'He's *listening* for me . . . ' One pin-point of hope at the tunnel-end: to get to Sara, to Theodora, to Muriel. Unmasked, incautious, with a long tearing sound of displaced air, Jocelyn leapt from the bed to the door.

But her door had been locked from the outside.

With a strange rueful smile, like an actress, Jocelyn, skirting the foot of the two beds, approached the door of the bathroom. 'At least I have still . . . my feet.' For for some time the heavy body of Mrs Bentley, tenacious of life, had been dragging itself from room to room. '*Harold!*' she said to the silence, face close to the door.

The door opened on Harold, looking more dreadfully at her than she had imagined. With a quick, vague movement he roused himself from his meditation. Therein he had assumed the entire burden of Harold Bentley. Forces he did not know of assembling darkly, he had faced for untold ages the imperturbable door to his wife's room. She would be there, densely, smotheringly there. She lay like a great cat, always, over the mouth of his life.

The Harolds, superimposed on each other, stood searching the bedroom strangely. Taking a step forward, shutting the door behind him:

'Here we are,' said Harold.

Jocelyn went down heavily. Harold watched.

Harold Wright was appalled. Jocelyn had fainted: Jocelyn never had fainted before. He shook, he fanned, he applied restoratives. His perplexed thoughts fled to Sara – oh, Sara certainly. 'Hi!' he cried, 'Sara!' and successively fled from each to each of the locked doors. There was no way out.

Across the passage a door throbbed to the maniac drumming of Sara Monkhouse. She had been locked in. For Talbot, agonized with solicitude, it was equally impossible to emerge from his dressing-room. Further down the passage, Edward Cartaret, interested by this nocturnal manifestation, wrenched and rattled his door-handle in vain.

Muriel, on her silent way through the house to Theodora's bedroom, had turned all the keys on the outside, impartially. She did not know which door might be Edward Cartaret's. Muriel was a woman who took no chances.

The Last Night in the Old Home

ANNABELLE, who had been searching about upstairs, pinching the corners of mattresses as though they ought to hold guineas and opening and shutting drawers, discovered a pair of gloves in the blue room wardrobe. So she came down to ask everyone whose these could be. From room to room she went: everyone soon learned to dread her step.

'It seems a pity,' she said, 'that they should be sold *with* the wardrobe. They are nice gloves – look.' They were fine suède gloves for narrow hands, worn at the finger-tips, doing up at the wrists with small pearl buttons. 'Someone should have the good of them.'

'Perhaps they're Delia's,' said Henry, her present victim.

'She says no. Hers don't *button* up.'

'I should keep them yourself.'

'Oh, no, Henry, I mustn't; besides, look, they are too small.'

Henry could have screamed. Throughout the house, disappearing in dusk, there reigned an unnatural silence that first he could not account for: all the clocks had been let run down. You cannot auction a ticking clock. The silence echoed, for against the dusty feet of tomorrow all carpets had been rolled up. Here in the morning-room hung a smell of stale note-paper; his mother had taken the family letters – from school, from London, from India – out of the bureau drawers to be read aloud. Now, thank God, they were burnt. Only the best, the jauntiest and most eloquent, had been put away in dispatch cases. All Adrian's had been kept, because he was dead. (With the dispatch-cases no one knew what to do.) Had Henry been dead, his might have acquired some kind of morbid value. As it was, they put up a poor show at the hearing by mother and sisters and had been unostentatiously burnt. Absent or present, he was constrained with his family: too civil, nervous. He was humiliated by Annabelle's oddness, that all the others took calmly. His embarrassment was unforgivable: Annabelle was not 'afflicted'; she simply did not grow up. Inside the big, bustling form of a woman she was a girl of ten. So she remained their home-girl.

After Annabelle, Delia looked into the morning-room. 'How funny it is,' she said briskly, 'with all the pictures down!' Smoke had dimmed, sun faded, the wallpaper; fresh flowery squares stared oddly.

Delia always put balm on the rawest of situations by saying something quite brilliantly superficial. She had been clicking round on her high heels, applying this happy touch to the family's nerves, all today and yesterday. Quite beautiful, she had married and left home young: she cared for no one at all. Henry liked her the best of them; she was as gay as a stranger; between these two convention was comfortably present. 'There's a fire,' she said, 'in the library.'

'Who's in there?'

'Mother and father and poor dear John.'

'Doing what?'

'That's the difficulty,' she said brightly; 'there's nothing much they *can* do. Oh, mother is trying to rub out the places where we all used to be measured against the door.'

Something more than her constant wish to be social accounted for Delia's brightness: she felt a profound relief. Something let go of her conscience. Delia was no good; to her husband, who bored her, she had for years been unfaithful; she was as light as a little cat. With home still going on here, some fiction of innocence had always unnerved her. Now mother and father and Annabelle would be people in a hotel; the cuckoo-clock, the scrap screen, the big chintz chairs rumpled by dogs, would all be auctioned to-morrow and carted away. There *it* went – pouf! Its grip relaxed on her spirit . . . Delia asked Henry to give her a cigarette, and, balancing with a hand on his shoulder as they stood over the grate cold with papery ashes, she began to tell him, amazingly, all about her life. Once or twice she glanced defiantly round the morning-room. Henry, having had no idea she was such a bad woman, violently registered shock.

She concluded: 'I've always wanted to ask you – do you have love-affairs?'

He looked at her queerly, 'No,' he said.

'How *wise*, but how silly.'

Annabelle went into the kitchen, where cook, for her final credit, was giving a final scrub to the copper and zinc saucepans, then ranging them back in their lots on the dresser and tables. All the other servants had wept and gone. Annabelle turned the handle of the mincing-machine and looked regretfully into a colander. 'Oh, dear,' she sighed. Cook took the mincing-machine firmly away from Annabelle and put it back on a shelf.

'I used to make cakes here, usen't I?'

'You did indeed, miss, and very nice cakes they were. Now let that strainer alone, there's a good girl!'

'Cook, whose gloves *can* these be? No one seems to care.'

No doubt, said cook, they had belonged to a visitor. Her eyes, always watery in their scorched lids from the heat of so many fires, looked smaller and dull, like a dead porcupine's; it was hard to tell if she had been crying. Tomorrow she was going straight on to another gentleman's family. If she felt at all, it was angry sorrow for John. He was her darling: it seemed a direct hit at cook that it should be John who had ruined the family. He had a way with him. He never told cook how much, these days, he detested apricot jam, or that her puddings and cakes made him flatulent.

Decency had required John's presence at the obsequies of the home. He felt this unduly hard; his parents' brave brightness affected him. Their silence from all reproach became sinister, like the silence of clocks. He felt prickly all over and drank a good deal of whisky. When Henry told him, that rationally, this was for the best, that the old place had no place now they were all grown up and there were no grandchildren, and that their parents would do much better out of this valley climate, John became very angry. He felt that it was in spirit Henry who ruined the home. Hard-hit, John felt really innocent. Not once had he been deliberate: if mess-bills ran up, horses he backed turned out rotten, cards he held worthless and women he loved exacting, was John to blame? He told himself he had had no real fun. It had always helped him to think of his old home; after a thick night it made him feel good and squashy.

The marks where the children were measured would not rub off the door; John suggested scratching them out with a pocket-knife, but his mother said that would spoil the paint. So he left the library, where the books were stacked up in lots, and went upstairs to look out of the landing window. Here the garden poplars were visible through the dusk, but he saw more plainly his figure reflected against the sky. He turned from the window; the gas was lit on the landing; outside the nursery door John saw the rocking-horse. So mounted, John as a little fellow had charged impressively, hurling himself on enemies. But, when you got off, those red-painted nostrils were always scoffing away. Maddened, John kicked the rocking-horse.

The rocking-horse, stirrups flying, bumped noisily on its rollers. 'Oh, you *mustn't*!' screamed Annabelle, darting out of the nursery, the suède gloves still in her hand. Kneeling, she crooned on the horse's neck. 'Darling . . . poor darling . . . Wicked, unkind John!'

'Damn!' muttered John, unnerved.

Annabelle heard him. Wild with affront, she scrambled heavily to her feet with a cowlike movement and dashed down the naked stairs. 'Mother, mother,' she wailed. Her mother came out of the library. 'Oh, mother, John said "Damn" to me!'

'Never mind,' said her mother, patting the convulsed home-girl.

'He *looked* so awful.'

'We must be kind to him.'

All the doors were open. Henry and Delia glanced at each other; she smiled at a crease in her sleeve, he fumbled a cigarette out and went quite white. They both felt home had lasted a day too long. John came downstairs; his hand shook on the banisters. He looked in at Delia, mouth twisted as though he wanted to laugh, then pushed past into the dining-room where the decanters were.

'He's right,' said Delia. 'I think I should like one too.'

'Our horse,' Annabelle wailed, 'our old darling horse . . . '

'This is intolerable,' said Henry. But their mother looked at him with expressionless eyes over Annabelle's heaving shoulder. 'Never mind,' she murmured, and Henry knew that he had been ordered away.

Only the drawing-room, where they were all always polite, remained unentered, untroubled. It was prepared for tomorrow, its last occasion, when crowds would bid for the piano, the sofas, the clock. The rugs were rolled up and numbered, the chairs stood in rows; statues' unwearied arms upheld unlit lamps on the mantel-piece. Twilight came in through the unshuttered windows, hung in drops from the chandeliers, and shone in the mirrors.

A wind came up; creepers began to tap on the south windows; draughts crept through the house, fluttering here and there a ticket on objects already bespoken. A door slammed upstairs. Henry went up to shut the windows; the rocking-horse was still rocking. A straw from some packing-case blew past his feet in the dark, which was melodramatic.

The Disinherited

AUTUMN had set in early. While the days were still glowing, the woods took on from a distance a yellow, unreal sheen, like a reflection from metal; their fretted outlines hardened against the blond open hills that the vibrations of summer no longer disturbed. In the early mornings, dew spread a bright white bloom between long indigo shadows; the afternoon air quickened, but after sunset mists diluted the moon. This first phase of autumn was lovely; decay first made itself felt as an extreme sweetness: with just such a touch of delicious morbidity a lover might contemplate the idea of death.

Later the rain came, and there were drenching monotone days; the leaves, rotting uncoloured, slid down through the rain. Mid-autumn set in mild, immobile and nerveless; the days had unclear margins, mists webbed the gardens all day, the sun slanting slowly through them to touch the brown pear trees and pale yellow currant-leaves, here and there a marigold or a sodden rose. There was no wind, and the woods stood heavily tense; against their darkness, in the toneless November evenings, the oaks were still yellow and shed a frightening glare. Everything rotted slowly. The dark, rain-swollen rivers flowed fast between bleaching sedges, with leaves caught on the current. After the rain, an unlit grey sky bound the earth, and pools threaded the grass and lay unglittering inside the brittle reeds. Now and then the skies were disturbed by a high-up swift rustling sigh: the summer birds flying south. The shredded last leaves still clung to the trees, as though they would not fall: eternity seemed to have set in at late autumn. Some way into November, a wind sprang up at nights.

Marianne Harvey was not aware of the autumn to which her friend Davina was becoming a prey. Since August, Marianne had been cheerfully busy, without a moment for any kind of reflection; the Harveys were nesting over again, after twelve years of marriage, making a new home. But all those weeks Davina Archworth had been idle with a melancholy and hollow idleness, with all day to kick the wet leaf-drifts and watch the birds go.

The Harveys had left London and come up to live on the new building estate, in a freshly built white rough-cast house with a touch of priggishness in its architecture. The estate, on a hill dominating from some distance a university city, was exclusive; lots here could only be purchased on the distinct condition that houses of a fixed value were to be put up. You undertook not to keep chickens, put up a frame garage or hang out clothes. Into the tone of this niceness the Harveys easily fell. Few houses had gone up so far; those there were stood apart, like Englishmen not yet acquainted, washed by clear upland air and each in its acre of wiry grass that had lost its nature, being no longer meadow and not yet lawn. Half-made roads, like the first knowing cuts of a scalpel, mapped the flank of the hill out, up to the concrete water-tower upon its crest. No buses approached, and there were and would be no shops.

At the foot of this genteel hill, at the river level, the old village frowsted inside its ring of elm trees, mouldy and snug. Its lichened barn-roofs were yellow, and from the church spire the weathercock now and then shot out one sharp gold ray; from the tower there came up, climbing the hill on Sundays, ponderous chimes. A clot of thin smoke hung melting in watery river light over the roofs of the village; after sunset a few dark lights outlined the three-cornered green. A wide pitch-black by-pass road with white kerbs swept south round the foot of the hill, cutting off the old village from the new building estate. On the far flank of the village the stretching brick-red tentacles of the city made their advance over water-meadows tufted with lines of willow; far off, the brittle city spires pricked at the skyline. The small, shallow river on which the village was built ran into another, grand one: a beetle-green gasometer stood at this point, and there was a steel bridge over which London expresses rumbled and rang. Sometimes a swan, disturbed, sailed up the back-water.

It enraged Davina that the new estate (no affair of her own, as she had not been asked to live there) should not have any shops. Naturally aristocratic, she loathed refinement. She especially liked little shops to be just a minute away from wherever she might be living, shops that are cheesy and mixed and stay open on Sundays, where you buy cigarettes, peppermints, shoelaces, picture papers, sardines, purgative pills and writing compendiums with pictures on the outside. She liked chatting late across counters in the dark lamplight and charming unauthorized people into selling her stamps. She had that kind of restless feeling for Marianne that makes one critical; she therefore despised Marianne's habit of shopping by telephone, which put her, she thought, out of touch with reality. The whole new estate with its rawness, its air at once hygienic and intellectual, revolted Davina. All the same, she was up there constantly, dropping in at all times of the day to see Marianne Harvey. Attraction, propinquity and, on Davina's part, idleness fostered this funny alliance.

Davina had come to live in the old village with and on her aunt – or, strictly, her uncle's widow – Mrs Walsingham Archworth. Her existence was temporary; though she had few prospects she was, or had been till lately, hoping for better times. Her aunt's house had been the manor, and Mrs Archworth, though she had by now disposed of all other property, still looked on herself as patroness of the village. Her house, backed by an ilex and flanked by lines of clipped hollies, had a high, narrow face, with dark inanimate windows, and looked like the frontispiece to a ghost-story. Inside, however, it was kindly, crimson and stuffy. Its front windows looked down a lawn, through wrought-iron gates, on to the village green, where the lime trees shed their leaves early . . . Davina could not enjoy living here, on her aunt; mortification and dullness ravaged her. But, at twenty-nine, she had no more money of any kind; she had run through her capital; love-affairs and her other expensive habits had ruined her. To earn was out of the question: she had no idea what to do. In an agony of impatience, she waited about indefinitely. Something that should have occurred – she was not sure what – had not occurred yet, and became every day more unlikely. She remained, angry, immobile, regretting that circumstances over which she had had really, at one time, every control, should have driven her into exploiting her aunt's affection.

This was too easy. In looks as well as in temperament Davina resembled her dead uncle, who, melancholy and dashing, had hung up his hat in this house with a gracious despondent gesture and had been loved to distraction by his dull, pink wife throughout the years of their marriage, in return for which he had given her scarcely a smile. Davina herself had, further, just that touch of the sombre romantic about her that appeals to all other women, even to relatives. She was adored by her aunt, now a puffy, huffy, formal, bewildered, charmless elderly widow. Davina was tall, with a head set strikingly on a dark-ivory neck; her springy dark hair, shortish, was tucked back behind her ears. Her features, well cut, were perhaps rather pronounced, but her sombreness and her unwilling smile could be enchanting. She could command that remarkable immobility possible only to nervously restless people, when only her dark eyes' intent and striking glitter betrayed the tension behind. She moved well, with an independent and colt-like carriage; her manner was, for a young woman's, decided, a shade overbearing, intimidating to lovers whom her appearance beguiled. Had she had sphere, space, ease of mind, she might have been generous, active and even noble; emotion need only have played a small part in her life. She was a woman born to make herself felt.

As things were, hurt pride distorted her memories; an inflamed sense of self isolated her; miscarried projects darkened her whole view. Her thoughts were almost all angry. 'If I had money — ' she said again and again. She walked miles a day, clicking her third left-hand finger angrily on her thumb, pacing the fields with a long nervy mannish stride. In this countryside she was a stranger; in the mild academic city she cared to know nobody. Friends, it appeared, had forgotten her. Indoors she smoked, kicked the fire up, tore the plots from crime novels, and switched the wireless scornfully on and off.

Mrs Archworth was sorry to see the hill she had known all her life, and sometimes walked with her husband, cut up for building plots. For several months this had made her huffy, distressed. She had to admit, however, that times were changing, and after some searchings of heart she decided to call on the newcomers. So her heavy Daimler ploughed uphill one afternoon through the mud of the half-made roads, swerving past rubble and bouncing her on the springs. Alas, the new houses were draughty, with sweating plaster, and she returned with a chill: it was unfortunate that she had found anybody at home. Marianne, for her part, had been gratified by Mrs Archworth's visit, for she took her to be county. It was in returning the call that Marianne had met Davina for the first time: she was shown by the parlourmaid into a morning-room dense with smoke and loud with the wireless, from which Davina, glowering, found no way to escape.

Six days after that, on the ridge of the hill by the water-tower, they met again. Marianne, hatless, was exercizing two dogs. Her thick honey-fair hair, ruffling away from her forehead, glinted in afternoon sunshine that fell on the unspoilt country beyond the hill. Rivery twists of mist lay along the river below. This was the first phase of autumn, the air agitating and sweet. When Marianne saw Davina she blushed with pleasure and shyness. They walked on the skyline, between the brambles that still gave out a morningish smell of dew: Marianne invited Davina back to her house for tea . . . She was house-proud, and led this new friend with a touch of emotion up the path to the porch, across the ambitious raw garden. Davina, however, looked neither to right nor left: indoors, she did give one glance of surprise rather than pleasure round the Harvey living-room, artfully pale and bare, where through steel-framed windows blue-pink afternoon light flooded the walls and waxy expanse of floor. It all looked to Davina nullish, with, here and there, the stigmata of intellectual good taste. The hearth was bare, but steam heating drew out sweat from the plaster while, to Davina's senses, devitalizing and parching the air. Ranged round the cold brick hearth, three low chairs with sailcloth cushions invited a confidence everything else forbade. A clock ticked, but the room had no pulse.

'My husband's not here,' said Marianne, looking uncertain. Davina simply said, 'Oh.' They sat down to tea.

'I am fifteen years younger than Matthew,' Marianne said later, apropos of something else.

Matthew had lately retired from the Civil Service owing to ill health. However, he felt better now. At the same time his aunt had died, leaving Matthew more money, so he had decided to live where he liked, and to build. Sentiment had drawn him back to the scene of his happiest years, Marianne having agreed that it would be interesting to live near a university. He was honorary secretary to a society here; in addition to this, he had some philanthropic work in connection with which he was quite often away. He was a member of the senior common-room of his college, and dined in hall three times a term. Once or twice a week the Harveys would dine early and motor into the city to attend the meetings of learned societies or soirées given by the Art Club. Life here was full of interest, Marianne said. Moreover, Matthew and Marianne were happy in each other's affection. After twelve years of marriage his wife still charmed him with her serenity, mild good spirits and love of home. And she had more than this: he took pride in that touch of the farouche about her beauty; she was big-limbed, wide-browed, and looked like a diffident goddess, but her eyebrows turned up to her temples like impatient wings and her alive hair in honey-dark ringlets fell every way. Her fairness and uncertain manner made her seem still quite young: in his friends here she stirred up a dusty sentiment. All this was dear to Matthew, who craved little more than refreshment: he was not a passionate man. Living closely, since they came back here, with the ghost of his own adolescence, raising the old evocations from the same poetry – out of one book slipped a grass-blade twenty-five years old, from another a pressed fritillary – taking the same river-walks, he saw how his friends grew greyer, how their sentiments creaked, and, with dismay for himself, dreaded to desiccate. He clung to his wife's ever-freshness, her touch of the vine-leaf . . . Cautious, well-read, tolerant, and inclined to be prosy, Matthew had fluffy pepper-and-salt hair thinning away from the temples, a rather too constant kind smile, and a nose veined at the bridge; he wore shell-rimmed spectacles with gold hook-on side-pieces, a Norfolk jacket of antique cut, and grey flannel trousers that always bulged at the knee. He and Marianne had two sons, Edwin and Luke; Luke had just joined

Edwin at a preparatory school. When the boys came back for their first Christmas in the new home they would be taken for walks by their father, who would describe his youth here and make them familiar with the antiquities of the city.

Davina had never learned how a poor relation behaves. She exacted, grumbled and ordered the servants around, walked mud into carpets, and stayed in bed overtime, rang bells all day long, and, till recently, took out the car when she chose. Her aunt's maids admired Davina's lordly habit of being unfair: their own mistress, with her affronted, muddled and rather tippeting manner, they had well in control . . . From the first, however, there had been trouble with the chauffeur.

Prothero, the chauffeur, lived in the coachman's room above what had been the stables, up a built-in staircase at the end of the yard. His window faced the Manor back-bedroom windows. He had been with Mrs Archworth four months, a few weeks more than Davina, having been engaged after good old Robinson died. He had come with a first-rate character; none of his former employers could write too highly of him. He was forbiddingly faultless, a careful driver; he did not grumble, make love to the maids or expect beer. Mrs Archworth could never be certain why she did not like him better, or why his proximity while he was tucking her into the car, his way of receiving orders, even the set of his shoulders and back of his ears as he drove, should fill her with a resentful uneasiness. There was something unlikely about him and she mistrusted the odd. Between his flat peaked blue cap and his blue collar his face was always shadowless, abstract, null; a face remembered as being unmemorable. The only look he gave you was level and unmoving. Though she got all she paid for, she could not feel he was hers. Her cook was 'my cook', but he remained 'the chauffeur'. His manner had not that alacrity to which she was accustomed; always on the polite side of surly, he was at the same time unsmiling and taciturn. Here, however, he was, and she dreaded change as in some way an ally of death . . . So that she liked to think his oddness was simply his surname; such an unusual name for a chauffeur, everyone said.

But one point against Prothero Mrs Archworth *could* fix: he burnt light too late. Her own nights were often disturbed by a windy form of dyspepsia; her long bedroom extended the depth of the house, and it was annoying to see, through the blind of her back window, Prothero's light still burning, behind the screen of the ilex, till one or two o'clock. It became her nervous habit to court the annoyance, to wake again and again to see if this were still so. Mrs Archworth would lie rigid with anger and speculation.

Finally, one morning, flushing with apprehension, she protested against this use of her electricity. Prothero bowed. That night, at ten o'clock, he flicked off his hanging light with sardonic promptness: a dimmer glow succeeded: he sat up by candlelight. She had to suppose, with an obscure sense of frustration, the candles might be his own. Night after night, as she still peered through the ilex, not a shadow moved on his blind. She suspected him, all the same, of bringing in women – but the yard gates were bolted and there was never a sound from the dog.

His life at the edge of this household of women remained inscrutable. But one thing they could all see: he could not do with Davina. She would take out the car when it pleased her, without a word to Prothero: she brought it in always dirty and sometimes late. Then one night she found the gates bolted against her; two days after that he had locked the garage. Davina went, stormy, for Prothero. No one knew what occurred, but after that she no longer took out the car. No word from either side reached Mrs Archworth direct. During this friction between her niece and her chauffeur she behaved like a terrified ostrich. After that week, things had quieted down for a bit.

One night in early November, Prothero, in reply to a whistle repeated on a rising note and each time with less caution, opened his door at the head of the built-in staircase and came half-way down, cigarette in his mouth. The stairs creaked as he padded, and came to a stop silently. Davina stood in the arch at the foot of the staircase, with Marianne Harvey behind her out in the yard. Their figures were silhouetted against a patch of yard lamplight. Both the young women were hatless and wore heavy overcoats. Against the night sky, clotted and dense, the papery ilex shivered; night wind, with a sinister flitter of dead leaves, raced round the yard, whose cobbles dappled away into leathery bat's-wing darkness beyond the lamp.

The two stood looking up; the staircase creaked again, and Prothero still said nothing. Davina advanced with a nervous swaggering movement and put one foot on the stairs. She began: 'Look here — '

He said uncivilly: 'Well?'

She dug her hands into her pockets. 'I want some more money,' she said with a casual air.

He shifted his cigarette. 'What,' he said, '*now*? Tonight?'

'Naturally,' said Davina, with some impatience. Outside the archway Mrs Harvey stepped back and glanced uneasily round her into the dark, as though she did not care at all for her company. An unseen smile hung in the dark of the stairs; Prothero let his cigarette drop and ground it out with his heel. 'For heaven's sake,' she said, '*hurry*'; and shifted her foot. The deliberate and endless silence was painful to Marianne. 'Right,' he said. 'Come on up.'

He turned back into his room, and Davina, with automatic swiftness and energy, went springing upstairs after him. His door stayed ajar; vibrations of heat from the stove came down through the arch to the horrified Marianne. Looking up at the dark sky, she fought for a feeling of everybody's nonentity. The clock in the church tower, not far away, struck nine: before the last stroke finished Davina was down again. She caught Marianne by the elbow and ran her across the yard. They paused by the lamp a minute; Davina held a crackling note close up to Marianne's face. 'That is that,' she said.

Wincing away from the note, with its smell of delinquency, Marianne, not for the first time, wished herself safe at home. But the wish was the merest moment's frightened retraction and not sincere: Marianne's heart was set on this evening's pleasure, this fantastic setting-out. In these weeks of knowing Davina her faculty for disapproval seemed to be all used up. She was under a spell. She blamed herself, and knew Davina despised her, for being too shy or too sly to ask Matthew for money before he started for London, where he would stay tonight.

She said faintly, 'Oh, how you *could* . . . '

Her friend looked satirical. She had seen Marianne's recoil from the servant's money. On the subject of class, she knew, Marianne felt as awkwardly and obscurely as people do about sex. Marianne said: 'But why not go to your aunt?'

'You have no idea of what's impossible and what's not! It would make *me* sick to ask Matthew — However, that's your affair. Now, for God's sake, my good girl, don't waste any more time!'

Marianne's brain hummed with frightening anticipation. Leaving the yard, they crept like a couple of cats round the unlit flank of the house, between the wall and the spiny flutter of hollies. Round at the front, an inch-wide slit of bright light fell on Davina's smile: secrecy quickened their breath as they stopped a minute to look in between the drawing-room curtains at Davina's aunt at bridge with three of her neighbours. In the dense red-shaded lamplight sealed in by the pane the two ladies' lace jabots, the two gentlemen's shirt-fronts, stood out like tombstones: the intent quartette, the glazed cabinets and woolly white rugs, all looked embedded in something transparent, solid and hot, like clarified red wax. Not a sound came through the pane. The two turned and crept away down the dark lawn.

Outside the gates, Marianne's coupé had been run up on to the rough grass of the green, with its lights out. Its air was lurking and crookish. They got in, and Marianne ran the car bumpily off the grass and away down a lane between blank end-walls of cottages, on to the by-pass road. Marianne's heart went up as they slid clear of the walls that had stared amazed in her headlights: the sweeping black irresistible river of road sucked at her will like a current; their speed heightened; with a swing of lights they swept south. Davina eyed the speedometer. 'Hurry,' she said.

Marianne had a flicker of spirit. 'If you bully me, I'll go home.'

'Let me *drive* — '

'No.'

'Oh, very well, Mrs Harvey.'

'This is a good beginning,' said Marianne, sore.

'Left!' said Davina sharply, and held to the lights of the dashboard, as they approached a cross-roads, a vague little pencilled map. After some minutes she said: 'If it makes you feel any better, he's not a chauffeur; he's a crook.'

'Don't be silly,' said Marianne. An impassable wall of good humour divides any lady from fact. But she could not resist saying, 'Besides, how do you know?'

'I know he knows I know. He's lying low here. I've seen his photograph somewhere – something once happened.'

'You get ideas in your head from reading those frightful books.'

'But things do happen, you know,' said Davina calmly. Sliding down in her seat and eyeing the flying darkness, she fingered the note in her pocket with cautious pleasure, like someone hugging a thought. Meanwhile Marianne thought of a smart little Jewish girl she used to go to tea with when she was nine years old and living at Dulwich. That little girl had declared there was a dead baby strapped up in a trunk in her family's cistern loft. After tea in the frightening Gothic house, they had crept up to the door, but Marianne would not go in, hearing with horror the cistern inside gurgle. But later her mother told her the little Jewish girl was not a lady, and ever since then Marianne had thought of the extraordinary with contempt. Pressing her chin down in the folds of her muffler, she made up her mind to ask no more about Prothero.

Prothero's pound note was soon changed, for Marianne had not filled up the car and they had to pull up for petrol: she ran the car into the bay of a filling station. While the man unlocked the pump, Marianne got out a minute, restlessly, from the car. Behind them, the last lights of streets were strung along the horizon; the thin glow above a provincial city hung on the sky. Marianne felt her face turned for ever to the unknown. But flight was life to Davina, with nothing to leave behind.

A friend's unknown friends are daemons or demigods with frightful attributes. Marianne's heart sank at the thought of the meeting ahead. The night air was uncalming and anxious: no moon but a rolling hurry of clouds: a circle of rotting flower-stalks outside the petrol station shivered under their headlights in the dark wind.

They drove on.

A glittering Neon sign like wolves' eyes read: OPEN ALL NIGHT, at which thought a dry weariness pervaded the brain. 'We shan't be staying *all* night,' said Davina easily. Here they were, and they tore up the pencilled map and scattered the scraps on the wind.

The road-house stood at the cross-roads, its row of Christmas-card windows shedding a fictitious glow. Four wide black roads had been levelled into the hill, and met in a kind of circus inside the clay banks of the cutting. The road-house stood high up; to the porch you mounted some steps up the high embankment; a car park was scooped out fifty yards further on. The wind moaned cheerlessly over the down behind, but the scene had a hard air of late night merriment, like a fixed grin . . . In the porch, Marianne pulled off a gauntlet to tuck back a strand of hair; Davina whipped out her lipstick and gave herself new, bright lips. 'We were once rather in love.'

But inside there was no one. A long row of swinging lanterns bobbed in their own horrid light as they pushed open the door. The lounge was empty and bald as the inside of a band-box, glazed with synthetic panelling. The chairs were askew, empty, with flattened cushions; ashtrays sent up a cold fume; the place wore an air of sudden, sheepish vacuity, as though a large party had just got up and gone out. The barman leaned, yawning, just inside the bar shutter. When they came in, he took no notice. Davina's friends had not come.

Davina, who had sauntered in with a smile on her fine reddened lips, dropped the smile and looked round her, utterly at a loss.

'Perhaps we are early,' said Marianne.

'No.'

'Perhaps they are late?'

'They can't be later than us.'

'Perhaps they've given us up?'

'They know I am always late — ' Davina broke off, crossed the room, and angrily questioned the barman. No, no one had asked for her; no one had waited; no one had telephoned. Sitting down by the shutter, she snapped out an order for bitter. 'I can't drink beer,' said Marianne, as it was brought.

'You'd better,' Davina said with a hollow look.

Marianne fingered her glass. 'This seems a funny place to be meeting anyone in . . . '

'Well, we're not, you see. Does that make it all right?'

A clock struck ten; someone bumped down the bar shutter and locked it. The barman came for their glasses. So that was that.

After some time Marianne said: 'You know, we can't wait all night.'

'I don't see why not.'

Lighting a cigarette, Davina said no more. An uneasy silence set in. Marianne, watching her friend's lips pulling at the cigarette, the once bold dark eyes that now crept to the door then dropped quickly to cover their mortification, felt pity go through her heart with a shameful pang. She also was mortified, and could have easily wept. She only half knew now all she had hoped of tonight. Girlish delicious expectancy went sour inside her. She was tragically sold. She had been, from the first, imposed on by something about Davina – her dashingness, curtness and air of experience. In these last weeks, Marianne's consciousness had been extended deliciously, painfully. A segment of bright unknown world had fallen across her path, where it shed prisms. Only she knew what formless excitement had racked her lately.

But where was Tonight?

Seeing Davina sitting, so much at a loss, with 'Forgotten' pasted across her, too proud to look up, Marianne felt the world contract again. In the next room, someone put a wailing blues on the gramophone. Marianne wished she were home, with her feet on the hot pipes and the cat on her stomach. Out here, draughts raced round the floor.

Davina shot up and said: 'I shall telephone!'

They drove on again. 'I'll tell you one thing,' Davina was saying. 'Somebody's double-crossed me. Unless Oliver's lying – and I don't think he'd be lying – I ought to have got his message at aunt's today.'

'Plans are changed?' quavered Marianne.

'Yes, don't you *see* — ' said Davina. Her spirits, however, were up. She sat smiling and silent, looking along the headlights. Things had changed for the better. They had swung east at the cross-roads, always further from home. After more miles of flying hypnotic light, Davina said it ought to be anywhere now. 'Any time now, on your right . . . ' On their right, they crept in between two Palladian lodges, unlit and staring, the wide gates standing apart. Beech-trunks raced past their lights and a sleek wettish avenue spattered under the tyres: three more gates were hooked back.

The immense façade of the house rushed glaring on to their headlamps: between high white-shuttered windows pilasters soared out of sight above an unlit fanlight like patterns of black ice.

Reaching across Marianne, Davina touched the horn, which sent up that face of coldness its peevish cry. The cry repeated – 'They can't even *hear!*' she groaned. But then the fanlight amazingly sprang into light, the hall door burst open on a perspective of pillars, and, with so much thrusting and force that this seemed a muffled riot, dark people shot out, surrounded the car, and pulled open both doors at once. Marianne ducked in a sweep of night air. Davina, peering, said: 'Oliver?'

'I've g-got this all to myself!' exclaimed an excitable voice.

'Where's Thingummy?'

'O-o-oh, he never turned up.'

'So he's not here,' said a woman.

'I am furious,' said Davina.

'That's too bad,' said Oliver, pulling Davina out of the car with a glass in his other hand. 'Never mind, you're here now.'

'It was too bad,' agreed someone. 'However, here we all are.'

They trooped back into the hall. A stout, speechless man who had pulled Marianne through the other door of the car looked at her in the light, closely, to see what he had got. He seemed satisfied. Indoors, the immense cold hall, all chequered pavement and pillars, wore an air of outrage, ravished by steps and voices. One door stood open, and light peered in at the glacial sheeted outlines of furniture and a chandelier that hung in a bag like a cheese and glittered inside the muslin. A chill came from the hearthstones; the house was masterless. Along a pathway of drugget over the marble, at a quick muffled shuffle as though conducting a funeral secretly, the revellers passed down the hall to a door at the far end. They shot through with a rush, each unwilling to be the last, and shut the door defiantly on the echoing house.

'Outside there gives you the creeps,' said the only woman who spoke. Davina's friend Oliver, dishevelled, fair, aquiline, and unnaturally tall, turned and shook hands with Marianne. 'I didn't see you,' he said. 'I'm so glad you came. I hope you had no trouble; I went down just now and opened the gates myself. Do you know if the sheep got out? They are grazing sheep; things are not what they used to be.'

Smoke and human stuffiness thickened the air of this room with its dead undertone of chill on which a snapping wood fire had little effect. It was a high, shabby, gilt-and-white octagonal ante-room, the naked shutters of three windows fortified by iron bars. Bottles crowded a top-heavy ornate table under the chandelier; panels of tarnished mirror kept multiplying the company, and on a red marble column a Psyche balanced with one hand over a breast. Oliver said: 'I brought her in here for company: I always liked the girl.' On a settee, pulled across the hearth at an angle, an enormous congested old lady slept with her feet apart, letting out stertorous breaths. Her wool coatee was pinned over the heaving ledge of her bust with a paste brooch in the form of a sailing-ship, and at each breath this winked out a knowing ray. Her hands, chapped and knouty, lay in the trough of her lap. Half under her skirts a black pair of kitchen bellows lay on the marble fire-kerb. There was not much more furniture in the room.

'That is Mrs Bennington, who takes care of me. She's so nice,' said Oliver. He rinsed a glass out at a siphon and brought Davina a drink. 'It's a nice house, too,' he said, 'till you get used to it.'

'It's all right once one's got here. Why not suggest this in the first place?'

'You see, I thought there'd be Thingummy.'

'Well, you certainly muddled things,' said Davina with less rancour, her nose inside her glass. When he and she had been younger, handsome, high-spirited, and still with something to spend, they had been in love, and expected to marry one day. Their May had been blighted. Now, each immobile from poverty, each frozen into their settings like leaves in the dull ice of different puddles, they seldom met. They had the dregs of tenderness left for each other, but, each time they met, less to say. It was best to meet in a crowd, as they met tonight. Tonight the crowd was not large, but things might have been worse.

Oliver shook the dregs from another glass and absently rinsed it, meanwhile looking at Marianne. He said to Davina: 'Will she enjoy herself?'

'She has a deadly life. Her standard is not high.'

'She looks most beautifully shy,' Oliver said wistfully.

Marianne felt very shy. The more the room settled down, the more strongly she felt she had no place here. She stood with a hand on the mantelpiece, looking blindly about with her wide-apart troubled eyes. The stout man who had her in charge snatched the glass Oliver had been so vaguely holding, filled it, and brought it to Marianne. 'Now you'll feel better,' he said. His name was Purdon. Marianne could not explain that she did not like whisky. The smell of spirits repelled and interested her; her nostrils quivered; she drank. '*That's* better,' said Purdon, and bustled up with a chair. Marianne sat down blinking and holding her glass. As though she had been a refugee, her coming in had seemed to constitute some kind of emergency.

'Where are we?' she said.

'Ah, *that's* just the fun,' said Purdon. 'Where we've no call to be!'

'As much call as anyone else,' said the platinum blonde oldish girl, Miriam. She knelt by the kerb and, pulling the bellows from under Mrs Bennington's skirts, began to puff at the fire. She coaxed the flames up knowingly; firelight flapped on her face and up Marianne's knees. An un-English man in a crimson high-necked pullover reached his drink from the floor and resettled himself on the settee, one arm around Mrs Bennington, with an air of content. These were all the people there really were in the room. The party resumed its tenor, illicit but not defiant. A low-spirited intimacy, an innocent kind of complicity, made itself felt. Little seemed worth saying, everything understood. What was said strayed up like bubbles from depths of interiority. They had the flat, wise air of a party of bandit children with their bravado put off, gathering in a cellar.

Marianne looked into her glass; where had all that gone? Her dilated eyes swam round the smoky gilt-and-white room with its tarnished reaches of mirror. She met Oliver's look that was like something swimming desperately on a heaving tide of light. Her throat pricked and she pulled at the scarf she still wore. She exclaimed to the fat man: 'This is nicer than where we were!'

'More homey?' he said nicely. She let him unwind her scarf and drape it about the Psyche. 'That poor girl,' he said, 'gives me the shivers.'

'It feels homey all right to me,' said Miriam, withdrawing her head from the grate. She wiped bellows-black from her fingers on to her black velvet skirt and went on: 'Which may throw some light on my pedigree, now that I come to think.'

No one knew who her father was; he might have been almost anyone. Owing her unkind and scandalous mother no duty, Miriam was always glad to air this uncertainty: it gave her a feeling of space and sometimes, to her mind, a slightly divine quality. She was herself a shady and bitter very good-hearted girl whom everyone liked and nobody seemed to want.

All Oliver's friends were like this. He was, like Davina, an enemy of society, having been led to expect what he did not get. His father had sold himself up and Oliver had had from him little but bad advice. Oliver despised the rich and disliked the poor and drank to the bloody extinction of the middle classes. He wished to call no man brother, and disbelieved with ferocity in himself. The old order left him stranded, the new offered him no place. He lived as he could, and thought well of Davina for settling herself on her aunt. His own relations had, under the suavity of their aspect, a mean kind of canniness, and were not to be imposed upon: they did what they could by imposing him on their friends. Perverse bad manners and clumsiness disqualified Oliver for the profession of being a guest, by which otherwise he might have victualled and housed himself. He had once or twice, on his uncle's recommendation, catalogued country-house libraries; his work was impatient, showy and incorrect, but no one had said so so far, for fear of offending his uncle. He was an ungracious beggar, and, handicapped by a stammer, uncertain health and excitable sensibility, an embarrassment to himself. With his height and fairness he was, in an overcast kind of way, magnificent-looking: a broken-spirited Viking. He was capable of fantastically disinterested affections. Not having been born for nothing into a privileged class, he was, like Davina, entirely unscrupulous.

Lord Thingummy – so Oliver called him, and it is good enough for the purposes of this tale – possessed a fine, mouldy, unreadable library. Inflated, one night at his club, by intellectual pride, he had let himself be persuaded by Oliver's uncle as to the existence, down at his house in the country, of possible unknown treasures in calf and vellum, and induced to hire Oliver to explore and catalogue these. For this he gave Oliver twenty pounds and his victuals. Lord Thingummy had been disposed to join Oliver for a few days in the country; but yesterday he had wired to put off. The very thought of the place had been too damp for him. His caretaker, Mrs Bennington, was put in charge of Oliver, with instructions not to make him too comfortable, for one had heard of Oliver as a dilatory chap . . . Lord Thingummy was thus, tonight, the party's unconscious host.

The man on the settee in a crimson pullover was a White Russian with little stake in the future. Tonight he was on a holiday; as a rule he lived rather drearily with a woman of means who had a feeling for Russians, in a maisonette just off Addison Road. Miriam was a girl he and Oliver knew. The stout man, Purdon, was a dentist who had won five thousand pounds in an Irish Sweep and shut up his surgery till this should all be spent: he regretted nothing. Tomorrow he went back to work. He was overflowing with friendliness and had bought the drinks for tonight.

Thingummy, said Oliver, was so damned mean he had had the heating turned off and taken the key of the cellar. The library, where he had said he had no doubt Oliver would be happy browsing about, smelt of must. 'He had the n-nerve,' said Oliver, 'to send me down here to live on chops in this ice-house. May his soul rot like his books!'

Purdon explained to Marianne by what a remarkable stroke of luck they all came to be here. When she understood, she had only one thought: she was agonized – the angry earl would appear. Her brain stopped like a clock; she had met few peers. She said unsteadily: 'I must be going home.'

'Rats,' said Purdon. Nobody else heard.

Davina and Oliver pulled cushions on to the parquet and sat with their shoulders against a corner of the settee. She said: 'How is the catalogue?'

'Getting on fast; I'm so anxious to get away.'

'Where shall you go next?'

'How should I know?'

'You might come and stay with my aunt.'

'That would depend,' he said. 'I must have a look at her first.'

Miriam tittered: 'He's put in the names of the stuck-on books on the doors.'

'He's as likely to read those as any others,' said Oliver.

Marianne trembled and stood up, eyeing her empty glass. She thought: 'Where am I?' put down her glass, and began to finger her way along the mantelpiece's swags and medallions. She thought the marble throbbed. In despair, she sat carefully down again, gripping the scrolled gold chair-arms. Looking across for Davina, she met Oliver's eyes once more. He immediately got up and came to her side. 'I've forgotten your name,' he said.

'Marianne,' she said. 'But I've got to be going home.'

He exclaimed in distress: 'Aren't you happy?'

She hesitated. 'I feel lost.'

'Why do you say that?' said Oliver miserably.

Her uncertain look turned away from him to the fire; he saw her cheeks burn and her trembling, obstinate grip on the arms of the chair. Feeling unutterably miserable and guilty, he turned and said to Davina: 'Don't let her go!'

'She's worn out,' said Davina, 'naturally.' Mortification came flooding back to her; she plucked angrily at a carnation she had taken from one of her aunt's vases and stuck in her buttonhole. 'That place was awful,' she said. '*You* simply thought, "No doubt they'll turn up here somehow." Message? I got no message. You seem to expect one to know where you are by instinct! People like you waste one's life!'

'Your aunt ought to be on the telephone.'

'You just hate trouble,' she said.

'Well, don't make it,' said Oliver.

'Please don't quarrel,' said the Russian. Their angry dialogue took place across the room. Through some seconds of silence Mrs Bennington wheezed.

'I took the message,' said Miriam, 'I, in my little fly – I mean, in my little car: I took the message. Purdon and I drove up to your aunt's house on the way from buying the drink. We snooped around the front lawn and just felt we couldn't face it, so we went round to the back and you still weren't there. They said you weren't anywhere. So we left word with a man who was polishing up a Daimler — '

'That is so,' said Purdon. 'We left word with the chauffeur.'

'We left word very particularly,' said Miriam. '*Don't* come where we said, we said, come straight to Thingummy's, here, because he's not here, so we can be. We even drew you a map,' said Miriam earnestly.

Davina pulled the carnation to pieces. 'I'd like to believe you,' she said, 'but I got no message.'

'Then somebody double-crossed you,' said Miriam.

By half-past ten Mrs Archworth's evening was over. The parlourmaid let out the retired Indian Civilian and his wife and the retired admiral, who pattered away round the green, with its dim lamps, to their cottages past the church. In the drawing-room the parrakeet, disturbed by the sudden silence, fidgeted under its red baize cover. Mrs Archworth turned two of the lamps out and stooped for a good night chat with the Pekinese. The parlourmaid came in to take out the tray of glasses.

'Shall I shut up, madam?' she said.

'Not till Miss Davina is in. She is dining at Mrs Harvey's; she won't be late. No doubt they will see her home. You must leave the door on the latch and come down later to bolt it.'

Kissing the Pekinese between the eyeballs, Mrs Archworth handed it over regretfully to the parlourmaid; she picked up her lozenge-box, her patience cards, and a paper-knife, and, with her usual air of unfocused indignation – for she seldom expected to sleep – went up to bed. The parlourmaid followed her up with a glass of hot water. Shaking her nightly powder into the glass and watching the water cloud, the aunt awaited, on the stretch and uneasy, Davina's step on the gravel. Outside two red rings of lamplight the darkness showed flat and empty; her thoughts groped around in it ignorantly, like tentacles, asking what everybody was doing, where everybody might be. She did not regret, however, that she was not on the telephone. Her axiom had been always: People can come to see one, or else people can write.

At ten o'clock to the minute Prothero lit four candles stuck into bottles and with satiric promptness flicked out the hanging light. So that Mrs Archworth, peering out later through her back window-curtains, found his blind pallid. His room, a man-servant's, with match-boarded ceiling, glazed cotton blind and fibre matting, was bare; the furniture showed by candlelight mean outlines on the whitewash. The man had no belongings; the place seemed to be to let. His chauffeur's tunic hung huddled against the back of the door. The stove through its mica front shed a dull red glow on the matting. The wind had dropped; inside its walls and high locked gates the yard down there was as still and deep as a well. Not a draught stirred those thin sheets of close-written paper shuffled over his table. Reaching the four candles closer to his left elbow, he went on writing again.

His hand with the twitching pen went rushing from line to line at a fever-high pace. He did not once pause. The pen rushed the hand along under some terrific compulsion, as though something, not thought, vital, were being drained out of him through the point of the pen. Words sprang to their places with deadly complicity, knowing each other too well . . . Once or twice when a clinker fell in the stove, or the outside staircase unaccountably creaked as though a foot were upon it, he looked up, the tyrannic pen staggered, he looked round the room with its immutable fixtures as though he were a ghost —

– grave to the N.N.E. of the church tower in the sunk bit by the wall. No stone yet as it's too soon, the earth is too soft, but a wire wreath frame left with some stalks of some sort of flowers, they were quite dead. Last month you must have got soaked through to what was your heart, rain comes hard on a grave with the earth not set yet. So now you must do without company. I went once.

You said once you thought you should like to die in a ward, for company. As much as you thought, you thought that. Well I was there. But you never thought much of that. Whatever you did want it wasn't that, whatever you did want you didn't seem to be getting. I never did know what you did want and I don't think you did. What you did get you didn't want, that was me. But you got what you didn't want. You got that and now I don't want any more.

I don't want you any more because I don't want any more. I don't want more of all that so I don't want you or see you. I don't see your eyes that you thought as much as you thought I should not forget. If you could think now you could not think how much I never want you and how much I forget. I don't go back to the bungalow. If you could see you could see how much I forget that time. You could see I don't see the picture of dogs' heads and the pink dotted curtain flapping or standing still or the moth bumping round the whole time or the magazine with the girl's face by your feet on the bed. You tried with eyes to say I should always see them but you were wrong. They are in a list, I can say them but I can't see them.

The bungalow is shut up, the papers call it a love nest but what you got there does no good to that kind of place. No woman would go there now and no one but a fool woman would have gone there in the first place. You said that yourself first thing when

I came, it was no good, it was mouldy, the trees drip on the roof and over the edge of the roof, that made green smears, the press was musty inside where you hung your dress and it was you said the sheets had a musty smell. If you wanted to be by the river you should have been by the river and not a field off, and then that might not have been such a lonely place. For all I know no one goes there and as I do not see it it may not be there, for all I know.

Now I don't want all that any more, now I don't want, I get on fine here with no more ants in my brain. The old woman's all right. She gets what she wants. I shut her into the hearse, it is like a hearse, with her rug and her dog and we go bumping along. My ears stick out like you said under my cap and the buttons have crests, a fist with a knife, and I click my heels when she talks. I give satisfaction here if you know what that means but you do not know what that means. She gets her money's worth.

I always was what I am, now I am what I always was, what you said that time. Flunkey. I like what I am, a free man. Up here I'm as snug as a monk with a stove with two hours' fuel, no pictures, no pictures of dogs. The bed squeaks when I turn so I lie still like you lie, only it's broader, with your arms down at your sides. My stairs are my stairs and no one comes up, if I did want they would come. I have that money you had, that was my money you had, a bad debt after all I did. The girl owes me seven pound ten and six, so I buy the kisses now. All the fun's in the deal now I know what I don't want.

They say when you've done what I've done you go back. But that's not true. I went once where you are to be sure you are there, but I don't go where we were that last time. I don't act any way they would think I would act. I act my own way now, only I act that way because it is my way. If I don't know what I will do, how can they know what I will do? I act now before I think, and I don't think after I act. I act how I like. You always knew what I would do, so I always had to do that. Now no one knows, I don't know, I act.

Love was just having to act in the one way. There was just one way we could go, like both being in a tram. We acted the way we had to. Slippings-off just us two and fake names and quarrels and all that fun. They all go that same way. Where the tram didn't take the points, where the bump was, was your way with that money you had. You had all the money. The clink in your gold chain bag that you always watched and always kept by your hand and the wallet you brought out when the bills came, smiling because it was you had the money to spend but not liking to spend your money and smiling at me that knowing way and pushing the notes back that we didn't want yet. You could pay for the fancies you had with all that money you had. Our bed smelt of all your money. I was a fool then to love you the way I did, I gave more than you paid for, you saw I was a fool and that you paid for a fool. You were not the big business man's daughter for nothing, Anita, and not the great big business man's wife.

No one saw so no one knew, we met first of all in the train so no one knew we had met, we didn't write letters, you were very smart that way, you were very sly. I saw you were no good. Your husband was a strict man. For some time we tricked your husband all over the place in a hurry, then you said there was no time, we had to have more time, we had to have some place. What with being so plotty, so damned smart, so careful no one would see us who would remember, a different place every time – that was not value, you thought. You had to have more time, you said. What did you have to have more time for? You'd torn me up by that time, in that first month, what more did you want? You went off and leased that bungalow in a fake name. By that time I was poison to you, and you were to me. It rained that first day that was the last time, when you told me I had to come there. I left my car in the garage outside the town up the river and then I walked down in the rain to where you were. I felt like lead, the wind bent the trees back on the hill on the far side, the rain hit the river, it was all dark grey like a photograph. No one was out, I didn't meet anyone. I felt like a stone. When I came round the trees I saw that was the place and I hated the place with trees dripping on the roof and streaks on the white gate. It looked a hole for a toad. When I came up the path a window blew open, a pink dotted curtain blew out in the wet. Your arm came out after the curtain and shut the window so I knew you were in there waiting. The trees up there lashed about. You had seen me, of course. Then, at that time, I couldn't see any way out. There was no air in the house. Though the place was alone with nobody going by you drew the pink curtain as soon as I came in. The whole time the windows rattled, the rain got lashed down by the trees on our roof.

At sunset the wind stopped and then the rain stopped, I got up and opened the window. There was a yellow light near the river, it was hot because it was July, now the wind had stopped and then everything steamed. The steam made everything hot, moths came out and bumped on the windows as it was getting darker, musty smells came out of the walls of the room where we were. We were done in by then. You began crying and I went off to open a can of corned beef to eat. I shut the door but you opened it, you went on talking at me while I was opening the can and that note came in your voice like the needle skidding on the inside of a record when the record is done. When I didn't answer you came into the kitchen the way you were and asked for a cigarette. I said I hadn't a cigarette, I'd been looking for yours. Then you said what you said. So I went out and walked.

I walked along by the river and didn't meet anyone, I thought I wouldn't go back but my hat was there and you had to have some answer to what you had said. I saw you had me bought up. A motor salesman who didn't do big business and didn't have money and started to have tastes he didn't have money for. A war gentleman after the war, you'd have liked me then in the war. I could see how things were. A man with the sort of face everybody forgot, that you said you mostly forgot. I walked some time by the same bit of the river. I didn't go far.

When I came back you had lit the lamp by the bed and lay smoking and reading a magazine with a girl's face on the front, you knew I would come back. I came and stood the other side of the lamp to wait till you had finished your magazine story. You stretched your arms past your head and yawned and arched up your back, then you smiled the way you smiled and said you'd been nervous. You said how much you liked company, like you had always said. But when I didn't say anything but just waited, without noticing you, you turned over slowly as though you were so comfortable and slid your hand slowly between your cheek and the pillow and said that again slowly. You said that again. You said what you meant. You said what you'd said before. I saw a red mist where your face was, just a mist on the pillow. I took the pillow and smothered you.

The moth bumped about the whole time I leaned on the pillow, then flew into the curtain. The picture of dogs' heads was over the bed and the magazine stayed by your feet on the bed, when you didn't move any more it was still there. Your eyes were looking at me when I lifted the pillow. I took the note-case out of your gold handbag and took your pearls off the table and took your rings and I left the lamp by you to burn out. I left fingerprints, I suppose. I took no trouble. I had taken trouble enough. I banked on no one knowing I knew you. I rubbed your face powder off the mirror with my elbow and had a good look, I thought at least I'd remember my own face. I went out leaving the door on the latch. You stayed there, that was all you knew. You stayed alone.

I took the gold bag that you always kept by your hand and dropped it in the river along the bank. Clouds came up again but everything was quite quiet, it was dark then. Walking away for always from where you were I didn't feel like me yet. Two swans went by but I didn't meet anyone by the river. It was past ten, I came to the town with the garage, I passed the cinema then, they were all coming out. I joined in with them all and walked to the

garage along with some people, we all took our cars out. I drove
south towards Newhaven, and pulled up the car by a wood and
slept for a bit, then I drove on. I put up the car at Newhaven when
it was light and crossed by the day boat the way it had been
arranged. I was crossing to France that day on the firm's business
anyhow. In Paris I sold your pearls and two of your rings, I kept
the third I liked best. I was at Le Mans when I saw they'd found
you, then the firm sent me on to Lyons and I saw your face in the
papers, you were the bungalow crime, the French papers had you
in because you were young and pretty and it looked like a man. It
seemed funny to think I knew you when I saw you in those papers.
Your husband covered our tracks, he thought more of being so
strict than of hanging anybody, he was just like you always said. He
said you'd taken the bungalow for yourself for a rest cure and he
had been going to join you. That didn't help the police so they
fixed robbery for the motive and pulled in a tramp but the fingerprints didn't fit, then they went after a deserter from Aldershot,
they're not so sharp as they say. For all everyone knew I might not
have been born.

This seemed odd to me, when I knew for the first time I had been
born and knew who I was now. I felt grand those weeks and fit to
lift a ton weight with nothing to lift but pennies. I felt so grand I
didn't know what to do. I was all alone. I didn't get thick with
anybody for fear of talking when there was only the one thing I
wanted to tell anybody. My head stayed very good and I saw the
sense of things I never had seen the sense of. Everything got
simple. So I began to like life and want a run for my money, else
what was the good of being the way I was? So I wasn't taxing my
good luck any more, I thought I would stage a get-out and start
new, the chance came when the firm sent me to Marseilles. Mutts
disappear there every day.

A man came along there that was what I wanted, a drunk,
Prothero, a chauffeur who'd been sacked from a villa near Antibes,
he'd drunk all his money in Marseilles, he was so tight he sold me
his passport for two hundred francs and threw in his references for
fifty more. His face fitted mine all right. I said if he'd meet me again
I'd give him the fifty francs that I hadn't on me the first time; he
turned up blind again. I walked him down by the quays where
there weren't so many lamps and then nudged him over into the
harbour, he wasn't giving a damn for what happened next anyhow,
so that was all right by him, he sank like a stone. I went back to his
place and checked out his luggage, I left mine where it was in my
hotel. The hotel people reported me missing, they found my papers
and passport along with my luggage and wrote back to the firm. I
wasn't just then owing the firm anything, so they didn't worry,

they concluded I'd been one more of those fool English who get themselves done in in the pleasure quarter and aren't heard of again. The French police poked round but they get sick of the English. I hadn't any family to make trouble, nobody cared so everyone let things drop. My photograph was in the French papers and in the English papers, and it must have been funny for people to think they had known me. No one remembered my face. No one went into mourning, no one felt that way. After a bit I came back to England and began to put Prothero's references into action. I was anxious to lie low, so applied here. The old woman considered herself lucky. So I got on without you, you see. You lie expecting me back, I don't come back.

You never considered yourself lucky. You considered you'd saddled yourself with a fool but you had to have me, I was a fool to love you that way, you were quite right. We are quit of each other, if that was what you wanted you got what you wanted, it was what I wanted, perhaps all the time we were wanting the same thing, and now I've got that I don't want anything more. You thought I had to have you, as much as you thought you thought that. You thought that when you said what you said then, and you thought that under the pillow. When I took the pillow off that was in your eyes. Well, unthink that. If I thought you thought that still, if I thought you lay thinking that where you are now, I'd break right through, I'd tear anything down to get at you and tear the thought out, I'd tear up the sunk earth. Yes, it makes me mad to see you don't see that I don't see you or want you, that you don't see when these stairs creak outside that I don't think 'Here she is,' that I lie as still as you lie with my bed not creaking any more than your sunk earth and don't think, 'She was here once.' If I were to write, '*I love you, I cannot bear this, I want you, come back*' – you might be tricked. You might come back to see me see you, then you would see me not see you, you would unthink the thought you thought under the pillow, as much as you thought. Yes, look, if I tricked you this way, you'd come back, you could not not come back, you could never resist that. Yes, so look, I'll trick you I'll write loud, like a scream would be if anyone was in the dark with nothing (but I am not in the dark) I'll write so loud you will hear though you can't hear, *Anita* —

The pen charged in his hand. Dragging his hand down to the foot of the paper, in staggering charging characters it wrote – '*Anita, I love you Anita, Anita, where are you? I didn't mean that, that was not me, I didn't, I can't bear you away. I see your eyes on my pillow, I can't lie alone, I cannot get through the night, come back, where are you, I won't hurt you, come back, come back, come back* — '

Prothero dropped the pen as though it were burning. He watched it, frightfully animate, roll to the edge of the table and over the edge. He stared at his right hand and spread out the fingers slowly; they reasserted his will. Shutting his eyes, he screwed round full to the light of the four candles a blank-lidded square fair face clammy with sweat. His hands meanwhile groped over the table, gathering up by feel the close-written sheets. Rising, an automatic and mindless movement, he flung open the lid of the stove with a pothook and thrust the papers in, heard for a minute the hot red roar of the stove, then dropped the lid on the roar.

So his nights succeeded each other. At the back of the Manor House, through the ilex, a light was still burning in Mrs Archworth's room. Downstairs, behind the red kitchen blind, a sleepy, indignant maid sat up for Davina. The village clock struck midnight with rolling strokes.

The wreathed gilt clock above Marianne's head struck midnight with brittle chimes, at which the air quivered like something stretched too tight. The chandelier glittering high up exhausted itself on the smoke, light losing quality as the evening wore on, and a sluggish chill crept over the party's wearied over-acute senses like a miasma. With drifts of cigarette ash in the lap of her black velvet skirt, Miriam sat talking introspectively to nobody in particular; she did not drink any more. The Russian played cat's cradle with a bit of gold cord from a chocolate-box. Purdon sat on a highish chair with his legs crossed, yawning at the chandelier. Mrs Bennington slept on.

'You see, I'm that way,' went on Miriam. 'I don't believe in anything. I don't believe anything really exists, you see.'

The Russian slipped the gold cord off the tips of his fingers and, frowning with concentration, started over again. 'But look here,' said Purdon, 'if you're not going to believe in anything, you have to have something not to believe *in*.'

'*I* don't have to,' said Miriam. 'I can believe in nothing. I always could; I was always funny that way.'

'Do you believe in progress?' said the Russian.

'Everything's talk,' said Miriam, 'and what does all that come to? I see through it.'

'I don't, either,' said the Russian.

'And look at all this fuss all the time. Every time you pick up a paper there's a fuss about something. What I want to know is, what are they getting at? Have you any idea?' she said to Davina.

'No,' said Davina.

'I daresay you've never thought; I daresay you're right, too. What do *you* do?'

'Nothing,' replied Davina. 'I can't.'

'Oh, well,' said Miriam kindly, 'perhaps you've got money?'

'No, not now.'

'Dear me,' said Miriam, 'none of us have any luck. If you'd had a hundred pounds I'd have taken you into partnership. I'm looking round for a partner. Or, strictly, I'm looking round for a hundred pounds, but I wouldn't mind a partner; it would be company. Have you heard about me?'

'No. What?'

'I keep a tea-and-cake parlour called The Cat and Kettle. If you like cakes it's all right, but it puts you off them. It's not far from here, at Warring – on the river, you know. I've got check blinds and an inglenook and olde-oak beams and a cat; it's nice till you get used to it. I do Devonshire Teas at one and six and Dainty Teas *à la carte*. I lose on the Devonshires, mostly; you've no idea how much a person can eat to spite you. Still, it's a draw, and you've got to consider that. I wouldn't mind so much if it weren't for the black beetles; I always think they try and run up my legs. My cat eats them, but you should see how they multiply; however, don't tell me a cat's not faithful. I bake the stuff myself; I'm a real home girl, I am; there's plenty of use for a gas-oven without putting one's head in it, as I always tell the girls. Every now and then my hand goes right out; I don't mind telling you, you could knock a man down with some of my gingerbread. But people would eat a boot if it was home made. They like getting caraways into their teeth and spitting out burnt currants; it feels like the old home. I've had customers drive thirty miles to see the dear old black kettle sit on the hob and kid themselves I made the tea out of it. Neurotic, that's what they are. I get mostly courting couples; the girls like it; there's something about that kettle that brings a man to the point. He mashes my comb honey about and goes soppy about his mother; it makes you sick. You'd think it would make a girl sick, but a girl goes through worse than that, as I always say. However, no times like the old times — Look in next time you're passing,' she said to Davina.

'I never am,' said Davina. 'I haven't got a car.'

'Well, you won't miss much,' said Miriam without rancour. 'It's a hole of a place where I am. Dishwater fogs all the winter and a slow motion High Street with no one about all day but the dear vicar. In summer it's like the inside of a hot pipe and you can't hear yourself think. Cars in a screaming jam all down the street, and punts jammed down the river till you couldn't drown a kitten between, and couples tie up all night, with ukuleles and portables, to the bank under my yard wall. You never know what goes on. It wouldn't be *your* cup of tea.'

'You know,' said Purdon to Miriam, 'you ought really to marry me.'

'Yes,' sighed the Russian, 'that's what I always say.' He put his head down on Mrs Bennington's shoulder and dropped the twist of gold cord despondently into her lap.

All this time, Oliver had been standing above Marianne, leaning against the mantelpiece. He had said nothing since the clock struck, but now he turned and said eagerly to Marianne: 'Come for a turn.'

The fire had 'caught' and danced fluttering up, throwing pink light on the kerb: Marianne sat so close that a faint smell of wool scorching came from her skirt. She fixed her eyes on the smiling, familiar flames and felt more herself. Once or twice with a sleepy unconscious movement she leaned her forehead against the cold marble upright of the mantelpiece. Remotely she had heard midnight strike on the gilt clock. All the time she was aware with some apprehension of Oliver standing silently tall above her, like a tree that might fall. When he did speak, she looked away from him round the room with her frightened eyes: everything seemed to vacillate. The table toppling with bottles seemed to be balancing anxiously, splaying its gilt claw feet out on the parquet like an animal on the ice.

'Won't you come?' said Oliver.

'It's so late. It's so cold.'

'We will walk round the house.'

He opened the door; she rose and, unwinding her scarf from the Psyche, walked through the door ahead of him in a dream. The others said nothing. Like children in a large temple the two walked through the hall and up the bare white stone staircase, ascending to meet themselves in a darkish mirror at the head of the first flight. Here the staircase divided and rose in two sweeps like antlers against the high wall that was hung each side of the mirror with pastoral tapestries. From the head of each flight ran a gallery, waxy and dark. The house's great vacant height and resounding unlit perspectives weighed upon Marianne. As they went from room to room she heard Oliver's fingers tap in the dark on the wall for the light switch, then Italianate ceilings and sheeted icebergs of furniture sprang into cold existence. 'Think of living here!' she said.

'Where *do* you live?'

She began to explain. But she was held up by something ardent and curious in his manner, the impatience with which, shaking his lock of fair hair back, he stared through her outline, not seeming to listen. What she was saying trailed off into unimportance. Tonight and his presence tightened their hold on her spirit; the everyday became cloudy and meaningless and, like a tapestry, full of arrested movement. At the tapestry she looked down – for they had come back to the gallery. She stood fixing her eyes on the subfusc temples on hills and the nymphs trailing dead garlands, inanimate in brown gloom.

'Shan't I see you again, then?'

She did not know what to say.

'You tell me you're married,' Oliver said accusingly.

Coming in tonight with Davina, quite unexplained, she had seemed to him as disconnected from fact as an angel or goddess. Her lost face, mild wild air, and, once or twice as they groped through the dark house, her anxious touch on his arm, had set up in him a violent solicitude. Now, outraged by what she had only begun to tell him, he exclaimed excitedly: 'Damn the natural affections!'

'Oh, you mustn't say that!'

'They are a ramp,' said Oliver. One angry hand on her elbow, he wheeled her right about to face a pair of heavily moulded doors. He flung one of these open on a resounding void, announcing: 'The grand saloon.' They went in. He flicked at a half-dozen switches but no light came. 'The bulbs are all gone; he's as poor as a rat,' said Oliver.

Reflections from outside touched the glass fronts of cabinets; a white path of canvas drugget led off into the dark. The room sounded enormous. He pulled the sheet from a sofa and they sat down; behind them the door swung to with a heavy click and Marianne caught a breath. Oliver swooped on her two hands in the dark and kissed the side of her cheek as she leaned wildly away.

'This isn't the way to behave — '

'It's how I behave!' he said with a touch of hysteria.

'I'd rather go home.'

'I've been missing you all my life!'

'We can't meet again now!'

'For God's sake don't play-act!' said he.

Excitement with Oliver took its most crippling form. Her wrists encircled in his tyrannic clutch, Marianne heard his hurried breathing check and gather into a sob. A tear, then another, splashed on the back of her hand. Speechless, he let go her hands to dash the tears from his face. In the large unknown room a ring of autumnal silence, sealike and desolate in its unbounded nature, bore in on Marianne their distance from everything fixed.

'What's the matter?' she said.

'You're the last straw.'

'Haven't you got any home?'

'Damn, damn,' said Oliver at a fresh burst of tears. Fumbling and trembling, she thrust her cambric handkerchief into his hand.

She put her arm round him, his head slid on to her shoulder, the sofa shook with a sob and he swore again.

'Why do you keep saying that?'

'This is not how I feel,' he said angrily.

'What can I do?'

Davina and Paul, the Russian, left the restless ante-room a few minutes later; they went for a turn, too, and wandered about the mansion, upstairs and down, knocking ash off their cigarettes. It was very cold; Davina stopped in the hall to put on her overcoat. They could see from lights on upstairs that the other two must be somewhere, and were uncertain whether to join them or not. They opened and shut doors without much curiosity. They sat down on a chest in the gallery, and Paul said how much mistaken Miriam was, not marrying Purdon, not believing in anything. Then he said he thought the end of the world would soon come.

'No doubt it's high time,' said Davina. 'But don't let's talk of it.'

'Who is your friend?'

'Marianne? She has a dull life. But look here, Paul: about me – I never know what to do.'

'Wait for something to happen.'

'I hate having no power. Tonight, for instance, I'm furious with someone.'

Not understanding, he looked at her sympathetically, got up and opened one of the grand saloon doors. They stood on the threshold and stared in at the dark. He said: 'The lights are not working.'

'Never mind, it's only a room.' They both turned away.

'All the same, we ought to find Oliver. It's high time Mrs Bennington went to bed.'

Next morning, pale milky sunshine flooded the façade of Lord Thingummy's house. In a bedroom behind the parapet Mrs Bennington, fully dressed under the eiderdown, lay breathing spirituously. The solitary housemaid, having risen at nine, opened the shutters all over the house, and long shafts of misty sunshine slid through the rooms. Patiently stooping, she picked up the cigarette-ends stamped out on the floors. In the grand saloon she sheeted up again an unsheeted sofa and picked up a lady's hand-kerchief and a striped woollen scarf. Downstairs, in the ante-room, the gilt clock had stopped at ten minutes to four: the hearth was white with cold wood-ash. The housemaid flung up a window and let out on to the morning the stale, cold fumes that hung like lead in the air. She sniffed each of the bottles and swept up some broken glass: a cigarette had burnt out in the trough of a brocade cushion. Fine dust lay everywhere; the sleepy housemaid bumped vaguely round with her broom, swirling the dust up and letting it settle again.

The housemaid's steps in the hollow house, her violence with the shutters and the knock of her broom, woke Oliver up. He woke saying 'She's gone,' and lay sprawled rigidly sideways across his bed with his eyes shut, unwilling to wake, while thoughts of his own ignobility raced through his brain . . . The grass of the park rolled fawn-pale to the horizon in the veiled sunshine; the lake stretched bright white against a brown belt of trees, fringed with papery pale windless reeds. A swan slowly turned on the lake and a man on horseback rode along the bare skyline: nothing else moved. The outdoor world lay reflected in the dark glass of Oliver's mind as he lay, with his eyes shut, sideways across his bed; he groaned at the still morning scene as though he stood at his window. For himself he could see no reason. He had, unwillingly, deluded her with his tears; one cannot weep all the time. He longed to see himself otherwise, like any other man, with a sound and passionate core. He thought of the grand saloon with alarm and pity, as though she lay dead in there. Opening his eyes a moment on the accusing daylight, he rolled over to reach for his first cigarette . . . He never finished Lord Thingummy's catalogue.

A thin veil of river-mist lay on the Archworth garden. Davina woke late, looked at the unclear trees, and thought: 'At least we are honest.' Getting up, she found she had circles under her eyes: one did not grow any younger. She thought with relief of last night's pleasure, because it was over, because it had been so slight. She and her friends had come to the same sad age when one can change no longer, and only become more oneself. They could enthrall and bluff each other no longer – but still, to meet is to meet. They had made some kind of hearth, and its warmth remained. Oliver with his dispirited Viking air, at once gallant and craven, and Paul with his placid and disenchanted smile, were renewed in her heart; she pictured Miriam on her high heels stepping over the beetles this morning and Purdon re-opening his surgery with a sigh. Combing back her springy dark hair and making up her mouth with pomegranate lipstick – alas! for no one – Davina thought of them kindly, regretting their premature autumn. 'We are not so bad,' she thought.

She went to her aunt's room.

Mrs Archworth sat propped up in bed in a hug-me-tight trimmed with marabout. Beside the hot bedroom fire the Pekinese snored and dribbled. As Davina tapped on the door and came in smartly, resentment fought with affection on her aunt's face: 'I was a little anxious — ' Mrs Archworth began.

'But just you wait till you hear — '

Mrs Archworth could not resist that flashing dark look. Poor plain pompous fussy old woman, no one else was at pains to fascinate her these days. She shifted her feet in bed, making room for Davina to sit, and patted the eiderdown with an uncertain smile. Davina explained with more than usual vividness how, Marianne's car having broken down, on a drive after dinner, outside unknown gates, the two had been for some hours the guests of Lord Thingummy.

'He would be kindness itself,' said her aunt. 'I once danced with him. And we dined there once, I remember, not long after your uncle and I were married. I am glad you should be making friends in the neighbourhood. This house, Davina, I'd like you to understand, is to be yours when I die.'

Davina said, startled: 'That's very good of you.'

Her aunt, with a wry and oddly dignified smile, said: 'My dear, *I* shall not need it.'

Marianne drove to meet Matthew at the 12.33 from London. The down platform was crowded, and for a moment or two of uncertain feeling she thought he had missed the train. Then he came ambling her way with light on his spectacles. His overcoat flapped and he carried a small dispatch-case. 'How is my girl?' he said, as they made their way through the barrier.

She was disorientated; she did not know. At home, she had not renewed the water in the bowls of chrysanthemums; it was a greenish colour, and stank faintly. The dogs, not yet exercized, fawned rather pointedly on the returning pair. The cat ran to meet them with its tail straight up; turned for no reason and ran away again. Mild unclear morning light filled the new white house with its evenly heated rooms. Matthew Harvey never kissed in a station, so half-way across the hall he put down his dispatch-case, closed the door to the kitchen, and kissed his wife. Colour rushed up her face, but he did not see.

He returned a book to the shelf and looked through a pile of letters. Meanwhile Marianne's look trailed wearily round the living-room, as though it were she who were just back from a journey and could still find no place to rest.

'I think,' said Matthew, 'I must get my glasses changed.'

'Changed?' said Marianne, starting.

'My glasses, yes,' said Matthew, leaning back in his chair and looking at her with affection. Then he stooped to pick up an end of white cotton from a hand-woven rug. He rolled this into a cocoon and flicked it into the fire. 'A bit of white cotton,' he said, 'but I picked it up.'

She stood with her back to him, looking out of the window, and said: 'The weathercock's pointing the other way.'

'The wind must have changed,' he said pleasantly.

She looked downhill, over the raw garden terraces, at the tops of the village trees with, in their heart, the glinting veering gold bird. Over the Archworths' chimneys a whorl of white smoke immobilized. Far off, across the flat water-meadows, the creeping red streets waited: beyond, a crowd of pale spires pricked the stooping grey sky. The world reflected itself in the vacant glass of her mind. Her hands, on which tears had fallen, vaguely clenched and unclenched in the pockets of her tweed coat.

'It is good to be back,' observed Matthew.

She did not reply.

'What's the matter?' he said. 'You're not quite yourself.'

'Perhaps I have got a slight chill.'

Davina looked over the net blind of Mrs Archworth's window, down into the yard. There was no one about in the yard, least of all Prothero. Biting her lip, she stared down at the white cobbles, the cement incline to the garage, the drifted leaves. A flush of angry intention appeared on her cheekbones. 'What's that?' exclaimed Mrs Archworth, struck by her rigid attitude. But the bedroom door had shut sharply: Davina was gone.

Inside its kennel, the foolish yard dog stirred with a rustle, dragging its chain in the straw; the pigeons rose wheeling on noisy wings. Davina slid back the garage door on its rollers, but found only the Daimler's wide polished back. The cook looked out of the back door and said that if it was Prothero anyone wanted, he had gone out.

'Why should he do that?'

'I couldn't tell you, I'm sure, miss. We're so independent, we are.'

Davina swung round and went out through the yard gate, down the lane to the village. Her tremendous anger made the village spread round the green, with its porches, dark little shop-fronts and stooping gables, look like a stage scene, a scene set for today. The raggy grass of the green was shredded with dead lime leaves, a smell of wood-smoke hung in the still air. Her look darted round the green; she had only one thought: 'He's gone.' That thought was bitter.

But Prothero came out of the grocer's opposite, with a felt hat pulled down over his forehead and a packet of candles under his arm. He stood in the shop door, not seeing Davina. Then, with his swinging, leisurely, damned independent stride, he started back round the green to the house again. Davina cut back before him to

the mouth of the lane. She waited; they came face to face and
Prothero pulled up patiently.

'Well?' said he.

'What about that message?'

'What about that money?'

'That's no way to talk – whoever you are.'

'It was good enough for you last night – whoever I am.'

She said contemptuously: 'I was in a hurry.'

'Oh, come,' said he, 'we had quite a pleasant chat.'

His light eyes and her dark eyes met implacably. Davina, driving
her hands down into her pockets, said: 'They gave you a message
for me. What became of it?'

'If your friends want to leave messages, they should go to the
front door, not hang round the yard like tinkers. I'm not here to
take messages; I am a busy man.'

'You'll be dismissed for this. You forget yourself.'

'I should like to,' he said, smiling without pleasure. 'But what
would your aunt say to our little bill? I wouldn't upset her now
you've feathered your nest so nicely. Besides, we should miss each
other, I daresay.'

'That's blackmail,' she said. 'You're a crook, aren't you?'

'I got even with someone.'

'That was grand,' she said bitterly.

'Yes, I'm right on top of the world.' He looked up at the
weathercock.

'You must be mad,' she said, looking at him intently. 'Else why
spoil my evening? Why make an enemy of me? Suppose I gave you
away?'

'You wouldn't do that if you could. For one thing, you haven't
the guts, and it wouldn't get you anywhere. Spoil your evening?'
He looked at her incuriously. 'How you do set your hearts on
things!'

'A monkey trick,' she said scornfully. 'Oh, you're a great man!'

'Mmn. I do what I want. And I take what I want, I don't hang
about for it. I wonder it doesn't sicken a girl like you, hanging
about here, waiting. You'd better get out. I'm through. Don't keep
coming after my money; it's not my money you want. I know
your sort. Well, I'm through with all that. I'm buying not selling,
these days. You keep your place, Miss Archworth, and I'll keep
mine. You can't have it both ways. Good day.'

Nodding, he walked away from her down the lane. She followed
him, at a distance, through the yard gates. He was mad, in plain
terms – her own. She watched him, with fascination, cross the
yard to his staircase. It was true she had, in some strange fashion,
fed her own pride by the hasty sale of her kisses, feeling set free of

herself each time those anonymous lips without pleasure had claimed her own, or those unseeing abstract cold eyes lit on her face. She went to the archway and called up the hollow staircase: 'Who *are* you?'

'My own man,' he said, and shut his door vigorously. Flakes of plaster slid from the staircase wall, and the steps creaked into silence after his tread. Davina felt in her pocket but found no cigarette. She called. 'I'm going,' and turned back to the house.

In the drawing-room, she filled up her case from the cigarette-box put out last night for the admiral and the Indian Civilian. The parrakeet wobbled on its perch; upstairs, she heard her aunt beginning to move about; she leaned on the mantelpiece thinking about Prothero: free men do not boast . . . She decided to walk up, now, at once, to the Harveys', to tell Marianne she was going away, would be quite gone in a week. But Matthew would be at home.

Davina walked up the hill, but not to the Harveys'; straight up between the ruts of the half-made road; then she struck out across the grass to the water-tower. Along the brambly skyline she walked rapidly, clicking her finger against her thumb and thinking: 'If I had money . . . '

She saw that events led nowhere, crisis was an illusion, and that passions of momentary violent reality were struck off like sparks from the spirit, only to die. One could precipitate nothing. One is empowered to live fully: occasion does not offer. The whole panorama of life seemed spread out under this hill: between the brambles, hitting an old tin can with her stick idly, Davina stood still to stare . . . Downhill from the tower the gentlemanly new houses reflected the autumn daylight in steel-framed windows. As the sky sharpened with clouds and over the landscape the morning darkened, the skyline spires went leaden, the gasometer and the far-off curve of the river took on a wary glint. An almost inaudible hum of wind rising began below in the trees.

Davina decided to throw off her dashing character and ask her aunt for the money to repay Prothero. Two men came uphill her way, stopped and debated: they were surveyors coming to peg out a new road.

Maria

'WE have girls of our own, you see,' Mrs Dosely said, smiling warmly.

That seemed to settle it. Maria's aunt Lady Rimlade relaxed at last in Mrs Dosely's armchair, and, glancing round once more at the Rectory drawing-room's fluttery white curtains, alert-looking photographs, and silver cornets spuming out pink sweet-pea, consigned Maria to these pleasant influences.

'Then that will be delightful,' she said in that blandly conclusive tone in which she declared open so many bazaars. 'Thursday *next*, then, Mrs Dosely, about tea-time?'

'That will be delightful.'

'It is *most* kind,' Lady Rimlade concluded.

Maria could not agree with them. She sat scowling under her hat-brim, tying her gloves into knots. Evidently, she thought, I *am* being paid for.

Maria thought a good deal about money; she had no patience with other people's affectations about it, for she enjoyed being a rich little girl. She was only sorry not to know how much they considered her worth; having been sent out to walk in the garden while her aunt had just a short chat, dear, with the Rector's wife. The first phase of the chat, about her own character, she had been able to follow perfectly as she wound her way in and out of some crescent-shaped lobelia beds under the drawing-room window. But just as the two voices changed – one going unconcerned, one very, very diffident – Mrs Dosely approached the window and, with an air of immense unconsciousness, shut it. Maria was baulked.

Maria was at one of those comfortable schools where everything is attended to. She was (as she had just heard her Aunt Ena explaining to Mrs Dosely) a motherless girl, sensitive, sometimes difficult, deeply reserved. At school they took all this, with her slight tendency to curvature and her dislike of all puddings, into loving consideration. She was having her character 'done' for her – later on, when she came out, would be time for her hair and complexion. In addition to this, she learnt swimming, dancing, some French, the more innocent aspects of history, and *noblesse oblige*. It was a really nice school. All the same, when Maria came home for the holidays they could not do enough to console her for being a motherless girl who had been sent away.

Then, late last summer term, with inconceivable selfishness, her Uncle Philip fell ill and, in fact, nearly died. Aunt Ena had written less often and very distractedly, and when Maria came home she was told, with complete disregard for her motherlessness, that her uncle and aunt would be starting at once for a cruise, and that she was 'to be arranged for'.

This was not so easy. All the relations and all the family friends (who declared when Sir Philip was ill they'd do anything in the world), wrote back their deep disappointment at being unable to have Maria just now, though there was nothing, had things been otherwise, that they would have enjoyed more. One to his farm in fact, said Mr MacRobert, the Vicar, when he was consulted, another to his merchandise. Then he suggested his neighbours, a Mr and Mrs Dosely, of Malton Peele. He came over to preach in Lent; Lady Rimlade had met him; he seemed such a nice man, frank, cheerful and earnest. *She* was exceedingly motherly, everyone said, and sometimes took in Indian children to make ends meet. The Doselys would be suitable, Maria's aunt felt at once. When Maria raged, she drew down urbane pink eyelids and said she did wish Maria would not be rude. So she drove Maria and the two little griffons over the next afternoon to call upon Mrs Dosely. If Mrs Dosely really seemed sympathetic, she thought she might leave the two little dogs with her too.

'And Mrs Dosely has girls of her own, she tells me,' said Lady Rimlade on the way home. 'I should not wonder if you made quite friends with them. I should not wonder if it was they who had done the flowers. I thought the flowers were done very nicely; I noticed them. Of course, I do not care myself for small silver vases like that, shaped like cornets, but I thought the effect in the Rectory drawing-room very cheerful and homelike.'

Maria took up the word skilfully. 'I suppose no one,' she said, 'who has not been in my position can be expected to realize what it feels like to have no home.'

'Oh, Maria darling . . . '

'I can't tell you what I think of this place you're sending me to,' said Maria. 'I bounced on the bed in that attic they're giving me and it's like iron. I suppose you realize that rectories are always full of diseases? Of course, I shall make the best of it, Aunt Ena. I shouldn't like you to feel I'd complained. But of course you don't realize a bit, do you, what I may be exposed to? So often carelessness about a girl at my age just ruins her life.'

Aunt Ena said nothing; she settled herself a little further down in the rugs and lowered her eyelids as though a strong wind were blowing.

That evening, on her way down to shut up the chickens, Mrs Dosely came upon Mr Hammond, the curate, rolling the cricket-pitch in the Rectory field. He was indefatigable, and, though more High Church than they cared for, had outdoor tastes. He came in to meals with them regularly, 'as an arrangement', because his present landlady could not cook and a young man needs to be built up, and her girls were still so young that no one could possibly call Mrs Dosely designing. So she felt she ought to tell him.

'We shall be one more now in the house,' she said, 'till the end of the holidays. Lady Rimlade's little niece Maria – about fifteen – is coming to us while her uncle and aunt are away.'

'Jolly,' said Mr Hammond sombrely, hating girls.

'We *shall* be a party, shan't we?'

'The more the merrier, I daresay,' said Mr Hammond. He was a tall young man with a jaw, rather saturnine; he never said much, but Mrs Dosely expected family life was good for him. 'Let 'em all come,' said Mr Hammond, and went on rolling. Mrs Dosely, with a tin bowl under one arm and a basket hooked on the other, stood at the edge of the pitch and watched him.

'She seemed a dear little thing – not pretty, but such a serious little face, full of character. An only child, you see. I said to her when they were going away that I expected she and Dilly and Doris would soon be inseparable, and her face quite lit up. She has no mother; it seems so sad.'

'*I* never had a mother,' said Mr Hammond, tugging the roller grimly.

'Oh, I do *know*. But for a young girl I do think it still sadder . . . I thought Lady Rimlade charming; so unaffected. I said to her that we all lived quite simply here, and that if Maria came we should treat her as one of ourselves, and she said that was just what Maria would love . . . In age, you see, Maria comes just between Dilly and Doris.'

She broke off; she couldn't help thinking how three years hence Maria might well be having a coming-out dance. Then she imagined herself telling her friend Mrs Brotherhood: 'It's terrible, I never seem to see anything of my girls nowadays. They seem always to be over at Lady Rimlade's.'

'We must make the poor child feel at home here,' she told Mr Hammond brightly.

The Doselys were accustomed to making the best of Anglo-Indian children, so they continued to be optimistic about Maria.

'One must make allowance for character', had become the watch-word of this warm-hearted household, through which passed a constant stream of curates with tendencies, servants with tempers, unrealized lady visitors, and yellow-faced children with no morale. Maria was forbearingly swamped by the family; she felt as though she were trying to box an eiderdown. Doris and Dilly had indelibly creased cheeks: they kept on smiling and smiling. Maria couldn't decide how best to be rude to them; they taxed her resourcefulness. She could not know Dilly had thought, 'Her face is like a sick monkey's,' or that Doris who went to one of those sensible schools, decided as soon that a girl in a diamond bracelet was shocking bad form. Dilly had repented at once of her unkind thought (though she had not resisted noting it in her diary), and Doris had simply said: 'What a pretty bangle. Aren't you afraid of losing it?' Mr Dosely thought Maria striking-looking (she had a pale, square-jawed little face, with a straight fringe cut above scowling brows), striking but disagreeable – here he gave a kind of cough in his thoughts and, leaning forward, asked Maria if she were a Girl Guide.

Maria said she hated the sight of Girl Guides, and Mr Dosely laughed heartily and said that this was a pity, because, if so, she must hate the sight of Doris and Dilly. The supper-table rocked with merriment. Shivering in her red *crêpe* frock (it was a rainy August evening, the room was fireless, a window stood open, and outside the trees streamed coldly), Maria looked across at the unmoved Mr Hammond, square-faced, set and concentrated over his helping of macaroni cheese. He was not amused. Maria had always thought curates giggled; she despised curates because they giggled, but was furious with Mr Hammond for not giggling at all. She studied him for some time, and, as he did not look up, at last said: 'Are you a Jesuit?'

Mr Hammond (who had been thinking about the cricket pitch) started violently; his ears went crimson; he sucked in one last streamer of macaroni. 'No,' he said, 'I am not a Jesuit. Why?'

'Oh, nothing,' said Maria. 'I just wondered. As a matter of fact, I don't know what Jesuits are.'

Nobody felt quite comfortable. It was a most unfortunate thing, in view of the nature of Mr Hammond's tendencies, for poor little Maria, in innocence, to have said. Mr Hammond's tendencies were so marked, and, knowing how marked the Doselys thought his tendencies were, he was touchy. Mrs Dosely said she expected Maria must be very fond of dogs. Maria replied that she did not care for any dogs but Alsatians. Mrs Dosely was glad to be able to ask Mr Hammond if it were not he who had told her that he had a cousin who bred Alsatians. Mr Hammond said that this was the case. 'But unfortunately,' he added, looking across at Maria, 'I dislike Alsatians intensely.'

Maria now realized with gratification that she had incurred the hatred of Mr Hammond. This was not bad for one evening. She swished her plateful of macaroni round with her fork then put the fork down pointedly. Undisguised wholesomeness was, in food as in personalities, repellent to Maria. 'This is the last supper but three – no, but two,' she said to herself, 'that I shall eat at this Rectory.'

It had all seemed so simple, it seemed so simple still, yet five nights afterwards found her going to bed once again in what Mrs Dosely called the little white nest that we keep for our girl friends. Really, if one came to look at it one way, the Dosely's were an experience for Maria, who had never till now found anybody who could stand her when she didn't mean to be stood. French maids, governesses, highly paid, almost bribed into service, had melted away. There was something marvellously, memorably un-winning about Maria . . . Yet here she still was. She had written twice to her aunt that she couldn't sleep and couldn't eat here, and feared she must be unwell, and Lady Rimlade wrote back advising her to have a little talk about all this with Mrs Dosely. Mrs Dosely, Lady Rimlade pointed out, was motherly. Maria told Mrs Dosely she was afraid she was unhappy and couldn't be well. Mrs Dosely exclaimed at the pity this was, but at all costs – Maria would see? – Lady Rimlade must not be worried. She had so expressly asked not to be worried at all.

'And she's so *kind*,' said Mrs Dosely, patting Maria's hand.

Maria simply thought, 'This woman is mad.' She said with a wan smile that she was sorry, but having her hand patted gave her pins and needles. But rudeness to Mrs Dosely was like dropping a pat of butter on to a hot plate – it slid and melted away.

In fact, all this last week Maria's sole consolation had been Mr Hammond. Her pleasure in Mr Hammond was so intense that three days after her coming he told Mrs Dosely he didn't think he'd come in for meals any more, thank you, as his landlady had by now learned to cook. Even so, Maria had managed to see quite a lot of him. She rode round the village after him, about ten yards behind, on Doris's bicycle; she was there when he offered a prayer with the Mothers' Union; she never forgot to come out when he was at work on the cricket-pitch ('Don't you seem to get rather hot' she would ask him feelingly, as he mopped inside his collar. 'Or are you really not as hot as you seem?'), and, having discovered that at six every evening he tugged a bell, then read Evensong in the church to two ladies, she came in alone every evening and sat in the front pew, looking up at him. She led the responses, waiting courteously for Mr Hammond when he lost his place.

But tonight Maria came briskly, mysteriously up to the little white nest, locking the door for fear Mrs Dosely might come in to kiss her good night. She could now agree that music was inspiring. For they had taken her to the Choral Society's gala, and the effect it had had on Maria's ideas was stupendous. Half-way through a rondo called '*Off to the Hills*' it had occurred to her that when she got clear of the Rectory she would go off to Switzerland, stay in a Palace Hotel, and do a little climbing. She would take, she thought, a hospital nurse, in case she hurt herself climbing, and an Alsatian to bother the visitors in the hotel. She had glowed – but towards the end of '*Hey, nonny, nonny*' a finer and far more constructive idea came along, eclipsing the other. She clapped her handkerchief to her mouth and, conveying to watchful Dilly that she might easily be sick at any moment, quitted the school-house hurriedly. Safe in her white nest, she put her candlestick down with a bump, got her notepaper out, and sweeping her hair-brushes off the dressing-table, sat down at it to write thus:

Dearest Aunt Ena: You must wonder why I have not written for so long. The fact is, all else has been swept from my mind by one great experience. I hardly know how to put it all into words. The fact is I love a Mr Hammond, who is the curate here, and am loved by him, we are engaged really and hope to be married quite shortly. He is a fascinating man, extremely High Church, he has no money but I am quite content to live with him as a poor man's wife as I shall have to do if you and Uncle Philip are angry, though you may be sorry when I bring my little children to your door to see you. If you do not give your consent we shall elope but I am sure, dear Aunt Ena, that you will sympathize with your little niece in her great happiness. All I beseech is that you will not take me away from the Rectory; I do not think I could live without seeing Wilfred every day – or every night rather, as we meet in the churchyard and sit on a grave with our arms round each other in the moonlight. The Doselys do not know as I felt it was my duty to tell you first, but I expect the village people may have noticed as unfortunately there is a right of way through the churchyard but we cannot think of anywhere else to sit. Is it not curious to think how true it was when I said at the time when you sent me to the Rectory, that you did not realize what you might be exposing me to? But now I am so thankful that you did expose me, as I have found my great happiness here, and am so truly happy in a good man's love. Goodbye, I must stop now as the moon has risen and I am just going out to meet Wilfred.

Your loving, full-hearted little niece,   MARIA

Maria, pleased on the whole with this letter, copied it out twice, addressed the neater copy with a flourish, and went to bed. The muslin frills of the nest moved gently on the night air; the moon rose beaming over the churchyard and the pale evening primroses fringing the garden path. No daughter of Mrs Dosely's could have smiled more tenderly in the dark or fallen asleep more innocently.

Mr Hammond had no calendar in his rooms: he was sent so many at Christmas that he threw them all away and was left with none, so he ticked off the days mentally. Three weeks and six long days had still to elapse before the end of Maria's visit. He remained shut up in his rooms for mornings together, to the neglect of the parish, and was supposed to be writing a book on Cardinal Newman. Postcards of arch white kittens stepping through rosy wreaths arrived for him daily; once he had come in to find a cauliflower labelled. 'From an admirer' on his sitting-room table. Mrs Higgins, the landlady, said the admirer must have come in by the window, as *she* had admitted no one, so recently Mr Hammond lived with his window hasped. This morning, the Saturday after the Choral Society's gala, as he sat humped over his table writing his sermon, a shadow blotted the lower window-panes. Maria, obscuring what light there was in the room with her body, could see in only with difficulty; her nose appeared white and flattened; she rolled her eyes ferociously round the gloom. Then she began trying to push the window up.

'*Go away!*' shouted Mr Hammond, waving his arms explosively, as at a cat.

'You must let me in, I have something awful to tell you,' shouted Maria, lips close to the pane. He didn't, so she went round to the front door and was admitted by Mrs Higgins with due ceremony. Mrs Higgins, beaming, ushered in the little lady from the Rectory who had come, she said, with an urgent message from Mrs Dosely.

Maria came in, her scarlet beret tipped up, with the jaunty and gallant air of some young lady intriguing for Bonny Prince Charlie.

'Are we alone?' she said loudly, then waited for Mrs Higgins to shut the door. 'I thought of writing to you,' she continued, 'but your coldness to me lately led me to think that was hopeless.' She hooked her heels on his fender and stood rocking backwards and forwards. 'Mr Hammond, I warn you: you must leave Malton Peele at once.'

'I wish *you* would,' said Mr Hammond, who, seated, looked past her left ear with a calm concentration of loathing.

'I daresay I may,' said Maria, 'but I don't want you to be involved in my downfall. You have your future to think of; you may be a bishop; I am only a woman. You see, the fact is, Mr

Hammond, from the way we have been going about together, many people think we must be engaged. I don't want to embarrass you, Mr Hammond.'

Mr Hammond was not embarrassed. 'I always have thought you a horrid little girl, but I never knew you were quite so silly,' he said.

'We've been indiscreet. I don't know what my uncle will say. I only hope you won't be compelled to marry me.'

'Get off that fender,' said Mr Hammond; 'you're ruining it . . . Well then, stay there; I want to look at you. I must say you're something quite new.'

'Yes, aren't I?' said Maria complacently.

'Yes. Any other ugly, insignificant-looking little girls I've known did something to redeem themselves from absolute un-attractiveness by being pleasant, say, or a little helpful, or some-times they were well bred, or had good table manners, or were clever and amusing to talk to. If it were not for the consideration of the Doselys for your unfortunate aunt – who is, I understand from Mr Dosely, so stupid as to be almost mentally deficient – they would keep you – since they really have guaranteed to keep you – in some kind of shed or loose-box at the bottom of the yard . . . I don't want to speak in anger,' went on Mr Hammond, 'I hope I'm not angry; I'm simply sorry for you. I always knew the Doselys took in Anglo-Indian children, but if I'd known they dealt in . . . cases . . . of your sort, I doubt if I'd have ever come to Malton Peele — Shut up, you little hell-cat! I'll teach you to pull my hair — '

She was on top of him all at once, tweaking his hair with science.

'You beastly Bolshevik!' exclaimed Maria, tugging. He caught her wrists and held them. 'Oh! Shut up – you hurt me, you beastly bully, you! Oh! how could you hurt a girl!' She kicked at his shin, weeping. 'I – I only came,' she said, 'because I was sorry for you. I needn't have come. And then you go and start beating me up like this — Ow!'

'It's your only hope,' said Mr Hammond with a vehement, grave, but very detached expression, twisting her wrist round further. 'Yes, go on, yell – I'm not hurting you. You may be jolly thankful I *am* a curate . . . As a matter of fact, I got sacked from my prep school for bullying . . . Odd how these things come back . . . '

They scuffled. Maria yelped sharply and bit his wrist. 'Ha, you would, would you? . . . Oh, yes, I know you're a little girl – and a jolly nasty one. The only reason I've ever seen why one wasn't supposed to knock little girls about is that they're generally supposed to be nicer – pleasanter – prettier – than little boys.' He parried a kick and held her at arm's length by her wrists. They glared at each other, both crimson with indignation.

'And you supposed to be a curate!'

'And you supposed to be a lady, you little parasite! This'll teach you — Oh!' said Mr Hammond, sighing luxuriously, 'how pleased the Doselys would be if they knew!'

'Big brute! You great hulking brute!'

'If you'd been my little sister,' said Mr Hammond, regretful, 'this would have happened before. But by this time, of course, you wouldn't be nearly so nasty . . . I should chivvy you round the garden and send you up a tree every day.'

'*Socialist!*'

'Well, get along now.' Mr Hammond let go of her wrists. 'You can't go out of the door with a face like that; if you don't want a crowd you'd better go through the window . . . Now you run home and snivel to Mrs Dosely.'

'*This* will undo your career,' Maria said, nursing wrists balefully. 'I shall have it put in the papers: "*Baronet's niece tortured by demon curate.*" That will undo your career for you, Mr Hammond.'

'I know, I *know*, but it's worth it!' Mr Hammond exclaimed exaltedly. He was twenty-four, and intensely meant what he said. He pushed up the window. 'Now get out,' he stormed, 'or I'll certainly kick you through it.'

'You are in a kind of a way like a brother to me, aren't you?' remarked Maria, lingering on the sill.

'I am not. Get out!'

'But oh, Mr Hammond, I came here to make a confession. I didn't expect violence, as no one's attacked me before. But I forgive you because it was righteous anger. I'm afraid we *are* rather compromised. You must read this. I posted one just the same to Aunt Ena three days ago.'

Maria handed over the copy of her letter.

'I may be depraved and ugly and bad, but you must admit, Mr Hammond, I'm not stupid.' She watched him read.

Half an hour later Mr Hammond, like a set of walking fire-irons, with Maria, limp as a rag, approached the Rectory. Maria hiccupped and hiccupped; she'd found Mr Hammond had no sense of humour at all. She was afraid he was full of vanity. 'You miserable little liar,' he'd said quite distantly, as though to a slug, and here she was being positively bundled along. If there'd been a scruff to her neck he would have grasped it. Maria had really enjoyed being bullied, but she did hate being despised. Now they were both going into the study to have yet another scene with Mr and Mrs Dosely. She was billed, it appeared, for yet another confession, and she had been so much shaken about that her technique faltered and she couldn't think where to begin. She wondered in a dim way what was going to happen next, and whether Uncle Philip would be coming to find Mr Hammond with a horse-whip.

Mr Hammond was all jaw; he wore a really disagreeable expression. Doris Dosely, up in the drawing-room window, gazed with awe for a moment, then disappeared.

'Doris!' yelled Mr Hammond. 'Where is your father? Maria has something to tell him.'

'Dunno,' said Doris and reappeared in the door. 'But here's a telegram for Maria – mother has opened it: something about a letter.'

'It would be,' said Mr Hammond. 'Give it me here.'

'I can't, I won't,' said Maria, backing away from the telegram. Mr Hammond, gritting his teeth audibly received the paper from Doris.

YOUR LETTER BLOWN FROM MY HAND OVERBOARD: [he read out] AFTER HAD READ FIRST SENTENCE WILD WITH ANXIETY PLEASE REPEAT CONTENTS BY TELEGRAM YOUR UNCLE PHILIP WISHES YOU JOIN US MARSEILLES WEDNESDAY AM WRITING DOSELYS AUNT ENA.

'How highly strung poor Lady Rimlade must be,' said Doris kindly.

'She is a better aunt than many people deserve,' said Mr Hammond.

'I think I may feel dull on that dreary old cruise after the sisterly, brotherly family life I've had here,' said Maria wistfully.

Her Table Spread

ALBAN had few opinions on the subject of marriage; his attitude to women was negative, but in particular he was not attracted to Miss Cuffe. Coming down early for dinner, red satin dress cut low, she attacked the silence with loud laughter before he had spoken. He recollected having heard that she was abnormal – at twenty-five, of statuesque development, still detained in childhood. The two other ladies, in beaded satins, made entrances of a surprising formality. It occurred to him, his presence must constitute an occasion: they certainly sparkled. Old Mr Rossiter, uncle to Mrs Treye, came last, more sourly. They sat for some time without the addition of lamplight. Dinner was not announced; the ladies by remaining on guard, seemed to deprecate any question of its appearance. No sound came from other parts of the Castle.

Miss Cuffe was an heiress to whom the Castle belonged and whose guests they all were. But she carefully followed the movements of her aunt, Mrs Treye; her ox-eyes moved from face to face in happy submission rather than expectancy. She was continually preoccupied with attempts at gravity, as though holding down her skirts in a high wind. Mrs Treye and Miss Carbin combined to cover her excitement; still, their looks frequently stole from the company to the windows, of which there were too many. He received a strong impression someone outside was waiting to come in. At last, with a sigh they got up: dinner had been announced.

The Castle was built on high ground, commanding the estuary; a steep hill, with trees, continued above it. On fine days the view was remarkable, of almost Italian brilliance, with that constant reflection up from the water that even now prolonged the too-long day. Now, in continuous evening rain, the winding wooded line of the further shore could be seen and, nearer the windows, a smothered island with the stump of a watch-tower. Where the Castle stood, a higher tower had answered the island's. Later a keep, then wings, had been added; now the fine peaceful residence had French windows opening on to the terrace. Invasions from the water would henceforth be social, perhaps amorous. On the slope down from the terrace, trees began again; almost, but not quite concealing the destroyer. Alban, who knew nothing, had not yet looked down.

It was Mr Rossiter who first spoke of the destroyer – Alban meanwhile glancing along the table; the preparations had been stupendous. The destroyer had come today. The ladies all turned to Alban: the beads on their bosoms sparkled. So this was what they had here, under their trees. Engulfed by their pleasure, from now on he disappeared personally. Mr Rossiter, rising a note, continued. The estuary, it appeared, was deep, with a channel buoyed up it. By a term of the Treaty, English ships were permitted to anchor in these waters.

'But they've been afraid of the rain!' chimed in Valeria Cuffe.

'Hush,' said her aunt, 'that's silly. Sailors would be accustomed to getting wet.'

But, Miss Carbin reported, that spring there *had* already been one destroyer. Two of the officers had been seen dancing at the hotel at the head of the estuary.

'So,' said Alban, 'you are quite in the world.' He adjusted his glasses in her direction.

Miss Carbin – blonde, not forty, and an attachment of Mrs Treye's – shook her head despondently. 'We were all away at Easter. Wasn't it curious they should have come then? The sailors walked in the demesne but never touched the daffodils.'

'As though I should have cared!' exclaimed Valeria passionately.

'Morale too good,' stated Mr Rossiter.

'But next evening,' continued Miss Carbin, 'the officers did not go to the hotel. They climbed up here through the trees to the terrace – you see, they had no idea. Friends of ours were staying here at the Castle, and they apologized. Our friends invited them in to supper . . . '

'Did they accept?'

The three ladies said in a breath: 'Yes, they came.'

Valeria added urgently, 'So don't you *think* — ?'

'So tonight we have a destroyer to greet you,' Mrs Treye said quickly to Alban. 'It is quite an event; the country people are coming down from the mountains. These waters are very lonely; the steamers have given up since the bad times; there is hardly a pleasure-boat. The weather this year has driven visitors right away.'

'You are beautifully remote.'

'Yes,' agreed Miss Carbin. 'Do you know much about the Navy? Do you think, for instance, that this is likely to be the same destroyer?'

'*Will they remember?*' Valeria's bust was almost on the table. But with a rustle Mrs Treye pressed Valeria's toe. For the dining-room also looked out across the estuary, and the great girl had not once taken her eyes from the window. Perhaps it was unfortunate that Mr Alban should have coincided with the destroyer. Perhaps it was unfortunate for Mr Alban too.

For he saw now he was less than half the feast; unappeased, the party sat looking through him, all grouped at an end of the table – to the other, chairs had been pulled up. Dinner was being served very slowly. Candles – possible to see from the water – were lit now; some wet peonies glistened. Outside, day still lingered hopefully. The bushes over the edge of the terrace were like heads – you could have sworn sometimes you saw them mounting, swaying in manly talk. Once, wound up in the rain, a bird whistled, seeming hardly a bird.

'Perhaps since then they have been to Greece, or Malta?'

'That would be the Mediterranean fleet,' said Mr Rossiter.

They were sorry to think of anything out in the rain tonight.

'The decks must be streaming,' said Miss Carbin.

Then Valeria, exclaiming. 'Please excuse me!' pushed her chair in and ran from the room.

'She is impulsive,' explained Mrs Treye. 'Have *you* been to Malta, Mr Alban?'

In the drawing-room, empty of Valeria, the standard lamps had been lit. Through their ballet-skirt shades, rose and lemon, they gave out a deep, welcoming light. Alban, at the ladies' invitation, undraped the piano. He played, but they could see he was not pleased. It was obvious he had always been a civilian, and when he had taken his place on the piano-stool – which he twirled round three times, rather fussily – his dinner-jacket wrinkled across the shoulders. It was sad they should feel so indifferent, for he came from London. Mendelssohn was exasperating to them – they opened all four windows to let the music downhill. They preferred not to draw the curtains; the air, though damp, being pleasant tonight, they said.

The piano was damp, but Alban played almost all his heart out. He played out the indignation of years his mild manner concealed. He had failed to love; nobody did anything about this; partners at dinner gave him less than half their attention. He knew some spring had dried up at the root of the world. He was fixed in the dark rain, by an indifferent shore. He played badly, but they were unmusical. Old Mr Rossiter, who was not what he seemed, went back to the dining-room to talk to the parlour maid.

Valeria, glittering vastly, appeared in a window.

'Come *in!*' her aunt cried in indignation. She would die of a chill, childless, in fact unwedded; the Castle would have to be sold and where would they all be?

But – 'Lights down there!' Valeria shouted above the music.

They had to run out for a moment, laughing and holding cushions over their bare shoulders. Alban left the piano; they looked boldly down from the terrace. Indeed, there they were: two lights like arc-lamps, blurred by rain and drawn down deep in reflection into the steady water. There were, too, ever so many portholes, all lit up.'

'Perhaps they are playing bridge,' said Miss Carbin.

'Now I wonder if Uncle Robert ought to have called,' said Mrs Treye. 'Perhaps we have seemed remiss – one calls on a regiment.'

'Patrick could row him out tomorrow.'

'He hates the water.' She sighed. 'Perhaps they will be gone.'

'Let's go for a row now – let's go for a row with a lantern,' besought Valeria, jumping and pulling her aunt's elbow. They produced such indignation she disappeared again – wet satin skirts and all – into the bushes. The ladies could do no more: Alban suggested the rain might spot their dresses.

'They must lose a great deal, playing cards throughout an evening for high stakes,' Miss Carbin said with concern as they all sat down again.

'Yet, if you come to think of it, somebody must win.'

But the naval officers who so joyfully supped at Easter had been, Miss Carbin knew, a Mr Graves, and a Mr Garrett: *they* would certainly lose. 'At all events, it is better than dancing at the hotel; there would be nobody of their type.'

'There is nobody there at all.'

'I expect they are best where they are . . . Mr Alban, a Viennese waltz?'

He played while the ladies whispered, waving the waltz time a little distractedly. Mr Rossiter, coming back, momentously stood: they turned in hope: even the waltz halted. But he brought no news. 'You should call Valeria in. You can't tell who may be round the place. She's not fit to be out tonight.'

'Perhaps she's not out.'

'She is,' said Mr Rossiter crossly. 'I just saw her racing past the window with a lantern.'

Valeria's mind was made up: she was a princess. Not for nothing had she had the dining-room silver polished and all set out. She would pace around in red satin that swished behind, while Mr Alban kept on playing a loud waltz. They would be dazed at all she had to offer – also her two new statues and the leopard-skin from the auction.

When he and she were married (she inclined a little to Mr

Garrett) they would invite all the Navy up the estuary and give them tea. Her estuary would be filled up, like a regatta, with loud excited battleships tooting to one another and flags flying. The terrace would be covered with grateful sailors, leaving room for the band. She would keep the peacocks her aunt did not allow. His friends would be surprised to notice that Mr Garrett had meanwhile become an admiral, all gold. He would lead the other admirals into the Castle and say, while they wiped their feet respectfully: 'These are my wife's statues; she has given them to me. One is Mars, one is Mercury. We have a Venus, but she is not dressed. And wait till I show you our silver and gold plates . . . ' The Navy would be unable to tear itself away.

She had been excited for some weeks at the idea of marrying Mr Alban, but now the lovely appearance of the destroyer put him out of her mind. He would not have done; he was not handsome. But she could keep him to play the piano on quiet afternoons.

Her friends had told her Mr Garrett was quite a Viking. She was so very familiar with his appearance that she felt sometimes they had already been married for years – though still, sometimes, he could not realize his good luck. She still had to remind him the island was hers too . . . Tonight, Aunt and darling Miss Carbin had so fallen in with her plans, putting on their satins and decorating the drawing-room, that the dinner became a betrothal feast. There was some little hitch about the arrival of Mr Garrett – she had heard that gentlemen sometimes could not tie their ties. And now he was late and would be discouraged. So she must now go half-way down to the water and wave a lantern.

But she put her two hands over the lantern, then smothered it in her dress. She had a panic. Supposing she should prefer Mr Graves?

She had heard Mr Graves was stocky, but very merry; when he came to supper at Easter he slid in the gallery. He would teach her to dance, and take her to Naples and Paris . . . Oh, dear, oh, dear, then they must fight for her; that was all there was to it . . . She let the lantern out of her skirts and waved. Her fine arm with bangles went up and down, up and down, with the staggering light; the trees one by one jumped up from the dark, like savages.

Inconceivably, the destroyer took no notice.

Undisturbed by oars, the rain stood up from the water; not a light rose to peer, and the gramophone, though it remained very faint, did not cease or alter.

In mackintoshes, Mr Rossiter and Alban meanwhile made their way to the boat-house, Alban did not know why. 'If that goes on,' said Mr Rossiter, nodding towards Valeria's lantern, 'they'll fire one of their guns at us.'

'Oh, no. Why?' said Alban. He buttoned up, however, the collar of his mackintosh.

'Nervous as cats. It's high time that girl was married. She's a nice girl in many ways, too.'

'Couldn't we get the lantern away from her?' They stepped on a paved causeway and heard the water nibble the rocks.

'She'd scream the place down. She's of age now, you see.'

'But if — '

'Oh, she won't do that; I was having a bit of fun with you.' Chuckling equably, Mrs Treye's uncle unlocked and pulled open the boat-house door. A bat whistled out.

'Why are we here?'

'She might come for the boat; she's a fine oar,' said Mr Rossiter wisely. The place was familiar to him; he lit an oil-lamp and, sitting down on a trestle with a staunch air of having done what he could, reached a bottle of whisky out of the boat. He motioned the bottle to Alban. 'It's a wild night,' he said. 'Ah, well, we don't have these destroyers every day.'

'That seems fortunate.'

'Well, it is and it isn't.' Restoring the bottle to the vertical, Mr Rossiter continued: 'It's a pity you don't want a wife. You'd be the better for a wife, d'you see, a young fellow like you. She's got a nice character; she's a girl you could shape. She's got a nice income.' The bat returned from the rain and knocked round the lamp. Lowering the bottle frequently, Mr Rossiter talked to Alban (whose attitude remained negative) of women in general and the parlourmaid in particular . . .

'*Bat!*' Alban squealed irrepressibly, and with his hand to his ear — where he still felt it — fled from the boat-house. Mr Rossiter's conversation continued. Alban's pumps squelched as he ran; he skidded along the causeway and balked at the upward steps. His soul squelched equally: he had been warned, he had been warned. He had heard they were all mad; he had erred out of headiness and curiosity. A degree of terror was agreeable to his vanity: by express wish he had occupied haunted rooms. Now he had no other pumps in this country, no idea where to buy them, and a ducal visit ahead. Also, wandering as it were among the apples and amphoras of an art school, he had blundered into the life room: woman revolved gravely.

'Hell,' he said to the steps, mounting, his mind blank to the outcome.

He was nerved for the jumping lantern, but half-way up to the Castle darkness was once more absolute. Her lantern had gone out; he could orientate himself — in spite of himself — by her sobbing. Absolute desperation. He pulled up so short that, for balance, he had to cling to a creaking tree.

'Hi!' she croaked. Then: 'You *are* there! I hear you!'

'Miss Cuffe — '

'How too bad you are! I never heard you rowing. I thought you were never coming — '

'Quietly, my dear girl.'

'Come up quickly. I haven't even seen you. Come up to the windows — '

'Miss Cuffe — '

'Don't you remember the way?' As sure but not so noiseless as a cat in the dark, Valeria hurried to him.

'Mr Garrett — ' she panted. 'I'm Miss Cuffe. Where have you been? I've destroyed my beautiful red dress and they've eaten up your dinner. But we're still waiting. Don't be afraid; you'll soon be there now. I'm Miss Cuffe; this is my Castle — '

'Listen, it's I, Mr Alban — .

'Ssh, ssh, Mr Alban: *Mr Garrett has landed.*'

Her cry, his voice, some breath of the joyful intelligence, brought the others on to the terrace, blind with lamplight.

'Valeria?'

'Mr Garrett has landed!'

Mrs Treye said to Miss Carbin under her breath, 'Mr Garrett has come.'

Miss Carbin, half weeping with agitation, replied, 'We must go in.' But uncertain who was to speak next, or how to speak, they remained leaning over the darkness. Behind, through the windows, lamps spread great skirts of light, and Mars and Mercury, unable to contain themselves, stooped from their pedestals. The dumb keyboard shone like a ballroom floor.

Alban, looking up, saw their arms and shoulders under the bright rain. Close by, Valeria's fingers creaked on her warm wet satin. She laughed like a princess, magnificently justified. Their unseen faces were all three lovely, and, in the silence after the laughter, such a strong tenderness reached him that, standing there in full manhood, he was for a moment not exiled. For the moment, without moving or speaking, he stood, in the dark, in a flame, as though all three said: 'My darling . . . '

Perhaps it was best for them all that early, when next day first lightened the rain, the destroyer steamed out – below the extinguished Castle where Valeria lay with her arms wide, past the boat-house where Mr Rossiter lay insensible and the bat hung masked in its wings – down the estuary into the open sea.

The Little Girl's Room

THIS was Geraldine's moment. At a nod from Mrs Letherton-Channing, carefully guarding the flame of her taper, she passed round the circle from cigarette to cigarette. The little girl's serious movements, the pretty shell of her hand, the soft braids of hair as she stooped, swinging over her shoulders, the soft creak of her plaited sandals as she stepped, cast some kind of spell on the talk: silence followed her like a shadow.

At first Clara Ellis frowned: talk of a first-rate scandalous quality had been held up. But: 'Why,' she exclaimed, glancing at Geraldine's arm, 'you freckle just like a cowslip!'

'Do I?' blushed Geraldine.

They all said 'Dear thing' . . . or 'How good of you, Geraldine dear.'

General Littlecote ducked to the flame in her hands rather grimly, as though the pleasure were bitter. Smoke began to go up in the afternoon light of the room; the green-panelled drawing-room, with bowls of lush yellow roses, ornate with Florentine furniture: smoke wreathed out of the high open windows across the magnolia flowering unseen. Geraldine reached her step-grandmother's chair and politely waited.

'Mr Scutcheon is late,' said Mrs Letherton-Channing.

'He's come,' said Geraldine gently. 'I saw him come up through the garden.'

'Really,' exclaimed Mrs Letherton-Channing. 'How should he know the way?' Her face became expressionless with annoyance. For who knew how this might end? Indeed, it would never do to have professors of Greek and Latin, Italian and German masters, mathematicians, historians and even Swedish exponents of physical culture, finding their way through her garden at every hour. Meditation and intimate talk became imperilled. For Geraldine was being highly educated at home.

'Perhaps Miss Weekes showed him,' said Geraldine. 'Ought I to go?' she added.

'Why, certainly, if he *is* here,' snapped Mrs Letherton-Channing. Her friends all realized that Mr Scutcheon had come too soon.

Mrs Letherton-Channing was a widow, with one step-son. The son's wife, Vivien, a difficult and rather derisive step-daughter-in-law, having died four years ago, the elder Mrs Letherton-Channing thereby succeeded to what she was determined to prove a wonder-child. Vivien had once kept her Geraldine very much to herself, but nowadays Mrs Letherton-Channing, in the strong position of being alive, could speak generously of her daughter-in-law, for Luke Letherton-Channing, distracted and set on flight to the ends of the earth, had, on his wife's death, immediately brought the eight-year-old to his step-mother's Italianate house in Berkshire.

Here Vivien, to whom such a question now became immaterial, had once declared that she could never breathe. 'Take Geraldine there?' she exclaimed. 'Why, she'd turn into a horrible little Verrocchio over a fountain!' But Vivien, whose departure from life had been despairing and hurried, had not tried to exact from Luke a promise he could not stand by. She died leaving bills unpaid, invitations unanswered, no word as to her child's future.

So the child came to Mrs Letherton-Channing's house, where one had the impression of dignified exile, where British integrity seemed to have camped on a Tuscan hill, where English mid-summer did not exceed Italian April – roses wearing into July an air of delicate pre-maturity – and high noon reflected upon the ceilings a sheen of ilex and olive. Here the very guests seemed expatriate, and coal-fires, ruddy ghosts of themselves, roared under mantles crusted and swagged with glazed Della Robbia lemons and bluish pears. Clara Ellis, who was at least sincerely malicious, professed to adore this little Italy from Wigmore Street. From any window, she said, the strong eye of faith could ride a Gozzoli distance while an English February sleeted or robins starved in the frost. When tea made its Georgian entrance or a sirloin appeared on the menu: 'Why,' Clara was pleased to exclaim, 'this is quite like England!'

Geraldine, fostered in this atmosphere, was tempted in all directions to be exceptional. Each young tendril put out found a wire waiting; she clung and blossomed, while, ambushed in gentleness, Mrs Letherton-Channing watched like a lynx for the most tentative emanations of young genius. Geraldine was certainly *something*. In preparation for her apotheosis she found herself very much guarded, very much educated, very much petted. There was sometimes a touch of reverence in her step-grandmother's manner. Though the child still danced with anxious clumsiness, sang with a false little clear voice, was listless behind the pencil, nerveless upon the keyboard, heavy upon the bow; her small intellectual flame stooped and wavered; she was docile, but incurious . . . while, in fact, at twelve she could still only claim the divine attribute through that shining vague look and constant abstention from effort in any direction. Nobody was encouraged to contradict Geraldine: it became penal to hurt her feelings. The Beautiful, in all possible concrete forms, was placed about for her contemplation, till life, for her wilful fancy, became an obstacle-race.

Mrs Letherton-Channing's afternoon visitors – old friends, aware of all this – were relieved on the whole when Geraldine left the room. Talk resumed its usual tenor of indiscretion. The child's presence had been like a flower put down in irrelevant purity alongside one's place at dinner, disconcerting to appetite. 'But what,' murmured a new-comer, a pretty foolish young mother, to Miss Ellis, 'does that poor little creature *do* with herself all day?'

Miss Ellis supposed that the child went into abeyance.

'But has she no governess?'

'Dear me, no: how prosaic!' exclaimed Miss Ellis. The child was no more to her at the moment than a thin little freckled arm.

Geraldine did not go immediately to the library where Mr Scutcheon, who had come out from Reading to instruct her in Greek, sat biting his nails. Waiting quietly in the hall, she intercepted another slice of the chocolate cake as it was carried out by the butler. She went down the garden: when she had finished her cake and licked her fingers she pulled a rose to pieces, plucking off even the stamens. She eyed the calyx with an obscure sensation of triumph, but had no thoughts. She made gargoyle faces; wishing that she could see herself, she ran to the pool, but the water was clotted with lily-leaves.

'*Old Miss Ellis,*' she said aloud, '*pink as hell is. General Littlecote . . . laughs like a little goat. Lady Miriam Glover . . . hops about like a plover.*' After reflection she added: '*That can't sit on her eggs . . . because of her long legs . . . Geraldine Letherton-Channing . . . ran in and ran in and ran in.*' Then she did run in, judging that Mr Scutcheon should by now have come to the boil and be cross enough.

She had achieved her purpose. In the library, Mr Scutcheon, bleak on a background of tooled and gilded book-backs, was furious. The library, with its opulence, revolted him. He was so hungry he could have eaten the books. Mrs Letherton-Channing never sent in tea: she appeared to believe that tutors were fed by ravens. It was an expensive fancy, that she could easily gratify, to have a step-granddaughter brought up like a Renaissance princess: she paid Mr Scutcheon an unusually high fee. This in itself tormented his angry and misanthropic honesty, for he considered Geraldine unteachable. At no time did he like teaching the rudiments of his subject; he was unfit, also, for the teaching of young children, for he was impatient and nervous. Geraldine approached Mr Scutcheon ecstatically, like a martyr approaching a lion.

'You're twenty-five minutes late,' he said snappily.

'Oh, I'm so *sorry*,' she said. 'But perhaps you were early?'

'Exactly: I made a point of being in time. I had been specially anxious to catch the 6.15 home.'

'We saw you come up through the garden: isn't it lovely?'

'A useful short cut,' he said.

He was a thin man, ugly: the very sight of Geraldine set him flushing with irritation just where his pince-nez clipped the bridge of his nose. She glanced at his wrists sticking out of his frayed shirt-cuffs, then at his thin chest. '*Mr Scutcheon*,' she said to herself, '*never has much on*.' Aloud she added, 'How is your little sister?' His little sister was an invalid.

'Much the same. Now, *please* — ' He jerked his chair to the table.

'Do you think I shall ever see her?'

Mr Scutcheon's sister wilted in a hot room in a hot street, overlooking the tramlines. 'I should think,' he said, 'that is unlikely.' He took quite a sharp displeasure in a picture she wished to present: Geraldine in a white dress on a merciful errand, with a bunch of – say – June lilies, stepping daintily from a car. 'I think,' he said, 'that is unlikely . . . You have crumbs round your mouth,' he added.

'Oh, dear,' fluttered Geraldine. She licked round her lips with the point of her tongue and glanced at him anxiously under her eyelashes. He seemed quite bound up in a resentment she could not fathom. He jerked his wrists further out of his cuffs; the flush on his nose deepened. His anger, his very presence, became delightful. He was the stupidest kind of scholar, without one word to jingle against another. Had he wished, had he dared imperil the flow of Mrs Letherton-Channing's guineas, he still could not have explained to Geraldine quite what he thought of her: that she was *low*, a sensationalist. He would have agreed that, in *this* sense, Mrs Letherton-Channing's husband had certainly grandfathered a prodigy.

Geraldine, sighing, took her exercise-books from the table drawer and seated herself beside him. She indicated her work. 'I'm afraid they are not very good,' she said socially, with the air of a lady submitting her drawings to visitors. They were not very good: his furious pencil jabbed and flickered. She caught breath after breath softly, leaning forward beside him. Her soft heavy plaits flopped on to the table: he started irritably. Head almost against his shoulder, she thought comfortably: 'He can't bear me!' She longed to return with Mr Scutcheon to Reading, a town which

– on account of a certain clangour about the streets, a civic rawness, an excess of some quality indigestible by the spirit – Geraldine was seldom allowed to visit.

'I'm not good at anything, am I?' said Geraldine wistfully.

'Possibly you can dance,' replied Mr Scutcheon. Quartered by silvery ejaculations from the clock, this most interesting hour of Geraldine's week went by too swiftly.

In the rose-clotted loggia, Mrs Letherton-Channing stood with Miss Ellis at about seven o'clock. Miss Ellis was staying in the house; the other visitors had departed.

'I think Geraldine's tired; she's not quite herself,' said Mrs Letherton-Channing.

'Her what?' inquired Miss Ellis, her indulgent cynical pouchy face deepening to coral-pink in the evening glow.

'Not quite herself,' repeated Mrs Letherton-Channing, who could flatten out any inference. 'I think I shall have to get rid of Mr Scutcheon. Perhaps she need not do Greek in summer? He has a sulky manner. And, do you know, he has taken to coming up through the garden?'

'Need she do Greek in winter?' said Miss Ellis. 'One could lock the bottom gate,' she added, appreciating the rigours of this unconscious siege.

'But then Miss Weekes could not get out to the village. As it is, she is always too glad of any excuse to come past the house.' Miss Weekes, the resident lady gardener, whose bothy, skilfully planted out by a hedge, was just by the wicket under discussion, remained in outlook resolutely Old English. She whistled; the smock and breeches in which she worked were an offence to Mrs Letherton-Channing, who had engaged her to look after the frames and hot-houses, not expecting her to emerge from these. She had discovered that Miss Weekes morris-danced, that she did rush-work, that she participated in every possible movement to build Jerusalem in this pleasant and green part of Berkshire. At no moment, when off duty, did Miss Weekes, darting here and there through the village, apparently cease from mental strife. Mrs Letherton-Channing could countenance a diluted reality but could not suffer a fellow fantasist. The woman was, moreover, un-friendly to Geraldine. It was clear that Miss Weekes *must* have let Mr Scutcheon in through the lower gate. But she had a wonderful way with asparagus.

'It is difficult,' sighed Mrs Letherton-Channing.

'It must be,' agreed Miss Ellis.

Mrs Letherton-Channing did not find her friend's satirical manner at all disconcerting. The appearance of Geraldine's step-grandmother was fine, even noble; she had presence, her white waved hair fitted her head like a cap. Her dark prominent eyes looked out at any margin of world beyond the domain of her own massive fancy without prejudice, almost without recognition. The mood of a d'Este princess dominated her interviews with the very cook. She was generous, and, feeling indebted to Geraldine's mother by her death, now spoke of her kindly. An etherealized grandmaternity, without the awkward preliminaries of motherhood, became her excellently; just as widowhood, after the exigencies of marriage, was at once the harbour and crown of her spirit. Her hands wrinkled slightly at the wrists like white kid gloves.

Miss Ellis, suddenly bored with composing a picture of ladies in a rosy sunset loggia, said innocently: 'I see in Geraldine now and then quite a touch of poor Vivien's manner. The real pretty woman's curtness.'

Mrs Letherton-Channing smiled. 'To me,' she said, 'she is like nobody but herself.'

'She'll meddle with life,' said Clara. She struck with her cushiony fingers several staccato chords on the stone balustrade of the loggia. 'I can't think,' she exclaimed, 'how they do it!'

'They?'

'Women – how they ever bring up their own children!'

Mrs Letherton-Channing pulled off one or two dead roses. 'Look how they fail,' she said placidly.

For less than a minute Geraldine's supper – the green goblet of milk, the Romary biscuits, the glossy strawberry-pyramid on a plate like a leaf – attracted Geraldine's eye, her look dark with secrecy, with some conspiracy with herself. Then she turned from it, pressing a strawberry to her bunched-up lips that slowly yielded as the fruit flattened and sweet red juice ran down her chin. 'The Enemies . . . ' she said aloud, in a tone of exaltation and terror, 'the *Enemies!*'

She was alone in her room, that, softly pale-pink and full of friendly light from the garden, seemed to be enclosed by more than material walls, by volutions of delicacy and sweet living shadows: the inner whorl of a shell, the heart of a flower. If stone sustained it, the very stone was kind. Here was the secret form of her little-girlhood, tenderly animate by the spirit. Here, round the smiling gold clock, time was captive, and only fluttered with little moth-wings; here, coming in, you distilled the whole sweetness of youth from a happy consciousness of mortality: the narrow bed was innocent as an early grave. By falling asleep here, the little girl gave herself back to the centuries, to touch, from their heart, the very heart of your fancy, like a little girl in an epitaph.

Geraldine's room had been furnished with discrimination. Botticelli wildflowers were woven into the curtains, garlands were painted over the furniture, and, on the bed-head, a fanciful picture of a sailing-ship. Over the bed hung a panel of leafy Perugian damask: at eye-level, opposite, Carpaccio's little St Ursula lay flat and calmly; even an angel did not disturb her, she was the very picture of afternoon sleep. Trees looked in at St Ursula's window: from Geraldine's window you saw the flagged path dropping terrace by terrace and the young tips of cypresses.

But here (you might notice) vacant little Geraldine seemed to exist with difficulty. Every time her reflection flitted out of the looking-glass the whole of Geraldine seemed to become mislaid. A huge rubber ball balanced on top of the bureau, Geraldine's stockings straggled over a chair; every day she trod biscuit-crumbs into the carpet. The air smelt faintly of peppermint, from her tooth-powder. Otherwise this was a guest-room: ready, but some-one never arrived.

'The enemies . . . ' she repeated. And at this evocation the pale walls contracted, the air darkened. With that soft creak of her sandals, pulling and pulling at the strawberry with her lips, Geraldine paced round that group of Imaginary Furious People occupying the centre of her floor.

They had just come in.

Mr Scutcheon, one of her grandmother's roses stuck defiantly into his button-hole, put in his nightly appearance. Miss Weekes, her hands in her breeches pockets, looked at Geraldine meditatively and contemptuously. Two more of her teachers were there, also the Angry Woman from the Village, the Little Boy from the Lodge, and, oddly enough, her own mother, who seemed to have some understanding with all the rest. (It was eight o'clock; downstairs, Mrs Letherton-Channing and Miss Ellis sat down to dinner.) In the enchanted half-light the Enemies stood glancing darkly at one another, urging each other on.

Geraldine, in elation, threw away the calyx of the strawberry. 'What do you want?' she whispered.

'*We've come,*' said Mr Thorne, who taught Geraldine mathematics. All the rest murmured.

'You must go,' she said haughtily.

'*We don't think,*' said the Little Boy from the Lodge, with an ugly look, while Miss Weekes, never taking her awful eyes from Geraldine, began to feel about for something in her pocket.

'*It's all up, Geraldine,*' said her mother, who seemed less interested, more indifferent than the rest, and wore her old ironical smile. All the same, she *had* some part in this, for Geraldine understood that in the last four years, since her mother died, the two had become strangers. Geraldine knotted her hands behind her and thrust her chin up.

'*There has been the Revolution,*' said Mr Scutcheon. The Enemies, drawing closer behind him, nodded. Geraldine saw them look round at the things about the room, wondering which to seize first. On Greek days, Mr Scutcheon was always promoted to be their leader. His eyes were bloodshot; he was wearing a black fur cap and carried a bottle. Evidently pistols were in his pocket. (Geraldine's fancy could hardly do more for anyone.)

'*Reading is running red with Blood,*' added Mr Thorne, who was nearly as vindictive. Geraldine, however, did not see him so plainly; his rage was inferior. '*And as for London . . .* ' went on Mr Thorne.

'*Hush,*' said Miss Weekes, but with a greedy look, as though she had been dwelling on this a long time. She took her pruning-knife from her pocket and turned it over.

Geraldine's mother said again with detachment, '*It's all up, Geraldine.*'

'*Mrs Letherton-Channing is loaded with chains,*' said the music mistress, who had at present a difficulty with her manner. For by day Miss Snipe's manner was at once obsequious and regretful: as an Enemy it was hard for her to behave. But Geraldine, glancing sidelong at her during a music lesson, as they sat elbow to elbow before the piano, had once seen her eyes go watery with malevolence. Miss Snipe, though wearing a fur cap, now appeared scared by success, and resentful, as though she felt she did not fully enjoy her triumph.

'*As for you —* ' began Mr Thorne. The Enemies' heads went together: the Angry Woman nodded. A delicious anticipation mounted in Geraldine.

Geraldine's mother glanced quizzically at the Enemies, but seemed, all the same, a little displeased by her strange company and their intention. So she had that same old smile, as much as to say, 'But what can one do?' During these years of death she must have forgotten all loving pity, as Geraldine had forgotten it. Each unspoken word by which Mrs Letherton–Channing estranged further mother and daughter must have been heard by the mother, who now returned each night with the Enemies, always a little colder, to her lost unfaithful child.

When the Enemies all moved forward steadily, resolute as one face, Geraldine's feeling took on such violence that even the birds became silent outside the window. Geraldine's excitement, courted with every sense, became unbearable. Through the dark flanks of the crowd she saw with ecstatic despair her goblet of milk, always waiting, solid and pale. She asked, 'General Littlecote?': they replied: '*He is massacred too.*' She saw his foolish old face lie in blood on a staircase, and spread out her hand to her side, in terror, close to her thumping heart. Her cheeks blazed. The rope of excitement she had been playing out guardedly, sparingly, now fled through her fingers, burning. She began to shout '*I defy* — !' and stamped on the mild carpet. (Downstairs, over the heads of Mrs Letherton-Channing, so placidly dining, and Miss Ellis, the chandelier blinked and tinkled.) Her Enemies, like a bubble swelling and darkening, a Menace beyond dimensions, Genii glaring and towering, showed how they would advance inch by inch with knives gleaming . . .

Geraldine dropped with a bump to her bare knees under their rush . . .

Geraldine got up from her knees, whistling, flushed, considerably embarrassed. She picked up the goblet and drank, bubbling into the milk: as she drank she glanced round the room as though it had been another child's nursery. The looking-glasses were innocent. There was now something about her at once cold and cryptic: she was thankful to be alone. She was, in fact, for herself a most unfriendly playmate, for she was treacherous. There remained, however, something in the air of the room that did not at once clear or dissolve or settle as dust settles, though the white drugget where *they* had all stood remained unwrinkled. There was still not quite silence after this nightly session of the red passions.

Mrs Letherton-Channing never entered her granddaughter's room without pleasure: pleasure shared or reflected tonight, for Miss Ellis accompanied her. They wore tea-gowns: their bodies, massive pillars of flesh, were softened about the outline and great wings of chiffon rose up with every gesture. Between them Geraldine lay curled in her bed sideways, a hand under her cheek.

'Somebody's tired,' said Mrs Letherton-Channing, stooping over the bed.

'Somebody's got a milky moustache,' said Miss Ellis.

Geraldine wiped her mouth.

Mrs Letherton-Channing stooped lower to look into Geraldine's eyes, which, as the child lay looking up, were exposed like pools to her. 'There's nothing you don't like . . . ?'

'Dear me,' said her friend, with satirical softness, 'we're all human.'

Mrs. Letherton-Channing took no notice. Moving softly, heavily, in her tea-gown, like something run on castors over the floor, she opened the window wider, to ask more night in. She put a bowl of flowers outside the door: by night flowers were enemies. Her own idea of peace filled the room: the child's bed became the very image of sleep. (Her own sleep came in tablets out of a bottle.) Night between these colourless walls became as spacious and pure as a sky, in which her own solid form and Clara's seemed miraculously to be suspended.

Even Miss Ellis, her face close to Geraldine, whispered: 'I wish I were your age!'

'Do you?'

It became clear to Geraldine (as she lay, without curiosity, eyes fixed on the curves of Miss Ellis's chin) – from the two ladies' manner and circumspect breathing, from the sound of wicker chairs being carried in from the terrace, from the gramophone jigging a dance, very faint, down in Miss Weekes's bothy, from, through trees, the sickle of light from a car that made the rest of the sky so suddenly dark – that the red Revolution was still delayed. Security, feeling for her in the dark, closed the last of its tentacles on her limbs, her senses. When the door shut, when they had gone, she sighed acquiescence into her frilly pillow and once more slept in her prison.

Firelight in the Flat

BOB ROBERTSON, sore from the morning's row with his wife, came home warily, step after step reluctantly up the fibre-carpeted stairs – the flats had no lift – with a stop on each of the floors as though his breath had morally given out.

Here, six floors up, was his door: red shone through the frosted panels where a strip of firelight reached over the hall.

Rattling the key in, he felt the lock slip round. Then – for the hall was jasminy with her scent – he tentatively called: 'Betty?' Before there was time for an answer, he felt her absence. She had gone out, certainly: she would be at the flicks. 'Damn,' said Robertson flatly. He'd meant to make things all right. This was what intentions came to. He hung up his hat in the dark.

Robertson was an ex-officer; as the war kept receding, this counted for less and less. Still, on the strength of this and of a school that was almost public, he travelled in high-class etchings and educational prints. His wife, Betty, bought shiny courageous stockings in bargain basements and regretted to friends that they could not afford children. Life disheartened her, really, and more and more of their food came back cooked from the *delikatessen* in paper bags.

Now the walls jumped in and out of shadow: a five-shilling clock struck a half-hour long ago past. Far down below, the traffic went past in jerks to the Great West Road, as though being pumped out of London. The sitting-room door was confidentially open: two armchair-backs, against the red waning fire, took off, somehow, one's idea of a home. Dull with patent fuelling, but in Mother's tradition, the open fire kept something inside alight. Bitterly retrospective, Robertson reached out for the switch. But there was no electricity. He felt round in his pocket: he had no shilling.

'Good Lord: *Bobbet*!' said Constance, turning in an armchair.

'Good *Lord*!' he replied, shaken. 'Constance? Don't do that again!'

'I was asleep.'

'Got a shilling?'

'No, spent it. I've got Betty's latchkey; she's with Diane. I'm waiting here to borrow my bus fare home.'

'You are the limit,' said he, and, having discovered her face looking up at him, kissed it – which was their way.

'Steady,' said she, rearranging the curl on her forehead. She was about seventeen.

'Got that job yet?'

'What *do* you expect?' said Constance sardonically.

'Better get married.'

'Oh, naturally,' agreed Constance. 'But, then, as I always say . . . ' She didn't, however, say it. He sat down in the other armchair, stretched out his legs, and sighed. 'You know,' he confided, 'I wasn't a bit keen, really, on getting back here this evening. Funny, wasn't it?'

Constance quite understood. Knees crossed, she swung one foot happily in the firelight. 'All you men are the same, all boys, really. You don't know what you want till you think you're not getting it.'

'I and Betty had a dust-up.' (She half listened, quite calmly.) 'You know, she's impossible, Constance; if I never say it again. It's really a bit stiff sometimes. Of course, I know things come hard on her. But she does muddle about so.' This was just; all day long she went clicking about the flat in those high-heeled old satin slippers with straps undone. She would crouch in front of the grate and groan at the messy grey ashes. He knew what was wrong with Betty: she wanted a gas fire. All day long she would sigh that she was done in.

'I wish you could see my fingers,' said Constance suddenly. 'I've just had a manicure.'

'Show!' She put her hands close to the fire; the nails glistened: they both bent over them.

'You are a funny kid, Constance.'

'Shut up.' She licked a finger and stamped three ripples back again on her forehead. 'You know,' she resumed, 'what I feel about a manicure: it does pull you together. I know a place where men come in to be manicured – wouldn't that make you sick!'

'It's snug sitting here in the dark. Just you and I, Constance . . . You don't know what I miss.'

'Bobbet, look here: I'm hungry,' she interrupted.

'So am I, damned hungry.' Robertson leaned towards Constance, across the fire, knocking his knuckles together between his knees. 'Do you know,' he said passionately, 'it's a year since I've had roast mutton? Betty won't touch cooking. All this muck out of paper bags — '

'Well, she does at least hot up things from the *delikatessen*. I should get stuff out of tins – you know, salmon. I suppose you haven't got any salmon here?'

He went to see; she followed; he struck matches; laughing they groped their way to the kitchenette. He dropped spent matches; she stamped them carefully out. Here was a half pork pie, chiefly pastry, there three split peaches floating syrupy in a Woolworth dish; some biscuits – one was nibbled along the edge. They laughed. But the food smelled strong in the close air; there was a smell of old gas from the cooker. All delicate fingertips, Constance fished up a peach, leaning forward to let the syrup drip clear of her tight black frock. He watched: flame crept unnoticed up the match to his fingers. He swore sharply; they were in the dark. They followed each other by touch, till a pale fluctuation of firelight led them back to the hall. Robertson had brought the pork pie with him.

'But Betty'll be coming in,' he said gloomily.

'Well, what of it? But she won't; not till eight. She and Diane went in about half-past five; they'll be seeing the programme round.' She knelt to poke the fire, making it light the room up. Then her voice changed to an odd note. I say . . . do you ever have any money?'

'Bus fare? Don't go yet, there's a good girl.'

'No, but I want some money: a good deal.'

'Marry money,' he said, intent on what he was at. He had settled down with the pie balanced on one knee and was hacking away at the crust with a pocket-knife. Constance's silence, her placid watching and waiting, suddenly filled the room: in fancy he saw a table pulled up to a window, a dish of gooseberries (why, he could not think), and, out there in the country dusk, high poplars vaguely and gravely swaying. The scene, in a sphere of desire, was round and perfect. So one would live if one kept a chicken farm. 'Marry money,' he went on waggishly, still intent. But he put out a hand for Constance's.

'But, you damn fool,' cried Constance, starting up very suddenly, standing beside the door and clicking the impotent switch up and down, up and down. 'I need money *now*. I want it at once – can't you *see*?'

He was unnerved by her outburst, as though a cold wind snatched open the doors of the flat. He contracted into himself, defensive and unfriendly. She had ruined their fun; he wished she would shut up. 'See?' he repeated, dividing the pie accurately. 'No, I don't specially see. We all want money like that.'

Her high heel rapped the floor. 'But I must have it now. Do you have to be told point-blank? I've got to get right out – *soon*.' Her heel stopped and she stood desperately still.

With a dull shock he understood, and said under his breath: '*Constance!*'

'Oo-er, you wicked girl,' said Constance, with hopeless frivolity.
'Go on: consider it said.'

Uneasy – for to what extent had she not already imposed on
him? – and with rising anger, he said, 'But why in hell's name
come to *me*? . . . Anyway,' he added quickly. 'I've *got* no money.
And if I had, my girl, think what Betty might think.'

'My mistake,' said Constance. 'It just occurred to me. As we
seemed to be getting along so well. I've got to *get* that money, so
any port in a storm.'

'So you thought it was worth trying?' Exasperated by her
contemptuous lightness, her irony, and this net of doom she was
casting about the flat, he glared in the firelight at his portion of pie.
She had ruined his appetite. At last he could say more gently: 'What
did you do it for?'

'New clothes,' said Constance loudly.

'Get out of here, you little — !'

'Yes, all right,' she said. 'I'm going.'

'No, look here. Stop. Do for God's sake be decent with me. I'm
not down on you, but I'm damned if I'll stand your attitude.
Whatever possessed you, you little fool?'

'I suppose I was balmy,' said Constance, turning away.

'Love?' he said, uneasy.

'I said, I suppose I was balmy . . . Only Bobbet, look here,
don't keep going on about marriage. Because it makes you sound
silly now, doesn't it?'

'But I don't see why you shouldn't,' he said eagerly. 'I'd marry
you . . . there'd be heaps of men; all men aren't such swine. *I'd*
marry you,' he repeated, with a growing security.

'I wouldn't marry *you*,' said Constance. 'Not for anything, now.
Not if it had *been* you: I'd rather walk into the Serpentine. Thanks
all the same.'

'Oh, well,' he said, and added, not quite in irony: 'But it's been a
nice evening, hasn't it?'

'Well then, listen,' she said. 'What about that money, really? You
needn't worry: I swear you'll get it back. I'll want about fifty
pounds: I think I could manage on that. Will you or won't you? I've
got no time to be sweet.'

'Well . . . ' he began. Because, when you come to think of
it . . . because after all . . . 'The thing is — ' he began again, with
a frankness that should have won her. 'Well, you see how I *stand*.
I've got Betty to think of.'

'Yes, you don't half think of Betty!'

'Well, damn it all, she's my wife — '

'Lucky girl!'

'I must say, Constance, you're a very poor gold-digger!'

She said drearily: 'I've never tried before.'

'What about – whoever it was?'

'I'd rather walk into the Serpentine.'

'Blast!' he said. 'You spoil everything.' And he sat huddled forward, his head in his hands. For, really, there seemed no peace for him anywhere. He did simply want a woman to cheer him up. Betty was weak and Constance was bad right through.

'Sorry I came?' she said, groping round for her hat.

He sat on, scrubbing his fingers up through his hair.

'It's no good about the money?' She listened, he listened; the fire snapped. 'Right-oh,' she said. 'I'm off.'

'I'll think out something,' he said. 'I'll write in a day or two. I swear I'll see you through — '

At this point, Betty, having lent Constance her latchkey, was forced to ring at the door of her own flat. She rang twice, eager to be at home. As Robertson sat on, stupefied, Constance went to the door.

'Hullo, Con,' he heard Betty greet her. 'Find your way in all right?'

'Yep. Bobbet's back. I've been trying to borrow money.'

'*I* don't know what you're thinking of,' Betty said languidly. '*We* don't have any money . . . Hullo, Bobbet . . . Hullo, what's up with the light?'

'We're right out of shillings.'

'Here are three in the cigarette-box; there're always some there. We're not so broke as you'd think,' Betty said, laughing, to Constance. 'How much do *you* want, Con?'

'Sixpence – I want my bus fare.'

'Well, take a shilling.'

Betty clinked the shilling into the meter. The flat sprang into sight: 'art' distemper, six of The World's Best Pictures, the dark sharp angles of antiqued oak. Constance strolled to a glass and made up her mouth scarlet, then pulled on her tight little hat with the jockey brim. She wrapped up her chin in her collar. 'I must be pushing along,' she said. 'Thanks for the shilling.'

'Sorry, darling, we can't keep you to supper. But the fact is, I don't think the galantine . . . '

'I must get along, anyhow; mother'll be raging. 'Sides, I've had some pig pie.'

'Splendid. Go on, Bobbet, go to the door with her!'

When he came back from the door, Robertson saw at once how battered Betty was looking. The fact was, she couldn't get on without him; she curled up under his anger and went to bits. She must have been crying, for the mascara had run right round her eyes. Now she was fluffing her hair up, for him specially. He could not know that her throat, under the tight pink pearls, was burning just at a point where the Dietrich's throat had been kissed some minutes before. Her fox fur slid off one shoulder, she sat just where Constance had sat, looking up at him. 'Oh, *Bobbet*,' she said, 'I've been so – oh, I don't know. But I do get so fed up.'

'Poor girl,' he said, touching her cheek. She sighed and caught at his hand, and sat fondling it, with her head back on his arm and her long lashes turned down. 'I feel rotten, she said, 'about everything.'

'Oh, well . . . You've been washing your hair.'

'Look at my pearls; Swan & Edgar: two and eleven-three. Was I awful? I had to have something.'

'I like you to have pretty things.'

'Yes, you *are* a sweet about that.'

'Constance is a funny girl,' she said later. 'So independent – I can't make her out. Did you talk much?'

'Not particularly.'

'I'm sorry for her in a way – oh, the fire's nearly out.' The fire, indeed, had gone dull in the brilliant glare. One had had, thought Robertson, half-heartedly poking it, quite enough of all that.

'It's wasted,' he said, 'when we're out. Blazing away all the time. How would it really be if we *had* a gas fire?'

'Oh, but I love the firelight: it's so homey. It's just doing the grate — Still, I do love the firelight.'

'How would it be,' he said, 'if we cleared right out of all this and started a chicken farm? I've got that bit saved. I'm just as fed up as you are. You know, in the country somewhere.'

'*Bobbet* – and a sweet cottage?'

They held hands to think of it: he thought of huts and chickens, she thought of children. A country silence crept into the flat: outside, there might have been poplars, vaguely and gravely swaying. They felt oddly secure.

'You and me. We've never had much of a break.'

'It's funny,' she said on their way to bed that night, 'the way that girl Constance never has the price of a bus fare, I often wonder what will become of her . . . '

The Man of the Family

'DEAR WILLIAM,' Mrs Peel kept exclaiming. '*Isn't* William wonderful?' She was his Aunt Luella, and because his talk was beyond her, and she could not always grasp what he was saying, she kept casting bright sceptical glances around the lunch-table. Her blonde shell-rimmed spectacles gave these glances a twinkle. Lady Lambe, his Aunt Héloïse, however, listened intently; she made little flapping gestures at the butler when he offered her things, as though she could not bear to be distracted. When she noticed the *soufflé* the others were eating she recalled the butler with an apology.

After each interruption William would raise his voice half a tone and continue patiently. He was on his way across London from Oxford. Patsey, beside him, sat with her hands on her lap twisting her rings about when she was not eating and taking no part in the talk. She was not modern at all and always seemed discouraged. Pretty Rachel sat smiling into the bowl of glass fruit, on which green sunshine, reflected back from the Regent's Park trees, twinkled and slid. The trees were in full June light, the dining-room in shadow. The table was round, with no 'head', so that any difficulty in placing William had been avoided.

Aunt Héloïse was also a Liberal: at the last three elections she had stood for Parliament: she meant to keep on standing. She was not original, but she was sound and receptive; when she came down to Oxford he took her to debates at the Union. Rachel Lambe never came with her mother; she said they all made her feel so terribly old (she was twenty-four). He too seldom saw her; she went out a great deal and seemed to have numerous friends; when they met she, though so naïve, contrived to be very mysterious. She had bronzy-gold hair, parted down the centre, that rippled smoothly against the line of her cheeks, and a smile – subtle, gentle, malicious – that sent curves up under her eyes: a da Vinci smile. An extraordinary daughter for one of one's aunts to have had.

William always lunched at his Aunt Luella's on his way across London. The Regent's Park house was his *pied-à-terre*; he could put up here even when the family were out of town, and bring friends in to meals – had he wished. Aunt Luella was an irritating, attractive woman; she was thin as a lath, wore a perpetual string of brown amber, and dressed to tone in with it. Her taste in interior decoration made him blush, but she kept an excellent table. She called him 'the man of the family' or 'the head of the family' (which he in fact was), and scoffed away gently at him. She scoffed at herself, her daughter and everyone else. Patsey was thirty-two, and looked like her mother's sister. She was statuesque, expensively dressed, and null; she had been engaged twice, but nothing had come of it. Quite a lot of life (he often longed to point out) was before her; interests still offered, but Patsey seemed blind to them. Her tomboyish name was unsuitable; Patsey was painfully womanly.

When William and Aunt Héloïse had settled the Government finally, they cleared their throats and there was a benign pause. Aunt Luella blinked. The butler came round with the Camembert. 'Do they *teach* you politics at Oxford?' Rachel said vaguely. William did not reply; he readjusted himself and turned sideways to Patsey.

'Well, Patsey, how goes it?' he said at last, genially.

She started violently. 'Goes what?' she said, flustered. 'It? Oh, very well, thank you. I've been having a lovely time.'

'Good,' said William. 'Splendid.'

'I've been helping at fêtes,' Patsey explained conscientiously. 'I went to the Chelsea Flower Show. I've been ever so many times to the Academy.'

'Splendid,' said William drearily. 'Nothing like going around. A man I know meant to go to the Academy only the other day, but I don't think he ever did.'

She looked at him, sidelong, out of her doglike brown eyes.

'I *adore* the Academy,' Rachel put in in her deep voice. 'I went to the private view and saw everyone. I *adore* the Academy.'

'Rachel "adores" anything to do with clothes,' said her mother. It was gratifying to her, as a plain intellectual woman to have produced something so pretty and frivolous. Yet neither 'pretty' nor 'frivolous' suited Rachel; they hung foolishly as pink muslin on her queer personality.

'Aren't I futile?' said Rachel, smiling down at her peach.

There certainly was no brandy like Aunt Luella's. William slid back in his chair with a good feeling inside. Catching her eye, he bowed an acknowledgment. 'And, oh, *William*,' said she, leaning suddenly forward. 'If you're not too busy today I'd love a little talk some time. Business.'

Business was Aunt Luella's forte. She loved to settle down at it for a stretch and bemuse William with documents. In her morning-room, with gold curtains and beetle-green walls blistered over with bluish patches like scum on a pool, he had put in hours of claustro-phobia and torment. The shining shagreen accoutrements of her desk disappeared early under a sea of parchments – deeds, securities, settlements – God could hardly know what. Dispatch-boxes yawned and pink tape littered the floor. When he was of age she meant him to be a Trustee – he felt even now she was fattening him up for one. She ran in and out of documents like a spider, at demoniacal speed. 'Of course,' she would say, 'I've really no *head* for these things. One's a lone woman – but don't let me bother you. Only it is such a help to talk things out with a man. Your father was marvellous; no one could know what a help to me! But you must be *sure* now and don't let me waste your time.'

Escape was always impossible. 'I wish I took after father,' William would mutter, scrubbing his hands through his hair.

'I think you've a *wonderful* grasp of things,' she would always say brightly. These were the only occasions when she took him – or anything – seriously. He never could think what the woman thought she was getting at – showing off, merely? He could bet any amount she hadn't allowed Uncle Henry within sight of those boxes; she had so thoroughly kept Uncle Henry down. William hated, however, to be a beast in any way about Aunt Luella.

This afternoon, however, no tin boxes appeared. She burrowed vaguely in one writing-table drawer, giving William time to finish his coffee and light one more of her excellent cigarettes. He wondered sadly if Rachel would have gone by the time she had finished; he had thought it might be pleasant to walk back with Rachel across the Park. He jumped when Aunt Luella, twisting round on her chair, leaned vivaciously towards him and, swinging out her string of beads on one finger, said: 'It's about *Patsey*. Didn't you notice her?'

'N-not particularly.'

'She's been looking really quite brilliant. The thing is: Patsey's just going to be engaged again – I don't say *married*, because really I'm getting so superstitious about the poor darling. Engaged. Well, she is now, really, only I mean it isn't announced.'

'How terribly nice,' said William, clattering down his coffee-cup. 'Shall I go and congratulate her?'

'*Just* one moment . . . He's really, the dearest old charming thing; "Chummy," we call him – his name's Everard. So *nice*, so nice-looking, such nice people. Patsey and I are delighted with him. It's ideal – just one thing's a pity. He is divorced, poor dear.'

'Oh . . . Did it, or had it done to him?'

'Oh, *did* it, of course. The wife was a little baggage. He's been worn to a shadow, had no sort of life. He wants somebody absolutely reposeful. Patsey's the very thing. It's lovely to see them together. Only people do ask such silly questions, and talk. "Wasn't he divorced?" they say, as if poor Chummy hadn't come out of it splendidly. So I just thought I'd tell you before you spoke to Patsey, so's you couldn't ask anything awkward. Not that you would. We're all quite full of it – Aunt Héloïse, Rachel, and all. Only do remember, it isn't really *announced*.'

Up in the Chinese drawing-room, Patsey and Rachel sat one at each end of a sofa, each glancing over a copy of *Vogue*. Rachel had the more recent. Aunt Héloïse sat in an upright chair by the window reading *The Times* thoroughly. Patsey kept re-settling her cushions behind her, and Rachel re-crossing her legs; the room was full of the amiable drooping silence of relatives who have nothing special to say. When William entered, all three of them brightened up. Rachel leaned back with her hands propping her head; Patsey, pinkly self-conscious, shuffled *Vogue* off her knee, then pulled it back and began to scan the advertisements.

William, congratulations nicely delivered, stayed looming above them, hands in his pockets. Rachel meanwhile gazed up at him, not unkindly. He was a nice-looking fairish youth, intelligent but bothered-looking. He had even some prestige; his own friends thought he disproved that one couldn't be brilliant *and* solid. 'I shall hope to meet Everard,' he was saying to Patsey encouragingly. He remembered how, centuries ago, when he was still at his prep school, Patsey had come down one afternoon in the car, very much engaged, very pink, very conscious, with her first young man, Gerald, very pink also. She seemed to be nearly always in this condition. 'Chummy's coming to tea,' she said proudly, with that old deprecating, absurd, rather touching glow in her cheeks. 'You *will* stay, won't you? I thought we might all get tickets for something tomorrow night.'

'Um-m,' said William. He glanced at Rachel – it rather depended on her. But Rachel did not respond: he was disconcerted at catching a flash of glances across him. Rachel and Rachel's mother were making faces – or something subtler: 'expressions' – at one another.

'I'm terribly much afraid,' he said, scenting danger, 'I can't be in town for more than a night this time. I'm so sorry, Patsey. But I'd love to stay for tea.'

Rachel could not stay for tea: she was seldom available. She must get back she said; she had some wretched people coming. Aunt Héloïse had a committee meeting at three. Lady Lambe had four afternoon committees a week, and on those afternoons Rachel was at home to friends. Lady Lambe and her daughter lived in Walpole Street, Chelsea. Rachel, getting up thoughtfully, invited William to

walk just across the Park with her. 'I think Regent's Park's so
shady; one never knows. Last time I got spoken to by a boy on a
scooter, and today I was followed by a repulsive Airedale. We
parted out on the doorstep; it's probably waiting still. I hate dogs,
you know.'

'Oh, poor old fellow,' cried Patsey; 'he must have got lost!'
Rachel thought this quite likely; she patted the top of Patsey's head,
kissed her hand to her mother, and went out, followed by William,
who felt pleased.

Rachel walked beautifully; people kept turning to look at her. Her
blue dress fled back from her figure in the light wind and the waves
of her gold hair flickered against her cheeks. William wore the grey
flannels and brown hat in which he had left Oxford. He decided
that if Rachel should happen to ask him to come back to tea with
her, Chummy might well keep. She walked in an absent silence,
but he felt she had something special to say. He glanced at her once
or twice, then said at a venture: 'What do *you* think of this person –
this Everard?'

She looked past him at the lake and said casually, 'I *don't* think
about him, but I know him, of course.'

'Oh, you do? Doesn't he bear thinking about?'

'Oh, I don't know whether he'd *bear* it – he's just not worth the
effort. I don't think often.'

'Aunt Luella and Pat seem pleased.'

'Yes, poor dears,' agreed Rachel, and wrinkled up her nose.
'Aren't women all pathetic?'

This had not struck him. 'So long as *they're* pleased,' he said, 'I
don't think we need think twice of it. Patsey's obviously got to
marry someone.'

'Oh, I know,' agreed Rachel. 'Babies and that sort of thing. But
she can't, I'm afraid, marry Chummy – so this has got to be
stopped.'

William pulled up short; his mind reeled. Rachel came to a stop
too, and stood eyeing him calmly.

'Why on earth? What's the matter with it? Or do *you* want to
marry him?'

This sounded unkind, but seemed to him only fair. Such
awkward clashes often occurred in novels. But Rachel shook her
head definitely 'Though I'd do quite a lot,' she said, 'for a really
good home. But that, as a matter of fact, is exactly what Everard's
after himself. I don't want to sound a brute, you know, William,
but of course Aunt Luella and Patsey are very well off; what you'd
call "warm". Everard values his comforts. After the first lunch he
must have seen points about Patsey, and after two or three dinners

and door-to-doors in the Daimler the best of her really nice character must have been perfectly clear. I don't mean that he probably isn't quite fond of her by this time – who wouldn't be, of Patsey? She's the dearest old slug.'

'Still, if they're both pleased,' William repeated. 'And, after all, people have to have *some* reason to marry. Aunt Luella may not be strong as a mother, but she's a born mother-in-law. Think what a time Chummy'll have with those black boxes!'

'That's just it. The poor woman's such a hopeless fool about money. She's as timid as a fowl by herself, and wouldn't re-invest tuppence, but she's probably been chatting to him about securities and he'll have been telling her she's the perfect woman of business. You know how weak her head is. I wouldn't mind him messing Aunt Luella's money about and losing it for her – she's got far too much – if he weren't also going to mess up Patsey's affections. But I cannot see why any one man should do both.'

Rachel said this so weightily that he stared.

'Do you hate him?' he asked. 'Or just know him fearfully well?'

'Wellish,' said Rachel. 'At least, I suppose you might say so. We nearly went abroad.'

They walked at uneven speed in the shade of the beeches, heads close for discretion's sake and talking in low tones. People veered to avoid them, for they looked anxious and pretty, like a young couple in love. Even William's friends, had they passed, might have thought this of him. Rachel paused at an empty seat and looked down at it hopelessly; William dusted a patch with his handkerchief and they both sat down. He stuck his feet out and glared at the toes of his shoes. Rachel brought out a mirror, studied her mouth, and applied a little more red.

'It was when I first grew up,' she said. 'I was fearfully bored. You know how hard up we were till grandfather died. Mother'd dropped all her friends who weren't on the right committees, and I never saw anyone, and had nothing to wear if I did. Mother never thought about anything but saving European children, and I used to take pleats in Patsey's cast-offs and wish I could die. Everyone seemed to be having a marvellous time, though I don't suppose they were really. Then a girl asked me down at the last moment to fill up a gap in a Hunt Ball party; Aunt Luella stood me a frock and I easily picked up Everard. I thought I was made.

'He seemed to be quite an experience. I had always suspected I must be all right really, but I never quite knew how nice I could be. He hadn't then come to the end of his wife's money, so he gave me a slap-up time. I wasn't a bit particular in those days. I saw he had mouldy patches, but that didn't bother me, till I met somebody else – but I hadn't then. Then he said, "Come abroad," and I didn't see why not. I'm sorry, William, but morals are like clothes and I'd scrapped one lot and hadn't found others to suit me. He said we'd go in his car. Mother was going to Serbia on a hunt of some kind. We fixed our start for the day after she was going – three weeks ahead. But in those three weeks Everard lost colour. One way and another . . . His wife put him on an allowance, and he got careful – not to say slightly morbid if he thought he was spending too much. So when he did take one out, he wanted his money's worth. He's not stupid, exactly; he's got a tongue. That's where I went right off him. In fact, he's not a nice man. That's where Patsey's heart would come in. You may think me cynical, William, but I honestly do believe that manners (or people not having them) undermine happiness far quicker than morals. A person, specially not a person like Patsey, can't expect her husband always to stay in her pocket, but she does expect him to be polite when he's there. It's these little remarks with an edge – you know, spiteful, cutting. He'd skin Patsey alive. He can't leave a person in peace once he doesn't like their face or thinks they're not keen on his. He never *hurt* me: you see, I wasn't really attached to him; but he merely annoyed me rather. I "kept him under observation" (as they say about measles), and when, the very last day, he turned nasty at having to pay an extra seven-and-six on my passport, I simply went home. I went down to Aunt Luella in Wales and wired from there that our trip was off, on grounds of economy.

'Now mind you, William, those three weeks he was in love with me and wanting me more than anything, and still he couldn't help being nasty. What he's wanting now is the key to Aunt Luella's black boxes – and, I daresay, the key of the cellar. What chance has Patsey got once they've settled him in?'

'You mean,' said William anxiously, 'that there's a distinction between being nasty and being simply immoral?'

'I do, of course,' said Rachel, with some impatience. 'Now you do see why this marriage is impossible?'

Her recital had given William all sorts of queer feelings. However, he felt he knew Rachel very much better. His theory that this sort of thing only happened to other people's relations broke down. 'What a lot goes on,' he thought. 'And how calmly women take it.' He felt Rachel underrated his own sex. All the same, he had this new, intimate feeling about her. 'But I can't quite see what you're going to do,' he said.

'It's a question of what you are going to do,' she said. 'You see, you will be expected to take a line about this.'

'My dear girl — '

'Why else do you think I told you?' said Rachel languidly, opening her eyes very wide.

'What do you expect me to do?' he asked. 'Rush back and kick Everard, shouting "Swine, swine, swine, swine?"'

Sitting with hands folded on her turquoise-blue bag, she shrugged her shoulders in absolute detachment. Beyond the Park, the white walls of Aunt Luella's house twinkled behind the screen of a drooping branch. Rachel's cheeks went up into charming curves; she was smiling at William.

'If you did,' she said, 'it wouldn't come off. Aunt Luella would blink and twiddle her beads and say "Listen to William; isn't he wonderful!" and Patsey and Everard would go on chastely squeezing each other's hands. I'm afraid you can't be direct. Besides, you really can't give them chapter and verse. Mother would be so upset. Besides, I don't want Everard made an idiot of. He's right according to his lights. The last thing I want is to score off the poor old thing. He did do me one good turn; he pulled me out of my hole, and, as I say, he did seem to be an experience. No, William, don't shoot him up. All we have to work for is the protection of Patsey. He must be quietly blighted. That's up to you, I feel. As the man of the family, you really do carry some weight with Aunt Luella. Simply be rather heavy. Tell her . . . tell her you've heard the most shocking things about Everard at Oxford. Say they're being said everywhere. If the worst comes to the worst, I'll support you, of course. But I think I should make the worst worse. You see, it's awkward for mother; she loathes Chummy instinctively; I think she must have some jungle instinct about him. But seeming to crab Patsey's marriage when she hasn't got me off — And whenever she tries to say anything about Everard, Aunt Luella goes off like an alarm clock.'

'Oxford,' said William annoyed. 'Who in God's name would have heard of Chummy there? He's quite obscure, isn't he?'

'Oh, I suppose you all gossip,' said his cousin, indifferent. 'Like men always do.' She laid her gloved hand with the diamond bracelet over his for a moment. 'William,' she said, 'be effective. I count on you absolutely. Do go back and be effective at once, *now*. Then come round and let's go out to dinner and hear how effective you've been.'

Shaking out her blue dress with a gesture, his cousin was gone. The June sun seemed to William paler; a very slight shiver went down his back.

As William paced round the morning-room, waiting for Aunt Luella, he asked himself once more what this fuss was about. He tried to pull out an antique-looking book from a rack, to discover this opened, revealing a vanity-box. He brushed his nose nervously over some prim yellow roses which were scentless and which, unbalanced, flopped heavily from the vase. He seated himself abruptly in an armchair which, mounted on springs, sank under him. Unnerved, he stood up with his back to the empty grate, repeating that values were relative. He glared at the children racing around in the Park and thought what a pity it was that the race need go on.

His Aunt Luella sent urgent messages, wanting to know why he wouldn't join them for tea. Perhaps she would never come. Suppose she sent Everard?

Then he heard her plunging along in that characteristic way, her necklace swinging against her belt-buckle. She shot in with the light on her spectacles, glittering at him reproachfully. 'William, you're *too* naughty! You mustn't be such a shy boy. Chummy is most disappointed. I never heard — '

'It's not that,' said her nephew. 'I never have been a shy boy. I've got heaps to say when I'm let get a word in edgeways. I've got heaps to say about Everard. Aunt Luella, this marriage — '

' – *Dear* Everard!' she exclaimed, and, as Rachel had said, went off like an alarm clock. Going on talking, she put out a hand for William's and made him sit down by her on the window-seat. 'Dear Chummy,' she finished, 'I do admire him so. Happiness makes him *solemn.*'

'He may have cause to be solemn. Do you really *know*, Aunt Luella, that he is in every way a suitable husband for Patsey?'

'Almost anyone would be – anyone *nice*. She'd make anyone into a good husband. That's her gift, I've always thought. It's sheer bad luck that it's never come into play. Dear Patsey . . . '

'I'm sorry,' said William, standing up with an effort. 'I'm afraid I've got to be a bit of a brute. It's up to me – I mean there seems no one else – I mean, as a man – I'm afraid Everard *isn't* nice. He won't do. Certain things have come to my knowledge — We must face facts.'

'Don't talk,' said his aunt with asperity, 'about what you know nothing about.'

'I'm sorry,' repeated William, 'but I've been given to understand — '

'My dear boy, you're too young to understand anything.'

'I merely happen to know,' said her nephew, scarlet, 'that he made improper suggestions to a young girl.'

'*My-dear-boy* — ' said his aunt. She looked from his chin to his shoes, blinked quickly behind her glasses, let out a small smothered hysterical sound like a whinny, then pressed her handkerchief violently to her lips. She was leaning back with her shoulder against the shuter: the shutter shook. William thrust his hands deep into his pockets and feelingly looked away from her.

The shutter still shook, and small noises exploded from his aunt's handkerchief. 'Aunt Luella,' said William, 'do pull yourself together. We've got to do something, haven't we?'

Aunt Luella meekly lowered her handkerchief from a mouth twisted in uncontrollable mirth. 'Dear William,' she faltered, 'I'm so awfully sorry. But you were so dramatic. Now, *who's* been giving our poor Rachel away?'

William froze by the table, opening the shagreen blotter. 'Oh so you've found out?'

'I know,' his aunt said grimly, 'the real *facts* of the matter. Who's been telling you fairy-tales? . . . I suppose,' she darted out at him, 'Rachel has?'

William nodded cautiously. Aunt Luella stared into the air between them. 'Oh!' she exclaimed. 'The *unscrupulous* girl she is!'

William gulped. 'I laughed for a moment,' his aunt explained indignantly. 'William, of course you are *wax* in that girl's hands. All boys are. Of course you don't know Rachel! If there ever was "still water!" Just one mass of jealous subtlety. She cannot bear to see Patsey happy this way. We all know she stops at nothing. But even so — '

'Didn't it rather shock you?'

'Shock me! My dear boy, at your age you cannot *imagine* what that poor Everard's been through. She's been his bad angel. Of course, she made a dead set at him. If ever a girl tried to wreck a man! And Chummy, being so conscientious and good all the time, trying to live his miserable marriage down. Told me? Of course he told me; he was so splendid about it, trying to shield that little minx all the way through. He was so distressed for us all when she walked in one day and he found she was Patsey's cousin. *She* never turned a hair. Of course he told me; Chummy and I are *friends*! He said he did feel, as things were, that I ought to know. But Chummy doesn't bear malice!'

'Anxious to get in first,' observed William gloomily.

His aunt, glaring, continued. ' "I only want," poor Everard said, "to shield Patsey. We must think first of her." That was of course what we both felt. And of course we kept poor dear Héloïse out of it. Though I must say it's what she deserves. Always saving Serbian children and looking superior. I could have told her Rachel would come to no good. But, really, her spite surprises me. And her effrontery. My first instinct was, of course, never to have her here again. But then dear Patsey'd have wondered. She asked him to take her abroad *in his wife's car!*'

'Aunt Luella,' said William, 'you shock me. How can you believe a swine who talks like that about Rachel! How can you let a person like that marry your Patsey!'

'I know the girl only too well,' his aunt said with gloomy triumph. 'For years I've seen this coming. I'm sorry for *you*, William. I don't like to disillusion a boy of your age. I wouldn't like you to feel you have made a fool of yourself.'

(Of this she gave small indication.) 'But there's only Rachel to thank. No, I'm not angry. I'm merely sorry for you.'

It struck William, whose relations with Aunt Luella had up to now been affable, suave and pleasant, that they were now in the thick of a raging row. She was rather certainly hating him. He felt like the dog in the Anstey story that inconveniently dug up the shot poodle. The familiar air of her beetle-green room reproached him. The cigarette-box recalled sharply arrears of her hospitality, their pleasant chats about documents. He gazed at his aunt, whose mauve colour rose steadily: he had never seen Aunt Luella change colour before. His heart dropped an inch.

'My God,' he thought, 'am I wrong?' He couldn't believe this was normal family life. 'Is this mother love? he wondered, and pictured a large red hen. Or could there be something subtler, nearer the quick, as it were, the matter with Aunt Luella? 'Confound all women,' he thought. He said obstinately: '*I* think Rachel comes out of this well. I'm sorry her name was ever brought into this. She simply wanted to save you and Patsey from — '

'She didn't,' snapped Aunt Luella; 'she wanted to wreck the marriage.' Frantic with indignation, she tugged at her amber string; the string snapped and the beads clattered about the floor. This gave William the sense of a last catastrophe; he went hopelessly down on his knees to gather the beads up.

'Stop crawling about,' said his aunt, 'and listen to me, William. I could have never believed that even a boy of your age could be so clumsy and stupid. You act like a child of five. You make it difficult for me ever to have you or Rachel about in this house again. If it were not for your Aunt Héloïse, I should advise you not to see Rachel again. She's an extremely bad influence.'

'Here are six of your beads,' said William with dignity. 'You'd be sorry to lose them. As it happens, I'm dining with her tonight.'

'Will you *listen* to what I'm saying?'

'I'm sorry this . . . outbreak . . . should have occurred, Aunt Luella. I'd no idea I'd upset you. But I can't regret having spoken. You seem to me on the verge of a fearful mistake. I feel bound, as the man of the family — '

'Man? My dear child, you've only just left school. Yes, I quite see you're sorry. But you really should learn you're too young to meddle with things. We won't say any more about it, only please try and remember another time that you don't know *every*thing yet. Now do go and flatten your hair down and wash your face and get cool. Then come and have tea and talk nicely to Patsey and Everard. Of course, we'll forget this. I'm sure you meant very well.' She approached and patted his shoulder.

William turned to the door. His aunt, now only too normal, looked after him quizzically. 'Yes, run along with you,' she said. 'And don't be so silly again. Stop; just come back and give your old auntie a kiss . . . There, *now* we're right again, aren't we? . . . Dear old William. How nice that we don't, as a family, ever have grievances.'

His aunt's kiss still damp on his cheek, he succeeded in leaving the room.

William rang up the Ivy to book a table for two. As he crossed the landing he heard, through the drawing-room door above a rich male voice talking affably. He heard a tinkle of glass and excited, delighted laughter from Aunt Luella and Patsey.

'Well, if I *must* — ' said the voice with beautiful resignation.

'Yes, you *must*, Everard; mustn't Everard, mummy?'

'Of course he must. Come along, don't be silly, Chummy!'

'Well, if I *must* . . . ' William heard a siphon go off.

'Mummy, where's that other table? It's higher.'

'No, wait, Chummy – let me!'

'Well, if you really *will* insist . . . ' Someone moved a table up for Everard's drink. 'No, let me light it!' cried Patsey. Later, she dropped the match-box. The Man of the Family was very much in possession.

'It really doesn't much matter,' thought William. 'They're all fools.'

The Needlecase

THE car was sent to the train – along the straight road between dykes in the late spring dusk – to bring back Miss Fox, who was coming to sew for a week. Frank, the second son of the house, had come suddenly back from town; he was pleased to find the car there, which was more than he hoped, but appalled to see Miss Fox, in black, like a jointed image, stepping in at the back. Frank had, and wished to have, no idea who she was. So he sat in front with the chauffeur, looking glumly left at the willows and dykes flitting by, while Miss Fox, from the back, looked as fixedly out at willows and dykes at the other side of the road. No one spoke. They turned in at the lodge gates and the avenue trees closed in.

When the car drew up at the hall door, Frank got out and shouted. It embarrassed him having come home, and he did not want to explain. His sister Angela, sitting up at her window, heard, shot downstairs, and flung her arms round his neck, nearly knocking him over, like far too big a dog, as though he had been away two years instead of two days. This pleasure she over-expressed was perfectly genuine; Angela was effusive because she was often depressed; she could not be bothered being subtle with Frank, whom she knew far too well, and whose chagrins she often shared. So she kept up this rowdy pretence that everything was for the best.

'Had-a-good-time?' she said.

'No.'

'I'm sure you did really,' said Angela.

'No doubt you know best,' said Frank. 'Who in God's name's that in there?'

'Oh, that's Miss *Fox*,' explained Angela, peering into the car, where Miss Fox sat like an image, waiting to be let out. Angela rang the bell wildly for someone to come and cope. The chauffeur carried Frank's bag and the sewing-woman's strapped-up brown paper suitcase up the wide steps. The front of the house loomed over them, massive and dark and cold: it was the kind of house that easily looks shut up, and, when shut up, looks derelict. Angela took Frank's arm and they went indoors, into the billiard-room, the only place they could be certain of meeting nobody else. The room had a dank, baizey smell, and a smell of cold anthracite from the unlit stove: four battered green shades hung low over the sheeted table. It was not cheery in here. Frank sat on the fender-stool with his shoulders up and stared through his sister Angela heavily, uninvitingly. Had he wished to be quite alone he would not, however, have shouted.

'What did you do?' said Angela.

'Nothing special,' Frank said. He had been up to London to meet a man who might get him a job if he liked the looks of him, and the man clearly had not. The man had seen Frank to do Arthur a good turn: unfortunately the brothers did not resemble each other. Everyone liked Arthur. And Frank had stayed up in London, and had hoped to stay longer, because of a girl, but that had been a flop too: he had run through his money; that was why he was home. Angela had the good sense to ask no more. Leaning against the table and screwing her left-hand white coral ear-ring tighter (she always looked rather well) she said nonchalantly: 'The Applebys have been over. Hermione's after Arthur. They want us for tennis on Monday. The vet. came about Reno; he says it's nothing – oh, and mother has heard from Arthur; he's coming down Friday week and bringing his new girl. So then mother wired to hurry on Miss Fox. She's going to make us all over – first the drawing-room covers, then mother's black lace, and then do up Toddy and me – cut some dresses and run up some tennis frocks. She's our one hope for the summer. No doubt she sews like hell, but we really couldn't look worse. Could we, Frank? I mean, could we?'

'Yes,' said Frank. 'I mean, no.'

'We heard of her through Aunt Doris,' said Angela, chatting away. 'She's one of the wonderfully brave – she's got a child to support that she shouldn't have. She trained somewhere or other, so I suppose she *can* make. She's been on these rounds for years, going down in the world a bit. She seems dirt cheap, so there must be something fishy. She used to work, years ago, for the Fotheringhams, but Aunt Doris only got on to her after she fell.'

'You surprise me,' said Frank, yawning drearily, wanting a drink more than anything in the world.

Miss Fox's arrival, though perfectly unassuming, had left quite a wake of noise: she had been taken up and put somewhere, but doors went on opening and shutting, Frank's mother stood out in the hall giving directions, and his elder sister Toddy began shouting for Angela. As Frank crossed the hall his mother broke off to give him her vivid mechanical smile and say, 'Oh, you're *back*.' The house – far too big but kept on for Arthur, who was almost always away but liked to think of it there – had many high

windows and a white stone well staircase that went, under a
skylight, up and up and up. This would have been an excellent
house for someone else to have lived in, and heated; Frank and
Angela could then have visited comfortably there. As it was, it was
like a disheartened edition of Mansfield Park. The country around
it was far too empty and flat.

Miss Fox was not to work tonight; they left her to settle in. But
Toddy was in such a hurry to get in first with her things that she
slipped upstairs, unobtrusively, as soon as dinner was over. She
found Miss Fox still smoking over her supper tray. She was of that
difficult class that has to have trays all the time. Too grand for the
servants, she had to be fed in her room – one of those top
bedrooms in any Georgian house with high ceilings and windows
down by the floor. It looked rather bleak in the light of two
hanging bulbs. A massive cheval glass, brought from downstairs
today, reflected Miss Fox's figure sitting upright at the table. Deal
presses stood round the walls, dress-boxes tottered in stacks and
two dressmaker's dummies – one stout and one slimmer – pro-
truded their glazed black busts. A sewing-machine with a treadle
awaited the dressmaker's onslaught. In the grate, a thin fire rather
uncertainly flapped. What should be done had been done to
acclimatize Miss Fox. But her purpose here could be never far from
her mind, for she rigidly sat at the table where she would work. A
folded-back magazine was propped on the coffee-pot: when Toddy
came in she lifted her eyes from this slowly, but did not attempt to rise.

Her meek, strong, narrow, expressionless face, with heavy
eyelids, high cheekbones and secretive mouth, framed in dusty fair
hair brushed flat and knotted behind, looked carven under the bleak
overhead light. Its immobile shadows were startling. Toddy
thought: 'She's important.' But this was absurd.

Toddy kicked the door to behind her and stood stock still, a
cascade of tired dance dresses flung over one arm, two bales of
gingham for tennis frocks balanced under the other. Success this
forthcoming summer was deadly important, for Toddy was now
twenty-four. She felt Miss Fox held her fate in the palm of her
hand. So she stood stock still and did not know how to begin. She
had quieter manners, a subtler air than Angela, but was in fact a
rather one-idea girl.

'I hope you have all you want,' she said helplessly.

'Yes, thank you, Miss Forrester.'

'I mustn't disturb you tonight. But I thought you might like
some idea — '

'Show me,' said Miss Fox politely, and pushed her chair back
from the table.

'My red tulle is ripped right round. It caught on a spur — '

She stopped, for Miss Fox was looking at her so oddly, as though she were a ghost, as though it were terror and pleasure to see her face. Toddy's looks were not startling, but were, like her brother Arthur's, pleasant enough. No one, no man, had been startled this way before.

'It caught on a spur,' she said, on a rising note.

Miss Fox's eyes went quite blank. 'Tch-tch-tch,' she said, and bent quickly over the stuff. She had unpacked and settled in – Toddy saw, looking round – screens hid her bed and washstand, the facts of her life, away, but one or two objects had appeared on the mantelpiece, and a fine, imposing work-basket stood at her elbow. Toddy, who loved work-baskets, had a touch of the jackdaw, so, while Miss Fox was examining the martyred red dress, she flicked back the hinged lid of the basket and with innocent, bird-like impertinence routed through its contents. All sorts of treasures were here; 'souvenir' tape-measures, tight velvet emery bags, button-bags, a pin-cushion inside a shell, scissors of all sorts in scabbards – and oh, such a needle-case! 'As large as a family Bible,' said Toddy, opening it, pleased. And, like a family Bible, it had a photo stuck inside. 'Oh, what a nice little boy!' – '*Thank you*,' exclaimed Miss Fox, and with irresistible quickness, a snatch, had the needlecase back. The movement so surprising, it seemed not to have happened.

'That looked such a dear little boy,' Toddy went on, impenitent.

'My little nephew,' Miss Fox said impenetrably.

It was odd to think she had a child, for with such a nun-like face she had looked all wrong, somehow, smoking a cigarette. The dusty look of her hair must be the effect of light, for Toddy, standing above her, looked down and saw how well brushed her hair was. Her fingers looked as though they would always be cold, and Toddy dreaded their touch on her naked spine when the time would come to try on her evening dresses. And felt frightened alone with her, at the top of this dark, echoing house. They saved light everywhere, you had to grope up the stairs, for this well of a house drank money. So its daughters, likely to wither, had few 'advantages'. Everyone knew, Arthur knew, that Arthur must marry money. Toddy was sick of the sacrifice. She was in love this year, baulked all the time, and her serene, squarish face concealed a constant, pricking anxiety.

'I've *got* to look nice,' she said suddenly.

'I'll do all I can,' said Miss Fox, flashing up once again that odd, reminiscent look.

'How *like* you, Toddy,' Angela cried at breakfast.

'What was like Toddy?' Frank asked, scrawling a maze among

the crumbs by his plate. He seldom listened to what his sisters were saying, but sat on at table with them because he had nowhere special to go next.

'Creeping up there, then poking about in her things. You really might give the poor old creature a break.'

'She's not so old,' said Toddy, serene. 'And the child looked about seven.'

'What was it like?'

'I only saw curls and a collar – I tell you, she snatched it away.'

'What child?' said Frank. He pushed his cup across vaguely and Angela gave him more coffee, but it was cold.

'The child she had,' said Toddy.

'Oh God,' said Frank, 'is she fallen?' But he did not care in the least.

'I told you she was, last night,' said Angela, hurt.

That morning, Miss Fox was put in the drawing-room to work. Bales of chintz were unrolled and she cut out the new covers, shaping them over the backs of the chairs with pins. In cold, windy April sunlight she crawled round and round the floor, with pins in her mouth. The glazed chintz looked horribly cold. Frank, kept so short of money, not only thought the rosy-and-scrolly pattern itself obscene, but found these new covers a frenzied extravagance. But now Arthur's most promising girl was coming to stay, and must at all costs be impressed. If she did marry Arthur, she'd scrap these covers first thing. Any bride would. Frank leaned in the doorway, letting a draught in that rustled under the chintz, to watch Miss Fox at work on her thankless task. She magnetized his idleness. Their silence was fascinating, for if he spoke she would have to spit out those pins. The drawing-room was full of tables covered with photographs: Arthur at every age. He watched Miss Fox dodge the tables and drag her lengths of chintz clear.

Then she sat back on her heels. 'How fast you get on,' Frank said.

'I give my whole mind to it.'

'Don't your hands get cold, touching that stuff?'

'They may do; I'm not particular.'

She put pins back in her mouth and Frank wondered how she had ever been seduced. He picked up her big scissors idly and snipped at the air with them. 'This house is like ice,' he said. 'Do you know this part of the world?'

She was round at the back of the sofa and nothing came for some time; she must be eyeing the pattern and chewing the pins. Then her voice came over the top. 'I've heard speak of it. It seems very quiet round here.'

'*Quiet* — ' began Frank.

But, hearing his voice, his mother looked in and said with her ready smile: 'Come, Frank, I want you a moment. We mustn't disturb Miss Fox.'

That same afternoon, the sun went in. Sharp dark clouds with steely white edges began bowling over the sky and their passing made the whole landscape anxious and taut. Frank went out riding with Angela; the wind, coming up and up, whistled among the willows; the dykes cut the country up with uneasy gleams. The grass was still fawn-coloured; only their own restlessness told them that it was spring. It *was* quiet round here. They jogged tamely along, and Angela said she saw no reason why things should ever happen, and yet they did. She wished they saw more of life. Even Miss Fox in the house was *something*, she said, something to talk about, something going on. 'And of course I do need those clothes. But when we *are* all dressed up, I don't know where we're to go. Oh hell, Frank. I mean, really.' She rode hatless, the wind stung her cheeks pink: Frank bitterly thought that she looked like some Academy picture about the Morning of Life.

'Do you think Arthur'll marry that girl?'

'I daresay he'll try,' said Frank.

'Oh, come. You know, Frank, our Arthur's a big success . . . It's terrible how we wonder about Miss Fox. Do you think we are getting prurient minds? But the idea's fantastic.'

'Fantastic,' Frank agreed, feeling his own despondency ironed into him. Angela shot off and galloped across the field.

That night, in a wind direct from the Ural mountains, the house began to creak and strain like a ship. The family sat downstairs with as few lights on as possible. It was Angela who slipped up to talk to Miss Fox. The handsome work-basket was present but hasped shut, and Angela, honourably, turned her eyes from it. She really did want to talk. She sat on the rug by the grate; the wind puffed down the chimney occasional gusts of smoke that made her eyes smart. Miss Fox sat at the table, puffing away at a cigarette with precision. Perhaps she was glad of company. Nothing showed she was not. Her head, sculptured by shadows, was one of the finest heads that Angela had ever seen.

'You must see a lot of funny things, going from house to house.'

'Well yes, I do. I do see some funny things.'

'Of course, so do hospital nurses. But people must be much funnier trying on clothes. And some families are mares' nests. I wish you'd tell me . . . '

'Oh well, that would hardly do.'

'You know nurses aren't discreet . . . My brother Frank thinks you're a witch.'

'Gentlemen will have their fun,' said Miss Fox, with an odd inflection, as though she were quoting. Meeting Angela's eye, she smiled her held-in, rigid smile. Angela thought with impatience of gentlemen's fun that they must have – and, in this connection, of Arthur, who had his share. She heard the wind gnaw at the corners of this great tomb of a house that he wouldn't let them give up.

'It's all right for Arthur,' she said.

'Those photographs in the drawing-room – they are all your Mr Arthur?'

'Of course,' said Angela crossly.

'Miss Toddy favours him, doesn't she?'

Angela hugged her knees and Miss Fox got no answer to this. So the sewing-woman reached out her cold hand across the table, shook out of the packet and lit with precision another thin cigarette. Then: 'I've seen Mr Arthur,' she said.

'Oh yes, I've seen Mr Arthur. He was staying one time in a lady's house where I worked. There were several young gentlemen there, and I wasn't, of course, in the way of hearing their names. They were a big party, ever so gay and high-spirited, dodging all over the house, they used to be, every night, and in and out of my workroom, playing some game. I used to be sitting alone, like I sit here, and they used to stop for a word as they went through, or sometimes get me to hide them. Pleasant, they all were. But I never did catch any names. Mr Arthur took a particular fancy to one of my dummies, and asked me to lend it him to dress up for some game. I should have known better; I ought to have known my place.

'But it was eight years ago. The last night, I let him take the dummy away. They did laugh, I heard. But there was an accident and Mr Arthur let it drop on the stairs. The pedestal broke and some of the skirt-wires bent. He came back, later, to tell me how sorry he was. He *was* sorry, too. He said he'd make it all right. But he went off next day, and I suppose something happened to put it out of his head. My lady was not at all pleased, as she had had the dummy made to her own figure, and her figure was difficult. I didn't work there again.'

'How like him!' exclaimed his sister, savagely reclasping her hands round her knees.

Miss Fox, immensely collected, let out a cloud of smoke. 'He meant no harm,' she said stonily.

Frank came upstairs in the dark, feeling his way by the handrail and calling, 'Angela?' It gave him the creeps when anyone disappeared. And downstairs Toddy was fumbling on the piano. 'Here,' called Angela. Frank knocked once, and came in. 'You look very snug,' he said, rather resentfully. This room's being inhabited gave the house a new focus. Soon they would all be up here. He came and stood by the fire and watched his sister rocking and hugging her knees. He saw by her face that he had cut in on a talk. His own superfluity bit him.

'Miss Fox once knew Arthur, Frank.'

'A ladder's run right down your stocking,' said Frank with angry irrelevance.

'Damn,' said Angela vaguely.

'Best catch it up,' said Miss Fox.

She looked from Frank to Angela. There was a pause. Then, in the most businesslike way, she put down her cigarette, opened her work-basket, glanced at Angela's stocking and, matching it with her eye, drew a strand from a mixed plait of darning silks. Then she took out the big black needlecase. 'Mr Frank . . . ' she said. He went over and, taking the case, brought it across to Angela. She knelt upon the hearthrug; he rested a hand on her shoulder and felt the shoulder go stiff. 'What a lot of needles,' she said mechanically. She and Frank both stared at the photograph of the child. They saw, as Toddy had seen, its curls and its collar. Like Arthur's collar and curls in old photographs downstairs. And between the collar and curls, Arthur's face stared back again at the uncle and aunt.

'I should take a number five needle,' said Miss Fox calmly.

'I have,' said Angela, closing the needlecase.

'Ladders down stockings break one's heart,' said Miss Fox.

The Apple Tree

'FRIGHTENED?' exclaimed Lancelot. 'Of her? Oh, nonsense – surely? She's an absolute child.'

'But *that's* what I mean,' said Mrs Bettersley, glancing queerly sideways at him over the collar of her fur coat. He still did not know what she meant, and did not think she knew either.

In a rather nerve-racking combination of wind and moonlight Simon Wing's week-end party picked its way back to his house, by twos and threes, up a cinder-path from the village. Simon, who entered with gusto into his new role of squire, had insisted that they should attend the Saturday concert in the village memorial hall, a raftered, charmless and icy building endowed by himself and only recently opened. Here, with numbing feet and spines creeping, they had occupied seven front seats, under a thin but constant spate of recitation, pianoforte duet and part-song, while upon them from all quarters draughts directed themselves like arrows. To restore circulation they had applauded vigorously, too often precipitating an encore. Simon, satisfied with his friends, with his evening, leant forward to beam down the row. He said this would please the village. Lancelot communicated to Mrs Bettersley a dark suspicion: this was really why Simon had asked them down.

'So I'm afraid,' she replied. 'And for church tomorrow.'

All the same, it had warmed them all to see Simon happy. Mounting the platform to propose a vote of thanks to the Vicar, the great ruddy man had positively expanded and glowed; a till now too palpable cloud rolled away from him. It was this recognition by his old friends of the old Simon – a recognition so instantaneous, poignant and cheerful that it was like a handshake, a first greeting – that now sent the party so cheerfully home in its two and threes, their host boisterously ahead. At the tail, lagging, Lancelot and Mrs Bettersley fell into a discussion of Simon (his marriage, his *ménage*, his whole aspect) marked by entire unrestraint; as though between these two also some shadow had dissipated. They were old friendly enemies.

'But a child — ' resumed Lancelot.

'Naturally I didn't mean to suggest that she was a werewolf!'

'You think she *is* what's the matter?'

'Obviously there's nothing funny about the *house.*'

Obviously there was nothing funny about the house. Under the eerie cold sky, pale but not bright with moonlight, among bare windshaken trees, the house's bulk loomed, honourably substantial. Lit-up windows sustained the party with promise of indoor comfort: firelight on decanters, room after room heavy-curtained, Simon's feeling for home made concrete (at last, after wandering years) in deep leather chairs, padded fenders, and sectional bookshelves, 'domes of silence' on yielding carpets: an unaspiring, comfortable sobriety.

'She does seem to me only half there,' confessed Lancelot. 'Not, of course, I mean mentally, but — '

'She had that frightful time – don't you know? *Don't* you know?' Mrs Bettersley brightened, approaching her lips to his ear in the moonlight. 'She was at that school – don't you remember? After all *that*, the school broke up, you know. She was sent straight abroad – she'd have been twelve at the time, I dare say; in a pretty state, I've no doubt, poor child! – to an aunt and uncle at Cannes. Her only relations; they lived out there in a villa, never came home – she stayed abroad with them. It was there Simon met her; then – all this.'

'School?' said Lancelot, stuttering with excitement. 'What – were they ill-treated?'

'Heavens, not that,' exclaimed Mrs Bettersley; 'worse — '

But just at this point – it was unbearable – they saw the party pull up and contract ahead. Simon was waiting to shepherd them through the gate, then lock the gate after them.

'I hope,' he said, beaming, as they came up, 'you weren't too bored?'

They could not fail to respond.

'It's been a marvellous evening,' said Mrs Bettersley; Lancelot adding, 'What wonderful talent you've got round here.'

'I don't think we're bad for a village,' said Simon modestly, clicking the gate to. 'The Choral Society are as keen as mustard. And I always think that young Dickinson ought to go on the stage. I'd pay to see him anywhere.'

'Oh, so would I,' agreed Lancelot cordially. 'It's too sad,' he added, 'your wife having missed all this.'

Simon's manner contracted. 'She went to the dress rehearsal,' he said quickly.

'Doesn't she act herself?'

'I can't get her to try . . . Well, here we are; here we are!' Simon shouted, stamping across the terrace.

Young Mrs Wing had been excused the concert. She had a slight chill, she feared. If she ever did cast any light on village society, it was tonight withheld. No doubt Simon was disappointed. His friends, filing after him through the French window into the library, all hoped that by now – it was half-past ten – young Mrs Simon might have taken her chill to bed.

But from the hearth her flat little voice said: 'Hullo!' There she stood, looking towards the window, watching their entrance as she had watched their exit. Her long silver sheath of a dress made her almost grown up. So they all prepared with philosophy to be nice to young Mrs Wing. They all felt this first week-end party, this incursion of old friends all so much knit up with each other, so much knit up round Simon, might well be trying for young Mrs Wing. In the nature even, possibly, of an ordeal. She was barely nineteen, and could not, to meet them, be expected to put up anything of 'a manner'. She had them, however, at a slight disadvantage, for Simon's marriage had been a shock for his friends. He had been known for years as a likely marrying man; so much so that his celibacy appeared an accident; but his choice of a wife – this mannerless, sexless child, the dim something between a mouse and an Undine, this wraith not considerable as a mother of sons, this cold little shadow across a hearth – had considerably surprised them. By her very passivity she attacked them when they were least prepared.

Mrs Wing, at a glance from her husband, raised a silver lid from some sandwiches with a gesture of invitation. Mrs Bettersley, whose appetite was frankly wolfish, took two, and, slipping out inch by inch from her fur coat, lined up beside her little hostess in the firelight, solid and brilliant. The others divided armchairs in the circle of warmth.

'Did you have a nice concert?' said Mrs Wing politely. No one could answer. 'It went off well on the whole,' said Simon gently, as though breaking sorrowful news to her.

Lancelot could not sleep. The very comfort of bed, the too exquisite sympathy with his body of springs and mattress, became oppressive. Wind had subsided; moonlight sketched a window upon his floor. The house was quiet, too quiet; with jealousy and nostalgia he pictured them all sleeping. Mrs Wing's cheek would scarcely warm a pillow. In despair Lancelot switched the light on; the amiable furniture stared. He read one page of *Our Mutual Friend* with distaste and decided to look downstairs for a detective story. He slept in a corridor branching off from the head of the main staircase.

Downstairs, the hall was dark, rank with cooling cigar-smoke. A clock struck three; Lancelot violently started. A little moon came in through the skylight; the library door was closed; stepping quietly, Lancelot made his way to it. He opened the door, saw red embers, then knew in a second the library was not empty. All the same, in there in the dark they were not moving or speaking.

Embarrassment – had he surprised an intrigue? – and abrupt physical fear – were these burglars? – held Lancelot bound on the threshold. Certainly someone in here was not alone; in here, in spite of the dark, someone was watching someone. He did not know whether to speak. He felt committed by opening the door, and, standing against the grey of the glass-roofed hall, must be certainly visible.

Finally it was Simon's voice that said defensively: 'Hullo?' Lancelot knew he must go away immediately. He had only one wish – to conceal his identity. But Simon apparently did not trust one; moving bulkily he came down the long room to the door, bumping, as though in a quite unfamiliar room, against the furniture, one arm stuck out ahead, as though pushing something aside or trying to part a curtain. He seemed to have no sense of space; Lancelot ducked, but a great hand touched his face. The hand was ice-cold.

'Oh, *you*?' said Simon. From his voice, his breath, he had been drinking heavily. He must still be holding a glass in his other hand – Lancelot heard whisky slopping about as the glass shook.

'It's all right,' said Lancelot; 'I was just going up. Sorry,' he added.

'You can't – come – in – here,' said Simon obstinately.

'No, I say: I was just going up.' Lancelot stopped; friendliness fought in him with an intense repulsion. Not that he minded – though this itself was odd: Simon hardly ever touched anything.

But the room was a trap, a *cul-de-sac*; Simon, his face less than a yard away, seemed to be speaking to him through bars. He was frightful in fear; a man with the humility of a beast; he gave off fear like some disagreeable animal smell, making Lancelot dislike and revolt at his own manhood, subject to such decay.

'Go away,' said Simon, pushing at him in the dark. Lancelot stepped back in alarm; a rug slipped under his foot; he staggered grasping at the jamb of the door. His elbow knocked a switch; immediately the hall, with its four powerful lamps, sprang into illumination. One was staggered by this explosion of light; Lancelot put his hands over his eyes; when he took them away he could see Simon's face was clammy, mottled; here and there a bead of sweat trembled and ran down. He was standing sideways, his shoulder against the door; past him a path of light ran into the library.

Mrs Simon stood just out of the light, looking fixedly up and pointing at something above her head. Round her Lancelot distinguished the big chairs, the table with the decanters, and faintly, the glazed bookcases. Her eyes, looking up, reflected the light but did not flicker; she did not stir. With an exclamation, a violent movement, Simon shut the library door. They both stood outside its white glossy panels. By contrast with what stood inside, staring there in the dark, Simon was once more human; unconsciously as much to gain as to impart reassurance, Lancelot put a hand on his arm.

Not looking at one another, they said nothing.

They were in no sense alone even here, for the slam of the door produced in a moment or two Mrs Bettersley, who looked down at them from the gallery over the zone of bright lights, her face sharpened and wolfish with vehement curiosity. Lancelot looked up; their eyes met.

'All right; only somebody sleep-walking,' he called up softly.

'All right,' she replied, withdrawing; but not, he guessed, to her room; rather to lean back in shadow against the wall of the gallery, impassive, watchful, arms folded over the breast of her dark silk kimono.

A moment later she still made no sign – he would have been glad of her presence, for the return to Simon of sensibility and intelligence, like circulation beginning again in a limb that had been tightly bound up, was too much for Simon. One side-glance that almost contained his horror, then – huge figure crumpling, swaying, sagging – he fainted suddenly. Lancelot broke his fall a little and propped him, sitting, against the wall.

This left Lancelot much alone. He noted details: a dog-collar lying unstrapped, ash trodden into a rug, a girl's gloves – probably Mrs Simon's – dropped crumpled into a big brass tray. Now drawn to the door – aware the whole time of his position's absurdity – he knelt, one ear to the keyhole. Silence. In there she must still stand in contemplation – horrified, horrifying – of something high up that from the not quite fixity of her gaze had seemed unfixed, pendent, perhaps swaying a little. Silence. Then – he pressed closer – a thud-thud-thud – three times, like apples falling.

This idea of apples entered his mind and remained, frightfully clear; an innocent pastoral image seen black through a dark transparency. This idea of fruit detaching itself and, from a leafy height, falling in the stale, shut-up room, had the sharpness of hallucination: he thought he was going mad.

'Come down,' he called up to the gallery.

Mrs Bettersley, with that expectant half-smile, appeared, looked over immediately, then came downstairs. Noting Simon's unconsciousness, for which she seemed to be grateful, she went to the library door. After a moment facing the panels she tried the handle, cautiously turning it.

'*She's* in there,' said Lancelot.

'Coming?' she asked.

He replied, 'No,' frankly and simply.

'Oh, well,' she shrugged; 'I'm a woman,' and entered the library, pushing the door to behind her. He heard her moving among the furniture. 'Now come,' she said. 'Come, my dear . . . ' After a moment or two of complete silence and stillness: 'Oh, my God, no – I can't!' she exclaimed. She came out again, very white. She was rubbing her hands together as though she had hurt them. 'It's impossible,' she repeated. 'One can't get past . . . it's like an apple tree.'

She knelt by Simon and began fumbling with his collar. Her hands shook. Lancelot watched the access of womanly busyness.

The door opened again and young Mrs Wing came out in her nightgown, hair hanging over her shoulders in two plaits, blinking under the strong light. Seeing them all, she paused in natural confusion.

'I walk in my sleep,' she murmured, blushed, and slipped past upstairs without a glance at her husband, still in confusion, like any young woman encountered by strangers in her nightgown; her appearance and disappearance the very picture of modest precipitancy.

Simon began to come to. Mrs Bettersley also retreated. The fewest possible people ought, they felt, to be in on this.

Sunday morning was milky-blue, mild and sunny. Mrs Bettersley appeared punctually for breakfast, beaming, pink, and impassible. Lancelot looked pale and puffy; Mrs Simon did not appear. Simon came in like a tempered Boreas to greet the party, rubbing his hands. After breakfast they stepped out through the window to smoke on the terrace. Church, said Simon pressingly, would be at eleven.

Mrs Bettersley revolted. She said she liked to write letters on Sunday morning. The rest, with a glance of regret at the shining November garden, went off like lambs. When they had gone, she slipped upstairs and tapped on Mrs Simon's door.

The young woman was lying comfortably enough, with a fire burning, a mild novel open face down on the counterpane. This pretty bride's room, pink and white, frilled and rosy, now full of church bells and winter sunshine, had for Mrs Bettersley, in all its appointments, an air of anxious imitation and of approximation to some idea of the grown-up. Simon's bed was made and the room in order.

'You don't mind?' said Mrs Bettersley, having sat down firmly. Mrs Simon said, nervously, she was so pleased.

'All right this morning?'

'Just a little chill, I think.'

'And no wonder! Do you often walk in your sleep?'

Mrs Simon's small face tightened, hardened, went a shade whiter among the pillows. 'I don't know,' she said. Her manner became a positive invitation to Mrs Bettersley to go away. Flattening among the bedclothes, she tried hard to obliterate herself.

Her visitor, who had not much time – for the bells had stopped; they would be back again in an hour – was quite merciless. 'How old were you,' she said, 'when *that* happened?'

'Twelve – please don't — '

'You never told anyone?'

'No – please, Mrs Bettersley – please not now. I feel so ill.'

'You're making Simon ill.'

'Do you think I don't know!' the child exclaimed. 'I thought he'd save me. I didn't think he'd ever be frightened. I didn't know any power could . . . Indeed, indeed, Mrs Bettersley, I had no idea . . . I felt so safe with him. I thought this would go away. Now when it comes it is twice as horrible. Do you think it is killing him?'

'I shouldn't wonder,' said Mrs Bettersley.

'Oh, oh,' moaned Mrs Wing, and, with wrists crossed over her face, shook all over, sobbing so that the bed-head rattled against the wall. 'He was so sorry for me,' she moaned; 'it was more than I could resist. He was so sorry for me. Wouldn't *you* feel Simon might save you?'

Mrs Bettersley, moving to the edge of the bed, caught the girl's wrists and firmly but not untenderly forced them apart, disclosing the small convulsed face and staring eyes. 'We've got three-quarters of an hour alone,' she said. 'You've got to tell me. Make it come into words. When it's once out it won't hurt any more – like a tooth, you know. Talk about it like anything. Talk to Simon. You never have, have you? You never do?'

Mrs Bettersley felt quite a brute, she told Lancelot later. She had, naturally, in taking this hard line, something to go on. Seven years ago, newspapers had been full of the Crampton Park School tragedy: a little girl's suicide. There had been some remarkable headlines, some details, profuse speculation. Influence from some direction having been brought to bear, the affair disappeared from the papers abruptly. Some suggestion of things having been 'hushed up' gave the affair, in talk, a fresh cruel prominence; it became a topic. One hinted at all sorts of scandal. The school broke up; the staff disappeared, discredited; the fine house and grounds, in the West Country, were sold at a loss. One pupil, Myra Conway, felt the shock with surprising keenness. She nearly died of brain fever; collapsing the day after the suicide, she remained at death's door for weeks, alone with her nurses in the horrified house, Crampton Park. All the other children were hurried away. One heard afterwards that her health, her nerves, had been ruined. The other children, presumably, rallied; one heard no more of them. Myra Conway became Myra Wing. So much they all knew, even Simon.

Myra Wing now lay on her side in bed, in her pink bedroom, eyes shut, cheek pressed to the pillow as though she were sleeping, but with her body rigid; gripping with both hands Mrs Bettersley's arm. She spoke slowly, choosing her words with diffidence as though hampered by trying to speak an unfamiliar language.

'I went there when I was ten. I don't think it can ever have been a very good school. They called it a home school, I suppose because most of us stayed for the holidays – we had no parents – and none of us was over fourteen. From being there so much, we began to feel that this was the world. There was a very high wall round the garden. I don't think they were unkind to us, but everything seemed to go wrong. Doria and I were always in trouble. I suppose that was why we knew each other. There were about eighteen other girls, but none of them liked us. We used to feel we had some disease – so much so, that we were sometimes ashamed to meet each other: sometimes we did not like to be together. I don't think we knew we were unhappy; we never spoke of that; we should have felt ashamed. We used to pretend we were all right; we got in a way to be quite proud of ourselves, of being different. I think, though, we made each other worse. In those days I was very ugly. Doria was as bad; she was very queer-looking; her eyes goggled and she wore big round glasses. I suppose if we had had parents it would have been different. As it was, it was impossible to believe anyone could ever care for either of us. We did not even care for each other; we were just like two patients in hospital, shut away from the others together because of having some frightful disease. But I suppose we depended on one another.

'The other children were mostly younger. The house was very large and dark-looking, but full of pictures to make it look homely. The grounds were very large, full of trees and laurels. When I was twelve, I felt if this was the world I could not bear it. When I was twelve I got measles: another girl of my age got the measles, too, and we were sent to a cottage to get well. She was very pretty and clever; we made friends; she told me she did not mind me but she could not bear Doria. When we both got well and went back to the others, I loved her so much I felt I could not bear to part from her. She had a home of her own; she was very happy and gay; to know her and hear about her life was like heaven. I took great trouble to please her; we went on being friends. The others began to like me; I ran away from Doria. Doria was left alone. She seemed to be all that was horrible in my life; from the moment we parted things began to go right with me. I laughed at her with the others.

'The only happy part of Doria's life and mine in the bad days had been the games we played and the stories we told in a lonely part of the garden, a slope of lawn with one beautiful old apple tree. Sometimes we used to climb up in the branches. Nobody else ever came there; it was like something of our own; to be there made us feel happy and dignified.

'Doria was miserable when I left her. She never wept; she used to walk about by herself. It was as though everything I had got free of had fallen on her, too: she was left with my wretchedness. When I was with the others I used to see her, always alone, watching me. One afternoon she made me come with her to the apple tree; I was sorry for her and went; when we got there I could not bear it. I was so frightened of being lost again; I said terrible things to her. I wished she was dead. You see, there seemed to be no other world outside the school.

'She and I still slept in the same room, with two others. That night – there was some moon – I saw her get up. She tied the cord of her dressing-gown – it was very thick – round her waist tightly; she looked once at me, but I pretended to be asleep. She went out and did not come back. I lay – there was only a little moon – with a terrible feeling, like something tight round my throat. At last I went down to look for her. A glass door to the garden was open. I went out to look for her. She had hanged herself, you know, in the apple tree. When I first got there I saw nothing. I looked round and called her, and shook the branches, but only – it was September – two or three apples fell down. The leaves kept brushing against my face. Then I saw her. Her feet were just over my head. I parted the branches to look – there was just enough moon – the leaves brushed my face. I crept back into bed and waited. No one knew; no steps came. Next morning, of course, they did not tell us anything. They said she was ill. I pretended to know no better. I could not think of anything but the apple tree.

'While I was ill – I was very ill – I thought the leaves would choke me. Whenever I moved in bed an apple fell down. All the other girls were taken away. When I got well, I found the house was empty. The first day I could, I crept out alone to look for the real apple tree. "It is only a tree," I thought; "if I could see it, I should be quite well." But the tree had been cut down. The place where it grew was filled with new turf. The nurse swore to me there had never been an apple tree there at all. She did not know – no one ever knew – I had been out that night and seen Doria.

'I expect you can guess the rest – you were there last night. You see, I am haunted. It does not matter where I am, or who I am with. Though I am married now, it is just the same. Every now and then – I don't know yet when or what brings it about – I wake to see Doria get up and tie the cord round her waist and go out. I have to go after her; there is always the apple tree. Its roots are in me. It takes all my strength, and now it's beginning to take Simon's.

'Those nights, no one can bear to be with me. Everyone who has been with me knows, but no one will speak of it. Only Simon tries to be there those times – you saw, last night. It is impossible to be with me; I make rooms impossible. I am not like a house that can be burnt, you see, or pulled down. You know how it is – I heard you in there last night, trying to come to me — '

'I won't fail again: I've never been more ashamed,' said Mrs Bettersley.

'If I stay up here the tree grows in the room; I feel it will choke Simon. If I go out, I find it darker than all the others against the sky . . . This morning I have been trying to make up my mind; I must go; I must leave Simon. I see quite well this is destroying him. Seeing him with you all makes me see how he used to be, how he might have been. You see, it's hard to go. He's my life. Between all this . . . we're so happy. But make me do this, Mrs Bettersley!'

'I'll make you do one thing. Come away with me – perhaps for only a month. My dear, if I can't do this, after last night, *I'm* ruined,' exclaimed Mrs Bettersley.

The passion of vanity has its own depths in the spirit, and is powerfully militant. Mrs Bettersley, determined to vindicate herself, disappeared for some weeks with the haunted girl. Lancelot, meanwhile, kept Simon company. From the ordeal their friend emerged about Christmas, possibly a little harder and brighter. If she had fought, there was not a hair displaced. She did not mention, even to Lancelot, by what arts, night and day, by what cynical vigilance, she had succeeded in exorcizing the apple tree. The victory aged her, but left her as disengaged as usual. Mrs Wing was returned to her husband. As one would expect, from then on less and less was seen of the couple. They disappeared into happiness: a sublime nonentity.

Reduced

THE Carbury's two little girls, Penny and Claudia, went upstairs again with their governess, Miss Rice, as soon as lunch was over; their steps could be heard retreating along the pitch-pine gallery round the hall. The visitors were disappointed – Mrs Laurie liked children and Frank Peele had been hoping to see more of the governess. Rain drummed on the hall skylight; still smoking their host Godwin Carbury's rather musty cigarettes, the grown-ups allowed themselves to be driven into the library. Here no chair invited you, the uninviting books must have been bought in lots, and looked gummed in the shelves. It could have been a pretty September day; the plum tree leaves in the tilting orchards round were bright yellow, but for days the Forest of Dene had been clouded and sodden.

Mrs Laurie, who was vivacious and had married at nineteen, and Mrs Carbury, who was muddled and dim, had been friends years ago in India when they were both young girls. They had kept in touch, Mrs Carbury having no other vivacious friend, life having taught Mrs Laurie that there was no knowing when anybody devoted might not come in useful – besides, she had always been sorry for Mima.

Mima's life had been unrewarding. She returned flatly from India after her friend's wedding, and it had not been till she was twenty-seven or eight that she met Godwin Carbury, who at forty was looking round for a wife. He had the reputation of being the most unpopular man in his part of the country, and that reputation followed him up to London. He was careful, savagely careful, about money and not careful enough about seeing this was not known. Added to this, he had a dour self-importance. It was understood that economy kept him single as long as his mother had lived to keep house at Pendlethwaite. Possibly Mima saw something in him that no one else saw; she was anxious to 'settle' suitably, and not herself accustomed to being liked. At all events, they married, and had had after some years these two thin, remote little girls. They had few neighbours at Pendlethwaite and Godwin's peculiarities cut them off more and more from anybody there was.

Whatever misgivings she had, Mima pandered to him blindly. On her own account she had just a little money, so once or twice a year she came up to London, gazed into shop windows, met Mrs Laurie (now widowed) and bought reduced coats and shoes for the little girls. She had begun lately to talk of giving up London; the girls' education would be a heavy expense, she said.

It surprised Mrs Laurie to find herself at Pendlethwaite, but she had been at a loose end, with nowhere to go for a week. So she thought, 'Try the Carburys', and had written to Mima. She was a shiftless woman, maintaining herself by the exercize of a good deal of charm: she could say daring things without sounding impertinent, and determined to get a little fun out of Godwin – apart from this, she did not expect very much.

Pendlethwaite was not a lovable house. Built about 1880 of unpleasing maroon brick, it creaked inside with pitch-pine; its church-like windows peered narrowly at the smiling landscape round; its grounds darkened a valley with belts of laurel and stiff, damp-looking clumps of unindigenous firs. The house looked dedicated to a perpetual January: sunnier seasons beat back from its walls. The bloomy red plums and mellow apples bending the boughs this month were pagan company for it. Indoors, there was no electricity; panels absorbed the lamplight; before October, no fires were lit till night. It had not even the insidious charm of decay, for Godwin had great ideas of keeping things up: the laurels were kept clipped, the thrifty meals served formally . . . Mrs Laurie had been diverted to find that she had a fellow guest, but this did not see her far. Frank Peele, just back on leave from Siam, was Mima's second cousin. He must have asked himself here because he had to be somewhere; she thought he was not a man you would scramble to entertain. At about thirty, he was a haggard schoolboy – shambling, facetious, huffy, forlorn, melancholic, with perhaps (she feared most of all) a romantic soul. She supposed Mima must enjoy being even sorrier for him than she need be for herself . . . Entertaining on this scale must be a plunge for the Carburys. Mrs Laurie could almost hear Godwin saying to Mima: 'Well then, in for a penny, in for a pound.' He went through with his duties as host with glum correctness. 'But if one stayed a day too long he'd cut off supplies.' As it was, his rigid economies hit you everywhere.

The one startling un-economy was the governess. Mrs Laurie, though unhappily childless, knew an expensive governess when she saw one. Miss Rice's technique was perfect. Her first appearance, at lunch, took Nella's breath away with its unobtrusiveness. Penny and Claudia – their dark eyes set close in, tucking their long, fair hair back behind their shoulders primly – clearly revolved round her. 'Those two little mice adore her,' thought Mrs Laurie, recalling the composed retreat after lunch: three people going back to a world of their own. But the adoration was kept within nice bounds. 'How does Mima *keep* the woman in this mausoleum? She might be anywhere. Mima can't be such a fool as I thought . . . I must find out.'

In the library, she lost no time in doing this. In the bow window, Frank Peele with his hands in his pockets stood looking out unexpectantly at the rain; Mima poured out thin coffee; Godwin glumly handed the cups round. Mrs Laurie said affably: 'So you got a governess? Last time we met, you were busy looking for one.'

'Yes, oh yes. We did,' Mima said in her flustered way.

'Miss Rice came in May,' said Godwin firmly.

'She seems a great success . . . '

Frank Peele grunted.

'When she first came in,' went on Mrs Laurie, 'I felt certain I'd seen her somewhere. I wonder where she was before? She's startlingly good-looking, but in such a tactful way. Hag-ridden – but that's the life, I suppose.'

'She appears content with us,' said Godwin, handing the sugar to Mrs Laurie bitterly. 'Mima, what are your plans for this afternoon?' His wife looked blank.

'Our guests should be entertained.'

'It struck me,' said Frank, wheeling round, 'as one of the few faces I had not seen before.'

'Really?' said Godwin.

Mima touched the coffee-tray clumsily; everything on it skidded. Did she not want Cousin Frank to fall for the governess? The nicest women like having unattached men around. 'She must be full of brains,' said Mrs Laurie vaguely.

'She teaches wonderfully; she's got the children on so. They seem to be learning everything.'

'Can we have them all down after tea to play Up Jenkin or something?'

'They do preparation then,' said Godwin repressively. ('Set,' thought his guest, 'on getting his money's worth.') Mima's eyes, oddly overwrought in her pink, creased face, stole to meet her husband's. 'Frank,' Godwin continued, 'I could show you those maps now.' Clearly, any discussion of Miss Rice was closed.

'Not today, thanks,' said Frank, 'I've got a crick in my neck.' Godwin, after one more forbidding look at Mima, left them, shutting the door reprovingly. Frank loafed along the bookshelves, pulled out *Monasteries of the Levant*, and folded himself in a chair with an air of resigned discomfort. A man with a book is practically not present. Mrs Laurie whipped out her *petit point*, and the two women, pulling their chairs together zestfully, settled down for a talk. Rain streamed down the windows, paper rustled inside the cold grate.

Mima saw so few friends that talk went to her head like wine. Evenly sing-song, the women's voices began rising and falling. After half an hour, Frank's book slipped on to his knee; his head rolled back, jaw dropping; he let out a sharp snore. 'Really . . .' exclaimed Mima, stopping the talk to titter. 'A tropical habit,' said Mrs Laurie. This was better than Frank with a book, they were quite alone. She hopped back to her topic.

'Mima, what's Godwin got up his sleeve about Miss Rice?'

'Miss Rice? – nothing,' Mima said, over-acting.

'His one wicked extravagance?'

'No,' faltered Mima. 'That's just the point – she's not.'

'A bargain? You amaze me. Can she be at all fishy?'

'My dear Nella – she's good with the children, isn't she?' Mima fixed her friend with such oddly imploring eyes that Mrs Laurie, startled, put down her work: 'She's made princesses of them,' she said extravagantly. 'How wise you have been, Mima!'

'You do really think so? Godwin and I wanted the best we could get, you see: he has such ideas for Penny and Claudia.'

'It does him credit,' said Mrs Laurie warmly.

'I suppose so — ' blurted out Mima – then, looking wretched, put her hand to her cheek. 'I've never quite liked – I mean if she – I can't help wondering — '

'Why did Godwin snap me up when I said I thought I knew her face?'

'We'd hoped no one would think that,' said Mima surprisingly. 'As a rule, you see, almost nobody comes here, and in every other way she seemed quite ideal: she is. In the ordinary way, we never could have afforded her. It did seem such an opportunity. You see, we could not offer a high salary.'

'That would narrow things down . . .'

'It did. All the ones I had interviewed were so vulgar and pushing, besides seeming to know nothing at all. The agency woman said, "For that, what can you expect?" I was in despair.'

'Oh? So then — ?'

'I came round more and more to Godwin's idea. As he said, it was practically a charity. It did seem unfair that the thing should count against her. When she had paid for her defence she hadn't a penny, and no other future, of course. And she was acquitted.'

'What on earth do you mean?'

Looking thoroughly frightened, Mima caught herself up. 'Oh dear, she said, 'and I swore never to speak of it. Nella, will you swear to let this go no further? It's such a relief to tell you: it's on my mind the whole time. You see, Godwin had followed all the evidence carefully. The witnesses gave her such magnificent testimonials, almost all her former employers were called. Even the Prosecution didn't make out she wasn't a good *governess*. And after all, she was cleared. (If only they'd found who'd done it . . .)'

'Begin at the beginning.'

'Well . . . Do you ever read murder trials?'

'Hardly ever miss one.'

'Do you remember that Sir Max Rant dying suddenly?'

'Mima – she's not *Henrietta Post*?'

'Sssh – sssh,' whispered Mima, glancing Frank's way cautiously. Then she nodded at Nella with frightened, important eyes.

Mrs Laurie stared, galvanized, at her hostess. Then: 'She's lucky to be alive,' she said. 'It was touch and go.'

'He was a dreadful old man, apparently. At the very worst, they said nothing against her *morals*.'

'No wonder she's haunted-looking. That was an appalling ordeal . . . But, after that, how on earth — ?'

'Godwin got me to write to her three weeks after the trial, offering her a new life and twenty-five pounds a year . . . '

'Godwin is on the spot! Well, they're your children, not mine – *Henrietta Post!*'

Immovably, without batting a closed eyelid, Frank said, 'Who is Henrietta Post?'

'Miss Rice's hands are cold again,' said Penny.

Claudia went on painting a moment longer, then, balancing her brush on the glass jar of paint-water, which gave out a prussic smell and had a red sediment, looked intently across the table at Penny, who stood by Miss Rice's chair, chafing her right hand. Their governess, with her book propped on the table, her pale cheek on her left hand, read on, smiling unnoticingly. Once she withdrew her hand from Penny's to turn over a page.

'Whatever will she do in winter?' said Claudia.

'There'll be fires then.'

'This fire never burns much.' They shared the same desperate thought: 'Suppose our darling should leave us?'

This afternoon, the black chill of the grate focused your fancy as firelight might have done. The schoolroom had a faded sea-blue wallpaper cut into by pitch-pine presses and two doors: not a colour warmed it; the high windows looked into a rain-blurred hill. Miss Rice had put nothing of her own on the mantelpiece, along which marched a file of plasticine animals modelled by the little girls. About the room were products of other hobbies good governesses encourage children to have – on the windowsill a nursery-garden in pots: pink-cheeked 'Bubbles' and 'Cherry Ripe' looked queerly down at the bleak room where these three people were living as best they could.

Miss Rice put away the book and with it her happy, forgetful smile – the book had been *Emma*. 'Have you stopped painting?' she said.

She had given them for their subject a Greek temple. Claudia's temple had a sunset behind it, Penny had filled in the columns with Mediterranean blue. Miss Rice came round and looked. 'A sunset like that would make reflections on white stone, Claudia. Penny, on such a fine day there would be shadows.' They saw. She always thought of something they had not thought of: they wrinkled up their foreheads in ecstatic despair. 'Penny, if you are stopping, wash that blue off your paint-brush.'

'Are paints poison?'

'Sometimes. Well, are you cold, too?'

They would admit nothing that could distress her.

'Then push the table back and get the skipping-ropes out.'

The little girls were alike, though there were two years between them, as though they could not decide to part in any particular. There was not much difference in size, as though Penny had waited for Claudia. Their voices were pitched on the same persuasive note; when their vehement dark eyes met they seemed to consult. What they thought of being alive their parents would never know; their characters were like batteries storing something up. Before Miss Rice was here, the doctor's sister had come in every morning to give them lessons. They had known before how to read and write, so all they had learnt from the doctor's sister was what everyone else knew: just why their house was avoided, how bitterly father was laughed at and mother pitied because of him. They learnt that it was wretched to be themselves. They marked the contempt with which every morning she bicycled up their avenue, and how insolently she ate what there was at lunch. Her raspy finger-tips, the pearls screwed tight in her fleshy ears, her horse-sense, all seemed part of her power to mortify them. She was the world and they prayed she might die, but she married. After that they waited, in armour. Then came Miss Rice.

'If you want to keep warm you must hurry,' said Miss Rice.

Claudia unwound the skipping-ropes and they took one each: they stood with their arms out, gripping the handles eagerly. 'One, two, three – go!' The ropes zip-zipped on the oilcloth. Penny stumbled at fifty-six, but Claudia kept in and skipped seventy-eight: her toes bounced and bounced, her hair flopped, her eyes started out of her head. At last the rope caught her toe. 'That's the record,' said Miss Rice, 'but Penny may beat it next time.' Both breathless they knelt on the hearthrug, life tingling up through them from their toes to their cheeks.

'If you skipped,' said Claudia, 'you might skip a hundred.'

'The rope is too short,' said Miss Rice.

'What else used you to do – dance?'

'Yes, once.'

They had never seen anyone dancing except in pictures of ballrooms; they preferred to imagine Miss Rice not on the crook of an arm but floating alone around a floor, with her ageless, shining white face, unfrivolous as an angel. At this happy moment, near her and warm from skipping, they felt on the edge of the story she did not tell . . . But *she* looked down at the skipping-ropes on the floor. 'Better put those away,' she said. Except when she was reading she never stayed quiet long: something they could feel creep up behind her chair would make her speaking eyes go suddenly cold and dark as the grate. Against this their love was powerless. This dreadful expectation seemed wrong in their darling – mother without her worries would not be anyone, father was there to stare and bite his moustache, but she seemed to them born to inherit light . . . Feeling their enemy here now the children, helpless, got up to put the skipping-ropes back in the press.

'Someone's coming!' said Penny. They heard the baize door at the far end of their passage swing to behind somebody, then a man's step. A knuckle rapped the door once, unconfidently: Miss Rice and the children waited. 'Come in,' she said.

Frank Peele peered round the door. 'Oh?' he said. 'May I come in? Sorry, I was exploring. Looking for secret passages. Exercise before tea.' Miss Rice smiled composedly. 'So here you all are,' he went on. He looked at the table. 'Painting?'

'Yes.'

'What a day!' he said to Miss Rice humbly. 'Very cheery up here, though. You believe in fresh air?' Then he saw that both windows were bolted: what he felt were the draughts. Miss Rice had moved to the table where she had been reading; Frank dropped into the wicker chair with a creak. The children shut their paint-boxes up. 'Must be getting on tea time,' remarked Frank.

'Are you hungry, Cousin Frank?' said Claudia gently.

Frank looked relieved at hearing someone say something. 'I don't deserve tea; I slept like a log in the library. Your mother and Mrs Laurie complain I snored.' He looked round the schoolroom wistfully, like a dog. 'They were talking nineteen to the dozen. When I dropped off they were well away about India; when I came to it was one Henrietta Post.'

Penny laughed. 'Who's Henrietta Post?' she said.

'Don't ask me,' said Frank. 'Miss Rice, who's Henrietta Post?'

Miss Rice pondered while the clock ticked several seconds and a cart rattled off into silence behind the wet orchards. The children turned to see how she took Frank's joke. She looked twice at him with steady, considering dark eyes. 'Surely you know?' she said at last.

'I don't know a soul,' said Frank, 'I've been in Siam.'

'But you get the papers there, don't you?'

'She's a celebrity, is she?'

'She was accused of murder,' said Miss Rice, as though giving a history lesson, 'tried last spring, acquitted, but never properly cleared. So she disappeared, hoping to be forgotten.'

'Good God,' exclaimed Frank. 'Where would a woman go to, after a show like that?'

'She is fortunate to be anywhere.'

'Stop: it's coming back!' Frank said, delighted to have a topic. 'Wasn't she that governess? The old swine whose house she was in had been making up to her, so when someone did him in they tried to fix it on her. I remember I thought at the time — '

Miss Rice's marked unresponse reminded Frank where he was. Chidden, he stopped awkwardly, with a glance at the children. *They* sat stone-still, clasped hands thrust down between their knees; you could not possibly tell what was going on in their heads, which were both turned intently away from their governess. Frank kicked himself. But for the life of him he couldn't stop blurting out: 'She was very good-looking, wasn't she?'

'You never saw any photographs?'

'Out where I am I only get *The Times*, you see. No pretty pictures in it.'

'I see.'

Frank went on violently: 'I know I thought at the time what a shocking, unfair thing to happen to any woman!' . . . Miss Rice with her cold smile looked thoughtfully into the grate as though there were a fire burning there: she said nothing more. Her charges' agonized tension became startling. Frank hummed and beat a nonplussed tattoo on his knee. They were waiting to see the last of him. Whatever brick one had dropped, they were all very odd up here . . .

This wet autumn evening closed in so early that the children had to stop work and wait for the lamp to come; when Mrs Carbury looked in they were all in the dark. 'Why, whatever are you doing?' she said nervously. 'Where's Miss Rice? Why doesn't she ring for the lamp?'

'It never comes any sooner.'

'Father wouldn't like you wasting your time like this. Where is Miss Rice?'

'In her room,' Penny said, so indifferently that there seemed to be something foolish about the fuss. At this point a band of light appeared in the passage; the housemaid brought in the lamp and Mima saw her daughters facing each other like images across the table of lesson books, their unchildish eyes dark in the sudden lamplight. She sat down, acting calm while the housemaid was in the room; all the same, her manner made the girl so jumpy that she went away again without drawing down the blinds. Mrs Carbury sat eyeing the other door; the children's bedroom opened off the schoolroom and Miss Rice's room was beyond, connecting with theirs. Her relief at not finding the governess was tremendous: all the same, she felt she was being defied.

'Does she always leave you to do preparation alone?'

'She's tired,' said Claudia. 'Cousin Frank was up here.'

'Oh? . . . Well, tell her I want to speak to her. Then you can leave your lessons, just for this evening, and go downstairs; Mrs Laurie says she will play games with you.'

The children looked at their books without stirring, and Mima for the first time felt mutiny in the air . . . Mima had had to brace herself to come in; twice already since tea she had started up to the schoolroom, then turned back before the baize door to that wing. Ever since her revelation to Mrs Laurie she had been in a fearful state: the way Mrs Laurie took it brought her own most persistent throttling fears to the top: 'Henrietta Post . . . Well, they're your children, not mine.' What Nella said was what anybody who knew would say. Mima had shrunk back from the schoolroom door, feeling: 'No, I really cannot face her.' Then she had been forced to think: 'But that is the woman my children are with the whole time . . . ' Once she had gone as far as Godwin's study to tell him he must agree to send Miss Rice away tomorrow, but the way he had looked up at her settled that. 'Nothing has changed since I agreed to engage her.' Mima knew too well that her husband found her a fool. 'I will give her notice first, then tell Godwin. It won't be so bad with Nella in the house here. Nella will back me up. *But when Godwin hears I've told Nella?* . . . He said before she came to stay: "Suppose your friend is inquisitive?" . . . What are they doing up there? What does she say to them? What goes on the whole time? My own children are strangers; they don't like being downstairs now. *What was it the prosecution said about influence?*'

Mima raised her voice. 'Run along now at once, children: Mrs Laurie is waiting.'

'We would much rather not, mother.'

'Then you're very ungrateful. Besides, I have got something to say to Miss Rice – Penny and Claudia, don't look at each other like that! It's rude to look at each other when mother speaks!'

'Miss Rice is tired,' repeated Claudia gently.

'If you give us the message,' said Penny, 'we'll tell her.'

'No, I want to talk to Miss Rice,' said Mima, her voice unnatural.

'Do you, mother?' said Penny. 'You don't generally.'

The wicker chair Mima sat in creaked convulsively. 'When we're alone again you may learn to make your mother happy. You may understand mother then and not be unkind to her. To-morrow, Miss Rice will be going away, children.'

Penny and Claudia looked at the chair their mother now sat in, then up at *Emma* left on the edge of the mantelpiece. Claudia looked at their row of young plants in the windowsill, sharp in the lamplight against the rain-lashed dark outside, Penny at the wrinkled rug where that afternoon they had knelt at their darling's feet. Then their gentle, vehement dark eyes, meeting, paused to consult again. They said in their quiet voices: 'Then we will go too.'

Tears, Idle Tears

FREDERICK burst into tears in the middle of Regent's Park. His mother, seeing what was about to happen, had cried: 'Frederick, you *can't* – in the middle of Regent's Park!' Really, this was a corner, one of those lively corners just inside a big gate, where two walks meet and a bridge starts across the pretty, winding lake. People were passing quickly; the bridge rang with feet. Poplars stood up like delicate green brooms; diaphanous willows whose weeping was not shocking quivered over the lake. May sun spattered gold through the breezy trees; the tulips though falling open were still gay; three girls in a long boat shot under the bridge. Frederick, knees trembling, butted towards his mother a crimson, convulsed face, as though he had the idea of burying himself in her. She whipped out a handkerchief and dabbed at him with it under his grey felt hat, exclaiming meanwhile in fearful mortification: 'You really haven't got to be such a *baby*!' Her tone attracted the notice of several people, who might otherwise have thought he was having something taken out of his eye.

He was too big to cry: the whole scene was disgraceful. He wore a grey flannel knickerbocker suit and looked like a schoolboy; though in fact he was seven, still doing lessons at home. His mother said to him almost every week: 'I don't know what they will think when you go to school!' His tears were a shame of which she could speak to no one; no offensive weakness of body could have upset her more. Once she had got so far as taking her pen up to write to the Mother's Advice Column of a helpful woman's weekly about them. She began: 'I am a widow; young, good tempered, and my friends all tell me that I have great control. But my little boy — ' She intended to sign herself 'Mrs D., Surrey.' But then she had stopped and thought no, no: after all, he is Toppy's son . . . She was a gallant-looking, correct woman, wearing today in London a coat and skirt, a silver fox, white gloves and a dark-blue toque put on exactly right – not the sort of woman you ought to see in a Park with a great blubbering boy belonging to her. She looked a mother of sons, but not of a son of this kind, and should more properly, really, have been walking a dog. 'Come on!' she said, as though the bridge, the poplars, the people staring were to be borne no longer. She began to walk on quickly, along the edge of the lake, parallel with the park's girdle of trees and the dark, haughty windows of Cornwall Terrace looking at her over the red may. They had meant to go to the Zoo, but now she had changed her mind: Frederick did not deserve the Zoo.

Frederick stumbled along beside her, too miserable to notice. His mother seldom openly punished him, but often revenged herself on him in small ways. He could feel how just this was. His own incontinence in the matter of tears was as shocking to him, as bowing-down, as annulling, as it could be to her. He never knew what happened – a cold, black pit with no bottom opened inside himself; a red-hot bellwire jagged up through him from the pit of his frozen belly to the caves of his eyes. Then the hot, gummy rush of tears, the convulsion of his features, the terrible, square grin he felt his mouth take all made him his own shameful and squalid enemy. Despair howled round his inside like a wind, and through his streaming eyes he saw everything quake. Anyone's being there – and most of all his mother – drove this catastrophe on him. He never cried like this when he was alone.

Crying made him so abject, so outcast from other people that he went on crying out of despair. His crying was not just reflex, like a baby's; it dragged up all unseemliness into view. No wonder everyone was repelled. There is something about an abject person that rouses cruelty in the kindest breast. The plate-glass windows of the lordly houses looked at him through the may trees with judges' eyes. Girls with their knees crossed, reading on the park benches, looked up with unkind smiles. His apathetic stumbling, his not seeing or caring that they had given up their trip to the Zoo, became more than Mrs Dickinson, his mother, could bear. She pointed out, in a voice tense with dislike: 'I'm not taking you to the Zoo.'

'Mmmph–mmph–mmph,' sobbed Frederick.

'You know, I so often wonder what your father would think.'

'Mmmph–mmph–mmph.'

'He used to be so proud of you. He and I used to look forward to what you'd be like when you were a big boy. One of the last things he ever said was: "Frederick will take care of you." You almost make me glad he's not here now.'

'Oough–oough.'

'What do you say?'

'I'm t-t-trying to stop.'

'Everybody's looking at you, you know.'

She was one of those women who have an unfailing sense of what not to say, and say it: despair, perversity or stubborn virtue

must actuate them. She had a horror, also, of the abnormal and had
to hit out at it before it could hit at her. Her husband, an R.A.F.
pilot who had died two days after a ghastly crash, after two or three
harrowing spaces of consciousness, had never made her ashamed or
puzzled her. Their intimacies, then even his death, had had a bold
naturalness.

'Listen, I shall walk on ahead,' said Frederick's mother, lifting
her chin with that noble, decided movement so many people liked.
'You stay here and look at that duck till you've stopped that noise.
Don't catch me up till you have. No, I'm really ashamed of you.'

She walked on. He had *not* been making, really, so very much
noise. Drawing choppy breaths, he stood still and looked at the
duck that sat folded into a sleek white cypher on the green, grassy
margin of the lake. When it rolled one eye open over a curve,
something unseeing in its expression calmed him. His mother
walked away under the gay tree-shadows; her step quickened
lightly, the tip of her fox fur swung. She thought of the lunch she
had had with Major and Mrs Williams, the party she would be
going to at five. First, she must leave Frederick at Aunt Mary's, and
what would Aunt Mary say to his bloated face? She walked fast; the
gap between her and Frederick widened: she was a charming
woman walking by herself.

Everybody had noticed how much courage she had; they said:
'How plucky Mrs Dickinson is.' It was five years since her tragedy
and she had not remarried, so that her gallantness kept on coming
into play. She helped a friend with a little shop called *Isobel* near
where they lived in Surrey, bred puppies for sale and gave the rest
of her time to making a man of Frederick. She smiled nicely and
carried her head high. Those two days while Toppy had lain dying
she had hardly turned a hair, for his sake: no one knew when he
might come conscious again. When she was not by his bed she was
waiting about the hospital. The chaplain hanging about her and the
doctor had given thanks that there were women like this; another
officer's wife who had been her friend had said she was braver than
could be good for anyone. When Toppy finally died the other
woman had put the unflinching widow into a taxi and driven back
with her to the Dickinsons' bungalow. She kept saying: 'Cry, dear,
cry· you'd feel better.' She made tea and clattered about, repeating:
'Don't mind me, darling: just have a big cry.' The strain became so
great that tears streamed down her own face. Mrs Dickinson
looked past her palely, with a polite smile. The empty-feeling
bungalow with its rustling curtains still smelt of Toppy's pipe; his
slippers were under a chair. Then Mrs Dickinson's friend, almost
tittering with despair, thought of a poem of Tennyson's she had
learnt as a child. She said: 'Where's Frederick? He's quiet. Do you

think he's asleep?' The widow, rising, perfectly automatic, led her into the room where Frederick lay in his cot. A nursemaid rose from beside him, gave them one morbid look and scurried away. The two-year-old baby, flushed, and drawing up his upper lip in his sleep as his father used to do, lay curved under his blue blanket, clenching one fist on nothing. Something suddenly seemed to strike his mother, who, slumping down by the cot, ground her face and forehead into the fluffy blanket, then began winding the blanket round her two fists. Her convulsions, though proper, were fearful: the cot shook. The friend crept away into the kitchen, where she stayed a half-hour, muttering to the maid. They made more tea and waited for Mrs Dickinson to give full birth to her grief. Then extreme silence drew them back to the cot. Mrs Dickinson knelt asleep, her profile pressed to the blanket, one arm crooked over the baby's form. Under his mother's arm, as still as an image, Frederick lay wide awake, not making a sound. In conjunction with a certain look in his eyes, the baby's silence gave the two women the horrors. The servant said to the friend: 'You would think he knew.'

Mrs Dickinson's making so few demands on pity soon rather alienated her women friends, but men liked her better for it: several of them found in her straight look an involuntary appeal to themselves alone, more exciting than coquetry, deeply, nobly exciting: several wanted to marry her. But courage had given her a new intractable kind of virgin pride: she loved it too much; she could never surrender it. 'No, don't ask me that,' she would say, lifting her chin and with that calm, gallant smile. 'Don't spoil things. You've been splendid to me: such a support. But you see, there's Frederick. He's the man in my life now. I'm bound to put him first. That wouldn't be fair, would it?' After that, she would simply go on shaking her head. She became the perfect friend for men who wished to wish to marry but were just as glad not to, and for married men who liked just a little pathos without being upset.

Frederick had stopped crying. This left him perfectly blank, so that he stared at the duck with abstract intensity, perceiving its moulded feathers and porcelain-smooth neck. The burning, swirling film had cleared away from his eyes, and his diaphragm felt relief, as when retching has stopped. He forgot his focus of grief and forgot his mother, but saw with joy a quivering bough of willow that, drooping into his gaze under his swollen eyelids, looked as pure and strong as something after the Flood. His thought clutched at the willow, weak and wrecked but happy. He knew he was now qualified to walk after his mother, but without feeling either guilty or recalcitrant did not wish to do so. He stepped over the rail – no park keeper being at hand to stop him – and, tenderly and respectfully, attempted to touch the white duck's tail. Without a blink, with automatic uncoyness, the duck slid away from Frederick into the lake. Its lovely white-china body balanced on the green glass water as it propelled itself gently round the curve of the bank. Frederick saw with a passion of observation its shadowy, webbed feet lazily striking out.

'The keeper'll eat you,' said a voice behind him.

Frederick looked cautiously round with his bunged-up eyes. The *individual* who had spoken sat on a park bench; it was a girl with a dispatch case beside her. Her big bony knee-joints stuck out through her thin crêpe-de-chine dress; she was hatless and her hair made a frizzy, pretty outline, but she wore spectacles, her skin had burnt dull red; her smile and the cock of her head had about them something pungent and energetic, not like a girl's at all. 'Whatcher mean, eat me?'

'You're on his grass. And putting salt on his duck's tail.'

Frederick stepped back carefully over the low rail. 'I haven't got any salt.' He looked up and down the walk: his mother was out of sight, but from the direction of the bridge a keeper was approaching, still distant but with an awesome gait. 'My goodness,' the girl said, 'what's been biting *you*?' Frederick was at a loss. 'Here,' she said, 'have an apple.' She opened her case, which was full of folded grease-paper that must have held sandwiches, and rummaged out an apple with a waxy, bright skin. Frederick came up, tentative as a pony, and finally took the apple. His breath was still hitching and catching; he did not wish to speak.

'Go on,' she said, 'swallow: it'll settle your chest. Where's your mother gone off to? What's all the noise about?' Frederick only opened his jaws as wide as they would go, then bit slowly, deeply into the apple. The girl re-crossed her legs and tucked her thin crêpe-de-chine skirt round the other knee. 'What had you done – cheeked her?'

Frederick swept the mouthful of apple into one cheek. 'No,' he said shortly. 'Cried.'

'I should say you did. Bellowed, I watched you all down the path.' There was something ruminative in the girl's tone that made her remark really not at all offensive; in fact, she looked at Frederick as though she were meeting an artist who had just done a turn. He had been standing about, licking and biting the apple, but now he came and sat down at the other end of the bench. 'How do you do it?' she said.

Frederick only turned away: his ears began burning again.

'What gets at you?' she said.

'Don't know.'

'Someone coming it over you? I know another boy who cries like you, but he's older. He knots himself up and bellows.'

'What's his name?'

'George.'

'Does he go to school?'

'Oh, lord, no; he's a boy at the place where I used to work.' She raised one arm, leaned back, and watched four celluloid bangles, each of a different colour, slide down it to her elbow joint, where they stuck. 'He doesn't know why he does it,' she said, 'but he's got to. It's as though he saw something. You can't ask him. Some people take him that way: girls do. I never did. It's as if he knew about something he'd better not. I said once, well, what just *is* it, and he said if he *could* tell me he wouldn't do it. I said, well, what's the *reason*, and he said, well, what's the reason not to? I knew him well at one time.'

Frederick spat out two pips, looked round cautiously for the keeper, then dropped the apple-core down the back of the seat. 'Whered's George live?'

'I don't know now,' she said, 'I often wonder. I got sacked from that place where I used to work, and he went right off and I never saw him again. You snap out of that, if you can, before you are George's age. It does you no good. It's all the way you see things. Look, there's your mother back. Better move, or there'll be *more* trouble.' She held out her hand to Frederick, and when he put his in it shook hands so cheerfully, with such tough decision, that the four celluloid bangles danced on her wrist. 'You and George,' she said. 'Funny to meet two of you. Well, goodbye, Henry: cheer up.'

'I'm Frederick.'

'Well, cheer up, Freddie.'

As Frederick walked away, she smoothed down the sandwich papers inside her dispatch case and snapped the case shut again. Then she put a finger under her hair at each side, to tuck her spectacles firmly down on her ears. Her mouth, an unreddened line across her harshly-burnt face, still wore the same truculent, homely smile. She crossed her arms under the flat chest, across her stomach, and sat there holding her elbows idly, wagging one foot in its fawn sandal, looking fixedly at the lake through her spectacles, wondering about George. She had the afternoon, as she had no work. She saw George's face lifted abjectly from his arms on a table, blotchy over his clerk's collar. The eyes of George and Frederick seemed to her to be wounds, in the world's surface, through which its inner, terrible unassuageable, necessary sorrow constantly bled away and as constantly welled up.

Mrs Dickinson came down the walk under the band of trees, carefully unanxious, looking lightly at objects to see if Frederick were near them: he had been a long time. Then she saw Frederick shaking hands with a sort of girl on a bench and starting to come her way. So she quickly turned her frank, friendly glance on the lake, down which, as though to greet her, a swan came swimming. She touched her fox fur lightly, sliding it up her shoulder. What a lovely mother to have. 'Well, Frederick,' she said, as he came into earshot, 'coming?' Wind sent a puff of red mayflowers through the air. She stood still and waited for Frederick to come up. She could not think what to do now: they had an hour to put in before they were due at Aunt Mary's. But this only made her manner calmer and more decisive.

Frederick gave a great skip, opened his mouth wide, shouted: 'Oo, I say, mother, I nearly caught a duck!'

'Frederick, dear, how silly you are: you couldn't.'

'Oo, yes, I could, I could. If I'd had salt for its tail!' Years later, Frederick could still remember, with ease, pleasure and with a sense of lonely shame being gone, that calm, white duck swimming off round the bank. But George's friend with the bangles, and George's trouble, fell through a cleft in his memory and were forgotten soon.

A Walk in the Woods

THE mysterious thing was that the woods were full of people –
though they showed a front of frondy depth and silence, inviolable
and sifted through with sun. They looked like a whole element,
like water, possible to behold but not to enter, in which only the
native creature can exist. But this was a deception. Once inside
them, it was only at a few moments that the solitary walker could
feel himself alone, and lovers found it hard to snatch unregarded
kisses. For those few moments when nobody was in sight, the
glades of bronze bracken, the wet, green rides leading off still
seemed to be the edge of another world. The brown distances, the
deep hollows welled with magic, forlorn silence, as though they
were untrodden. But what was likely to be the last fine Sunday of
autumn had brought Londoners, or people from suburbs on this
side of the city, in hundreds into these woods, which lay open, the
People's property – criss-crossed by tarmac roads on which yellow
leaves stuck. The people who came here were mostly well-to-do,
for you needed a car to get here without effort. So saloon cars, run
off the roads between the wide-apart birch-trees, were packed flank
to flank, like shining square-rumped tin pigs, in the nearby glades.
Inside a few of these cars people remained sitting with the wireless
on – but mostly they had got out, yawned, stretched, and scattered
in threes and fours.

Most of the Londoners lacked a sense of direction. Directly they
were out of the sight of the road, an atavistic fear of the woods
invaded them. Willing or unwilling they walked in circles, coming
back again and again to make certain they had not lost their
cars – in which had often been left a tea-basket, an overcoat of
some value, or an old lady, an aunt or a grandmother. Not to be
sure where one is induces panic – and yet the sensation of being lost
was what they unconsciously looked for on this holiday – they had
come to the woods. The sounds of bolder people whistling to dogs,
of mackintoshes rustling against the bracken reassured them and
made them strike in deeper.

Walking between the pillars of the trees, the men squared their
shoulders – as though they inherited savage dignity. The matronly

women, heavy in fur coats – which, just taken out after the summer, shed a smell of camphor – protestingly rolled as they walked on their smart heels. They looked about them, dissatisfied, acquisitive, despising the woods because they belonged to everyone. Had they not profoundly dreaded to trespass, they would have preferred the property of some duke. Now and then, recalling a pottery vase at home, they would strip off their gloves and reach for a fanlike spray of gold beech leaves. Or, unwillingly stooping, they tugged at a frond of bracken – but that is hard to pick. Their faces stayed unrelaxed: there is no poetry for the middle-class woman in her middle years. Nature's disturbing music is silent for her; her short phase of instinctive life is over. She is raising, forcing upward the children she has, and driving her man on. Her features become bleak with narrow intention: she is riveted into society. Still, to touch the edge of Nature stands for an outing – you pack baskets and throng to the edge of forest or sea. The still, damp, glittering woods, the majestic death of the year were reflected in the opaque eyes of these women – hardly more human, very much less pathetic, than the glass eyes of the foxes some of them wore. In family parties the women and men parted; they did not speak to each other. The women walked more slowly to act as a brake. Where tracks narrowed between thickets or bracken the families went in files. The children escaped and kept chasing each other, cat-calling, round the trees. They were not allowed to run down the wet green rides.

Sometimes the thud of hooves was heard, and young people on horseback crossed the end of a glade – in coloured jerseys, with chins up, flaunting their bold happiness. The walkers, with a sort of animal envy, lowered their eyes and would not look after them. From couples of lovers crashing through the bracken, or standing suspended in love, fingers touching, in patches of sun, eyes were averted in a commenting way.

The riders thudding across a glade were heard, not seen, by a couple in a thicket. These two, in a secret clearing at the foot of an oak, sat on a mackintosh eating sandwiches. They were very hungry. They had come to the edge of the woods in a Green Line bus, struck in and wandered for a long time now, looking for the place their fancy wanted. The woman, a city woman, refused to believe the woods had no undiscovered heart, if one could only come on it. Each time she had sighted the black of another tarmac road she had let out a persecuted sigh. The young man saw she was flagging, and he was hungry. He had found what she wanted by fighting through this thicket to the foot of the oak, then pulling her after him. In here they at least *saw* no one. They had spread the mackintosh, kissed, and opened the sandwiches.

'Listen,' she said. 'There go people riding.'

'Did you ever ride?'

'I did once.'

'On that farm?'

'Yes, that time,' she said, smiling quickly, touched that he should remember. She spoke often about her childhood, never about her girlhood – which was past, for she was ten years older than he. And her girlhood had been brief: she had married young. She watched him reach out for another sandwich, then gently and wilfully detained him by making her thumb and finger into a bracelet round his thin wrist. He pulled his wrist up to his lips and kissed the joint of her thumb. They enjoyed this play as seriously as lions. She shut her eyes, dropped her head back to let the sun through the branches fall on her forehead – then let his wrist go. He took the sandwich he wanted; she opened her eyes and saw him.

'You greedy boy.'

'Yes, I *am* greedy,' he said. '*You* know I'm greedy.'

She thrust both hands up her cheeks and said: 'That's no good – *here*.'

'No, we've struck unlucky. I thought woods in winter — '

'It's still autumn. It's the fine Sunday.' Her face went narrow, as though she heard the crack of a whip: she opened a gap in their thicket by bending a branch back. With cautious, angry eyes they both looked through. A party of five people were filing through the bracken, about ten yards away. 'There they go,' she said. 'There go the neighbours. That's my life. Oh, God! Henry — '

'They can't hurt us.'

'You know they can. Look, eat that last sandwich, do.'

'What about you?'

'I don't want it: I cut them for you. Turkey and ham, that should be.'

'*I'm* a spoilt boy,' said Henry, taking the sandwich without any more fuss. She crumbled up the paper, drove it with the point of his stick into the soft earth at the foot of the oak and earthed it up alive. Then she brushed crumbs from the mackintosh with a downcast face, making a bed in which they dare not lie. But Henry drew his long legs up, scrambled round like a dog and lay across the mackintosh with his head in Carlotta's lap. She stroked his stubborn dark hair back, leaned her bosom over his face and stroked his forehead with a terrible held-in tenderness. The whole weight of his body seemed to have gone into his head, which lay as heavy as a world on her thighs. His clerk's face was exposed to her touch and to the sky – generally so intent, over-expressive, nervous, the face was wiped into blank repose by her touch. He flung one hand across his chest and held a fold of her skirt. His spectacles, by reflecting the sky's light, hid his eyes from her, so she leaned over further and lifted them off gently. She looked into the blotted darkness of his pupils which, from being exposed like this, looked naked. Then he shut his eyes and put on the withdrawn smile of someone expecting sleep. 'You are so good,' he said.

'Sleep then . . . go on, sleep . . . '

'Will you?'

'Maybe. Sleep . . . '

But she watched, with the bend of her spine against the tree, while he lay with his eyes shut. She saw that his will to sleep was a gentle way of leaving her for a little. She felt a tide of peace coming in – but then the tide turned: his forehead twitched. A bird trilled its unhopeful autumn song. He opened his eyes and said: 'It's awful, having no place.'

'But we make a place of our own.'

'But I get so tired – all this doesn't seem natural.'

'Oh, Henry – what's the good?'

'Well, *you've* often said that.'

'Then *you've* said, what's the good?'

'It was all very well at first,' he said, 'just knowing you. Just coming round to your place. Seeing you before Joe got back, or even with Joe. I used to like you to have a place of your own – that was why I'd rather go with you than a girl.'

'That's what you want,' she said, 'just mothering. That's what Joe thinks; he doesn't think any harm. "Here comes your boy," he says. I think he's right, too: that's all you're really after.' She gently outlined his mouth with one of her fingertips.

But his mouth tightened. 'No, it's more than that now,' he said. '*You* know it's more than that.' He stared at the sky with his unfocused eyes – like a hare's eyes. 'I wanted what I've got; I wanted that all the time; I wanted that from the first – though it may once have been mixed up in the other thing. But ever *since* that, ever since we — '

'Do you wish we hadn't?'

'You don't know what you're saying. But I used to like your home; it was such a snug little place. I was happy there in a way: that's all gone now. I used to like Joe, too, one time. And now – it's awful . . . *This* isn't what I imagined the first time I saw you. Hiding in woods like this – it isn't fit for you . . . really.'

'It's my only life. You're my only life. My only way out. Before you came, I was walled in alive. I didn't know where to turn. I was burning myself out . . . I don't mind where we go, so long as we get *away* from them . . . And we do have these days when Joe's gone to his mother's.'

'But we've got no place . . . When I was young I used to believe there was really some tremendous world, and that one would get to it. A sort of a Shakespeare world. And I heard it in music, too. And I lived there for three days after I first met you. I once used to believe — '

'But you're young still.'

'Well, perhaps I do still.'

'I always have. That's our place.'

'But we ought to have some real place – I mean, I want you.'

'Oh, shut up,' she said. 'I — '

'Look, come on,' he said, getting up. 'Better walk on. This does no good. Let's walk on into the woods.'

'They're so full.'

'But they look empty.'

'Kiss once — '

They kissed. It was he who pulled apart. He gathered up her mackintosh on his arm and began to fight a way out for her through the thickets. As she stepped between the branches he held back, her lips shook and she looked quite blind. Her look attracted the notice of Muffet and Isabella, two schoolgirls who, walking arm-in-arm through the woods, had already started to stare and nudge each other on seeing the thicket of purple leaves shake. Any man and woman together made them giggle. They saw a haggard woman with dark red hair and a white face: something in her expression set them off giggling all the more. Henry disentangled the mackintosh from the last of the thicket; his consciousness of the girls staring and giggling made him look very young. His pride in Carlotta was wounded; his pity for her abased him. She was a married woman out with her neighbour's lodger. They both came from a newly developed suburb, and had met at the local debating society.

As he saw the girls' pink faces stuck open with laughter he saw why Carlotta hated her life. He saw why she towered like a statue out of place. She was like something wrecked and cast up on the wrong shore. When they met she had been one of these women going through life dutifully, and at the same time burning them-selves up. Across the hall where they met, her forehead like no other woman's forehead, her impatient carriage, her deep eyes and held-in mouth, had been like a signal to him. He could not turn away. When they had talked, she excited, released, soothed him. Pride and a bitter feeling of misdirection had, up to that meeting, isolated them both. Passion broke down a wall in each of their lives. But her spirit was stronger than his, and so he was frightened of her . . . Carlotta stumbled stepping out of the thicket, and put a hand on his elbow for support. Henry twitched his elbow away and strode ahead of her, lashing round at the bracken with his stick.

'Henry — '

'Look out, they're looking. Those girls behind. *Don't* look round — '

'All right,' she said. 'We can't be too careful, can we.' Henry did not know if she spoke in irony or sheer pain.

Muffet was spending the Sunday with Isabella, whose family lived not far from the Green Line bus stop. The girls were friends at the High School. They both wore dark-blue overcoats and walked bare-headed; their lively faces showed no particular character. They were allowed by their mothers to walk in the woods so long as they did not get talking to men: they had been told what happens to girls who do that – their minds were bulging with cautionary horrors. They had neither of them got boys yet: when they had got boys they would stop walking together. At present their walks were gay and enjoyable – on fine Sundays the woods were a great show for them: too soon this would be over, winter silence would fall.

This afternoon, in a fairly retired glade, they had come on a lonely car in which a couple embraced. They also inspected cars parked nearer the roadside, squinting in at grandmothers and the picnic baskets, running away in alarm from pairs of well-got-up women, upright in backs of cars like idols under glass cases, discontentedly waiting for their men to return. Or, intercepting a bar of wireless music, Isabella and Muffet would take a few dancing steps. They envied the thundering riders, the young lovers, the imperious owners of well-bred dogs . . . Isabella and Muffet, anything but reluctant, hopped with impatience where brook and river meet. They were fifteen. They stared at everyone. At the same time they had a sense of propriety which was very easily offended.

They peered at the broken thicket, then turned to stare after the couple.

'My goodness,' said Isabella, '*she* looked silly!'

'Breaking trees, too,' said Muffet. 'That's against the law.'

'Besides being old enough to be his mother. She *was* old. Did you see her?'

'Perhaps she was his mother.'

'Mother my eye! But he gave her the push all right – did you see that? Did you see?'

'Going on at him like that.'

'Well, I call it a shame. It's a shame on him. He's a nice boy.'

'No, I call him sappy. I mean, at her age. Fancy him letting her.'

'Well, I tell you, I call it a shame.'

'Well, I tell you, it makes me laugh . . . Look, let's go down there: I see people down there.' Isabella dug a bag of sweets out of her pocket and they sauntered on, both sucking, talking with cheeks blocked. 'Supposing you got offered a fur coat, what kind would you go for, nutria or kolinsky? . . . If a boy that always went racing but that you were sweet on asked you to marry him, would you? . . . Supposing you were going with a boy, then found out he was a trunk murderer . . . '

'Oh, there's such a sweet dog, such a sweet fellow. Come, then!'

'My goodness,' said Isabella, 'it isn't half getting dark.'

'Well, what *do* you expect?'

'No, but the sun's gone in. And that's not mist, now; that's fog, that is.'

'They're starting two of those cars up.'

'Mother'll be starting to worry. Better be getting home.'

Yes, mist that had been the natural breath of the woods was thickening to fog, as though the not-distant city had sent out an infection. At dusk coming so suddenly and so early, the people felt a touch of animal fear – quickening their steps, they closed on each other in a disordered way, as though their instinct were to bolt underground. Wind or thunder, though more terrible in woods, do not hold this same threat of dissolution. The people packed back into their cars; the cars lurched on to the roads and started back to London in a solid stream. Down the rides, beginning to be deserted, the trees with their leaves still clinging looked despoiled and tattered. All day the woods had worn an heroic dying smile; now they were left alone to face death.

But this was still somebody's moment. There was still some daylight. The small lake, or big pool, clearly reflected in its black mirror the birches and reeds. A tall girl, with a not quite young porcelain face, folding her black fur collar round her throat with both hands, stood posing against a birch, having her photograph taken across the water by two young men at the other side of the lake. Bob, busy over the camera on a portable tripod, was an 'art' photographer: he could photograph Nature in the most difficult light. Therefore he could go far in search of her strange moods. He felt, thought, loved, even, in terms of the Lens. He sold his work to papers, where it appeared with lines of poetry underneath. This girl over the water in the fog-smudged woods was to be called 'Autumn Evening'. Cecil, an old friend, behind Bob's shoulder, looked across at the girl.

Without breaking her pose, a born model's, she coughed, and shook under her fur coat. Cecil said cautiously: 'She's getting a bit cold, Bob.'

'*Tsssss!*' said Bob sharply. He had become his camera. His whole temperament crouched over his subject, like a lion over a bit of meat.

'Won't be long,' Cecil called across the lake.

'I'm all right,' said the girl, coughing again.

'Tell her not to grab her collar up,' Bob muttered. 'She's not supposed to look cold. She's got her coat all dragged up; it spoils the figure.'

'He says, not to grab your collar,' Cecil shouted.

'Right-o.' She let her collar fall open. Turning her head inside the fur corolla, she looked more obliquely across the lake. 'Is that better?'

'O.K. . . . *Ready!*' The slow exposure began.

People taking photographs in this half-light, this dream-light, made Carlotta and Henry stop to wonder. They stood back among the birches to be out of the way. Then the artistic tensity broke up; signals were exchanged across the water; the girl came round the lake to join the two young men. 'What's that floating?' she said. But they were busy packing up the camera. 'Should that be all right?' she said, but no one answered. Bob handed Cecil the tripod, shouldered his camera, and they walked away from the lake with Bob's hand on his girl's shoulder.

'Do you think that photo will ever come out?' said Carlotta.

'I suppose he knows what he's doing . . . I'd like to try with a camera . . . '

'I'd sooner paint,' said Carlotta. They walked round the edge of the lake, looking across to where the girl had stood. 'She was pretty,' Carlotta said. She thought: 'She'll get her death. But I'd like to stand like that. I wish Henry *had* a camera. I wish I could give him one . . . ' Against the photographer's shoulder-blade eternalized minutes were being carried away. Carlotta and Henry were both tired: what they saw seemed to belong in the past already. The light seemed to fade because of their own nerves. And still water in woods, in any part of the world, continues an everlasting terrible fairy tale, in which you are always lost, in which giants oppress. Now the people had gone, the lovers saw that this place was what they had been looking for all today. But they were so tired, each stood in an isolated dream.

'What *is* that floating?' she said.

Henry screwed up his eyes. 'A thermos.' He picked up a broken branch and, with an infinity of trouble, started to claw in, with the tip of the branch, the floating flask towards himself. Its cap was gone.

'But we don't want it, Henry.'

She might never have spoken – Henry's face was intent; he

recklessly stood with one toe in the water. The ribbed aluminium cylinder, twirling under the touches of the branch, rode reluctantly in. Henry reached it eagerly out of the water, shook it. Its shattered inner glass coating rattled about inside – this, the light hollowness, the feel of the ribs in his grasp made Henry smile with almost crazy pleasure. 'Treasure!' he said, with a checked, excited laugh.

Carlotta smiled, but she felt her throat tighten. She saw Henry's life curve off from hers, like one railway line from another, curve off to an utterly different and far-off destination. When she trusted herself to speak, she said as gently as possible: 'We'll have to be starting back soon. You know it's some way. The bus — '

'No, we won't miss that,' said Henry, rattling the flask and smiling.

A Love Story
1939

MIST lay over the estuary, over the terrace, over the hollows of the
gummy, sub-tropical garden of the hotel. Now and then a soft,
sucking sigh came from the water, as though someone were
turning over in his sleep. At the head of the steps down to the boat-
house, a patch of hydrangeas still flowered and rotted, though it
was December. It was now six o'clock, dark – chinks of light from
the hotel lay yellow and blurred on the density. The mist's muffling
silence could be everywhere felt. Light from the double glass doors
fell down the damp steps. At the head of the steps the cast-iron
standard lamps were unlit.

Inside the double glass doors, the lounge with its high curtained
bow windows was empty. Brilliantly hotly lit by electric light, it
looked like a stage on which there has been a hitch. Light blared on
the *vieux rose* curtains and on the ocean of carpet with its jazz
design. The armchairs and settees with their taut stuffing had an air
of brutal, resilient strength. Brass ashtrays without a segment of
ash stood on small tables dotted over the lounge. A glass screen
kept the lounge from any draughts from the door; a glass screen
protected the lounge from the stairs. But there was nothing to
dread: the heating was on, only a smell of tinder-dry turkey carpet,
ivory paint, polish and radiators came downstairs from the empty
floors above. In the immense tiled fireplace a fire burned with a
visible, silent roar.

From a cabinet came a voice announcing the six o'clock news. In
the middle of this, three berries fell from a vase of holly and
pattered noisily into a brass tray. The temperate voice of the
announcer paused for a moment, half-way through a disaster, as
though disturbed by the noise. A spurt of gas from a coal sent a
whicker up through the fire. The unheard news came to an end.

Two women came up the steps and pushed in at the glass doors.
Their hair was sticky from the damp of the mist. The girl steered
her mother round the screen to the fire, then went across and
turned off the wireless. The mother unbuttoned her leather coat

and threw it back from her handsome, full chest. Keyed up by the sudden electric light, her manner was swaggering and excitable. She looked with contempt at the wireless cabinet and said: 'I don't care what I hear – now!'

'Do shut up, mother. Do sit down.'

'Do stop being so nervous of me, Teresa. Whatever do you think I'm going to do?'

Teresa took off her trenchcoat and slung it over a chair, then crossed the lounge with her loose, cross walk, in her slacks. 'I know what you want,' she said flatly, ringing the bell. She sat down in an armchair by the fire and stuck her young slender jaw out and crossed her legs. Her mother stayed standing up, with her shoulders braced back; she kept pushing her hair back from her forehead with her long, plump, fine-wristed ringed hand. 'I daresay you're right to be so nervous,' she said. 'I don't know myself what I'll do, from minute to minute. Why did I have to come here – can you tell me that? Why was this the only thing I could do? Do you know when I was last here – who I was with?'

'I suppose I know,' said Teresa, defensively. 'You know you don't want me to understand you, mother, so I'm not trying to.'

'It's a terrible thing to say,' said Mrs Massey, 'but it would be better if this had happened to you. I'd rather see you suffer than have no feelings. You're not like a woman, Teresa. And he was your age, not my age.'

'Is that so?' Teresa said, in a voice too lifeless for irony.

Mrs Massey looked angrily round the lounge and said: 'They've changed the chairs round, since.' She pointed to an empty space on the carpet and said: '*That* was where he sat . . . There isn't even his chair.'

Teresa looked pointedly off down the corridor. 'Michael's coming,' she said. A boy in a white cotton coat, with a dark, vivid, Kerry face, beamed at them through the glass screen, then came round the screen for orders. 'Good evening, Michael,' said Teresa.

'Good evening, miss. Good evening to you, ma'am.'

'It's not a good evening for me, I'm afraid, Michael.'

Michael lowered his eyes. 'I'm sorry to hear that,' he said, in a trembling and feeling voice. 'It's a long time since we saw you.'

'Does it seem so — ?' Mrs Massey began wildly. But Teresa put up her hand and in a curt, raised voice ordered her mother's drink . . . 'But I wanted a double,' objected Mrs Massey, when Michael had gone.

'You know you had that at home,' said Teresa, 'and more than once.' More coldly, she added: 'And how fed up Teddy used to get.'

Frank and Linda, their fingers loosely linked, came downstairs on their way to their private sitting-room. They glanced vacantly through the screen and turned left down the corridor. 'We missed the news again,' she said, as he shut the door. 'We always seem to run late.' 'We can't help that, darling,' he said. Their fire had been made up while they were upstairs. She gave it an unnecessary kick with her heel, and said: 'Did you see those two making a scene in the lounge?'

'I sort of did see the girl,' Frank said. 'Which was the other?'

'I thought they looked like locals in for a drink. Or I daresay they came round here to make a scene. I do think the Irish are exhibitionists.'

'Well, we can't help that, darling, can we?' said Frank, ringing the bell. He sat down in a chair and said: 'Oh, my God . . . ' Linda dropping into the chair opposite. 'Well, really . . . ' Frank said. 'However, I feel fine. I don't care what time it is.'

Up in a sitting-room on the first floor, the Perry-Duntons' two dogs slept in front of the fire, bellies taut to the heat. Legs rigid, they lay in running attitudes, like stuffed dogs knocked over on to their sides. On the sofa pulled up opposite the fire was Clifford – feet braced against one end, backbone against the other, knees up, typewriter in the pit of his stomach, chin tucked down into his chest. With elbows in to his ribs in a trussed position, he now and then made a cramped dash at the keys. When the keys stopped, he stayed frowning at them. Sheet after sheet, completed without conviction, fluttered on to the hearthrug between the dogs.

Polly Perry-Dunton's armchair was pushed up so that one arm made telepathic contact with Clifford's sofa. Curled up childishly in the cushions, she held a Penguin volume a little above her face. She kept the stiff Penguin open by means of an anxious pressure from her thumb. She read like someone told to pose with a book, and seemed unable to read without holding her breath.

Crackles came now and then from the *Daily Sketch* that Clifford had folded under his feet. Light blazed on their two heads from a marble bowl near the ceiling. The top of the mantelpiece was stacked with Penguins; the other armchair was stacked with American magazines. Polly's portable wireless in its shagreen cover stood silent on the floor by her chair. An art photograph of Clifford and Polly, profiles just overlapping like heads on a coin, was propped on the whatnot and kept from slipping by Polly's toy panda from Fortnum's.

Clifford reached out his right hand, apparently vaguely: Polly uncoiled like a spring from the armchair, knelt on the hearthrug and lit him a cigarette. Cigarette pressed tightly between his lips, Clifford turned back to frown at the keys again. She sat back on her heels to adore his frown, his curls, his fresh skin – then she locked her arms tightly around his neck. The impulsive, light little-girlishness of the movement let him still say nothing, not even turn his head.

She said into his cheek: 'May Polly say one thing?'

'Mm-mm.'

'I've left my pussy gloves in the car.'

'Mm-mm . . . You don't want them, do you?'

'No, not indoors. I wouldn't want gloves indoors. But let's remember tomorrow . . . Look, you crumpled one sheet right up. Did you mean to?'

'I meant to.'

Polly reverently uncrumpled the sheet. 'Pity,' she said. 'It's beautifully typed. Do you mean you're *not* going to say all that?'

'No. I'm trying to think of something else.'

'I should think most people could never think of so much that they were even not going to say.'

Clifford waited a minute, then he unfastened Polly's arms from his neck with as little emotion as a woman undoing a boa. He then typed five or six lines in a sort of rush. She returned with a glutted sigh to her chair, thumbed her book, held her breath and thought of her pussy gloves.

Clifford's voice to Polly was always the same: resignation or irony kept it on one note. The two of them had been over here on honeymoon when the war began; here they still were, because of the war. Some days he went out with his gun along the foot of the mountain, some days they ran the motor-boat in and out of white inlets or to an island, some days they went out in Polly's big car. When they had run the car back into the lock-up they would walk back, her hand creeping inside his, down the tarmac curve to the hotel between walls of evergreen. At this hour, the tarmac gleamed wet-white in the lasting, luminous Irish dusk. From this hour, claustrophobia resumed its sway. Polly hardly reached up to Clifford's shoulders; she walked beside him with her little skip-and-jump. She felt that his being so tall, she so little, cancelled out their adverse difference in age. She was thirty-two, he twenty-four. Her trim little sexless figure, her kilted skirts, socks and little-girl snooded hair that flopped forward so softly could make her look fourteen. Without the ring of technicians who got her up she could have easily looked faded and sluttish, like a little girl in Wool-worth's wilting behind the goods. But she had a childish hard will, and by day she never looked old.

She grew up when she was asleep. Then, a map of unwilling adult awareness – lines, tensions and hollows – appeared in her exposed face. Harsh sleep froze her liquidity; her features assembled themselves and became austere. An expression of watching wrote itself on the lids of her shut eyes. The dread she denied all day came out while she slept and stood in the door. The flittering of a palm tree, the bump of a moored boat as the tide rose, the collapse of a last coal in their grate went straight to the nerves upright under her sleep. She slept tenaciously, late into the daylight – but Clifford never looked at her long.

Her rape of Clifford – with his animal muteness, nonchalance, mystery and the charm of the obstination of his wish to write – had been the climax of Polly's first real wish. Her will had detected the flaw in his will that made the bid possible. Her father had bought him for her. Till they met, her wealth and her years of styleless, backgroundless dullness had atrophied Polly. The impulse with which she first put her arms round Clifford's neck and told him never to leave her had been, however, unforced and pure. Rain – a little rain, not much – fell on her small parched nature at Clifford's tentative kiss. There had seemed no threat to Polly in Clifford's nature till the war came, with its masculine threat. Their sequestration now, here, remained outwardly simple: Clifford handled no money, Polly drew all the cheques.

They stayed on here where they were hidden and easy – any move might end in some fatal way. The Perry-Duntons knew almost nothing of the hotel. They had meals served in their suite, and only went down or upstairs or through the lounge on their way outdoors or in. During such appearances, Polly's service-flat temperament sheathed her in passive, moronic unseeingness. Her blindness made everything negative – Clifford saw nothing, either. He walked out or in through the public rooms beside her, tense, persecuted by the idea of notice, with his baited, defensive frown. The hotel had come to return the Perry-Duntons' indifference. The out-of-season skeleton staff of servants served them without interest, acting the automata Polly took them to be. Servants love love and money, but the Perry-Duntons bored the servants, by now. By now even Mrs. Coughlan, the manageress, thought and spoke of them with apathy. The Perry-Duntons deadened the air round them with their static, depleting intimacy.

Now, Clifford twitched one more sheet off the machine. Leaning sideways over from the sofa, he, with absorption, began to tickle a dog's belly with an edge of the sheet. The dog bent itself further backward, into a bow. Watchful, Polly judged that this meant a break. She got up and began to tug like a bird at the *Daily Sketch* under Clifford's feet. 'What's that there for?' she said. 'I don't think I've looked at it yet.'

'Sorry,' said Clifford, raising his feet.

'But what's it *there* for, Clifford?'

'I was taught not to put my boots up on things – not straight up on things, that is.'

'How funny, because you generally do. I wonder what made you just think of that?'

Clifford could not tell her. He swung his feet off the sofa on to the hearthrug between the dogs. Sitting forward on the edge of the sofa, elbows on his wide-apart knees, he dug his heels slowly, without passion, into the rug. He looked slowly down from his hands with their hanging bunches of fingers to the oriental pattern under them. Polly picked up a sheet of type-writing and began to read. 'Goodness,' she said, after an interval, 'I hope you're not going to *throw* this one away! . . . What's the matter?'

'I'm going out for your gloves.'

'Oh, but I don't want them.'

'I'd like to go out for them, rather. I'd like a stretch.'

'*Alone*, Clifford?'

'There's a mist.'

'You might get lost. You might walk into the water. Do you really *want* to go out?'

At this, the dogs got up and looked eager. He pushed at them with his feet. 'No, stay with Polly,' he said. 'I won't be long.'

'You do promise?' She folded herself away from him in an abandon of puzzled sadness. Clifford kicked the dogs back again and went quietly round the door.

Frank stepped across the corridor to the office to get a stamp for Linda. The plate-glass and mahogany front of the office was framed in tariffs of summer trips, sets of view postcards printed in dark blue and a bill of the working-hours of the Protestant church. The glass hatch was down: Frank put his face against it and looked flirtatiously into the back recess. On an inside ledge, the register was just out of view. Mrs Coughlan put up the glass hatch, like a lady playing at keeping shop. She received the full blast of Frank's full-blooded charm. 'Stamp?' she said. 'Oh dear, now Miss Heally knows where they are. To tell you the truth, I'm afraid I don't, and Miss Heally's just upstairs having a little rest. We're very quiet just now. Don't you find it terribly quiet – Major Mull?'

'Mr Mull,' said Frank. 'Oh, we love it,' he said.

'Still, it's not like the season, is it? Will you be back with us then?'

'Will I not!' said Frank, using his eyes.

'Is the stamp for yourself?'

'Well, it's not: it's for my cousin.'

'Ah yes,' said Mrs Coughlan, not batting an eyelid. 'The post went, you know; it went about five minutes. But I tell you what – Were you never in the last war?' – 'I was,' said Frank. 'But I'm not in this one, thank God.' – 'Now Miss Heally thought you had some military rank – I tell you what I could do, I could let you have a stamp I have, if I could trouble you to step this way.'

She pressed with her corsets against the door of the counter, and Frank let her out. She preceded him down the warm, half-lit, spongey-carpeted corridor to the door of her sitting-room: from this, she recoiled on to Frank's toe, at the same time blowing a whisper in at his right ear. 'I won't ask you in here,' she said, 'if you don't mind. I've a lady in here who is a little upset.' As she spoke, the door of the sitting-room opened, and the, to Frank's eye, snappy form of Teresa appeared, outlined in electric light. Teresa glowered at Frank, then said: 'We'll be going now, Mrs Coughlan. I think my mother would really rather be home.'

'I would not rather!' exclaimed unseen Mrs Massey. 'For God's sake, Teresa, let me alone.'

'No, don't let me barge in,' said Frank, standing firmly just where he was. Mrs Coughlan flashed at him the recognition that *he* would be always the gentleman. 'Well, if you'll excuse me,' she said, 'for just a jiffy, I'll bring the stamp along to your sitting-room.'

Frank went back to Linda. He left their door an inch open and, while they were waiting, rang for a glass of port. 'What's that for?' said Linda. 'I wanted a stamp.'

'That's for Mrs Coughlan. You'll get your stamp to play with. But of course you know that the post's gone?' 'Then hell, what is the good of a stamp?' 'You said you wanted a stamp, so I'm getting a stamp for you. I love getting you anything that you want.' 'Then what's the point of me having written this letter?' 'None, darling; I told you that. Writing letters is just fidgets. Never mind, it will come in some time when you want a letter to post.'

Disengaging herself from Frank's kiss, Linda propped the letter up on the mantelpiece, on a carton of cigarettes. While he kissed her again, she looked at it out of one eye. This made Frank look too. 'Oh, *that's* who it's to,' he said. He made faces at it, while Linda, still held pressed to his chest, giggled contentedly. 'I sort of had to,' she said, 'or he wouldn't know where I am.'

Mrs Coughlan came in with the stamp. The port was brought in by Michael and put on the mantelpiece. She started at it, but after a certain amount of fuss was induced to lift her glass daintily. 'Well, here's to you,' she said. 'And to you too,' she said to Linda. 'But isn't this really dreadful, at this hour.'

'Good for the heart,' said Frank. 'Not that your heart needs it, I'm sure. But your caller sounded to me a bit off.'

'Oh, Mrs Massey's had bad news. She came round here with her daughter, then didn't feel well.'

'Was she in the lounge?' said Linda.

'She was first, but it didn't seem fit for her, so Miss Teresa made her come in to me. You don't know who might come into a public room. So I said, to come in to me for a little rest, while I kept an eye on the office while Miss Heally was up. We are all devoted to Mrs Massey,' said Mrs Coughlan, meeting the eye of Linda just a shade stonily. 'I was saying to Miss Heally only this morning, wasn't it too long since we'd seen Teresa or her. They're in and out, as a rule, with the friends Mrs Massey has staying. They're quite near to here, through the woods, though it's longer if you take the two avenues. They've a sweet place, there, but it's lonely; they've nothing there but the sea.'

'Through the woods?' said Linda. 'Then, do you mean that pink house? – That's that house *we* want,' she said to Frank. Mrs Coughlan glanced primly midway between the two of them. 'Yes, it's a sweet place, Palmlawn,' said Mrs Coughlan. 'We often say, she seems quite wedded to it.'

Frank said: 'Is Teresa the tiger cat?'

Far too much won by Frank's eye and manner, Mrs Coughlan had to pause to prop up her loyalties. 'Well, her manner's just a weeshy bit short,' she said. 'And this evening, of course, *she's* upset, too.'

'She sounded more fed up.'

Mrs Coughlan, replacing her glass on the mantelpiece, dabbed her mouth with an *eau de nil* handkerchief charged with *Muguet de Coty*. Reassembling herself as manageress, she threw an inventorial glance round their sitting-room. 'I hope,' she said, 'you have everything? Everything comfy? Ring if it isn't, won't you?' 'Yes, thanks,' said Linda, 'we're very cosy in here.' Mrs Coughlan, whose business it was to know how to take everything, knew perfectly well how to take this. 'Well, I must be running along. Thank you very much, Major Mull – Mr Mull – I hope you'll join *me* for a minute or two this evening, unless, of course, you're engaged . . . Isn't this war shocking?'

'Shocking,' said Frank. 'I sell cars.'

'Very,' said Linda. 'Why?'

'I can't help thinking,' said Mrs Coughlan, 'of poor Mrs Massey's friend. A flying man. He was often in here, you know.'

Fumbling with the slimy lock in the mist, Clifford unlocked the lock-up. He reached into the Alvis, switched the dashboard lights on and got in and sat in the car to look for Polly's gloves. Mist came curdling into the lock-up after him. He put the wrist-length, fluffy gloves in one pocket. Then he checked up on the petrol: there were six gallons still. Then he plunged his hand slowly into another of his pockets, touched the pennies, thumbed the two half-crowns. In the dark his body recorded, not for the first time, yet another shock of the recurrent idea. The shock, as always, dulled out. He switched the lights off, folded his arms, slid forward and sat in the dark deflated – completely deflated, a dying pig that has died.

Frank and Linda, intently, silently cosy in front of their sitting-room fire in the dark, heard people break into the passage from Mrs Coughlan's room. At this Frank, with pussy-cat stealth and quickness, raised his face from the top of Linda's head. His clean ears, close to his head, might have been said to prick up. 'Damn,' said Linda, missing Frank, 'something is always happening.' The concourse passed their door. 'That's Mrs Massey, that was.' Frank at once pressed his hands on Linda's shoulders. But he said: 'Should I just have a look-see?' He got up, padded across the room, opened the door an inch and put one eye to the inch.

Mrs Coughlan had not gone far. She immediately came back and put her mouth into the inch of door. 'Mr Mull, could I trouble you just a minute?' she said. Frank edged round the door and Linda was left alone.

Mrs Massey was not equal to the walk back. This – only felt by herself as an additional rush of sorrow – was clear to Teresa, and also to Mrs Coughlan, as a predicament. There had been talk, before they left Mrs Coughlan's parlour, of telephoning to the village for a car. Mrs Massey would not brook the idea. 'I won't give trouble,' she said. 'There's trouble enough already.' Magnificent with protest, she now stood trembling and talking loudly and sweeping her hair back at the foot of the stairs. 'I should never have come,' she said. 'But how could I stay where I was? We'll go home now; we'll just go quietly home – Are you gummed there, Teresa? Come home: we've been here quite long enough.' She gave Frank a haunted look as Mrs Coughlan brought him up. 'This is Mr Mull, Mrs Massey,' said Mrs Coughlan. 'Mr Mull says he'll just get his car out and run you home.'

Mrs Massey said: 'I don't know what you all think.'

Teresa, taking no notice, put on her trenchcoat and tightly buckled the belt. 'That is good of you,' she said to Frank slightingly. 'Aren't you busy?' 'Not in the world,' said Frank. 'Hold on while I get the car round.'

'You needn't do that, thank you: Mother and I can walk as far as the car.'

Teresa and Frank, with Mrs Massey between them, started off

down the aisle of carpet to the glass doors. 'Aren't the steps dreadfully dark for her!' helped Miss Heally, who was there with the rest – she shot ahead to switch on the outdoor lamps. The three passed down the steps in the blur of a blaze of lights, as though leaving a ball. 'Good night now. Safe home, Mrs Massey dear!' called Miss Heally and Mrs Coughlan from the top of the steps. Linda, hearing the noise, hearing Frank's step on the gravel, threw a window up and leaned into the mist. She called: 'Frank?' He replied if at all, with a gesture that she could not see: he was busy steering the party. 'Left turn,' he said, patting at Mrs Massey's elbow. The mother and daughter wheeled docilely.

'Do you know where we are, at all?'

'Oh, I'm used to all this.'

'Do you come from London, then?' Teresa said.

'I've come back from London.'

'On leave?' said Teresa quickly.

'No, thank God. I sell cars.'

'You won't sell many just now.' Teresa's trenchcoat brushed on the evergreens. Majestic and dazed between her escort, Mrs Massey stumbled along in a shackled way. In the yard, the open doors of the lock-up beside Frank's stuck out clammy into the mist: they almost walked into them. 'That lunatic's taken that Alvis out,' said Frank. Teresa, in her not encouraging way, said: 'Well, you'll be another lunatic, in a minute.' Mrs Massey, ignoring the dialogue, detached herself quietly from Teresa. While Frank and his torch and key were busy over a padlock, Mrs Massey passed quietly into the open lock-up next door. She bumped her knee on the Alvis and started to climb round it. 'It's all right, Teresa, the car's in here,' she called back, with quite an approach to her usual gaiety.

Clifford's reflex to the bump on the car was to blaze all his lights on. Inside, his lock-up became one curdled glare; his tail light spread a ruby stain on the mist. He turned his head sharply and stayed with his coinlike profile immobilized against the glaring end wall. Mrs Massey came scrambling into view. Clifford put down one window. 'I beg your pardon?' he said.

'Better back out a little,' said Mrs Massey. 'I can't get in this side while you're in here.' Clifford started his engine and backed out. But then he pulled up, got up and got half out of the car. 'I'm afraid this is not your car,' he said.

'How could it be my car,' said Mrs Massey, 'when my car's at home? This is so kind of you – I don't know what you must think. Let me in now, though.' Clifford shrank back; she got in and settled herself by him contentedly. 'There's my daughter to come,' she said, 'and a man from the hotel. Just wait, now, and they'll show you the way.'

Frank had only just got his lock-up open when Teresa was at his elbow again. 'We'll hang on a minute,' he said, 'and let this other chap out. I'll start up. Be getting your mother in at the back.'

'My mother's got into the other car.'

'Which car?'

'I don't know. Don't dawdle there – are you mad? Mother might be off anywhere!'

Frank went out to blink. The Alvis, almost silently turning, swept a choked glare through the mist. 'Oh, *that* chap,' Frank said. 'That chap won't eat anyone. Cut along, Teresa – look, he's waiting for you.'

'I don't know him.'

'Mother knows him by now.'

'You're well out of us,' said Teresa, standing still bitterly.

'If that's what you think,' Frank said, 'I'll come along too.'

Linda was told of Frank's kindness in volunteering to drive the Masseys home. Mrs Coughlan was very much pleased and could not praise him enough. He should be back at the hotel in twenty minutes – but Linda knew he would not be. Frank's super-abundance of good feeling made Linda pretty cross – his gusto, his sociability, his human fun, and his conquering bossiness. He liked life, and wherever he was things happened. This evening, first Mrs Coughlan, now Mrs Massey . . . Except in bed, one was seldom alone with Frank. Having interfered once more, and got one more kind act in, he would come back like a cat full of rabbit again. Linda felt quite suspended. She wished there were pin tables in this high-class hotel. She rang for a drink, and two packs of cards and sat down and laid out a complex patience on the octagonal table below the sitting-room light. She thanked God she was not as young as she had been and no longer fell into desperations or piques. It was not that Frank did not concentrate, but he did not concentrate consecutively. She looked up once from her patience at her stamped letter, and half thought of tearing it up and writing a warmer one.

Mrs Coughlan and Miss Heally returned to their sitting-room: opening the piano they began to play a duet.

Polly Perry-Dunton, as well as Linda, heard the piano. Every three minutes Polly looked at her watch. After ten minutes, Polly left her sitting-room and went and lay on her bed in a sort of rigour. She pulled Clifford's pyjamas out from under the pillow and buried her face in them.

The Alvis, dip lights squinting along the row of sticky trees on the left, nosed its way through the mist down the avenue. Mrs Massey, in absolute quiescence, leaned back by Clifford's shoulder: he drove in silence. Frank, in the back of the car beside Teresa, had non-committally drawn her arm through his. Teresa did not take her eyes from the back of her mother's head. When the open white gates loomed up, Teresa leaned forward and told Clifford which way to turn. About a mile down the main road Teresa again spoke up. Clifford turned through more gates, and the four of them passed with well-sprung smoothness over the bumps of a peaty wet avenue. An uneasy smell of the sea came up the mist. Rhododendrons lolled and brushed the sides of the car. The left wheels mounted an edge of lawn. Clifford took a sweep and undipped his lights on veranda-posts and the pallid walls of a house.

'Teresa,' said Mrs Massey, 'tell them to come in.'

Teresa lit the two oil lamps under their dark pink shades. Mrs Massey, one hand on her drawing-room mantelpiece, swayed with the noble naturalness of a tree. Her form, above a smoulder of peat fire, was reflected in a mirror between the two dark windows – a mirror that ran from ceiling to floor. The room with its possessions, its air of bravura and slipshod moodiness, its low, smoked ceiling, armchairs with sunk seats, cabinets of dull glass began to be seen in the dark light. Clifford's scraggy Nordic figure, and Frank's thick-set springy figure, firmly poised on its heels, were also seen in the mirror, making a crowd.

'Sit down,' said Mrs Massey, 'I feel more like standing. I'm afraid I'm restless – I had bad news, you know.'

'That is frightfully tough,' said Frank.

'I feel bad,' said Mrs Massey, 'at not knowing your names. Yes, it's tough to be dead isn't it? He was about your age,' she said to Clifford. ' – Teresa dear, are you gummed there? Go and look for the drinks.'

Through the shadows in which they were all still standing up, Clifford threw a quick, begging look at Frank. Frank had to defer to Clifford's panic, and to Clifford's being unable to speak. 'Look, we must be pushing along,' Frank reluctantly, firmly said. Clifford bowed his heroic head sharply and took two steps to the door: the nightmare of being wanted was beginning, in this room, to close in round him again.

Mrs Massey only removed her eyes from Clifford to attend to a cigarette she was lighting over a lamp. Obliterated in shadows round the unglowing fire, Teresa, crouching, puffed at peat with a bellows. 'Teresa,' said her mother, 'do *you* see who he's so like — ?'

' – There's no drink left, as you know,' said Teresa quickly. 'I could make some tea, but they're just off.'

Clifford said: 'I'm afraid we *are* just off!'

In reply, Mrs Massey lifted the lamp from its low table to hold it, unsteadily, on a level with Clifford's face. She took a step or two forward, with the lamp. 'It's extraordinary,' she said, 'though you don't know it, that you should be in this house *tonight*. You mustn't mind what I say or do: I'm upset – you're English, too, aren't you? He looks like a hero, doesn't he?' she said appealingly to Frank.

'Now we've all had a look at each other,' said Frank firmly, 'let me take this out of your way.' Taking the wobbling lamp from Mrs Massey, he put it safely back on its table again.

'I wish I were proud of my country,' said Mrs Massey. 'But I'm ashamed of this country to tell you the truth.'

'Oh, come,' said Frank. 'We have much to be thankful for.'

Teresa crashed the bellows into the grate and went out of the room through the open door. Outside, she pulled up a chair and stood on it to light the lamp in the hall. Frank strolled after her and leaned in the door to watch. He said: 'Are you very fed up?' The hanging lamp spun round, and Teresa's eyes, fixed on the burner, glittered. 'Is it bad?' Frank said. 'You don't tell me anything. Did *you* love the poor chap?'

'Did I get a chance?'

The chair she stood on wobbled on the uneven flagstones: Frank came and stood close up to steady the chair. 'Come down off that,' he said, 'like a good girl.' Teresa stepped down off the chair into Frank's arms – but she stood inside them like steel. He let her go, and watched her pick up her trenchcoat and walk off down a stone passage to hang it up. There she stayed, as though she were falling and could fall no further, with her breast and face thrust into the hanging coats. Her shoulder-blades showed through her sweater, and Frank, coming up gently, put his two hands on them. 'She'd rather him dead,' said Teresa into the coats, 'she'd rather him dead than gone from her.' She kept moving her shoulders under Frank's hands.

'Could you cry? Could you have a cry if I took you off now in that car?'

Teresa, into the coats, said something he could not hear. 'And leave those two?' she said in a louder voice.

Frank had to agree: he looked back at the drawing-room door.

Mrs Massey and Clifford, waiting for Frank, now sat in two armchairs opposite the fire. 'I don't understand,' she said. 'How did we come in your car?'

'You got in . . . ' he said tentatively.

'And where had you been going?'

'Nowhere; I was looking for my wife's gloves.' He pulled the pussy gloves out of his pocket and showed them, to show he spoke the truth. Looking intently at the pussy gloves, Mrs Massey's eyes for the first time filled with tears. The access of some new feeling, a feeling with no context, resculptured her face. In the musty dark of her drawing-room, the dark round the dull fire, her new face looked alabaster and pure. The outline of her mist-clotted fair hair shook, as though shaken by the unconscious silent force of her tears.

'Aren't they small!' she said. 'Is your wife quite a little thing? Are you two very happy, then?'

'Very.'

'Take her gloves back safe . . . How English you are.'

Frank came in and said they must be pushing along. Teresa did not come in; she was opening the hall door. Out there on the sweep above the lawn and the sea, Clifford's lights were still blazing into the mist. Teresa went out and examined, as much by touch as anything, the wonderful car. An idea of going away for ever lifted and moved her heart, like a tide coming in. A whiteness up in the mist showed where there should have been the moon; the sleep-locked sea of the bay sighed. A smell of fern-rot and sea-water and gravel passed by Teresa into the house. Frank came to the hall door and saw her in the mist close to the car. He thought, calmly, of Linda wondering where he was, and wanted to go, and wanted to stay, and conceived how foolish it was, in love, to have to differentiate between women. In love there is no right and wrong, only the wish. However, he left Teresa alone and, going back into the drawing-room, said something further to Clifford about dinner.

Mrs Massey was just detaching her arms from Clifford's neck. 'I had to kiss him,' she said. 'He'll never understand why.' She went slowly ahead of the two men out to the car. 'Dinner?' she said. 'Is that really what time it is? . . . Teresa?'

But there was no reply.

Up the mist between the formless rhododendrons the Alvis, with Frank and Clifford, crawled back to the main road. 'If you thought of turning this car in before leaving this country,' Frank said, 'you might let me know first? My name's Mull – Mull, Cork always finds me.'

'My name is Perry-Dunton,' said Clifford, after a pause.

'Yes, I thought it might be.'

'Why?' said Clifford, alarmed.

'Caught my eye on the register. You two seem to like it here. And how right you are. Staying on?'

'Well, we're not quite sure of our plans.'

'I wish I wasn't – we've only got the week-end. Look, why don't you two drop down for a drink with us after dinner? My cousin would be delighted.'

'It is most awfully nice of you, but I don't think — '

'Right-o,' said Frank, nodding his head.

Look at All Those Roses

Lou exclaimed at that glimpse of a house in a sheath of startling flowers. She twisted round, to look back, in the open car, till the next corner had cut it out of sight. To reach the corner, it struck her, Edward accelerated, as though he were jealous of the rosy house – a house with gables, flat-fronted, whose dark windows stared with no expression through the flowers. The garden, with its silent, burning gaiety, stayed in both their minds like an apparition.

One of those conflicts between two silent moods had set up, with Lou and Edward, during that endless drive. Also, there is a point when an afternoon oppresses one with fatigue and a feeling of unreality. Relentless, pointless, unwinding summer country made nerves ache at the back of both of their eyes. This was a late June Monday; they were doubling back to London through Suffolk by-roads, on the return from a week-end. Edward, who detested the main roads, had traced out their curious route before starting, and Lou now sat beside him with the map on her knees. They had to be back by eight, for Edward, who was a writer, to finish and post an article: apart from this, time was no object with them. They looked forward with no particular pleasure to London and unlocking the stuffy flat, taking in the milk, finding bills in the letter-box. In fact, they looked forward to nothing with particular pleasure. They were going home for the purely negative reason that there was nowhere else they could as cheaply go. The week-end had not been amusing, but at least it had been 'away'. Now they could foresee life for weeks ahead – until someone else invited them – the typewriter, the cocktail-shaker, the telephone, runs in the car out of London to nowhere special. Love when Edward got a cheque in the post, quarrels about people on the way home from parties – and Lou's anxiety always eating them. This future weighed on them like a dull burden . . . So they had been glad to extend today.

But under a vacant sky, not sunny but full of diffused glare, the drive had begun to last too long: they felt bound up in the tired impotence of a dream. The stretches of horizon were stupefying. The road bent round wedges of cornfield, blocky elms dark with summer: for these last ten miles the countryside looked abandoned;

they passed dropping gates, rusty cattle-troughs and the thistly, tussocky, stale grass of neglected farms. There was nobody on the roads; perhaps there was nobody anywhere . . . In the heart of all this, the roses looked all the odder.

'They were extraordinary,' she said (when the first corner was turned) in her tired, little, dogmatic voice.

'All the more,' he agreed, 'when all the rest of the country looks something lived in by poor whites.'

'I wish we lived *there*,' she said. 'It really looked like somewhere.'

'It wouldn't if we did.'

Edward spoke with some tartness. He had found he had reason to dread week-ends away: they unsettled Lou and started up these fantasies. Himself, he had no illusions about life in the country: life without people was absolutely impossible. What would he and she do with nobody to talk to but each other? Already, they had not spoken for two hours. Lou saw life in terms of ideal moments. She found few ideal moments in their flat.

He went on: 'You know you can't stand ear-wigs. And we should spend our lives on the telephone.'

'About the earwigs?'

'No. About ourselves.'

Lou's smart little monkey face became dolorous. She never risked displeasing Edward too far, but she was just opening her mouth to risk one further remark when Edward jumped and frowned. A ghastly knocking had started. It seemed to come from everywhere, and at the same time to be a special attack on them. Then it had to be traced to the car's vitals: it jarred up Lou through the soles of her feet. Edward slowed to a crawl and stopped. He and she confronted each other with that completely dramatic lack of expression they kept for occasions when the car went wrong. They tried crawling on again, a few tentative yards: the knocking took up again with still greater fury.

'Sounds to me like a big end gone.'

'Oh my goodness,' she said.

All the same, she was truly glad to get out of the car. She stretched and stood waiting on the grass roadside while Edward made faces into the bonnet. Soon he flung round to ask what she would suggest doing: to his surprise (and annoyance) she had a plan ready. She would walk back to that house and ask if they had a telephone. If they had not, she would ask for a bicycle and bicycle to the place where the nearest garage was.

Edward snatched the map, but could not find where they were. Where they were seemed to be highly improbable. 'I expect you,' Lou said, 'would rather stay with the car.' 'No, I wouldn't,' said Edward, 'anybody can have it . . . You like to be sure where I am, don't you?' he added. He locked their few odd things up in the boot of the car with the suitcases, and they set off in silence. It was about a mile.

There stood the house, waiting. Why should a house wait? Most pretty scenes have something passive about them, but this looked like a trap baited with beauty, set ready to spring. It stood back from the road. Lou put her hand on the gate and, with a touch of bravado, the two filed up the paved path to the door. Each side of the path, hundreds of standard roses bloomed, over-charged with colour, as though this were their one hour. Crimson, coral, blue-pink, lemon and cold white, they disturbed with fragrance the dead air. In this spell-bound afternoon, with no shadows, the roses glared at the strangers, frighteningly bright. The face of the house was plastered with tea-roses: waxy cream when they opened but with vermilion buds.

The blistered door was propped open with a bizarre object, a lump of quartz. Indoors was the dark, cold-looking hall. When they had come to the door they found no bell or knocker: they could not think what to do. 'We had better cough,' Lou said. So they stood there coughing, till a door at the end of the hall opened and a lady or woman looked out – they were not sure which. 'Oh?' she said, with no expression at all.

'We couldn't find your bell.'

'There they are,' she said, pointing to two Swiss cow-bells that hung on loops of string by the door she had just come out of. Having put this right, she continued to look at them, and out through the door past them, wiping her powerful-looking hands vaguely against the sides of her blue overall. They could hardly see themselves as intruders when their intrusion made so little effect. The occupying inner life of this person was not for an instant suspended by their presence. She was a shabby amazon of a woman, with a sculptural clearness about the face. She must have lost contact with the outer world completely: there was now nothing to 'place' her by. It is outside attachments – hopes, claims, curiosities, desires, little touches of greed – that put a label on one to help strangers. As it was, they could not tell if she were rich or poor, stupid or clever, a spinster or a wife. She seemed prepared, not anxious, for them to speak. Lou, standing close beside Edward, gave him a dig in a rib. So Edward explained to the lady how they found themselves, and asked if she had a telephone or a bicycle.

She said she was sorry to say she had neither. Her maid had a bicycle, but had ridden home on it. 'Would you like some tea?' she said. 'I am just boiling the kettle. Then perhaps you can think of something to do.' This lack of grip of the crisis made Edward decide the woman must be a moron: annoyance contused his face.

But Lou, who wanted tea and was attracted by calmness, was entirely won. She looked at Edward placatingly.

'Thank you,' he said. 'But I must do something at once. We haven't got all night; I've got to be back in London. Can you tell me where I can telephone from? I must get through to a garage – a good garage.'

Unmoved, the lady said: 'You'll have to walk to the village. It's about three miles away.' She gave unexpectedly clear directions, then looked at Lou again. 'Leave your wife here,' she said. 'Then she can have tea.'

Edward shrugged; Lou gave a brief, undecided sigh. How much she wanted to stop. But she never liked to be left. This partly arose from the fact that she was not Edward's wife: he was married to someone else and his wife would not divorce him. He might some day go back to her, if this ever became the way of least resistance. Or he might, if it were the way of even less resistance, move on to someone else. Lou was determined neither should ever happen. She did love Edward, but she also stuck to him largely out of contentiousness. She quite often asked herself why she did. It seemed important – she could not say why. She was determined to be a necessity. Therefore she seldom let him out of her sight – her idea of love was adhesiveness . . . Knowing this well, Edward gave her a slightly malign smile, said she had far better stay, turned, and walked down the path without her. Lou, like a lost cat, went half-way to the door. 'Your roses are wonderful . . . ' she said, staring out with unhappy eyes.

'Yes, they grow well for us, Josephine likes to see them.' Her hostess added: 'My kettle will be boiling. Won't you wait in there?'

Lou went deeper into the house. She found herself in a long, low and narrow parlour, with a window at each end. Before she could turn round, she felt herself being looked at. A girl of about thirteen lay, flat as a board, in a wicker invalid carriage. The carriage was pulled out across the room, so that the girl could command the view from either window, the flat horizons that bounded either sky. Lying there with no pillow she had a stretched look. Lou stood some distance from the foot of the carriage: the dark eyes looked at her down thin cheekbones, intently. The girl had an unresigned, living face; one hand crept on the rug over her breast. Lou felt, here was the nerve and core of the house . . . The only movement was made by a canary, springing to and fro in its cage.

'Hullo,' Lou said, with that deferential smile with which one approaches an invalid. When the child did not answer, she went on: 'You must wonder who I am?'

'I don't now; I did when you drove past.'

'Then our car broke down.'

'I know, I wondered whether it might.'

Lou laughed and said: 'Then you put the evil eye on it.'

The child ignored this. She said: 'This is not the way to London.'

'All the same, that's where we're going.'

'You mean, where you were going . . . Is that your husband who has just gone away?'

'That's Edward: yes. To telephone. He'll be back.' Lou, who was wearing a summer suit, smart, now rather crumpled, of honey-yellow linen, felt Josephine look her up and down. 'Have you been to a party?' she said, 'or are you going to one?'

'We've just been staying away,' Lou walked nervously down the room to the front window. From here she saw the same roses Josephine saw: she thought they looked like forced roses, magnetized into being. Magnetized, buds uncurled and petals dropped. Lou began to wake from the dream of the afternoon: her will stirred; she wanted to go; she felt apprehensive, threatened. 'I expect you like to lie out of doors, with all those roses?' she said.

'No, not often: I don't care for the sky.'

'You just watch through the window?'

'Yes,' said the child, impatiently. She added: 'What are the parts of London with most traffic?'

'Piccadilly Circus. Trafalgar Square.'

'Oh, I would like to see those.'

The child's mother's step sounded on the hall flags: she came in with the tea-tray. 'Can I help you?' said Lou, glad of the interim.

'Oh, thank you. Perhaps you'd unfold that table. Put it over here beside Josephine. She's lying down because she hurt her back.'

'My back was hurt six years ago,' said Josephine. 'It was my father's doing.'

Her mother was busy lodging the edge of the tray on the edge of the tea-table.

'Awful for him,' Lou murmured, helping unstack the cups.

'No, it's not,' said Josephine. 'He has gone away.'

Lou saw why. A man in the wrong cannot live where there is no humanity. There are enormities you can only keep piling up. He had bolted off down that path, as Edward had just done. Men cannot live with sorrow, with women who embrace it. Men will suffer a certain look in animals' eyes, but not in women's eyes. And men dread obstinacy, of love, of grief. You could stay with burning Josephine, not with her mother's patient, exalted face . . . When her mother had gone again, to fetch the teapot and kettle, Josephine once more fastened her eyes on Lou. 'Perhaps your husband will be some time,' she said. 'You're the first new person I have seen for a year. Perhaps he will lose his way.'

'Oh, but then I should have to look for him!'

Josephine gave a fanatical smile. 'But when people go away they sometimes quite go,' she said. 'If they always come back, then what is the good of moving?'

'I don't see the good of moving.'

'Then stay here.'

'People don't just go where they want; they go where they must.'

'Must you go back to London?'

'Oh, I have to, you know.'

'Why?'

Lou frowned and smiled in a portentous, grown-up way that meant nothing at all to either herself or Josephine. She felt for her cigarette case and, glumly, found it empty – Edward had walked away with the packet of cigarettes that he and she had been sharing that afternoon. He also carried any money she had.

'You don't know where he's gone to,' Josephine pointed out. 'If you had to stay, you would soon get used to it. We don't wonder where my father is.'

'What's your mother's name?'

'Mrs Mather. She'd like you to stay. Nobody comes to see us; they used to, they don't now. So we only see each other. They may be frightened of something — '

Mrs Mather came back, and Josephine looked out of the other window. This immediate silence marked a conspiracy, in which Lou had no willing part. While Mrs Mather was putting down the teapot, Lou looked round the room, to make sure it was ordinary. This window-ended parlour was lined with objects that looked honest and worn without having antique grace. A faded room should look homely. But extinct paper and phantom cretonnes gave this a gutted air. Rooms can be whitened and gutted by too-intensive living, as they are by a fire. It was the garden, out there, that focused the senses. Lou indulged for a minute the astounding fancy that Mr Mather lay at the roses' roots . . . Josephine said sharply: 'I don't want any tea,' which made Lou realize that she would have to be fed and did not want to be fed in front of the stranger Lou still was. Mrs Mather made no comment: she drew two chairs to the table and invited Lou to sit down. 'It's rather sultry,' she said. 'I'm afraid your husband may not enjoy his walk.'

'How far did you say it was?'

'Three miles.'

Lou, keeping her wrist under the table, glanced down covertly at her watch.

'We are very much out of the way,' said Mrs Mather.

'But perhaps you like that?'

'We are accustomed to quiet,' said Mrs Mather, pouring out tea. 'This was a farm, you know. But it was an unlucky farm, so since my husband left I have let the land. Servants seem to find that the place is lonely – country girls are so different now. My present servant is not very clear in her mind, but she works well and does not seem to feel lonely. When she is not working she rides home.'

'Far?' said Lou, tensely.

'A good way,' said Mrs Mather, looking out of the window at the horizon.

'Then aren't you rather . . . alone? – I mean, if anything happened.'

'Nothing more can happen,' said Mrs Mather. 'And there are two of us. When I am working upstairs or am out with the chickens, I wear one of those bells you see in the hall, so Josephine can always hear where I am. And I leave the other bell on Josephine's carriage. When I work in the garden she can see me, of course.' She slit the wax-paper top off a jar of jam. 'This is my last pot of last year's damson,' she said. 'Please try some; I shall be making more soon. We have two fine trees.'

'You should see mother climb them,' said Josephine.

'Aren't you afraid of falling?'

'Why?' said Mrs Mather, advancing a plate of rather rich bread and butter. 'I never eat tea, thank you,' Lou said, sitting rigid, sipping round her cup of tea like a bird.

'She thinks if she eats she may have to stay here for ever,' Josephine said. Her mother, taking no notice, spread jam on her bread and butter and started to eat in a calmly voracious way. Lou kept clinking her spoon against the teacup: every time she did this the canary started and fluttered. Though she knew Edward could not possibly come yet, Lou kept glancing down the garden at the gate. Mrs Mather, reaching out for more bread and butter, saw, and thought Lou was looking at the roses. 'Would you like to take some back to London?' she said.

Josephine's carriage had been wheeled out on the lawn between the rosebeds. She lay with eyes shut and forehead contracted, for overhead hung the dreaded space of the sky. But she had to be near Lou while Lou cut the roses. In a day or two, Lou thought, I should be wearing a bell. What shall I do with these if I never do go? she thought, as she cut through the strong stems between the thorns and piled the roses on the foot of the carriage. I shall certainly never want to look at roses again. By her wrist watch it was six o'clock – two hours since Edward had started. All round, the country under the white, stretched sky was completely silent. She went once to the gate.

'Is there any way from that village?' she said at last. 'Any 'bus to anywhere else? Any taxi one could hire?'

'I don't know,' said Josephine.

'When does your servant come back?'

'Tomorrow morning. Sometimes our servants never come back at all.'

Lou shut the knife and said: 'Well, those are enough roses.' She supposed she could hear if whoever Edward sent for the car came to tow it away. The car, surely, Edward would not abandon? She went to the gate again. From behind her Josephine said: 'Then please wheel me indoors.'

'If you like. But I shall stay here.'

'Then I will. But please put something over my eyes.'

Lou got out her red silk handkerchief and laid this across Josephine's eyes. This made the mouth more revealing: she looked down at the small resolute smile. 'If you want to keep on listening,' the child said, 'you needn't talk to me. Lie down and let's pretend we're both asleep.'

Lou lay down on the dry, cropped grass alongside the wheels of the carriage: she crossed her hands under her head, shut her eyes and lay stretched, as rigid as Josephine. At first she was so nervous, she thought the lawn vibrated under her spine. Then slowly she relaxed. There is a moment when silence, no longer resisted, rushes into the mind. She let go, inch by inch, of life, that since she was a child she had been clutching so desperately – her obsessions about this and that, her obsession about keeping Edward. How anxiously she had run from place to place, wanting to keep everything inside her own power. I should have stayed still: I shall stay still now, she thought. What I want must come to me: I shall not go after it. People who stay still generate power. Josephine stores herself up, and so what she wants happens, because she knows what she wants. I only think I want things; I only think I want Edward. (He's not coming and I don't care, I don't care.) I feel life myself now. No wonder I've been tired, only half getting what I don't really want. Now I want nothing; I just want a white circle.

The white circle distended inside her eyelids and she looked into it in an ecstasy of indifference. She knew she was looking at nothing – then knew nothing . . .

Josephine's voice, from up in the carriage, woke her. 'You were quite asleep.'

'Was I?'

'Take the handkerchief off: a motor's coming.'

Lou heard the vibration. She got up and uncovered Josephine's eyes. Then she went to the foot of the carriage and got her roses together. She was busy with this, standing with her back to the gate, when she heard the taxi pull up, then Edward's step on the path. The taxi driver sat staring at the roses. 'It's all right,' Edward shouted, 'they're sending out from the garage. They should be here any moment. But what people – God! – Look here, have you been all right?'

'Perfectly, I've been with Josephine.'

'Oh, hullo, Josephine,' Edward said, with a hasty exercise of his charm. 'Well, I've come for this woman. Thank you for keeping her.'

'It's quite all right, thank you . . . Shall you be going now?'

'We must get our stuff out of the car: it will have to be towed to the garage. Then when I've had another talk to the garage people we'll take this taxi on and pick up a train . . . Come on, Lou, come on! We don't want to miss those people! And we've got to get that stuff out of the car!'

'Is there such a hurry?' she said, putting down the roses.

'Of course, there's a hurry . . . ' He added, to Josephine: 'We'll look in on our way to the station, when I've fixed up all this, to say goodbye to your mother.' He put his hand on Lou's shoulder and punted her ahead of him down the path. 'I'm glad you're all right,' he said, as they got into the taxi. 'You're well out of that, my girl. From what I heard in the village — '

'What, have you been anxious?' said Lou, curiously.

'It's a nervy day,' said Edward, with an uneasy laugh. 'And I had to put in an hour in the village emporium, first waiting for my call, then waiting for this taxi. (And this is going to cost us a pretty penny.) I got talking, naturally, one way and another. You've no idea what they said when they heard where I had parked you. Not a soul round there will go near the place. I must say – discounting gossip – there's a story there,' said Edward. 'They can't fix any-thing, but . . . Well, you see, it appears that this Mather woman . . . ' Lowering his voice, so as not to be heard by the driver, Edward began to tell Lou what he had heard in the village about the abrupt disappearance of Mr Mather.

Attractive Modern Homes

NO SOONER were the Watsons settled into their new home than Mrs Watson was overcome by melancholy. The actual settling-in was over only too soon. They had bought the house before it was done building, which had meant putting in time in rooms nearby; she had looked forward to having her own things round her again, and come, perhaps, to expect too much of them. The day the last workman left, the Watsons took possession. He screwed the bronze name-plate on to the gate, while she immediately put up the orange style curtains to give the façade style and keep strangers from looking in. But her things appeared uneasy in the new home. The armchairs and settee covered in jazz tapestry, the sideboard with mirror panel, the alabaster light bowls, even the wireless cabinet looked sulky, as though they would rather have stayed in the van. The semi-detached house was box-like, with thin walls: downstairs it had three rooms and a larder, upstairs, three rooms and a bath. The rooms still smelled of plaster, the bath of putty. The stairs shook when the wardrobe was carried up: the whole structure seemed to be very frail.

Shavings and trodden paper littered the unmade garden and a persistent hammering from unfinished houses travelled over the fence. Even after dark these hollow echoes continued, for Eagles, the builder, was selling houses as fast as he put them up, and his men worked overtime, hammering on in the raw brick shells by candlelight. Earthy emanations and smells of shavings, singing and the plonk of boards being dropped filled the autumn darkness on the estate. The gored earth round the buildings looked unfriendly with pain. Outside the gates, drain trenches had been filled in roughly, but the roads were not made yet – they were troughs of mud, harrowed by builders' lorries this wet autumn, and bounded only by kerbs, along which you picked your way. It would not be possible yet to get a car out.

The Watsons' house, which they had called Rhyll, stood at the far edge of the estate, facing a row of elms along a lane that used to be called Nut Lane. Between the trees, one hedge had been broken down, leaving a flank of the lane bare to the new road alongside the row of villa gates. The Watsons' best room windows stared between the trees at a field that rose beyond them: a characterless hill. Almost no one passed, and nobody looked in.

Mr Watson considered the trees an advantage. He was quick to point out any advantage, with a view to cheering his wife up. His promotion in business, so querulously awaited, came hard on her now it had come, for it entailed a transfer to another branch of the firm and the move here from the place they had always known. Here they were utter strangers; they had not a soul to speak to; no one had heard of them. The eighty miles they had travelled might have been eight hundred. Where they came from they had been born: there had been his people and her people and the set they had grown up with. Everyone took them for granted and thought well of them, so their ten years of marriage had been rich with society. Mrs Watson enjoyed society and esteem and was dependent upon them, as women naturally are. When she heard they must move she had said at once: 'We might as well go straight to the Colonies,' though after that she enjoyed the melancholy importance the prospect of moving gave her among her friends. Yes, where they came from many people were sorry, if not seriously upset, when the Watsons left: they said it was too bad. But their having come here made no difference to anyone. No one remarked their curtains, no one glanced at their door.

This new town they had come to had a mellow, ancient core, but was rapidly spreading and filling up with workers. The Watsons had been edged out to this new estate, the only place where they could find a house. And how un-ideal it was. An estate is not like a village, it has no heart; even the shops are new and still finding their own feet. It has not had time to take on the prim geniality of a suburb. The dwellers are pioneers unennobled by danger. Everybody feels strange and has no time for curiosity. Nothing has had time to flower in this new place.

For instance, the Watsons had neighbours – the houses on either side were already done and lived in. But it had struck her that when they were moving in – while their van stood at the gate and her imposing furniture jolted up the unmade path – not a next-door curtain twitched; nobody took note. No one asked her in for a cup of tea, that first day, or even offered a cup over the fence. Where she came from, it had been customary to do this for newcomers who had not yet unpacked the kettle.

'It seems odd to me,' she had remarked to her husband.

He had been glad to have no one coming around to stare. But he was sorry to have her taking against the neighbours, this would make for no good: 'They're newcomers themselves,' was all he could find to say.

'Then you would think they might think.'

He looked worried, and she mistook his expression for crossness. 'Oh, all right,' she said. 'I merely passed the remark. There's no harm in my passing a remark occasionally, I suppose.'

She had never needed imagination herself, but now felt for the first time its absence in other people. Soon she suspected everyone but herself to be without natural feeling. For instance, she had worked on the children's feelings about the move, pointing out that they were leaving their little friends for ever and that their grannies, who loved them, would now be far away. So that Freddie and Vera wept when they got into the train and whined a good deal during the time in rooms. But now they were delighted with their surroundings; they enjoyed squelching in the deep mud. The half-built houses with their skeleton roofs, scaffolding, tubs of mortar, stacks of piping, and salmon-pink window-frames magnetized Freddie, who wished to become a builder. Where they came from, everything had been complete for years. He explored the uphill reaches of Nut Lane where hedges still arched over to make a tunnel. Vera liked tossing her curls and showing off at her new school, where, her mother warned her, the children were common. Vera was a child with naturally nice ways who would throw anything off, but Mrs Watson kept watching Freddie closely to see he did not pick his nose, drop 'h's or show any other signs of having been in bad company. There was only one school near here: they had no choice . . . Seeing the children's horrible good spirits, Mrs Watson said to her husband, 'How children do forget!' Her manner to Freddie and Vera became reproachful and wan. The old gentleman in the house they were semi-detached from gave Vera a peppermint over the fence, but did not speak to her mother.

To realize one's unhappiness as a whole needs some largeness, even of an ignoble kind. Mrs Watson pitched upon details. The estate was a mile and a half out of the town and buses only ran every twenty minutes. By the time you got anywhere it was time to start home again. And what is the good of shops with nobody to walk round with? Also, back where they came from she was accustomed to have a girl in daily to work, but here there was no way of hearing of any girl, so she had to work alone. Being alone all day, she never heard any news except what was in the paper. Back where they came from hardly a morning passed without someone dropping in, or out shopping you met someone, or when you went down the road you knew from the look of windows that people knew Mrs Watson was going by. Whatever she bought or did invited some heartfelt comment. And he and she had been often invited out. Here they did not even go to the movies; to leave the house after dark fell was not tempting, for lamps along the estate roads were few and dim, making it hard to pick your way on the kerb, and her dread of stepping into the deep mud became neurotic.

Mr Watson had a vice: he was a reader. And he was also always happy messing about with the wireless. He was out all day and talked to men at the office. At week-ends he got on with making the garden; the children played up the lane and she spent most of Saturday wiping mud off the line. Once, after tea, Freddie came in with a white face to say he had seen something funny up Nut Lane. Though his mother told him at once not to be so naughty, this made her come over queerish, later, herself. She got to dread the country left dingily at their door.

Up to now she had been happy without knowing, like a fortunate sheep or cow always in the same field. She was a woman who did not picture herself. She had looked into mirrors only to pat her perm down or smooth a jumper nicely over her bust. Everything that had happened to her seemed natural – love, marriage, the birth of Freddie, then Vera – for she had seen it happen to someone else. She never needed to ask what was happening really. No wonder the move had been like stepping over a cliff. Now no one cared any more whether she existed; she came to ask, without words, if she did exist. Yes, she felt sure there *must* be a Mrs Watson. Asking why she felt sure, she fell prey to every horror of the subjective world. Wandering, frightened, there, she observed with apathy that the perm was growing out of her hair; some days she never took off her overall. She fell into a way of standing opposite the mantel mirror in the front room on heavy afternoons. The room was made water-grey by the elms opposite, that had not yet shed their rotting autumn leaves – there was no frost, no wind, no reason why they should ever fall. There are no words for such dismay. Her blue eyes began to dilate oddly; her mouth took on an uncertain stubborn twist. The hammering from behind the house continued; now and then a gate down the road clicked and somebody walked past without knowing her.

In all Eagles' houses the married bedroom is at the front. At this time of year the sun rose behind the hill, casting shadows of elms across the blanket about the moment that Mrs Watson woke. The orange curtains would flame, the bedroom dazzle with sunshine. Though rain often set in later and almost all nights were wet, the early mornings were brilliant. She used to sit up, pull off her shingle-cap and shake out her short, blonde hair, seeing light burn its tips. The empty promise of morning shot a pang through her heart to tell her she was awake again. Mr Watson slept late with determination; you saw his dread of waking under his lids. He lay beside her in a pre-natal attitude, legs crossed and drawn up, one cheek thrust into the pillow. The ripple his wife's getting up sent across the mattress did not ever disturb him. When she had lit the geyser, set breakfast and started the children dressing she would come back and shake the end of the bed. The first thing he always saw was his wife at the bed's foot, gripping the brass with sun flaming round the tips of her hair. A Viking woman, foreign to all he knew of Muriel, with eyes remorseless as the remorseless new day, fixed on him a stare that he did not dare to plumb.

She had given up grumbling and seldom passed remarks now. Something behind her silence he learned to dread.

Saturdays were his half-days. One Saturday, when they had been there about eight weeks, he suddenly stuck his fork upright into the garden soil, eased the palms of his townish hands which had blistered, scraped off clods from his insteps on to the fork and went indoors to the kitchen to run the tap. He did all this in the decisive manner of someone acting on impulse, shy of himself. Towelling his face and hands on the roller he instinctively listened. Rhyll was a sounding box and she could be heard not there. She did say something, he thought, about going into town. Freddie and Vera were out about the estate. So there was no one to wonder . . . So he stepped round the house and out at the front gate. Since they came, he had had no secret pleasure. Today he would start up Nut Lane which, unknown, edged the estate with savageness.

Standing between the stumps of broken-down hedges he looked back at their road. A single twist of smoke from a chimney melted into the thin November grey, but the houses with close 'art' curtains looking unliving – what should animate them? Behind, scaffolding poles, squares more of daylight being entombed there . . . Inside, the lane was full of builders' rubbish. He started uphill, stepping from rib to rib of slimy hardness over chasms of mud. Rotting leaves made silent whole reaches of lane. Recoiling from branches in the thickety darkness, he thought he had not asked what Freddie said he had seen. The idea of a ghost's persistent aliveness comforted some under part of his mind.

The slope slackened, the lane was running level through a scrubby hazel wood with the sky behind. This must be round the other side of the hill. He looked into the wood which, because he had not known it existed, looked as though no one had ever seen it before. Part of its strangeness was a woman's body face down on the ground. Her arms were stretched out and she wore a mackintosh. With a jump of vulgar excitement he wondered if she were dead. Then the fair hair unnaturally fallen forward and red belt of the mackintosh showed him this was his wife, who could not be dead. Her manner of being here made his heart stop; then he felt hot colour come up his neck. He foresaw her shame at lying like this here; having heard steps she was keeping her face hidden. He could not have been more stricken in his idea of her if he had found her here with another man. He did not like to see her embrace the earth.

Waiting to bolt if she stirred, he stood where he was, eyeing her figure; its fiercely abject line. He stepped sharply up the bank into the wood. Her not stiffening as he approached shocked him. He pulled up and saw her contract one hand.

He heard himself say: 'So you didn't go to town?'

'No.'

'Feeling bad?'

'I'm all right.'

'Then look here,' he said, his voice humping a tone, 'you oughtn't to be like that in a place like this. I might have been anyone.'

'What of it?' she said, her mouth muffled by grass.

'Besides, look here . . . That grass is reeking wet.'

'That's up to me,' she said. 'Get out. Why keep on coming after me?'

'How should I know? I was simply taking a turn.'

'Well, take your turn,' said her dead voice.

He took an angry forward step, looking down at her violently. Nothing appears more wanton than despair. 'I won't have it,' he said, 'it isn't decent. Get up.'

She drew her arms in, pushed herself on to her knees and got right up in one slow, disdainful movement, keeping her face away. 'Decent?' she said. 'This place isn't anywhere.'

'It's round where we live.'

'Live?' she said, 'What do you mean, live?'

'Well, we — '

'What do you mean, we?'

'You and I,' he said, looking sideways at her shoulder.

'Yes,' she said. 'It's fine for me having you. Sometimes anyone would almost think you could speak.'

'Well, what is there to say?'

'Don't ask me.'

'Well, you've got a home.'

'Oh, yes,' she said, 'I have, haven't I? Yes, it's sweet, isn't it? Like you see in advertisements.' She thrust her thumbs under the belt of her mackintosh.

'You've no business . . . ' he said. 'Suppose Freddie or Vee had happened to come up here. That'd have been a nice . . . '

'Well, it'd show Vera . . . '

'Look here,' he said, 'You're batty!'

'No; I'm just noticing.'

Catching at her near shoulder he pulled her round to face him.

His excitement, unfamiliar, excited him; he saw his rage tower. She stood stock still in her buttoned mackintosh, staring woodenly past his shoulder at the bleak wood, unconscious as any dummy of being touched. She said: 'Why is it awful?'

'It's a new place.'

'Yes. But it oughtn't to be awful, not awful like this.'

'Awful?'

'You know it is.'

'We've got each other.'

She gave him that glazed, unironic, really terrible look. Throat nervously filling up, he objected again – 'But, people . . . '

'Yes, I know they do. Even right in the country miles off. They seem to get on all right. So what I want to know is . . . '

'You expect such a whole lot . . . '

'No. Only what's natural.'

He frowned down at the form she had left in the crushed, autumny grass for so long that she looked down at it too. 'There must be some way,' he said. 'To keep going, I mean.'

'Yes, there ought to be,' she said. 'If you ask me, I don't know what a house like that is meant for. You can't think what it's like when you're in it the whole time. I can't understand, really.'

'We're the same as we've been always.'

'Yes,' she said, 'but it didn't notice before.'

He changed colour and said, 'You know I . . . I think the world of you.'

'Well, you've sort of got to, haven't you?' she replied unmovedly. 'Why aren't the two of us having a better time?'

'Well, we don't know anyone yet.'

'I wonder,' she said. 'Do you think there's so much in that?'

He looked at the wood's dead glades and emasculate, sparse leaves thin with afternoon light. 'You know,' he said, 'this place will be nice in spring. We might come here quite a lot.'

But, not listening, she said, 'The way we live, we never know anyone. All that crowd back at home, they've forgotten us. It was all coming in for coffee, or else whist. It doesn't get you anywhere. I mean, you get used to it, but that doesn't make it natural. What I mean is . . . '

However, she broke off there and began to walk away, stepping down the low bank into the lane. 'Yes,' she said in a different voice, 'it's a nice wood. The kids know it quite well.'

'What d'you think Freddie saw?' he said rapidly, following her downhill.

'Oh, I don't know. I daresay he saw himself.' Tilted on wobbling heels she went downhill ahead of him, low branches thwacking against the thighs of her mackintosh. A crimpled dead leaf caught in her hair, over her turned-up collar. He followed, eyes on the leaf, doggedly striding, stumbling between the ruts. It was going on tea-time: in the tunnel of lane the twilight was pretty deep and a dull, lightish glimmer came from her mackintosh. Coming down, the lane was shorter; the wood was near their door, too near their door.

When, one behind the other, they stepped through the broken hedge opposite Rhyll, a youngish woman stood at Rhyll gate, at a loss, looking about. She was hatless and wore a brick woollen three-piece suit. Her air was neighbourly.

She said, 'Oh, Mrs Watson?'

Mrs Watson replied guardedly.

'I hope I may introduce myself. I am Mrs Dawkins from just along there. Kosy Kot. I was sorry to find you out. I am sure you won't mind my taking the liberty, but your Vera and my Dorothy have been playing together recently and I called in to ask if you'd think of kindly allowing Vera to stop to tea with Dorothy this afternoon. Mr Dawkins and I would be most glad that she should.'

'Well, really, that's most kind of you, I'm sure. If Vera's a good girl, and comes home at half-past six . . . '

'I did hope you would not think it a liberty, I have to be careful with Dorothy, as we are quite newcomers, but Vera is such a sweet, nice little thing – I understand that you are newcomers also?'

'So to speak,' said Mrs Watson. 'We've lived here about eight weeks. But the newer houses are lived in now, I see.'

'It's a nice estate,' said Mrs Dawkins, 'isn't it? Convenient and yet in a way countrified. I shall be glad when they make the roads up; at present Mr Dawkins cannot get his car out, which is disappointing for him.' She glanced at the blank beside Rhyll where there could be a baby garage.

'We've delayed getting our car till the roads were made,' said Mrs Watson at once. 'The 'buses being so frequent and everything.'

Mr Watson, looking surprised, edged past them in at Rhyll gate. Both ladies turned and watched him up to the path.

'I always say,' continued Mrs Dawkins, 'that it takes time to settle into a place. Gentlemen, being out so much, don't feel it the same way.'

'It's hardly to be expected,' said Mrs Watson. Putting a hand up to pat all round the shingle, she plucked the leaf from her hair. 'Still, I've no doubt a place grows on one. It's really all habit, isn't it?'

The Easter Egg Party

THEIR object was to restore her childhood to her. They were simple and zealous women, of an integrity rooted in flawless sentiment; they bowed to nothing but their own noble ideas, and flinched from nothing but abandoning these. They issued the invitation on an impulse but awaited the answer with no drop in morale. They did not shrink from facts, for they attended committees for the good of the world – most facts, however, got to West Wallows a little bit watered down: such things did happen, but not to people one knew. So that when their eye was drawn – they were un-married sisters, with everything in common, and had, in regard to some things, one eye between them – when their eye was drawn by a once-quite-familiar name to an obscure paragraph in their daily paper, their hearts (or their heart) stopped. The case was given in outline, with unusual reticence. When they saw what had either happened or nearly happened – they were not quite clear which – to the little girl of a friend they had known as a little girl, shyness and horror drove a wedge between them; they became two people whose looks could not quite meet. Across the breakfast table of their large cottage, in the half-acre garden already gladey and glittering with the first greens of spring, they failed to discuss the matter. After a day of solitary side-by-side reflection it came up with them in its happier practical aspect: 'Could one *do* anything now? . . . Is there any way one could help?'

Eunice and Isabelle Evers were both just over fifty: their unperplexed lives showed in their faces, lined only by humour, and in their frank, high foreheads. They were Amazons in homespuns, Amazons, without a touch of deprivation or pathos; their lives had been one long vigorous walk. Like successful nuns, they both had a slightly married air. An unusual number of people in Gloucester-shire knew and respected them, and they cut ice in the village of West Wallows. They thought the world of children, of any children; and children, in consequence, thought the world of them: they were past mistresses at blowing that bubble world that is blown for children by children-loving grown-ups – perhaps, also the dearest of their own pleasures lay there. If they had any fantasies, these centred round ponies and bread-and-jam on the beach, and they still received intimations of immortality.

Therefore, any unspeakable thing happening to any child was more upsetting to them than if they had been mothers. It was against their natures to judge Dorothea (the friend they had known as a little girl) in any way. All the same, across what line, into what world had she wandered in these years since her marriage, since they had lost sight of her, that her little girl should be exposed to such things as this? Dorothea's marriage had failed. Must one own she failed as a mother? They knew, vaguely, Dorothea was 'on the stage' – though one never saw her name on the programme of any play.

Dorothea's answer to their invitation took so long in coming that they had begun to fear she was out of reach. But when she did answer, Dorothea accepted with alacrity. She said that it really was truly sweet of them, and she only hoped they would find Hermione good. 'She's really as good as gold, but she's always rather reserved. I am sure it might do her good to be away from me for a bit; you see, I am really very upset these days. I suppose that's only natural; my nerves have always been awful, and now *this* coming, on top of everything else. It's nearly killed me, of course. I suppose one will get over it. Well, it really is dear of you; you always were such dears. *Oh*, how far away all those happy days seem now! . . . I will send Hermione down on April 12th. Yes, I think she's fond of animals; at all events you could try. Of course she's never had any, poor little soul.'

So they began to prepare for Hermione.

West Wallows was more than a village: it was a neighbourhood. From the wide street branched roads that led past the white gates of many homes. The rector was tactful and energetic, the squire unusually cultivated; there were a number of moderate-sized dwellings – some antique, some quite recently built. Inexpensive sociability, liberal politics, shapely antique family furniture, 'interests', enlightened charity set the note of the place. No one was very rich; nobody was eccentric, and, though few people hunted, nobody wrote letters against blood sports. The local families harmonized with the pleasant retired people who had settled here. Probably few neighbourhoods in England have such a nice atmosphere as West Wallows. In the holidays all the children had a jolly time . . . The Easter holidays were in progress now, and this created a slight predicament: how much should Hermione be with other children?

The Misses Evers decided to wait and see.

They decided to wait for grace and see what line things took.

They hinted at nothing to anyone. In the week before Hermione came, the tortoiseshell cat Barbara was persuaded to wean her two patchy kittens, who learnt to lap prettily from an Umbrian saucer. The honeysuckle up the south front of the cottage unfolded the last of its green shoots, and in the garden and in the strip of orchard the other side of the brook daffodils blew their trumpets.

The first afternoon was windy. Every time a sucker of honeysuckle swung loose and tapped the window Hermione jumped. This was the only sign she gave of having grown-up nerves. She was not quite a pretty child; her face was a long, plump oval; her large dark-grey eyes were set rather close together, which gave her an urgent air. Her naturally curly dark hair had grown too long for a bob and swung just clear of her shoulders. She sat in the dark glass dome of her own inside world, just too composedly eating bread and honey. Now and then she glanced, with mysterious satisfaction, at the bangles on one or the other of her wrists.

'This is honey from our own bees, Hermione.'

'Goodness.'

'It tastes quite different from other honey, we think.'

'Yes; Mummy said you kept bees. Do you keep doves too?'

Eunice glanced at the white forms that whirled rather frighteningly over the wind-teased garden. 'Those are the next-door pigeons; they keep on flying over, so we have the fun of them.'

'The next-door cat in London keeps getting into our larder. I do hate cats.'

'Oh, but you must like Barbara – and she's got two kittens.'

'Cats always do that, don't they?'

After tea Eunice took her up to what was to be her room, the spare-room over the porch, snug as a ship's cabin and frilly with sprigged stuff. She showed her the sampler worked by another little girl of eleven, just a hundred years ago, and some framed photographs of Italy. 'That's Assisi, where St Francis lived.'

'Goodness,' said Hermione, biting her thumb vaguely. She looked through the loops of dotted muslin curtain at the tops of the apple trees. 'It's just like on a calendar,' she said. She sat on the bed, with her tongue feeling round one cheek, while Eunice unpacked her two suitcases for her. 'Oh, what pretty clothes and things,' said Eunice deprecatingly. 'But I don't think you'll have a chance to wear most of them here. You'll want to wear old clothes and simply tumble about.'

'I haven't got any old clothes. Mummie gives them away.'

In her tweed skirt, with her knotted oak walking-stick, lifting her forehead to the sweet spring air Isabelle, next morning, swung down the village street, and Hermione walked beside her, changing step now and then with a queer little dancing hop. In her raspberry-woollen dress, her turn-up hat with the Donald Duck clip and her long, white, carefully pulled-up socks, the child looked like a stage child half-way through a tour: nothing would tone her down. Isabelle pointed out the village pond with its white ducks, the saddle-back church tower, the Beacon on the top of the steep, green, nursery-rhyme hill, the quaint old sign of the Spotted Cow, which made all children laugh – Hermione did not smile. A street is a street, and the point of a street is, people: looking boldly up, she challenged whoever passed with her dusky, gelatinous dark-grey eyes. It was their attention she wanted; she collected attention like twists of silver paper or small white pebbles. Her search for attention was so arduous that she gave less than half her mind to whatever Isabelle said. Whenever Isabelle turned into a shop, Hermione would ferret along the counter. In the chemist's she said she would like to buy that green celluloid box to keep her tooth-brush in.

'Have you brought your pocket-money?' said Isabelle brightly.

'Oh – but I haven't any.'

'Then I'm afraid the green box will have to wait,' said Isabelle still more brightly, with an inspiring smile. She did not approve of buying hearts with small gifts: besides, one must teach Hermione not to 'hint'. Hermione gave the green box a last look, the first fully human look she had spent on anything since she came to West Wallows. She slowly dragged her eyes from it and followed Isabelle out of the chemist's shop.

'This afternoon,' said Isabelle, 'we'll go primrosing.'

'I think those lambs are pretty,' said Hermione, suddenly pointing over a wall. 'I should like a pet lamb of my own; I should call it Percy.'

'Well, perhaps you can make a friend of one of these lambs. If you go every day very quietly into the field — '

'But I want it to be my own; I want to call it Percy.'

'Well, let's call "Percy", and see which of them comes . . . Percy, Percy, Percy!' called Isabelle, leaning over the wall. None of the lambs took any notice: one of the sheep gave her a long, reproving look. Hermione, meanwhile, had frigidly walked away.

Eunice and Isabelle took it in turns to what they called take Hermione out of herself. They did not confess how unnerved they sometimes were by their sense of intense attention being focused on nothing. They took her in to see the neighbour who kept the pigeons; Eunice taught her to climb the safe apple trees; Isabelle took her out in a pair of bloomers and dared her to jump the brook.

Hermione jumped in and was pulled out patient and very wet. They borrowed a donkey for her, and the run of a paddock, but she fell off the donkey three times. This child stayed alone the whole time and yet was never alone; their benevolent spying on her, down the orchard or through windows, always showed them the same thing – Hermione twirling round her silver bangles at some unseen person, or else tossing her hair. They took her primrosing three times; then they took her bird's nesting in the Hall grounds. In the great hollow beech hedges, in the dense ivy, the secret nests excited her: she stood up on tiptoes; her cheeks flamed. But all this waned when she might not touch the eggs. She could not understand why. The glossy blues, the faint greens, the waxy buff-pinks, the freckles seemed to her to be for nothing: while the sisters, breathless, held apart the branches she now looked only glumly into the nests. When they found a brood of fledglings she ran six yards back and said: 'Ugh! Fancing leaving eggs just for *that!*'

'But they're alive, dear. Next Spring they'll be singing away, like all the birds we hear now, or laying eggs of their own.'

'Well, I don't see why.'

The sisters bound each other to silence with quick glances.

Hermione said: 'I'd sooner have sugar eggs.'

It was from this rather baffling afternoon that the idea of the Easter egg party arose.

Hermione ought now, they felt, if ever, to be fit for younger society. Perhaps she might find friends – how they doubted this! At all events, one must see. And since she was to meet children, why should she not meet all the West Wallows children at once? About a quite large party there should be something kind and ambiguous: if she failed to hit it off with Maisie or Emmeline, she might hit it off with Harriet or Joanna. (The fact was, they felt, in a way they rather dreaded to face, that in a large party she would stand out less.) The Misses Evers were well known for their juvenile parties, but up to now these had always been held at Christmas, when guessing games could be played, or at Midsummer, when they got permission for their young guests to help to make someone's hay. An Easter party was quite a new idea and looked like running them in for more expense – they did not jib at this, but they dreaded the ostentation. Isabelle bicycled into Market Chopping and bought three dozen sweet eggs – a little reduced in price, as Easter was just over. Some were chocolate, wrapped in brilliant metallic paper; some were marzipan, with the most naturalistic freckles; some were cardboard, containing very small toys. That same afternoon, Eunice, at her bureau, wrote out invitations to the fourteen young guests, ranging in age from fourteen down to six. As she addressed each envelope she would pause, to give Hermione, entrancedly doing nothing on the sofa beside her, a biography of each possible child.

The afternoon of the party was, happily, very fine. From three o'clock on the garden gate clicked incessantly: unaccompanied by grown-ups the guests in their coloured jerseys or very clean blouses came up the path – to be mustered by Eunice and Isabelle on the patch of lawn by the sundial. They were already tanned or freckled by the spring sun, and all wore an air of stolid elation. 'Now, finding *ought* to be keeping,' said Isabelle, 'but we think that if any one of you people finds more than three, he or she might hand the rest back, to go at the end to some other person who may not have been so clever.'

Eunice put in: 'And we shall be giving a prize: this Easter rabbit' (she held up a china ornament) 'to whoever hands in most eggs by the end of the afternoon.'

Isabelle took up: 'They are hidden about the garden and in the orchard the other side of the stream. To make things just a little easier we have tied a piece of pink wool *somewhere near* every place where an egg is. And whoever finds each egg must untie the pink wool, please, or it will be so difficult. Now, are we all here? Oh, no: we are still waiting for Poppy. The moment she's here I'm going to blow this whistle, then – off with you all! At five o'clock I shall blow the whistle for tea.'

At this moment the late-comer bolted in at the gate, whereupon Isabelle blew the whistle piercingly. The children – the boys were small, the girls larger-sized, some of them quite lumpy – glanced at each other, tittered and moved off. For some distance they stayed in compact formation, like explorers advancing in dangerous territory; though all the time their sharp eyes were glancing left and right. Then, in the glittering sunshine of the garden, shreds of pink wool began to be discerned. One by one children bounded off from the others, glancing jealously round to see that no one was on their tracks.

Hermione had lagged a little behind the party that moved off. She had been introduced to all the children by name, but after the 'how-d'you-do's no one had spoken to her. She had secured by the wrist the only other child that tagged behind the party, a small, dumb little boy: she gripped this child by the wrist as though he were not human – he appeared in some way to give her countenance. From the beginning she had been difficult: she had been reluctant to come down from her room at all: from the lawn below Eunice had called and waved; Hermione had answered but not come. Ghostly just inside her shut window, or like a paper figure pasted against the glass, she had watched strange children invade the garden she knew. She had gone on like a kitten that somehow gets up a tree, panics, and cannot be got down again – till Eunice ran up to dislodge her with some well-chosen words. But alas, once one had got her on to the lawn, her up-a-tree air only became more noticeable. She shook hands with a rigid arm, on which all the bracelets jumped. She looked straight at everyone, but from a moody height: what was evident was not just fear or shyness but a desperate, cut-off haughtiness. In her eyes existed a world of alien experience. The jolly, tallish girls with their chubbed hair, the straddling little boys with their bare knees, apt to frown at the grass between their sandshoes, rebounded from that imperious stare. Either she cared too much or she did not care a fig for them – and in either case they did not know how to meet her.

Sloping south to the brook, the garden was made devious by swastika hedges: it was all grots and plots. Japanese plums caught light in their ethereal petals; flowering currants sent out their sweet, hot smell. The waving shreds of pink wool made round themselves centres of magnetic attraction in which children hummed and jostled, like the bees round the currants. The garden, the orchard became tense with the search: now and then yelps of triumph struck their silence like sharp bells. By the end of a half-hour everyone seemed to have found at least one egg. Children met to compare their spoils, then pounced jealously off again.

Only Hermione and the doomed little boy that she would not let go of had not yet found an egg. She sometimes shifted her grip on his hot wrist. In her haze of self-consciousness, weighted by that deep-down preoccupation, she moved too slowly, dragging the little boy. Once or twice she did see pink wool, but when she got to the spot it was always being untied by the child who had found the egg. Disgraced by their failure, she and the little boy said not a word to each other; they moved about in silence of deepening animosity. Now they stood on the bridge, between the garden and orchard: Hermione looked from one shore to the other with eyes that held incredulity and despair. She had not found *any* egg.

Without warning the little boy went rigid all over, braced himself against the rail of the bridge, threw open his cave of a mouth and yelled: 'Oh *Mais-see*, I wanner go with you!'

A girl bustling contentedly through the orchard, three bright eggs shining on the palm of her hand, stopped and lifted her nose like a mother dog. Then she approached the bridge. 'I say,' she said to Hermione, 'would you mind letting my little brother go? He'd like to look by himself.'

'He and I are looking together.'

'Oh. How many have you each found?'

'Somebody else always finds the ones we are looking for.'

'Good gracious,' said Maisie, 'then haven't you found *any*?

Someone says that Harriet's got six, and everyone else here has found at least two. Do you mean to say poor Simon hasn't got *any*? . . . Never mind, Simon; come and look with me. *We'll* soon find some.'

'I don't see why he should. Why should I be the only person left who hasn't got any egg?'

'Well, I can't help that, can I? You'd better look more properly . . . Come along Simon.'

Hermione let him go.

When she found herself quite alone on the bridge she shaded her eyes (because the sun was descending) to peer at the round, white object under one apple tree. It was a panama hat, last seen on the girl Harriet: now it sat on the grass. As though something inside her answered a magnet, Hermione left the bridge and ran to that apple tree. The general search had ebbed back to the garden: in the orchard no one shouted; no one swished through the long grass – the place was deserted suddenly. Hermione knelt down, cautiously raised the hat, and saw the clutch of six supernatural eggs – two gold, one red, one silver and two blue. They lay tilted together in their nest in the grass. Trembling with satisfaction, she regarded them steadily. Then she made a pouch of her skirt and gathered the eggs up into it. Clumsily, cautiously rising, she made off at a trot for a hedge that cut off the orchard from Church Lane.

She was not missed till the five o'clock whistle sounded and the children trooped in through the french window for tea. Then Eunice and Isabelle combined to pass the contretemps over as smoothly as possible. While Eunice poured out, and kept the chatter going, Isabelle, with the whistle, slipped out for a thorough look. Sadly, sadly, she saw some trampled daffodils – the nicer the set of children, the larger their feet. When she got to the end of the orchard she saw the gap forced through the hedge, and her heart sank.

The big scandal only broke at the end of tea-time, when Eunice began to check up the eggs found. Throughout tea the outraged Harriet had not suffered in silence: there had been a good deal of mumbling at her end of the table, but Eunice did not know what the matter was. When the loss came out Eunice put two and two together with disheartening rapidity – so did everyone else. Speaking looks were cast by the West Wallows children at the place where Hermione did not sit. There was nothing for it but to present the china rabbit to Harriet with as much haste, and still as much pomp, as possible and to suggest we should now all play prisoners' base on the lawn.

Seven strokes from the church clock fell on the sad, clear evening. The Easter egg party guests had been sent home an hour ago; the sisters had returned from their desperate search up and down the village, in the fields, in the near woods. Something made Eunice go up to Hermione's room – there *was* Hermione, sitting on the bed. She must have slipped back while nobody was about. In the deep dusk she was sitting across the bed, legs stuck out and back stuck to the wall, in the attitude in which one props up a doll. She was, presumably, waiting: the moment the door opened, she said, without looking up: 'I want to go home now.'

'But Hermione — '

'Mummy said I needn't stay if I didn't like it. She said I could come straight home.'

'Dear, this isn't because you think *we* are . . . upset about anything?'

'I can't help *what* you are,' said Hermione, quite dispassionate. 'Couldn't you get some other girl to stay with you? There's nothing for me to do here; I mean, I can't do anything. And all those girls were awful to me today; nobody cared if I found an egg or not. That girl Maisie wouldn't let me play with her brother. No one has ever been so awful to me as they all were; they took all the eggs, and I never found even one. And you never let me talk, all the time, you never let me touch anything. You keep on making me take an interest in things, and you never take the slightest interest in me. Mummy said you were interested in me, but now I don't believe her. I feel just as if I was dead, and I do want to go home. Oh, and I took those six old eggs.'

'Well, hush now, dear: we're all tired. Hop into bed, like a good girl, and I'll bring you some biscuits and milk. Would you like me to bring up one of the kittens too?'

'No, thank you; your kittens scratch. Well, can I go home tomorrow?'

'We'll see about that tomorrow.'

Eunice sighed and went downstairs. She filled a beaker with milk and put out a plate of biscuits, then she looked into the parlour for a word with Isabelle. The lamps were lit, but the curtains were not drawn yet: outside there was a dark twitter of birds. Isabelle, reading the look on her sister's face, came round the table, saying: 'Oh, Eunice . . . '

'I know,' Eunice said. 'It apparently can't be helped. Her mind's set now on going home. I wonder whether she'd better . . . '

'Eunice, that's not like you!' cried Isabelle, with a burst of their old heroic energy.

'I know,' said Eunice, putting down the biscuits. Absently, she began to sip the milk. 'But you see, this is really not like anything else. There are times when being like one's self, however much one's self, does not seem much help. Well, there it is, Isabelle.

We've always known life was difficult, but I must confess, till today I'd never really believed it. I don't see quite where we failed: she *is* a child, after all.'

'I suppose, once a child has been the centre of things . . . '

'Oh, look – I'm drinking this milk. It really was for Hermione.'

Hermione left next day: perhaps it was for the best. They never speak of her to the children at West Wallows, and the West Wallows children do not ask about her. The sisters seldom speak of her even between themselves; she has left a sort of scar, like a flattened grave, in their hearts. It rained the day she left, but cleared up again at sunset. When Isabelle, in her gum-boots, walking in the orchard, found the six Easter eggs under the original apple tree, the chocolate under the paper had gone to a pulp, and the gold and colours of the paper had run.

Love

IT WAS a funny experience, it was really – not like a thing that
happened, more like a dream. Sometimes I think I did dream it –
for all I can get out of Edna, I might have done. It's like Edna to put
the whole thing on me – she does that by keeping on saying
nothing. So of course I can never refer to it. And I don't know
that I want to – not to Edna. Anyhow, Edna's shut up, just like
a clam.

The minute we came round the rocks into that bay I felt there
was something . . . The day, with that sea glare and at the same
time no sun, made everything look unnatural, and we were dead
beat. We'd kept slogging along in that loose sand: our shoes were
full of it. For miles we hadn't seen anything you could call
anything – only rocks, and slopes coming down, and the same sea.
So when we came round that rock and saw the hotel, it gave us
quite a shock. The bay was ever so narrow, it looked private; the
hotel stood back but sand came right up to it. There was a sort of
jetty, but that had rotted. The hotel must have been pink, with a
name painted across it, but the name and the colour had faded right
out. All the shutters were up, but for one window: it looked like a
dead person winking at you. I never did like being stared at. I said,
'Why, Edna, it's shut up.'

She said, 'Well, it *is* a poor-looking place!'

The hotel (I can see it now) had only two storeys, but it was quite
long. And at one side they'd tacked on a sort of a wooden annexe,
maybe for a dance-hall or restaurant. That was all shuttered up,
too, inside the coloured glass. Along the front of it, though, went a
great iron veranda, that looked as though it had come from some
other place. Quite massive, it was, all pillars and scrolls and
lace-work: it looked heavy enough to pull the whole annexe down.
There were great steps, with the bottom buried in sand. What drew
my eye to it was the bright blue dress of the lady sitting up there.
She was not the sort of person you'd see anywhere. She sat up
there, simply looking at us.

So Edna, to show she was within her rights, bumped down there
on the sand and took her shoes off and shook all the sand out of

them, one after the other. 'That's better,' she said. 'Why don't you? Go on,' but somehow I didn't like to. 'You are a silly,' she said. 'It's only just an hotel!'

I looked sideways and saw a board with 'Luncheons, Teas, Suppers', stuck there in the sand – but the writing ever so faint. 'I daresay it's all right,' I said. 'We might have come for our teas.'

'You and your tea,' she said. 'You're always on about tea.'

But I saw she wanted her tea as much as I did, from the way she whacked the sand out of her skirt. You can't help getting to notice a person's character when you work in the same office and go on holidays with them. If you asked me how I liked Edna I wouldn't know how to answer, but a girl on her own like I am has to put up with some things, and it's slow to go on your holiday all alone. I wouldn't mind keeping on noticing Edna's character if she wouldn't keep on saying she keeps on noticing mine. Still, we'd booked our room, so we had to get along somehow – and it was only the fortnight, after all. You get better value for money in quiet places, so she and I had picked on a quiet place. Edna and I aren't like some other girls in business, always off where you can pick up a boy. For one thing, Edna hasn't got much appeal – and I always was one to keep myself to myself. It was quite a nice place Edna and I had picked on, it was refined – but I must say it was a bit slow. No other place up or down the coast for ever so many miles; we really did ought to have brought bikes. We sunbathed a bit, but we somehow only burned red. It was nice, safe bathing, but when it was cold for that, or too windy for deck-chairs, there was nothing to do but go for a trudge on the sands. That suited Edna all right – she always was quite a hiker – and I didn't like to be left. We never walked much inland, as you'll understand, because of the awful cows. I often said I did wish the sand wasn't so soft, and Edna'd say, 'Whatever do you expect?'

This day I'm talking about was the last day but one of our holiday – that may have been the reason that, once we'd started off walking, we'd come further along than we ever had. I'd been wanting my tea some time, though I wasn't going to say so, to make Edna start picking at me.

'I doubt they serve teas,' I said. 'The place looks shut up, to me.' 'Then what they want to leave that board for?' said Edna. 'If they say teas, they've got to serve teas.' She got quite red. 'Besides, look,' she said, sort of spying at the veranda, 'besides, look; they've got a visitor there.' So she started marching towards the place. I went too – though it somehow didn't seem right.

The person on the veranda sat as still as an image. Only her eyes kept moving, following us. She let us come on till we were near up, then said, 'Oh, no, you mustn't go in!'

I must say Edna did jump, too, but she said, 'Well, this is an hotel all right, isn't it?'

The person looked sort of puzzled: she just said, 'You mustn't; they wouldn't like you to.'

'What are you up to, then?' said Edna, ever so sharp.

That gave the lady even more of a puzzle. Then she said, 'But I always sit outside.'

Being interfered with settled the thing for Edna; she just gave my elbow a sort of pull, and we walked away from the lady, past all those shut shutters, round the end of the hotel. We made a guess that the front door must be on the inland side. The last we saw of the lady, she'd shot up and was banging ever so frightenedly on the window behind her, calling, 'Oh, mind, oh, mind!' 'If you ask me,' said Edna, 'this is a loony-bin. But if so, why do they put up "Teas"?'

On the land side of the hotel, the grass went sloping quite steep up. Awful cows had trodden and messed up all over the place. We looked round but we didn't see any cows. There was the hall door, all right, under a glass porch with one pane gone. The door was ever so shut and the bell out of its socket so nothing would do Edna but to start hammering, I'd have ten times sooner gone missing my tea; I could have slapped Edna, being stubborn like that.

'Oh give over, do, Edna,' I was starting to say – when quite of a sudden the door opened and a young fellow looked out – in his shirt-sleeves, he was. He'd come ever so quiet, in those rubber-soled shoes. He didn't smile or frown, he just looked at us – the way he had no expression was quite rude. He held the door half-shut, keeping his hand on it.

'We want tea for two,' said Edna – right out flat.

'Sorry,' he said, 'we don't serve teas.' He stepped back and started shutting the door. But Edna pushed in her shoulder as quick as quick. She started to say, 'Well, what I want to know is — ' and I started to ask her to come off it. Then, though, something made me look round at the hill, and – oh, my goodness, I could have dropped! There were those awful cows, the pack of them, awful black cows, with their horns and everything, coming downhill behind us ever so stealthy ready to spring on us. I grabbed Edna, and she saw – before we half knew what had happened, we'd fought past the young man in at the door. Edna snatched the door from him and gave it a slam shut. I felt her shake all over, just like a piece of paper. She said, 'My girl friend doesn't like cows.'

The first minute, it was so dark we couldn't see anything, it was so dark in there. The place smelled ever so musty. There must have been an archway through to the front; there were chinks of light round the shutters on the sea side. When I started to see, I saw what looked like a row of corpses, all hanging along on the one wall. Later, I noticed these were gentlemen's mackintoshes. I should have told that first go off, by the smell. There they all hung, not moving – why should they move?

Edna said, 'Those cows of yours are not safe.'

He said, 'Those aren't my cows. Are you two from town?'

I daresay Edna gave him one of her looks. She shrilled up and said, 'Then what about that board?' 'Which board? – Oh, that,' he said, as easy as anything. He walked off like a cat, in his rubber shoes, and began unbolting the shutter we'd seen the light come through. So we saw the sea out through the window, and felt better – a bit. And we saw through there, through the arch, now he'd got the shutter open, a lounge – but no palms, and dust over the mirrors, and wicker chairs and tables all coming untwined. We did serve teas, all right,' he said, 'but it isn't convenient now.' He went on, 'Then you two came round by the sea?'

I don't think he meant to cheek us, it was just his manner, I don't think he more than half knew we were there. After a bit he said, 'It seems a shame, doesn't it? Did you come from far?' I told him where we'd come from. Then he said, 'Have you two got friends, where you are?'

'What's that to you?' said Edna.

He simply went on, 'If you've got friends, or anyone that you talk to, where you're staying – well, just *don't* talk this time – see? I don't serve teas any more, and I don't serve anything, and I don't want locals or visitors coming nosing round here after teas or anything else that I don't serve.' He stood with his arms crossed and his thumbs tucked under his elbows, looking at Edna and me in the calmest way. 'You've no right in here,' he said. 'This place isn't even open. You wouldn't come pushing in if you were a nice pair of girls. All the same, though' (he said to us like an emperor), 'I'll give you your teas, all right, *if you won't go off and talk.*'

So then I piped up (I could see no harm in it, really) and said, how Edna and I always kept ourselves to ourselves. And I told him we'd be back in London the day after tomorrow. Edna said she wasn't sure that she did fancy her tea now, after one thing and another and what had been said. 'Oh yes, you do,' he said. 'Women always fancy their teas.' He rubbed one hand on a table and rubbed some dust off, then stood and watched the dust on his hand. Then he did something queerer – he went and opened the window and stuck his head right out and looked up and down. Whatever he thought he'd see, it didn't seem to be there. So then he pulled his head in and shut the window and said, 'O.K.; I'll go and see what I've got.'

'You mean, tea?' we said.

'Tea,' he said. 'If you'll sit in those two chairs.' He pulled two chairs out – they were ever so dusty – and stuck the two of us down in a chair each. 'If you move out of those,' he said, 'you won't get any tea. See? And if a lady should pass, you don't have to talk to her – see? The lady's like you, she keeps herself to herself.'

That was the way he went on – as if we'd been a pair of kids. I and Edna dared hardly look at each other – but she put her finger up and gave her forehead a tap. Still, whatever were we to do, just two girls like her and me – and with those cows waiting just outside the door? He got as far as the archway, to give a last look at us. Then he frowned – and we all three looked at the window. There *she* was, the one in blue, with her eyes starting out of her head. She saw him, and began to bang on the glass. I and Edna were sitting back, and so she couldn't see us. We could see her talking away, but we couldn't hear what she said. In the glare out there her blue dress looked ever so queer. She kept banging harder and harder, with the flat of her hands. 'If you don't watch out,' said Edna, 'she'll smash your window. Not that it's my affair.'

For the minute, he seemed to me to quite lose his head. Then he gave us each such a look – like an awful warning, it was – then made a dart at the window and threw it up. Then we *did* hear her – her voice came out in a wail. 'Oh, Oswald, oh, my darling Oswald!' she said.

Before he could step away from the window she reached in, as quick as quick, and got her arms round his neck. 'Oh, I did watch,' she said. 'I *did*! But they got in. Oh, Oswald, forgive me. Forgive me, Oswald,' she said. 'What's going to happen? They'll take you away. I've failed you!' He wriggled his head, but she held on ever so tight. Her wrists were as thin as wire, with gold bracelets slipping into her cuff.

'That's all right, Miss Tope,' he said. 'Nothing's happened; I'm safe, really I am.'

'But they got in. Where are they?'

'They didn't,' he said. 'They've gone.'

She glared past him in at the window – and I tell you, I and Edna stiffened back in our chairs. 'But what did they see?' she said. 'What did they guess? Suppose they're somewhere? Let me come in and look.'

'Ah,' he said, 'but if you come in, who's going to keep look-out? Go back and keep look-out. You know I depend on you.' That made her let him go and come over puzzled for a minute. She stood there puzzling it out, with her eyes fixed on his face. 'I'm *depending* on you,' he said – he was like a father to her. And she could have been his mother – as years go. She looked ready to cry. 'Are you really safe?' she said.

'I'm always safe,' he said, 'while you keep watch.' He gave her a sort of nod, and she crinkled her whole face up and gave him the same sort of nod – then she went away. He waited another minute, then shut the window and walked off, as calm as anything, through the arch.

Well, Edna and I just sat; we stayed in those two chairs and didn't utter or even look at each other. I don't know how that time ever went by. We heard Oswald off somewhere, putting out china, and we could smell the oil stove – he must have left the door open; *he* was listening, all right. Then when he came back and put the tray down he said, 'Well, here you are.' Edna reached for the pot, but he'd got to it first; he pulled up a chair and sat down, ever so at his ease. That was his way of showing we weren't to pay: it was not our tea, it was his. Edna hates being put under compliment – how she did flush up. And I'm sure I was glad to keep my face in my cup. He cut me and Edna each a slice off the loaf. I saw Edna ready to fire up.

'It's all very fine to say not to talk,' she said. 'But how are my friend and me to know what not to talk about? That Miss Tope, I daresay? Whatever is eating her?'

He said, 'She thinks I did a murder.'

'Does she?' said Edna. 'Did you?'

'No,' says he, as offhand as anything. 'But she thinks every minute they'll be coming for me. The fact is, I don't want them coming round after *her*. Her people are all on to get her shut up. They wouldn't care what she suffered. She gave them the slip once, though, and now they don't know she's here. If they did, they'd be round here for her in a jiffy – they don't care *what* she might suffer, wouldn't care if it killed her. But I'd see them all to blazes before I'd let them touch her. I'm the one friend she's got.'

'I must say,' said Edna, 'you take a lot on yourself. Why, she's bats, she is really. She might do anyone harm. Look at those hands of hers – they're as strong as strong.'

'She won't do me harm,' said Oswald.

'She might do herself harm, too.'

'Not while she's with me.'

'Where did she get that, then, about that murder you did?'

Oswald went all quite different when he talked of Miss Tope; he wasn't cool and please-yourself any longer. You might think he was a mother just had her first. 'I kidded her that,' he said. 'If they weren't to come and take her she and I were bound to keep lying low. And when she first came back here she was out all over the place – along the main road, round the village – just like a child, so trustful, talking away to everyone. Of course she got remarked on – how could she not be? Her people would have been here for her in a week. So I had to think up some way to keep her quiet without letting on it was *her*: she'd have died of that. So I told her I'd done something awful, and that they'd be coming for me, and that she'd have to hide me, and keep watch. Since then, she's never budged from this place.'

'Poor soul,' I said.

He said, 'You don't know her. She's as sweet and lovely as she was when a girl.'

'No doubt,' said Edna, 'she is the perfect lady. All the same, she's willing to stay where she thinks there's been a murder done. Do you mean to say *that* didn't give her a turn against you?'

'Why, no,' Oswald said. 'She'd never judge what *I* did. She just sometimes cries and calls me her poor thing. She and I have been like that – friends with each other – since I was a little kid and she was the loveliest girl. You see her and my fathers, they were so thick – though her father was a rich gentleman; at one time he could have bought England; he had a yacht and all. It was her father set my father up in this business, this hotel. Then they were always coming here, Miss Meena and him. And where Major Tope came, in those days, his crowd used to follow him. Ever so many gentlemen, and Miss Meena – they used to call this their head-quarters – my father's place. I remember all these windows blazing down on the sand, and Miss Meena in her lace dress on that veranda, singing to her guitar. She was like a queen to them all – and she was my queen all right. They used to laugh at me, always round after her. But in those days I was only a little kid. When Major Tope's crash came, all that crowd that used to come here melted away like snow. I guess they lost money, too. Major Tope had invested for *my* father all my father had made out of this place. So when the crash came, my father went down too. Major Tope couldn't stand it all; he put himself out. My father wasn't left long after that lot went: I was left with this place, and I did carry on for a bit, just with teas and that, but when Miss Tope came back I shut down. It wouldn't do – not with her.'

'Then you didn't ought to have left that board up, with "Teas"!'

'That's for her,' he said. 'I did try taking it down, once, but how she did take on – she won't see a thing changed. The day she came back she said, "Here I am, back, Oswald. Now we'll be happy. We've always been happy here." She hates to see anything go – I couldn't hurt like that.'

'That's all very well,' said Edna, 'but how ever do you make out? With no custom or anything? You've got your own life to think of – a young fellow like you.'

He said, as stand-offish as anything, 'Oh, I make out all right. This premises is still mine, and I get a bit for the grass.'

'Still, you can't keep on,' Edna said. He said: 'Leave that to her and me.'

He got up and piled back the things on the tray. 'Well, if you must go . . . ' he said. 'Thanks for your company.' So she and I got up. When he saw Edna eyeing out of the window he said, 'No, not that way; you're going back inland.' He got us out through the hall – oh, it echoed, it did sound empty – past the mackintoshes all those people had left. 'Well, I'm sure you've been very kind,' I said, 'giving us tea and everything. Thank you, I'm sure.'

'The way to thank me,' he said, 'is by keeping your mouths shut.'

While he was opening the door I said, 'Oh, Edna, the cows!' He gave a sort of grin and said he'd make that all right. As a matter of fact, the cows were off up another hill. Oswald started us off up a path that he said would bring us down again on the sands in the next bay. (And it did.) He stayed, with a stick, as he'd promised, between us and that other hill where the cows were. We walked fast and were ever so out of breath. I looked back once and saw Oswald, looking quite little, and his hotel down there looking just like a little box. I thought when we got our breaths we were bound to start saying something. Then I saw Edna'd put on one of her funny manners, so I didn't say anything – I didn't want to, either. Because what can you say when you don't know what you think. And what can you think when a thing doesn't make sense?

No. 16

To approach Medusa Terrace by its east corner, on a first visit to the Maximilian Bewdons, was to fancy oneself, for an unnerving minute, the victim of a hoax. Maximilian's only visitors, nowadays, were of the type least able to bear this – idealistic, friendless, new from the provinces: accordingly, unaware of the slump in him. One can make for oneself a pretty picture of the distinguished writer's St John's Wood home – jasmine outside, *objets d'art* within. Maximilian had not, in fact, been distinguished for fifteen years. But the last circle from the splash he had once made faded slowly – and meanwhile he was able to make a living. The masks on Medusa Terrace had lost their features; the pilasters crumbled; front doors were boarded up.

The differing fortunes of St John's Wood house property give that uphill landscape a dreamlike inconsistency. To walk there is to have a crazy architectural film, with no music, reeled past. Every corner brings you to something out of the scheme – even without a touch of fever on you (and Jane Oates had more than a touch of fever) some starts of taste or fancy look like catastrophes. Pale tan brick blocks of flats, compressed cities, soar up over studios all trellis and vine. There are gashes and pitted gardens where villas have been torn down. Criss-cross go roads of dun silent stucco, frosted glass porches, grills. A perspective gallops downhill all jade-and-whiteness and bird-song – but you may turn off into a by-street as mean, faded and airless as any in Pimlico. Dotted among the bosky gothic love-nests are vita-glassed mansions, avid for sun and money, still on the agent's lists. Here, a once bewitching villa, now scabrous, awaits the knacker for some obscure shame – next door, its twin is all paintpots and whistling workmen, being dolled up again. The straight roads string all this on an old plan. The stranger feels abnormally keyed up; he finds himself in a sort of nightmare of whim.

Jane Oates's troubled sensations *were* heightened by fever: she had a temperature, had only got up this morning and should have been still in bed. But today – now – she was to meet Maximilian Bewdon for the first time: she would not have failed if she'd had to come from the tomb. Not only influenza but hero worship made her pulses race. His letter, with the invitation to lunch, had been brought to her the first day she was ill, and her thought then had been: I must go if I die. So images had swum through her drowsy days and made her delirious nights ecstatic. Here she was, on her way to Medusa Terrace – too eager, she had got off the bus too soon. Her feet were lead, her spine ached, her head sang, glassily clear.

The thaw had left London glistening, supine, sunny. From gardens the snow, swept up into mounds, had not gone yet. Jane had come on buses from Battersea Park; she was not a Londoner; she had not been up here before. Everything, in this maze of trees and doorways as she walked towards Maximilian, gave her its message or mystery. The sun still hurt her still rather weak eyes. She had the stolid, untroubled beauty of a mature country girl, and a touch of old-fashioned style.

In the autumn, about three months ago, Jane's book had been published. It was a naïve book, but sufficiently disconcerting, and *new* – too new to go far unless it should happen to catch some important eye. She had no friends (in London), no one to make a splash. So the publisher gave the book an agreeable format, a vermilion cover with a chalky surface, gave one or two luncheons for Jane (at which she could not speak) and hoped for a *succès d'estime*. Maximilian, reviewing for an obscure paper, had not only 'done' the book but had made a feature of it. The publisher shrugged when he got the cutting and saw Maximilian's name. But Jane's cup was full. She got the column by heart and, for days, sang a Magnificat. That *he* should have written this – and that he should have written *this*. Her liberation into this sudden book could have been all: but now she was truly crowned. She wrote Maximilian a humble letter, confessing the hero worship of years. Since she was seventeen (she was now thirty) she had hardly missed a word Maximilian signed. She was deeply feeling; she lived alone in the country. She was a true enough artist to have false taste – for the ignorant artist, like the savage, is attracted by what is glittering: by the time he learns what is what, some virtue is gone already.

Maximilian Bewdon, after about a week, had replied to Jane's letter: they started to correspond. Though her book was prose she wrote poems also, she told him, but she was shy of those. She learned that he was married; he asked her if she were married; she answered that she had never been in love. Before Christmas, she was able to write and tell him she was coming to London, to share a flat for three months with a friend who lived in Battersea Park. When she got to Battersea Park, already ill, she got his letter, bidding her bring the poems to lunch.

So here they were, in a folder under her arm. She was not nervous; fever floated her or distilled her out of herself. But when she turned the corner into Medusa Terrace, Jane Oates stopped – like everyone else. She instinctively put her hand up, then took her hand from her eyes to see the same thing again – that north-facing terrace of cracked stucco, dank in its own shadow, semi-ruinous, hollow, full of sealed-up echoes. Doors nailed up, windows boarded or stony with grime. In the gardens, the snow was trodden black. The place so much expected an instant doom, one felt unsafe standing near it.

'Am I — ? Or, *could* he have — ?'

Jane looked up at the numbers stuck on the broken fanlights. Still at the 1's and 2's – he had said, No. 16. Plunging into the shadow with a shiver – she had kept to the sunny sides of the streets – she walked the length of the façade. At the end she dared look up: the last house *was* No. 16. Through less dusty panes she saw curtains like orange ghosts. A shaft of sun struck through from a back window, through a bunch of balloons hung in an arch. This one end house was tacked, living, to the hulk of the terrace. She turned up the steps and rang.

When she had rung twice, a lady came to the door, knocking back a strand of grey hair from her eyes. She eyed Jane and eyed the folder of poems. 'Oh dear – I hope you are not Miss Oates?'

'I — '

'Oh dear. I had wired to put you off: you did not seem to be on the telephone. My husband has been ill for several days; he's just up, but not fit to see anyone. He only remembered this morning that you were coming, or I should have – I *am* sorry. Oh dear.'

At these words Jane, in her feverish weakness, sweated: she saw sweat and a flush break out on the lady's forehead, and Mrs Bewdon put up a hand and said: 'We've had influenza.' 'I've had it too.' 'It seems to be everywhere.' 'I'm sorry I didn't get your telegram: I started early, it was a long way — '

'Nancy,' said a voice from inside a room, 'let Miss Oates come in.'

So Jane, unable to say anything further, was let into the shabby, decent hall – an oak chest with letters stamped for posting, prints hung on the paper seamed with damp, a humid smell of broth. She turned through a door to face Maximilian, who stood in the archway, underneath the bunch of coloured balloons. She heard the roar of two antique gasfires, one in the dark front room, one in the sunny back, and saw Maximilian's figure crucified on the sunshine in an extravagance of apology. 'What must you think?' he said. She stood blind, the sun in her eyes, and could not think anything. There was a moment's silence, while Jane shifted the folder, pressing it with the thumb of her woollen glove. Then he said: 'Thank you for missing the telegram.'

'But I must go.'

'No, you mustn't go. There *is* lunch.' He reached out – the act seemed vague and belated like an act in a dream – and shook Jane's hot, dry hand in his hotter and drier hand. 'Now you're here,' he said.

'But you're ill.'

'Still, I'm here,' he said, with an obstinate frown. They sat down beside each other on the sofa, and she saw his exposed-looking forehead, the spectacles through which he sent, obliquely, a look at once baited and fiery, the short hands wasting their force in uneasy, fleeting, nervous touches on things. Maximilian looked about fifty; he looked frustrated and spent. His hair, weak as fur, flowed back and he wore a little moustache. He said, with an accusing smile: 'You thought I had gone.'

'Yes, I did, when I first came to the Terrace.'

'That's what they all think – that lets them out, don't you see. They take one look and go home. "He'd gone," they say to the others. Lots don't start at all. "We don't know where he is now. They've pulled down where he once was. There's no tracing him — "'

'How *can* you?' Jane said gently. Maximilian repeated: 'It lets them out. That's my tact.'

Jane, looking apprehensively round at the room, said: 'But some day, I suppose, it *will* happen?'

'Oh, we'll be pulled down all right,' said Maximilian, pressing his forehead.

'If the idea upsets you — '

Mrs Bewdon, laying the front room table, said: 'The idea does not upset my husband at all. When we move, he will miss it. We are let keep this house on from week to week: when the men come, they'll begin at the other end. They work fast, I daresay, and it will be so noisy. So *then* we shall have to think — '

'I am so sorry,' said Jane.

'I shan't be sorry,' said Mrs Bewdon. 'That will be something settled.' She bent to straighten a fork. 'But he – I – we cannot bear to decide . . . '

Her husband said: 'One decides quickly enough when there is any question of desire.'

'It's so long since the last of our neighbours left: they expected something to happen, but nothing has, as you see. At the same time, it's still a shock to find *nobody* else. It is not as though this house stood by itself. When we cannot sleep, or when we are at all ill . . . For instance, since my husband has been ill he keeps hearing the piano next door. "Go in," he said to me yesterday, "and tell her how much I like her playing. Ask her to go on playing —— " 'Yes, you *did*, Maximilian, but No. 15 is empty; it's nailed up; there is a crack under the balcony.'

She looked through the arch at her husband, laughing not altogether kindly.

'The house suits me,' he said. 'Are we going to have no lunch?' Mrs Bewdon picked up her tray and floundered out of the room.

A slight steam came from the dishes. Jane Oates could taste nothing: she scalded her mouth with the broth, and the fish pie lay on her tongue like wadding. The Bewdons put up an even less good show. She no longer heard what was said, or heard if anything *was* said: before the end of lunch she had to stop and rest her brow on her hands. Maximilian poured himself out a glass of water. The sun wheeled off the face of the extinct terrace opposite: reflections no longer entered the north room. Someone left the table, and when Jane raised her forehead Maximilian said, 'Nancy has gone to make the coffee.'

'Oh, it will be too hot.'

Maximilian agreed: 'This is the worst time of day.'

She looked: behind his and her figures she saw book-shelves, in the flat, fading light. She looked up, at the cracks across the ceiling and at the bunch of balloons – air must have escaped from them, for they were already flaccid like old grapes. 'Why are those balloons there?'

'A man peddled them up and down the terrace, so I had to buy them all.'

'That was kind.'

'He held me responsible.' Maximilian hitched one elbow over the back of his chair; he turned away from Jane with a quick, rather frenzied movement.

'Mr Bewdon, I ought not to make you talk.'

'We shan't meet again like this – for the first time. We shan't meet again when we don't know what we are saying.'

Birds and waterfalls sounded in Jane's head, so that when Mrs Bewdon brought in the tray of coffee and poured out, talking, Jane sat not listening but smiling. 'Maximilian, you're not drinking your coffee. It's no use to sit twisting round from the light. Miss Oates will excuse you: you must go and lie down.'

'Miss Oates must stay with me, to read her poems.'

'Well you may read, Miss Oates, but he must not say anything. When he goes to sleep, creep away, if you don't mind. I'm going up to lie down in my own room. It will do me good.'

Maximilian went through the arch and lay down on the sofa in the back room: Mrs Bewdon tucked a rug over his feet, and soon the gas fire drew a scorched smell from the rug. For some time one heard Mrs Bewdon walking about upstairs; then a spring cracked in her bed as *she* lay down. Maximilian crossed his hands over his eyes; Jane undid the folder of poems and sat on a low chair, one elbow on the typewriting table so that she could prop her cheek on her hand. The wintry sun no longer afflicted them; it sent rays obliquely across the garden, through the boughs of a tree. Jane did not know she knew her poems by heart, but now she heard herself speak them as though she had been hypnotized. It frightened her not to know what was coming next – and she felt something mounting up round her in the dusk, was again frightened, did not know where it came from. Whenever she stopped, the outdoor silence pressed as close as suspense: you had the sensation of a great instrument out there in London, unstruck.

Jane kept her eyes down as though she were reading, but when she paused she looked towards Maximilian – at his face pitched up unkindly by the end of the sofa, and at his eye-bandage of knotted hands. All at once he said: 'Stop.'

She broke off a line.

'You're so beautiful.'

'But your hands are over your eyes.'

'I remember you coming in and standing there in the sun. So ill, when I am so ill. You might be a lovely neighbour. You played the piano yesterday.'

'I was ill yesterday.'

'Then you did play the piano – Come over here, Jane.'

Jane dropped the poems and knelt by the sofa. Maximilian uncovered his eyes – after a moment he caught at her two wrists and held them so that her fingers were pressed to his temples. 'Fever and pain,' he said. 'You make me hear the piano. What do you hear?'

'A waterfall in my head.' She felt her pulse jumping inside his grip and said: 'We are making each other iller.' He had shut his eyes; she looked at his face and said: 'I wish I had cool hands.'

'If you had cool hands you would go away. I shall lose you when you are well.' Pressing her fingers close to his temples he said: 'All this will be gone – where we are – not a rack left. There'll be no "here" left – how can you come back?' Then he let go her wrists roughly. 'But I don't want you to come again.'

'Why?'

'You'd soon see why.'

'But my poems . . .'

'Take them away. Burn them. You'll only lose your way.'

'Are you lost?'

'Yes, I'm lost. You don't understand yet. We only know when we're ill – the piano inside my head, the waterfall inside yours. My image of you, that neighbourly image. Eternity is inside us – it's a secret that we must never, never try to betray. Look where just *time* has brought me; look at where it's left me. When you make friends, don't talk about me.'

'You praised my book,' she said wildly starting up.

'I've got to live. How could I write, in a paper, "She should have burned her hands off before she wrote"?'

'Are we not to believe in each other?'

'Come back here; put your head beside me.' Maximilian rolled his head sideways on the end of the sofa, and, sitting back on her heels on the ground beside him, Jane laid her head where he had made room. Maximilian's voice went drowsy; his eyes closed. 'You sweet neighbour,' he said. 'You sweet, distempered friend.'

'But Shakespeare . . . '

'Go to sleep, Jane, never mind, go to sleep.'

Mrs Bewdon woke and came down to make tea. She fumbled her way to the kitchen, where she put on the kettle, then into the back room, where she turned the light on and saw Jane and Bewdon asleep with their foreheads together: he lying, she kneeling twisted beside the sofa. They looked like a suicide pact. The room smelled of the scorching of Bewdon's rug. Mrs Bewdon, when she had drawn the curtains, stooped and gave Jane's shoulder a light pat. 'Tea-time,' she said.

Jane opened her eyes, and Mrs Bewdon gave her a hand up. Maximilian went on breathing stertorously.

'I ought to go.'

'Oh, I should have something hot first. You don't look really fit to be out at all. He'll sleep on,' she said, without a glance at the sofa, 'so you can slip away just when you like.'

The two women, at tea in the front room, talked low, so as not to wake Maximilian. They did not want to wake him for their peace sake. Jane learned, from the way Mrs Bewdon spoke of her husband, that she felt a dogged, loyal, unsmiling, unloving pity for him. Mrs Bewdon's demoralized manner seemed to come from her opinion that she did not live with a real man. She must have married during some delusion of youth.

Mrs Bewdon's kindness to Jane was profoundly chagrining. Mrs Bewdon said: 'It's been kind of you to have come. Such a long way – I hope it has been worth while. I'm sorry my husband was not more himself, but you know what influenza is. He's always interested in young writers, though I'm afraid he's inclined to discourage them. He likes to say to them "Don't write".'

'Do they mind?'

'They think it is just his fun,' said Mrs Bewdon, looking round for the sugar. 'Or else they think he is jealous. But he does really take an interest in them. He's disappointed they don't come back.'

Jane tried to feel sorry for the sleeping man. She still felt herself closely bound to him – he had done no more than hold her wrists, but she was a girl who had never been touched. Now, the indifference in Mrs Bewdon's voice, and her half-understanding, brought everything low. He has lost me, too, she thought. I shall be unhappy when I am well again.

'Oh, must you be going?' said Mrs Bewdon. 'Perhaps you are right, though: your eyes look rather ill. Shall I ring up a taxi?'

'No thank you; I can't afford one.'

'Don't forget your poems,' said Mrs Bewdon, running back for the folder, 'I expect they are good.' Jane heard Bewdon, the other side of the archway, turn over and exclaim something in his sleep – one of those sleeping protests. Running quickly away from his helplessness, she followed Mrs Bewdon into the hall. The hall door, opened by Mrs Bewdon, showed cracked steps dropping into the dark. 'You must walk past some day,' said Mrs Bewdon, 'and see if we are still here.'

The terrace gave out a hundred hollow echoes and, as the door shut, just perceptibly shook. The lamplight picked out its sad face. Not a step but Jane's on the pavement; not a note from the piano. They stared at Jane when she got into the bus . . . On the Battersea Park hall table she found the telegram: she pushed away her poems behind her bureau but took the telegram to her cold bed. Through the night, she kept starting up, switching her lamp on: she re-read *Should not see anyone.* In the dark again she heard Bewdon's voice saying 'Sleep . . . ' Her pillow sounded hollow with notes and knockings, notes and knockings you hear in condemned rooms.

A Queer Heart

MRS CADMAN got out of the bus backwards. No amount of practice ever made her more agile; the trouble she had with her big bulk amused everyone, and herself. Gripping the handles each side of the bus door so tightly that the seams of her gloves cracked, she lowered herself cautiously, like a climber, while her feet, overlapping her smart shoes, uneasily scrabbled at each step. One or two people asked why the bus made, for one passenger, such a long, dead stop. But on the whole she was famous on this line, for she was constantly in and out of town. The conductor waited behind her, smiling, holding her basket, arms wide to catch her if she should slip.

Having got safe to the ground, Mrs Cadman shook herself like a satisfied bird. She took back her shopping-basket from the conductor and gave him a smile instead. The big, kind, scarlet bus once more ground into movement, off up the main road hill: it made a fading blur in the premature autumn dusk. Mrs Cadman almost waved after it, for with it went the happy part of her day. She turned down the side road that led to her gate.

A wet wind of autumn, smelling of sodden gardens, blew in her face and tilted her hat. Leaves whirled along it, and one lime leaf, as though imploring shelter, lodged in her fur collar. Every gust did more to sadden the poor trees. This was one of those roads outside growing provincial cities that still keep their rural mystery. They seem to lead into something still not known. Traffic roars past one end, but the other end is in silence: you see a wood, a spire, a haughty manor gate, or your view ends with the turn of an old wall. Here some new, raw-looking villas stood with spaces between them; in the spaces were orchards and market-gardens. A glasshouse roof reflected the wet grey light; there was a shut chapel farther along. And, each standing back in half an acre of ground, there were two or three stucco houses with dark windows, sombre but at the same time ornate, built years ago in this then retired spot. Dead lime leaves showered over their grass plots and evergreens. Mrs Cadman's house, Granville, was one of these: its name was engraved in scrolls over the porch. The solid house was not large, and Mrs Cadman's daughter, Lucille, could look after it with a daily help.

The widow and her daughter lived here in the state of cheerless meekness Lucille considered suitable for them now. *Mr* Cadman had liked to have everything done in style. But twelve years ago he had died, travelling on business, in an hotel up in the North. Always the gentleman, he had been glad to spare them this upset at home. He had been brought back to the Midlands for his impressive funeral, whose size showed him a popular man. How unlike Mr Cadman was Rosa proving herself. One can be most unfriendly in one's way of dying. Ah, well, one chooses one's husband; one's sister is dealt out to one by fate.

Mrs Cadman, thumb on the latch of her own gate, looked for a minute longer up and down the road – deeply, deeply unwilling to go in. She looked back at the corner where the bus had vanished, and an immense sigh heaved up her coat lapels and made a cotton carnation, pinned to the fur, brush a fold of her chin. Laced, hooked, buttoned so tightly into her clothes, she seemed to need to deflate herself by these sudden sighs, by yawns or by those explosions of laughter that often vexed Lucille. Through her face – embedded in fat but still very lively, as exposed, as ingenuous as a little girl's – you could see some emotional fermentation always at work in her. Her smiles were frequent, hopeful and quick. Her pitching walk was due to her tight shoes.

When she did go in she went in with a sort of rush. She let the door bang back on the hall wall, so that the chain rattled and an outraged clatter came from the letter-box. Immediately, she knew she had done wrong. Lucille, appalled, looked out of the dining-room. '*Shissssh!* How can you, mother?' she said.

'Ever so sorry, dear,' said Mrs Cadman, cast down.

'She's just dropped off,' said Lucille. 'After her bad night and everything. It really does seem hard.'

Mrs Cadman quite saw that it did. She glanced nervously up the stairs, then edged into the dining-room. It was not cheerful in here: a monkey puzzle, too close to the window, drank the last of the light up; the room still smelt of dinner; the fire smouldered resentfully, starved for coal. The big mahogany furniture lowered, with no shine. Mrs Cadman, putting her basket down on the table, sent an uncertain smile across at Lucille, whose glasses blankly gleamed high up on her long face. She often asked herself where Lucille could have come from. *Could* this be the baby daughter she had borne, and tied pink bows on, and christened a pretty name? In the sun in this very bow window she had gurgled into sweet-smelling creases of Lucille's neck – one summer lost in time.

'You *have* been an age,' Lucille said.

'Well, the shops were quite busy. I never *saw*,' she said with irrepressible pleasure, 'I never *saw* so many people in town!'

Lucille, lips tighter than ever shut, was routing about, unpacking the shopping basket, handling the packages. Chemist's and grocer's parcels. Mrs Cadman watched her with apprehension. Then Lucille pounced; she held up a small, soft parcel in frivolous wrappings. 'Oho,' she said. 'So you've been in at Babbington's?'

'Well, I missed one bus, so I had to wait for the next. So I just popped in there a minute out of the cold. And, you see, I've been wanting a little scarf — '

'Little scarf!' said Lucille. 'I don't know what to make of you, mother. I don't really. How *could* you, at such a time? How you ever could have the heart!' Lucille, standing the other side of the table, leaned across it, her thin weight on her knuckles. This brought her face near her mother's. 'Can't you understand?' she said. 'Can't you take *anything* in? The next little scarf *you'll* need to buy will be black!'

'What a thing to say!' exclaimed Mrs Cadman, profoundly offended. 'With that poor thing upstairs now, waiting to have her tea.'

'Tea?' She can't take her tea. Why, since this morning she can't keep a thing down.'

Mrs Cadman blenched and began unbuttoning her coat. Lucille seemed to feel that her own prestige and Aunt Rosa's entirely hung on Aunt Rosa's approaching death. You could feel that she and her aunt had thought up this plan together. These last days had been the climax of their complicity. And there was Mrs Cadman – as ever, as usual – put in the wrong, frowned upon, out of things. Whenever Rosa arrived to stay Mrs Cadman had no fun in her home, and now Rosa was leaving for ever it seemed worse. A perverse kick of the heart, a flicker of naughtiness, made Mrs Cadman say: 'Oh, well, while there's life there's hope.'

Lucille said: 'If you won't face it, you won't. But I just say it does fall heavy on me . . . We had the vicar round here this afternoon. He was up with Aunt for a bit, then he looked in and said he did feel I needed a prayer too. He said he thought I was wonderful. He asked where you were, and he seemed to wonder you find the heart to stay out so long. I thought from his manner he wondered a good deal.'

Mrs Cadman, with an irrepressible titter, said: 'Give him something to think about! Why if I'd ha' shown up that vicar'd have popped out as fast as he popped in. Thinks I'd make a mouthful of him. Why, I've made him bolt down the street. Well, well. He's not *my* idea of a vicar. When your father and I first came here we had a rural dean. Oh, he was as pleasant as anything.'

Lucille, with the air of praying for Christian patience, folded her lips. Jabbing her fingers down the inside of her waistbelt, she more tightly tucked in her tight blouse. She liked looking like Mrs Noah – no, *Miss* Noah. 'The doctor's not been again. We're to let him know of any change.'

'Well, let's do the best we can,' said Mrs Cadman. 'But don't keep on *talking*. You don't make things any better, keeping on going on. My opinion is one should keep bright to the last. When my time comes,oh, I would like a cheery face.'

'It's well for you . . . ' began Lucille. She bit the remark off and, gathering up the parcels, stalked scornfully out of the dining-room. Without comment she left exposed on the table a small carton of goodies Mrs. Cadman had bought to cheer herself up with and had concealed in the toe of the shopping bag. Soon, from the kitchen came the carefully muffled noises of Lucille putting away provisions and tearing the wrappings off the chemist's things. Mrs Cadman, reaching out for the carton, put a peppermint into each cheek. She, oh so badly, wanted a cup of tea but dared not follow Lucille into the kitchen in order to put the kettle on.

Though, after all, Granville *was* her house . . .

You would not think it was her house – not when Rosa was there. While Lucille and her mother were *tête à tête* Lucille's disapproval was at least fairly tacit. But as soon as Rosa arrived on one of these yearly autumn visits – always choosing the season when Mrs Cadman felt in her least good form, the fall of the leaf – the aunt and niece got together and found everything wrong. Their two cold natures ran together. They found Mrs Cadman lacking; they forbade the affection she would have offered them. They censured her the whole time. Mrs Cadman could date her real alienation from Lucille from the year when Rosa's visits began. During Mr Cadman's lifetime Rosa had never come for more than an afternoon. Mr Cadman had been his wife's defence from her sister – a great red kind of rumbustious fortification. He had been a man who kept every chill wind out. Rosa, during those stilted afternoon visits, had adequately succeeded in conveying that she found marriage *low*. She might just have suffered a pious marriage; she openly deprecated this high living, this state of fleshly bliss. In order not to witness it too closely she lived on in lodgings in her native town . . . But once widowhood left her sister exposed, Rosa started flapping round Granville like a doomful bird. She instituted these yearly visits, which, she made plain at the same time, gave her not much pleasure. The journey was tedious, and by breaking her habits, leaving her lodgings, Rosa was, out of duty, putting herself about. Her joyless and intimidating visits had, therefore, only one object – to protect the interests of Lucille.

Mrs Cadman had suspected for some time that Rosa had something the matter with her. No one looks as yellow as that for nothing. But she was not sufficiently intimate with her sister to get down to the cosy subject of insides. This time, Rosa arrived looking worse than ever, and three days afterwards had collapsed. Lucille said now she had known her aunt was poorly. Lucille said now she had always known. 'But of course you wouldn't notice, mother,' she said.

Mrs Cadman sat down by the fire and, gratefully, kicked off her tight shoes. In the warmth her plump feet uncurled, relaxed, expanded like sea-anemones. She stretched her legs out, propped her heels on the fender and wiggled her toes voluptuously. They went on wiggling of their own accord: they seemed to have an independent existence. Here, in her home, where she felt so 'put wrong' and chilly, they were like ten stout, confidential friends. She said, out loud: 'Well, *I* don't know what I've done.'

The fact was: Lucille and Rosa resented her. (She'd feel better when she had had her tea.) She should *not* have talked as she had about the vicar. But it seemed so silly, Lucille having just him. She did wish Lucille had a better time. No young man so much as paused at the gate. Lucille's aunt had wrapped her own dank virginity round her like someone sharing a mackintosh.

Mrs Cadman had had a good time. A real good time always lasts: you have it with all your nature and all your nature stays living with it. She had been a pretty child with long, blonde hair that her sister Rosa, who was her elder sister, used to tweak when they were alone in their room. She had grown used, in that childish attic bedroom, to Rosa's malevolent silences. Then one had grown up, full of great uppish curves. Hilda Cadman could sing. She had sung at parties and sung at charity concerts, too. She had been invited from town to town, much fêted in business society. She had sung in a dress cut low at the bosom, with a rose or carnation tucked into her hair. She had drunk port wine in great red rooms blazing with chandeliers. Mr Cadman had whisked her away from her other gentlemen friends, and not for a moment had she regretted it. Nothing had been too good for her: she had gone on singing. She had felt warm air on her bare shoulders; she still saw the kind, flushed faces crowding round. Mr Cadman and she belonged to the jolly set. They all thought the world of her, and she thought the world of them.

Mrs Cadman, picking up the poker, jabbed the fire into a spurt of light. It does not do any good to sit and think in the dark.

The town was not the same now. They had all died, or lost their money, or gone. But you kept on loving the town for its dear old sake. She sometimes thought: Why not move and live at the seaside, where there would be a promenade and a band? But she knew her nature clung to the old scenes; where you had lived, you lived – your nature clung like a cat. While there was *something* to look at she was not one to repine. It kept you going to keep out and about. Things went, but then new things came in their place. You can't cure yourself of the habit of loving life. So she drank up the new pleasures – the big cafés, the barging buses, the cinemas, the shops dripping with colour, almost all built of glass. She could be perfectly happy all alone in a café, digging into a cream bun with a fork, the band playing, smiling faces all round. The old faces had not gone: they had dissolved, diluted into the ruddy blur through which she saw everything.

Meanwhile, Lucille was hard put to it, living her mother down. Mother looked ridiculous, always round town like that.

Mrs Cadman heard Lucille come out of the kitchen and go upstairs with something rattling on a tray. She waited a minute more, then sidled into the kitchen, where she cautiously started to make tea. The gas-ring, as though it were a spy of Lucille's, popped loudly when she applied the match.

'Mother, she's asking for you.'

'Oh, dear – do you mean she's — ?'

'She's much more herself this evening,' Lucille said implacably.

Mrs Cadman, at the kitchen table, had been stirring sugar into her third cup. She pushed her chair back, brushed crumbs from her bosom and followed Lucille like a big, unhappy lamb. The light was on in the hall, but the stairs led up into shadow: she had one more start of reluctance at their foot. Autumn draughts ran about in the top storey: up there the powers of darkness all seemed to mobilize. Mrs Cadman put her hand on the banister knob. 'Are you sure she *does* want to see me? Oughtn't she to stay quiet?'

'You should go when she's asking. You never know . . .'

Breathless, breathing unevenly on the top landing, Mrs Cadman pushed open the spare-room – that was the sick-room – door. In there – in here – the air was dead, and at first it seemed very dark. On the ceiling an oil-stove printed its flower-pattern; a hooded lamp, low down, was turned away from the bed. On that dark side of the lamp she could just distinguish Rosa, propped up, with the sheet drawn to her chin.

'Rosa?'

'Oh, it's you?'

'Yes; it's me, dear. Feeling better this evening?'

'Seemed funny, you not coming near me.'

'They said for you to keep quiet.'

'My own sister . . . You never liked sickness, did you? Well, I'm going. I shan't trouble you long.'

'Oh, don't talk like that!'

'I'm glad to be going. Keeping on lying here . . . We all come to it. Oh, give over crying, Hilda. Doesn't do any good.'

Mrs Cadman sat down, to steady herself. She fumbled in her lap with her handkerchief, perpetually, clumsily knocking her elbows against the arms of the wicker chair. 'It's such a shame,' she said. 'It's such a pity. You and me, after all . . . '

'Well, it's late for all that now. Each took our own ways.' Rosa's voice went up in a sort of ghostly sharpness. 'There were things that couldn't be otherwise. I've tried to do right by Lucille. Lucille's a good girl, Hilda. You should ask yourself if you've done right by her.'

'Oh, for shame, Rosa,' said Mrs Cadman, turning her face through the dark towards that disembodied voice. 'For shame, Rosa, even if you *are* going. You know best what's come between her and me. It's been you and her, you and her. I don't know where to turn sometimes — '

Rosa said: 'You've got such a shallow heart.'

'How should you know? Why, you've kept at a distance from me ever since we were tots. Oh, I know I'm a great silly, always after my fun, but I never took what was yours; I never did harm to you. I don't see what call we have got to judge each other. You didn't want my life that I've had.'

Rosa's chin moved: she was lying looking up at her sister's big rippling shadow, splodged up there by the light of the low lamp. It is frightening, having your shadow watched. Mrs Cadman said: 'But what did I do to you?'

'I *could* have had a wicked heart,' said Rosa. 'A vain, silly heart like yours. I could have fretted, seeing you take everything. One thing, then another. But I was shown. God taught me to pity you. God taught me my lesson . . . You wouldn't even remember that Christmas tree.'

'What Christmas tree?'

'No, you wouldn't even remember. Oh, I thought it was lovely. I could have cried when they pulled the curtains open, and there it was, all blazing away with candles and silver and everything — '

'Well, isn't that funny? I — '

'No; you've had all that pleasure since. All of us older children couldn't take it in, hardly, for quite a minute or two. It didn't look real. Then I looked up, and there was a fairy doll fixed on the top, right on the top spike, fixed on to a star. I set my heart on her. She had wings and long, fair hair, and she was shining away. I couldn't take my eyes off her. They cut the presents down; but she wasn't for anyone. In my childish blindness I kept praying to God. If I am not to have her, I prayed, let her stay there.'

'And what did God do?' Hilda said eagerly.

'Oh, He taught me and saved me. You were a little thing in a blue sash; you piped up and asked might you have the doll.'

'Fancy me! Aren't children awful!' said Mrs Cadman. 'Asking like that.'

'They said: "Make her sing for it." They were taken with you. So you piped up again, singing. You got her, all right. I went off where they kept the coats. I've thanked God ever since for what I had to go through! I turned my face from vanity from that very night. I had been shown.'

'Oh, what a shame!' said Hilda. 'Oh, I think it was cruel; you poor little mite.'

'No; I used to see that doll all draggled about the house till no one could bear the sight of it. I said to myself: that's how those things end. Why, I'd learnt more in one evening than you've ever learnt in your life. Oh, yes, I've watched you, Hilda. Yes, and I've pitied you.'

'Well, you showed me no pity.'

'You asked for no pity – all vain and set up.'

'No wonder you've been against me. Fancy me not knowing. I didn't *mean* any harm – why, I was quite a little thing. I don't even remember.'

'Well, you'll remember one day. When you lie as I'm lying you'll find that everything comes back. And you'll see what it adds up to.'

'Well, if I do?' said Hilda. 'I haven't been such a baby; I've seen things out in my own way; I've had my ups and downs. It hasn't been all jam.' She got herself out of the armchair and came and stood uncertainly by the foot of the bed. She had a great wish to reach out and turn the hooded lamp round, so that its light could fall on her sister's face. She felt she should *see* her sister, perhaps for the first time. Inside the flat, still form did implacable disappointment, then, stay locked? She wished she could give Rosa some little present. Too late to give Rosa anything pretty now: she looked back – it had always, then, been too late? She thought: you poor queer heart; you queer heart, eating yourself out, thanking God for the pain. She thought: I did that to her; then what have I done to Lucille?

She said: 'You're ever so like me, Rosa, really, aren't you? Setting our hearts on things. When you've got them you don't notice. No wonder you wanted Lucille . . . You did ought to have had that fairy doll.'

The Girl with the Stoop

A SMALL summer town, seaside, in the late rainy autumn has a left-behind air. Simply to live here is not fully to live – and Tibbie, a summer girl, a born holiday-maker, had not learnt yet how to feel like a resident. Very few things ruffled her calm nature, but she did not feel at ease in her aunt's house. In this villa, everyone except Tibbie seemed to be always going up or down the stairs: Tibbie felt she could seldom fully relax . . . This was a Wednesday morning, about eleven; she had washed three pairs of silk stockings and written a picture postcard, and that seemed to be all she had to do. For some time she watched the rain from the bow window, while desultorily teasing her aunt's cat. Then, though it did not stop raining, the sky lightened a little; brighter reflections appeared on the wet bushes, the wet asphalt garden path. Tibbie feared to linger in the drawing-room – her aunt might come down and find something for her to do. So she heaved herself out of the armchair with a sigh, unhung her mackintosh from the hall rack, buttoned herself to the chin, tucked her curls inside an oil-silk hood, and went out – went out with no object at all.

The residential road led straight down to the sea. Behind their neat, white gates the villas were in a torpor: all the people in them might have died in their sleep. She did not even wonder whether they had. The fishmonger's boy, in a glistening mackintosh cape, bicycled slowly past her, whistling a little flat. He just gave her a look, but she did not even see him. The wet, salt air met her forehead, creeping under her hood. Her face, with the long nose dustily freckled, the sweet, mild, crumpled, indeterminate mouth, lolled a little forward over her high collar, like a flower without the sense to grow up straight.

Tibbie was staying here with her Aunt Cara simply to put in time. She was engaged to be married; she should be making her trousseau; she had brought lengths of pink ninon to sew. The young man was in India; he had proposed by letter; in April he would return to claim his inert bride. Aunt Cara, in common with the other relations, supposed marriage might pull Tibbie together. She was sorry to see so few letters go to the mail, fearing Tibbie might let the young man slip. She pointed out to Tibbie how many nice English girls were to be met in India, and how neglect tries the most faithful young man's heart. But Tibbie would say: 'Oh, no, Tom loves me, I'm sure.'

This morning, the sea front was void and dejected-looking. The tide was out, leaving stretches of dead sand. The empty bandstand dripped; drops slipped through the slats of seats. Tibbie's equable little heart sank. But one reach of the promenade she always walked down with pleasure – she looked forward to passing the Palace Hotel. This great de luxe hotel, dazzlingly white and lofty, all glass lounges, balconies, boxes of flowers, and with its cascade of marble steps, was the chief glory of the quiet resort. Even in autumn it had a sort of season: rich convalescents stayed there, or people who played golf. At tea time a band played; all day long maroon pages could be seen at attention inside the revolving door. Yes, even to dawdle past the Palace Hotel was to feel oneself lapped by its sumptuous mystery . . . Ungloved hands plunged shyly in her mackintosh pockets, Tibbie, unbending her stoop a little, threw up the look of a dreamer at the sun lounge windows, those great steamy vistas of plate-glass.

Francis, leaning forward against the plate-glass window, gripping the arms of his cripple's chair, cried: 'There she goes! There goes that girl with the stoop!'

'Does she?' said Geoff, unmoved, inside *Esquire*. Then he remembered he ought to humour Francis; he looked politely over the magazine. Indoor hotel life made Geoff apathetic; this morning the too-rich breakfast lay on his stomach; the steam heating put a band round his head.

'She looked at us, too,' said Francis. He added, knitting his forehead: 'I wonder where she's off to?'

'She isn't in any hurry. Where could a girl be off to, in this hole?'

Francis flushed and immediately said, stiffly: 'Oh, all right, all right; I know it's a frightful place. For God's sake get out if you're bored. Why don't you get back to London? I don't want anyone martyred because of me.'

'Oh, shut up. I didn't mean it like that.'

Geoff said to himself that that was the worst of Francis – things kept being so tricky the whole time. You never knew where you might put your foot next. Francis had been sent down here by his rich father for a blow of sea air before the winter set in, and Geoff, his big, ordinary first cousin, was there, too, as a guest, to cheer Francis up. The boys were the same age, but matters of health and money created a rather cruel contrast between them. Geoff, born hard up, had been glad to accept the place in the family business that should have been Francis's. He had been given a week's leave from the business to come down here and live like a fighting cock. But his animal charm and his animal spirits wilted; he failed to cheer Francis up, and he did not have much fun. He longed to go off to golf, but that seemed shabby: not part of the bargain of being here. Altogether, he felt rather a flop. It was Francis who had first called this place a hole, but Geoff saw now he had been wrong to agree . . . On fine days they would go up and down the sea front, Francis adeptly steering his motor chair. This morning it was too wet to do even that. Anxious to make amends, Geoff put down *Esquire* and looked politely after his cousin's girl with the stoop. 'Well, she's not my type,' he said, as nicely as ever. 'But, of course, you can't really judge, in a mackintosh.'

'She blinks like that at us every time we see her. She's so shy and vague – she's exactly perfect, I think.'

'Well, that seems too bad – I don't see what one can do. She's not quite the sort of girl one could — '

Francis said, with his sad, unkind, mocking smile: 'I thought you once said you could pick anyone up . . . ?'

'Well, a girl's a girl, of course. But — '

'Oh, all right, all right,' said Francis. 'Don't think any more of it. Sorry I ever spoke. I detest asking people to do things . . . ' Perversely, he reached across for *Esquire*, and Geoff knew one would not see it again. He said to himself that really there were limits. At the same time, he knew the matter would not be dropped; Francis never forgot anything he had set his heart on. Being crippled made him a difficult child. But what a tough time he had, what a tough time, really. This was the first thing he'd asked for that he had really wanted. It did seem a shame; it did seem rather a shame . . . Geoff stretched and stood up against the sun lounge window. He looked thoughtfully at Tibbie walking away.

Tibbie knew it was odd, but she could not see any harm. She would, naturally, not speak of this to her aunt – this really whirl-wind invitation to tea.

For, the following morning, which was even wetter, Geoff had picked Tibbie up, in the Tudor Café, where she sat listlessly drinking her morning coffee, listening to wireless music, looking out at the sea. Geoff picked her up with an ease combined with faultless propriety that left them both decidedly gratified. He had come across to her table – she had taken her hood off and her curls were pressed flat to her head. He said: 'Have you dropped a glove?' and she, knowing she wore none, said: 'Have you found one?' diffidently raising her lashes. 'Well, not this morning,' Geoff said, with his most disarming smile. 'But the fact is, I've got a message for you.' 'Oh – who from?' 'Someone you don't know yet – unless you know him by sight. He feels he knows you by sight . . . My cousin's a cripple,' Geoff concluded. 'It's pretty dull for him here. It would be ever so nice of you if you'd come to tea . . . '

So here was Tibbie, at half-past four on a Thursday, going up in the Palace Hotel lift. She wore gloves today and wore her prettiest hat. She was ever so slightly disappointed at being sucked upstairs, away from the band. Geoff had not told her they had a private suite. This made everything much more dashing, grander – but was it quite so respectable, having tea upstairs? But this time next year I shall be in India, she thought.

Into the luxurious small room, with its wide sea view, Tibbie advanced nose first. Francis ran his chair forward to meet her. 'I'm sorry I cannot get up,' he said. He nodded to where Geoff stood by the window and said: 'You've met my cousin, I think?' On satinwood tables stood vases of tawny flowers, to match the curtains of apricot silk. Francis spun round his chair to face a great big armchair into which Tibbie, hypnotized, found herself sinking down. Her face was now below his: she found herself looking up at a boy of about twenty, who was levelling on her his power of making natural people unnaturally shy. His eyes were brilliant. A dark lock fell forward over his forehead; she looked at his oversensitive hands on the arms of his chair. Dipping her face down, Tibbie looked round the parlour under her lashes that were as soft as moths. 'What lovely flowers,' she said.

'They're for you – they were the best I could get: the shops are so rotten here. Oh, but I beg your pardon – you live here, perhaps?'

'No, only my aunt does. I — '

'Then it doesn't matter,' said Francis. 'Look, do take your gloves off, your hat – do look as though you would stay!' So Tibbie pulled her gloves off, lifted her hat off her curls. Francis stared sharply; he said: 'What's that ring? Why do you wear that?'

'Oh, my engagement ring,' she said, modestly. Francis let this little confident statement sink into the masculine silence of the room. Then he twitched his head round at Geoff and said: 'Why isn't tea coming? Ring for tea.' Reaching out, he switched on a table-lamp; the dusk outside looked desolate, dark as ink. Tea came rattling cheerfully in on a little trolley; Geoff brought his engaging presence up to the trolley; Francis invited Tibbie to pour out. She could not help peeping at the under-ledge of the trolley – really, she had never seen such a tea! They were all three of them getting on very nicely when Francis said with his self-torturing smile: 'Where are you going to live when you are married?'

'India', she smiled. 'Doesn't that seem funny?'

'No. You'll hate it. It's very hot.'

'Oh, come,' Geoff said, 'India sounds quite a lot of fun. I should jump at going out to India myself.' 'Pity you can't,' Francis threw at him, slightingly. But Tibbie, biting into a grape tartlet, fluttered in Geoff's direction a grateful look. Geoff went on: 'Francis never thinks much of anyone's plans, you know.'

Francis stonily said: 'I don't need to plan; I plot. I don't believe in plans.' He jerked back his lock of hair and said, directly, to Tibbie: 'Neither do you.' Which made her send Geoff (not Francis) a little look of surprise. Francis said: 'You don't care if you go to India . . .'

'Oh, but I do.'

'You may not get there,' said Francis.

Geoff started laughing and flushing. 'Oh, shut up,' he said. 'Shut up. You'll make this girl sorry she came to tea; you'll upset her.'

'Are you upset, Tibbie?' said Francis, lightly. She could not speak; she was laughing – real laughter, not awkward, forbidding laughter like Geoff's. Vibrating gently all over, like a small cat emitting a great purr, she unsteadily folded her tea napkin and put back her plate on the trolley. A flake of pastry still clung to her chin; she curved forward over her mirth. 'You sound so funny,' she said. 'You seem to think I have no character. It's so funny, when I've only just come to tea. Why, I've got my destiny lines all over my hand. I've had my hand told three times and it always comes out the same – I am to cross the sea and live in a sunny clime.'

'The sun shines almost everywhere except here. You could live in a villa in Italy.'

'Oh, but you see, I don't know anyone there.'

'I'm going to live in a villa in Italy.'

'I thought you said you never made any plans!' crowed Tibbie, contentedly, looking round her at the lamps, the flowers, the apricot curtains that had been softly drawn. 'But, of course, it's different for you,' she said.

'Yes,' said Francis. 'It's different for me.'

Geoff saw Tibbie down in the lift. He went through the white-pillared lounge with her and pushed her gently ahead of him through the revolving door. In the door she turned round to say something, but it was cut off. When they both came out on the steps and stood where the light streamed through the dark, mild rain, he said: 'Shall I see you home?' 'I don't think so, because . . . All right.' she unfurled her umbrella, then turned her profile away to the dark sea. 'I can't sometimes believe I shall be in India,' she said. 'So I couldn't think what to say when your cousin talked about it. But, of course, I believe in my destiny.'

'I hope you didn't think Francis impertinent?'

'Oh, no; things are different for him aren't they? Always stuck there like that. I should have thought he'd have liked a more lively person than me.'

'All the same, we are meeting again, aren't we?'

'Well, he only said, "Don't go." He didn't say to come back . . . '

Next morning the sun shone; the sea shone like white glass. The promenade glistened; the curve of the bay, the promenade gardens, with their few wet roses, wore the smile of November, pallidly gay. Francis and his chair went down in the lift and were deferentially bumped by the pages down the hotel steps – then he cruised about in the sun, all by himself, looking for an advantageous position. He had sent Geoff off to play golf with a man they had met last night. Francis stopped his chair by a seat on the promenade. He wore a dark red, high-necked sweater, an expensive tweed coat; a camel-hair rug was tucked over his knees. His cheek-bones were stained by a slight flush; he sat looking sideways out to sea, his whole nervous attention fixed on the promenade. For some time he sat listening for Tibbie's step; then she came round his chair and stood beside him, blinking her eyelashes in the sun.

'Well,' said Francis, 'here is your sunny clime.'

Tibbie looked at the bench and said: 'Where's Geoff gone?'

'Golf,' said Francis, sharply. 'Why?'

'I just wondered,' she said. She dithered, then sat down. She was wearing no gloves again, so when she spread her hands on her lap, palms upward, she could frown down thoughtfully at the lines on them. Francis said: 'Well? Are they different since yesterday?' 'Oh, how could they change; they are me.' 'Did you like coming to tea?'

'Oh, yes. But you made me feel such a silly.'

'Was that why you kept laughing the whole time? . . . You can write about that in your letter to India, can't you? – "Oh, I went out to tea with a funny boy." Do you write to India often?'

'Well, I do when I can. But so little happens here, there's not much to write about.'

'*About?*' said Francis. 'But you write love letters, don't you?' Tibbie looked quite mystified; Francis continued: 'Have you and that young man got nothing to say?'

'You see, when I used to know him we were not engaged, really. So I don't know what we said. We played tennis most of the time.'

A contraction shook Francis's chair, and made Tibbie turn round. Perplexed she watched something playing over his face: was it pain, or was it light from the sea? He returned to himself and said in a steady voice: 'You wouldn't play tennis at all well.'

'No, but Tom likes me to try . . . Why are you so sharp with me?'

'I didn't sleep last night.'

'Oh, dear, that does seem a pity, when it's such a lovely morning today. How did you know I didn't play tennis well?'

'I know all about you: I knew you before we met. You knew I knew you, Tibbie? What made you so foolish? You're a sweet, dreadful funk, with no backbone at all. How dared you laugh when I asked you to marry me – when I'm like – *this*?' cried Francis, striking his chair.

'Oh, I *didn't* know you meant that. The whole tea was so funny. I didn't know where I was.'

'You never know where you are.'

'I don't understand. Do you really . . . I mean, *do* you . . . '

'Yes, I naturally love you. I want you always by me. Haven't I just told you I didn't sleep? Listen, Tibbie: I don't ask you to love me; all I want is that you should be always there. All those mornings you've walked past and looked up at the window I've wanted to bang the glass and shout: "Stop, you idiot: stay!" I'm sick and spoilt and impossible and I torment everyone, but now you torment me whenever you go away. Yes, I sent Geoff out yesterday morning to pick you up, like I'd send him out for a newspaper or a bunch of flowers. Yes, I though it could all be as easy as that. But when you'd gone I knew it was terrible. I've always hated people because I've hated their pity. But I love you: you show me how to be kind . . . '

Francis checked himself, stooped: he reached out a hand to Tibbie, and she uncertainly let her hand fall into his. She sat looking slantwise past him at the sun-painted sea front, the shining, unreal scene. They both seemed to be somewhere else. Then she drew her hand away, nervous. She said: 'You are kind in such a funny way.'

'Because you are always walking away, going. I want you always by me just as you are, not different. I want you in rooms with me. Stay with me all the time!'

'I'd, I'd be afraid, Francis. You sort of eat me up. Besides — '

'There is no besides. I'm all will and you've no will. I know you don't understand. But I could make you so happy. Look how you liked my room, how you liked the flowers. You understand those, perhaps? I'm rich; I could give you all those small, silly things. Oh, I could shelter you, Tibbie. It's *my* life-line that's in your hand.'

'Yes, but you see . . . '

'But what?'

'But you see, I'm going away today . . . ' She said this looking away, and he did not say anything. 'I'm going away; I got the letter this morning. Tom's mother's come to London; I've got to go up to her. You see, Tom's mother has never seen me, and they say I must certainly go to her.'

Francis said, in a voice that seemed to come from a distance: 'All right, all right, then: go, then, go: then come back.'

But Tibbie knitted her forehead. 'But Tom's mother lives right up in Scotland. And, you see, I'm to go back to Scotland with her. They all say I must. They say Tom would like me to . . .'

'You can't go,' Francis said, in a perfectly dead voice. 'All that's out of the question – don't you understand?'

'No, I don't – *you* told me I didn't.'

'Yes, but *look!*' cried Francis, striking his chair again. 'You can't leave me when I cannot come after you! You don't *want* to leave me, Tibbie, do you? . . . For God's sake, look straight at me: stop drooping your head!'

But she only bent down more; she curled up like an anemone in an unkind wind. At the same time, with a frightened obstinacy, her soft lashes stayed down on her cheek. Then she said in her mild voice, without even a falter: 'But it's all settled, this morning. My aunt's sent the telegrams; she has ordered the taxi. The taxi's coming at three.'

Francis paused for the last time – the unusual hesitation of someone facing the whole of life. He said: 'But you and I cannot have met for nothing.' But she only raised her hands, which were trembling ever so slightly, and looked again at what had been written there. 'I can't change what's all settled,' she said.

'At the same time you can't go.'

'But I can.' Getting up, she looked in surprise at him – surprised to find herself getting up. It was as though wires moved her. As she turned the end of the bench she heard Francis, behind her, give a wrench at his chair. Her thought was: 'He must not come after me – on wheels, on wheels: wheels turn very fast.' She broke into a run. She ran down the promenade, stooping, breathless, not looking back once, not daring to listen. The cold sea flashed alongside of her. She reached the corner; then she lagged slowly, slowly back to her aunt's gate.

When the promenade was quite empty Francis drove his chair, slowly, in the other direction, to the Palace Hotel.

The War Years

Unwelcome Idea

ALONG Dublin bay, on a sunny July morning, the public gardens along the Dalkey tramline look bright as a series of parasols. Chalk-blue sea appears at the ends of the roads of villas turning downhill – but these are still the suburbs, not the seaside. In the distance, floating across the bay, buildings glitter out of the heat-haze on the neck to Howth, and Howth Head looks higher veiled. After inland Ballsbridge, the tram from Dublin speeds up; it zooms through the residential reaches with the gathering steadiness of a launched ship. Its red velvet seating accommodation is seldom crowded – its rival, the quicker bus, lurches ahead of it down the same road.

After Ballsbridge, the ozone smell of the bay sifts more and more through the smell of chimneys and pollen and the July-darkened garden trees as the bay and line converge. Then at a point you see the whole bay open – there are nothing but flats of grass and the sunk railway between the running tram and the still sea. An immense glaring reflection floods through the tram. When high terraces, backs to the tramline, shut out the view again, even their backs have a salted, marine air: their cotton window-blinds are pulled half down, crooked; here and there an inner door left open lets you see a flash of sea through a house. The weathered lions on gate posts ought to be dolphins. Red, low-lying villas have been fitted between earlier terraces, ornate, shabby, glassy hotels, bow-fronted mansions all built in the first place to stand up over spaces of grass. Looks from trams and voices from public gardens invade the old walled lawns with their grottos and weeping willows. Spit-and-polish alternates with decay. But stucco, slate and slate-fronts, blotched Italian pink-wash, dusty windows, lace curtains and dolphin-lions seem to be the eternity of this tram route. Quite soon the modern will sag, chip, fade. Change leaves everything at the same level. Nothing stays bright but mornings.

The tram slides to stops for its not many passengers. The Blackrock bottleneck checks it, then the Dun Laoghaire. These are the shopping centres strung on the line: their animation congests them. Housewives with burnt bare arms out of their cotton dresses mass blinking and talking among the halted traffic, knocking their shopping-bags on each other's thighs. Forgotten Protestant ladies from 'rooms' near the esplanade stand squeezed between the kerb and the shops. A file of booted children threads its way through the crush, a nun at the head like a needle. Children by themselves curl their toes in their plimsoles and suck sweets and disregard everything. The goods stacked in the shops look very static and hot. Out from the tops of the shops on brackets stand a number of clocks. As though wrought up by the clocks the tram-driver smites his bell again and again, till the checked tram noses its way through.

By half-past eleven this morning one tram to Dalkey is not far on its way. All the time it approaches the Ballsbridge stop Mrs Kearney looks undecided, but when it does pull up she steps aboard because she has seen no bus. In a slither of rather ungirt parcels, including a dress-box, with a magazine held firmly between her teeth, she clutches her way up the stairs to the top. She settles herself on a velvet seat: she is hot. But the doors at each end and the windows are half-open, and as the tram moves air rushes smoothly through. There are only four other people and no man smokes a pipe. Mrs Kearney has finished wedging her parcels between her hip and the side of the tram and is intending to look at her magazine when she stares hard ahead and shows interest in someone's back. She moves herself and everything three seats up, leans forward and gives a poke at the back. 'Isn't that you?' she says.

Miss Kevin jumps round so wholeheartedly that the brims of the two hats almost clash. 'Why, for goodness' sake! . . . Are you on the tram?' She settled round in her seat with her elbow hooked over the back – it is bare and sharp, with a rubbed joint: she and Mrs Kearney are of an age, and the age is about thirty-five. They both wear printed dresses that in this weather stick close to their backs; they are enthusiastic, not close friends but as close as they are ever likely to be. They both have high, fresh, pink colouring; Mrs Kearney could do with a little less weight and Miss Kevin could do with a little more.

They agree they are out early. Miss Kevin has been in town for the July sales but is now due home to let her mother go out. She has parcels with her but they are compact and shiny, having been made up at the counters of shops. 'They all say, buy now. You never know.' She cannot help looking at Mrs Kearney's parcels, bursting out from their string. 'And aren't you very laden, also,' she says.

'I tell you what I've been doing,' says Mrs Kearney. 'I've been saying goodbye to my sister Maureen in Ballsbridge, and who knows how long it's to be for! My sister's off to County Cavan this morning with the whole of her family and the maid.'

'For goodness' sake,' says Miss Kevin. 'Has she relatives there?'

'She has, but it's not that. She's evacuating. For the holidays they always go to Tramore, but this year she says she should evacuate.' This brings Mrs Kearney's parcels into the picture. 'So she asked me to keep a few of her things for her.' She does not add that Maureen has given her these old things, including the month-old magazine.

'Isn't it well for her,' says Miss Kevin politely. 'But won't she find it terribly slow down there?'

'She will, I tell you,' says Mrs Kearney. 'However, they're all driving down in the car. She's full of it. She says we should all go somewhere where we don't live. It's nothing to her to shift when she has the motor. But the latest thing I hear they say now in the paper is that we'll be shot if we don't stay where we are. They say now we're all to keep off the roads – and there's my sister this morning with her car at the door. Do you think they'll halt her, Miss Kevin?'

'They might,' says Miss Kevin. 'I hear they're very suspicious. I declare, with the instructions changing so quickly it's better to take no notice. You'd be upside down if you tried to follow them all. It's of the first importance to keep calm, they say, and however would we keep calm doing this, then that? Still, we don't get half the instructions they get in England. I should think they'd really pity themselves . . . Have you earth in your house, Mrs Kearney? We have, we have three buckets. The warden's delighted with us: he says we're models. We haven't a refuge, though. Have you one?'

'We have a kind of pump, but I don't know it is much good. And nothing would satisfy Fergus till he turned out the cellar.'

'Well, you're very fashionable!'

'The contents are on the lawn, and the lawn's ruined. He's crazy,' she says glumly, 'with A.R.P.'

'Aren't men very thorough,' says Miss Kevin with a virgin detachment that is rather annoying. She has kept thumbing her sales parcels, and now she cannot resist undoing one. 'Listen,' she says, 'isn't this a pretty delaine?' She runs the end of a fold between her finger and thumb. 'It drapes sweetly. I've enough for a dress and a bolero. It's French: they say we won't get any more now.'

'And that Coty scent – isn't that French?'

Their faces flood with the glare struck from the sea as the tram zooms smoothly along the open reach – wall and trees on its inland side, grass and bay on the other. The tips of their shingles and the thoughts in their heads are for the minute blown about and refreshed. Mrs Kearney flutters in the holiday breeze, but Miss Kevin is looking inside her purse. Mrs Kearney thinks she will take the kids to the strand. 'Are you a great swimmer, Miss Kevin?'

'I don't care for it: I've a bad circulation. It's a fright to see me go blue. They say now the sea's full of mines,' she says, with a look at the great, innocent bay.

'Ah, they're tethered; they'd never bump you.'

'I'm not nervous at any time, but I take a terrible chill.'

'My sister Maureen's nervous. At Tramore she'll never approach the water: it's the plage she enjoys. I wonder what will she do if they stop the car – she has all her plate with her in the back with the maid. And her kiddies are very nervous: they'd never stand it. I wish now I'd asked her to send me a telegram. Or should I telegraph her to know did she arrive? . . . Wasn't it you said we had to keep off the roads?'

'That's in the event of invasion, Mrs Kearney. In the event of not it's correct to evacuate.'

'She's correct all right, then,' says Mrs Kearney, with a momentary return to gloom. 'And if nothing's up by the finish she'll say she went for the holiday, and I shouldn't wonder if she still went to Tramore. Still, I'm sure I'm greatly relieved to hear what you say . . . Is that your father's opinion?'

Miss Kevin becomes rather pettish. 'Him?' she says, 'oh gracious, I'd never ask him. He has a great contempt for the whole war. My mother and I daren't refer to it – isn't it very mean of him? He does nothing but read the papers and roar away to himself. And will he let my mother or me near him when he has the news on? You'd think,' Miss Kevin says with a clear laugh, 'that the two of us originated the war to spite him: he doesn't seem to blame Hitler at all. He's really very unreasonable when he's not well. We'd a great fight to get in the buckets of earth, and now he makes out they're only there for the cat. And to hear the warden praising us makes him sour. Isn't it very mean to want us out of it all, when they say the whole country is drawn together? He doesn't take any pleasure in A.R.P.'

'To tell you the truth I don't either,' says Mrs Kearney. 'Isn't it that stopped the Horse Show? Wouldn't that take the heart out of you – isn't that a great blow to national life? I never yet missed a Horse Show – Sheila was nearly born there. And isn't that a terrible blow to trade? I haven't the heart to look for a new hat. To my mind this war's getting very monotonous: all the interest of it is confined to a few . . . Did you go to the Red Cross Fête?'

The tram grinds to a halt in Dun Laoghaire Street. Simultaneously Miss Kevin and Mrs Kearney move up to the window ends of their seats and look closely down on the shop windows and shoppers. Town heat comes off the street in a quiver and begins to pervade the immobile tram. 'I declare to goodness,' exclaims Miss Kevin, 'there's my same delaine! French, indeed! And watch the figure it's on – it would sicken you.'

But with parallel indignation Mrs Kearney has just noticed a clock. 'Will you look at the time!' she says, plaintively. 'Isn't this an awfully slow tram! There's my morning gone, and not a thing touched at home, from attending evacuations. It's well for her! She expected me on her step by ten – "It's a terrible parting," she says on the p.c. But all she does at the last is to chuck the parcels at me, then keep me running to see had they the luncheon basket and what had they done with her fur coat . . . I'll be off at the next stop, Miss Kevin dear. Will you tell your father and mother I was inquiring for them?' Crimson again at the very notion of moving, she begins to scrape her parcels under her wing. 'Well,' she says, 'I'm off with the *objets d'art*.' The heels of a pair of evening slippers protrude from a gap at the end of the dress box. The tram-driver, by smiting his bell, drowns any remark Miss Kevin could put out: the tram clears the crowd and moves down Dun Laoghaire Street, between high flights of steps, lace curtains, gardens with round beds. 'Bye-bye, now,' says Mrs Kearney, rising and swaying.

'Bye-bye to you,' said Miss Kevin. 'Happy days to us all.'

Mrs Kearney, near the top of the stairs, is preparing to bite on the magazine. 'Go on!' she says. 'I'll be seeing you before then.'

Oh, Madam . . .

OH, madam . . . Oh, *madam*, here you are!

I don't know what you'll say. Look, sit down just for a minute, madam; I dusted this chair for you. Yes, the hall's all right really; you don't see so much at first – only, our beautiful fanlight gone. No, there's nothing in here to hurt: I swept up the glass. Oh, *do* sit a minute, madam; you look quite white . . . This is a shock for you, isn't it! I was in half a mind to go out and meet you, but I didn't rightly like to leave everything. Not with the windows gone. They can see in.

Oh, *I'm* quite all right, madam. I made some tea this morning . . . Do I? Oh well, that's natural, I suppose. I'd be quite all right if I wasn't feeling so bad. Well, you know how I always was – I don't like a cup to go. And now . . . If you'll only sit still, madam, I'll go and get you something. I know you don't take tea, not in the regular way, but it really is wonderful what tea does for you . . . Sherry? I'll go and try, but I really don't know – the dining-room door won't – I'm *afraid*, madam, I'm afraid it's the ceiling in there gone . . . And as you know, Johnson's got the key to the cellar, and Johnson went off after the all clear. I said, 'You did ought to stay till madam's with us.' But he didn't seem quite himself – he *did* have a bad night, madam, and you know how men are, nervous . . . I don't know where – back to his wife's, I daresay: he didn't vouchsafe . . . The girls? Oh, *they're* quite well, I'm thankful to say. They were very good through it, really, better than Johnson. They'll be back for their things, that is, if — Well, oh *dear*, madam, wait till you see . . .

No, I'm all *right*, madam, really . . . Do I? Not more than you do, I'm sure. This *is* a home-coming for you – after that nice visit. I don't know what to say to you – your beautiful house! There usen't to be a thing wrong in it, used there, madam? I took too much pride in it, I daresay . . . I *know*, madam, the stairs – all plaster. I took the dustpan and brush to them, but as fast as you work it keeps flaking down. It's all got in my hair, under my cap. I caught a sight of myself in Johnson's mirror and I said to myself, 'Why, madam will think I've turned white in the night!' . . . Yes, there it goes; watch it. It's the shock to the house. Like snow? The things you think of! You *are* brave!

Oh *no*, madam. No, you get through it somehow. You'd have been wonderful . . . We'd have done what we could to make you comfortable, madam, but it would not have been fit for you – not last night. If I said once I said a dozen times, to the others, 'Well, thank goodness *madam's* not here tonight; thank goodness madam's away' . . . Yes, we all sat down in our sitting-room. It *is* a strong basement. It does rock, but not like the rest of the house . . . It was that one they dropped in the cinema that did our damage, madam. They say what went on the cinema weighed a ton. They should never have put a cinema, not in this neighbourhood. However – poor thing, it's not there now . . . No, *I* haven't, madam; I haven't been out this morning. I only just saw what I saw from the back. And I'm only glad *you* didn't – it would only distress you. I expect your taxi brought you the other way. All I know I heard from the warden. He seemed to consider we'd had quite an escape.

Well, I suppose we did, madam – that's if you come to think of it. They did seem to have quite set their hearts on us. I don't know how many went in the park. When it was not the bangs it was the hums . . . Well, I don't know, really – what *could* we do? As I say, all things come to an end. It would have sickened you, madam, to hear our glass going. Well, you've *seen* the front. No wonder you came in white. Then that ceiling down. I know *I* thought, 'Well, there does go the house!' Of course I ran up at once, but I couldn't do anything . . . The wardens were nice; they were very nice gentlemen. I don't know how they think of it all, I'm sure.

You won't take *anything*, madam? . . . You'll need your fur coat, excuse me, madam, you will. There's the draught right through the house. You don't want to catch cold, not on top of everything . . . No, it's useless; you *can't* move that dining-room door . . . But the house has been wonderful, madam, really – you really have cause to be proud of it. Yes, it's all right here in the little telephone room – that is – well, you can see for yourself . . . What is it – an ashtray, madam? . . . No, I don't wonder, really: I'm sure if I were a smoker – you have to have *something*, don't you, to fall back on? I'll bring the ashtray upstairs with us for the rest of the stumps . . . Yes, madam, I'll follow, madam. As you say, get it over . . . Oh dear, madam, you *are* upset.

You can't help that; you can't but walk in the plaster. I'll have it all off in a day or two.

Airy? Well yes, if you call it that. I'd sooner our landing window, I must say. You see, what the warden said happened, the blast passed through. Well, I don't know, I'm sure: that was what he said. You have to have names for things, I suppose.

The drawing-room? Oh, *madam* . . . Very well . . . *There!*
I don't know what to say: really . . . You know, madam, I'd
rather last night again than have to show you all this. It's a piece in
the Bible, isn't it, where they say not to set your heart on anything
on this earth. But that's not nature, not when you care for things
. . . Haven't you, madam? It's good of you to say so. I know how
I'd have felt if I'd thought there ever *was* dust in here. It used to sort
of sparkle, didn't it, in its way . . . As it is – why, look, madam:
just this rub with my apron and the cabinet starts to come up again,
doesn't it? Like a mirror – look – as though nothing had happened
. . . If I could get started in here – but what am I talking about! The
windows gone – it doesn't look decent, does it . . . Oh, I *know*,
madam, I know: your satin curtains, madam! Torn and torn, like a
maniac been at them. Well, he *is* a maniac, isn't he? . . . Yes, it did
look worse – I swept up a bit in here. But I don't seem to have any
head – I didn't know where to start.

That's right, madam, go on the balcony. You won't see so much
different from there. To look at the park, you wouldn't hardly
believe . . . Sun shining . . . Well, it may do good, I suppose. But
this doesn't rightly feel like a day to me . . . All that mess there?
That was one of those last night. Yes, it *sounded* near us, all right: I
hadn't properly looked . . . Oh dear, madam, did that give you a
turn?

No, I don't know yet, madam; I haven't heard. I didn't care to go
asking out on the street. I expect I'd hear in good time, if — It
doesn't do to meet trouble. No, not Kentish Town, madam,
Camden Town . . . Well, I have been wondering, naturally. It did
pass through my mind that my sister'd telephone me . . . Well, I
would like to – just run up there for a minute? That is, if my sister
doesn't telephone me. Just run up there for a minute this afternoon?
That always has been my home . . . It's very kind of you, madam:
I hope so, too . . .

Little houses aren't strong, madam. You always worry a bit.
When I looked out at the back this morning at some of those little
houses, where the mews used to be – (no, don't *you* look out that
way, madam; you can't do anything; better look at the park) – I
thought, 'Well, they're paper, aren't they.' They're not built to
stand up. That was the big bomb they got, the cinema bomb . . .
Yes, they always seemed to be nice people: the girls and I used to
go through that way to shop. Very quiet; you wouldn't know they
were there. I don't think this terrace has ever had to complain . . .
Didn't you, madam? No, I hardly suppose you did . . . Well,
perhaps they were, madam. Let's hope that they were.

That's right madam, turn up your coat collar. The draught
comes right through.

What with you being so good about everything, and now I take another look – well, it might be worse, mightn't it! When we just get the windows back in again – why, madam, I'll have the drawing-room fit for you in no time! I'll sheet my furniture till we're thoroughly swept, then take the electro to the upholstery. Because, look, madam, I don't think anything's *stained* . . . The clock's going: listen – would you believe that? We mustn't go crying after the curtains, must we? . . . Well, I did, first thing this morning: I couldn't *but* cry. It all seemed to come over me all at once. But now *you're* back – such a difference I feel! Hitler can't beat you and me, madam, can he? If I can just get these glaziers – they expect you to whistle. It's not good for a trade to be too much in demand, is it? It makes the working people ever so slow.

No such great hurry? – I don't understand – I – you – why, madam? *Wouldn't* you wish — ?

Why no, I suppose not, madam . . . I hadn't thought.

You feel you don't really . . . Not after all this.

But you couldn't ever, not this beautiful house! You couldn't ever . . . I know many ladies *are*. I know many ladies feel it is for the best. You can't but notice all those good houses shut. But, madam, this seemed so much your home —

You must excuse me, madam. I had no right – It was the shock, a minute. I should have thought. The whole thing come on so sudden . . . Why yes, madam; I've not doubt that you should. It will be nice for you down at her ladyship's. All that nice quiet country and everything. We should all wish you to be where it's safe, I'm sure . . . You mean, for the duration? . . . *I* see, madam. I am sure you'll only decide what's right. Only . . . this lovely house, madam. We've all cared for it so . . . I *am* a silly: I was upset this morning, but somehow I never saw us not starting again . . .

I suppose it might, yes. Happen another night . . .

All the same, I should like, if you didn't object, madam, to stay on here for the month and get things straight. I'd like to leave things as I found them – fancy, ten years ago! . . . That's very good of you, madam, but it's been my own satisfaction. If it has made any difference I'm only glad . . . I daresay I'm funny in ways, madam, but it's been quite my life here, really it has . . . I *should* prefer that, if it would suit you. I couldn't think of workmen round in here without me . . . I've been through so much with this place . . . In *any* event, madam, I should rather be here.

Tonight? . . . *I* see, madam, I'm sure they'll be glad to see you. I'm sure you should lose no time, not after a shock like this.

We should think of your packing, then, shouldn't we? If we went up now to your room perhaps you'd just show me what . . . Oh, yes, I see. I hadn't properly thought. Of course you would need to take everything. When it's for so long, and – Well, good clothes should be where it's safe.

The plaster's worse on the second flight, I'm afraid.

Yes . . . I was really dreading bringing you up here, madam. But now you won't want to sleep here for some time. Your luck's not hurt – look; there's not a mirror got cracked . . . It was that old blast got the little lamp . . . I can't picture you, if I may say so, madam, waking up in the mornings anywhere not here. Oh, you've travelled, I know, but you have always been back. Still, nothing goes on for ever, does it . . . Your dresses, madam – I've been over them: not a speck. There must be some merciful Providence, mustn't there?

You won't find such good-fitting cupboards, not at her ladyship's.

Yes, look at the sun out there. Autumn's always the nicest season just around here, I think.

Excuse me, madam – Madam, it's nothing, really. I – I – I – I'm really not taking on. I daresay I – got a bit of dust in my eye . . . You're too kind – you make me ashamed, really . . . Yes, I daresay it's the lack of sleep . . . The sun out there . . . If you'll excuse me, madam – I'll give my nose a good blow – that clears a thing off . . . Yes, I will try, when I've just run up to my sister's. I'll try a good nap. But to tell you the truth madam, I shan't truly sleep till I've started to get things straight . . . I'm quite myself now, really. Hope I didn't upset you . . . I'll just run up to the boxroom after the trunks and cases – they'll need some brushing, I *should* think . . .

That really is what I'd rather, if you have no objection. Johnson and the girls will be round tomorrow, and as you won't be here, madam, no doubt you would like me to . . . And I couldn't leave this house empty, the whole night . . . I know, madam; I know that must come in time . . . Lonely? No; no, *I* don't feel lonely. And this never did feel to me a lonely house.

Summer Night

As the sun set its light slowly melted the landscape, till everything was made of fire and glass. Released from the glare of noon, the haycocks now seemed to float on the aftergrass: their freshness penetrated the air. In the not far distance hills with woods up their flanks lay in light like hills in another world – it would be a pleasure of heaven to stand up there, where no foot ever seemed to have trodden, on the spaces between the woods soft as powder dusted over with gold. Against those hills, the burning red rambler roses in cottage gardens along the roadside looked earthy – they were too near the eye.

The road was in Ireland. The light, the air from the distance, the air of evening rushed transversely through the open sides of the car. The rims of the hood flapped, the hood's metal frame rattled as the tourer, in great bounds of speed, held the road's darkening magnetic centre streak. The big shabby family car was empty but for its small driver – its emptiness seemed to levitate it – on its back seat a coat slithered about, and a dressing-case bumped against the seat. The driver did not relax her excited touch on the wheel: now and then while she drove she turned one wrist over, to bring the watch worn on it into view, and she gave the mileage marked on the yellow signposts a flying, jealous, half-inadvertent look. She was driving parallel with the sunset: the sun slowly went down on her right hand.

The hills flowed round till they lay ahead. Where the road bent for its upward course through the pass she pulled up and lighted a cigarette. With a snatch she untwisted her turban; she shook her hair free and threw the scarf behind her into the back seat. The draught of the pass combed her hair into coarse strands as the car hummed up in second gear. Behind one brilliantly-outlined crest the sun had now quite gone; on the steeps of bracken in the electric shadow, each frond stood out and climbing goats turned their heads. The car came up on a lorry, to hang on its tail, impatient, checked by turns of the road. At the first stretch the driver smote her palm on the horn and shot past and shot on ahead again.

The small woman drove with her chin up. Her existence was in her hands on the wheel and in the sole of the foot in which she felt through the sandal, the throbbing pressure of the accelerator. Her face, enlarged by blown-back hair, was as overbearingly blank as the face of a figure-head; her black eyebrows were ruled level, and her eyes, pupils dilated, did little more than reflect the slow burn of daylight along horizons, the luminous shades of the half-dark.

Clear of the pass, approaching the county town, the road widened and straightened between stone walls and burnished, showering beech. The walls broke up into gateways and hoardings and the suburbs began. People in modern building estate gardens let the car in a hurry through their unseeing look. The raised footpaths had margins of grass. White and grey rows of cottages under the pavement level let woodsmoke over their half-doors: women and old men sat outside the doors on boxes, looking down at their knees; here and there a bird sprang in a cage tacked to a wall. Children chasing balls over the roadway shot whooping right and left of the car. The refreshed town, unfolding streets to its centre, at this hour slowly heightened, cooled; streets and stones threw off a grey-pink glare, sultry lasting ghost of the high noon. In this dayless glare the girls in bright dresses, strolling, looked like colour-photography.

Dark behind all the windows: not a light yet. The in-going perspective looked meaning, noble and wide. But everybody was elsewhere – the polished street was empty but cars packed both the kerbs under the trees. What was going on? The big tourer dribbled, slipped with animal nervousness between the static, locked cars each side of its way. The driver peered left and right with her face narrow, glanced from her wrist-watch to the clock in the tower, sucked her lip, manoeuvred for somewhere to pull in. The A.A. sign of the hotel hung out from under a balcony, over the steps. She edged in to where it said *Do Not Park*.

At the end of the hotel hall one electric light from the bar shone through a high-up panel: its yellow sifted on to the dusty desk and a moth could be seen on the glass pane. At the door end came in street daylight, to fall weakly on prints on the oiled walls, on the magenta announcement-strip of a cinema, on the mahogany bench near the receptionist's office, on the hatstand with two forgotten hats. The woman who had come breathlessly up the steps felt in her face a wall of indifference. The impetuous click of her heeled sandals on the linoleum brought no one to the receptionist's desk, and the drone of two talkers in the bar behind the glass panel seemed, like the light, to be blotted up, word by word. The little woman attacked the desk with her knuckles. 'Is there nobody there – I say? Is there nobody *there*?'

'I am, I am. Wait now,' said the hotel woman, who came

impassively through the door from the bar. She reached up a hand and fumbled the desk light on, and by this with unwondering negligence studied the customer – the childish, blown little woman with wing-like eyebrows and eyes still unfocused after the long road. The hotel woman, bust on the desk, looked down slowly at the bare legs, the crumple-hemmed linen coat. 'Can I do anything for you?' she said, when she had done.

'I want the telephone – want to put through a call!'

'You can of course,' said the unmoved hotel woman. 'Why not?' she added after consideration, handing across the keys of the telephone cabinet. The little woman made a slide for the cabinet: with her mouth to the mouthpiece, like a conspirator, she was urgently putting her number through. She came out then and ordered herself a drink.

'Is it long distance?'

'Mm-mm . . . What's on here? What are all those cars?'

'Oh, this evening's the dog racing.'

'Is it?'

'Yes, it's the dog racing. We'd a crowd in here, but they're all gone on now.'

'I wondered who they were,' said the little woman, her eyes on the cabinet, sippeting at her drink.

'Yes, they're at the dog racing. There's a wonderful crowd. But I wouldn't care for it,' said the hotel woman, fastidiously puckering up her forehead. 'I went the one time, but it didn't fascinate me.'

The other forgot to answer. She turned away with her drink, sat down, put the glass beside her on the mahogany bench and began to chafe the calves of her bare legs as though they were stiff or cold. A man clasping sheets of unfurled newspaper pushed his way with his elbow through the door from the bar. 'What it says here,' he said, shaking the paper with both hands 'is identically what I've been telling you.'

'That proves nothing,' said the hotel woman. 'However, let it out of your hand.' She drew the sheets of the paper from him and began to fold them into a wad. Her eyes moved like beetles over a top line. 'That's an awful battle . . . '

'What battle?' exclaimed the little woman, stopping rubbing her legs but not looking up.

'An awful air battle. Destroying each other,' the woman added, with a stern and yet voluptuous sigh. 'Listen, would you like to wait in the lounge?'

'She'd be better there,' put in the man who had brought the paper. 'Better accommodation.' His eyes watered slightly in the electric light. The little woman, sitting upright abruptly, looked defiantly, as though for the first time, at the two watching her from

the desk. 'Mr Donovan has great opinions,' said the hotel woman.
'Will you move yourself out of here?' she asked Mr Donovan. 'This
is very confined – *There's* your call, now!'

But the stranger had packed herself into the telephone box like a
conjuror's lady preparing to disappear. '*Hullo?*' she was saying.
'Hullo! I want to speak to — '

' — You are,' the other voice cut in. 'All right? Anything
wrong?'

Her face flushed all over. 'You sound nearer already! I've got to
C — .'

The easy calm voice said: 'Then you're coming along well.'

'Glad, are you?' she said, in a quiver.

'Don't take it too fast,' he said. 'It's a treacherous light. Be easy,
there's a good girl.'

'You're a fine impatient man.' His end of the line was silent. She
went on: 'I might stay here and go to the dog racing.'

'Oh, is that tonight?' He went on to say equably (having
stopped, as she saw it, and shaken the ash off the tip of his
cigarette), 'No, I shouldn't do that.'

'Darling . . . '

'Emma . . . How is the Major?'

'He's all right,' she said, rather defensively.

'I see,' he said. 'Everything quite O.K.?'

'In an hour, I'll be . . . where you live.'

'First gate on the left. Don't kill yourself, there's a good girl.
Nothing's worth that. Remember we've got the night. By the way,
where are you talking?'

'From the hotel.' She nursed the receiver up close to her face and
made a sound into it. Cutting that off she said: 'Well, I'll hang up. I
just . . . '

'Right,' he said – and hung up.

Robinson, having hung up the receiver, walked back from the hall
to the living-room where his two guests were. He still wore a
smile. The deaf woman at the table by the window was pouring
herself out another cup of tea. 'That will be very cold!' Robinson
shouted – but she only replaced the cosy with a mysterious smile.
'Let her be,' said her brother. 'Let her alone!'

The room in this uphill house was still light: through the open
window came in a smell of stocks from the flower beds in the lawn.
The only darkness lay in a belt of beech trees at the other side of the
main road. From the grate, from the coal of an unlit fire came the
fume of a cigarette burning itself out. Robinson still could not help
smiling: he reclaimed his glass from the mantelpiece and slumped
back with it into his leather armchair in one of his loose, heavy,

good-natured attitudes. But Justin Cavey, in the armchair opposite, still look crucified at having the talk torn. 'Beastly,' he said, 'you've a beastly telephone.' Though he was in Robinson's house for the first time, his sense of attraction to people was marked, early, by just this intransigence and this fretfulness.

'It is and it's not,' said Robinson. That was that. 'Where had we got to?' he amiably asked.

The deaf woman, turning round from the window, gave the two men, or gave the air between them, a penetrating smile. Her brother, with a sort of lurch at his pocket, pulled out a new packet of cigarettes: ignoring Robinson's held-out cigarette case he frowned and split the cellophane with his thumbnail. But, as though his sister had put a hand on his shoulder, his tension could be almost seen to relax. The impersonal, patient look of the thinker appeared in his eyes, behind the spectacles. Justin was a city man, a black-coat, down here (where his sister lived) on holiday. Other summer holidays before this he had travelled in France, Germany, Italy: he disliked the chaotic 'scenery' of his own land. He was down here with Queenie this summer only because of the war, which had locked him in: duty seemed to him better than failed pleasure. His father had been a doctor in this place; now his sister lived on in two rooms in the square – for fear Justin should not be comfortable she had taken a room for him at the hotel. His holiday with his sister, his holiday in this underwater, weedy region of memory, his holiday on which, almost every day, he had to pass the doors of their old home, threatened Justin with a pressure he could not bear. He had to share with Queenie, as he shared the dolls' house meals cooked on the oil stove behind her sitting-room screen, the solitary and almost fairylike world created by her deafness. Her deafness broke down his only defence, talk. He was exposed to the odd, immune, plumbing looks she was for ever passing over his face. He could not deflect the tilted blue of her eyes. The things she said out of nowhere, things with no surface context, were never quite off the mark. She was not all solicitude; she loved to be teasing him.

In her middle-age Queenie was very pretty: her pointed face had the colouring of an imperceptibly fading pink-and-white sweet-pea. This hot summer her artless dresses, with their little lace collars, were mottled over with flowers, mauve and blue. Up the glaring main street she carried a *poult-de-soie* parasol. Her rather dark first-floor rooms faced north, over the square with its grass and lime trees: the crests of great mountains showed above the opposite façades. She would slip in and out on her own errands, as calm as a cat, and Justin, waiting for her at one of her windows, would see her cross the square in the noon sunshine with hands laced over her forehead into a sort of porch. The little town, though strung on a through road, was an outpost under the mountains: in its quick-talking, bitter society she enjoyed, to a degree that surprised Justin, her privileged place. She was woman enough to like to take the man Justin round with her and display him; they went out to afternoon or to evening tea, and in those drawing-rooms of tinted lace and intently-staring family photographs, among octagonal tables and painted cushions, Queenie, with her cotton gloves in her lap, well knew how to contribute, while Justin talked, her airy, brilliant, secretive smiling and looking on. For his part, he was man enough to respond to being shown off – besides, he was eased by these breaks in their *tête-à-tête*. Above all, he was glad, for these hours or two of chatter, not to have to face the screen of his own mind, on which the distortion of every one of his images, the war-broken towers of Europe, constantly stood. The immolation of what had been his own intensely had been made, he could only feel, without any choice of his. In the heart of the neutral Irishman indirect suffering pulled like a crooked knife. So he acquiesced to, and devoured, society: among the doctors, the solicitors, the auctioneers, the bank people of this little town he renewed old acquaintanceships and developed new. He was content to bloom, for this settled number of weeks – so unlike was this to his monkish life in the city – in a sort of tenebrous popularity. He attempted to check his solitary arrogance. His celibacy and his studentish manner could still, although he was past forty, make him acceptable as a young man. In the mornings he read late in his hotel bed; he got up to take his solitary walks; he returned to flick at his black shoes with Queenie's duster and set off with Queenie on their tea-table rounds. They had been introduced to Robinson, factory manager, in the hall of the house of the secretary of the tennis club.

Robinson did not frequent drawing-rooms. He had come here only three years ago, and had at first been taken to be a bachelor – he was a married man living apart from his wife. The resentment occasioned by this discovery had been aggravated by Robinson's not noticing it: he worked at very high pressure in his factory office, and in his off times his high-powered car was to be seen streaking too gaily out of town. When he was met, his imperturbable male personality stood out to the women unpleasingly, and stood out most of all in that married society in which women aspire to break the male in a man. Husbands slipped him in for a drink when they were alone, or shut themselves up with him in the dining-room. Justin had already sighted him in the hotel bar. When Robinson showed up, late, at the tennis club, his manner with women was easy and teasing, but abstract and perfectly automatic.

From this had probably come the legend that he liked women 'only in one way'. From the first time Justin encountered Robinson, he had felt a sort of anxious, disturbed attraction to the big, fair, smiling, offhand, cold-minded man. He felt impelled by Robinson's unmoved physical presence into all sorts of aberrations of talk and mind; he committed, like someone waving an anxious flag, all sorts of absurdities, as though this type of creature had been a woman; his talk became exaggeratedly cerebral, and he became prone, like a perverse person in love, to expose all his own piques, crotchets and weaknesses. One night in the hotel bar with Robinson he had talked until he burst into tears. Robinson had on him the touch of some foreign sun. The acquaintanceship – it could not be called more – was no more than an accident of this narrowed summer. For Justin it had taken the place of travel. The two men were so far off each other's beat that in a city they would certainly not have met.

Asked to drop in some evening or any evening, the Caveys had tonight taken Robinson at his word. Tonight, the night of the first visit, Justin's high, rather bleak forehead had flushed from the moment he rang the bell. With Queenie behind his shoulder, in muslin, he had flinched confronting the housekeeper. Queenie, like the rest of the town ladies, had done no more till now than go by Robinson's gate.

For her part, Queenie showed herself happy to penetrate into what she had called 'the china house'. On its knoll over the main road, just outside the town, Bellevue did look like china up on a mantelpiece – it was a compact, stucco house with mouldings, recently painted a light blue. From the lawn set with pampas and crescent-shaped flower-beds the hum of Robinson's motor mower passed in summer over the sleepy town. And when winter denuded the trees round them the polished windows, glass porch and empty conservatory sent out, on mornings of frosty sunshine, a rather mischievous and uncaring flash. The almost sensuous cleanness of his dwelling was reproduced in the person of Robinson – about his ears, jaw, collar and close clipped nails. The approach the Caveys had walked up showed the broad, decided tyre-prints of his car.

'Where had we got to?' Robinson said again.

'I was saying we should have to find a new form.'

'Of course you were,' agreed Robinson. 'That was it.' He nodded over the top of Justin's head.

'A new form for thinking and feeling . . . '

'But one thinks what one happens to think, or feels what one happens to feel. That is as just so happens – I should have thought. One either does or one doesn't?'

'One doesn't!' cried Justin. 'That's what I've been getting at. For some time we have neither thought nor felt. Our faculties have slowed down without our knowing – they had stopped without our knowing! We know now. Now that there's enough death to challenge being alive we're facing it that, anyhow, we don't live. We're confronted by the impossibility *of* living – unless we can break through to something else. There's been a stop in our senses and in our faculties that's made everything round us so much dead matter – and dead matter we couldn't even displace. We can no longer express ourselves: what we say doesn't even approximate to reality; it only approximates to what's been said. I say, this war's an awful illumination; it's destroyed our dark; we have to see where we are. Immobilized, God help us, and each so far apart that we can't even try to signal each other. And our currency's worthless – our "ideas", so on, so on. We've got to mint a new one. We've got to break through to the new form – it needs genius. We're pre-cipitated, this moment, between genius and death. I tell you, we must have genius to live at all.'

'I am certainly dished, then,' said Robinson. He got up and looked for Justin's empty glass and took it to the sideboard where the decanters were.

'We have it!' cried Justin, smiting the arm of his chair. 'I salute your genius, Robinson, but I mistrust my own.'

'That's very nice of you,' said Robinson. 'I agree with you that this war makes one think. I was in the last, but I don't remember thinking: I suppose possibly one had no time. Of course, these days in business one comes up against this war the whole way through. And to tell you the truth,' said Robinson, turning round, 'I do like my off times to *be* my off times, because with this and then that they are precious few. So I don't really think as much as I might – though I see how one might always begin. You don't think thinking gets one a bit rattled?'

'I don't think!' said Justin violently.

'Well, you should know,' said Robinson, looking at his thumb-nail. 'I should have thought you did. From the way you talk.'

'I couldn't think if I wanted: I've lost my motivation. I taste the dust in the street and I smell the limes in the square and I beat round inside this beastly shell of the past among images that all the more torment me as they lose any sense that they had. As for feeling — '

'You don't think you find it a bit slow here? Mind you, I haven't a word against this place but it's not a place I'd choose for an off time — '

' — My dear Robinson,' Justin said, in a mincing, school-masterish tone, 'you seem blind to our exquisite sociabilities.'

'Pack of old cats,' said Robinson amiably.

'You suggest I should get away for a bit of fun?'

'Well, I did mean that.'

'I find my own fun,' said Justin, 'I'm torn, here, by every single pang of annihilation. But that's what I look for; that's what I want completed; that's the whole of what I want to embrace. On the far side of the nothing – my new form. Scrap "me"; scrap my wretched identity and you'll bring to the open some bud of life. I *not* "I" – I'd be the world . . . You're right: what you would call thinking does get me rattled. I only what you call think to excite myself. Take myself away, and I'd *think*. I might see; I might feel purely; I might even love — '

'Fine,' agreed Robinson, not quite easy. He paused and seemed to regard what Justin had just said – at the same time, he threw a glance of perceptible calculation at the electric clock on the mantelpiece. Justin halted and said: 'You give me too much to drink.'

'You feel this war may improve us?' said Robinson.

'What's love like?' Justin said suddenly.

Robinson paused for just less than a second in the act of lighting a cigarette. He uttered a shortish, temporizing and, for him, unnaturally loud laugh.

Queenie felt the vibration and turned round, withdrawing her arm from the windowsill. She had been looking intently, between the clumps of pampas, down the lawn to the road: cyclists and walkers on their way into town kept passing Robinson's open gate. Across the road, above the demesne wall, the dark beeches let through glitters of sky, and the colour and scent of the mown lawn and the flowers seemed, by some increase of evening, lifted up to the senses as though a new current flowed underneath. Queenie saw with joy in her own mind what she could not from her place in the window see – the blue china house, with all its reflecting windows, perched on its knoll in the brilliant, fading air. They are too rare – visions of where we are.

When the shock of the laugh made her turn round, she still saw day in Robinson's picture-frames and on the chromium fingers of the clock. She looked at Robinson's head, dropped back after the laugh on the leather scroll of his chair: her eyes went from him to Justin. 'Did you two not hit it off?'

Robinson laughed again, this time much more naturally: he emitted a sound like that from inside a furnace in which something is being consumed. Letting his head fall sideways towards Queenie, he seemed to invite her into his mood. 'The way things come out is sometimes funny,' he said to Justin, 'if you know what I mean.'

'No, I don't,' Justin said stonily.

'I bet your sister does.'

'You didn't know what I meant. Anything I may have said about your genius I do absolutely retract.'

'Look here, I'm sorry,' Robinson said, 'I probably took you up all wrong.'

'On the contrary: the mistake was mine.'

'You know, it's funny about your sister: I never can realize she can't hear. She seems so much one of the party. Would she be fond of children?'

'You mean, why did she not marry?'

'Good God, no – I only had an idea . . . '

Justin went on: 'There was some fellow once, but I never heard more of him. You'd have to be very oncoming, I daresay, to make any way with a deaf girl.'

'No, I meant my children,' said Robinson. He had got up, and he took from his mantelpiece two of the photographs in silver frames. With these he walked down the room to Queenie, who received them with her usual eagerness and immediately turned with them to the light. Justin saw his sister's profile bent forward in study and saw Robinson standing above her leaning against the window frame. When Robinson met an upward look from Queenie he nodded and touched himself on the chest. 'I can see that – aren't they very like you?' she said. He pointed to one picture then held up ten fingers, then to the other and held up eight. 'The fair little fellow's more like you, the bold one. The dark one has more the look of a girl – but he will grow up manly, I daresay . . . ' With this she went back to the photographs: she did not seem anxious to give them up, and Robinson made no movement to take them from her – with Queenie the act of looking was always reflective and slow. To Justin the two silhouettes against the window looked wedded and welded by the dark. 'They are both against me,' Justin thought. 'She does not hear with her ears, he does not hear with his mind. No wonder they can communicate.'

'It's a wonder,' she said, 'that you have no little girl.'

Robinson went back for another photograph – but, standing still with a doubtful look at Queenie, he passed his hand, as though sadly expunging something, backwards and forwards across the glass. 'She's quite right; we did have a girl,' he said. 'But I don't know how to tell her the kid's dead.'

Sixty miles away, the Major was making his last round through the orchards before shutting up the house. By this time the bronze-green orchard dusk was intense; the clumped curves of the fruit were hardly to be distinguished among the leaves. The brilliance of evening, in which he had watched Emma driving away, was now gone from the sky. Now and then in the grass his foot knocked a dropped apple – he would sigh, stoop rather stiffly, pick up the apple, examine it with the pad of his thumb for bruises and slip it, tenderly as though it had been an egg, into a baggy pocket of his tweed coat. This was not a good apple year. There was something standardized, uncomplaining about the Major's movements – you saw a tall, unmilitary-looking man with a stoop and a thinnish, drooping moustache. He often wore a slight frown, of doubt or preoccupation. This frown had intensified in the last months.

As he approached the house he heard the wireless talking, and saw one lamp at the distant end of the drawing-room where his aunt sat. At once, the picture broke up – she started, switched off the wireless and ran down the room to the window. You might have thought the room had burst into flames. 'Quick!' she cried. 'Oh, gracious, quick! – I believe it's the telephone.'

The telephone was at the other side of the house – before he got there he heard the bell ringing. He put his hands in his pockets to keep the apples from bumping as he legged it rapidly down the corridor. When he unhooked on his wife's voice he could not help saying haggardly: 'You all right?'

'Of course. I just thought I'd say good night.'

'That was nice of you,' he said, puzzled. 'How is the car running?'

'Like a bird,' she said in a singing voice. 'How are you all?'

'Well, I was just coming in; Aunt Fran's in the drawing-room listening to something on the wireless, and I made the children turn in half an hour ago.'

'You'll go up to them?'

'Yes, I was just going.' For a moment they both paused on the line, then he said: 'Where have you got to now?'

'I'm at T — now, at the hotel in the square.'

'At T — ? Aren't you taking it rather fast?'

'It's a lovely night; it's an empty road.'

'Don't be too hard on the car, she — '

'Oh, I know,' she said, in the singing voice again. 'At C — I did try to stop, but there was a terrible crowd there: dog racing. So I came on. Darling . . . ?'

'Yes?'

'It's a lovely night, isn't it?'

'Yes, I was really quite sorry to come in. I shall shut up the house now, then go up to the children; then I expect I'll have a word or two with Aunt Fran.'

'I see. Well, I'd better be pushing on.'

'They'll be sitting up for you, won't they?'

'Surely,' said Emma quickly.

'Thank you for ringing up, dear: it was thoughtful of you.'

'I was thinking about you.'

He did not seem to hear this. 'Well, take care of yourself. Have a nice time.'

'Good night,' she said. But the Major had hung up.

In the drawing-room Aunt Fran had not gone back to the wireless. Beside the evening fire lit for her age, she sat rigid, face turned to the door, plucking round and round the rings on her left hand. She wore a foulard dress, net jabot and boned-up collar, of the type ladies wear to dine in private hotels. In the lamplight her waxy features appeared blurred, even effaced. The drawing-room held a crowd of chintz-covered chairs, inlaid tables and wool-worked stools; very little in it was antique, but nothing was strikingly up-to-date. There were cabinets of not rare china, and more blue-and-white plates, in metal clamps, hung in lines up the walls between water-colours. A vase of pink roses arranged by the governess already dropped petals on the piano. In one corner stood a harp with two broken strings – when a door slammed or one made a sudden movement this harp gave out a faint vibration or twang. The silence for miles around this obscure country house seemed to gather inside the folds of the curtains and to dilute the indoor air like a mist. This room Emma liked too little to touch already felt the touch of decay; it threw lifeless reflections into the two mirrors – the walls were green. Aunt Fran's body was stranded here like some object on the bed of a pool that has run dry. The magazine that she had been looking at had slipped from her lap to the black fur rug.

As her nephew appeared in the drawing-room door Aunt Fran fixed him urgently with her eyes. *'Nothing wrong?'*

'No, no – that was Emma.'

'What's happened?'

'Nothing. She rang up to say good night.'

'But she had said good night,' said Aunt Fran in her troubled way. 'She said good night to us when she was in the car. You remember, it was nearly night when she left. It seemed late to be starting to go so far. She had the whole afternoon, but she kept putting off, putting off. She seemed to me undecided up to the very last.'

The Major turned his back on his aunt and began to unload his pockets, carefully placing the apples, two by two, in a row along the chiffonier. 'Still, it's nice for her having this trip,' he said.

'There was a time in the afternoon,' said Aunt Fran, 'when I thought she was going to change her mind. However, she's there now – did you say?'

'Almost,' he said, 'not quite. Will you be all right if I go and shut up the house? And I said I would look in on the girls.'

'Suppose the telephone rings?'

'I don't think it will, again. The exchange will be closing, for one thing.'

'This afternoon,' said Aunt Fran, 'it rang four times.'

She heard him going from room to room, unfolding and barring the heavy shutters and barring and chaining the front door. She could begin to feel calmer now that the house was a fortress against the wakeful night. 'Hi!' she called, 'don't forget the window in here' – looking back over her shoulder into the muslin curtains that seemed to crepitate with dark air. So he came back, with his flat, unexpectant step. I'm not cold,' she said, 'but I don't like dark coming in.'

He shuttered the window. 'I'll be down in a minute.'

'Then we might sit together?'

'Yes, Aunt Fran: certainly.'

The children, who had been talking, dropped their voices when they heard their father's step on the stairs. Their two beds creaked as they straightened themselves and lay silent, in social, expectant attitudes. Their room smelled of toothpaste; the white presses blotted slowly into the white walls. The window was open, the blind up, so in here darkness was incomplete – obscured, the sepia picture of the Good Shepherd hung over the mantelpiece. 'It's all right,' they said, 'we are quite awake.' So the Major came round and halted between the two beds. 'Sit on mine,' said Di nonchalantly. 'It's my turn to have a person tonight.'

'Why did Mother ring up?' said Vivie, scrambling up on her pillow.

'Now how on earth did *you* know?'

'We knew by your voice – we couldn't hear what you said. We were only at the top of the stairs. Why did she?'

'To tell me to tell you to be good.'

'She's said that,' said Vivie, impatient. 'What did she say truly?'

'Just good night.'

'Oh. Is she there?'

'Where?'

'Where she said she was going to.'

'Not quite – nearly.'

'Goodness!' Di said; 'it seems years since she went.' The two children lay cryptic and still. Then Di went on: 'Do you know what Aunt Fran said because Mother went away without any stockings?'

'No,' said the Major, 'and never mind.'

'Oh, *I* don't mind,' Di said, 'I just heard.' 'And I heard,' said

Vivie: she could be felt opening her eyes wide, and the Major could just see, on the pillow, an implacable miniature of his wife's face. Di went on: 'She's so frightened something will happen.'

'Aunt Fran is?'

'She's always frightened of that.'

'She is very fond of us all.'

'Oh,' burst out Vivie, 'but Mother likes things to happen. She was whistling all the time she was packing up. Can't *we* have a treat tomorrow?'

'Mother'll be back tomorrow.'

'But *can't* we have a treat?'

'We'll see; we'll ask Mother,' the Major said.

'Oh yes, but suppose she didn't come back?'

'Look, it's high time you two went to sleep.'

'We can't: we've got all sorts of ideas . . . *You* say something Daddy. Tell us something. Invent.'

'Say what?' said the Major.

'Oh goodness,' Vivie said; '*something*. What do you say to Mother?'

He went downstairs to Aunt Fran with their dissatisfied kisses stamped on his cheek. When he had gone Di fanned herself with the top of her sheet. 'What makes him so disappointed, do you know?'

'I know, he thinks about the war.'

But it was Di who, after the one question, unlocked all over and dropped plumb asleep. It was Vivie who, turning over and over, watched in the sky behind the cross of the window the tingling particles of the white dark, who heard the moth between the two window-sashes, who fancied she heard apples drop in the grass. One arbitrary line only divided this child from the animal: all her senses stood up, wanting to run the night. She swung her legs out of bed and pressed the soles of her feet on the cool floor. She got right up and stepped out of her nightdress and set out to walk the house in her skin. From each room she went into the human order seemed to have lapsed – discovered by sudden light, the chairs and tables seemed set round for a mouse's party on a gigantic scale. She stood for some time outside the drawing-room door and heard the unliving voices of the Major and aunt. She looked through the ajar door to the kitchen and saw a picked bone and a teapot upon the table and a maid lumped mute in a man's arms. She attempted the front door, but did not dare to touch the chain: she could not get out of the house. She returned to the schoolroom, drawing her brows together, and straddled the rocking-horse they had not ridden for years. The furious bumping of the rockers woke the canaries under their cover: they set up a wiry springing in their cage. She dismounted, got out the box of chalks and began to tattoo her chest, belly and thighs with stars and snakes, red, yellow and blue. Then, taking the box of chalks with her, she went to her mother's room for a look in the long glass – in front of this she attempted to tattoo her behind. After this she bent right down and squinted, upside down between her legs, at the bedroom – the electric light over the dressing-table poured into the vacantly upturned mirror and on to Emma's left-behind silver things. The anarchy she felt all through the house tonight made her, when she had danced in front of the long glass, climb up to dance on the big bed. The springs bounced her higher and higher; chalk-dust flew from her body on to the fleece of the blankets, on to the two cold pillows that she was trampling out of their place. The bed-castors lunged, under her springing, over the threadbare pink bridal carpet of Emma's room.

Attacked by the castors, the chandelier in the drawing-room tinkled sharply over Aunt Fran's head.

She at once raised her eyes to the ceiling. 'Something has got in,' she said calmly – and, rising, made for the drawing-room door. By reflex, the Major rose to stop her: he sighed and put his weak whisky down. 'Never mind,' he said, 'Aunt Fran. It's probably nothing. I'll go.'

Whereupon, his Aunt Fran wheeled round on him with her elbows up like a bird's wings. Her wax features sprang into stony prominence. 'It's never me, never me, never me! Whatever *I* see, whatever I hear it's "nothing", though the house might fall down. You keep everything back from me. No one speaks the truth to me but the man on the wireless. Always things being said on the telephone, always things being moved about, always Emma off at the end of the house singing, always the children hiding away. I am never told, never told, never told. I get the one answer, "nothing". I am expected to wait here. No one comes near the drawing-room. I am never allowed to go and see!'

'If that's how you feel,' he said, 'do certainly go.' He thought: it's all right, I locked the house.

So it was Aunt Fran's face, with the forehead lowered, that came by inches round Emma's door. She appeared to present her forehead as a sort of a buffer, obliquely looked from below it, did not speak. Her glance, arriving gradually at its object, took in the child and the whole room. Vivie paused on the bed, transfixed, breathless, her legs apart. Her heart thumped; her ears drummed; her cheeks burned. To break up the canny and comprehensive silence she said loudly: 'I am all over snakes.'

'So this is what . . . ' Aunt Fran said. 'So this is what . . . '

'I'll get off this bed, if you don't like.'

'The bed you were born in,' said Aunt Fran.

Vivie did not know what to do; she jumped off the bed saying: 'No one told me not to.'

'Do you not know what is wicked?' said Aunt Fran – but with no more than estranged curiosity. She approached and began to try to straighten the bed, her unused hands making useless passes over the surface, brushing chalk-dust deeper into the fleece. All of a sudden, Vivie appeared to feel some majestic effluence from her aunt's person: she lagged round the bed to look at the stooping, set face, at the mouth held in a curve like a dead smile, at the veins in the downcast eyelids and the backs of the hands. Aunt Fran did not hurry her ceremonial fumbling; she seemed to exalt the moment that was so fully hers. She picked a pillow up by its frill and placed it high on the bolster.

'That's mother's pillow,' said Vivie.

'Did you say your prayers tonight?'

'Oh, *yes*.'

'They didn't defend you. Better say them again. Kneel down and say to Our Lord — '

'In my skin?'

Aunt Fran looked directly at, then away from, Vivie's body, as though for the first time. She drew the eiderdown from the foot of the bed and made a half-blind sweep at Vivie with it, saying: 'Wrap up, wrap up.' 'Oh, they'll come off – my snakes!' said Vivie, backing away. But Aunt Fran, as though the child were on fire, put into motion an extraordinary strength – she rolled, pressed and pounded Vivie up in the eiderdown until only the prisoner's dark eyes, so like her mother's, were left free to move wildly outside the great sausage, of padded taffeta, pink.

Aunt Fran, embracing the sausage firmly, repeated: 'Now say to Our Lord — '

Shutting the door of her own bedroom, Aunt Fran felt her heart beat. The violence of the stranger within her ribs made her sit down on the ottoman – meanwhile, her little clock on the mantelpiece loudly and, it seemed to her, slowly ticked. Her window was shut, but the pressure of night silence made itself felt behind the blind, on the glass.

Round the room, on ledges and brackets, stood the fetishes she travelled through life with. They were mementoes – photos in little warped frames, musty, round straw boxes, china kittens, palm crosses, the three Japanese monkeys, *bambini*, a Lincoln Imp, a merry-thought pen-wiper, an ivory spinning-wheel from Cologne. From these objects the original virtue had by now almost evaporated. These gifts' givers, known on her lonely journey, were by now faint as their photographs: she no longer knew, now, where anyone was. All the more, her nature clung to these objects that moved with her slowly towards the dark.

Her room, the room of a person tolerated, by now gave off the familiar smell of herself – the smell of the old. A little book wedged the mirror at the angle she liked. When she was into her ripplecloth dressing-gown she brushed and plaited her hair and took out her teeth. She wound her clock and, with hand still trembling a little, lighted her own candle on the commode, then switched off her nephew's electric light. The room contracted round the crocus of flame as she knelt down slowly beside her bed – but while she said the Lord's Prayer she could not help listening, wondering what kept the Major so long downstairs. She never felt free to pray till she had heard the last door shut, till she could relax her watch on the house. She never could pray until they were *all* prostrate – loaned for at least some hours to innocence, sealed by the darkness over their lids.

Tonight she could not attempt to lift up her heart. She could, however, abase herself, and she abased herself for them all. The evil of the moment down in the drawing-room, the moment when she had cried, 'It is never me!' clung like a smell to her, so closely that she had been eager to get her clothes off, and did not like, even now, to put her hands to her face.

Who shall be their judge? Not I.

The blood of the world is poisoned, feels Aunt Fran, with her forehead over the eiderdown. Not a pure drop comes out at any prick – yes, even the heroes shed black blood. The solitary watcher retreats step by step from his post – who shall stem the black tide coming in? There are no more children: the children are born knowing. The shadow rises up the cathedral tower, up the side of the pure hill. There is not even the past: our memories share with us the infected zone; not a memory does not lead up to this. Each moment is everywhere, it holds the war in its crystal; there is no elsewhere, no other place. Not a benediction falls on this apart house of the Major; the enemy is within it, creeping about. Each heart here falls to the enemy.

So this is what goes on . . .

Emma flying away – and not saying why, or where. And to wrap the burning child up did not put out the fire. You cannot look at the sky without seeing the shadow, the men destroying each other. What is the matter tonight – is there a battle? This is a threatened night.

Aunt Fran sags on her elbows; her knees push desperately in the woolly rug. She cannot even repent; she is capable of no act; she is undone. She gets up and eats a biscuit, and looks at the little painting of Mont Blanc on the little easel beside her clock. She still does not hear the Major come up to bed.

Queenie understood that the third child, the girl, was dead: she gave back the photograph rather quickly, as though unbearable sadness emanated from it. Justin, however, came down the room and looked at the photograph over Robinson's shoulder – at the rather vulgar, frank, blonde little face. He found it hard to believe that a child of Robinson's should have chosen the part of death. He then went back to the table and picked up, with a jerky effrontery, the photographs of the two little boys. 'Do they never come here?' he said. 'You have plenty of room for them.'

'I daresay they will; I mean to fix up something. Just now they're at Greystones,' Robinson said – he then looked quite openly at the clock.

'With their mother?' Justin said, in a harsh impertinent voice.

'Yes, with my wife.'

'So you keep up the two establishments?'

Even Robinson glanced at Justin with some surprise. 'If you call it that,' he said indifferently. 'I rather landed myself with this place, really – as a matter of fact, when I moved in it looked as though things might work out differently. First I stopped where you are, at the hotel, but I do like to have a place of my own. One feels freer, for one thing.'

'There's a lot in that,' said Justin, with an oblique smile. 'Our local ladies think you keep a Bluebeard's castle up here.'

'What, corpses?' Robinson said, surprised.

'Oh yes, they think you're the devil.'

'Who, me?' replied Robinson, busy replacing photographs on the mantelpiece. 'That's really very funny: I'd no idea. I suppose they may think I've been pretty slack – but I'm no good at teafights, as a matter of fact. But I can't see what else can be eating them. What ought I to do, then? Throw a party here? I will if your sister'll come and pour out tea – but I don't think I've really got enough chairs . . . I hope,' he added, looking at Queenie, '*she* doesn't think it's not all above board here?'

'You're forgetting again: she misses the talk, poor girl.'

'She doesn't look very worried.'

'I daresay she's seldom been happier. She's built up quite a romance about this house. She has a world to herself – I could envy her.'

Robinson contrived to give the impression that he did not wish to have Queenie discussed – partly because he owned her, he understood her, partly because he wished to discuss nothing: it really was time for his guests to go. Though he was back again in his armchair, regard for time appeared in his attitude. Justin could not fail to connect this with the telephone and the smile that had not completely died. It became clear, staringly clear, that throughout the evening his host had been no more than marking time. This made Justin say 'Yes' (in a loud, pertinacious voice), 'this evening's been quite an event for us. Your house has more than its legend, Robinson; it has really remarkable character. However, all good things — ' Stiff with anger, he stood up.

'Must you?' said Robinson, rising. 'I'm so sorry.'

Lighting-up time, fixed by Nature, had passed. The deaf woman, from her place in the window, had been watching lights of cars bend over the hill. Turning with the main road, that had passed the foot of the mountains, each car now drove a shaft of extreme brilliance through the dark below Robinson's pampas-grass. Slipping, dropping with a rush past the gate, illuminating the dust on the opposite wall, car after car vanished after its light – there was suddenly quite a gust of them, as though the mountain country, before sleeping, had stood up and shaken them from its folds. The release of movement excited Queenie – that and the beat of light's wings on her face. She turned round very reluctantly as Justin approached and began to make signs to her.

'Why, does Mr Robinson want us to go?' she said.

'That's the last thing I want!' shouted Robinson.

('She can't hear you.')

'Christ . . . ' said Robinson, rattled. He turned the lights on – the three, each with a different face of despair, looked at each other across the exposed room, across the tea-tray on the circular table and the superb leather backs of the chairs. 'My brother thinks we've kept you too long,' she said – and as a lady she looked a little shaken, for the first time unsure of herself. Robinson would not for worlds have had this happen; he strode over and took and nursed her elbow, which tensed then relaxed gently inside the muslin sleeve. He saw, outdoors, his window cast on the pampas, saw the whole appearance of shattered night. She looked for reassurance into his face, and he saw the delicate lines in hers.

'And look how late it's got, Mr Robinson!'

'It's not that,' he said in his naturally low voice, 'But — '

A car pulled up at the gate. Alarmed by the lit window it cut its lights off and could be felt to crouch there, attentive, docile, cautious, waiting to turn in. 'Your friend is arriving,' Justin said.

On that last lap of her drive, the eighteen miles of flat road along the base of the mountains, the last tingling phase of darkness had settled down. Grassy sharpness passed from the mountains' out-line, the patches of firs, the gleam of watery ditch. The west sky had gradually drunk its yellow and the ridged heights that towered over her right hand became immobile cataracts, sensed not seen. Animals rising out of the ditches turned to Emma's headlamps green lamp-eyes. She felt the shudder of night, the contracting bodies of things. The quick air sang in her ears; she drove very fast. At the crossroads above Robinson's town she pulled round in a wide swerve: she saw the lemon lights of the town strung along under the black trees, the pavements and the pale, humble houses below her in a faint, mysterious glare as she slipped down the funnel of hill to Robinson's gate. (The first white gate on the left, you cannot miss it, he'd said.) From the road she peered up the lawn and saw, between pampas-tufts, three people upright in his lit room. So she pulled up and switched her lights and her engine off and sat crouching in her crouching car in the dark – night began to creep up her bare legs. Now the glass porch sprang into prominence like a lantern – she saw people stiffly saying goodbye. Down the drive came a man and woman almost in flight; not addressing each other, not looking back – putting the back of a fist to her mouth quickly Emma checked the uprush of an uncertain laugh. She marked a lag in the steps – turning their heads quickly the man and woman looked with involuntary straightness into the car, while her eyes were glued to their silhouettes. The two turned down to the town and she turned in at the gate.

Farouche, with her tentative little swagger and childish, pleading air of delinquency, Emma came to a halt in Robinson's living-room. He had pulled down the blind. She kept recoiling and blinking and drawing her fingers over her eyes, till Robinson turned off the top light. 'Is that that?' there was only the reading-lamp.

She rested her shoulder below his and grappled their enlaced fingers closer together as though trying to draw calmness from him. Standing against him, close up under his height, she held her head up and began to look round the room. 'You're whistling something,' she said, after a moment or two.

'I only mean, take your time.'

'Why, am I nervous?' she said.

'Darling, you're like a bat in out of the night. I told you not to come along too fast.'

'I see now, I came too early,' she said. 'Why didn't you tell me you had a party? Who were they? What were they doing here?'

'Oh, they're just people in this place. He's a bit screwy and she's deaf, but I like them, as a matter of fact.'

'They're mackintoshy sort of people,' she said. 'But I always thought you lived all alone . . . Is there anyone else in the house now?'

'Not a mouse,' said Robinson, without change of expression. 'My housekeeper's gone off for the night.'

'I see,' said Emma. 'Will you give me a drink?'

She sat down where Justin had just been sitting, and, bending forward with a tremulous frown, began to brush ash from her arm of the chair. You could feel the whole of her hesitate. Robinson, without hesitation, came and sat easily on the arm of the chair from which she had brushed the ash. 'It's sometimes funny,' he said, 'when people drop in like that. "My God," I thought when I saw them, "what an evening to choose."' He slipped his hand down between the brown velvet cushion and Emma's spine, then spread the broad of his hand against the small of her back. Looking kindly down at her closed eyelids he went on: 'However, it all went off all right. Oh, and there's one thing I'd like to tell you – that chap called me a genius.'

'How would he know?' said Emma, opening her eyes.

'We never got that clear. I was rather out of my depth. His sister was deaf . . . ' here Robinson paused, bent down and passed his lips absently over Emma's forehead. 'Or did I tell you that?'

'Yes, you told me that . . . Is it true that this house is blue?'

'You'll see tomorrow.'

'There'll hardly be time, darling; I shall hardly see this house in the daylight. I must go on to – where I'm supposed to be.'

'At any rate, I'm glad that was all O.K. They're not on the telephone, where you're going?'

'No, it's all right; they're not on the telephone . . . *You'll* have to think of something that went wrong with my car.'

'That will keep,' said Robinson. 'Here you are.'

'Yes, here I am.' She added: 'The night was lovely,' speaking more sadly than she knew. Yes, here she was, being settled down to as calmly as he might settle down to a meal. Her naïvety as a lover . . . She could not have said, for instance, how much the authoritative male room – the electric clock, the sideboard, the unlit grate, the cold of the leather chairs – put, at every moment when he did not touch her, a gulf between her and him. She turned her head to the window. 'I smell flowers.'

'Yes, I've got three flower-beds.'

'Darling, for a minute could we go out?'

She moved from his touch and picked up Queenie's tea-tray and asked if she could put it somewhere else. Holding the tray (and given countenance by it) she halted in front of the photographs. 'Oh . . . ' she said. 'Yes. Why?' 'I wish in a way you hadn't got any children.' 'I don't see why I shouldn't have: you have.'

'Yes, I . . . But Vivie and Di are not so much *like* children — '

'If they're like you,' he said, 'those two will be having a high old time, with the cat away — '

'Oh darling, I'm not the cat.'

In the kitchen (to put the tray down) she looked round: it shone with tiling and chromium and there seemed to be switches in every place. 'What a whole lot of gadgets you have,' she said. 'Look at all those electric . . . ' 'Yes I like them.' 'They must cost a lot of money. My kitchen's all over blacklead and smoke and hooks. My cook would hate a kitchen like this.'

'I always forget that you have a cook.' He picked up an electric torch and they went out. Going along the side of the house, Robinson played a mouse of light on the wall. 'Look, really blue.' But she only looked absently. 'Yes – But have I been wrong to come?' He led her off the gravel on to the lawn, till they reached the edge of a bed of stocks. Then he firmly said: 'That's for you to say, my dear girl.'

'I know it's hardly a question – I hardly know you, do I?'

'We'll be getting to know each other,' said Robinson.

After a minute she let go of his hand and knelt down abruptly beside the flowers: she made movements like scooping the scent up and laving her face in it – he, meanwhile, lighted a cigarette and stood looking down. 'I'm glad you like my garden,' he said. 'You feel like getting fond of the place?'

'You say you forget that I have a cook.'

'Look, sweet, if you can't get that off your mind you'd better get in your car and go straight home . . . But you will.'

'Aunt Fran's so old, too old; it's not nice. And the Major keeps thinking about the war. And the children don't think I am good; I regret that.'

'You have got a nerve,' he said, 'but I love that. You're with me. Aren't you with me? – Come out of that flower-bed.'

They walked to the brow of the lawn; the soft feather-plumes of the pampas rose up a little over her head as she stood by him overlooking the road. She shivered. 'What are all those trees?' 'The demesne – I know they burnt down the castle years ago. The demesne's great for couples.' 'What's in there?' 'Nothing, I don't think; just the ruin, a lake . . . '

'I wish — '

'Now, what?'

'I wish we had more time.'

'Yes: we don't want to stay out all night.'

So taught, she smothered the last of her little wishes for consolation. Her shyness of further words between them became extreme; she was becoming frightened of Robinson's stern, experienced delicacy on the subject of love. Her adventure became the quiet practice with him. The adventure (even, the pilgrimage) died at its root, in the childish part of her mind. When he had headed her off the cytherean terrain – the leaf-drowned castle ruin, the lake – she thought for a minute he had broken her heart, and she knew now he had broken her fairytale. He seemed content – having lit a new cigarette – to wait about in his garden for a few minutes longer: not poetry but a sort of tactile wisdom came from the firmness, lawn, under their feet. The white gateposts, the boles of beeches above the dust-whitened wall were just seen in reflected light from the town. There was no moon, but dry, tense, translucent darkness: no dew fell.

Justin went with his sister to her door in the square. Quickly, and in their necessary silence, they crossed the grass under the limes. Here a dark window reflected one of the few lamps, there a shadow crossed a lit blind, and voices of people moving under the trees made a reverberation in the box of the square. Queenie let herself in; Justin heard the heavy front door drag shut slowly across the mat. She had not expected him to come in, and he did not know if she shared his feeling of dissonance, or if she recoiled from shock, or if she were shocked at all. Quitting the square at once, he took the direct way to his hotel in the main street. He went in at the side door, past the bar in which he so often encountered Robinson.

In his small, harsh room he looked first at his bed. He looked, as though out of a pit of sickness, at his stack of books on the mantelpiece. He writhed his head round sharply, threw off his coat and begun to unknot his tie. Meanwhile he beat round, in the hot light, for some crack of outlet from his constriction. It was at his dressing-table, for he had no other, that he began and ended his letter to Robinson: the mirror screwed to the dressing-table constituted a witness to this task – whenever his look charged up it met his own reared head, the flush heightening on the bridge of the nose and forehead, the neck from which as though for an execution, the collar had been taken away.

My dear Robinson: Our departure from your house (Bellevue, I think?) tonight was so awkwardly late, and at the last so hurried, that I had inadequate time in which to thank you for your hospitality to my sister and to myself. That we exacted this hospitality does not make its merit, on your part, less. Given the inconvenience we so clearly caused you, your forbearance with us was past praise. So much so that (as you may be glad to hear) my sister does not appear to realize how very greatly we were *de trop*. In my own case – which is just – the same cannot be said.

I am conscious that, in spite of her disability, she did at least prove a less wearisome guest than I.

My speculations and queries must, to your mind, equally seem absurd. This evening's fiasco has been definitive: I think it better our acquaintance should close. You will find it in line with my usual awkwardness that I should choose to state this decision of mine at all. Your indifference to the matter I cannot doubt. My own lack of indifference must make its last weak exhibition in this letter – in which, if you have fine enough nostrils (which I doubt) every sentence will almost certainly stink. In attempting to know you I have attempted to enter, and to comport myself in, what might be called an area under your jurisdiction. If my inefficacies appeared to you ludicrous, my curiosities (as in one special instance tonight) appeared more – revolting. I could gauge (even before the postscript outside your gate) how profoundly I had offended you. Had we either of us been gentlemen, the incident might have passed off with less harm.

My attempts to know you I have disposed of already. My wish that you should know me has been, from the first, ill found. You showed yourself party to it in no sense, and the trick I played on myself I need not discuss. I acted and spoke (with regard to you) upon assumptions you were not prepared to warrant. You cannot fail to misunderstand what I mean when I say that a year ago this might not have happened to me. But – the assumptions on which I acted, Robinson, are becoming more general in a driven world than you yet (or may ever) know. The extremity to which we are each driven must be the warrant for what we do and say.

My extraordinary divagation towards you might be said to be, I suppose, an accident of this summer. But there are no accidents. I have the fine (yes) fine mind's love of the fine plume, and I meet no fine plumes down my own narrow street. Also, in this place (birthplace) you interposed your solidity between me and what might have been the full effects of an exacerbating return. In fact, you had come to constitute for me a very genuine holiday. As things are, my five remaining days here will have to be seen out. I shall hope not to meet you, but must fear much of the trap-like size of this town. (You need not, as I mean to, avoid the hotel bar.) Should I, however, fail to avoid you, I shall again, I suppose, have to owe much, owe any face I keep, to your never-failing imperviousness. Understand that it will be against my wish that I re-open this one-sided account.

I wish you good night. Delicacy does not deter me from adding that I feel my good wish to be superfluous. I imagine that, incapable of being haunted, you are incapable of being added to. Tomorrow (I understand) you will feel fine, but you will not

know any more about love. If the being outside your gate came
with a question, it is possible that she should have come to me.
If I had even seen her she might not go on rending my heart. As
it is, as you are, I perhaps denounce you as much on her behalf as
my own. Not trying to understand, you at least cannot misunderstand the mood and hour in which I write. As regards my
sister, please do not discontinue what has been your even kindness to her: she might be perplexed. She has nothing to fear, I
think.

Accept, my dear Robinson (without irony) my kind regards,

J.C.

Justin, trembling, smote a stamp on this letter. Going down as he
was, in the hall he unhooked his mackintosh and put it over his
shirt. It was well past midnight; the street, empty, lay in dusty
reaches under the few lamps. Between the shutters his step raised
an echo; the cold of the mountains had come down; two cats in his
path unclinched and shot off into the dark. On his way to the
letterbox he was walking towards Bellevue; on his way back he still
heard the drunken woman sobbing against the telegraph pole. The
box would not be cleared till tomorrow noon.

Queenie forgot Justin till next day. The house in which her rooms
were was so familiar that she went upstairs without a pause in the
dark. Crossing her sitting-room she smelled oil from the cooker
behind the screen: she went through an arch to the cubicle where
she slept. She was happy. Inside her sphere of silence that not a
word clouded, the spectacle of the evening at Bellevue reigned.
Contemplative, wishless, almost without an 'I', she unhooked her
muslin dress at the wrists and waist, stepped from the dress and
began to take down her hair. Still in the dark, with a dreaming
sureness of habit, she dropped hairpins into the heart-shaped tray.

This was the night she knew she would find again. It had stayed
living under a film of time. On just such a summer night, once
only, she had walked with a lover in the demesne. His hand, like
Robinson's, had been on her elbow, but she had guided him, not
he her, because she had better eyes in the dark. They had gone
down walks already deadened with moss, under the weight of July
trees; they had felt the then fresh aghast ruin totter above them;
there was a moonless sky. Beside the lake they sat down, and while
her hand brushed the ferns in the cracks of the stone seat
emanations of kindness passed from him to her. The subtle deaf girl
had made the transposition of this nothing or everything into an
everything – the delicate deaf girl that the man could not speak to
and was afraid to touch. She who, then so deeply contented, kept in

her senses each frond and breath of that night, never saw him again and had soon forgotten his face. That had been twenty years ago, till tonight when it was now. Tonight it was Robinson who, guided by Queenie down leaf tunnels, took the place on the stone seat by the lake.

The rusted gates of the castle were at the end of the square. Queenie, in her bed facing the window, lay with her face turned sideways, smiling, one hand lightly against her cheek.

In the Square

AT ABOUT nine o'clock on this hot bright July evening the square looked mysterious: it was completely empty, and a whitish reflection, ghost of the glare of midday, came from the pale-coloured façades on its four sides and seemed to brim it up to the top. The grass was parched in the middle; its shaved surface was paid for by people who had gone. The sun, now too low to enter normally, was able to enter brilliantly at a point where three of the houses had been bombed away; two or three of the may trees, dark with summer, caught on their tops the illicit gold. Each side of the breach, exposed wallpapers were exaggerated into viridians, yellows and corals that they had probably never been. Elsewhere, the painted front doors under the balconies and at the tops of steps not whitened for some time stood out in the deadness of colour with light off it. Most of the glassless windows were shuttered or boarded up, but some framed hollow inside dark.

The extinct scene had the appearance of belonging to some ages ago. Time having only been thrust forward for reasons that could no longer affect the square, this still was a virtual eight o'clock. One taxi did now enter at the north side and cruise round the polish to a house in a corner: a man got out and paid his fare. He glanced round him, satisfied to find the shell of the place here. In spite of the dazzling breach, the square's acoustics had altered very little: in the confined sound of his taxi driving away there was nothing to tell him he had not arrived to dinner as on many summer evenings before. He went up familiar steps and touched the chromium bell. Some windows of this house were not shuttered, though they were semi-blinded by oiled stuff behind which the curtains dimly hung: these windows fixed on the outdoors their tenacious look; some of the sashes were pushed right up, to draw this singular summer evening – parched, freshening and a little acrid with ruins – into the rooms in which people lived. When the bell was not answered, the man on the steps frowned at the jade green front door, then rang again. On which the door was opened by an unfamiliar person, not a maid, who stood pushing up her top curls. She wore a cotton dress and studied him with the coldly intimate look he had found new in women since his return.

By contrast with the fixed outdoor silence, this dark interior was a cave of sound. The house now was like a machine with the silencer off it; there was nothing muted; the carpets looked thin. One got a feeling of functional anarchy, of loose plumbing, of fittings shocked from their place. From the basement came up a smell of basement cooking, a confident voice and the sound of a shutting door. At the top of the house a bath was being run out. A tray of glasses was moved, so inexpertly that everything on it tinkled, somewhere in the drawing-room over his head.

'She's expecting you, is she?' said the sceptical girl. He saw on the table behind her only a couple of leaflets and a driver's cap.

'I think so.'

'You know I'm expecting you!' exclaimed Magdela, beginning to come round the turn of the stairs.

'Sorry,' said the girl, stepping back to speak up the staircase. 'I didn't know you were in.' Turning, she disappeared through a waiting door, the door behind the dining-room, which she shut. 'Do come up, Rupert,' said Magdela, extending her hand to him from where she stood. 'I'm sorry; I meant to come down myself.'

Of the three drawing-room windows two stood open, so she must have heard the taxi; her failure to get to the door in time had been due to some inhibition or last thought. It would have been remarkable if she *had* yet arrived at the manner in which to open her own door – which would have to be something quite different from the impulsive informality of peacetime. The tray of glasses she had been heard moving now stood on a pedestal table beside a sofa. She said: 'These days, there is no one to . . . ' Indeed the expanse of parquet, though unmarked, no longer showed watery gloss and depth. Though it may have only been by the dusk that the many white lampshades were discoloured, he saw under one, as he sat down beside her, a film of dust over the bulb. Though they were still many, the lamps were fewer; some had been put away with the bric-à-brac that used to be on the tables and in the alcoves – and these occasional blanks were the least discomforting thing in the dead room. The reflections in from the square fell on the chairs and sofas already worn rough on their satin tops and arms, and with grime homing into their rubbed parts.

This had been the room of a hostess; the replica of so many others that you could not count. It had never had any other aspect, and it had no aspect at all tonight. The chairs remained so many, and their pattern was now so completely without focus that, had Magdela not sat down where she did sit, he would not have known in which direction to turn.

'How nice it was of you to ring me up,' she said. 'I had no idea you were back in London. How did you know I was here? No one else is.'

'I happened to hear . . . '

'Oh, did you?' she said, a little bit disconcerted, then added quickly: 'Were you surprised?'

'I was delighted, naturally.'

'I came back,' she said. 'For the first year I was away, part of the time in the country, part of the time in the north with Anthony – he has been there since this all started, you know. Then, last winter, I decided to come back.'

'You are a Londoner.'

She said mechanically: 'Yes, I suppose so – yes. It's so curious to see you again, like this. Who would think that this was the same world?' She looked sideways out of the window, at the square. 'Who would have thought this could really happen? The last time we – how long ago was that? Two years ago?'

'A delightful evening.'

'Was it?' she said, and looked round the room. 'How nice. One has changed so much since then, don't you think? It is quite . . . '

At this point the door opened and a boy of about sixteen came in, in a dressing-gown. Not only was his hair twisted in tufts of dampness but a sort of humidity seemed to follow him, as though he were trailing the bathroom steam. 'Oh, sorry,' he said, but after a glance at Rupert he continued his way to the cigarette box. 'Bennet,' said Magdela, 'I feel sure you ought not to smoke – Rupert, this is my nephew, Bennet; I expect we sometimes talked about him. He is here just for the night, on his way from school.'

'That reminds me,' said Bennet, 'would you very much mind if I stayed tomorrow?' Rupert watched Bennet squinting as he lighted a cigarette. 'They say everyone's smoking more, now,' said Bennet. 'Actually, I hardly smoke at all.' He dropped the match into the empty steel grate. 'I took a bath,' he said to Magdela. 'I'm just going out.'

'Oh, Bennet, have you had anything to eat?'

'Well, I had tea at six,' he said, 'with an egg. I expect I'll pick up something at a Corner House.' He stooped to pull up a slipper on one heel and said: 'I didn't know you had visitors. As a matter of fact, I didn't know you were in. But everyone seems to be in tonight.' When he went out he did not shut the door behind him, and they could hear him slip-slopping upstairs. 'He's very independent,' said Magdela. 'But these days I suppose everyone is?'

'I must say,' he said, 'I'm glad you are not alone here. I should not like to think of your being that.'

'Wouldn't you?' she said. 'Well, I never am. This is my only room in the house – and, even so, as you see, Bennet comes in. The house seems to belong to everyone now. That was Gina who opened the front door.'

'Yes,' he said, 'who is she?'

'She used to be Anthony's secretary, but she wanted to come to London to drive a car for the war, so he told her she could live in this house, because it was shut up at that time. So it seemed to be quite hers, when I came back. She is supposed to sit in the back dining-room; that was why I couldn't ask you to dinner. But also, there is nobody who can cook – there is a couple down in the basement, but they are independent; they are only supposed to be caretakers. They have a son who is a policeman, and I know he sometimes sleeps somewhere at the top of the house – but caretakers are so hard to get. They have a schoolgirl daughter who comes in here when she thinks I am not about.'

'It seems to me you have a lot to put up with. Wouldn't you be more comfortable somewhere else?'

'Oh,' she said, 'is that how you think of me?'

'I do hope you will dine with me, one night soon.'

'Thank you,' she said, evasively. 'Some night that would be very nice.'

'I suppose the fact is, you are very busy?'

'Yes, I am. I am working, doing things quite a lot.' She told him what she did, then her voice trailed off. He realized that he and she could not be intimate without many other people in the room. He looked at the empty pattern of chairs round them and said: 'Where are all those people I used to meet?' 'Whom do you mean, exactly?' she said, startled. ' . . . Oh, in different places, different places, you know. I think I have their addresses, if there's anyone special . . . ?'

'You hear news of them?'

'Oh yes; oh yes, I'm sure I do. What can I tell you that would be interesting? I'm sorry,' she said suddenly, shutting her eyes, 'but so much has happened.' Opening her eyes to look at him, she added: 'So much more than you know.'

To give point to this, the telephone started ringing: the bell filled the room, the sounding-box of the house, and travelled through windows into the square. Rupert remembered how, on other summer evenings, you had constantly heard the telephones in the houses round. It was tonight startling to hear a telephone ring. Magdela stared at the telephone, at a distance from her – not as though she shared this feeling that Rupert had, but as though something happened out of its time. She seemed to forbid the bell with her eyes, with that intent fixed warning intimate look, and, seeming unwilling to leave the sofa, contracted into stone-stillness by Rupert's side. At a loss, he said: 'Like me to see who it is?'

'No, I will; I must,' her voice hardened. 'Or they will be answering from downstairs.'

This evidently did happen; the bell stopped an instant before her fingers touched the receiver. She raised it, listened into it, frowned. 'It's all right, Gina,' she said. 'Thank you: you needn't bother. I'm here.'

She stood with her back to Rupert, with her head bent, still warily listening to the receiver. Then: 'Yes, it's me now,' she said, in an all at once very much altered tone, 'but . . . '

After Gina had let in Rupert she went back to continue to wait for her telephone call. *She* always answered from the foot of the stairs. Before sitting down again, or not sitting down, she went through from the back to the front dining-room, to open the window overlooking the square. The long table and the two sideboards were, as she always remembered them, sheeted up, and a smell of dust came from the sheets. Returning to the room that was hers to sit in, she left the archway doors open behind her, so that, before the blackout, air might pass through. The perspective of useless dining-room through the archway, the light fading from it through the bombed gap, did not affect her. She had not enough imagination to be surprised by the past – still less, by its end. When, the November after the war started, she first came to sleep in the closed house, she had, as Anthony's mistress, speculated as to this former part of his life. She supposed he had gained something by entertaining, though it did not seem to her he had much to show. While she stayed faithful to him she pitied him for a number of reasons she did not let appear. Now that she had begun to deceive him she found only that one reason to pity him. Now she loved someone else in a big way, she supposed it was time to clear out of this house. She only thought this; she did not feel it; her feelings were not at all fine. She did not know how to move without bringing the whole thing up, which would be tough on Anthony while he was in the north.

As to her plans for tonight – she never knew. So much depended – or, she might hear nothing. She wondered if she should put in time by writing to Anthony; she got out her pad and sat with it on her knee. Hearing Bennet's bath continue to run out she thought, that's a funny time for a bath. Underneath where she sat, the caretaker's wife was washing up the supper dishes and calling over her shoulder to her policeman son: the voice came out through the basement window and withered back on the silence round.

She wrote words on the pad:

'Since I came here one thing and another seems to have altered my point of view. I don't know how to express myself, but I think under the circum-stances I ought to tell you. Being here has started to get me down; for one thing it is such a way from the bus. Of course it has been a help; but don't you think it would be better if your wife had the place all to herself? As far as I can see she means to stay. Naturally she and I do not refer to this. But, for instance, if she had two nephews there would be no place for the other to sleep . . .'

. . . And looked at them with her head on one side. She heard Bennet come down the flights of staircase, rigidly dropping his feet from step to step. He pulled up with a jingle of the things in his pockets and thought of something outside her door. O God, don't let him come bothering in here, you see I might get this done. But he did: leaning his weight on the door handle, and with the other hand holding the frame of the door, he swung forward at her, with damp-flattened hair.

'Sorry,' he said, 'but shall you be going out?' She kept a hold on her letter-pad and said fiercely: 'Why?'

'If not, I might have your key.'

'Why not ask your aunt?'

'She's got someone there. You mean, you might go out, but you don't know?'

'No. Don't come bothering here, like a good boy. What's the matter with you, have you got a date?'

'No,' he said. 'I just want some food in some place.'

He walked away from her through the archway and looked out at the square from the end of the dining-room. The lampless dusk seemed to fascinate him. 'There are quite a lot of people standing about,' he said. 'Couples. This must be quite a place. Do you suppose they go into the empty houses?'

'No, they're all locked up.'

'What's the good of that, I don't see?'

'They're property.'

'I should say they were cracked; I shouldn't say they'd ever be much use. Oh, sorry, are you writing a letter? I say, I thought they were taking the railings away from squares; I thought the iron was some good. You think this place will patch up? I suppose it depends who wants it. Anybody can have it as far as I'm concerned. You can't get to anywhere from here.'

'Hadn't you better push off? Everywhere will be shut.'

'I know, but what about the key?'

But her head turned sharply: the telephone started ringing at the foot of the stairs. Bennet's expression became more hopeful. 'Go on, why don't you,' he said, 'then we might know where we are.'

Gina came back to him from the telephone, with one hand pushing her curls up. 'So what?' said Bennet.

'That was for her,' she said. 'It would be. I got my head bitten off. No place for me on that line. You'd think she was the only one in the house.' She picked up her bag and gave him the key out of it. 'Oh, all right,' she said. 'Here you are. Run along.'

He thumbed the key and said: 'Oh, then it wasn't your regular?'

'Nothing of mine,' she said. 'Regular if you like . . . Look, I thought you were going to run along?'

Just before Bennet shut the front door behind him he heard a ghostly click from the telephone at the foot of the stairs – in the drawing-room the receiver had been put back. Whatever there had been to say to his aunt must have been said – or totally given up. He thought, so what was the good of *that*? Stepping down into the dusk of the square, that lay at the foot of the steps like water, he heard voices above his head. His aunt and her visitor stood at one of the open windows, looking down, or seeming to look down, at the lovers. Rupert and Magdela for the moment looked quite intimate, as though they had withdrawn to the window from a number of people in the room behind them – only in that case the room would have been lit up.

Bennet, going out to hunt food, kept close along under the fronts of the houses with a primitive secretiveness. He made for the north outlet of the square, by which Rupert's taxi had come in, and at last in the distance heard the sound of a bus.

Magdela smiled and said to Rupert: 'Yes, look. Now the place seems to belong to everyone. One has nothing except one's feelings. Sometimes I think I hardly know myself.'

'How curious that light is,' he said, looking across at the gap.

'You know, I am happy.' This was her only reference to the words he had heard her say to the telephone. 'Of course, I have no plans. This is no time to make plans, now. But do talk to me – perhaps you have no plans, either? I have been so selfish, talking about myself. But to meet you after so much has happened – in one way, there seemed nothing to talk about. Do tell me how things strike you, what you have thought of things – coming back to everything like you have. Do you think we shall all see a great change?'

Sunday Afternoon

'SO HERE you are!' exclaimed Mrs Vesey to the newcomer who joined the group on the lawn. She reposed for an instant her light, dry fingers on his. 'Henry has come from London,' she added. Acquiescent smiles from the others round her showed that the fact was already known – she was no more than indicating to Henry the role that he was to play. 'What are your experiences? – Please tell us. But nothing dreadful: we are already feeling a little sad.'

'I am sorry to hear that,' said Henry Russel, with the air of one not anxious to speak of his own affairs. Drawing a cane chair into the circle, he looked from face to face with concern. His look travelled on to the screen of lilac, whose dark purple, pink-silver, and white plumes sprayed out in the brilliance of the afternoon. The late May Sunday blazed, but was not warm: something less than a wind, a breath of coldness, fretted the edge of things. Where the lilac barrier ended, across the sun-polished meadows, the Dublin mountains continued to trace their hazy, today almost colourless line. The coldness had been admitted by none of the seven or eight people who, in degrees of elderly beauty, sat here full in the sun, at this sheltered edge of the lawn: they continued to master the coldness, or to deny it, as though with each it were some secret *malaise*. An air of fastidious, stylized melancholy, an air of being secluded behind glass, characterized for Henry these old friends in whose shadow he had grown up. To their pleasure at having him back among them was added, he felt, a taboo or warning – he was to tell a little, but not much. He could feel with a shock, as he sat down, how insensibly he had deserted, these last years, the aesthetic of living that he had got from them. As things were, he felt over him their suspended charm. The democratic smell of the Dublin bus, on which he had made the outward journey to join them, had evaporated from his person by the time he was half-way up Mrs Vesey's chestnut avenue. Her house, with its fanlights and tall windows, was a villa in the Italian sense, just near enough to the city to make the country's sweetness particularly acute. Now, the sensations of wartime, that locked his inside being, began as surely to be dispelled – in the influence of this eternalized Sunday afternoon.

'Sad?' he said, 'that is quite wrong.'

'These days, our lives seem unreal,' said Mrs Vesey – with eyes that penetrated his point of view. 'But, worse than that, this afternoon we discover that we all have friends who have died.'

'Lately?' said Henry, tapping his fingers together.

'Yes, in all cases,' said Ronald Cuffe – with just enough dryness to show how much the subject had been beginning to tire him. 'Come, Henry, we look to you for distraction. To us, these days, you are quite a figure. In fact, from all we have heard of London, it is something that you should be alive. Are things there as shocking as they say – or are they more shocking?' he went on, with distaste.

'Henry's not sure,' said someone, 'he looks pontifical.'

Henry, in fact, was just beginning to twiddle this far-off word 'shocking' round in his mind, when a diversion caused some turning of heads. A young girl stepped out of a window and began to come their way across the lawn. She was Maria, Mrs Vesey's niece. A rug hung over her bare arm: she spread out the rug and sat down at her aunt's feet. With folded arms, and her fingers on her thin pointed elbows, she immediately fixed her eyes on Henry Russel. 'Good afternoon,' she said to him, in a mocking but somehow intimate tone.

The girl, like some young difficult pet animal, seemed in a way to belong to everyone there. Miss Ria Store, the patroness of the arts who had restlessly been refolding her fur cape, said: 'And where have *you* been, Maria?'

'Indoors.'

Someone said, 'On this beautiful afternoon?'

'Is it?' said Maria, frowning impatiently at the grass.

'Instinct,' said the retired judge, 'now tells Maria it's time for tea.'

'No, this does,' said Maria, nonchalantly showing her wrist with the watch on it. 'It keeps good time, thank you, Sir Isaac.' She returned her eyes to Henry. 'What have you been saying?'

'You interrupted Henry. He was just going to speak.'

'*Is* it so frightening?' Maria said.

'The bombing?' said Henry. 'Yes. But as it does not connect with the rest of life, it is difficult, you know, to know what one feels. One's feelings seem to have no language for anything so preposterous. As for thoughts – '

'At that rate,' said Maria, with a touch of contempt, 'your thoughts would not be interesting.'

'Maria,' said somebody, 'that is no way to persuade Henry to talk.'

'About what is important,' announced Maria, 'it seems that no one can tell one anything. There is really nothing, till one knows it oneself.'

'Henry is probably right,' said Ronald Cuffe, 'in considering that this – this outrage is *not* important. There is no place for it in human experience; it apparently cannot make a place of its own. It will have no literature.'

'Literature!' said Maria. 'One can see, Mr Cuffe, that *you* have always been safe!'

'Maria,' said Mrs Vesey, 'you're rather pert.'

Sir Isaac said, 'What does Maria expect to know?'

Maria pulled off a blade of grass and bit it. Something calculating and passionate appeared in her; she seemed to be crouched up inside herself. She said to Henry sharply: 'But you'll go back, of course?'

'To London? Yes – this is only my holiday. Anyhow, one cannot stay long away.'

Immediately he had spoken Henry realized how subtly this offended his old friends. Their position was, he saw, more difficult than his own, and he could not have said a more cruel thing. Mrs Vesey, with her adept smile that was never entirely heartless, said: 'Then we must hope your time here will be pleasant. Is it so very short?'

'And be careful, Henry,' said Ria Store, 'or you will find Maria stowed away in your baggage. And there would be an embarrassment, at an English port! We can feel her planning to leave us at any time.'

Henry said, rather flatly: 'Why should not Maria travel in the ordinary way?'

'Why should Maria travel at all? There is only one journey now – into danger. We cannot feel that that is necessary for her.'

Sir Isaac added: 'We fear, however, that this is the journey Maria wishes to make.'

Maria, curled on the lawn with the nonchalance of a feline creature, through this kept her eyes cast down. Another cold puff came through the lilac, soundlessly knocking the blooms together. One woman, taken quite unawares, shivered – then changed this into a laugh. There was an aside about love from Miss Store, who spoke with a cold, abstracted knowledge – 'Maria has no experience, none whatever; she hopes to meet heroes – she meets none. So now she hopes to find heroes across the sea. Why, Henry, she might make a hero of you.'

'It is not that,' said Maria, who had heard. Mrs Vesey bent down and touched her shoulder; she sent the girl into the house to see if tea were ready. Presently they all rose and followed – in twos and threes, heads either erect composedly or else deliberately bowed in thought. Henry knew the idea of summer had been relinquished: they would not return to the lawn again. In the dining-room – where the white walls and the glass of the pictures held the reflections of summers – burned the log fire they were so glad to see. With her shoulder against the mantelpiece stood Maria, watching them take their places at the round table. Everything Henry had heard said had fallen off her – in these few minutes all by herself she had started in again on a fresh phase of living that was intact and pure. So much so, that Henry felt the ruthlessness of her disregard for the past, even the past of a few minutes ago. She came forward and put her hands on two chairs – to show she had been keeping a place for him.

Lady Ottery, leaning across the table, said: 'I must ask you – we heard you had lost everything. But that cannot be true?'

Henry said, unwillingly: 'It's true that I lost my flat, and everything in my flat.'

'*Henry*,' said Mrs Vesey, 'all your beautiful things?'

'Oh dear,' said Lady Ottery, overpowered, 'I thought that could not be possible. I ought not to have asked.'

Ria Store looked at Henry critically. 'You take this too calmly. What has happened to you?'

'It was some time ago. And it happens to many people.'

'But not to everyone,' said Miss Store. 'I should see no reason, for instance, why it should happen to me.'

'One cannot help looking at you,' said Sir Isaac. 'You must forgive our amazement. But there was a time, Henry, when I think we all used to feel that we knew you well. If this is not a painful question, at this juncture, why did you not send your valuables out of town? You could have even shipped them over to us.'

'I was attached to them. I wanted to live with them.'

'And now,' said Miss Store, 'you live with nothing, for ever. Can you really feel that that is life?'

'I do. I may be easily pleased. It was by chance I was out when the place was hit. You may feel – and I honour your point of view – that I should have preferred, at my age, to go into eternity with some pieces of glass and jade and a dozen pictures. But, in fact, I am very glad to remain. To exist.'

'On what level?'

'On any level.'

'Come, Henry,' said Ronald Cuffe, 'that is a cynicism one cannot like in you. You speak of your age: to us, of course, that is nothing. You are at your maturity.'

'Forty-three.'

Maria gave Henry an askance look, as though, after all, he were not a friend. But she then said. 'Why should he wish he was dead?'

Her gesture upset some tea on the lace cloth, and she idly rubbed it up with her handkerchief. The tug her rubbing gave to the cloth shook a petal from a Chinese peony in the centre bowl on to a plate of cucumber sandwiches. This little bit of destruction was watched by the older people with fascination, with a kind of appeasement, as though it were a guarantee against something worse.

'Henry is not young and savage, like you are. Henry's life is – or was – an affair of attachments,' said Ria Store. She turned her eyes, under their lids, on Henry. 'I wonder how much of you *has* been blown to blazes.'

'I have no way of knowing,' he said. 'Perhaps you have?'

'Chocolate cake?' said Maria.

'Please.'

For chocolate layer cake, the Vesey cook had been famous since Henry was a boy of seven or eight. The look, then the taste, of the brown segment linked him with Sunday afternoons when he had been brought here by his mother; then, with a phase of his adolescence when he had been unable to eat, only able to look round. Mrs Vesey's beauty, at that time approaching its last lunar quarter, had swum on him when he was about nineteen. In Maria, child of her brother's late marriage, he now saw that beauty, or sort of physical genius, at the start. In Maria, this was without hesitation, without the halting influence that had bound Mrs Vesey up – yes and bound Henry up, from his boyhood, with her – in a circle of quizzical half-smiles. In revenge, he accused the young girl who moved him – who seemed framed, by some sort of anticipation, for the new catastrophic *outward* order of life – of brutality, of being without spirit. At his age, between two generations, he felt cast out. He felt Mrs Vesey might not forgive him for having left her for a world at war.

Mrs Vesey blew out the blue flame under the kettle, and let the silver trapdoor down with a snap. She then gave exactly one of those smiles – at the same time, it was the smile of his mother's friend. Ronald Cuffe picked the petal from the sandwiches and rolled it between his fingers, waiting for her to speak.

'It is cold, *indoors*,' said Mrs Vesey. 'Maria, put another log on the fire – Ria, you say the most unfortunate things. We must remember Henry has had a shock. – Henry, let us talk about something better. You work in an office, then, since the war?'

'In a Ministry – in an office, yes.'

'Very hard? – Maria, that is all you would do if you went to England: work in an office. This is not like a war history, you know.'

Maria said: 'It is not in history yet.' She licked round her lips for the rest of the chocolate taste, then pushed her chair a little back from the table. She looked secretively at her wrist-watch. Henry wondered what the importance of time could be.

He learned what the importance of time was when, on his way down the avenue to the bus, he found Maria between two chestnut trees. She slanted up to him and put her hand on the inside of his elbow. Faded dark-pink stamen from the flowers above them had moulted down on to her hair. 'You have ten minutes more, really,' she said. 'They sent you off ten minutes before your time. They are frightened someone would miss the bus and come back; then everything would have to begin again. As it is always the same, you would not think it would be so difficult for my aunt.'

'Don't talk like that; it's unfeeling; I don't like it,' said Henry, stiffening his elbow inside Maria's grasp.

'Very well, then: walk to the gate, then back. I shall be able to hear your bus coming. It's true what they said – I'm intending to go away. They will have to make up something without me.'

'Maria, I can't like you. Everything you say is destructive and horrible.'

'Destructive? – I thought you didn't mind.'

'I still want the past.'

'Then how weak you are,' said Maria. 'At tea I admired you. The past – things done over and over again with more trouble than they were ever worth? – However, there's no time to talk about that. Listen, Henry: I must have your address. I suppose you *have* an address now?' She stopped him, just inside the white gate with the green drippings: here he blew stamen off a page of his notebook, wrote on the page and tore it out for her. 'Thank you,' said Maria, 'I might turn up – if I wanted money, or anything. But there will be plenty to do: I can drive a car.'

Henry said: 'I want you to understand that I won't be party to this – *in any way*.'

She shrugged and said. 'You want *them* to understand' – and sent a look back to the house. Whereupon, on his entire being, the suspended charm of the afternoon worked. He protested against the return to the zone of death, and perhaps never ever seeing all this again. The cruciform lilac flowers, in all their purples, and the colourless mountains behind Mrs Vesey's face besought him. The moment he had been dreading, returning desire, flooded him in this tunnel of avenue, with motors swishing along the road outside and Maria standing staring at him. He adored the stoicism of the group he had quitted – with their little fears and their great doubts – the grace of the thing done over again. He thought, with nothing left but our brute courage, we shall be nothing but brutes.

'What is the matter?' Maria said. Henry did not answer: they turned and walked to and fro inside the gates. Shadow played over her dress and hair: feeling the disenchantedness of his look at her she asked again, uneasily, 'What's the matter?'

'You know,' he said, 'when you come away from here, no one will care any more that you are Maria. You will no longer be Maria, as a matter of fact. Those looks, those things that are said to you – they make you, you silly little girl. You are you only inside their spell. You may think action is better – but who will care for you when you only act? You will have an identity number, but no identity. Your whole existence has been in contradistinction. You may think you want an ordinary fate – but there is no ordinary fate. And that extraordinariness in the fate of each of us is only recognized by your aunt. I admit that her view of life is too much for me – that is why I was so stiff and touchy today. But where shall we be when nobody has a view of life?'

'You don't expect me to understand you, do you?'

'Even your being a savage, even being scornful – yes, even that you have got from them. – Is that my bus?'

'At the other side of the river: it has still got to cross the bridge. – Henry – ' she put her face up. He touched it with kisses thoughtful and cold. 'Goodbye,' he said, 'Miranda.'

' – Maria – '

'Miranda. This is the end of *you*. Perhaps it is just as well.'

'I'll be seeing you – '

'You'll come round my door in London – with your little new number chained to your wrist.'

'The trouble with you is, you're half old.'

Maria ran out through the gates to stop the bus, and Henry got on to it and was quickly carried away.

The Inherited Clock

'YES, I can see you now,' said Aunt Addie, 'skipping about the terrace at Sandyhill in your little scarlet highwayman coat. I think I had never seen you in such high spirits. It was such a beautiful March day, hazy, but warm and sunny, and Cousin Rosanna and your mother and I were in the winter-garden with the door open. Each time you came dancing down our end of the terrace you would toss your curls and go dancing away again. Your mother feared you were over-excited; I said, "It's the spring, perhaps", but Cousin Rosanna said, "Not at all: it's the clock". We three had come down for the day; Paul was staying with her. I don't remember where *he* was at the time: I'm afraid probably sulking somewhere about the place.'

'I remember my coat,' said her niece Clara, 'but I don't remember the day. What has made you think of it?'

'As you know, I was at Sandyhill yesterday: they are taking two more of Cousin Rosanna's servants, so she has decided to close some more of the house, including that little ante-room through to the library. She had been hesitating whether to move the clock: before I left, after tea, she had made up her mind not to – that might have meant some unnecessary jolt or jar. "How it is to travel to Clara's, ultimately", she said, "is not my affair. I am taking no risks with it during my own lifetime."'

Clara surprised, said: 'Travel to me?'

'That will have to be thought of, of course, dear.'

'But what clock are you talking about?'

Miss Detter began to say something, tripped up, glanced askance at her niece, then turned an unhappy red, as though Clara had said something irreligious. 'Why, yours – the one she is leaving to you,' she said. 'You know she refers to that constantly, in your presence. That skeleton clock that you like so much. How can you look so blank? Cousin Rosanna would be quite hurt if she thought it meant as little as that to you. It was the discussion yesterday, whether or not to move it, that brought back that day when you wore – '

'My scarlet coat. Yes, but why?'

'As we watched you through the door of the winter-garden, Cousin Rosanna turned and said to your mother, "I have been telling Clara that, ultimately, she is to have the clock". Your mother, knowing what a part the clock had played in Rosanna's life, was much touched. There was a good deal of bustle, I remember, about getting us off to the train, it being discovered, just before we started, that you had hurt the poor little forefinger of your right hand. It was really rather a shocking sight: black and blue with several small ugly cuts. You were loyally mum about what had happened, but we all suspected that Master Paul had been up to some more cruel tricks. This, naturally, made you a little nervous in the train. So your mother, hoping to cheer you up, said, "So, Clara, when Cousin Rosanna goes to Heaven she is going to send you her lovely skeleton clock". I don't know whether it was the idea of Cousin Rosanna going away to Heaven, or whether the word "skeleton" frightened you, but you burst into tears and became almost hysterical. Not liking to see you cry in a railway carriage, I said, "You know the reason Cousin Rosanna loves it? It has not stopped ticking for more than a hundred years!" But that only seemed to unsettle you still more.'

'Well, if you say this happened, Aunt Addie, of course it did,' Clara said – with a somehow encaged and rebellious feeling. 'I know I was six the winter I had that coat: I am thirty now – one cannot expect to remember everything.'

'Yes, I remember you before you remember yourself,' said Aunt Addie, looking at her affectionately. 'Of course, I have always taken an interest in you – but then, you have always taken an interest in yourself. I don't mean that unkindly: why shouldn't you? You have an exceptional character.'

'Only to you, I think.'

'At least,' Aunt Addie said, in a brisker tone, 'you will make a point, won't you, next time you're at Sandyhill, of saying something enthusiastic about the clock? Let her see how much you are looking forward to it.'

'Might that not seem – ?'

'Why, Clara? You know Cousin Rosanna likes you and Paul to be perfectly natural about the money, and if about money why not about the clock, when she so much connects it with you in her own mind?'

There was, it was true, a singular lack of nonsense about Rosanna Detter's relations with her two young heirs. She had named them as such early on in their infancy, made a point of having them frequently at her house, and insisted that their expectations should be discussed and defined. The contents of her will had long ago been made known, and she proposed, she said, in ordinary fairness to make no changes in it without warning. Apart from bequests to charities, legacies to old servants and £5000 for Addie Detter (who had declared fervently this was much too much) Rosanna's fortune was to be divided equally between Paul Ardeen and Clara Detter, respectively son and daughter of two of her first cousins, and thus, second cousins to one another. Clara lived, as a child, with her widowed mother in a small house in Ealing; Paul with his not prosperous doctor father on the outskirts of an industrial town: the two young people's surroundings, as well as their temperaments, could not fail to attach them to their auspicious future. Meanwhile, Cousin Rosanna made them no allowances and few presents – though there were times when the watchful Clara suspected that Rosanna paid the more pressing of Paul's debts.

It gratified Cousin Rosanna, herself an only child, to watch these two high-spirited only children quarrel. Their co-heirship had not created a happy tie. Dark bullet-headed Paul, at once cool and bragging, and blonde fine-strung Clara, with her fairy-like affectations, seldom relaxed, during visits to Sandyhill, their resourceful campaign against one another. Cousin Rosanna, in packing them off to play (for she could tolerate neither for very long at a time) could assure herself that they were equally tough. The children worked on each other like two indestructible pieces of sand-paper. It might have been thought that Rosanna, in selecting heirs near in age and of opposite sexes, entertained some romantic spinsterish project that they should marry, and that their declared hostility pleased her as being, admittedly, the first phase of love. This cannot have been so, for Paul's marriage, at twenty-two, was, by all showing, not adversely seen. It was Clara, surprisingly, who was piqued. She perceived, if Rosanna chose to ignore, a touch of Paul's usual insolence in the choice. The fortunate Edmée – blonde like Clara, but of how different a type – was to be recognized, at the first glance, as being just one more in the succession of fancies with whom Paul by habit went round town: nor did she show any reason why she should be the last. Summoned for the occasion to Sandyhill, Clara stood by at the presentation of the heavy-lidded bride. She was able to watch Paul fold, with expressionless satisfaction, preparatory to slipping into his wallet, Rosanna's five-hundred-pound cheque for the honeymoon.

It had been two years later, when she was twenty-one, that Clara met her fate in the person of Henry Harley; who, already a married man, was forced to tell her that he saw little prospect of changing his way of life. He was not well off; his wife had been irreproachable; the payment of alimony would cripple him, and he was not disposed to let scandal prejudice his career. She chose to continue obstinate in her feeling, and in her hopes of things taking a better turn. Her poverty, to which one dared set no term, meanwhile made everything more difficult: the circumstances under which their affair was conducted constantly alarmed Henry and oppressed her. This had gone on now for nine years, and provided the reason why Clara at thirty was unmarried. As the years went by, she became increasingly grateful to Cousin Rosanna for either her resolute ignorance or her tolerance, and she had reproached herself, before the war started, for not going down more often to Sandyhill. Since the war, she was tied to exacting work; also, the closing of that coastal area interdicted visits from London – except, of course, on the plea of family business that could from time to time be produced. Cousin Rosanna's influence in her neighbourhood was more considerable than one ought, these days, to admit. The officially dangerous position of Sandyhill disqualified the house as a hospital or a repository for children; but also, so far no soldiers had been billeted there. And she had kept intact, until very lately, her staff of middle-aged servants.

Sandyhill itself was to go to Paul, who did not conceal his intention of selling it. It might do well, he expected, for a private asylum, when peace should bring back happier days. The house *had*, it is true, already in some ways, the look of an institution, though of an expensive kind: it stood among pleasure-grounds dark with ilex, girt by a high flint wall. The avenue ran downhill between ramparts of evergreen, to debouch into the main street of an unassuming seaside resort. Sandyhill had been built by Rosanna's great-uncle, from whom (fairly late in her own life) she had inherited it, with substantial wealth: cleverly sheltered by trees from the sea winds, it faced south and enjoyed a good deal of sunshine. From the terrace, from the adjoining winter-garden and from the plate-glass windows upstairs and down, you also enjoyed, if this were your pleasure, a view of the Channel above the ilex groves. Indoors, the rooms were powerfully heated, brocade-papered, and so planned that you looked through an enfilade of pine-framed doorways. They composed a museum of discredited *objets d'art* which, up to now, had been always specklessly kept.

In one of the hollows about the grounds had been placed a small lake, sunless most of the day and overlooked by a kiosk. Into this lake had dropped, since Clara's last visit, what had so far been Sandyhill's only bomb; the blast had wrenched the shutters off the kiosk, and, by a freak of travel, obliterated the glass winter-garden projecting west of the house . . . This day of Clara's return, not long after the conversation with Aunt Addie, was an almost eerie extension of her aunt's memory: it was in March, 'hazy, but warm and sunny'. Clara and Cousin Rosanna lunched in the morning-room. 'As Addie no doubt will have told you, they've taken Preeps and Marchant, so I have closed the dining-room and the library.' Nodding towards a door on her left hand, Cousin Rosanna added: 'Therefore the house stops there.'

'May I look, later?'

Cousin Rosanna stared. 'By all means, if you are interested in dust-sheets.' Her eyes, always prominent, were today more so: about her face and her manner appeared the something you less at the time observe than afterwards recollect – *then*, you say you saw the beginning of the end. At sixty-five, the big woman was to be felt contracting, withdrawing from life with the same heavy indifference with which she withdrew her life from room after room. Clara did notice that her dictatorial 'ultimatelys' were fewer. Though lunch was served with most of its old formality the dried-egg omelette was rubbery: the contempt with which Cousin Rosanna ate it had been, more, a contempt for her own palate, that with impunity one could now insult.

She now, by abruptly turning her chair to the fire, implied she had left the table: her guest could do as she liked. Clara, accordingly, rose and went frankly straight to the door where the house had been forced by war to stop. This led to the ante-room which, in its turn, led to the library. At once, she could hear a clock expectantly ticking. The ante-room french window was shuttered up: only cracks of light from the terrace fell on the shrouded sofa and on the sheet tucked bibwise over the bookcase on which the clock stood. The gleam of the glass of the dome inside which the ticking proceeded was just, but only just, to be seen.

'What are you up to in there?' called out Cousin Rosanna. 'Looking at your clock?'

'I can't see it, yet.'

'Well, you ought to know what it looks like, goodness knows!'

Clara did not reply. Her cousin, restless, repeated: 'What are you doing *now*?'

'Opening a shutter – may I?'

'If you shut it again. You haven't got Preeps and Marchant to dance round clearing up after you now, you know.'

The skeleton clock, in daylight, was threatening to a degree its oddness could not explain. Looking through the glass at its wheels, cogs, springs and tensions, and at its upraised striker, awaiting with a sensible quiver the finish of the hour that was in force, Clara tried to tell herself that it was, only, shocking to see the anatomy of time. The clock was without a face, its twelve numerals being welded on to a just visible wire ring. As she watched, the minute hand against its background of nothing made one, then another, spectral advance. This was enough: if she did not yet feel she could anticipate feeling her sanity being demolished, by one degree more, as every sixtieth second brought round this unheard click. Retreating, she looked round the walls of the ante-room: she saw the dark-patterned oblongs where the pictures had hung. She could remember which picture used to hang in each oblong; she remembered the names of the books in the bookcase under the sheet.

But as far as she knew she had not seen the clock before.

'None the worse, you see,' vouchsafed Cousin Rosanna, as Clara returned to the morning-room.

'You mean,' Clara said with an effort, 'the same as ever?'

'No, I don't; I mean none the worse for the bomb. As it stood up to that, it should see *you* out, we may hope. So you can take it for granted, as I have done, instead of rushing to look for it every time you come here.' Cousin Rosanna, however, did not seem wholly displeased.'

'Do I really?' said Clara, trying to smile this off.

'Unless you walk in your sleep, and sleep in daytime, in which case you had better go to the doctor. – Have you seen the winter-garden?'

'Not yet: I –'

'It isn't there. – By the way, you will have to see that that clock's attended to. I have had the same man, out from Southstone, to wind it for twenty-four years: he took on when that previous poor fellow – shocking affair that was! – And another thing: keep a careful eye on Paul, or he'll get his hands on it before you can say knife. However, you don't need me to tell you *that!*'

'No, no, of course not, Cousin Rosanna . . . He wants it so much,' Clara added, as though musingly.

'For the reason we know,' said Rosanna, with a protuberant meaning stare. 'You know really, Clara, in view of all, you ought not to begrudge Paul that one bit of fun. Dear me, a cat would have laughed, and I must say I did. I can see you now – '

'I was wearing my scarlet coat?'

'Scarlet? Good heavens no; at least, I should hope not: you were fat to be wearing scarlet at fourteen. Not that, with you standing there with that glass thing over your head, one looked twice at whatever else you had on. However – "Now then, Paul," I said, "that's enough. She can't breathe in there: take it off her." – However,' concluded Cousin Rosanna, who for the first time today showed genuine pleasure, 'easier said than done'. Her mood changed; she looked at Clara with moody boredom. 'Did you say you wanted to go for a turn?' she said. 'Because if that's what you want you had better go.'

Clara was fat no longer: that growing phase had been brief. Today her step on the terrace, if more assertive, was not much heavier than it had been as a child's. Her height and her feverish fair good looks were set off by clothes that showed an expensive taste – taste that she could not fully indulge, yet. She glanced, without shock as without feeling, at the site of the winter-garden – here some exotic creepers had already perished against the exposed wall. Then she slanted downwards across the lawn, into one of the paths that entered the woods of ilex. These sombre pleasure-grounds, unchanging as might have been a photograph of themselves, were charged for her with a past that, though discontinuous, maintained a continuous atmosphere of its own. To these she had sometimes escaped; they had equally been the scene of those inescapable games with Paul. She could have thought she heard what war had suspended – still dead leaves being brushed from hard paths with stiff brooms. To each cut-out of a branch against the diluted sky attached some calculation or fear or unhopeful triumph. Every glade, every seat, every vista at the turn of a path only drew out the story. To be coming, for instance, into view of the lake, and of the kiosk reflected in its apathetic water, was to breathe the original horror of Paul's telling her that 'they' kept the headless ladies locked up in there. He had looked in, he told her, between the slats of the shutters, but could not advise her to do the same. Now, with the shutters gone, she saw mildewed inside walls: as she stared at the kiosk, like someone performing an exercise, even lungfuls of horror seemed salutary. No, there was nothing, no single thing, in the history of Clara at Sandyhill that she could not remember. – Yet, was there?

With regard to no place other than Sandyhill could this opening and splitting wider of a crevasse in her memory have alarmed her more. At its deepness, she dared not attempt to guess; its extent, if it ever did stop, must simply wait to be seen.

That, as things turned out, was to be Clara's last visit to Sandyhill, except for the day of Cousin Rosanna's funeral. Neither Clara nor Paul received any deathbed summons: their cousin's loss of interest must have been so entire that she could not be bothered putting them through the last hoop. The funeral was correct but for one detail – Paul failed to be there. Stationed far up north, he had (his telegram told them) missed the necessary train. Clara returned to London that same evening, leaving Aunt Addie at Sandyhill to console the servants and to receive Paul whenever he should arrive. A week later, fairly late in the evening, Aunt Addie came stagger-ing into Clara's St John's Wood flat with the clock embraced inside her exhausted arms. It was not packed – in a packing-case it might have got knocked about, in which case it might have stopped. As it was, it had gone on ticking, and had struck twice in the train, to the interest of everyone, and once again in the lift, coming up here to Clara's flat.

'I took the precaution of travelling first class,' Aunt Addie said. 'I knew you would want to have it as soon as possible. Look, I am putting it *here*, for the time being' – (that meant, the only table the size of the room allowed) – 'but when I get my breath back, we'll put it where you intend. You must often have seen it here, in your mind's eye. – Not, I hope, on anything it could fall off?'

'In that case, I can only think of the floor.'

'Oh,' said Aunt Addie, preoccupied, 'I seem to have left fingerprints on the dome.' She breathed on the glass and began to polish them off. 'Naturally, you have had a good deal to think about. In fact, I should not be surprised if this changed the course of your life.'

'A clock – how could it?' said Clara wildly.

'No, I was referring to Cousin Rosanna's death, dear. I could already see some little changes in Paul.'

' . . . By the way, did Paul say anything when you took the clock?'

'Er, no,' said Aunt Addie, colouring faintly. 'He was not about, as it happened; he was so busy.'

Clara's life, ever since she had been told of the will (which was practically as far back as she could remember) had, of course, hinged on the prospect of this immense change. Not unreasonably, she expected everything to go better. She perceived that her nature was of the kind that is only able to flower in clement air: either wealth or reciprocal love, ideally both, were necessary. To begin with, she intended to buy herself surroundings that suited her, that would set her off. But chiefly, as her obsessive love for Henry became, in the course of nine years, the centre of everything, she had quite simply looked to her coming money for the one consummation of this, marriage. The humiliating uncertainties of their relationship, and, still more, the thought of him living there with his wife, were more of a torment than she had dared to allow. Humble about herself with regard to him, and humbly bare of illusions regarding Henry, she believed that her, Clara's, coming into her money would be the one thing needed to make him break with his wife. Should his career show damage from the divorce proceedings, he could afford to abandon it: she could compensate him. She could buy open some other door for his ambition. As for love – so far Henry had only loved her, as you might say, on trust. She had yet to gain him wholly by showing what she could, in the whole, be. Now she could feel the current of her nature stirring strongly under the thinning ice. Had it been the strength of the current that thinned the ice? Or had the ice had to be thinned by the breath of financial summer before the current, however strong, could be felt?

When Aunt Addie had gone, Clara tried again to realize all that was now, since last week, within her reach. She went across to the mirror and stood and stared at herself imperiously. But the current, without warning, ceased to be felt: no kind of exultation was possible. The newly-arrived clock, chopping off each second to fall and perish, recalled how many seconds had gone to make up her years, how many of these had been either null or bitter, how many had been void before the void claimed them. She had been subject to waiting as to an illness; the tissues of her being had been consumed by it. Was it impossible that the past should be able to injure the future irreparably? Turning away from the mirror, she made herself face the clock; she looked through into the nothing behind its hands. Turning away from the clock, she went to the telephone.

Henry's reply, at the same time cautious and social, warned her that, as so often at his hour, he was not alone. – All the same: 'What do you think? My clock has arrived,' she said. 'Aunt Addie has just brought it, from Sandyhill.'

'Indeed. Which is that?'

'Which clock? Surely you know, Henry. The one I must have so often told you about . . . Didn't I? Well, it's with me now, in this room. Can you hear it ticking?'

'No, I'm afraid not.'

She got up, pulling the telephone with her as far as the cord would go, then stretched the receiver at arm's length towards the glass dome. After some seconds she went on: 'You heard it *that* time? I like to think we are hearing the same thing. They say it has never stopped for more than a hundred years: don't you think it sounds like that? Cousin Rosanna insisted I was to have this clock.'

'Thrown in,' Henry said, 'with the pound of tea.' But his voice, besides being ironical, was distrait: all the time, he was thinking up some story that could account for his end of the conversation, and was being careful to make, in his wife's hearing, no remark that would not fit in with that.

'Yes,' said Clara, quivering, 'with, with my pound of tea. Do you think that could mean she did really care for me? I wish I could think so. There is something frightening about the death of someone who always kept one so near her, without love. Still, there it is: she's dead. And because of that – Henry, tell me again that you're glad?'

'Of course.'

'For both our sakes – yours and mine?'

'Of course . . . Well, this has been nice, but I fear I must say good night. We were thinking of listening to the European news.'

'Stop, wait, don't go for a minute! I can't bear this clock! I dread it; I can't stay with it in the room! What am I to do this evening? Where can I go?'

'I'm afraid I can't think, really.'

'There's no *possible* chance you . . . ?'

'No, I'm afraid not.'

'But you do love me?'

'Of course.'

So Clara, to stop herself thinking, rang up two or three friends, but not one of them answered: their telephones went on ringing. Therefore she put on her overcoat, found her torch, dropped down in the lift and went for a walk in the black-out. It was late enough for the streets to be almost empty. Clara, walking at high speed into the solid darkness, was surprised all over her body to feel no impact: she seemed to pass like a ghost through an endless wall. No segment of moon peered at her, no stars guided. Brought to a halt for breath, she began to spy with her torch at the things round her – a post-box, a corner with no railing, the white plate of a street-name. Nothing told her anything, except one thing – unless she had lost her memory, she had lost her way. She dived into a wardens' post to ask where this was, or where she was, and in the glare in there they all stared at her. 'Where did you want to get back to?' someone said, and for either a second or an eternity she fancied she might be unable to tell him . . . When Clara once again found herself at the portico of the block of flats where she lived, tomorrow had begun to curdle the sky. Having hesitated with her key in her own door she let herself in and went quickly through to her bedroom. But the wall between herself and the clock was thin. Getting up, lying down, getting up, she continued, until her telephone called her, her search for the ear-plugs that Aunt Addie had given her when first the raids began.

When Aunt Addie rang up, two mornings later, it was to announce that, after a search of London, she *had* succeeded in finding an old man to wind the clock. 'I knew you'd be anxious; I know I was! Providentially, however, I am in time.'

'In time for what?'

'For the day it is always wound. So you will know when to expect the man,' said Aunt Addie.

Therefore Clara, who started for work at cock-crow, not to return till some time on in the evening, told the porter to admit, on whichever day he should come, an old man to wind the clock in her flat. The day must have been Friday, for that evening she came home to find a door ajar. There was somebody, besides the clock, in possession – this turned out to be Paul. Having arranged the black-out and turned the lights on, he was comfortably sitting on her sofa, smoking one of his superior cigarettes. He was, of course, in khaki. 'Really, what hours you keep!' he said. 'However, I've had my dinner. I trust you have?' At this point, as though recollecting himself, Paul sprang up and smote Clara matily on the shoulder. He then stood back to inspect her. 'Radiant – and can one wonder?' he added. 'By the way, I was sorry to miss you the other day. I hope I wasn't missed?'

'At the funeral? Everyone thought that looked pretty queer; and Cousin Rosanna, of course, would have been furious.'

'If so, most unfairly. I missed my train that morning because I had made a night of it, and I made a night of it because I felt like hell. You might not think so, and I was surprised myself. After all, she had never wanted anything.'

'Never wanted us to love her?'

'Well, if you put it that way – never gave us a chance. However, I snapped out of that. I feel fine now.'

'How nice . . . How is Edmée?'

'I thought her looking wonderfully herself. And how is Henry? As nice as ever?'

Clara said frigidly: 'How did you get in?'

'A civil old burglar, or somebody, let me in. He said nothing to me, so I said nothing to him. He put the glass back on the clock and went away quietly, so I decided to wait.'

Paul, whose way of standing about was characteristic, did not seem disposed to sit down again. Having flicked ash into a shell not meant for an ashtray, he remained with his back to the mantelpiece, fixing on nothing particular his tolerant, narrow-eyed, level look. His uniform fitted and suited him just a degree too well, and gave him the air of being on excellent terms with war. He had thickened slightly: otherwise, little change appeared in the dark bullet-head, rather Mongolian features and compact, tactile hands that had made him by turns agreeably disagreeable and disagreeably agreeable as a little boy. 'Tick-tock, tick-tock,' he said, out of the blue. 'Sounds louder than ever, in here; though as nice as ever, of course. You don't think it's a little large for the room?'

'I shall be moving soon, I expect,' said Clara, who had not only sat down but put her feet up on her sofa, to show that Paul's presence affected her in no sort of way.

'Oh, shall you really? How right.' Paul glanced down at the toe of one shoe, lifted his eyebrows and went on: 'This isn't, of course, a point I should ever bother to raise, but you do of course realize that nothing should have left Sandyhill until the valuation had been made for probate?'

'I don't suppose Aunt Addie understood that. You could always have stopped her!'

'On the contrary: the devoted creature nipped off to the train with the clock while my back was turned. When I thought of your face at this end, I must say I had to smile.'

'Really,' said Clara touchily, 'why?'

Paul not only looked at his cousin but, somehow, gave the impression that only indolence kept him from looking harder. 'It is just as well, as we both see now,' he observed, 'that the point of that joke *is* known only to you and me. That you have never enjoyed it seems unfair. Still, I suppose it is partly in view of that that I've come round this evening to do the handsome thing – '

'Yes, I wondered what you had come about.'

'I make you an offer, Clara. I'll buy you out of the clock. Cash down – as soon as I touch the cash.'

Clara, not so much as raising her eyes from her rather too delicate ringless hands, said: 'Cousin Rosanna warned me this might happen.'

'What you mean – and how stupid of me, and how right you are – is that cash is no longer an object with you, either? Look, I'll go one better: I'll take the clock away for nothing. And better still, I'll take it away tonight.'

Clara went rigid immediately: her cheeks flamed and her voice shot into the particular note for so long familiar to her and Paul.

'Why should you take it simply because you want it?'

'Why should you keep it when you don't want it, simply because I do?' Even Paul's imperturbability showed, as of old, a crack. 'Well, we both know why – and better leave it at that. All the same, Clara, have some sense. It's one thing to cut your nose off to spite my face. But is it really worth going crackers?'

'Crackers – what do you mean?'

'Well, look at yourself in the glass.'

The mirror being exactly opposite the sofa, Clara had looked before she could stop herself. As quickly, she said: 'I don't see anything wrong. And didn't you say I was looking radiant?'

'Because, frankly, my one thought was, "We must keep her calm".' Paul, having ground out his cigarette with an air at once resigned and concerned, came to sit down on the sofa beside Clara. He pushed her feet off gently to make room for himself. Leaning a little towards her, he placed one hand, like a hostage, or like an invitation to read his entire motive, palm upwards on the brocade between them. His nearness enveloped Clara in a sense of complicity, frightening because it was acutely familiar, more frightening because she could not guess at its source. While his eyes expressed no more than good-natured fondness, and his manner

regretful conciliation, both conveyed a threat for which no
memory could account. 'I hate,' he said, 'to see you all shot
up. Doesn't Henry?'

'Why should he? I haven't asked him.'

Her cousin, at once quickly and darkly, said: 'Possibly better not.
I'm all, if we can, for keeping this in the family.'

'The clock?'

'No, I mean its effect on you. When you think it's only three
days since Aunt Addie imported it. – And to think how well she
meant, the old dear!'

Rearing up among the cushions at her end of the sofa, Clara
exclaimed: 'You think that will work? Cousin Rosanna intended
the clock for me. So this is just one thing you must do without. I
would sooner drop it out of the window . . . '

'I am sure you would,' said Paul. 'In fact, I expect you've tried?'

He was right. Once in the small hours of a sleepless night, once
on the occasion of an unnerving return home, that solution had
already offered itself. Clara had turned the lights out, opened her
eighth-floor window, found her way to the clock by the noise it
made in the dark and gone so far as to balance it on the
window-sill. In her finger-tips, as they supported it, could be felt
its confident vibration – through the dome, through the stand
projecting some inches into the night. She had awaited in vain
some infinitesimal check, some involuntary metallic shudder with
which the clock should anticipate its last second, the first it would
not consume for a hundred years. Annihilation waited – the
concrete roadway under the block of flats. By the concrete roadway
the clock would be struck, not to strike again. Towards the dawn
of the coming, unthreatened day, some early goer to work would
halt, step back and bend his torch on the cogs, uncoiled springs and
incomprehensible splinters that had startled him by crunching
under his boot. – But, suppose not. Suppose gravity failed? Or
suppose the tick stayed up here without the clock, or the nothing
that had shown through its skeleton form continued to bear its
skeleton shadow? If what she purposed to do could *be* done, how
was it it had never been done before? . . . Clara, quailing, hoped
that she only did so before the conventionality of her own nature.
She was not the woman, it seemed (if there were indeed such a
woman) who could drop a clock from the window of a St John's
Wood flat. The chance of somebody passing at the decisive second,
the immediate alarm to be raised by what would sound like a
bomb, the likelihood of the affair being traced to her, the attention
already drawn to the clock by its sentimental arrival with Aunt
Addie and her own talk about it with the flats porter – all these
Clara, too gladly, let weigh with her. She reprieved not so much

the clock as her own will. She had returned the clock to its place on the table – twice.

'However,' Paul said, 'if that's how you feel . . . I let you see that I want it – apparently, that's enough.' He shrugged his shoulders, and slowly withdrew his hand: the interlude of frankness could be taken as over. Getting up, he strolled across to the clock, and, taking up his stand between it and Clara, could be felt to hold communication with it. Intently stooping, he squinted into its works. 'Yes,' he said remotely, 'I am stuck on this clock. Always have been, and I suppose always shall.'

'Why?'

'Why should there be any why?' said Paul, without turning round. 'I am simply stuck on this clock. One is bound to be stuck on something: what is wrong with a clock? *Your* trouble seems to be that you are stuck on the past.'

Clara, eyes indecisively on Paul's khaki back, licked her lips once or twice before she actually spoke. Then she cried: 'Have you *no* idea that I've no idea what you mean? Or Cousin Rosanna, or Aunt Addie either? Unless you three are combining to send me mad, someone had better tell me what this is all about. As far as I know, the first time I saw that clock was the last day I spent with Rosanna at Sandyhill. I detest it, and should be glad if you'd tell me why. Every time I am told I remember something I don't remember, it turns out to be something about that clock; and there's such high feeling about it I don't know which way to turn. – Did you, for instance, once put the clock-glass over my head, and did I get stuck inside it?'

This engaged Paul's attention: he turned round slowly, gained time by soundlessly whistling, then said: 'You're not serious?' He considered her. 'But what a thing to forget! We damn' nearly chipped your face off. Besides, that came quite late on.'

'But late on in what?'

'In our story. If you'll tell me how much you've forgotten, I'll tell you where we begin. If you *have* forgotten, you must have some rather too good reason – in which case, don't I err in bringing the whole thing up? . . . Very well. Yes, I popped that thing over your head because it was time to stop you, and I thought that might do it. Stop you what? Stop you blackmailing me. We were by then no longer in the Garden of Eden, and I observed Rosanna showing the red light.' – At this point, Paul gave Clara a final suspicious look: what he saw appeared to convince him, for he went on: 'Since the day we did that with the clock you had almost never let up. It was, "Oh, Paul, I feel so wicked; we've been so wicked; I have simply got to confess to Cousin Rosanna!" Then, "Very well, kiss me, then perhaps I'll feel better, then perhaps I won't have to tell

Cousin Rosanna *this* time." And this year in, year out, my sweet, every holiday you and I were at Sandyhill. Castor oil got to be lovely compared to your upturned face. Your particular *mise en scène* was the ante-room: you used to put your ear to the clock glass and say, "You know, it *still* doesn't sound the same." That meant your feeling bad and my having to come across. To make things more interesting, one could never be certain that Rosanna might not pop in at one or the other door, not to speak of her passing the terrace window. You and me on such close terms (she wasn't to know the reason) and, of all places, right there by her precious clock – that *would* have finally torn it, for you and me.'

'You don't mean, she'd have cut us out of the will?'

'Well, Clara, ask yourself – would she not? Given, I mean, that peculiar obsession *she* had.'

'If Rosanna had an obsession, I don't remember that, either.' She attempted a wintry smile, and added: 'This seems to be like a whole continent that's submerged, you know.'

'Poetic idea,' Paul conceded, with a glance to the left of his cousin's ear. 'To return to Cousin Rosanna – you know how when you are waiting you have to look back and back again at the clock? Now our friend, as it happened, had been Rosanna's from girlhood, so it was this clock she connected with her particular habit – a habit she'd had every reason to form. There was nothing Rosanna did not know about waiting. Great-uncle, from whom she got Sandyhill and the money, did not quit the stage till she was well on in life. Therefore Rosanna waited, throughout what are called one's best years – not only for money, exactly like you and me, but for a young man, like, if I may say so, you. The young man – not a nice character, unlike Henry – wasn't moving till Rosanna could declare the bank open. Great-uncle, unfriendly to romance, lived just too long: by the time the money came to Rosanna the man had lost heart and married somebody else. And in those days, if you remember, that was considered final. So Rosanna, like the great girl she was, in her way, cut her losses in the romance direction and went all out to make the money her big thing. She felt free, all things considered, to buy what she liked with it; she jingled her new purse and looked around for her fun. You and I were her fun. Can't you see how the thing worked out? The younger the heirs you name, the longer they have to wait, and the more the waiting can do to them. Again, *she'd* expected both love and money, and got money only: can you blame her if she was damned if she'd contemplate you and me, or you or me, having both? So my marriage – than which I'm sure there are many worse – and your, er, stalemate with regard to Henry, suited her book ideally – couldn't have suited better. As for you and me, biting bits out of each other all over Sandyhill – how her dear old good face used to light up! The better we loathed each other, the better she liked us. But then came what looked like our interlude – that *that* was no more than a new and more subtle manifestation of mutual hate was, I suppose unavoidably lost on her. Therefore that, as I tell you, did damn' nearly cook our goose.'

'How ironical,' supplied Clara, 'that would have been, we well know. – All the same, what made her so set on my having to have the clock?'

'I can only think, because you were a fellow-woman. It was Rosanna's way of saying, "Over to you!"'

'But, so equally set on the clock never being yours?'

'*That* couldn't be clearer. I'd more than shown that I liked it; I'd asked her for it point-blank. I was a man, so she liked my going without. Yes, I did get those cheques, I know – as you also noted. She liked me to make a fool of myself *qua* man. I wanted the clock, so you were to have it – could the mental process be more straight-forward? . . . Yes, I tell you, I asked for it. I was a fool, at nine, and that clock was the only thing in that god-awful house I liked. So I piped up. That was the day our bit of trouble began.

'It was one of those typical headachy Sandyhill March mornings – house heated to bursting-point and a livery sun outdoors. A family gathering was in progress – you and your aunt and your mother had come down for the day. I mouldered off by myself, as I frequently did do, to watch the old clock at its cheering work. Rosanna came in and said, "You like that, don't you?" to which I said, "Yes, I should like to have it." To which she said, "Yes, I daresay you would." At which point you came prancing into the room. I suppose you were about six, and your mother had got you up in a perfectly sickening little scarlet coat, like a monkey wears on a barrel-organ. The moment was jam for Rosanna: she turned to you and she said, "Clara, one day I intend *you* to have that clock. Do you know it has never stopped, and it never will?" You registered pleasure, and I went off down the woods. – *None* of this comes back?'

'Nothing,' said Clara firmly – with growing fear.

'So that really you don't remember my catching you, later on, in the ante-room, you having glided back for a private gloat at your clock? Or what I said, or we did, or what happened then?'

'No, *no.* Why? What do you mean? Paul you're simply making me worse. – And what are you *doing*? Leave that alone: *it's mine!*'

'That's just why I'm asking you to step over here,' said Paul, who was lifting the dome with becoming care, to place it on the table beside the clock. 'Why? To make an experiment. Let's face it. Either this works – which it may not – or I take you by hand tomorrow to a psychiatrist. Blood is thicker than water, after all. Come on – I can't wait all night; I have got a date.'

Hooking his arm round Clara's reluctant waist, Paul approached his cousin relentlessly to the clock. After four or five seconds of this enforced staring into the diligent works, Clara began to relax – was she hypnotized? In the absolute nothing behind the clock's anatomy there appeared and began to dilute, like colour dropped into water, the red of the Sandyhill ante-room wallpaper: meanwhile, there crept on another sense the smell of pitched pine exasperated by heating. There could be felt the stare of a draped and open door-window, in which, from moment to moment, somebody might appear. The murmur of voices out of the winter-garden hung on the hazy terrace behind Paul's voice.

'*I'll tell you something, Clara. Have you ever* SEEN *a minute? Have you actually had one wriggling inside your hand? Did you know if you keep your finger inside a clock for a minute, you can pick out that very minute and take it home for your own?*' So it is Paul who stealthily lifts the dome off. It is Paul who selects the finger of Clara's that is to be guided, shrinking, then forced wincing into the works, to be wedged in them, bruised in them, bitten into and eaten up by the cogs. '*No, you have got to keep it there, or you will lose the minute. I am doing the counting – the counting up to sixty.*' . . . But there is to be no sixty. The ticking stops.

We have stopped the clock.

The hundred years are all angry. '*Stop crying, idiot: that won't start it again!*' . . . But oh, oh but, it won't let my finger go! . . . O-o-h! . . . '*Suck it, be quiet, don't make a noise!*' . . . What have you made me do?' '*You wanted to.*' You made me want to . . . What shall we, what shall we, what shall we do, do, *do?* . . . '*You go out and skip about on the terrace, make them keep on watching you, then they won't come in.*' But what will you do? '*Something.*' But it's stopped ticking! . . . '*I tell you, go out and skip about on the terrace.*'

For the second time, Paul withdrew Clara's finger, with a painful jerk, from the clock which had stopped ticking. Her finger was bitten, but not so badly: it had grown too big to go in so deep this time. He was, meanwhile, going on smoothly: 'We were in luck that Friday – because it *was* a Friday, of course. All I did was put the glass back and walk away. But half an hour later, the regular chap from Southstone turned up to wind it. With a mouth that butter couldn't possibly melt in, I tailed him into the ante-room, just to see. The clock stopped and that half-hour missing made even him turn pale. He sent me to find Rosanna. I was unable to. I came back to watch him put through a long and amazing job. The ladies were upstairs, tying up your finger. By the time he had got the clock set and going, he found he had run things fine for his bus home. He decided, therefore, as Rosanna was missing, not to report the occurrence till the following week. Owing to hurry or worry, the poor brute, he shot out of Sandyhill gate and across the main street in time to be flattened out by a bus coming the other way. Any evidence perished with him: Rosanna was spared the knowledge. In gratitude, you and I subscribed sixpence each towards the funeral wreath. But of course you would never remember *that?*'

'I remember giving the sixpence for the wreath,' said Clara slowly, not looking up from her finger.

'But only that?'

'No, *not* only that – thank you, Paul.' There ensued an unavoidable pause, at the end of which Clara said: 'I expect you would like to go now? I think I heard you say you had got a date?'

'Nothing need stand, if you'd rather not be alone?'

'Thank you very much; I, I shall sit with my memories. I expect to spend some time getting to know them.' Turning away, with all the detachment possible, she occupied herself in emptying Paul's ash from the shell into a more suitable tray. 'Oh, by the way, Paul,' she added, 'do by all means have the clock. Aunt Addie ought to have known that you wanted it. And, apart from any sentiment of Rosanna's, it means nothing to me. Won't you take it along now?'

'Thanks, that is nice of you, Clara,' said Paul promptly. 'Actually, under the circumstances, I could not very easily take it along this evening; and in fact I have nowhere to put it for the duration. Could you keep it for me, or would it be in your way?'

'There is no reason why it should be in my way; as I say, I expect to move to a larger flat. It is not very useful at present to tell the time by, but apart from that I should never know it was there.'

The Cheery Soul

On arriving, I first met the aunt of whom they had told me, the aunt who had not yet got over being turned out of Italy. She sat resentfully by the fire, or rather the fireplace, and did not look up when I came in. The acrid smell that curled through the drawing-room could be traced to a grate full of sizzling fir cones that must have been brought in damp. From the mantelpiece one lamp, with its shade tilted, shed light on the parting of the aunt's hair. It could not be said that the room was cheerful: the high, curtained bow windows made draughty caves; the armchairs and sofas, pushed back against the wall, wore the air of being renounced for ever. Only a row of discreet greeting-cards (few with pictures) along the top of a bureau betrayed the presence of Christmas. There was no holly, and no pieces of string.

I coughed and said: 'I feel I should introduce myself,' and followed this up by giving the aunt my name, which she received with apathy. When she did stir, it was to look at the parcel that I coquettishly twirled from its loop of string. 'They're not giving presents, this year,' she said in alarm. 'If I were you, I should put that back in my room.'

'It's just – my rations.'

'In that case,' she remarked, 'I really don't know what you had better do.' Turning away from me she picked up a small bent poker, and with this began to interfere with the fir cones, of which several, steaming, bounced from the grate. 'A good wood stove,' she said, 'would make all the difference. At Sienna, though they say it is cold in winter, we never had troubles of this kind.'

'How would it be,' I said, 'if I sat down?' I pulled a chair a little on to the hearthrug, if only for the idea of the thing. 'I gather our hosts are out. I wonder where they have gone to?'

'Really, I couldn't tell you.'

'My behaviour,' I said, 'has been shockingly free-and-easy. Having pulled the bell three times, waited, had a go at the knocker . . .'

'. . . I heard,' she said, slightly bowing her head.

'I gave *that* up, tried the door, found it unlocked, so just marched in.'

'Have you come about something?' she said with renewed alarm.

'Well, actually, I fear that I've come to stay. They have been so very kind as to . . . '

' . . . Oh, I remember – someone *was* coming.' She looked at me rather closely. 'Have you been here before?'

'Never. So this is delightful,' I said firmly. 'I am billeted where I work' (I named the industrial town, twelve miles off, that was these days in a ferment of war production), 'my landlady craves my room for these next two days for her daughter, who is on leave, and, on top of this, to be frank, I'm a bit old-fashioned: Christmas alone in a strange town didn't appeal to me. So you can see how I sprang at . . . '

'Yes, I can see,' she said. With the tongs, she replaced the cones that had fallen out of the fire. 'At Orvieto,' she said, 'the stoves were so satisfactory that one felt no ill effects from the tiled floors.'

As I could think of nothing to add to this, I joined her in listening attentively to the hall clock. My entry into the drawing-room having been tentative, I had not made so bold as to close the door behind me, so a further coldness now seeped through from the hall. Except for the clock – whose loud tick was reluctant – there was not another sound to be heard: the very silence seemed to produce echoes. The Rangerton-Karneys' absence from their own house was becoming, virtually, ostentatious. 'I understand,' I said, 'that they are tremendously busy. Practically never not on the go.'

'They expect to have a finger in every pie.'

Their aunt's ingratitude shocked me. She must be (as they had hinted) in a difficult state. They had always spoken with the most marked forbearance of her enforced return to them out of Italy. In England, they said, she had no other roof but theirs, and they were constantly wounded (their friends told me) by her saying she would have preferred internment in Italy.

In common with all my fellow-workers at — , I had a high regard for the Rangerton-Karneys, an admiration tempered, perhaps, with awe. Their energy in the promotion of every war effort was only matched by the austerity of their personal lives. They appeared to have given up almost everything. That they never sat down could be seen from their drawing-room chairs. As 'local people' of the most solid kind they were on terms with the bigwigs of every department, the key minds of our small but now rather important town. Completely discreet, they were palpably 'in the know'.

Their house in the Midlands, in which I now so incredibly found myself, was largish, built of the local stone, *circa* 1860 I should say from its style. It was not very far from a railway junction, and at a still less distance from a canal. I had evaded the strictures on Christmas travel by making the twelve-mile journey by bicycle – indeed, the suggestion that I should do this played a prominent part in their invitation. So I bicycled over. My little things for the two nights were contained in one of those useful American-cloth suitcases, strapped to my back-wheel carrier, while my parcel of rations could be slung, I found, from my handlebar. The bumping of this parcel on my right knee as I pedalled was a major embarrassment. To cap this, the misty damp of the afternoon had caused me to set off in a mackintosh. At the best of times I am not an expert cyclist. The grateful absence of hills (all this country is very flat) was cancelled out by the greasiness of the roads, and army traffic often made me dismount – it is always well to be on the safe side. Now and then, cows or horses loomed up abruptly to peer at me over the reeking hedgerows. The few anonymous villages I passed through all appeared, in the falling dusk, to be very much the same: their inhabitants wore an air of war-time discretion, so I did not dare risk snubs by asking how far I had come. My pocket map, however, proved less unhelpful when I found that I had been reading it upside down. When, about half way, I turned on my lamp, I watched mist curdle under its wobbling ray. My spectacles dimmed steadily; my hands numbed inside my knitted gloves (the only Christmas present I had received so far) and the mist condensed on my muffler in fine drops.

I own that I had sustained myself through this journey on thoughts of the cheery welcome ahead. The Rangerton-Karneys' invitation, delivered by word of mouth only three days ago, had been totally unexpected, as well as gratifying. I had had no reason to think they had taken notice of me. We had met rarely, when I reported to the committees on which they sat. That the brother and two sisters (so much alike that people took them for triplets) had attracted *my* wistful notice, I need not say. But not only was my position a quite obscure one; I am not generally sought out; I make few new friends. None of my colleagues had been to the Rangerton-Karneys' house: there was an idea that they had given up guests. As the news of their invitation to me spread (and I cannot say I did much to stop it spreading) I rose rapidly in everyone's estimation.

In fact, their thought had been remarkably kind. Can you wonder that I felt myself favoured? I was soon, now, to see their erstwhile committee faces wreathed with seasonable and genial smiles. I never was one to doubt that people unbend at home. Perhaps a little feverish from my cycling, I pictured blazing hearths through holly-garlanded doors.

Owing to this indulgence in foolish fancy, my real arrival rather deflated me.

'I suppose they went out after tea?' I said to the aunt.

'After lunch, I think,' she replied. 'There was no tea.' She picked up her book, which was about Mantegna, and went on reading, pitched rather tensely forward to catch the light of the dim-bulbed lamp. I hesitated, then rose up saying that perhaps I had better deliver my rations to the cook. 'If you can,' she said, turning over a page.

The whirr of the clock preparing to strike seven made me jump. The hall had funny acoustics – so much so that I strode across the wide breaches from rug to rug rather than hear my step on the stone flags. Draught and dark coming down a shaft announced the presence of stairs. I saw what little I saw by the flame of a night-light, palpitating under a blue glass inverted shade. The hall and the staircase windows were not blacked out yet. (Back in the drawing-room, I could only imagine, the aunt must have so far bestirred herself as to draw the curtains.)

The kitchen was my objective – as I had said to the aunt. I pushed at a promising baize door: it immediately opened upon a vibration of heat and rich, heartening smells. At these, the complexion of everything changed once more. If my spirits, just lately, had not been very high, this was no doubt due to the fact that I had lunched on a sandwich, then had not dared leave my bicycle to look for a cup of tea. I was in no mood to reproach the Rangerton-Karneys for this Christmas break in their well-known austere routine.

But, in view of this, the kitchen was a surprise. Warm, and spiced with excellent smells, it was in the dark completely but for the crimson glow from between the bars of the range. A good deal puzzled, I switched the light on – the black-out, here, had been punctiliously done.

The glare made me jump. The cook must have found, for her own use, a quadruple-power electric bulb. This now fairly blazed down on the vast scrubbed white wood table, scored and scarred by decades of the violent chopping of meat. I looked about – to be staggered by what I did not see. Neither on range, table, nor outsize dresser were there signs of the preparation of any meal. Not a plate, not a spoon, not a canister showed any signs of action. The heat-vibrating top of the range was bare; all the pots and pans were up above, clean and cold, in their places along the rack. I went so far as to open the oven door – a roasting smell came out, but there was nothing inside. A tap drip-drop-dripped on an upturned bowl in the sink – but nobody had been peeling potatoes there.

I put my rations down on the table and was, dumbfounded,

preparing to turn away, when a white paper on the white wood caught my eye. This paper, in an inexpert line of block-printing, bore the somewhat unnecessary statement: I AM NOT HERE. To this was added, in brackets: 'Look in the fish kettle.' Though this be no affair of mine, could I fail to follow it up? Was this some new demonstration of haybox cookery; was I to find our dinner snugly concealed? I identified the fish kettle, a large tin object (about the size, I should say, of an infant's bath) that stood on a stool half-way between the sink and range. It wore a tight-fitting lid, which came off with a sort of plop: the sound in itself had an ominous hollowness. Inside, I found, again, only a piece of paper. This said: 'Mr & the 2 Misses Rangerton-Karney can boil their heads. This holds 3.'

I felt that the least I could do for my hosts the Rangerton-Karneys was to suppress the unkind joke, so badly out of accord with the Christmas spirit. I *could* have dropped the paper straight into the kitchen fire, but on second thoughts I went back to consult the aunt. I found her so very deep in Mantegna as to be oblivious of the passage of time. She clearly did not like being interrupted. I said: 'Can you tell me if your nephew and nieces had any kind of contretemps with their cook today?'

She replied: 'I make a point of not asking questions.'

'Oh, so do I,' I replied, 'in the normal way. But I fear . . . '

'You fear what?'

'She's gone,' I said. 'Leaving this . . . '

The aunt looked at the paper, then said: 'How curious.' She added: 'Of course, she has gone: that happened a year ago. She must have left several messages, I suppose. I remember that Etta found one in the mincing machine, saying to tell them to mince their gizzards. Etta seemed very much put out. That was *last* Christmas Eve, I remember – dear me, what a coincidence . . . So you found this, did you?' she said, re-reading the paper with less repugnance than I should have wished to see. 'I expect, if you went on poking about the kitchen . . . '

Annoyed, I said tartly: 'A reprehensible cook!'

'No worse than other English cooks,' she replied. 'They all declare they have never heard of a *pasta*, and that oil in cookery makes one repeat. But I always found her cheerful and kind. And of course I miss her – Etta's been cooking since.' (This was the elder Miss Rangerton-Karney.)

'But look,' I said, 'I was led to *this* dreadful message, by another one, on the table. *That* can't have been there a year.'

'I suppose not,' the aunt said, showing indifference. She picked up her book and inclined again to the lamp.

I said: 'You don't think some other servant . . . '

She looked at me like a fish.

'They *have* no other servants. Oh no: not since the cook . . . '

Her voice trailed away. 'Well, it's all very odd, I'm sure.'

'It's worse than odd, my dear lady: there won't be any dinner.'

She shocked me by emitting a kind of giggle. She said: 'Unless they *do* boil their heads.'

The idea that the Rangerton-Karneys might be out on a cook-hunt rationalized this perplexing evening for me. I am always more comfortable when I can tell myself that people are, after all, behaving accountably. The Rangerton-Karneys always acted in trio. The idea that one of them should stay at home to receive me while the other two went ploughing round the dark country would, at this crisis, never present itself. The Rangerton-Karneys' three sets of thoughts and feelings always appeared to join at the one root: one might say that they had a composite character. One thing, I could reflect, about misadventures is that they make for talk and often end in a laugh. I tried in vain to picture the Rangerton-Karneys laughing – for that was a thing I had never seen.

But if Etta is now resigned to doing the cooking . . . ? I thought better not to puzzle the thing out.

Screening my electric torch with my fingers past the uncurtained windows, I went upstairs to look for what might be my room. In my other hand I carried my little case – to tell the truth, I was anxious to change my socks. Embarking on a long passage, with doors ajar, I discreetly projected my torch into a number of rooms. All were cold; some were palpably slept in, others dismantled. I located the resting-places of Etta, Max and Paulina by the odour of tar soap, shoe-leather and boiled woollen underclothes that announced their presences in so many committee rooms. At an unintimate distance along the passage, the glint of my torch on Florentine bric-à-brac suggested the headquarters of the aunt. I did at last succeed, by elimination, in finding the spare room prepared for me. They had put me just across the way from their aunt. My torch and my touch revealed a made-up bed, draped in a glacial white starched quilt, two fringed towels straddling the water-jug, and virgin white mats to receive my brushes and comb. I successively bumped my knee (the knee still sore from the parcel) on two upright chairs. Yes, this must be the room for me. Oddly enough, it was much less cold than the others – but I did not think of that at the time. Having done what was necessary to the window, I lit up, to consider my new domain.

Somebody had been lying on my bed. When I rest during the day, I always remove the quilt, but whoever it was had neglected to do this. A deep trough, with a map of creases, appeared. The

creases, however, did not extend far. Whoever it was had lain here
in a contented stupor.

I worried – Etta might blame me. To distract my thoughts, I
opened my little case and went to put my things on the dressing-
table. The mirror was tilted upwards under the light, and something was written on it in soap: DEARIE, DON'T MIND ME. I at once
went to the washstand, one corner blunted by writing. On my way
back, I kicked over a black bottle, which, so placed on the floor as to
be in easy reach from the bed, now gaily and noisily bowled away.
It was empty – I had to admit that its contents, breathed out again,
gave that decided character to my room.

The aunt was to be heard, pattering up the stairs. Was this
belated hostess-ship on her part? She came into view of my door,
carrying the night-light from the hall table. Giving me a modest,
affronted look she said: 'I thought I'd tidy my hair.'

'The cook has been lying on my bed.'

'That would have been very possible, I'm afraid. She was
often a little – if you know what I mean. But, she left last
Christmas.'

'She's written something.'

'I don't see what one can do,' the aunt said, turning into her
room. For my part, I dipped a towel into the jug and reluctantly
tried to rub out the cook's message, but this only left a blur all over
the glass. I applied to this the drier end of the towel. Oddly enough
(perhaps) I felt fortified: this occult good feeling was, somehow,
warming. The cook was supplying that touch of nature I had
missed since crossing the Rangerton-Karneys' threshold. Thus,
when I stepped back for another look at the mirror, I was barely
surprised to find that a sprig of mistletoe had been twisted around
the cord of the hanging electric light.

My disreputable psychic pleasure was to be interrupted. Downstairs, in the caves of the house, the front door bell jangled, then
jangled again. This was followed by an interlude with the knocker:
an imperious rat-a-tat-tat. I called across to the aunt: 'Ought one of
us to go down? It might be a telegram.'

'I don't think so – why?'

We heard the glass door of the porch (the door through which I
had made my so different entry) being rattled open; we heard the
hall traversed by footsteps with the weight of authority. In
response to a mighty '*Anyone there?*' I defied the aunt's judgment
and went hurrying down. Coming on a policeman outlined in the
drawing-room door, my first thought was that this must be about
the black-out. I edged in, silent, just behind the policeman: he
looked about him suspiciously, then saw me. 'And who might you
be?' he said. The bringing out of his notebook gave me stage fright

during my first and other replies. I explained that the Rangerton-Karneys had asked me to come and stay.

'Oh, they did?' he said. 'Well, that is a laugh. Seen much of them?'

'Not so far.'

'Well, you won't.' I asked why: he ignored my question, asked for all my particulars, quizzed my identity card. 'I shall check up on all this,' he said heavily. 'So they asked you for Christmas, did they? And just *when*, may I ask, was this invitation issued?'

'Well, er – three days ago.'

This made me quite popular. He said: 'Much as I thought. Attempt to cover their tracks and divert suspicion. I daresay you blew off all round about them having asked you here?'

'I may have mentioned it to one or two friends.'

He looked pleased again and said: 'Just what they reckoned on. Not a soul was to guess they had planned to bolt. As for you – *you're* a cool hand, I must say. Just walked in, found the place empty and dossed down. Never once strike you there was anything fishy?'

'A good deal struck me,' I replied austerely. 'I took it however, that my host and his sisters had been unexpectedly called out – perhaps to look for a cook.'

'Ah, cook,' he said. 'Now what brought that to your mind?'

'Her whereabouts seemed uncertain, if you know what I mean.'

Whereupon, he whipped over several leaves of his notebook. 'The last cook employed here,' he said, 'was in residence here four days, departing last Christmas Eve, December 24th, 194–. We have evidence that she stated locally that she was unable to tolerate certain goings-on. She specified interference in her department, undue advantage taken of the rationing system, mental cruelty to an elderly female refugee . . . '

I interposed: 'That would certainly be the aunt.'

' . . . and failure to observe Christmas in the appropriate manner. On this last point she expressed herself violently. She further adduced (though with less violence of feeling) that her three employers were "dirty spies with their noses in everything". Subsequently, she withdrew this last remark; her words were, "I do not wish to make trouble, as I know how to make trouble in a way of my own." However, certain remarks she had let drop have been since followed up, and proved useful in our inquiries. Unhappily, we cannot check up on them, as the deceased met her end shortly after leaving this house.'

'The *deceased*?' I cried, with a sinking heart.

'Proceeding through the hall door and down the approach or avenue, in an almost total state of intoxication, she was heard singing "God rest you merry, gentlemen, let nothing you dismay". She also shouted: "Me for an English Christmas!" Accosting several pedestrians, she informed them that in her opinion times were not what they were. She spoke with emotion (being intoxicated) of turkey, mince pies, ham, plum pudding, etc. She was last seen hurrying in the direction of the canal, saying she must get brandy to make her sauce. She was last heard in the vicinity of the canal. The body was recovered from the canal on Boxing Day, December 26th, 194–.'

'But what,' I said, 'has happened to the Rangerton-Karneys?'

'Now, now!' said the policeman, shaking his finger sternly. 'You *may* hear as much as is good for you, one day – or you may not. Did you ever hear of the Safety of the Realm? I don't mind telling you one thing – you're lucky. You might have landed yourself in a nasty mess.'

'But, good heavens – the *Rangerton-Karneys*! They know everyone.'

'Ah!' he said, 'but it's that kind you have to watch.' Heavy with this reflection, his eye travelled over the hearth-rug. He stooped with a creak and picked up the aunt's book. 'Wop name,' he said, 'propaganda: sticks out a mile. Now, don't you cut off anywhere, while I am now proceeding to search the house.'

'Cut off?' I nearly said, 'What do you take me for?' Alone, I sat down in the aunt's chair and dropped a few more fir cones into the extinct fire.

Songs My Father Sang Me

'WHAT's the matter,' he asked, 'have I said something?'

Not troubling to get him quite into focus, she turned her head and said, 'No, why – did you say anything?'

'Or p'r'aps you don't like this place?'

'I don't mind it – why?' she said, looking round the night club, which was not quite as dark as a church, as though for the first time. At some tables you had to look twice, to see who was there; what lights there were were dissolved in a haze of smoke; the walls were rather vaultlike, with no mirrors; on the floor dancers drifted like pairs of vertical fish. He, meanwhile, studied her from across their table with neither anxiety nor acute interest, but with a dreamlike caricature of both. Then he raised the bottle between them and said, 'Mm-mm?' to which she replied by placing the flat of her hand mutely, mulishly, across the top of her glass. Not annoyed, he shrugged, filled up his own and continued, 'Then anything isn't really the matter, then?'

'This tune, this song, is the matter.'

'Oh – shall we dance?'

'No.' Behind her agelessly girlish face, sleekly framed by the cut of her fawn-blonde hair, there passed a wave of genuine trouble for which her features had no vocabulary. 'It's what they're playing – this tune.'

'It's pre-war,' he said knowledgeably.

'It's last war.'

'Well, last war's pre-war.'

'It's the tune my father remembered he used to dance to; it's the tune I remember him always trying to sing.'

'Why, is your father dead?'

'No, I don't suppose so; why?'

'Sorry,' he said quickly, 'I mean, if . . . '

'Sorry, why are you sorry?' she said, raising her eyebrows. 'Didn't I ever tell you about my father? I always thought he made me rather a bore. Wasn't it you I was telling about my father?'

'No. I suppose it must have been someone else. One meets so many people.'

'Oh, what,' she said, 'have I hurt your feelings? But you haven't got any feelings about me.'

'Only because you haven't got any feelings about me.'

'Haven't I?' she said, as though really wanting to know. 'Still, it hasn't seemed all the time as though we were quite a flop.'

'Look,' he said, 'don't be awkward. Tell me about your father.'

'He was twenty-six.'

'When?'

'How do you mean, "when"? Twenty-six was my father's age. He was tall and lean and leggy, with a casual sort of way of swinging himself about. He was fair, and the shape of his face was a rather long narrow square. Sometimes his eyes faded in until you could hardly see them; sometimes he seemed to be wearing a blank mask. You really only quite got the plan of his face when it was turned halfway between a light and a shadow – *then* his eyebrows and eyehollows, the dints just over his nostrils, the cut of his upper lip and the cleft in his chin, and the broken in-and-out outline down from his temple past his cheekbone into his jaw all came out at you, like a message you had to read in a single flash.'

She paused and lighted a cigarette. He said, 'You sound as though you had never got used to him.'

She went on, 'My father was one of the young men who were not killed in the last war. He was a man in the last war until that stopped; then I don't quite know what he was, and I don't think he ever quite knew either. He got his commission and first went out to France about 1915, I think he said. When he got leaves he got back to London and had good times, by which I mean something larky but quite romantic, in the course of one of which, I don't know which one, he fell in love with my mother and they used to go dancing, and got engaged in that leave and got married the next. My mother was a flapper, if you knew about flappers? They were the pin-ups *de ses jours*, and at the same time inspired idealistic feeling. My mother was dark and fluffy and as slim as a wraith; a great *glacé* ribbon bow tied her hair back and stood out like a calyx behind her face, and her hair itself hung down in a plume so long that it tickled my father's hand while he held her while they were dancing and while she sometimes swam up at him with her violet eyes. Each time he had to go back to the front again she was miserable, and had to put her hair up, because her relations said it was high time. But sometimes when he got back again on leave she returned to being a flapper again, to please him. Between his leaves she had to go back to live with her mother and sisters in West Kensington; and her sisters had a whole pack of business friends who had somehow never had to go near the front, and all these combined in an effort to cheer her up, but, as she always wrote to

my father, nothing did any good. I suppose everyone felt it was for
the best when they knew there was going to be the patter of little
feet. I wasn't actually *born* till the summer of 1918. If you remember, I told you my age last night.

'The first thing *I* remember, upon becoming conscious, was
living in one of those bungalows on the flats near Staines. The river
must have been somewhere, but I don't think I saw it. The only
point about that region is that it has no point and that it goes on and
on. I think there are floods there sometimes, there would be
nothing to stop them; a forest fire would be what is needed really,
but that would not be possible as there are no trees. It would have
looked better, really, just left as primeval marsh, but someone had
once said, "Let there be bungalows". If you ever motored anywhere near it you probably asked yourself who lives there, and why.
Well, my father and mother and I did, and why? – because it was
cheap, and there was no one to criticize how you were getting on.
Our bungalow was tucked well away in the middle, got at by a sort
of maze of in those days unmade roads. I'm glad to say I've
forgotten which one it was. Most of our neighbours kept themselves to themselves for, probably, like ours, the best reasons; but
most of them kept hens also; we didn't even do that. All round us,
nature ran riot between corrugated iron, clothes-lines and creosoted
lean-to sheds.

'I know that our bungalow had been taken furnished; the only
things we seemed to have of our own were a number of satin
cushions with satin fruits stitched on. In order to dislodge my
biscuit crumbs from the satin apples my mother used to shake the
cushions out of the window on to the lawn. Except for the
prettiness of the dandelions, our lawn got to look and feel rather
like a hearthrug; I mean, it got covered with threads and cinders
and shreds; once when I was crawling on it I got a pin in my hand,
another time I got sharp glass beads in my knee. The next-door
hens used to slip through and pick about; never, apparently, quite
in vain. At the far end, some Dorothy Perkins roses tried to climb
up a pergola that was always falling down. I remember my father
reaching up in his shirt-sleeves, trying to nail it up. Another thing
he had to do in our home was apply the whole of his strength to the
doors, french window and windows, which warped until they
would not open nor shut. I used to come up behind him and push
too.

'The war by now, of course, had been over for some years; my
father was out of the British Army and was what was called taking
his time and looking around. For how long he had been doing so I
can't exactly tell you. He not only read all the "post vacant"
advertisements every day but composed and succeeded in getting

printed an advertisement of himself, which he read aloud to me: it said he was prepared to go anywhere and try anything. I said, "But what's an ex-officer?," and he said, "I am." Our dining-room table, which was for some reason, possibly me, sticky, was always spread with new newspapers he had just brought home, and he used to be leaning over them on his elbows, biting harder and harder on the stem of his pipe. I don't think I discovered for some years later that the principal reason for newspapers is news. My father never looked at them for that reason – just as he always lost interest in any book in which he had lost his place. Or perhaps he was not in the mood for world events. My mother had never cared much for them at the best of times. "To think of all we expected after the war," she used to say to my father, from day to day.

'My mother, by this time, had had her hair shingled – in fact, *I* never remember her any other way than with a dark shaved point tapered down the back of her neck. I don't know when she'd begun to be jealous of him and me. Every time he came back from an interview that he hadn't got to or from an interview that hadn't come to anything, he used to bring me back something, to cheer himself up, and the wheels off all the mechanical toys got mixed with the beads and the threads and the cinders into our lawn. What my mother was really most afraid of was that my father would bundle us all off into the great open spaces, in order to start fresh somewhere and grow something. I imagine he knew several chaps who had, or were going to. After one or two starts on the subject he shut up, but I could see she could see he was nursing it. It frustrated her from nagging at him all out about not succeeding in getting a job in England: she was anxious not to provide an opening for him to say, "Well, there's always one thing we *could* do . . ." The hard glassy look her eyes got made them look like doll's eyes, which may partly have been what kept me from liking dolls. So they practically never talked about anything. I don't think she even knew he minded about her hair.

'You may be going to ask when my father sang. He often *began* to sing – when he hammered away at the pergola, when something he thought of suddenly struck him as good, when the heave he gave at the warped french window sent it flying open into the garden. He was constantly starting to sing, but he never got very far – you see, he had no place where he could sing unheard. The walls were thin and the lawn was tiny and the air round the bungalow was so silent and heavy that my mother was forced to listen to every note. The lordly way my father would burst out singing, like the lordly way he cocked his hat over one eye, had come to annoy her, in view of everything else. But the still more unfortunate thing was that my father only knew, or else only liked, two tunes, which were two tunes out of the bygone years which made him think of the war and being in love. Yes, they were dance tunes; yes, we have just heard one; yes, they also reminded my mother of war and love. So when he had got to the fourth or fifth bar of either, she would call out to know if he wanted to drive her mad. He would stop and say, "Sorry," but if he was in the mood he'd be well away, the next minute, with the alternative tune, and she would be put to the trouble of stopping that.

'Mother did not know what to look like now she was not a flapper. Mostly she looked like nothing – I wonder whether she knew. Perhaps that was what she saw in the satin cushions: they looked like something – at least, to her. The day she and I so suddenly went to London to call on her sister's friend she did certainly manage, however, to look like something. My father, watching us down the garden path, ventured no comment on her or my appearance. However, which ought to have cheered me up, we created quite a furore in the train. We went sailing into the richly-appointed office of mother's sister's friend, who was one of those who, during the war, had felt mother should be cheered up. Can I, need I, describe him? The usual kind of business pudge, in a suit. He looked in a reluctant way at my mother, and reluctantly, slightly morbidly, at me. I don't know how I got the impression mother held all the cards. The conversation, of course, flowed over my head – I just cruised round and round the room, knocking objects over. But the outcome – as I gathered when we got home – was that mother's sister's friend said he'd give my father a job. He had said he could use an ex-officer, provided it was an ex-officer with charm. What my father would have to do was to interest housewives, not in himself but in vacuum cleaners. If it helped to interest some housewives in vacuum cleaners, he could interest them just a little bit in himself. Mother's sister's friend called this using judgment of character.

'When my mother, that evening, put all this to my father, he did not say anything but simply stood and stared. *She* said, "Then I suppose you want us to starve?"

'So my father stopped being a problem and became a travelling salesman. The best part was that the firm allowed him a car.

'I must say for my mother that she did not ask my father how he was getting on. At least she had much less trouble about the singing: sometimes he'd be away for two or three days together; when he was home he simply sprawled in his chair, now and then asking when there'd be something to eat, as unmusical as a gramophone with the spring broken. When I came filtering in he sometimes opened one eye and said. "And what have *you* been doing?" – as though he'd just finished telling me what he'd been doing himself. He garaged the car some way down the next road, and in the mornings when he was starting off I used to walk with him to the garage. He used to get into the car, start up the engine, back out, then look round at me and say, "Like to come out on the job? – yes, I bet you would," then let the clutch in and whizz off. Something about this always made me feel sick.

'I don't of course clearly remember when this began, or how long it went on for; but I know when it stopped. The night before my seventh birthday was a June night, because my birthdays are in June. The people who lived all round us were sitting out, on the verandas or on their lawns, but my mother had sent me to bed early because she was having a party for me next day and did not want to get me over-excited. My birthday cake which had arrived from the shop was on the dining-room sideboard, with a teacloth over it to keep the flies off, and my father and mother were in the lounge with the french windows shut, because she had several things to say to him that she did not want the people all round to hear. The heat travelled through the roof into all the rooms, so that I could not sleep: also, my bed was against the wall of my room, and the lounge was the other side of the wall. My mother went on like someone who has been saving up – just some touch, I suppose, had been needed to set her off. She said she would like to know why there was not more money – my father's job, I suppose now, was on a commission basis. Or, she said, was he keeping another woman? – a thing she had heard that most travelling salesmen did. She said she really felt quite ashamed of having foisted my father on to her sister's friend, and that she only wondered how long the firm would stand for it. She said her sisters pitied her, though she had tried to conceal from them that her life was hell. My father, who had as usual got home late and as usual had not yet had any supper, could not be heard saying anything. My mother then said she wished she knew why she had married him, and would like still more to know why he had married her.

'My father said, "You were so lovely – you've no idea."

'Next morning there was a heat-haze over everything. I bustled into the dining-room to see if there was anything on my plate. I forget what my mother had given me, but her richest sister had sent me a manicure-set in a purple box: all the objects had purple handles and lay in grooves on white velvet. While I was taking them out and putting them back again, my father suddenly looked up from his coffee and said *his* present for me was in the car, and that I'd have to come out and fetch it. My mother could hardly say no to this, though of course I saw her opening her mouth. So out we set, I gripping the manicure-set. I don't think my father seemed odder than usual, though he was on the point of doing an unexpected thing – when he had got the car started and backed out he suddenly held open the other door and said, "Come on, nip in, look sharp; my present to you is a day trip." So then I nipped in and we drove off, as though this were the most natural thing in the world.

'The car was a two-seater, with a let-down hood . . . No, of course I cannot remember what make it was. That morning, the hood was down. Locked up in the dickie behind my father kept the specimen vacuum cleaner he interested women in. He drove fast, and as we hit the bumps in the road I heard the parts of the cleaner clonking about. As we drove, the sun began to burn its way through the haze, making the roses in some of the grander gardens look almost impossibly large and bright. My bare knees began to grill on the leather cushion, and the crumples eased out of the front of my cotton frock.

'I had never been with my father when he was driving a car – it felt as though speed and power were streaming out of him, and as if he and I were devouring everything that we passed. I sat slumped round with my cheek against the hot cushion and sometimes stared at his profile, sometimes stared at his wrists, till he squinted round and said, "Anything wrong with *me*?" Later on, he added, "Why not look at the scenery?" By that time there *was* some scenery, if that means grass and trees; in fact, these had been going on for some time, in a green band streaming behind my father's face. When I said, "Where are we going?" he said, "Well, where *are* we going?" At that point I saw quite a large hill, in fact a whole party of them, lapping into each other as though they would never stop, and never having seen anything of the kind before I could not help saying, "Oh, I say, look!"

'My father gave a nod, without stopping singing – I told you he had begun to sing? He had not only started but gone on: when he came to the end of his first tune he said, "Pom-*pom*", like a drum, then started through it again; after that he worked around to the second, which he sang two or three times, with me joining in. We both liked the second still better, and how right we were – and it's worn well, hasn't it? That's what this band's just played.'

'Oh, what they've just played?' he said, and looked narrowly at the band; while, reaching round for the bottle on the table between them he lifted it to replenish her glass and his. This time she did not see or did not bother to stop him: she looked at her full glass vaguely, then vaguely drank. After a minute she went on:

'Ginger beer, sausage rolls, chocolate – that was what we bought when we stopped at the village shop. Also my father bought a blue comb off a card of combs, with which he attempted to do my hair, which had blown into tags and ratstails over my eyes and face. He looked at me while he combed in a puzzled way, as though something about me that hadn't struck him became a problem to him for the first time. I said, "Aren't we going to sell any vacuum cleaners?" and he said, "We'll try and interest the Berkshire Downs." I thought that meant, meet a family; but all we did was turn out of the village and start up a rough track, to where there could not be any people at all. The car climbed with a slow but exciting roar: from the heat of the engine and the heat of the sun the chocolate in the paper bag in my hands was melting by the time we came to the top.

'From the top, where we lay on our stomachs in the shade of the car, we could see – oh well, can't you imagine, can't you? It was an outsize June day. The country below us looked all colours, and was washed over in the most reckless way with light; going on and on into the distance the clumps of trees and the roofs of villages and the church towers had quivering glimmers round them; but most of all there was space, sort of moulded space, and the blue of earth ran into the blue of sky.

'My father's face was turned away from me, propped up on his hand. I finally said to him, 'What's that?"

'"What's what?" he said, startled.

'"What we're looking at."

'"England," he said, "that's England. I thought I'd like to see her again."

'"But don't we live in England?"

'He took no notice. "How I loved her," he said.

'"Oh, but don't you now?"

'"I've lost her," he said, "or she's lost me; I don't quite know which; I don't understand what's happened." He rolled round and looked at me and said, "But *you* like it, don't you? I thought I'd like you to see, if just once, what I once saw."

'I was well into the third of my sausage rolls: my mouth was full, I could only stare at my father. He said, "And there's something else down there – see it?" I screwed my eyes up but still only saw the distance. "Peace," he said. "Look hard at it; don't forget it."

'"What's peace?" I said.

'"An idea you have when there's a war on, to make you fight well. An idea that gets lost when there isn't a war."

'I licked pastry-crumbs off my chin and began on chocolate. By this time my father lay on his back, with his fingers thatched together over his eyes: he talked, but more to the sky than me. None of the things he was saying now went anywhere near my brain – a child's brain, how could they? – his actual words are gone as though I had never heard them, but his meaning lodged itself in some part of my inside and is still there and has grown up with me.

He talked about war and how he had once felt, and about leaves and love and dancing and going back to the war, then the birth of me – "Seven years ago today," he said, "seven years; I remember how they brought me the telegram."

'Something else, on top of the sausage and heat and chocolate suddenly made me feel sick and begin to cry. "Oh please, oh please don't," I said, "it's my birthday."

'"Don't what?" he said. I, naturally, didn't know. My father again looked at me, with the same expression he had worn when attempting to comb my hair. Something about me – my age? – was a proposition. Then he shut his eyes, like – I saw later, not at the time – somebody finally banishing an idea. "No; it wouldn't work," he said. "It simply couldn't be done. You can wait for me if you want. I can't wait for you."

'Then he began acting like somebody very sleepy: he yawned and yawned at me till I yawned at him. I didn't feel sick any more, but the heat of the afternoon came down like a grey-blue blanket over my head. "What you and I want," my father said, watching me, "is a good sleep."

'I wish I could tell you at *which* moment I fell asleep, and stopped blurrily looking at him between my eyelids, because *that* was the moment when I last saw my father.

'When I woke, there was no more shadow on my side of the car; the light had changed and everything looked bright yellow. I called to my father but he did not answer, for the adequate reason that he was not there. He was gone. For some reason I wasn't at all frightened; I thought he must have gone to look for something for us for tea. I remembered that I was not at my birthday party, and I must say I thought twice about that pink cake. I was more bored than anything, till I remembered my manicure-set, which owing to the funniness of the day I had not been able to open a second time. I took the objects out of their velvet bedding and began to prod at my nails, as I'd seen my mother do. Then I got up and walked, once more, all the way round the car. It was then that I noticed what I had missed before: a piece of white paper twisted into the radiator. I couldn't read handwriting very well, but did at last make out what my father had put. *"The car and the vacuum cleaner are the property of Messrs X and X"* (the firm of my mother's sister's friend), *"the child is the property of Mrs So-and-So, of Such-and such"* (I needn't bother to give you my mother's name and the name of our bungalow), *"the manicure-set, the comb and anything still left in the paper bags are the property of the child. Signed — "*
It was signed with my father's name.

'The two dots I saw starting zigzag up the side of the down turned out to be two sweating policemen. What happened when they came to where I was was interesting at the moment but is not interesting now. They checked up on the message on the front of the car, then told me my father had telephoned to the police station, and that I was to be a good girl and come with them. When they had checked up on the cleaner, we all drove down. I remember the constable's knobbly, sticky red hands looked queer on the wheel where my father's had lately been . . . At the police station, someone or other's wife made quite a fuss about me and gave me tea, then we piled into another car and drove on again. I was soon dead asleep; and I only woke when we stopped in the dark at the gate of the bungalow.

'Having tottered down the path, in the light from the front door, my mother clawed me out of the car, sobbing. I noticed her breath smelt unusual. We and the policeman then trooped into the lounge, where the policeman kept nodding and jotting things on a pad. To cheer up my mother he said that England was very small – "And he's not, so far as you know, in possession of a passport?" I sucked blobs of chocolate off the front of my frock while my mother described my father to the policeman. "But no doubt," the policeman said, "he'll be thinking better of this. A man's home is a man's home, I always say."

'When my mother and I were left alone in the lounge, we stared at each other in the electric light. While she asked if I knew how unnatural my father was, she kept pouring out a little more from the bottle: she said she had to have medicine to settle her nerves, but it seemed to act on her nerves just the opposite way. That I wouldn't say what my father had said and done set her off fairly raving against my father. To put it mildly, she lost all kind of control. She finished up with: "And such a fool, too – a fool, a fool!"

'"He is not a fool," I said, "he's my father."

'"He is not your father,' she screamed, "and he is a fool."

'That made me stare at her, and her stare at me.

'"How do you mean," I said, "my father is not my father?"

'My mother's reaction to this was exactly like as if someone had suddenly pitched a pail of cold water over her. She pulled herself up and something jumped in her eyes. She said she had not said anything of the sort, and that if I ever said she had I was a wicked girl. I said I hadn't said she had, but she had said so. She put on a worried look and put a hand on my forehead and said she could feel I'd got a touch of the sun. A touch of the sun, she said, would make me imagine things – and no wonder, after the day I'd had.

'All next day I was kept in bed; not as a punishment but as a kind of treat. My mother was ever so nice to me; she kept coming in to put a hand on my forehead. The one thing she did not do was get the doctor. And afterwards, when I was let get up, nothing was good enough for me; until really anyone would have thought that my mother felt she was in my power. Shortly after, her rich sister came down, and my mother then had a fine time, crying, talking and crying; the sister then took us back with her to London, where my mother talked and cried even more. Of course I asked my aunt about what my mother had said, but my aunt said that if I imagined such wicked things they would have to think there was something wrong with my brain. So I did not re-open the subject, and am not doing so now. In the course of time my mother succeeded in divorcing my father for desertion; she was unable to marry her sister's friend because he was married and apparently always had been, but she did marry a friend of her sister's friend's, and was soon respectably settled in Bermuda, where as far as I know she still is.'

'But your father?' he said.

'Well, what about my father?'

'You don't mean you never heard anything more of him?'

'I never said so – he sent me two picture postcards. The last' – she counted back – 'arrived fourteen years ago. But there probably have been others that went astray. The way I've always lived, I'm not long at any address.'

He essayed, rashly, 'Been a bit of a waif?'

The look he got back for this was halfway between glass and ice. 'A waif's the first thing I learned not to be. No, more likely my father decided, better leave it at that. People don't, on the whole, come back, and I've never blamed them. No, why should he be dead? Why should not he be – any place?'

'Here, for instance?'

'Tonight, you mean?'

'Why not?' he said. 'Why not – as you say?'

'Here?' She looked round the tables, as though she hardly knew where she was herself. She looked round the tables, over which smoke thickened, round which khaki melted into the khaki gloom. Then her eyes returned, to fix, with unsparing attention, an addled trio of men round the fifty-mark. 'Here?' she repeated, 'my father? – I hope not.'

'But I thought,' he said, watching her watching the old buffers, 'I thought we were looking for someone of twenty-six?'

'Give me a cigarette,' she said, 'and, also, don't be cruel.'

'I wouldn't be,' he said, as he lighted the cigarette, 'if you had any feeling for me.'

The Demon Lover

TOWARDS the end of her day in London Mrs Drover went round to
her shut-up house to look for several things she wanted to take
away. Some belonged to herself, some to her family, who were by
now used to their country life. It was late August; it had been a
steamy, showery day: at the moment the trees down the pavement
glittered in an escape of humid yellow afternoon sun. Against the
next batch of clouds, already piling up ink-dark, broken chimneys
and parapets stood out. In her once familiar street, as in any unused
channel, an unfamiliar queerness had silted up; a cat wove itself in
and out of railings, but no human eye watched Mrs Drover's
return. Shifting some parcels under her arm, she slowly forced
round her latchkey in an unwilling lock, then gave the door, which
had warped, a push with her knee. Dead air came out to meet her as
she went in.

The staircase window having been boarded up, no light came
down into the hall. But one door, she could just see, stood ajar, so
she went quickly through into the room and unshuttered the big
window in there. Now the prosaic woman, looking about her, was
more perplexed than she knew by everything that she saw, by
traces of her long former habit of life – the yellow smoke-stain up
the white marble mantelpiece, the ring left by a vase on the top of
the escritoire; the bruise in the wallpaper where, on the door being
thrown open widely, the china handle had always hit the wall. The
piano, having gone away to be stored, had left what looked like
claw-marks on its part of the parquet. Though not much dust had
seeped in, each object wore a film of another kind; and, the only
ventilation being the chimney, the whole drawing-room smelled of
the cold hearth. Mrs Drover put down her parcels on the escritoire
and left the room to proceed upstairs; the things she wanted were in
a bedroom chest.

She had been anxious to see how the house was – the part-time
caretaker she shared with some neighbours was away this week on
his holiday, known to be not yet back. At the best of times he did
not look in often, and she was never sure that she trusted him.
There were some cracks in the structure, left by the last bombing,

on which she was anxious to keep an eye. Not that one could do anything –

A shaft of refracted daylight now lay across the hall. She stopped dead and stared at the hall table – on this lay a letter addressed to her.

She thought first – then the caretaker *must* be back. All the same, who, seeing the house shuttered, would have dropped a letter in at the box? It was not a circular, it was not a bill. And the post office redirected, to the address in the country, everything for her that came through the post. The caretaker (even if he *were* back) did not know she was due in London today – her call here had been planned to be a surprise – so his negligence in the manner of this letter, leaving it to wait in the dusk and the dust, annoyed her. Annoyed, she picked up the letter, which bore no stamp. But it cannot be important, or they would know . . . She took the letter rapidly upstairs with her, without a stop to look at the writing till she reached what had been her bedroom, where she let in light. The room looked over the garden and other gardens: the sun had gone in; as the clouds sharpened and lowered, the trees and rank lawns seemed already to smoke with dark. Her reluctance to look again at the letter came from the fact that she felt intruded upon – and by someone contemptuous of her ways. However, in the tenseness preceding the fall of rain she read it: it was a few lines.

> Dear Kathleen: You will not have forgotten that today is our anniversary, and the day we said. The years have gone by at once slowly and fast. In view of the fact that nothing has changed, I shall rely upon you to keep your promise. I was sorry to see you leave London, but was satisfied that you would be back in time. You may expect me, therefore, at the hour arranged. Until then . . .   K.

Mrs Drover looked for the date: it was today's. She dropped the letter on to the bed-springs, then picked it up to see the writing again – her lips, beneath the remains of lipstick, beginning to go white. She felt so much the change in her own face that she went to the mirror, polished a clear patch in it and looked at once urgently and stealthily in. She was confronted by a woman of forty-four, with eyes starting out under a hat-brim that had been rather carelessly pulled down. She had not put on any more powder since she left the shop where she ate her solitary tea. The pearls her husband had given her on their marriage hung loose round her now rather thinner throat, slipping in the V of the pink wool jumper her sister knitted last autumn as they sat round the fire. Mrs Drover's most normal expression was one of controlled worry, but of assent.

Since the birth of the third of her little boys, attended by a quite serious illness, she had had an intermittent muscular flicker to the left of her mouth, but in spite of this she could always sustain a manner that was at once energetic and calm.

Turning from her own face as precipitately as she had gone to meet it, she went to the chest where the things were, unlocked it, threw up the lid and knelt to search. But as rain began to come crashing down she could not keep from looking over her shoulder at the stripped bed on which the letter lay. Behind the blanket of rain the clock of the church that still stood struck six – with rapidly heightening apprehension she counted each of the slow strokes. 'The hour arranged . . . My God,' she said, '*what* hour? How should I . . . ? After twenty-five years . . . '

The young girl talking to the soldier in the garden had not ever completely seen his face. It was dark; they were saying goodbye under a tree. Now and then – for it felt, from not seeing him at this intense moment, as though she had never seen him at all – she verified his presence for these few moments longer by putting out a hand, which he each time pressed, without very much kindness, and painfully, on to one of the breast buttons of his uniform. That cut of the button on the palm of her hand was, principally what she was to carry away. This was so near the end of a leave from France that she could only wish him already gone. It was August 1916. Being not kissed, being drawn away from and looked at intimidated Kathleen till she imagined spectral glitters in the place of his eyes. Turning away and looking back up the lawn she saw, through branches of trees, the drawing-room window alight: she caught a breath for the moment when she could go running back there into the safe arms of her mother and sister, and cry: 'What shall I do, what shall I do? He has gone.'

Hearing her catch her breath, her fiancé said, without feeling: 'Cold?'

'You're going away such a long way.'

'Not so far as you think.'

'I don't understand?'

'You don't have to,' he said. 'You will. You know what we said.'

'But that was – suppose you – I mean, suppose.'

'I shall be with you,' he said, 'sooner or later. You won't forget that. You need do nothing but wait.'

Only a little more than a minute later she was free to run up the silent lawn. Looking in through the window at her mother and sister, who did not for the moment perceive her, she already felt that unnatural promise drive down between her and the rest of all human kind. No other way of having given herself could have made her feel so apart, lost and foresworn. She could not have plighted a more sinister troth.

Kathleen behaved well when, some months later, her fiancé was reported missing, presumed killed. Her family not only supported her but were able to praise her courage without stint because they could not regret, as a husband for her, the man they knew almost nothing about. They hoped she would, in a year or two, console herself – and had it been only a question of consolation things might have gone much straighter ahead. But her trouble, behind just a litle grief, was a complete dislocation from everything. She did not reject other lovers, for these failed to appear: for years she failed to attract men – and with the approach of her 'thirties she became natural enough to share her family's anxiousness on this score. She began to put herself out, to wonder; and at thirty-two she was very greatly relieved to find herself being courted by William Drover. She married him, and the two of them settled down in this quiet, arboreal part of Kensington: in this house the years piled up, her children were born and they all lived till they were driven out by the bombs of the next war. Her movements as Mrs Drover were circumscribed, and she dismissed any idea that they were still watched.

As things were – dead or living the letter-writer sent her only a threat. Unable, for some minutes, to go on kneeling with her back exposed to the empty room, Mrs Drover rose from the chest to sit on an upright chair whose back was firmly against the wall. The desuetude of her former bedroom, her married London home's whole air of being a cracked cup from which memory, with its reassuring power, had either evaporated or leaked away, made a crisis – and at just this crisis the letter-writer had, knowledgeably, struck. The hollowness of the house this evening cancelled years on years of voices, habits and steps. Through the shut windows she only heard rain fall on the roofs around. To rally herself, she said she was in a mood – and for two or three seconds shutting her eyes, told herself that she had imagined the letter. But she opened them – there it lay on the bed.

On the supernatural side of the letter's entrance she was not permitting her mind to dwell. Who, in London, knew she meant to call at the house today? Evidently, however, this had been known. The caretaker, *had* he come back, had had no cause to expect her: he would have taken the letter in his pocket, to forward it, at his own time, through the post. There was no other sign that the caretaker had been in – but, if not? Letters dropped in at doors of deserted houses do not fly or walk to tables in halls. They do not sit on the dust of empty tables with the air of certainty that they will be found. There is needed some human hand – but nobody but the caretaker had a key. Under circumstances she did not care to consider, a house can be entered without a key. It was possible that she was not alone now. She might be being waited for, downstairs. Waited for – until when? Until 'the hour arranged'. At least that was not six o'clock: six has struck.

She rose from the chair and went over and locked the door.

The thing was, to get out. To fly? No, not that: she had to catch her train. As a woman whose utter dependability was the keystone of her family life she was not willing to return to the country, to her husband, her little boys and her sister, without the objects she had come up to fetch. Resuming work at the chest she set about making up a number of parcels in a rapid, fumbling-decisive way. These, with her shopping parcels, would be too much to carry; these meant a taxi – at the thought of the taxi her heart went up and her normal breathing resumed. I will ring up the taxi now; the taxi cannot come too soon: I shall hear the taxi out there running its engine, till I walk calmly down to it through the hall. I'll ring up – But no: the telephone is cut off . . . She tugged at a knot she had tied wrong.

The idea of flight . . . He was never kind to me, not really. I don't remember him kind at all. Mother said he never considered me. He was set on me, that was what it was – not love. Not love, not meaning a person well. What did he do, to make me promise like that? I can't remember – But she found that she could.

She remembered with such dreadful acuteness that the twenty-five years since then dissolved like smoke and she instinctively looked for the weal left by the button on the palm of her hand. She remembered not only all that he said and did but the complete suspension of *her* existence during that August week. I was not myself – they all told me so at the time. She remembered – but with one white burning blank as where acid has dropped on a photograph: *under no conditions* could she remember his face.

So, wherever he may be waiting, I shall not know him. You have no time to run from a face you do not expect.

The thing was to get to the taxi before any clock struck what could be the hour. She would slip down the street and round the side of the square to where the square gave on the main road. She would return in the taxi, safe, to her own door, and bring the solid driver into the house with her to pick up the parcels from room to room. The idea of the taxi driver made her decisive, bold: she unlocked her door, went to the top of the staircase and listened down.

She heard nothing – but while she was hearing nothing the *passé* air of the staircase was disturbed by a draught that travelled up to her face. It emanated from the basement: down there a door or window was being opened by someone who chose this moment to leave the house.

The rain had stopped; the pavements steamily shone as Mrs Drover let herself out by inches from her own front door into the empty street. The unoccupied houses opposite continued to meet her look with their damaged stare. Making towards the thoroughfare and the taxi, she tried not to keep looking behind. Indeed, the silence was so intense – one of those creeks of London silence exaggerated this summer by the damage of war – that no tread could have gained on hers unheard. Where her street debouched on the square where people went on living, she grew conscious of, and checked, her unnatural pace. Across the open end of the square two buses impassively passed each other: women, a perambulator, cyclists, a man wheeling a barrow signalized, once again, the ordinary flow of life. At the square's most populous corner should be – and was – the short taxi rank. This evening, only one taxi – but this, although it presented its blank rump, appeared already to be alertly waiting for her. Indeed, without looking round the driver started his engine as she panted up from behind and put her hand on the door. As she did so, the clock struck seven. The taxi faced the main road: to make the trip back to her house it would have to turn – she had settled back on the seat and the taxi *had* turned before she, surprised by its knowing movement, recollected that she had not 'said where'. She leaned forward to scratch at the glass panel that divided the driver's head from her own.

The driver braked to what was almost a stop, turned round and slid the glass panel back: the jolt of this flung Mrs Drover forward till her face was almost into the glass. Through the aperture driver and passenger, not six inches between them, remained for an eternity eye to eye. Mrs Drover's mouth hung open for some seconds before she could issue her first scream. After that she continued to scream freely and to beat with her gloved hands on the glass all round as the taxi, accelerating without mercy, made off with her into the hinterland of deserted streets.

Careless Talk

'How good, how kind, *how* thoughtful!' said Mary Dash. 'I can't tell you what a difference they will make! And you brought them like this all the way from Shepton Mallet in the train?' She looked helpless. 'Where do you think I had better put them? This table's going to be terribly small for four, and *think*, if one of Eric Farnham's sweeping gesticulations . . . ' She signalled a waiter. 'I want these put somewhere for me till the end of lunch. *Carefully*,' she added. 'They are three eggs.' The waiter bowed and took the parcel away. 'I do hope they will be all right,' said Mrs Dash, looking suspiciously after him. 'But at least they'll be quieter with the hats, or something. I expect you see how crowded everywhere is?'

Joanna looked round the restaurant and saw. The waiters had to melt to get past the backs of the chairs; between the net-curtained windows, drowsy with August rain, mirrors reflected heads in smoke and electric light and the glitter of buttons on uniforms. Every European tongue struck its own note, with exclamatory English on top of all. As fast as people went wading out people came wading in, and so many greeted each other that Joanna might easily have felt out of it. She had not lunched in London for four months and could not resist saying so to her friend.

'Honestly, you haven't deteriorated,' said Mary. Herself, she was looking much as ever, with orchids pinned on to her last year's black. 'Then how lucky I caught you just today! And I'm glad the others will be late. The only men one likes now are always late. While it's still just you and me, there's so much to say. I don't know what I've done without you, Joanna.' She fixed enraptured eyes on Joanna's face. 'For instance, can *you* tell me what's become of the Stones?'

'No, I'm afraid I can't. I . . . '

'And Edward and I were wondering if you could tell us about the Hickneys. I know they are somewhere in Dorset or Somerset. They're not by any chance anywhere near you? . . . Well, never mind. Tell me about yourself.'

But at this point Eric Farnham joined them. 'You don't know how sorry I am,' he said. 'I was kept. But you found the table all right. Well, Joanna, this couldn't be nicer, could it?'

'Isn't she looking radiant?' said Mary Dash. 'We have been having the most tremendous talk.'

Eric was now at the War Office, and Joanna, who had not seen him in uniform before, looked at him naïvely, twice. He reminded her of one of the pictures arrived at in that paper game when, by drawing on folded-over paper, you add to one kind of body an intriguingly wrong kind of head. He met her second look kindly through his shell-rimmed glasses. 'How do you think the war is going?' she said.

'Oh, we mustn't ask him things' said Mary quickly. 'He's doing most frightfully secret work.' But this was lost on Eric, who was consulting his wristwatch. 'As Ponsonby's later than I am,' he said, 'that probably means he'll be pretty late. Though God knows what they do at that Ministry. I propose not waiting for Ponsonby. First of all, what will you two drink?'

'Ponsonby?' Joanna said.

'No, I don't expect you'd know him. He's only been about lately,' said Mary. 'He's an expert; he's very interesting.'

'He could be,' said Eric. 'He was at one time. But he's not supposed to be interesting just now.' The drinks came; then they got together over the *cartes du jour.* Ponsonby did not arrive till just after the potted shrimps. 'This is dreadful,' he said. 'I do hope you'll forgive me. But things keep on happening, you know.' He nodded rapidly round to several tables, then dropped exhausted into his place. 'Eat?' he said. 'Oh, really, anything – shrimps. After that, whatever you're all doing.'

'Well, Mary's for grouse,' said Eric. Ponsonby, after an instant of concentration, said, 'In that case, grouse will do me fine.'

'Now you must talk to Joanna,' said Mary Dash. 'She's just brought me three eggs from the country and she's longing to know about everything.'

Ponsonby gave Joanna a keen, considering look. 'Is it true,' he said, 'that in the country there are no cigarettes at all?'

'I believe there are sometimes some. But I don't – '

'There are. Then that alters everything,' said Ponsonby. 'How lucky you are!'

'I got my hundred this morning,' said Eric, 'from my regular man. But those will have to last me to Saturday. I can't seem to cut down, somehow. Mary, have you cut down?'

'I've got my own, if that's what you mean,' said she. 'I just got twenty out of my hairdresser.' She raised her shilling-size portion of butter from its large bed of ice and spread it tenderly over her piece of toast. 'Now, what is your news?' she said. 'Not that I'm asking anything, of course.'

'I don't think anything's happened to me,' said Eric, 'or that anything else has happened that you wouldn't know about. When I say happened I mean *happened*, of course. I went out of London for one night; everywhere outside London seemed to me very full. I must say I was glad to be home again.' He unlocked his chair from the chair behind him, looked at the grouse on his plate, then took up his knife and fork.

'Eric,' said Mary, after a minute, 'the waiter's trying to tell you there's no more of that wine *en carafe*.'

'Bring it in a bottle then. I wonder how much longer – '

'Oh, my dear, so do I,' said Mary. 'One daren't think about that. Where we were dining last night they already had several numbers scratched off the wine list. Which reminds me. Edward sent you his love.'

'Oh, how *is* Edward?' Joanna said. 'What is he doing?'

'Well, I'm not strictly supposed to say. By the way, Eric, I asked Joanna, and she doesn't know where the Stones *or* the Hickneys are.'

'In the case of the Hickneys, I don't know that it matters.'

'Oh, don't be inhuman. You know you're not!'

'I must say,' said Eric, raising his voice firmly, 'I do like London now a lot of those people have gone. Not *you*, Joanna; we all miss you very much. Why don't you come back? You've no idea how nice it is.'

Joanna, colouring slightly, said, 'I've got no place left to come back to. Belmont Square – '

'Oh, my Lord, yes,' he said. 'I did hear about your house. I was so sorry. Completely? . . . Still, you don't want a house, you know. None of us live in houses. You could move in on someone. Sylvia has moved in on Mona – '

'That's not a good example,' said Mary quickly. 'Mona moved out almost at once and moved in on Isobel, but the worst of that is that now Isobel wants her husband back, and meanwhile Sylvia's taken up with a young man, so Mona can't move back to her own flat. But what would make it difficult for Joanna is having taken on all those hens. Haven't you?'

'Yes, and I have evacuees – '

'But we won't talk about those, will we?' said Mary quickly. 'Any more than you would want to hear about bombs. I think one great rule is never to bore each other. Eric, *what's* that you are saying to Ponsonby?'

Eric and Ponsonby had seized the occasion to exchange a few rapid remarks. They stopped immediately. 'It was quite boring,' Ponsonby explained.

'I don't believe you,' said Mary. 'These days everything's frightfully interesting. Joanna, you must be feeling completely dazed. Will everyone ask you things when you get home?'

'The worst of the country these days,' said Joanna, 'is everyone gets so wrapped up in their own affairs.'

'Still, surely they must want to know about us? I suppose London is too much the opposite,' said Mary. 'One lives in a perfect whirl of ideas. Ponsonby, who was that man I saw you with at the Meunière? I was certain I knew his face.'

'That was a chap called Odgers. Perhaps he reminded you of somebody else? We were talking shop. I think that's a nice place, don't you? I always think they do veal well. That reminds me, Eric. Was your friend the other evening a Pole, or what?'

'The fact is I hardly know him,' said Eric. 'I'm never quite sure of his name myself. He's a Pole all right, but Poles aren't really my thing. He was quite interesting, as a matter of fact; he had quite a line of his own on various things. Oh, well, it was nothing particular . . . No, I can't do you Poles, Mary. Warrington's really the man for Poles.'

'I know he is, but he keeps them all up his sleeve. You do know about Edward and the Free French? I hope it didn't matter my having told you that, but Edward took it for granted that you already knew.'

Ponsonby recoiled from his wristwatch. 'Good heavens,' he said, 'it *can't* be as late as this? If it is, there's someone waiting for me.'

'Look,' said Eric, 'I'll hurry on coffee.'

'You know,' Mary added anxiously, 'you really can't concentrate without your coffee. Though I know we mustn't be difficult. It's like this all the time,' she said to Joanna. 'Have *you* got to hurry, Eric?'

'I needn't exactly hurry. I just ought to keep an eye on the time.'

'I'll do that for you,' Mary said. 'I'd love to. You see you've hardly had a word with Joanna, and she's wanting so much to catch up with life. I tell you one thing that *is* worrying me: that waiter I gave Joanna's lovely eggs to hasn't been near this table again. Do you think I put temptation right in his way? Because, do you know, all the time we've been talking I've been thinking up a new omelette I want to make. One's mind gets like that these days,' she said to Joanna. 'One seems able to think of twenty things at one time. Eric, do you think you could flag the *maître d'hôtel*? I don't know how I'd feel if I lost three eggs.'

The Happy Autumn Fields

THE family walking party, though it comprised so many, did not
deploy or straggle over the stubble but kept in a procession of
threes and twos. Papa, who carried his Alpine stick, led, flanked by
Constance and little Arthur. Robert and Cousin Theodore, locked
in studious talk, had Emily attached but not quite abreast. Next
came Digby and Lucius, taking, to left and right, imaginary aim at
rooks. Henrietta and Sarah brought up the rear.

It was Sarah who saw the others ahead on the blond stubble, who
knew them, knew what they were to each other, knew their names
and knew her own. It was she who felt the stubble under her feet,
and who heard it give beneath the tread of the others a continuous
different more distant soft stiff scrunch. The field and all these
outlying fields in view knew as Sarah knew that they were Papa's.
The harvest had been good and was now in: he was satisfied – for
this afternoon he had made the instinctive choice of his most
womanly daughter, most nearly infant son. Arthur, whose hand
Papa was holding, took an anxious hop, a skip and a jump to every
stride of the great man's. As for Constance – Sarah could often see
the flash of her hat-feather as she turned her head, the curve of her
close bodice as she turned her torso. Constance gave Papa her
attention but not her thoughts, for she had already been sought in
marriage.

The landowner's daughters, from Constance down, walked with
their beetle-green, mole or maroon skirts gathered up and carried
clear of the ground, but for Henrietta, who was still ankle-
free. They walked inside a continuous stuffy sound, but left silence
behind them. Behind them, rooks that had risen and circled, sun
striking blue from their blue-black wings, planed one by one to the
earth and settled to peck again. Papa and the boys were dark-clad as
the rooks but with no sheen, but for their white collars.

It was Sarah who located the thoughts of Constance, knew what
a twisting prisoner was Arthur's hand, felt to the depths of Emily's
pique at Cousin Theodore's inattention, rejoiced with Digby and
Lucius at the imaginary fall of so many rooks. She fell back,
however, as from a rocky range, from the converse of Robert and

Cousin Theodore. Most she knew that she swam with love at the nearness of Henrietta's young and alert face and eyes which shone with the sky and queried the afternoon.

She recognized the colour of valediction, tasted sweet sadness, while from the cottage inside the screen of trees wood-smoke rose melting pungent and blue. This was the eve of the brothers' return to school. It was like a Sunday; Papa had kept the late afternoon free; all (all but one) encircling Robert, Digby and Lucius, they walked the estate the brothers would not see again for so long. Robert, it could be felt, was not unwilling to return to his books; next year he would go to college like Theodore; besides, to all this they saw he was not the heir. But in Digby and Lucius aiming and popping hid a bodily grief, the repugnance of victims, though these two were further from being heirs than Robert.

Sarah said to Henrietta: 'To think they will not be here to-morrow!'

'*Is* that what you are thinking about?' Henrietta asked, with her subtle taste for the truth.

'More, I was thinking that you and I will be back again by one another at table . . . '

'You know we are always sad when the boys are going, but we are never sad when the boys have gone.' The sweet reciprocal guilty smile that started on Henrietta's lips finished on those of Sarah. 'Also,' the young sister said, 'we know this is only something happening again. It happened last year, and it will happen next. But oh how should I feel, and how should you feel, if it were something that had not happened before?'

'For instance, when Constance goes to be married?'

'Oh, I don't mean *Constance*!' said Henrietta.

'So long,' said Sarah, considering, 'as, whatever it is, it happens to both of us?' She must never have to wake in the early morning except to the birdlike stirrings of Henrietta, or have her cheek brushed in the dark by the frill of another pillow in whose hollow did not repose Henrietta's cheek. Rather than they should cease to lie in the same bed she prayed they might lie in the same grave. 'You and I will stay as we are,' she said, 'then nothing can touch one without touching the other.'

'So you say; so I hear you say!' exclaimed Henrietta, who then, lips apart, sent Sarah her most tormenting look. 'But I cannot forget that you chose to be born without me; that you would not wait — ' But here she broke off, laughed outright and said: 'Oh, *see!*'

Ahead of them there had been a dislocation. Emily took advantage of having gained the ridge to kneel down to tie her bootlace so abruptly that Digby all but fell over her, with an exclamation. Cousin Theodore had been civil enough to pause beside Emily, but Robert, lost to all but what he was saying, strode on, head down, only just not colliding into Papa and Constance, who had turned to look back. Papa, astounded, let go of Arthur's hand, whereupon Arthur fell flat on the stubble.

'Dear me,' said the affronted Constance to Robert.

Papa said. 'What is the matter there? May I ask, Robert, where you are going, sir? Digby, remember that is your sister Emily.'

'Cousin Emily is in trouble,' said Cousin Theodore.

Poor Emily, telescoped in her skirts and by now scarlet under her hatbrim, said in a muffled voice: 'It is just my bootlace, Papa.'

'Your bootlace, Emily?'

'I was just tying it.'

'Then you had better tie it. – Am I to think,' said Papa, looking round them all, 'that you must all go down like a pack of ninepins because Emily has occasion to stoop?'

At this Henrietta uttered a little whoop, flung her arms round Sarah, buried her face in her sister and fairly suffered with laughter. She could contain this no longer; she shook all over. Papa, who found Henrietta so hopelessly out of order that he took no notice of her except at table, took no notice, simply giving the signal for the others to collect themselves and move on. Cousin Theodore, helping Emily to her feet, could be seen to see how her heightened colour became her, but she dispensed with his hand chillily, looked elsewhere, touched the brooch at her throat and said: 'Thank you, I have not sustained an accident.' Digby apologized to Emily, Robert to Papa and Constance. Constance righted Arthur, flicking his breeches over with her handkerchief. All fell into their different steps and resumed their way.

Sarah, with no idea how to console laughter, coaxed, 'Come, come, come,' into Henrietta's ear. Between the girls and the others the distance widened; it began to seem that they would be left alone.

'And why not?' said Henrietta, lifting her head in answer to Sarah's thought.

They looked around them with the same eyes. The shorn uplands seemed to float on the distance, which extended dazzling to tiny blue glassy hills. There was no end to the afternoon, whose light went on ripening now they had scythed the corn. Light filled the silence which, now Papa and the others were out of hearing, was complete. Only screens of trees intersected and knolls made islands in the vast fields. The mansion and the home farm had sunk for ever below them in the expanse of woods, so that hardly a ripple showed where the girls dwelled.

The shadow of the same rook circling passed over Sarah then

over Henrietta, who in their turn cast one shadow across the stubble. 'But, Henrietta, we cannot stay here for ever.'

Henrietta immediately turned her eyes to the only lonely plume of smoke, from the cottage. 'Then let us go and visit the poor old man. He is dying and the others are happy. One day we shall pass and see no more smoke; then soon his roof will fall in, and we shall always be sorry we did not go today.'

'But he no longer remembers us any longer.'

'All the same, he will feel us there in the door.'

'But can we forget this is Robert's and Digby's and Lucius's goodbye walk? It would be heartless of both of us to neglect them.'

'Then how heartless Fitzgeorge is!' smiled Henrietta.

'Fitzgeorge is himself, the eldest and in the Army. Fitzgeorge I'm afraid is not an excuse for us.'

A resigned sigh, or perhaps the pretence of one, heaved up Henrietta's still narrow bosom. To delay matters for just a moment more she shaded her eyes with one hand, to search the distance like a sailor looking for a sail. She gazed with hope and zeal in every direction but that in which she and Sarah were bound to go. Then – 'Oh, but Sarah, here *they* are, coming – they are!' she cried. She brought out her handkerchief and began to fly it, drawing it to and fro through the windless air.

In the glass of the distance, two horsemen came into view, cantering on a grass track between the fields. When the track dropped into a hollow they dropped with it, but by now the drumming of hoofs was heard. The reverberation filled the land, the silence and Sarah's being; not watching for the riders to reappear she instead fixed her eyes on her sister's handkerchief which, let hang limp while its owner intently waited, showed a bitten corner as well as a damson stain. Again it became a flag, in furious motion. – 'Wave too, Sarah, wave too! Make your bracelet flash!'

'They must have seen us if they will ever see us,' said Sarah, standing still as a stone.

Henrietta's waving at once ceased. Facing her sister she crunched up her handkerchief, as though to stop it acting a lie. 'I can see you are shy,' she said in a dead voice. 'So shy you won't even wave to *Fitzgeorge*?'

Her way of not speaking the *other* name had a hundred meanings; she drove them all in by the way she did not look at Sarah's face. The impulsive breath she had caught stole silently out again, while her eyes – till now at their brightest, their most speaking – dulled with uncomprehending solitary alarm. The ordeal of awaiting Eugene's approach thus became for Sarah, from moment to moment, torture.

Fitzgeorge, Papa's heir, and his friend Eugene, the young neighbouring squire, struck off the track and rode up at a trot with their hats doffed. Sun striking low turned Fitzgeorge's flesh to coral and made Eugene blink his dark eyes. The young men reined in; the girls looked up at the horses. 'And my father, Constance, the others?' Fitzgeorge demanded, as though the stubble had swallowed them.

'Ahead, on the way to the quarry, the other side of the hill.'

'We heard you were all walking together,' Fitzgeorge said, seeming dissatisfied.

'We are following.'

'What, alone?' said Eugene, speaking for the first time.

'Forlorn!' glittered Henrietta, raising two mocking hands.

Fitzgeorge considered, said 'Good' severely, and signified to Eugene that they would ride on. But too late: Eugene had dismounted. Fitzgeorge saw, shrugged and flicked his horse to a trot; but Eugene led his slowly between the sisters. Or rather, Sarah walked on his left hand, the horse on his right and Henrietta the other side of the horse. Henrietta, acting like somebody quite alone, looked up at the sky, idly holding one of the empty stirrups. Sarah, however, looked at the ground, with Eugene inclined as though to speak but not speaking. Enfolded, dizzied, blinded as though inside a wave, she could feel his features carved in brightness above her. Alongside the slender stepping of his horse, Eugene matched his naturally long free step to hers. His elbow was through the reins; with his fingers he brushed back the lock that his bending to her had sent falling over his forehead. She recorded the sublime act and knew what smile shaped his lips. So each without looking trembled before an image, while slow colour burned up the curves of her cheeks. The consummation would be when their eyes met.

At the other side of the horse, Henrietta began to sing. At once her pain, like a scientific ray, passed through the horse and Eugene to penetrate Sarah's heart.

We surmount the skyline: the family come into our view, we into theirs. They are halted, waiting, on the decline to the quarry. The handsome statufied group in strong yellow sunshine, aligned by Papa and crowned by Fitzgeorge, turn their judging eyes on the laggards, waiting to close their ranks round Henrietta and Sarah and Eugene. One more moment and it will be too late; no further communication will be possible. Stop oh stop Henrietta's heartbreaking singing! Embrace her close again! Speak the only possible word! Say – oh, say what? Oh, the word is lost!

'Henrietta . . . '

A shock of striking pain in the knuckles of the outflung hand –

Sarah's? The eyes, opening, saw that the hand had struck, not been struck: there was a corner of a table. Dust, whitish and gritty, lay on the top of the table and on the telephone. Dull but piercing white light filled the room and what was left of the ceiling; her first thought was that it must have snowed. If so, it was winter now.

Through the calico stretched and tacked over the window came the sound of a piano: someone was playing Tchaikowsky badly in a room without windows or doors. From somewhere else in the hollowness came a cascade of hammering. Close up, a voice: 'Oh, *awake*, Mary?' It came from the other side of the open door, which jutted out between herself and the speaker – he on the threshold, she lying on the uncovered mattress of a bed. The speaker added: 'I had been going away.'

Summoning words from somewhere she said: 'Why? I didn't know you were here.'

'Evidently – Say, who is "Henrietta"?'

Despairing tears filled her eyes. She drew back her hurt hand, began to suck at the knuckle and whimpered, 'I've hurt myself.'

A man she knew to be 'Travis', but failed to focus, came round the door saying: 'Really I don't wonder.' Sitting down on the edge of the mattress he drew her hand away from her lips and held it: the act, in itself gentle, was accompanied by an almost hostile stare of concern. 'Do listen, Mary,' he said. 'While you've slept I've been all over the house again, and I'm less than ever satisfied that it's safe. In your normal senses you'd never attempt to stay here. There've been alerts, and more than alerts, all day; one more bang anywhere near, which may happen at any moment, could bring the rest of this down. You keep telling me that you have things to see to – but do you know what chaos the rooms are in? Till they've gone ahead with more clearing, where can you hope to start? And if there *were* anything you could do, you couldn't do it. Your own nerves know that, if you don't: it was almost frightening, when I looked in just now, to see the way you were sleeping – you've shut up shop.'

She lay staring over his shoulder at the calico window. He went on: 'You don't like it here. Your self doesn't like it. Your will keeps driving your self, but it can't be driven the whole way – it makes its own get-out: sleep. Well, I want you to sleep as much as you (really) do. But *not* here. So I've taken a room for you in a hotel; I'm going now for a taxi; you can practically make the move without waking up.'

'No, I can't get into a taxi without waking.'

'Do you realize you're the last soul left in the terrace?'

'Then who is that playing the piano?'

'Oh, one of the furniture-movers in Number Six. I didn't count the jaquerie; of course *they're* in possession – unsupervised, teeming, having a high old time. While I looked in on you in here ten minutes ago they were smashing out that conservatory at the other end. Glass being done in in cold blood – it was brutalizing. You never batted an eyelid; in fact, I thought you smiled.' He listened. 'Yes, the piano – they are highbrow all right. You know there's a workman downstairs lying on your blue sofa looking for pictures in one of your French books?'

'No,' she said, 'I've no idea who is there.'

'Obviously. With the lock blown off your front door anyone who likes can get in and out.'

'Including you.'

'Yes. I've had a word with a chap about getting that lock back before tonight. As for you, you don't know what is happening.'

'I did,' she said, locking her fingers before her eyes.

The unreality of this room and of Travis's presence preyed on her as figments of dreams that one knows to be dreams can do. This environment's being in semi-ruin struck her less than its being some sort of device or trap; and she rejoiced, if anything, in its decrepitude. As for Travis, he had his own part in the conspiracy to keep her from the beloved two. She felt he began to feel he was now unmeaning. She was struggling not to contemn him, scorn him for his ignorance of Henrietta, Eugene, her loss. His possessive angry fondness was part, of course, of the story of him and Mary, which like a book once read she remembered clearly but with indifference. Frantic at being delayed here, while the moment awaited her in the cornfield, she all but afforded a smile at the grotesquerie of being saddled with Mary's body and lover. Rearing up her head from the bare pillow, she looked, as far as the crossed feet, along the form inside which she found herself trapped: the irrelevant body of Mary, weighted down to the bed, wore a short black modern dress, flaked with plaster. The toes of the black suède shoes by their sickly whiteness showed Mary must have climbed over fallen ceilings; dirt engraved the fate-lines in Mary's palms.

This inspired her to say: 'But I've made a start; I've been pulling out things of value or things I want.'

For answer Travis turned to look down, expressively, at some object out of her sight, on the floor close by the bed. '*I* see,' he said, 'a musty old leather box gaping open with God knows what – junk, illegible letters, diaries, yellow photographs, chiefly plaster and dust. Of all things, Mary! – after a missing will?'

'Everything one unburies seems the same age.'

'Then what are these, where do they come from – family stuff?'

'No idea,' she yawned into Mary's hand. 'They may not even be mine. Having a house like this that had empty rooms must have made me store more than I knew, for years. I came on these, so I wondered. Look if you like.'

He bent and began to go through the box – it seemed to her, not unsuspiciously. While he blew grit off packets and fumbled with tapes she lay staring at the exposed laths of the ceiling, calculating. She then said: 'Sorry if I've been cranky, about the hotel and all. Go away just for two hours, then come back with a taxi, and I'll go quiet. Will that do?'

'Fine – except why not now?'

'*Travis* . . . '

'Sorry. It shall be as you say . . . You've got some good morbid stuff in this box, Mary – so far as I can see at a glance. The photographs seem more your sort of thing. Comic but lyrical. All of one set of people – a beard, a gun and a pot hat, a schoolboy with a moustache, a phaeton drawn up in front of mansion, a group on steps, a *carte de visite* of two young ladies hand-in-hand in front of a painted field — '

'*Give that to me!*'

She instinctively tried and failed, to unbutton the bosom of Mary's dress: it offered no hospitality to the photograph. So she could only fling herself over on the mattress, away from Travis, covering the two faces with her body. Racked by that oblique look of Henrietta's she recorded, too, a sort of personal shock at having seen Sarah for the first time.

Travis's hand came over her, and she shuddered. Wounded, he said: 'Mary . . . '

'Can't you leave *me* alone?'

She did not move or look till he had gone out saying: 'Then, in two hours.' She did not therefore see him pick up the dangerous box, which he took away under his arm, out of her reach.

They were back. Now the sun was setting behind the trees, but its rays passed dazzling between the branches into the beautiful warm red room. The tips of the ferns in the jardinière curled gold, and Sarah, standing by the jardinière, pinched at a leaf of scented geranium. The carpet had a great centre wreath of pomegranates, on which no tables or chairs stood, and its whole circle was between herself and the others.

No fire was lit yet, but where they were grouped was a hearth. Henrietta sat on a low stool, resting her elbow above her head on the arm of Mamma's chair, looking away intently as though into a fire, idle. Mamma embroidered, her needle slowed down by her thoughts; the length of tatting with roses she had already done overflowed stiffly over her supple skirts. Stretched on the rug at

Mamma's feet, Arthur looked through an album of Swiss views, not liking them but vowed to be very quiet. Sarah, from where she stood, saw fuming cataracts and null eternal snows as poor Arthur kept turning over the pages, which had tissue paper between.

Against the white marble mantelpiece stood Eugene. The dark red shadows gathering in the drawing-room as the trees drowned more and more of the sun would reach him last, perhaps never: it seemed to Sarah that a lamp was lighted behind his face. He was the only gentleman with the ladies: Fitzgeorge had gone to the stables, Papa to give an order; Cousin Theodore was consulting a dictionary; in the gunroom Robert, Lucius and Digby went through the sad rites, putting away their guns. All this was known to go on but none of it could be heard.

This particular hour of subtle light – not to be fixed by the clock, for it was early in winter and late in summer and in spring and autumn now, about Arthur's bed-time – had always, for Sarah, been Henrietta's. To be with her indoors or out, upstairs or down, was to share the same crepitation. Her spirit ran on past yours with a laughing shiver into an element of its own. Leaves and branches and mirrors in empty rooms became animate. The sisters rustled and scampered and concealed themselves where nobody else was in play that was full of fear, fear that was full of play. Till, by dint of making each other's hearts beat violently, Henrietta so wholly and Sarah so nearly lost all human reason that Mamma had been known to look at them searchingly as she sat instated for evening among the calm amber lamps.

But now Henrietta had locked the hour inside her breast. By spending it seated beside Mamma, in young imitation of Constance the Society daughter, she disclaimed for ever anything else. It had always been she who with one fierce act destroyed any toy that might be outgrown. She sat with straight back, poising her cheek remotely against her finger. Only by never looking at Sarah did she admit their eternal loss.

Eugene, not long returned from a foreign tour, spoke of travel, addressing himself to Mamma, who thought but did not speak of her wedding journey. But every now and then she had to ask Henrietta to pass the scissors or tray of carded wools, and Eugene seized every such moment to look at Sarah. Into eyes always brilliant with melancholy he dared begin to allow no other expression. But this in itself declared the conspiracy of still undeclared love. For her part she looked at him as though he, transfigured by the strange light, were indeed a picture, a picture who could not see her. The wallpaper now flamed scarlet behind his shoulder. Mamma, Henrietta, even unknowing Arthur were in no hurry to raise their heads.

Henrietta said: 'If I were a man I should take my bride to Italy.'

'There are mules in Switzerland,' said Arthur.

'Sarah,' said Mamma, who turned in her chair mildly, 'where are you, my love; do you never mean to sit down?'

'To Naples,' said Henrietta.

'Are you not thinking of Venice?' said Eugene.

'No,' returned Henrietta, 'why should I be? I should like to climb the volcano. But then I am not a man, and am still less likely ever to be a bride.'

'Arthur . . . ' Mamma said.

'Mamma?'

'Look at the clock.'

Arthur sighed politely, got up and replaced the album on the circular table, balanced upon the rest. He offered his hand to Eugene, his cheek to Henrietta and to Mamma; then he started towards Sarah, who came to meet him. 'Tell me, Arthur,' she said, embracing him, 'what did you do today?'

Arthur only stared with his button blue eyes. 'You were there too; we went for a walk in the cornfield, with Fitzgeorge on his horse, and I fell down.' He pulled out of her arms and said: 'I must go back to my beetle.' He had difficulty, as always, in turning the handle of the mahogany door. Mamma waited till he had left the room, then said: 'Arthur is quite a man now; he no longer comes running to me when he has hurt himself. Why, I did not even know he had fallen down. Before we know, he will be going away to school too.' She sighed and lifted her eyes to Eugene. 'Tomorrow is to be a sad day.'

Eugene with a gesture signified his own sorrow. The sentiments of Mamma could have been uttered only here in the drawing-room, which for all its size and formality was lyrical and almost exotic. There was a look like velvet in darker parts of the air; sombre window draperies let out gushes of lace; the music on the piano-forte bore tender titles, and the harp though unplayed gleamed in a corner, beyond sofas, whatnots, armchairs, occasional tables that all stood on tottering little feet. At any moment a tinkle might have been struck from the lustres' drops of the brighter day, a vibration from the musical instruments, or a quiver from the fringes and ferns. But the towering vases upon the consoles, the albums piled on the tables, the shells and figurines on the flights of brackets, all had, like the alabaster Leaning Tower of Pisa, an equilibrium of their own. Nothing would fall or change. And everything in the drawing-room was muted, weighted, pivoted by Mamma. When she added: 'We shall not feel quite the same,' it was to be understood that she would not have spoken thus from her place at the opposite end of Papa's table.

'Sarah,' said Henrietta curiously, 'what made you ask Arthur what he had been doing? Surely you have not forgotten today?'

The sisters were seldom known to address or question one another in public; it was taken that they knew each other's minds. Mamma, though untroubled, looked from one to the other. Henrietta continued: 'No day, least of all today, is like any other – Surely that must be true?' she said to Eugene. 'You will never forget my waving my handkerchief?'

Before Eugene had composed an answer, she turned to Sarah: 'Or *you*, them riding across the fields?'

Eugene also slowly turned his eyes on Sarah, as though awaiting with something like dread her answer to the question he had not asked. She drew a light little gold chair into the middle of the wreath of the carpet, where no one ever sat, and sat down. She said: 'But since then I think I have been asleep.'

'Charles the First walked and talked half an hour after his head was cut off,' said Henrietta mockingly. Sarah in anguish pressed the palms of her hands together upon a shred of geranium leaf.

'How else,' she said, 'could I have had such a bad dream?'

'That must be the explanation!' said Henrietta.

'A trifle fanciful,' said Mamma.

However rash it might be to speak at all, Sarah wished she knew how to speak more clearly. The obscurity and loneliness of her trouble was not to be borne. How could she put into words the feeling of dislocation, the formless dread that had been with her since she found herself in the drawing-room? The source of both had been what she must call her dream. How could she tell the others with what vehemence she tried to attach her being to each second, not because each was singular in itself, each a drop condensed from the mist of love in the room, but because she apprehended that the seconds were numbered? Her hope was that the others at least half knew. Were Henrietta and Eugene able to understand how completely, how nearly for ever, she had been swept from them, would they not without fail each grasp one of her hands? – She went so far as to throw her hands out, as though alarmed by a wasp. The shred of geranium fell to the carpet.

Mamma, tracing this behaviour of Sarah's to only one cause, could not but think reproachfully of Eugene. Delightful as his conversation had been, he would have done better had he paid this call with the object of interviewing Papa. Turning to Henrietta she asked her to ring for the lamps, as the sun had set.

Eugene, no longer where he had stood, was able to make no gesture towards the bell-rope. His dark head was under the tide of dusk; for, down on one knee on the edge of the wreath, he was feeling over the carpet for what had fallen from Sarah's hand. In the inevitable silence rooks on the return from the fields could be heard streaming over the house; their sound filled the sky and even the room, and it appeared so useless to ring the bell that Henrietta stayed quivering by Mamma's chair. Eugene rose, brought out his fine white handkerchief and, while they watched, enfolded carefully in it what he had just found, then returning the handkerchief to his breast pocket. This was done so deep in the reverie that accompanies any final act that Mamma instinctively murmured to Henrietta: 'But you will be my child when Arthur has gone.'

The door opened for Constance to appear on the threshold. Behind her queenly figure globes approached, swimming in their own light: these were the lamps for which Henrietta had not rung, but these first were put on the hall tables. 'Why, Mamma,' exclaimed Constance, 'I cannot see who is with you!'

'Eugene is with us,' said Henrietta, 'but on the point of asking if he may send for his horse.'

'Indeed?' said Constance to Eugene. 'Fitzgeorge has been asking for you, but I cannot tell where he is now.'

The figures of Emily, Lucius and Cousin Theodore criss-crossed the lamplight there in the hall, to mass behind Constance's in the drawing-room door. Emily, over her sister's shoulder, said: 'Mamma, Lucius wishes to ask you whether for once he may take his guitar to school.' – 'One objection, however,' said Cousin Theodore, 'is that Lucius's trunk is already locked and strapped.' 'Since Robert is taking his box of inks,' said Lucius, 'I do not see why I should not take my guitar.' – 'But Robert,' said Constance, 'will soon be going to college.'

Lucius squeezed past the others into the drawing-room in order to look anxiously at Mamma, who said: 'You have thought of this late; we must go and see.' The others parted to let Mamma, followed by Lucius, out. Then Constance, Emily and Cousin Theodore deployed and sat down in different parts of the drawing-room, to await the lamps.

'I am glad the rooks have done passing over,' said Emily, 'they make me nervous.' – 'Why?' yawned Constance haughtily, 'what do you think could happen?' Robert and Digby silently came in.

Eugene said to Sarah: 'I shall be back tomorrow.'

'But, oh – ' she began. She turned to cry: 'Henrietta!'

'Why, what is the matter?' said Henrietta, unseen at the back of the gold chair. 'What could be sooner than tomorrow?'

'But something terrible may be going to happen.'

'There cannot fail to be tomorrow,' said Eugene gravely.

'*I* will see that there is tomorrow,' said Henrietta.

'You will never let me out of your sight?'

Eugene, addressing himself to Henrietta, said: 'Yes, promise her what she asks.'

Henrietta cried: 'She *is* never out of my sight. Who are you to ask me that, you Eugene? Whatever tries to come between me and Sarah becomes nothing. Yes, come tomorrow, come sooner, come – when you like, but no one will ever be quite alone with Sarah. You do not even know what you are trying to do. It is *you* who are making something terrible happen. – Sarah, tell him that this is true! Sarah — '

The others, in the dark on the chairs and sofas, could be felt to turn their judging eyes upon Sarah, who, as once before, could not speak –

– The house rocked: simultaneously the calico window split and more ceiling fell, though not on the bed. The enormous dull sound of the explosion died, leaving a minor trickle of dissolution still to be heard in parts of the house. Until the choking stinging plaster dust had had time to settle, she lay with lips pressed close, nostrils not breathing and eyes shut. Remembering the box, Mary wondered if it had been again buried. No, she found, looking over the edge of the bed: that had been unable to happen because the box was missing. Travis, who must have taken it, would when he came back no doubt explain why. She looked at her watch, which had stopped, which was not surprising; she did not remember winding it for the last two days, but then she could not remember much. Through the torn window appeared the timelessness of an impermeably clouded late summer afternoon.

There being nothing left, she wished he would come to take her to the hotel. The one way back to the fields was barred by Mary's surviving the fall of ceiling. Sarah was right in doubting that there would be tomorrow: Eugene, Henrietta were lost in time to the woman weeping there on the bed, no longer reckoning who she was.

At last she heard the taxi, then Travis hurrying up the littered stairs. 'Mary, you're all right, Mary – *another*?' Such a helpless white face came round the door that she could only hold out her arms and say: 'Yes, but where have *you* been?'

'You said two hours. But I wish — '

'I have missed you.'

'Have you? Do you know you are crying?'

'Yes. How are we to live without natures? We only know inconvenience now, not sorrow. Everything pulverizes so easily because it is rot-dry; one can only wonder that it makes so much noise. The source, the sap must have dried up, or the pulse must have stopped, before you and I were conceived. So much flowed through people; so little flows through us. All we can do is imitate love or sorrow. – Why did you take away my box?'

He only said: 'It is in my office.'

She continued: 'What has happened is cruel: I am left with a fragment torn out of a day, a day I don't even know where or when; and now how am I to help laying that like a pattern against the poor stuff of everything else? – Alternatively, I am a person drained by a dream. I cannot forget the climate of those hours. Or life at that pitch, eventful – not happy, no, but strung like a harp. I have had a sister called Henrietta.'

'And I have been looking inside your box. What else can you expect? – I have had to write off this day, from the work point of view, thanks to you. So could I sit and do nothing for the last two hours? I just glanced through this and that – still, I know the family.'

'You said it was morbid stuff.'

'Did I? I still say it gives off something.'

She said: 'And then there was Eugene.'

'Probably. I don't think I came on much of his except some notes he must have made for Fitzgeorge from some book on scientific farming. Well, there it is: I have sorted everything out and put it back again, all but a lock of hair that tumbled out of a letter I could not trace. So I've got the hair in my pocket.'

'What colour is it?'

'Ash-brown. Of course, it is a bit – desiccated. Do you want it?'

'No,' she said with a shudder. 'Really, Travis, what revenges you take!'

'I didn't look at it that way,' he said puzzled.

'Is the taxi waiting?' Mary got off the bed and, picking her way across the room, began to look about for things she ought to take with her, now and then stopping to brush her dress. She took the mirror out of her bag to see how dirty her face was. 'Travis – ' she said suddenly.

'Mary?'

'Only, I — '

'That's all right. Don't let us imitate anything just at present.'

In the taxi, looking out of the window, she said: 'I suppose, then, that I am descended from Sarah?'

'No,' he said, 'that would be impossible. There must be some reason why you should have those papers, but that is not the one. From all negative evidence Sarah, like Henrietta, remained unmarried. I found no mention of either, after a certain date, in the letters of Constance, Robert or Emily, which makes it seem likely both died young. Fitzgeorge refers, in a letter to Robert written in his old age, to some friend of their youth who was thrown from his horse and killed, riding back after a visit to their home. The young man, whose name doesn't appear, was alone; and the evening, which was in autumn, was fine though late. Fitzgeorge wonders, and says he will always wonder, what made the horse shy in those empty fields.'

Ivy Gripped the Steps

IVY gripped and sucked at the flight of steps, down which with such a deceptive wildness it seemed to be flowing like a cascade. Ivy matted the door at the top and amassed in bushes above and below the porch. More, it had covered, or one might feel consumed, one entire half of the high, double-fronted house, from the basement up to a spiked gable: it had attained about half-way up to the girth and more than the density of a tree, and was sagging outward under its own weight. One was left to guess at the size and the number of windows hidden by looking at those in the other side. But these, though in sight, had been made effectively sightless: sheets of some dark composition that looked like metal were sealed closely into their frames. The house, not old, was of dull red brick with stone trimmings.

To crown all, the ivy was now in fruit, clustered over with fleshy pale green berries. There was something brutal about its fecundity. It was hard to credit that such a harvest could have been nourished only on brick and stone. Had not reason insisted that the lost windows must, like their fellows, have been made fast, so that the suckers for all their seeking voracity could not enter, one could have convinced oneself that the ivy must be feeding on something inside the house.

The process of strangulation could be felt: one wondered how many more years of war would be necessary for this to complete itself. And, the conventionality of the house, the remains, at least, of order in its surroundings made what was happening more and more an anomaly. Mrs Nicholson's house had always enjoyed distinction – that of being detached, while its neighbours, though equally 'good', had been erected in couples or even in blocks of four; that of being the last in the avenue; that of having on one hand as neighbour the theatre, to whose façade its front was at right angles. The theatre, set back behind shallow semi-circular gardens, at once crowned and terminated the avenue, which ran from it to the Promenade overhanging the sea. And the house, apart from the prestige of standing just where it stood, had had the air of reserving something quite of its own. It was thus perhaps just, or not unfitting, that it should have been singled out for this gothic fate.

This was, or had been, one of the best residential avenues in Southstone, into which private hotels intruded only with the most breathless, costly discretion: if it was not that now it was nothing else, for there was nothing else for it to be. Lines of chestnut trees had been planted along the pavements, along the railed strip of lawn that divided the avenue down the middle – now, the railings were, with all other ironwork, gone; and where the lawn was very long rusty grass grew up into the tangles of rusty barbed wire. On to this, as on to the concrete pyramids — which, in the course of four years of waiting to be pushed out to obstruct the invader, had sunk some inches into the soil – the chestnuts were now dropping their leaves.

The decline dated from the exodus of the summer of 1940, when Southstone had been declared in the front line. The houses at the sea end of the avenue had, like those on the Promenade, been requisitioned; but some of those at the theatre end stayed empty. Here and there, portions of porches or balustrades had fallen into front gardens, crushing their overgrowth; but there were no complete ruins; no bomb or shell had arrived immediately here, and effects of blast, though common to all of Southstone, were less evident than desuetude and decay. It was now the September of 1944; and, for some reason, the turn of the tide of war, the accumulation of the Invasion victories, gave Southstone its final air of defeat. The withdrawal of most of the soldiers, during the summer, had drained off adventitious vitality. The A.A. batteries, this month, were on the move to another part of the coast. And, within the very last few days, the silencing of the guns across the Channel had ended the tentative love affair with death: Southstone's life, no longer kept to at least a pitch by shelling warnings, now had nothing but an etiolated slowness. In the shuttered shopping streets along the Promenade, in the intersecting avenues, squares and crescents, vacuum mounted up. The lifting of the ban on the area had, so far, brought few visitors in.

This afternoon, for minutes together, not a soul, not even a soldier, crossed the avenue: Gavin Doddington stood to regard the ivy in which was, virtually, solitude. The sky being clouded, though not dark, a timeless flat light fell on to everything. Outside the theatre a very few soldiers stood grouped about; some moodily, some in no more than apathy. The theatre gardens had been cemented over to make a lorry park; and the engine of one of the lorries was being run.

Mrs Nicholson could not be blamed for the ivy: *her* absence from Southstone was of long standing, for she had died in 1912 – two years before the outbreak of what Gavin still thought of as Admiral

Concannon's war. After her death, the house had been put up for auction by her executors: since then, it might well have changed hands two or three times. Probably few of the residents dislodged in 1940 had so much as heard Mrs Nicholson's name. In its condition, today, the house was a paradox: having been closed and sealed up with extreme care, it had been abandoned in a manner no less extreme. It had been nobody's business to check the ivy. Nor, apparently, had there been anybody to authorize a patriotic sacrifice of the railings – Gavin Doddington, prodding between the strands of ivy, confirmed his impression that that iron lacework still topped the parapet of the front garden. He could pursue with his finger, thought not see, the pattern that with other details of the house, outside and in, had long ago been branded into his memory. Looking up at the windows in the exposed half he saw, still in position along the sills, miniature reproductions of this pattern, for the support of window boxes. Those, which were gone, had been flowery in her day.

The assumption was that, as lately as 1940, Mrs Nicholson's house *had* belonged to someone, but that it belonged to nobody now. The late owner's death in some other part of England must have given effect to a will not brought up to date, by which the property pased to an heir who could not be found – to somebody not heard of since Singapore fell or not yet reported anything more than 'missing' after a raid on London or a battle abroad. Legal hold-ups dotted the world-wide mess . . . So reasoning, Gavin Doddington gave rein to what had been his infant and was now his infantile passion for explanation. But also he attached himself to the story as to something nothing to do with him; and did so with the intensity of a person who must think lest he should begin to feel.

His passion for explanation had been, when he knew Mrs Nicholson, raised by her power of silently baulking it into the principal reason for suffering. It had been among the stigmata of his extreme youth – he had been eight when he met her, ten when she died. He had not been back to Southstone since his last stay with her.

Now, the lifting of the official ban on the area had had the effect of bringing him straight back – why? When what one has refused is put out of reach, when what one has avoided becomes forbidden, some lessening of the inhibition may well occur. The ban had so acted on his reluctance that, when the one was removed, the other came away with it – as a scab, adhering, comes off with a wad of lint. The transmutation, due to the fall of France, of his '*I* cannot go back to Southstone' into '*One* cannot go there' must have been salutary, or, at least, exteriorizing. It so happened that when the ban came off he had been due for a few days' leave from the

Ministry. He had at once booked a room at one of the few hotels that remained at the visitor's disposition.

Arriving at Southstone yesterday evening, he had confined his stroll in the hazy marine dusk to the cracked, vacant and wire-looped Promenade – from which he returned with little more than the wish that he had, after all, brought somebody down here with him. Amorist since his 'teens, he had not often set off on a holiday uncompanioned. The idea of this as a pilgrimage revolted him: he remained in the bar till the bar closed. This morning he had no more than stalked the house, approaching it in wavering closing circles through the vaguer Southstone areas of association. He had fixed for the actual confrontation that hour, deadline for feeling, immediately after lunch.

The story originated in a friendship between two young girls in their Dresden finishing year. Edith and Lilian had kept in touch throughout later lives that ran very widely apart – their letters, regularly exchanged, were perhaps more confidential than their infrequent meetings. Edith had married a country gentleman, Lilian a business man. Jimmie Nicholson had bought the South-stone house for his wife in 1907, not long before his death, which had been the result of a stroke. He had been senior by about fifteen years: their one child, a daughter, had died at birth.

Edith Doddington, who had never been quite at ease on the subject of Lilian's marriage, came to stay more often now her friend was a widow, but still could not come as often as both would have liked. Edith's own married life was one of contrivance and of anxiety. After money, the most pressing of Edith's worries centred round the health of her second son: Gavin had been from birth a delicate little boy. The damp of his native county, inland and low-lying, did not suit him: there was the constant question of change of air – till his health stabilized, he could not go away to school. It was natural that Lilian, upon discovering this, should write inviting Gavin to stay at Southstone – ideally, of course, let his mother bring him; but if Edith could not be free, let him come alone. Mrs Nicholson hoped he and she, who had not yet met, would not, or would not for long, be shy of each other. Her maid Rockham was, at any rate, good with children.

Gavin had heard of Southstone as the scene of his mother's only exotic pleasures. The maid Rockham was sent to London to meet him: the two concluded their journey with the absurdly short drive, in an open victoria, from the station to Mrs Nicholson's house. It was early in what was a blazing June: the awnings over the windows rippled, the marguerites in the window-boxes undulated, in a hot breeze coming down the avenue from the sea. From the awnings the rooms inside took a tense bright dusk. In the sea-blue drawing-room, up whose walls reared mirrors framed in ivory brackets, Gavin was left to await Mrs Nicholson. He had time to marvel at the variety of the bric-à-brac crowding brackets and tables, the manyness of the cut-crystal vases, the earliness of the purple and white sweet pea – at the Doddingtons', sweet pea did not flower before July. Mrs Nicholson then entered: to his surprise she did not kiss him.

Instead, she stood looking down at him – she was tall – with a glittering, charming uncertainty. Her head bent a little lower, during consideration not so much of Gavin as of the moment. Her *coiffeur* was like spun sugar: that its crisp upward waves should seem to have been splashed with silvery powder added, only, marquise-like glowing youth to her face.

The summery light-like fullness of her dress was accentuated by the taut belt with coral-inlaid clasp: from that small start the skirts flowed down to dissipate and spread where they touched the floor. Tentatively she extended her right hand, which he, without again raising his eyes, shook. 'Well . . . Gavin,' she said. 'I hope you had a good journey? I am so very glad you could come.'

He said: 'And my mother sends you her love.'

'Does she?' Sitting down, sinking an elbow into the sofa cushions, she added: 'How *is* Edith – how is your mother?'

'Oh, she is very well.'

She vaguely glanced round her drawing-room, as though seeing it from his angle, and, therefore, herself seeing it for the first time. The alternatives it offered could be distracting: she soon asked him her first intimate question – 'Where do you think you would like to sit?'

Not that afternoon, nor indeed, until some way on into this first visit did Gavin distinguish at all sharply between Mrs Nicholson and her life. Not till the knife of love gained sufficient edge could he cut out her figure from its surroundings. Southstone was, for the poor landowner's son, the first glimpse of the enchanted existence of the *rentier*. Everything was effortless; and, to him, consequently, seemed stamped with style. This society gained by smallness: it could be comprehended. People here, the company that she kept, commanded everything they desired, were charged with nothing they did not. The expenditure of their incomes – expenditure calculated so long ago and so nicely that it could now seem artless – occupied them. What there was to show for it showed at every turn; though at no turn too much, for it was not too much. Such light, lofty, smooth-running houses were to be found, quite likely, in no capital city. A word to the livery stables brought an imposing carriage to any door: in the afternoons one drove, in a little party, to reflect on a Roman ruin or to admire a village church. In the Promenade's glare, at the end of the shaded avenue, parasols passed and repassed in a rhythm of leisure. Just inland were the attentive shops. There were meetings for good causes in cool drawing-rooms, afternoon concerts in the hotel ballrooms; and there was always the theatre, where applause continued long after Gavin had gone to bed. Best of all, there were no poor to be seen.

The plan of this part of Southstone (a plateau backed by the downs and overhanging the sea) was masterful. Its architecture was ostentatious, fiddling, bulky and mixed. Gavin was happy enough to be at an age to admire the one, to be unaware of the other – he was elated, rather than not, by this exhibition of gimcrack size; and bows, bays, balustrades, glazed-in balconies and French-type mansardes not slowly took up their parts in the fairy tale. As strongly was he impressed by the strong raying out, from such points as station and theatre, of avenues; each of which crossed, obliquely, just less wide residential roads. Lavishness appeared in the public flowers, the municipal seats with their sofa-like curving backs, the flagpoles, cliff grottoes, perspectives of lawn. There was a climate here that change from season to season, the roughest Channel gale blowing, could not disturb. This town without function fascinated him – outside it, down to the port or into the fishing quarter, 'old Southstone', he did not attempt to stray. Such tameness might have been found odd in a little boy: Mrs Nicholson never thought of it twice.

Gavin's estimation of Southstone – as he understood much later – coincided with that of a dead man. When Jimmie Nicholson bought the house for his wife here, Southstone was the high dream of his particular world. It was as Lilian's husband he made the choice: alone, he might not have felt capable of this polished leisure. His death left it uncertain whether, even *as* Lilian's husband, he could have made the grade. The golf course had been his object: failing that he was not, perhaps, so badly placed in the cemetery, which was also outside the town. For, for Southstone dividends kept their mystic origin: they were as punctual as Divine grace, as unmentioned as children still in wombs. Thickset Jimmie, with his pursuant reek of the City, could have been a distasteful reminder of money's source.

Gavin, like his dead host, beheld Southstone with all the ardour of an outsider. His own family had a touch of the brutishness that comes from any dependence upon land. Mr and Mrs Doddington were constantly in wet clothes, constantly fatigued, constantly depressed. Nothing new appeared in the squire's home; and what was old had acquired a sort of fog from being ignored. An austere, religious idea of their own standing not so much inspired as preyed upon Gavin's parents. Caps touched to them in the village could not console them for the letters they got from their bank. Money for them was like a spring in a marsh, feebly thrusting its way up to be absorbed again: any profit forced from the home farm, any rents received for outlying lands went back again into upkeep, rates, gates, hedging, draining, repairs to cottages and renewal of stock. There was nothing, no nothing ever, to show. In the society round them they played no part to which their position did not compel them: they were poor gentry, in fact, at a period when poverty could not be laughed away. Their lot was less enviable than that of any of their employees or tenants, whose faces, naked in their dejection, and voices pitched to complaints they could at least utter, had disconcerted Gavin, since babyhood, at the Hall door. Had the Doddingtons been told that their kind would die out, they would have expressed little more than surprise that such complicated troubles could end so simply.

Always towards the end of a stay at Southstone Gavin's senses began to be haunted by the anticipation of going back. So much so that to tread the heat-softened asphalt was to feel once more the suck of a sticky lane. *Here*, day and night he breathed with ease that was still a subconscous joy: the thought of the Midlands made his lungs contract and deaden – such was the old cold air, sequestered by musty baize doors, of the corridors all the way to his room at home.

His room *here* was on the second floor, in front, looking on to the avenue. It had a frieze of violets knotted along a ribbon: as dusk deepened, these turned gradually black. Later, a lamp from the avenue cast a tree's shifting shadow on to the ceiling above his bed; and the same light pierced the Swiss skirts of the dressing-table. Mrs Nicholson, on the first occasion when she came as far as his door to say good night, deprecated the 'silliness' of this little room. Rockham, it seemed, had thought it suitable for his age – she, Rockham, had her quarters on the same floor – Mrs Nicholson, though she did not say so, seemed to feel it to be unsuitable for his sex. 'Because I don't suppose,' she said, 'that you really ever *are* lonely in the night?'

Propped upright against his pillows, gripping his glass of milk, he replied: 'I am never frightened.'

'But, lonely – what makes you lonely, then?'

'I don't know. I suppose, thoughts.'

'Oh, but why,' she said, 'don't you like them?'

'When I am here the night seems a sort of waste, and I don't like to think what a waste it is.'

Mrs Nicholson, who was on her way out to dinner, paused in the act of looping a gauze scarf over her hair and once again round her throat. 'Only tell me,' she said, 'that you're not more lonely, Gavin, because I am going out? Up here, you don't know if I am in the house or not.'

'I do know.'

'Perhaps,' she suggested humbly, 'you'll go to sleep? They all say it is right for you, going to bed so early, but I wish it did not make days so short. – I must go.'

'The carriage hasn't come round yet.'

'No, it won't: it hasn't been ordered. It is so lovely this evening, I thought I would like to walk.' She spoke, though, as though the project were spoiled for her: she could not help seeing, as much as he did, the unkindness of leaving him with this picture. She came even further into the room to adjust her scarf at his mirror, for it was not yet dark. 'Just once, one evening perhaps, you could stay up late. Do you think it would matter? I'll ask Rockham.'

Rockham remained the arbiter: it was she who was left to exercise anything so nearly harsh as authority. In even the affairs of her own house Mrs Nicholson was not heard giving an order: what could not be thought to be conjured into existence must be part of the clockwork wound up at the start by Jimmie and showing no sign of beginning to run down yet. The dishes that came to table seemed to surprise her as much, and as pleasingly, as they did Gavin. Yet the effect she gave was not of idleness but of pre-occupation: what she did with her days Gavin did not ask himself – when he did ask himself, later, it was too late. They continued to take her colour – those days she did nothing with.

It was Rockham who worked out the daily programme, devised to keep the little boy out of Madam's way. 'Because Madam,' she said, 'is not accustomed to children.' It was by Rockham that, every morning, he was taken down to play by the sea: the beach, undulations of orange shingle, was fine-combed with breakwaters, against one of which sat Rockham, reading a magazine. Now and then she would look up, now and then she would call. These relegations to Rockham sent Gavin to angry extremes of in-fantilism: he tried to drape seaweed streamers around her hat; he plagued to have pebbles taken out of his shoe. There was a literal feeling of degradation about this descent from the plateau to the cliff's foot. From close up, the sea, with its heaving mackerel vacancy, bored him – most of the time he stood with his back to it, shading his eyes and staring up at the heights. From right down here, though Southstone could not be seen – any more than objects set back on a high shelf can be seen by somebody standing immediately underneath it – its illusion, its magical artificiality, was to be savoured as from nowhere else. Tiny, the flags of the

Promenade's edge, the figures leaning along the railings, stood out against a dazzle of sky. And he never looked up at these looking down without an interrupted heartbeat – might she not be among them?

The rule was that they, Rockham and Gavin, walked zigzag down by the cliff path, but travelled up in the lift. But one day fate made Rockham forget her purse. They had therefore to undertake the ascent. The path's artful gradients, hand-railed, were broken by flights of steps and by niched seats, upon every one of which Rockham plumped herself down to regain breath. The heat of midday, the glare from the flowered cliff beat up Gavin into a sort of fever. As though a dropped plummet had struck him between the eyes he looked up, to see Mrs Nicholson's face above him against the blue. The face, its colour rendered transparent by the transparent silk of a parasol, was inclined forward: he had the experience of seeing straight up into eyes that did not see him. Her look was pitched into space: she was not only not seeing him, she was seeing nothing. She was listening, but not attending, while someone talked.

Gavin, gripping the handrail, bracing his spine against it, leaned out backwards over the handrail into the void, in the hopes of intercepting her line of view. But in vain. He tore off clumps of sea pinks and cast the too-light flowers outwards into the air, but her pupils never once flickered down. Despair, the idea that his doom must be never, never to reach her, not only now but ever, gripped him and gripped his limbs as he took the rest of the path – the two more bends and few more steps to the top. He clawed his way up the rail, which shook in its socket.

The path, when it landed Gavin on to the Promenade, did so some yards from where Mrs Nicholson and her companion stood. Her companion was Admiral Concannon. 'Hello, hello!' said the Admiral, stepping back to see clear of the parasol. 'Where have *you* sprung from?'

'Oh, but Gavin,' exclaimed Mrs Nicholson, also turning, 'why not come up in the lift? I thought you liked it.'

'Lift?' said the Admiral. 'Lift, at his age? What, has the boy got a dicky heart?'

'No indeed!' she said, and looked at Gavin so proudly that he became the image of health and strength.

'In that case,' said the Admiral, 'do him good.' There was something, in the main, not unflattering about this co-equal masculine brusqueness. Mrs Nicholson, looking over the railings, perceived the labouring top of her maid's hat. 'It's poor Rockham,' she said, 'that I am thinking about; she hasn't got a heart but she has attacks. – How hazy it is!' she said, indicating the horizon with a gloved hand. 'It seems to be days since we saw France. I don't believe Gavin believes it is really there.'

'It is there all right,' said the Admiral, frowning slightly.

'Why, Rockham,' she interposed, 'you look hot. Whatever made you walk up on a day like this?'

'Well, I cannot fly, can I, madam; and I overlooked my purse.'

'Admiral Concannon says we may all be flying. – What are you waiting for?'

'I was waiting for Master Gavin to come along.'

'I don't see why he should, really – which would you rather, Gavin?'

Admiral Concannon's expression did not easily change, and did not change now. His features were severely clear cut; his figure was nervy and spare; and he had an air of eating himself – due, possibly, to his retirement. His manners of walking, talking and standing, though all to be recognized at a distance, were vehemently impersonal. When in anything that could be called repose he usually kept his hands in his pockets – the abrupt extraction of one hand, for the purpose of clicking thumb and finger together, was the nearest thing to a gesture he ever made. His voice and step had become familiar, among the few nocturnal sounds of the avenue, some time before Gavin had seen his face; for he escorted Mrs Nicholson home from parties to which she had been wilful enough to walk. Looking out one night, after the hall door shut, Gavin had seen the head of a cigarette, immobile, pulsating sharply under the dark trees. The Concannons had settled at Southstone for Mrs Concannon's health's sake: their two daughters attended one of the schools.

Liberated into this blue height, Gavin could afford to look down in triumph at the sea by whose edge he had lately stood. But the Admiral said: 'Another short turn, perhaps?' – since they were to *be* three, they had better be three in motion. Mrs Nicholson raised her parasol, and the three moved off down the Promenade with the dignified aimlessness of swans. Ahead, the distance dissolved, the asphalt quivered in heat; and she, by walking between her two companions, produced a democracy of masculine trouble into which age did not enter at all. As they passed the bandstand she said to Gavin: 'Admiral Concannon has just been saying that there is going to be a war.'

Gavin glanced across at the Admiral, who remained in profile. Unassisted and puzzled, he said: 'Why?'

'Why indeed?' she agreed. – 'There!' she said to the Admiral. 'It's no good trying to tease me, because I never believe you.' She glanced around her and added: 'After all, we live in the present day! History is quite far back; it is said, of course, but it does seem silly. I never even cared for history at school; I was glad when we came to the end of it.'

'And when, my dear, did you come to the end of history?'

'The year I put up my hair. It had begun to be not so bad from the time we started catching up with the present; and I was glad I had stayed at school long enough to be sure that it had all ended happily. But oh, those unfortunate people in the past! It seems unkind to say so, but can it have been their faults? They can have been no more like us than cats and dogs. I suppose there *is* one reason for learning history – one sees how long it has taken to make the world nice. Who on earth could want to upset things now? – No one could want to,' she said to the Admiral. 'You forget the way we behave now, and there's no other way. Civilized countries are polite to each other, just as you and I are to the people we know, and uncivilized countries are put down – but, if one thinks, there are beautifully few of those. Even savages really prefer wearing hats and coats. Once people wear hats and coats and can turn on electric light, they would no more want to be silly than you or I do. – Or *do* you want to be silly?' she said to the Admiral.

He said: 'I did not mean to upset you.'

'You don't,' she said. 'I should not dream of suspecting *any* civilized country!'

'Which civilized country?' said Gavin. 'France?'

'For your information,' said the Admiral coldly, 'it is Germany we should be preparing to fight, for the reason that she is preparing to fight us.'

'I have never been happier anywhere,' said Mrs Nicholson, more nearly definitely than usual. 'Why,' she added, turning to Gavin, 'if it were not for Germany, now I come to think of it, you would not be here!'

The Admiral, meanwhile, had become intent on spearing on the tip of his cane a straying fragment of paper, two inches torn off a letter, that was defiling the Promenade. Lips compressed, he crossed to a little basket (which had till then stood empty, there being no litter) and knocked the fragment into it off his cane. He burst out: 'I should like to know what this place is coming to – we shall have trippers next!'

This concern his beautiful friend *could* share – and did so share that harmony was restored. Gavin, left to stare out to sea, reflected on one point in the conversation: he could never forget that the Admiral had called Mrs Nicholson, 'My dear'.

Also, under what provocation had the Admiral threatened Mrs Nicholson with war? . . . Back at Gavin's home again, once more with his parents, nothing was, after all, so impossible: this was outside the zone of electric light. As late summer wore slowly over the Midlands, the elms in the Doddingtons' park casting lifeless slate-coloured shadows over sorrel, dung, thistles and tufted grass, it was born in on Gavin that this existence belonged, by its nature, to *any* century. It was unprogressive. It had stayed as it was while, elsewhere, history jerked itself painfully off the spool; it could hardly be more depressed by the fateful passage of armies than by the flooding of tillage or the failure of crops: it was hardly capable, really, of being depressed further. It was an existence mortgaged to necessity; it was an inheritance of uneasiness, tension and suspicion. One could preassume the enmity of weather, prices, mankind, cattle. It was this dead weight of existence that had supplied to history not so much the violence or the futility that had been, as she said, apparent to Mrs Nicholson, but its repetitive harshness and its power to scar. This existence had no volition, but could not stop; and its never stopping, because it could not, made history's ever stopping the less likely. No signs of even an agreeable pause were to be seen round Doddington Hall. Nor could one, at such a distance from Southstone, agree that time had laboured to make the world nice.

Gavin now saw his mother as Mrs Nicholson's friend. Indeed, the best of the gowns in which Edith went out to dinner, when forced to go out to dinner, had been Lilian's once, and once or twice worn by her. Worn by Edith, they still had the exoticism of gifts, and dispelled from their folds not only the giver's sachets, but the easy pitiful lovingness of the giver's mood. In them, Gavin's mother's thin figure assumed a grace whose pathos was lost to him at the time. While the brown-yellow upward light of the table oil-lamp unkindly sharpened the hollows in Mrs Doddington's face and throat, Gavin, thrown sideways out of his bed, fingered the mousseline or caressed the satin of the skirts with an adoring absorption that made his mother uneasy – for fetishism is still to be apprehended by these for whom it has never had any name. She would venture: 'You like, then, to see me in pretty clothes?' . . . It was, too, in the first of these intermissions between his visits to Southstone that he, for the first time, took stock of himself, of his assets – the evident pleasingness of his manner; his looks – he could take in better and better part his elder brother's jibes at his pretty-prettiness – his quickness of mind, which at times made even his father smile; and his masculinity, which, now he tried it out, gave him unexpected command of small situations. At home, nights were not a waste: he attached himself to his thoughts, which took him, by seven-league strides, onward to his next visit. He rehearsed, using his mother, all sorts of little gratuities of behaviour, till she exclaimed: 'Why, Lilian has made quite a little page of you!' At her heels round the garden or damp extensive offices of the Hall, at her elbow as she peered through her letters or resignedly settled to her accounts, he reiterated: 'Tell me about Germany.'

'Why Germany?'

'I mean, the year you were there.'

A gale tore the slates from the Hall stables, brought one tree down on to a fence and another to block the drive, the night before Gavin left for Southstone. This time he travelled alone. At Southstone, dull shingly roaring thumps from the beach travelled as far inland as the railway station; from the Promenade – on which, someone said, it was all but impossible to stand upright – there came a whistling strain down the avenues. It was early January. Rockham was kept to the house by a nasty cold; so it was Mrs Nicholson who, with brilliantly heightened colour, holding her muff to the cheek on which the wind blew, was on the station platform to meet Gavin. A porter, tucking the two of them into the waiting carriage, replaced the foot-warmer under the fur rug. She said: 'How different this is from when you were with me last. Or do you like winter?'

'I like anything, really.'

'I remember one thing you don't like: you said you didn't like thoughts.' As they drove past a lighted house from which music came to be torn about by the wind, she remembered: 'You've been invited to several parties.'

He was wary: 'Shall you be going to them?'

'Why, yes; I'm sure I *could* go,' she said.

Her house was hermetic against the storm: in the drawing-room, heat drew out the smell of violets. She dropped her muff on the sofa, and Gavin stroked it – 'It's like a cat,' he said quickly, as she turned round. 'Shall I have a cat?' she said. 'Would you like me to have a cat?' All the other rooms, as they went upstairs, were tawny with fires that did not smoke.

Next morning, the wind had dropped; the sky reflected on everything its mild brightness; trees, houses and pavements glistened like washed glass. Rockham, puffy and with a glazed upper lip, said: 'Baster Gavid, You've brought us better weather.' Having blown her nose with what she seemed to hope was exhaustive thoroughness, she concealed her handkerchief in her bosom as guiltily as though it had been a dagger. 'Badam,' she said, 'doesn't like be to have a cold. – Poor Bisses Codcaddod,' she added, 'has been laid up agaid.'

Mrs Concannon's recovery must be timed for the little dinner party that they were giving. Her friends agreed that she ought to reserve her strength. On the morning of what was to be the day, it was, therefore, the Admiral whom one met out shopping: Gavin and Mrs Nicholson came on him moodily selecting flowers and fruit. Delayed late autumn and forced early spring flowers blazed, under artificial light, against the milder daylight outside the florist's plate glass. 'For tonight, for the party?' exclaimed Mrs Nicholson. 'Oh, let us have carnations, scarlet carnations!'

The Admiral hesitated. 'I think Constance spoke of chrysanthemums, white chrysanthemums.'

'Oh, but these are so washy, so like funerals. They will do poor Constance no good, if she still feels ill.'

Gavin, who had examined the prices closely, in parenthesis said: 'Carnations are more expensive.'

'No, wait!' cried Mrs Nicholson, gathering from their buckets all the scarlet carnations that were in reach, and gaily shaking the water from their stems, 'you must let me send these to Constance, because I am so much looking forward to tonight. It will be delightful.'

'I hope so,' the Admiral said. 'But I'm sorry to say we shall be an uneven number: we have just heard that poor Massingham has dropped out. Influenza.'

'Bachelors shouldn't have influenza, should they. – But then, why not ask somebody else?'

'So very much at the last moment, that might seem a bit – informal.'

'Dear me,' she teased, 'have you really *no* old friend?'

'Constance does not feel . . .'

Mrs Nicholson's eyebrows rose: she looked at the Admiral over the carnations. This was one of the moments when the Admiral could be heard to click his finger and thumb. 'What a pity,' she said. 'I don't care for lopsided parties. *I* have one friend who is not touchy – invite Gavin!'

To a suggestion so completely outrageous, who was to think of any reply? It was a *coup*. She completed, swiftly: 'Tonight, then? We shall be with you at about eight.'

Gavin's squiring Mrs Nicholson to the Concannons' party symptomized this phase of their intimacy; without being, necessarily, its highest point. Rockham's cold had imperilled Rockham's prestige: as intervener or arbiter she could be counted out. There being no more talk of these odious drops to the beach, Gavin exercised over Mrs Nicholson's mornings what seemed a conqueror's rights to a terrain; while with regard to her afternoons she showed a flattering indecision as to what might not please him or what he could not share. At her tea-table, his position was made subtly manifest to her guests. His bedtime was becoming later and later; in vain did Rockham stand and cough in the hall; more than once or twice he had dined downstairs. When the curtains were drawn, it was he who lit the piano candles, then stood beside her as she played – ostensibly to turn over the music, but forgetting the score to watch her hands. At the same time, he envisaged their two figures as they would appear to someone – his other self – standing out there in the cold dark of the avenue, looking between the curtains into the glowing room. One evening, she sang 'Two Eyes of Grey that used to be so Bright.'

At the end, he said: 'But that's supposed to be a song sung by a man to a woman.'

Turning on the stool, she said: 'Then you must learn it.'

He objected: 'But your eyes are not grey.'

Indeed they were never neutral eyes. Their sapphire darkness, with that of the sapphire pendant she was wearing, was struck into by the Concannons' electric light. That round fitment on pulleys, with a red silk frill, had been so adjusted above the dinner table as to cast down a vivid circle, in which the guests sat. The stare and sheen of the cloth directly under the light appeared supernatural. The centrepiece was a silver or plated pheasant, around whose base the carnations – slightly but strikingly 'off' the red of the shade, but pre-eminently flattering in their contrast to Mrs Nicholson's orchid *glacé* gown – were bunched in four silver cornets. This was a party of eight: if the Concannons had insisted on stressing its 'littleness', it was, still, the largest that they could hope to give. The evident choiceness of the guests, the glitter and the mathematical placing of the silver and glass, the prompt, meticulous service of the dishes by maids whose suspended breath could be heard – all, all bespoke art and care. Gavin and Mrs Nicholson were so placed as to face one another across the table: her glance contained him, from time to time, in its leisurely, not quite attentive play. He wondered whether she felt, and supposed she must, how great had been the effrontery of their entrance.

For this dinner-party lost all point if it were not *de rigueur*. The Concannon daughters, even (big girls, but with hair still down their backs) had, as not qualified for it, been sent out for the evening. It, the party, had been balanced up and up on itself like a house of cards: built, it remained as precarious. Now the structure trembled, down to its base, from one contemptuous flip at its top story – Mrs Nicholson's caprice of bringing a little boy. Gavin perceived that night what he was not to forget: the helplessness, in the last resort, of society – which he was never, later, to be able to think of as a force. The pianola-like play of the conversation did not drown the nervousness round the table.

At the head of the table the Admiral leaned just forward, as though pedalling the pianola. At the far end, an irrepressible cough from time to time shook Mrs Concannon's décolletage and the crystal pince-nez which, balanced high on her face, gave her a sensitive blankness. She had the *dévote* air of some sailors' wives; and was heroic in pale blue without a wrap – arguably, nothing could make her iller. The Admiral's pride in his wife's courage passed like a current over the silver pheasant. For Mrs Concannon, joy in sustaining all this for his sake, and confidence in him, provided a light armour: she possibly did not feel what was felt for her. To Gavin she could not have been kinder; to Mrs Nicholson she had only and mildly said: 'He will not be shy, I hope, if he does not sit beside you?'

Rearrangement of the table at the last moment could not but have disappointed one or other of the two gentlemen who had expected to sit, and were now sitting, at Mrs Nicholson's right and left hand. More and more, as course followed course, these two showed how highly they rated their good fortune – indeed, the censure around the rest of the table only acted for them, like heat drawing out scent, to heighten the headiness of her immediate aura. Like the quick stuff of her dress her delinquency, even, gave out a sort of shimmer: while she, neither arch nor indolent, turned from one to the other her look – if you like, melting; for it dissolved her pupils, which had never been so dilated, dark, as tonight. In this look, as dinner proceeded, the two flies, ceasing to struggle, drowned.

The reckoning would be on the way home. Silent between the flies' wives, hypnotized by the rise and fall of Mrs Nicholson's pendant, Gavin ate on and on. The ladies' move to the drawing-room sucked him along with it in the wake of the last skirt . . . It was without a word that, at the end of the evening, the Admiral saw Mrs Nicholson to her carriage – Gavin, like an afterthought or a monkey, nipping in under his host's arm extended to hold open the carriage door. Light from the porch, as they drove off, fell for a moment longer on that erect form and implacable hatchet face. Mrs Nicholson seemed to be occupied in gathering up her skirts to make room for Gavin. She then leaned back in her corner, and he in his: not a word broke the tension of the short dark drive home. Not till she had dropped her cloak in front of her drawing-room fire did she remark: 'The Admiral's angry with me.'

'Because of me?'

'Oh dear no; because of her. If I did not think to be angry was very silly, I'd almost be a little angry with him.'

'But you meant to make him angry, didn't you?' Gavin said.

'Only because he's silly,' said Mrs Nicholson. 'If he were not so silly, that poor unfortunate creature would stop coughing: she would either get better or die.' Still standing before her mantel-piece, she studied some freesias in a vase – dispassionately, she pinched off one fading bloom, rolled it into a wax pill between her thumb and finger, then flicked it away to sizzle in the heart of the fire. 'If people,' she said, 'give a party for no other reason but to show off their marriage, what kind of evening can one expect? – However, I quite enjoyed myself. I hope you did?'

Gavin said: 'Mrs Concannon's quite old. But then, so's the Admiral.'

'He quite soon will be, at this rate,' said Mrs Nicholson. 'That's why he's so anxious to have that war. One would have thought a man could just be a man. – What's the matter, Gavin; what are you staring at?'

'That is your most beautiful dress.'

'Yes; that's why I put it on.' Mrs Nicholson sat down on a low blue velvet chair and drew the chair to the fire: she shivered slightly. 'You say such sweet things, Gavin: what fun we have!' Then, as though, within the seconds of silence ticked off over her head by the little Dresden clock, her own words had taken effect with her, she turned and, with an impulsive movement, invited him closer to her side. Her arm stayed round him; her short puffed sleeve, disturbed by the movement, resulted down into silence. In the fire a coal fell apart, releasing a seam of gas from which spurted a pale tense quivering flame. 'Aren't you glad we are back?' she said, 'that we are only you and me? – Oh, why endure such people when all the time there is the whole world! Why do I stay on and on here; what am I doing? Why don't we go right away somewhere, Gavin; you and I? To Germany, or into the sun? Would that make you happy?'

'That – that flame's so funny,' he said, not shifting his eyes from it.

She dropped her arm and cried, in despair: 'After all, what a child you are!'

'I am not.'

'Anyhow, it's late; you must go to bed.'

She transmuted the rise of another shiver into a slight yawn.

Overcharged and trembling, he gripped his way, flight by flight, up the polished banister rail, on which his palms left patches of mist; pulling himself away from her up the staircase as he had pulled himself towards her up the face of the cliff.

After that midwinter visit there were two changes: Mrs Nicholson went abroad, Gavin went to school. He overheard his mother say to his father that Lilian found Southstone this winter really too cold to stay in. 'Or, has made it too hot to stay in?' said Mr Doddington, from whose disapproval the story of Gavin and the Concannons' party had not been able to be kept. Edith Doddington coloured, loyal, and said no more. During his first term Gavin received at school one bright picture postcard of Mentone. The carefully chosen small preparatory school confronted him, after all, with fewer trials than his parents had feared and his brother hoped. His protective adaptability worked quickly; he took enough colour, or colourlessness, from where he was to pass among the others, and along with them – a civil and indifferent little boy. His improved but never quite certain health got him out of some things and secured others – rests from time to time in the sick-room, teas by the matron's fire. This spectacled woman was not quite unlike Rockham; also, she was the most approachable edge of the grown-up ambience that connected him, however remotely, with Mrs Nicholson. At school, his assets of feeling remained, one would now say, frozen.

His Easter holidays had to be spent at home; his summer holidays exhausted their greater part in the same concession to a supposed attachment. Not until September was he dispatched to Southstone, for a week, to be set up before his return to school.

That September was an extension of summer. An admirable company continued its season of light opera at the theatre, in whose gardens salvias blazed. The lawns, shorn to the roots after weeks of mowing, were faintly blond after weeks of heat. Visitors were still many; and residents, after the fastidious retreat of August, were returning – along the Promenade, all day long, parasols, boater hats and light dresses flickered against the dense blue gauze backdrop that seldom let France be seen. In the evenings the head of the pier was a lighted musical box above the not yet cooling sea. Rare was the blade of chill, the too crystal morning or breathlike blur on the distance that announced autumn. Down the avenues the dark green trees hardened but did not change: if a leaf did fall, it was brushed away before anyone woke.

If Rockham remarked that Gavin was now quite a little man, her mistress made no reference to his schoolboy state. She did once ask whether the Norfolk jacket that had succeeded his sailor blouse were not, in this weather, a little hot; but that he might be expected to be more gruff, mum, standoffish or awkward than formerly did not appear to strike her. The change, if any, was in her. He failed to connect – why should he? – her new languor, her more marked contrarieties and her odd little periods of askance musing with the illness that was to be her death. She only said, the summer had been too long. Until the evenings she and Gavin were less alone, for she rose late; and, on their afternoon drives through the country, inland from the coast or towards the downs, they were as often as not accompanied by, of all persons, Mrs Concannon. On occasions when Mrs Concannon returned to Mrs Nicholson's house for tea, the Admiral made it his practice to call for her. The Concannons were very much occupied with preparations for another social event: a Southstone branch of the Awaken Britannia League was to be inaugurated by a drawing-room meeting at their house. The daughters were busy folding and posting leaflets. Mrs Nicholson, so far, could be pinned down to nothing more than a promise to send cakes from her own, or rather her cook's, kitchen.

'But at least,' pleaded Mrs Concannon, at tea one afternoon, 'you should come if only to hear what it is about.'

By five o'clock, in September, Mrs Nicholson's house cast its shadow across the avenue on to the houses opposite, which should otherwise have received the descending sun. In revenge, they cast shadow back through her bow window: everything in the drawing-room seemed to exist in copper-mauve glass, or as though reflected into a tarnished mirror. At this hour, Gavin saw the pale walls, the silver lamp stems, the transparent frills of the cushions with a prophetic feeling of their impermanence. At her friend's words, Mrs Nicholson's hand, extended, paused for a moment over the cream jug. Turning her head she said: 'But I know what it is about; and I don't approve.'

With so little reference to the Admiral were these words spoken that he might not have been there. There, however, he was, standing drawn up above the low tea table, cup and saucer in hand. For a moment, not speaking, he weighed his cup with a frown that seemed to ponder its exact weight. He then said: 'Then, logically, you should not be sending cakes.'

'Lilian,' said Constance Concannon fondly, 'is never logical with regard to her friends.'

'Aren't I?' said Mrs Nicholson.—'But cake, don't you think, makes everything so much nicer? You can't offer people nothing but disagreeable ideas.'

'You are too naughty, Lilian. All the League wants is that we should be alert and thoughtful. – Perhaps Gavin would like to come?'

Mrs Nicholson turned on Gavin a considering look from which complicity seemed to be quite absent; she appeared, if anything, to be trying to envisage him as alert and thoughtful. And the Admiral, at the same moment, fixed the candidate with a measuring eye. 'What may come,' he said, 'is bound, before it is done, to be his affair.' Gavin made no reply to the proposition – and it was found, a minute or two later, that the day fixed for the drawing-room meeting was the day fixed for his return home. School began again after that. 'Well, what a pity,' Mrs Concannon said.

The day approached. The evenings were wholly theirs, for Mrs Nicholson dined out less. Always, from after tea, when any guests had gone, he began to reign. The apartnesses and frustrations of the preceding hours, and, most of all, the occasional dissonances that those could but produce between him and her, sent him pitching towards the twilight in a fever that rose as the week went on. This fever, every time, was confounded by the sweet pointlessness of the actual hour when it came. The warmth that lingered in the exhausted daylight made it possible for Mrs Nicholson to extend

herself on the *chaise longue* in the bow window. Seated on a stool at
the foot of the *chaise longue*, leaning back against the frame of the
window, Gavin could see, through the side pane of the glass
projection in which they sat, the salvias smouldering in the theatre
gardens. As it was towards these that her chair faced, in looking at
them he was looking away from her. On the other hand, they were
looking at the same thing. So they were on the evening that was his
last. At the end of a minute or two of silence she exclaimed: 'No, I
don't care, really, for scarlet flowers. – You do?'

'Except carnations?'

'I don't care for public flowers. And you look and look at them
till I feel quite lonely.'

'I was only thinking, *they* will be here tomorrow.'

'Have you been happy this time, Gavin? I haven't sometimes
thought you've been quite so happy. Has it been my fault?'

He turned, but only to finger the fringe of the Kashmir shawl
that had been spread by Rockham across her feet. Not looking up,
he said: 'I have not seen you so much.'

'There are times,' she said, 'when one seems to be at the other
side of glass. One sees what is going on, but one cannot help it. It
may be what one does not like, but one cannot feel.'

'Here, I always feel.'

'Always feel what?' she remotely and idly asked.

'I just mean, here, I feel. I don't feel, anywhere else.'

'And what is "here"?' she said, with tender mocking obtuseness.
'Southstone? What do you mean by "here"?'

'Near you.'

Mrs Nicholson's attitude, her repose, had not been come at
carelessly. Apparently relaxed, but not supine, she was supported
by six or seven cushions – behind her head, at the nape of her neck,
between her shoulders, under her elbows and in the small of her
back. The slipperiness of this architecture of comfort enjoined
stillness – her repose depended on each cushion staying just where
it was. Up to now, she had lain with her wrists crossed on her
dress: a random turn of the wrist, or flexing of fingers, were the
nearest things to gestures she permitted herself – and indeed, these
had been enough. *Now*, her beginning to say, 'I wonder if they
were right . . .' must, though it sounded nothing more than
reflective, have been accompanied by an incautious movement, for
a cushion fell with a plump to the ground. Gavin went round,
recovered the cushion and stood beside her: they eyed one another
with communicative amazement, as though a third person had
spoken and they were uncertain if they had heard aright. She arched
her waist up and Gavin replaced the cushion. He said: 'If who were
right?'

'Rockham . . . The Admiral. She's always hinting, he's always saying, that I'm in some way thoughtless and wrong with you.'

'Oh, him.'

'I know,' she said. 'But you'll say goodbye to him nicely?'

He shrugged. 'I shan't see him again – this time.'

She hesitated. She was about to bring out something that, though slight, must be unacceptable. 'He *is* coming in,' she said, 'for a moment, just after dinner, to fetch the cakes.'

'Which cakes?'

'The cakes for tomorrow. I had arranged to send them round in the morning, but that would not do; no, that would not be soon enough. Everything is for the Admiral's meeting to make us ready, so everything must be ready in good time.'

When, at nine o'clock, the Admiral's ring was heard, Mrs Nicholson, indecisively, put down her coffee cup. A wood fire, lit while they were at dinner, was blazing languidly in the already warm air: it was necessary to sit at a distance from it. While the bell still rang, Gavin rose, as though he had forgotten something, and left the drawing-room. Passing the maid on her way to open the front door, he made a bolt upstairs. In his bedroom, Rockham was in possession: his trunk waited, open, bottom layer packed; her mending-basket was on the bureau; she was taking a final look through his things – his departure was to be early tomorrow morning. 'Time flies,' she said. 'You're no sooner come than you're gone.' She continued to count handkerchiefs, to stack up shirts. 'I'd have thought,' she said, 'you'd have wanted to bring your school cap.'

'Why? Anyway, it's a silly beastly old colour.'

'You're too old-fashioned,' she said sharply. 'It was high time somebody went to school. – Now you *have* come up, just run down again, there's a good boy, and ask Madam if there's anything for your mother. If it's books, they ought to go in here among your boots.'

'The Admiral's there.'

'Well, my goodness, you know the Admiral.'

Gavin played for time, on the way down, by looking into the rooms on every floor. Their still only partial familiarity, their fullness with objects that, in the half light coming in from the landing, he could only half perceive and did not yet dare touch, made him feel he was still only at the first chapter of the mystery of the house. He wondered how long it would be before he saw them again. Fear of Rockham's impatience, of her calling down to ask what he was up to, made him tread cautiously on the thickly carpeted stairs; he gained the hall without having made a sound. Here he smelled the fresh-baked cakes, waiting in a hamper on the hall table. The drawing-room door stood ajar, on, for a minute, dead silence. The Admiral must have gone, without the cakes.

But then the Admiral spoke. 'You must see, there is nothing more to be said. I am only sorry I came. I did not expect you to be alone.'

'For once, that is not my fault,' replied Mrs Nicholson, unsteadily. 'I do not even know where the child is.' In a voice that hardly seemed to be hers she cried out softly: 'Then this is to go on always? What more do you ask? What else am I to be or do?'

'There's nothing more you can do. And all you must be is, happy.'

'How easy,' Mrs Nicholson said.

'You have always said that that was easy, for you. For my own part, I never considered happiness. There you misunderstood me, quite from the first.'

'Not quite. Was I wrong in thinking you were a man?'

'I'm a man, yes. But I'm not that sort.'

'That is too subtle for me,' said Mrs Nicholson.

'On the contrary, it is too simple for you. You ignore the greater part of my life. You cannot be blamed, perhaps; you have only known me since I was cursed with too much time on my hands. Your – your looks, charm and gaiety, my dear Lilian, I'd have been a fool not to salute at their full worth. Beyond that, I'm not such a fool as I may have seemed. Fool? – all things considered, I could not have been simply that without being something a good deal viler.'

'I have been nice to Constance,' said Mrs Nicholson.

'Vile in my own eyes.'

'I know, that is all you think of.'

'I see, now, where you are in your element. You know as well as I do what your element is; which is why there's nothing more to be said. Flirtation's always been off my beat – so far off my beat, as a matter of fact, that I didn't know what it was when I first saw it. There, no doubt, I was wrong. If you can't live without it, you cannot, and that is that. If you have to be dangled after, you no doubt will be. But don't, my dear girl, go for that to the wrong shop. It would have been enough, where I am concerned, to watch you making a ninnie of that unfortunate boy.'

'Who, poor little funny Gavin?' said Mrs Nicholson. 'Must I have nothing? – I have no little dog. You would not like it, even, if I had a real little dog. And you expect me to think that you do not care . . .'

The two voices, which intensity more than caution kept pitched low, ceased. Gavin pushed open the drawing-room door.

The room, as can happen, had elongated. Like figures at the end of a telescope the Admiral and Mrs Nicholson were to be seen standing before the fire. Of this, not a glint had room to appear between the figures of the antagonists. Mrs Nicholson, head bent as though to examine the setting of the diamond, was twisting round a ring on her raised left hand – a lace-edged handkerchief, like an abandoned piece of stage property, had been dropped and lay on the hearthrug near the hem of her skirts. She gave the impression of having not moved: if they had not, throughout, been speaking from this distance, the Admiral must have taken a step forward. But this, on his part, must have been, and must be, all – his head was averted from her, his shoulders were braced back, and behind his back he imprisoned one of his own wrists in a handcuff grip that shifted only to tighten. The heat from the fire must have made necessary, probably for the Admiral when he came, the opening of a window behind the curtains; for, as Gavin advanced into the drawing-room, a burst of applause entered from the theatre, and continued, drowning the music which had begun again.

Not a tremor recorded the moment when Mrs Nicholson knew Gavin was in the room. Obliquely and vaguely turning her bowed head she extended to him, in an unchanged look, what might have been no more than an invitation to listen, also, to the music. 'Why, Gavin,' she said at last, 'we were wondering where you were.'

Here he was. From outside the theatre, stink still travelled to him from the lorry whose engine was being run. Nothing had changed in the colourless afternoon. Without knowing, he had plucked a leaf of the ivy which now bred and fed upon her house. A soldier, passing behind him to join the others, must have noticed his immobility all the way down the avenue; for the soldier said, out of the side of his mouth: 'Annie doesn't live here any more.' Gavin Doddington, humiliated, affected to study the ivy leaf, whose veins were like arbitrary vulgar fate-lines. He thought he remembered hearing of metal ivy; he knew he had seen ivy carved round marble monuments to signify fidelity, regret, or the tomb-defying tenaciousness of memory – what you liked. Watched by the soldiers, he did not care to make the gesture involving the throwing of the leaf: instead, he shut his hand on it, as he turned from the house. Should he go straight to the station, straight back to London? Not while the impression remained so strong. On the other hand, it would be a long time before the bars opened.

Another walk round Southstone, this afternoon, was necessary: there must be a decrescendo. From his tour of annihilation, nothing out of the story was to be missed. He walked as though he were carrying a guide-book.

Once or twice he caught sight of the immune downs, on the ascent to whose contours war had halted the villas. The most open view was, still, from the gates of the cemetery, past which he and she had so often driven without a thought. Through those gates, the extended dulling white marble vista said to him, only, that the multiplicity of the new graves, in thirty years, was enough in itself to make the position of hers indifferent – she might, once more, be lying beside her husband. On the return through the town towards the lip of the plateau overhanging the sea, the voidness and the air of concluded meaning about the plan of Southstone seemed to confirm her theory: history, after this last galvanized movement forward, had come, as she expected, to a full stop. It had only not stopped where or as she foresaw. Crossing the Promenade obliquely, he made, between wire entanglements, for the railings; to become one more of the spaced-out people who leaned along them, willing to see a convoy or gazing with indifference towards liberated France. The path and steps up the cliff face had been destroyed; the handrail hung out rotting into the air.

Back in the shopping centre, he turned a quickening step, past the shuttered, boarded or concave windows, towards the corner florist's where Mrs Nicholson had insisted on the carnations. But this had received a direct hit: the entire corner was gone. When time takes our revenges out of our hands it is, usually, to execute them more slowly: her vindictiveness, more thorough than ours, might satisfy us, if, in the course of her slowness, we did not forget. In this case, however, she had worked in the less than a second of detonation. Gavin Doddington paused where there was no florist – was he not, none the less, entitled to draw a line through this?

Not until after some time back in the bar did it strike him – there had been one omission. He had not yet been to the Concannons'. He pushed his way out: it was about seven o'clock, twenty minutes or so before the black-out. They had lived in a crescent set just back from a less expensive reach of the Promenade. On his way, he passed houses and former hotels occupied by soldiers or A.T.S. who had not yet gone. These, from top to basement, were in a state of naked, hard, lemon-yellow illumination. Interposing dark hulks gave you the feeling of nothing more than their recent military occupation. The front doors of the Concannons' crescent opened, on the inland side, into a curved street, which, for some military reason now probably out of date, had been blocked at the near end: Gavin had to go round. Along the pavements under the front doorsteps there was so much wire that he was thrust out into the road – opposite only one house was there an inviting gap in the loops. Admiral Concannon, having died in the last war, could not have obtained this as a concession – all the same this *was*, as the number faintly confirmed, his house. Nobody now but Gavin recognized its identity or its importance. Here had dwelled, and here continued to dwell, the genius of the Southstone that now was. Twice over had there been realized the Admiral's alternative to love.

The Concannons' dinning-room window, with its high triple sashes, was raised some distance above the street. Gavin, standing opposite it, looked in at an A.T.S. girl seated at a table. She faced the window, the dusk and him. From above her head, a naked electric light bulb, on a flex shortened by being knotted, glared on the stripped, whitish walls of the room and emphasized the fact that she was alone. In her khaki shirt, sleeves rolled up, she sat leaning her bare elbows on the bare table. Her face was abrupt with youth. She turned one wrist, glanced at the watch on it, then resumed her steady stare through the window, downwards at the dusk in which Gavin stood.

It was thus that, for the second time in his life, he saw straight up into the eyes that did not see him. The intervening years had given him words for trouble: a phrase, *'l'horreur de mon néant'*, darted across his mind.

At any minute, the girl would have to approach the window to do the black-out – for that, along this coast, was still strictly enforced. It was worth waiting. He lighted a cigarette: she looked at her watch again. When she did rise it was, first, to unhook from a peg beside the dining-room door not only her tunic but her cap. Her being dressed for the street, when she did reach up and, with a succession of movements he liked to watch, begin to twitch the black stuff across the window, made it his object *not* to be seen – just yet. Light staggered, a moment longer, on the desiccated pods of the wall-flowers that, seeded from the front garden, had sprung up between the cracks of the pavement, and on the continuous regular loops or hoops of barbed wire, through all of which, by a sufficiently long leap, one *could* have projected oneself head foremost, unhurt. At last she had stopped the last crack of light. She had now nothing to do but to come out.

Coming smartly down the Concannons' steps, she may just have seen the outline of the civilian waiting, smoking a cigarette. She swerved impassively, if at all. He said: 'A penny for your thoughts.' She might not have heard. He fell into step beside her. Next, appearing to hear what he had not said, she replied: 'No, I'm *not* going your way.'

'Too bad. But there's only one way out – can't get out, you know, at the other end. What have *I* got to do, then – stay here all night?'

'*I* don't know, I'm sure.' Unconcernedly humming, she did not even quicken her light but ringing tramp on the curved street. If he kept abreast with her, it was casually, and at an unpressing distance: this, and the widening sky that announced the open end of the crescent, must have been reassuring. He called across to her: 'That house you came out of, I used to know people who lived there. I was just looking round.'

She turned, for the first time – she could not help it. 'People lived there?' she said. 'Just fancy. I know I'd sooner live in a tomb. And that goes for all this place. Imagine anyone coming here on a holiday!'

'I'm on a holiday.'

'Goodness. What do you do with yourself?'

'Just look around.'

'Well, I wonder how long you stick it out. – Here's where we go different ways. Good night.'

'I've got nobody to talk to,' Gavin said, suddenly standing still in the dark. A leaf flittered past. She was woman enough to halt, to listen, because this had not been said to her. If her 'Oh yes, we girls have heard that before' was automatic, it was, still more, wavering. He cast away the end of one cigarette and started lighting another: the flame of the lighter, cupped inside his hands, jumped for a moment over his features. Her first thought was: yes, he's quite old – that went along with his desperate jauntiness. Civilian, yes: too young for the last war, too old for this. A gentleman – they were the clever ones. But he had, she perceived, forgotten about her thoughts – what she saw, in that moment before he snapped down the lighter, stayed on the darkness, puzzling her somewhere outside the compass of her own youth. She had seen the face of somebody dead who was still there – 'old' because of the presence, under an icy screen, of a whole stopped mechanism for feeling. Those features had been framed, long ago, for hope. The dints above the nostrils, the lines extending the eyes, the lips' grimacing grip on the cigarette – all completed the picture of someone wolfish. A preyer. But who had said, preyers are preyed upon?

His lower lip came out, thrusting the cigarette up at a debonair angle towards his eyes. 'Not a soul,' he added – this time with calculation, and to her.

'Anyway,' she said sharply, 'I've got a date. Anyway, what made you pick on this dead place? Why not pick on some place where you know someone?'

Pink May

'YES, it was funny,' she said, 'about the ghost. It used to come into my bedroom when I was dressing for dinner – when I was dressing to go out.'

'*You were frightened?*'

'I was in such a hurry; there never was any time. When you have to get dressed in such a hell of a hurry any extra thing is just one thing more. And the room at the times I'm talking about used to be full of daylight – sunset. It had two french windows, and they were on a level with the tops of may trees out in the square. Then may was in flower that month, and it was pink. In that sticky sunshine you have in the evenings the may looked sort of theatrical. It used to be part of my feeling of going out.' She paused, then said, 'That was the month of my life.'

'*What month?*'

'The month we were in that house. I told you, it was a furnished house that we took. With rents the way they are now, it cost less than a flat. They say a house is more trouble, but this was no trouble, because we treated it like a flat, you see. I mean, we were practically never in. I didn't try for a servant because I know there aren't any. When Neville got up in the mornings he percolated the coffee; a char came in to do the cleaning when I'd left for the depot, and we fixed with the caretaker next door to look after the boiler, so the baths were hot. And the beds were comfortable, too. The people who really lived there did themselves well.'

'*You never met them?*'

'No, never – why should we? We'd fixed everything through an agent, the way one does. I've an idea the man was soldiering somewhere, and she'd gone off to be near him somewhere in the country. They can't have had any children, any more than we have – it was one of those small houses, just for two.'

'*Pretty?*'

'Y-yes,' she said. 'It was chintzy. It was one of those oldish houses made over new inside. But you know how it is about other people's belongings – you can't ever quite use them, and they seem to watch you the whole time. Not that there was any question of settling down – how could we, when we were both out all day? And at the beginning of June we moved out again.'

'*Because of the* . . . *?*'

'Oh no,' she said quickly. 'Not that reason, at all.' She lighted a cigarette, took two puffs and appeared to deliberate. 'But what I'm telling you *now* is about the ghost.'

'*Go on.*'

'I was going on. As I say, it used to be funny, dressing away at top speed at the top of an empty house, with the sunset blazing away outside. It seems to me that all those evenings were fine. I used to take taxis back from the depot: you must pay money these days if you want time, and a bath and a change from the skin up was essential – you don't know how one feels after packing parcels all day! I couldn't do like some of the girls I worked with and go straight from the depot on to a date. I can't go and meet someone unless I'm feeling special. So I used to hare home. Neville was never in.'

'*I'd been going to say* . . . '

'No, Neville worked till all hours, or at least he had to hang round in case something else should come in. So he used to dine at his club on the way back. Most of the food would be off by the time he got there. It was partly that made him nervy, I dare say.'

'*But you weren't nervy?*'

'I tell you,' she said, 'I was happy. Madly happy – perhaps in rather a nervy way. Whatever you are these days, you are rather more so. That's one thing I've discovered about this war.'

'*You were happy* . . . '

'I had my reasons – which don't come into the story.'

After two or three minutes of rapid smoking she leaned forward to stub out her cigarette. 'Where was I?' she said, in a different tone.

'*Dressing* . . . '

'Well, first thing when I got in I always went across and opened my bedroom windows, because it seemed to me the room smelled of the char. So I always did that before I turned on my bath. The glare on the trees used to make me blink, and the thick sort of throaty smell of the may came in. I was never certain if I liked it or not, but it somehow made me feel like after a drink. Whatever happens tomorrow, I've got tonight. You know the feeling? Then I turned on my bath. The bathroom was the other room on that floor, and a door led through to it from one side of the bed. I used to have my bath with that door ajar, to let light in. The bathroom black-out took so long to undo.

'While the bath ran in I used to potter about and begin to put out what I meant to wear, and cold-cream off my old make-up, and so on. I say "potter" because you cannot hurry a bath. I also don't mind telling you that I whistled. Well, what's the harm in *some-body's* being happy? Simply thinking things over won't win this war. Looking back at that month, I whistled most of the time. The way they used to look at me, at the depot! The queer thing is, though, I remember whistling but I can't remember when I happened to stop. But I must *have* stopped, because it was then I heard.'

'*Heard?*'

She lit up again, with a slight frown. 'What was it I heard first, that first time? I suppose, the silence. So I must have stopped whistling, mustn't I? I was lying there in my bath, with the door open behind me, when the silence suddenly made me sit right up. Then I said to myself, "My girl, there's nothing queer about *that*. What else would you expect to hear, in an empty house?" All the same, it made me heave the other way round in my bath, in order to keep one eye on the door. After a minute I heard what wasn't a silence – which immediately made me think that Neville had come in early, and I don't mind telling you I said "Damn".'

'*Oh?*'

'It's a bore being asked where one is going, though it's no bother to say where one has been. If Neville *was* in he'd be certain to search the house, so I put a good face on things and yelled "Hoi". But he didn't answer, because it wasn't him.'

'*?*'

'No, it wasn't. And whatever was in my bedroom must have been in my bedroom for some time. I thought, "A wind has come up and got into that damned chintz!" Any draught always fidgets me; somehow it gets me down. So I got out of my bath and wrapped the big towel round me and went through to shut the windows in my room. But I was surprised when I caught sight of the may trees – all their branches were standing perfectly still. That seemed queer. At the same time, the door I'd come through from the bathroom blew shut, and the lid fell off one of my jars of face cream on to the dressing-table, which had a glass top.

'No, I didn't see what it was. The point was, whatever it was saw me.

'That first time, the whole thing was so slight. If it had been only that one evening, I dare say I shouldn't have thought of it again. Things only get a hold on you when they go on happening. But I always have been funny in one way – I especially don't like being watched. You might not think so from my demeanour, but I don't really like being criticized. I don't think I get my knife into other people: why should they get their knife into me? I don't like it when my ear begins to burn.

'I went to put the lid back on the jar of cream and switch the lights on into the mirror, which being between the two windows never got the sort of light you would want. I thought I looked odd in the mirror – rattled. I said to myself, "Now what have I done to *someone?*" but except for Neville I literally couldn't think. Anyway, there was no time – when I picked up my wristwatch I said, "God!" So I flew round, dressing. Or rather, I flew round as much as one could with something or somebody getting in the way. That's all I remember about that *first* time, I think. Oh yes, I did notice that the veil on my white hat wasn't all that it ought to be. When I had put that hat out before my bath the whole affair had looked as crisp as a marguerite – a marguerite that has only opened today.

'You know how it is when a good deal hangs on an evening – you simply can't afford to be not in form. So I gave myself a good shake on the way downstairs. "Snap out of that!" I said. "You've got personality. You can carry a speck or two on the veil."

'Once I got to the restaurant – once I'd met him – the whole thing went out of my mind. I was in twice as good form as I'd ever been. And the turn events took . . .

'It was about a week later that I had to face it. I was up against something. The more the rest of my life got better and better, the more that one time of each evening got worse and worse. Or rather, it wanted to. But I wasn't going to let it. With everything else quite perfect – well, would *you* have? There's something exciting, I mean, some sort of a challenge about knowing someone's *trying* to get you down. And when that someone's another woman you soon get a line on her technique. She was jealous, that was what was the matter with her.

'Because, at all other times the room was simply a room. There wasn't any objection to me and Neville. When I used to slip home he was always asleep. I could switch all the lights on and kick my shoes off and open and shut the cupboards – he lay like the dead. He *was* abnormally done in, I suppose. And the room was simply a room in somebody else's house. And the mornings, when he used to roll out of bed and slip-slop down to make the coffee, without speaking, exactly like someone walking in his sleep, the room was no more than a room in which you've just woken up. The may outside looked pink-pearl in the early sunshine, and there were some regular birds who sang. Nice. While I waited for Neville to bring the coffee I used to like to lie there and think my thoughts.

'If he was awake at all before he had left the house, he and I exchanged a few perfectly friendly words. I had *no* feeling of anything blowing up. If I let him form the impression that I'd been spending the evenings at movies with girl friends I'd begun to make at the depot, then going back to their flats to mix Ovaltine – well, that seemed to me the considerate thing to do. If he'd even

been more *interested* in my life – but he wasn't interested in anything but his work. I never picked on him about that – I must say, I
do know when a war's a war. Only men are so different. You see,
this other man worked just as hard but *was* interested in me. He
said he found me so restful. Neville never said that. In fact, all the
month we were in that house, I can't remember anything Neville
said at all.

'No, what *she* couldn't bear was my going out, like I did. She was
either a puritan, with some chip on her shoulder, or else she'd once
taken a knock. I incline to that last idea – though I can't say why.

'No, I can't say why. I have never at all been a subtle person. I
don't know whether that's a pity or not. I must say I don't care for
subtle people – my instinct would be to give a person like that a
miss. And on the whole I should say I'd succeeded in doing so. But
that, you see, was where her advantage came in. You can't give
a . . . well, I couldn't give *her* a miss. She was there. And she
aimed at encircling me.

'I think maybe she had a poltergeist that she brought along with
her. The little things that happened to my belongings . . . Each
evening I dressed in that room I lost five minutes – I mean, each
evening it took me five minutes longer to dress. But all that was
really below her plane. That was just one start at getting me down
before she opened up with her real technique. The really subtle
thing was the way her attitude changed. That first time (as I've told
you) I felt her disliking me – well, really "dislike" was to put it
mildly. But after an evening or two she was through with that. She
conveyed the impression that she had got me taped and was simply
so damned sorry for me. She was sorry about every garment I put
on, and my hats were more than she was able to bear. She was
sorry about the way I did up my face – she used to be right at my
elbow when I got out my make-up, absolutely silent with despair.
She was sorry I should never again see thirty, and sorry I should kid
myself about that . . . I mean to say, she started pitying me.

'Do you see what I mean when I say her attitude could have been
quite infectious?

'And that wasn't all she was sorry for me about. I mean, there are
certain things that a woman who's being happy keeps putting out
of her mind. (I mean, when she's being happy about a man.) And
other things you keep putting out of your mind if your husband is
not the man you are being happy about. There's a certain amount
you don't ask yourself, and a certain amount that you might as well
not remember. Now those were exactly the things she kept bringing
up. She liked to bring those up better than anything.

'What I don't know is, and what I still don't know – *why* do all
that to a person who's being happy? To a person who's living the

top month of her life, with the may in flower and everything? What
had I ever done to her? She was dead – I suppose? . . . Yes, I see
now, she must have taken a knock.'

'What makes you think that?'

'I know now how a knock feels.'

'Oh . . . ?'

'Don't look at me such a funny way. I haven't changed, have I?
You wouldn't have noticed anything? . . . I expect it's simply this
time of year: August's rather a tiring month. And things end without warning, before you know where you are. I hope the war will
be over by next spring; I do want to be abroad, if I'm able to.
Somewhere where there's nothing but pines or palms. I don't want
to see London pink may in flower again – *ever*.'

'Won't Neville . . . ?'

'Neville? Oh, didn't you really realize? Didn't I . . . ? He, I,
we've – I mean, we're living apart.' She rose and took the full,
fuming ash-tray across to another table, and hesitated, then
brought an empty tray back. 'Since we left that house,' she said. 'I
told you we left that house. That was why. We broke up.

'It was the *other* thing that went wrong,' she said. 'If I'd still kept
my head with Neville, he and I needn't ever – I mean, one's
marriage *is* something . . . I'd thought I'd always be married,
whatever else happened. I ought to have realized Neville was in a
nervy state. Like a fool I spilled over to Neville; I lost my head. But
by that time I hadn't any control left. When the one thing you've
lived for has crashed to bits . . .

'Crashed was the word. And yet I see now, really, that things
had been weakening for some time. At the time I didn't see, any
more than I noticed the may was fading out in the square – till one
morning the weather changed and I noticed the may was brown.
All the happiness stopped like my stopping whistling – but at what
particular moment I'm never sure.

'The beginnings of the end of it were so small. Like my being a
bit more unpunctual every evening we met. That made us keep
losing our table at restaurants – you know how the restaurants are
these days. Then I somehow got the idea that none of my clothes
were becoming; I began to think he was eyeing my hats unkindly,
and that made me fidget and look my worst. Then I got an idiot
thing about any girl that he spoke of – I didn't like anyone being
younger than me. Then, at what had once been our most perfect
moments, I began to ask myself if I *was* really happy, till I said to
him – which was fatal – "Is there so much in this?" . . . I should
have seen more red lights – when, for instance, he said, "You
know, *you're* getting nervy." And he quite often used to say
"Tired?" in rather a tired way. I used to say, it was just getting

718   *Collected Stories*

dressed in a rush. But the fact is, a man hates the idea of a woman rushing. One night I know I did crack: I said, "Hell, I've got a ghost in my room!" He put me straight into a taxi and sent me – not took me – home.

'I did see him several times after that. So his letter – his letter was a complete surprise . . . The joke was, I really had been out with a girl that evening I came in, late, to find his letter.

'If Neville had not been there when I got the letter, Neville and I might still – I suppose – be married. On the other hand – there are always two ways to see things – if Neville had *not* been there I should have gone mad . . . So now,' she said, with a change of tone, 'I'm living in an hotel. Till I see how things turn out. Till the war is over, or something. It isn't really so bad, and I'm out all day. Look, I'll give you my address and telephone number. It's been wonderful seeing you, darling. You promise we'll meet again? I do really need to keep in touch with my friends. And *you* don't so often meet someone who's seen a ghost!'

'*But look, did you ever see it?*'

'Well, not exactly. No, I can't say I *saw* it.'

'*You mean, you simply heard it?*'

'Well, not exactly that . . . '

'*You saw things move?*'

'Well, I never turned round in time. I . . .

'If you don't understand – I'm sorry I ever told you the story! Not a ghost – when it ruined my whole life! Don't you see, can't you see there must have been *something*? Left to oneself, one doesn't ruin one's life!'

Green Holly

MR RANKSTOCK entered the room with a dragging tread: nobody looked up or took any notice. With a muted groan, he dropped into an armchair – out of which he shot with a sharp yelp. He searched the seat of the chair, and extracted something. '*Your* holly, I think, Miss Bates,' he said, holding it out to her.

Miss Bates took a second or two to look up from her magazine. 'What?' she said. 'Oh, it must have fallen down from that picture. Put it back, please; we haven't got very much.'

'I regret,' interposed Mr Winterslow, 'that we have any: it makes scratchy noises against the walls.'

'It is seasonable,' said Miss Bates firmly.

'You didn't do this to us last Christmas.'

'Last Christmas,' she said, 'I had Christmas leave. This year there seems to be none with berries: the birds have eaten them. If there were not a draught, the leaves would not scratch the walls. I cannot control the forces of nature, can I?'

'How should I know?' said Mr Rankstock, lighting his pipe.

These three by now felt that, like Chevalier and his Old Dutch, they had been together for forty years: and to them it did seem a year too much. Actually, their confinement dated from 1940. They were Experts – in what, the Censor would not permit me to say. They were accounted for by their friends in London as 'being somewhere off in the country, nobody knows where, doing something frightfully hush-hush, nobody knows what.' That is, they were accounted for in this manner if there were still anybody who still cared to ask; but on the whole they had dropped out of human memory. Their reappearances in their former circles were infrequent, ghostly and unsuccessful: their friends could hardly disguise their pity, and for their own part they had not a word to say. They had come to prefer to spend leaves with their families, who at least showed a flattering pleasure in their importance.

This Christmas, it so worked out that there was no question of leave for Mr Rankstock, Mr Winterslow or Miss Bates: with four others (now playing or watching ping-pong in the next room) they composed in their high-grade way a skeleton staff. It may be wondered why, after years of proximity, they should continue to address one another so formally. They did not continue; they had begun again; in the matter of appellations, as in that of intimacy, they had by now, in fact by some time ago, completed the full circle. For some months, they could not recall in which year, Miss Bates had been engaged to Mr Winterslow; before that, she had been extremely friendly with Mr Rankstock. Mr Rankstock's deviation towards one Carla (now at her ping-pong in the next room) had been totally uninteresting to everybody; including, apparently, himself. If the war lasted, Carla might next year be called Miss Tongue; at present, Miss Bates was foremost in keeping her in her place by going on addressing her by her Christian name.

If this felt like their fortieth Christmas in each other's society, it was their first in these particular quarters. You would not have thought, as Mr Rankstock said, that one country house could be much worse than any other; but this had proved, and was still proving, untrue. The Army, for reasons it failed to justify, wanted the house they had been in since 1940; so they – lock, stock and barrel and files and all – had been bundled into another one, six miles away. Since the move, tentative exploration (for they were none of them walkers) had established that they were now surrounded by rather more mud but fewer trees. What they did know was, their already sufficient distance from the market town with its bars and movies had now been added to by six miles. On the other side of their new home, which was called Mopsam Grange, there appeared to be nothing; unless, as Miss Bates suggested, swineherds, keeping their swine. Mopsam village contained villagers, evacuees, a church, a public-house on whose never-open door was chalked 'No Beer, No Matches, No Teas Served', and a vicar. The vicar had sent up a nice note, saying he was not clear whether Security regulations would allow him to call; and the doctor had been up once to lance one of Carla's boils.

Mopsam Grange was neither old nor new. It replaced – unnecessarily, they all felt – a house on this site that had been burned down. It had a Gothic porch and gables, french windows, bow windows, a conservatory, a veranda, a hall which, puce-and-buff tiled and pitch-pine-panelled, rose to a gallery: in fact, every advantage. Jackdaws fidgeted in its many chimneys – for it had, till the war, stood empty: one had not to ask why. The hot-water system made what Carla called rude noises, and was capricious in its supplies to the (only) two mahogany-rimmed baths. The electric light ran from a plant in the yard; if the batteries were not kept charged the light turned brown.

The three now sat in the drawing-room, on whose walls, mirrors and fitments, long since removed, left traces. There were, however, some pictures: General Montgomery (who had just shed his holly) and some Landseer engravings that had been found in an attic. Three electric bulbs, naked, shed light manfully; and in the grate the coal fire was doing far from badly. Miss Bates rose and stood twiddling the bit of holly. 'Something,' she said, 'has got to be done about this.' Mr Winterslow and Mr Rankstock, the latter sucking in his pipe, sank lower, between their shoulder-blades, in their respective armchairs. Miss Bates, having drawn a breath, took a running jump at a table, which she propelled across the floor with a grating sound. *'Achtung!'* she shouted at Mr Rankstock, who, with an oath, withdrew his chair from her route. Having got the table under General Montgomery, Miss Bates – with a display of long, slender leg, clad in ribbed scarlet sports stockings, that was of interest to no one – mounted it, then proceeded to tuck the holly back into position over the General's frame. Meanwhile, Mr Winterslow, choosing his moment, stealthily reached across her empty chair and possessed himself of her magazine.

What a hope!–Miss Bates was known to have eyes all the way down her spine. 'Damn you, Mr Winterslow,' she said, 'put that down! Mr Rankstock, interfere with Mr Winterslow: Mr Winterslow has taken my magazine!' She ran up and down the table like something in a cage; Mr Rankstock removed his pipe from his mouth, dropped his head back, gazed up and said: 'Gad, Miss Bates; you look fine . . . '

'It's a pretty *old* magazine,' murmured Mr Winterslow flicking the pages over.

'Well, *you're* pretty old,' she said. 'I hope Carla gets you!'

'Oh, I can do better, thank you; I've got a ghost.'

This confidence, however, was cut off by Mr Rankstock's having burst into song. Holding his pipe at arm's length, rocking on his bottom in his archair, he led them:

'"Heigh-ho! sing Heigh-ho! unto the green holly:
  Most friendship is feigning, most loving mere folly – "'

'"*Mere folly, mere folly*,"' contributed Mr Winterslow, picking up, joining in. Both sang:

'"*Then, heigh ho, the holly!
   This life is most jolly*."'

'Now – *all!*' said Mr Rankstock, jerking his pipe at Miss Bates. So all three went through it once more, with degrees of passion: Miss Bates, when others desisted, being left singing 'Heigh-ho! sing heigh-ho! sing – ' all by herself. Next door, the ping-pong came to an awe-struck stop. 'At any rate,' said Mr Rankstock, 'we all like Shakespeare.' Miss Bates, whose intelligence, like her singing, tonight seemed some way at the tail of the hunt, looked blank, began to get off the table, and said, 'But I thought that was a Christmas carol?'

Her companions shrugged and glanced at each other. Having taken her magazine away from Mr Winterslow, she was once more settling down to it when she seemed struck. 'What was that you said, about you had got a ghost?'

Mr Winterslow looked down his nose. 'At this early stage, I don't like to say very much. In fact, on the whole, forget it; if you don't mind – '

'Look,' Mr Rankstock said, 'if you've started seeing things – '

'I am only sorry,' his colleague said, 'that I've spoke.'

'Oh no, you're not,' said Miss Bates, 'and we'd better know. Just what *is* fishy about this Grange?'

'There is nothing "fishy",' said Mr Winterslow in a fastidious tone. It was hard, indeed, to tell from his manner whether he did or did not regret having made a start. He had reddened – but not, perhaps, wholly painfully – his eyes, now fixed on the fire, were at once bright and vacant; with unheeding, fumbling movements he got out a cigarette, lit it and dropped the match on the floor, to slowly burn one more hole in the fibre mat. Gripping the cigarette between tense lips, he first flung his arms out, as though casting off a cloak; then pressed both hands, clasped firmly, to the nerve-centre in the nape of his neck, as though to contain the sensation there. 'She was marvellous,' he brought out – 'what I could see of her.'

'Don't talk with your cigarette in your mouth,' Miss Bates said. ' – Young?'

'Adorably, not so very. At the same time, quite – oh well, you know what I mean.'

'Uh-hu,' said Miss Bates. 'And wearing – ?'

'I am certain she had a feather boa.'

'You mean,' Mr Rankstock said, 'that this brushed your face?'

'And when and where did this happen?' said Miss Bates with legal coldness.

Cross-examination, clearly, became more and more repugnant to Mr Winterslow in his present mood. He shut his eyes, sighed bitterly, heaved himself from his chair, said: 'Oh, well – ' and stood indecisively looking towards the door. 'Don't let us keep you,' said Miss Bates. 'But one thing I don't see is: if you're being fed with beautiful thoughts, why you wanted to keep on taking my magazine?'

'I wanted to be distracted.'

'?'

'There *are* moments when I don't quite know where I am.'

'You surprise me,' said Mr Rankstock. – 'Good *God* man, what is the matter?' For Mr Winterslow, like a man being swooped around by a bat, was revolving, staring from place to place high up round the walls of the gaunt, lit room. Miss Bates observed: 'Well, now we *have* started something.' Mr Rankstock, considerably kinder, said: 'That is only Miss Bates's holly, flittering in the wind.'

Mr Winterslow gulped. He walked to the inch of mirror propped on the mantelpiece and, as nonchalantly as possible, straightened his tie. Having done this, he said: 'But there isn't a wind tonight.'

The ghost hesitated in the familiar corridor. Her visibleness, even on Christmas Eve, was not under her own control; and now she had fallen in love again her dependence upon it began to dissolve in patches. This was a concentration of every feeling of the woman prepared to sail downstairs *en grande tenue*. Flamboyance and agitation were both present. But between these, because of her years of death, there cut an extreme anxiety: it was not merely a matter of, how was she? but of, *was* she – tonight – at all? Death had left her to be her own mirror; for into no other was she able to see.

For tonight, she had discarded the feather boa; it had been dropped into the limbo that was her wardrobe now. Her shoulders, she knew, were bare. Round their bareness shimmered a thousand evenings. Her own person haunted her – above her forehead, the crisped springy weight of her pompadour; round her feet the frou-frou of her skirts on a thick carpet; in her nostrils the scent from her corsage; up and down her forearm the glittery slipping of bracelets warmed by her own blood. It is the haunted who haunt.

There were lights in the house again. She had heard laughter, and there had been singing. From those few dim lights and untrue notes her senses, after their starvation, set going the whole old grand opera. She smiled, and moved down the corridor to the gallery, where she stood looking down into the hall. The tiles of the hall floor were as pretty as ever, as cold as ever, and bore, as always on Christmas Eve, the trickling pattern of dark blood. The figure of the man with the side of his head blown out lay as always, one foot just touching the lowest step of the stairs. It was too bad. She had been silly, but it could not be helped. They should not have shut her up in the country. How could she not make hay while the sun shone? The year round, no man except her husband, his uninterest-ing jealousy, his dull passion. Then, at Christmas, so many men that one did not know where to turn. The ghost, leaning further over the gallery, pouted down at the suicide. She said: 'You should have let me explain.' The man made no answer: he never had.

Behind a door somewhere downstairs, a racket was going on: the house sounded funny, there were no carpets. The morning-room door was flung open and four flushed people, headed by a young woman, charged out. They clattered across the man and the trickling pattern as though there were nothing there but the tiles. In the morning-room, she saw one small white ball trembling to stillness upon the floor. As the people rushed the stairs and fought for place in the gallery the ghost drew back – a purest act of repugnance, for this was not necessary. The young woman, to one of whose temples was strapped a cotton-wool pad, held her place and disappeared round a corner exulting: '*My* bath, *my* bath!' 'Then may you freeze in it, Carla!' returned the scrawniest of the defeated ones. The words pierced the ghost, who trembled – they did not know!

Who were they? She did not ask. She did not care. She never had been inquisitive: information had bored her. Her schooled lips had framed one set of questions, her eyes a consuming other. Now the mills of death with their catching wheels had stripped her of semblance, cast her forth on an everlasting holiday from pretence. She was left with – nay, had become – her obsession. Thus is it to be a ghost. The ghost fixed her eyes on the other, the drawing-room door. He had gone in there. He would have to come out again.

The handle turned; the door opened; Winterslow came out. He shut the door behind him, with the sedulous slowness of an uncertain man. He had been humming, and now, squaring his shoulders, began to sing, ' . . . *Mere folly, mere folly* – ' as he crossed the hall towards the foot of the staircase, obstinately never raising his eyes. 'So it is you,' breathed the ghost, with unheard softness. She gathered about her, with a gesture not less proud for being tormentedly uncertain, the total of her visibility – was it possible diamonds should not glitter now, on her rising-and-falling breast – and swept from the gallery to the head of the stairs.

Winterslow shivered violently, and looked up. He licked his lips. He said: 'This cannot go on.'

The ghost's eyes, with tender impartiality and mockery, from above swept Winterslow's face. The hair receding, the furrowed forehead, the tired sag of the jowl, the strain-reddened eyelids, the blue-shaved chin – nothing was lost on her, nothing broke the spell. With untroubled wonder she saw his handwoven tie, his coat pockets shapeless as saddle-bags, the bulging knees of his flannel trousers. Wonder went up in rhapsody: so much chaff in the fire. She never had had illusions: *the* illusion was all. Lovers cannot be choosers. He'd do. He would have to do. – 'I know!' she agreed, with rapture, casting her hands together. 'We are mad – you and I.

Oh, what is going to happen? I entreat you to leave this house tonight!'

Winterslow, in a dank, unresounding voice, said: 'And anyhow, what made you pick on me?'

'It's Kismet,' wailed the ghost zestfully. 'Why did you have to come here? Why you? I had been so peaceful, just like a little girl. People spoke of love, but I never knew what they meant. Oh, I could wish we had never met, you and I!'

Winterslow said: 'I have been here for three months; we have all of us been here, as a matter of fact. Why all this all of a sudden?'

She said: 'There's a Christmas Eve party, isn't there, going on? One Christmas Eve party, there was a terrible accident. Oh, comfort me! No one has understood. – Don't stand *there*; I can't bear it – not just *there!*'

Winterslow, whether he heard or not, cast a scared glance down at his feet, which were in slippers, then shifted a pace or two to the left. 'Let me up,' he said wildly. 'I tell you, I want my spectacles! I just want to get my spectacles. Let me by!'

'*Let* you up!' the ghost marvelled. 'But I am only waiting . . . '

She was more than waiting: she set up a sort of suction, an icy indrawing draught. Nor was this wholly psychic, for an isolated holly leaf of Miss Bates's, dropped at a turn of the staircase, twitched. And not, you could think, by chance did the electric light choose this moment for one of its brown fade-outs: gradually, the scene – the hall, the stairs and the gallery – faded under this fog-dark but glass-clear veil of hallucination. The feet of Winterslow, under remote control, began with knocking unsureness to mount the stairs. At their turn he staggered, steadied himself, and then stamped derisively upon the holly leaf. 'Bah,' he neighed – '*spectacles!*'

By the ghost now putting out everything, not a word could be dared.

'Where are you?'

Weakly, her dress rustled, three steps down: the rings on her hand knocked weakly over the panelling. 'Here, oh here,' she sobbed. 'Where I was before . . . '

'Hell,' said Miss Bates, who had opened the drawing-room door and was looking resentfully round the hall. 'This electric light.'

Mr Rankstock, from inside the drawing-room, said: 'Find the man.'

'The man has gone to the village. Mr Rankstock, if *you* were half a man – . Mr Winterslow, what are you doing, kneeling down on the stairs? Have you come over funny? Really, this is the end.'

At the other side of a baize door, one of the installations began ringing. 'Mr Rankstock,' Miss Bates yelled implacably, 'yours, this time.' Mr Rankstock, with an expression of hatred, whipped out a pencil and pad and shambled across the hall. Under cover of this Mr Winterslow pushed himself upright, brushed his knees and began to descend the stairs, to confront his colleague's narrow but not unkind look. Weeks of exile from any hairdresser had driven Miss Bates to the Alice-in-Wonderland style: her snood, tied at the top, was now thrust back, adding inches to her pale, polished brow. Nicotine stained the fingers she closed upon Mr Winterslow's elbow, propelling him back to the drawing-room. 'There is always drink,' she said. 'Come along.'

He said hopelessly: 'If you mean the bottle between the filing cabinets, I finished that when I had to work last night. – Look here, Miss Bates, why should she have picked on *me*?'

'It has been broken off, then?' said Miss Bates. 'I'm sorry for you, but I don't like your tone. I resent your attitude to my sex. For that matter, why did you pick on her? Romantic, nostalgic, Blue-Danube-fixated – hein? There's Carla, an understanding girl, unselfish, getting over her boils; there are Avice and Lettice, due back on Boxing Day. There is me, as you have ceased to observe. But oh dear no; *we* do not trail feather boas – '

' – She only wore that in the afternoon.'

'Now let me tell you something,' said Miss Bates. 'When I opened the door, just now, to have a look at the lights, what do you think *I* first saw there in the hall?'

'Me,' replied Mr Winterslow, with returning assurance.

'O-*oh* no; oh indeed no,' said Miss Bates. 'You – why should I think twice of that, if you *were* striking attitudes on the stairs? You? – no, I saw your enchanting inverse. Extended, and it is true stone dead, I saw the man of my dreams. From his attitude, it was clear he had died for love. There were three pearl studs in his boiled shirt, and his white tie must have been tied in heaven. And the hand that had dropped the pistol had dropped a white rose; it lay beside him brown and crushed from having been often kissed. The ideality of those kisses, for the last of which I arrived too late – ' here Miss Bates beat her fist against the bow of her snood – 'will haunt, and by haunting satisfy me. The destruction of his features, before I saw them, made their former perfection certain, where I am concerned. – And here I am, left, left, left, to watch dust gather on Mr Rankstock and you; to watch – yes, I who saw in a flash the ink-black perfection of *his* tailoring – mildew form on those clothes that you never change; to remember how both of you had in common that way of blowing your noses before you kissed me. He had been deceived – hence the shot, hence the fall. But who was *she*, your feathered friend, to deceive him? Who could have deceived him more superbly than I? – *I* could be fatal,' moaned Miss Bates, pacing the drawing-room. '*I* could be fatal – only give me a break!'

'Well, I'm sorry,' said Mr Winterslow, 'but really, what can I do, or poor Rankstock do? We are just ourselves.'

'You put the thing in a nutshell,' said Miss Bates. 'Perhaps I could bear it if you just got your hairs cut.'

'If it comes to that, Miss Bates, you might get yours set.'

Mr Rankstock's re-entry into the drawing-room – this time with brisker step, for a nice little lot of new trouble was brewing up – synchronized with the fall of the piece of holly, again, from the General's frame to the Rankstock chair. This time he saw it in time, '*Your* holly, I think, Miss Bates,' he said, holding it out to her.

'We must put it back,' said Miss Bates. 'We haven't got very much.'

'I cannot see,' said Mr Winterslow, 'why we should have any. I don't see the point of holly without berries.'

'The birds have eaten them,' said Miss Bates. 'I cannot control the forces of nature, can I?'

'*Then heigh-ho! sing heigh-ho! –* ' Mr Rankstock led off.

'Yes,' she said, 'let us have that pretty carol again.'

Mysterious Kôr

FULL moonlight drenched the city and searched it; there was not a niche left to stand in. The effect was remorseless: London looked like the moon's capital – shallow, cratered, extinct. It was late, but not yet midnight; now the buses had stopped the polished roads and streets in this region sent for minutes together a ghostly unbroken reflection up. The soaring new flats and the crouching old shops and houses looked equally brittle under the moon, which blazed in windows that looked its way. The futility of the black-out became laughable: from the sky, presumably, you could see every slate in the roofs, every whited kerb, every contour of the naked winter flowerbeds in the park; and the lake, with its shining twists and tree-darkened islands would be a landmark for miles, yes, miles, overhead.

However, the sky, in whose glassiness floated no clouds but only opaque balloons, remained glassy-silent. The Germans no longer came by the full moon. Something more immaterial seemed to threaten, and to be keeping people at home. This day between days, this extra tax, was perhaps more than senses and nerves could bear. People stayed indoors with a fervour that could be felt: the buildings strained with battened-down human life, but not a beam, not a voice, not a note from a radio escaped. Now and then under streets and buildings the earth rumbled: the Underground sounded loudest at this time.

Outside the now gateless gates of the park, the road coming downhill from the north-west turned south and became a street, down whose perspective the traffic lights went through their unmeaning performance of changing colour. From the promontory of pavement outside the gates you saw at once up the road and down the street: from behind where you stood, between the gateposts, appeared the lesser strangeness of grass and water and trees. At this point, at this moment, three French soldiers, directed to a hostel they could not find, stopped singing to listen derisively to the waterbirds wakened up by the moon. Next, two wardens coming off duty emerged from their post and crossed the road diagonally, each with an elbow cupped inside a slung-on tin hat.

The wardens turned their faces, mauve in the moonlight, towards the Frenchmen with no expression at all. The two sets of steps died in opposite directions, and, the birds subsiding, nothing was heard or seen until, a little way down the street, a trickle of people came out of the Underground, around the anti-panic brick wall. These all disappeared quickly, in an abashed way, or as though dissolved in the street by some white acid, but for a girl and a soldier who, by their way of walking, seemed to have no destination but each other and to be not quite certain even of that. Blotted into one shadow he tall, she little, these two proceeded towards the park. They looked in, but did not go in; they stood there debating without speaking. Then, as though a command from the street behind them had been received by their synchronized bodies, they faced round to look back the way they had come.

His look up the height of a building made his head drop back, and she saw his eyeballs glitter. She slid her hand from his sleeve, stepped to the edge of the pavement and said: 'Mysterious Kôr.'

'What is?' he said, not quite collecting himself.

'This is –

> *"Mysterious Kôr thy walls forsaken stand,*
> *Thy lonely towers beneath a lonely moon – "*
>
> – this is Kôr.'

'Why,' he said, 'it's years since I've thought of that.'

She said: 'I think of it all the time –

> *"Not in the waste beyond the swamps and sand,*
> *The fever-haunted forest and lagoon,*
> *Mysterious Kôr thy walls —— "*

– a completely forsaken city, as high as cliffs and as white as bones, with no history —— '

'But something must once have happened: why had it been forsaken?'

'How could anyone tell you when there's nobody there?'

'Nobody there since how long?'

'Thousands of years.'

'In that case, it would have fallen down.'

'No, not Kôr,' she said with immediate authority. 'Kôr's altogether different; it's very strong; there is not a crack in it anywhere for a weed to grow in; the corners of stones and the monuments might have been cut yesterday, and the stairs and arches are built to support themselves.'

'You know all about it,' he said, looking at her.

'I know, I know all about it.'

'What, since you read that book?'

'Oh, I didn't get much from that; I just got the name. I knew that must be the right name; it's like a cry.'

'Most like the cry of a crow to me.' He reflected, then said: 'But the poem begins with "Not" – "*Not in the waste beyond the swamps and sand —* " And it goes on, as I remember, to prove Kôr's not really anywhere. When even a poem says there's no such place — '

'What it tries to say doesn't matter: I see what it makes me see. Anyhow, that was written some time ago, at that time when they thought they had got everything taped, because the whole world had been explored, even the middle of Africa. Every thing and place had been found and marked on some map; so what wasn't marked on any map couldn't be there at all. So *they* thought: that was why he wrote the poem. "*The world is disenchanted,*" it goes on. That was what set me off hating civilization.'

'Well, cheer up,' he said; 'there isn't much of it left.'

'Oh, yes, I cheered up some time ago. This war shows we've by no means come to the end. If you can blow whole places out of existence, you can blow whole places into it. I don't see why not. They say we can't say what's come out since the bombing started. By the time we've come to the end, Kôr may be the one city left: the abiding city. I should laugh.'

'No, you wouldn't,' he said sharply. '*You* wouldn't – at least, I hope not. I hope you don't know what you're saying – does the moon make you funny?'

'Don't be cross about Kôr; please don't, Arthur,' she said.

'I thought girls thought about people.'

'What, these days?' she said. 'Think about people? How can anyone think about people if they've got any heart? I don't know how other girls manage: I always think about Kôr.'

'Not about me?' he said. When she did not at once answer, he turned her hand over, in anguish, inside his grasp. 'Because I'm not there when you want me – is that my fault?'

'But to think about Kôr *is* to think about you and me.'

'In that dead place?'

'No, ours – we'd be alone here.'

Tightening his thumb on her palm while he thought this over, he looked behind them, around them, above them – even up at the sky. He said finally: 'But we're alone here.'

'That was why I said "Mysterious Kôr".'

'What, you mean we're there now, that here's there, that now's then? . . . *I* don't mind,' he added, letting out as a laugh the sigh he had been holding in for some time. 'You ought to know the place, and for all I could tell you we might be anywhere: I often do have it, this funny feeling, the first minute or two when I've come up out of the Underground. Well, well: join the Army and see the world.' He nodded towards the perspective of traffic lights and said, a shade craftily: 'What are those, then?'

Having caught the quickest possible breath, she replied: 'Inexhaustible gases; they bored through to them and lit them as they came up; by changing colour they show the changing of minutes; in Kôr there is no sort of other time.'

'You've got the moon, though: that can't help making months.'

'Oh, and the sun, of course; but those two could do what they liked; we should not have to calculate when they'd come or go.'

'We might not have to,' he said, 'but I bet I should.'

'I should not mind what you did, so long as you never said, "What next?"'

'I don't know about "next", but I do know what we'd do first.'

'What, Arthur?'

'Populate Kôr.'

She said: 'I suppose it would be all right if our children were to marry each other?'

But her voice faded out; she had been reminded that they were homeless on this his first night of leave. They were, that was to say, in London without any hope of any place of their own. Pepita shared a two-roomed flatlet with a girl friend, in a by-street off the Regent's Park Road, and towards this they must make their half-hearted way. Arthur was to have the sitting-room divan, usually occupied by Pepita, while she herself had half of her girl friend's bed. There was really no room for a third, and least of all for a man, in those small rooms packed with furniture and the two girls' belongings: Pepita tried to be grateful for her friend Callie's forbearance – but how could she be, when it had not occurred to Callie that she would do better to be away tonight? She was more slow-witted than narrow-minded – but Pepita felt she owed a kind of ruin to her. Callie, not yet known to be home later than ten, would be now waiting up, in her house-coat, to welcome Arthur. That would mean three-sided chat, drinking cocoa, then turning in: that would be that, and that would be all. That was London, this war – they were lucky to have a roof – London, full enough before the Americans came. Not a place: they would even grudge you sharing a grave – that was what even married couples complained. Whereas in Kôr . . .

In Kôr . . . Like glass, the illusion shattered: a car hummed like a hornet towards them, veered, showed its scarlet tail-light, streaked away up the road. A woman edged round a front door and along the area railings timidly called her cat; meanwhile a clock near, then another set further back in the dazzling distance, set about striking midnight. Pepita, feeling Arthur release her arm with an abruptness that was the inverse of passion, shivered; whereat he asked brusquely: 'Cold? Well, Which way? – we'd better be getting on.'

Callie was no longer waiting up. Hours ago she had set out the three cups and saucers, the tins of cocoa and household milk and, on the gas-ring, brought the kettle to just short of the boil. She had turned open Arthur's bed, the living-room divan, in the neat inviting way she had learnt at home – then, with a modest impulse, replaced the cover. She had, as Pepita foresaw, been wearing her cretonne housecoat, the nearest thing to a hostess gown that she had; she had already brushed her hair for the night, rebraided it, bound the braids in a coronet round her head. Both lights and the wireless had been on, to make the room both look and sound gay: all alone, she had come to that peak moment at which company should arrive – but so seldom does. From then on she felt welcome beginning to wither in her, a flower of the heart that had bloomed too early. There she had sat like an image, facing the three cold cups, on the edge of the bed to be occupied by an unknown man.

Callie's innocence and her still unsought-out state had brought her to take a proprietary pride in Arthur; this was all the stronger, perhaps, because they had not yet met. Sharing the flat with Pepita, this last year, she had been content with reflecting the heat of love. It was not, surprisingly, that Pepita seemed very happy – there were times when she was palpably on the rack, and this was not what Callie could understand. 'Surely you owe it to Arthur,' she would then say, 'to keep cheerful? So long as you love each other — ' Callie's calm brow glowed – one might say that it glowed in place of her friend's; she became the guardian of that ideality which for Pepita was constantly lost to view. It was true, with the sudden prospect of Arthur's leave, things had come nearer to earth: he became a proposition, and she would have been as glad if he could have slept somewhere else. Physically shy, a brotherless virgin, Callie shrank from sharing this flat with a young man. In this flat you could hear everything: what was once a three-windowed Victorian drawing-room had been partitioned, by very thin walls, into kitchenette, living-room, Callie's bedroom. The living-room was in the centre; the two others open off it. What was once the conservatory, half a flight down, was now converted into a draughty bathroom, shared with somebody else on the girl's floor. The flat, for these days, was cheap – even so, it was Callie, earning more than Pepita, who paid the greater part of the rent: it thus became up to her, more or less, to express good will as to Arthur's making a third. 'Why, it will be lovely to have him here,' Callie said. Pepita accepted the good will without much grace – but then, had she ever much grace to spare? – she was as restlessly

secretive, as self-centred, as a little half-grown black cat. Next
came a puzzling moment: Pepita seemed to be hinting that Callie
should fix herself up somewhere else. 'But where would I go?'
Callie marvelled when this was at last borne in on her. 'You know
what London's like now. And, anyway' – here she laughed, but
hers was a forehead that coloured as easily as it glowed – 'it
wouldn't be proper, would it, me going off and leaving just you
and Arthur; I don't know what your mother would say to me. No,
we may be a little squashed, but we'll make things ever so homey. I
shall not mind playing gooseberry, really, dear.'

But the hominess by now was evaporating, as Pepita and Arthur
still and still did not come. At half-past ten, in obedience to the rule
of the house, Callie was obliged to turn off the wireless, whereupon silence out of the stepless street began seeping into the
slighted room. Callie recollected the fuel target and turned off her
dear little table lamp, gaily painted with spots to make it look like a
toadstool, thereby leaving only the hanging light. She laid her hand
on the kettle, to find it gone cold again and sigh for the wasted gas
if not for her wasted thought. Where are they? Cold crept up her
out of the kettle; she went to bed.

Callie's bed lay along the wall under the window: she did not like
sleeping so close up under glass, but the clearance that must be left
for the opening of door and cupboards made this the only possible
place. Now she got in and lay rigidly on the bed's inner side, under
the hanging hems of the window curtains, training her limbs not to
stray to what would be Pepita's half. This sharing of her bed with
another body would not be the least of her sacrifice to the lovers'
love; tonight would be the first night – or at least, since she was an
infant – that Callie had slept with anyone. Child of a sheltered
middle-class household, she had kept physical distances all her life.
Already repugnance and shyness ran through her limbs; she was
preyed upon by some more obscure trouble than the expectation
that she might not sleep. As to *that*, Pepita was restless; her tossings
on the divan, her broken-off exclamations and blurred pleas had
been to be heard, most nights, through the dividing wall.

Callie knew, as though from a vision, that Arthur would sleep
soundly, with assurance and majesty. Did they not all say, too, that
a soldier sleeps like a log? With awe she pictured, asleep, the face
that she had not yet, awake, seen – Arthur's man's eyelids, cheekbones and set mouth turned up to the darkened ceiling. Wanting to
savour darkness herself, Callie reached out and put off her bedside
lamp.

At once she knew that something was happening – outdoors, in
the street, the whole of London, the world. An advance, an extraordinary movement was silently taking place; blue-white beams

overflowed from it, silting, dropping round the edges of the
muffling black-out curtains. When, starting up, she knocked a fold
of the curtain, a beam like a mouse ran across her bed. A search-
light, the most powerful of all time, might have been turned full
and steady upon her defended window; finding flaws in the black-
out stuff, it made veins and stars. Once gained by this idea of
pressure she could not lie down again; she sat tautly, drawn-up
knees touching her breasts, and asked herself if there were anything
she should do. She parted the curtains, opened them slowly wider,
looked out – and was face to face with the moon.

Below the moon, the houses opposite her window blazed back in
transparent shadow; and something – was it a coin or a ring? –
glittered half-way across the chalk-white street. Light marched in
past her face, and she turned to see where it went: out stood the
curves and garlands of the great white marble Victorian mantelpiece of that lost drawing-room; out stood, in the photographs
turned her way, the thoughts with which her parents had faced the
camera, and the humble puzzlement of her two dogs at home. Of
silver brocade, just faintly purpled with roses, became her house-
coat hanging over the chair. And the moon did more: it exonerated
and beautified the lateness of the lovers' return. No wonder, she
said herself, no wonder – if this was the world they walked in, if
this was whom they were with. Having drunk in the white
explanation, Callie lay down again. Her half of the bed was in
shadow, but she allowed one hand to lie, blanched, in what would
be Pepita's place. She lay and looked at the hand until it was no
longer her own.

Callie woke to the sound of Pepita's key in the latch. But no
voices? What had happened? Then she heard Arthur's step. She
heard his unslung equipment dropped with a weary, dull sound,
and the plonk of his tin hat on a wooden chair. 'Sssh-sssh!' Pepita
exclaimed, 'she *might* be asleep!'

Then at last Arthur's voice: 'But I thought you said — '

'I'm not asleep; I'm just coming!' Callie called out with rapture,
leaping out from her form in shadow into the moonlight, zipping
on her enchanted house-coat over her nightdress, kicking her shoes
on, and pinning in place, with a trembling firmness, her plaits in
their coronet round her head. Between these movements of hers
she heard not another sound. Had she only dreamed they were
there? Her heart beat: she stepped through the living-room,
shutting her door behind her.

Pepita and Arthur stood the other side of the table; they gave the
impression of being lined up. Their faces, at different levels – for
Pepita's rough, dark head came only an inch above Arthur's khaki
shoulder – were alike in abstention from any kind of expression; as

though, spiritually, they both still refused to be here. Their features looked faint, weathered – was this the work of the moon? Pepita said at once: 'I suppose we are very late?'

'I don't wonder,' Callie said, 'on this lovely night.'

Arthur had not raised his eyes; he was looking at the three cups. Pepita now suddenly jogged his elbow, saying, 'Arthur, wake up; say something; this is Callie – well, Callie, this is Arthur, of course.'

'Why, yes of course this is Arthur,' returned Callie, whose candid eyes since she entered had not left Arthur's face. Perceiving that Arthur did not know what to do, she advanced round the table to shake hands with him. He looked up, she looked down, for the first time: she rather beheld than felt his red-brown grip on what still seemed her glove of moonlight. 'Welcome, Arthur,' she said. 'I'm so glad to meet you at last. I hope you will be comfortable in the flat.'

'It's been kind of you,' he said after consideration.

'Please do not feel that,' said Callie. 'This is Pepita's home, too, and we both hope – don't we, Pepita? – that you'll regard it as yours. Please feel free to do just as you like. I am sorry it is so small.'

'Oh, I don't know,' Arthur said, as though hypnotized; 'it seems a nice little place.'

Pepita, meanwhile, glowered and turned away.

Arthur continued to wonder, though he had once been told, how these two unalike girls had come to set up together – Pepita so small, except for her too-big head, compact of childish brusqueness and of unchildish passion, and Callie, so sedate, waxy and tall – an unlit candle. Yes, she was like one of those candles on sale outside a church; there could be something votive even in her demeanour. She was unconscious that her good manners, those of an old fashioned country doctor's daughter, were putting the other two at a disadvantage. He found himself touched by the grave good faith with which Callie was wearing that tartish house-coat, above which her face kept the glaze of sleep; and, as she knelt to relight the gas-ring under the kettle, he marked the strong, delicate arch of one bare foot, disappearing into the arty green shoe. Pepita was now too near him ever again to be seen as he now saw Callie – in a sense, he never *had* seen Pepita for the first time: she had not been, and still sometimes was not, his type. No, he had not thought of her twice; he had not remembered her until he began to remember her with passion. You might say he had not seen Pepita coming: their love had been a collision in the dark.

Callie, determined to get this over, knelt back and said: 'Would Arthur like to wash his hands?' When they had heard him stumble down the half-flight of stairs, she said to Pepita: 'Yes, I was so glad you had the moon.'

'Why?' said Pepita. She added: 'There was too much of it.'

'You're tired. Arthur looks tired, too.'

'How would you know? He's used to marching about. But it's all this having no place to go.'

'But, Pepita, you — '

But at this point Arthur came back: from the door he noticed the wireless, and went direct to it. 'Nothing much on now, I suppose?' he doubtfully said.

'No; you see it's past midnight; we're off the air. And, anyway, in this house they don't like the wireless late. By the same token,' went on Callie, friendly smiling, 'I'm afraid I must ask you, Arthur, to take your boots off, unless, of course, you mean to stay sitting down. The people below us — '

Pepita flung off, saying something under her breath, but Arthur, remarking, 'No, I don't mind,' both sat down and began to take off his boots. Pausing, glancing to left and right at the divan's fresh cotton spread, he said: 'It's all right is it, for me to sit on this?'

'That's my bed,' said Pepita. 'You are to sleep in it.'

Callie then made the cocoa, after which they turned in. Preliminary trips to the bathroom having been worked out, Callie was first to retire, shutting the door behind her so that Pepita and Arthur might kiss each other good night. When Pepita joined her, it was without knocking: Pepita stood still in the moon and began to tug off her clothes. Glancing with hate at the bed, she asked: 'Which side?'

'I expected you'd like the outside.'

'What are you standing about for?'

'I don't really know: as I'm inside I'd better get in first.'

'Then why not get in?'

When they had settled rigidly, side by side, Callie asked: 'Do you think Arthur's got all he wants?'

Pepita jerked her head up. 'We can't sleep in all this moon.'

'Why, you don't believe the moon does things, actually?'

'Well, it couldn't hope to make some of us *much* more screwy.'

Callie closed the curtains, then said: 'What do you mean? And – didn't you hear? – I asked if Arthur's got all he wants.'

'That's what I meant – have you got a screw loose, really?'

'Pepita, I won't stay here if you're going to be like this.'

'In that case, you had better go in with Arthur.'

'What about me?' Arthur loudly said through the wall. 'I can hear practically all you girls are saying.'

They were both startled – rather that than abashed. Arthur, alone in there, had thrown off the ligatures of his social manner: his voice held the whole authority of his sex – he was impatient, sleepy, and he belonged to no one.

'Sorry,' the girls said in unison. Then Pepita laughed soundlessly, making their bed shake, till to stop herself she bit the back of her hand, and this movement made her elbow strike Callie's cheek. 'Sorry,' she had to whisper. No answer: Pepita fingered her elbow and found, yes, it was quite true, it was wet. 'Look, shut up crying, Callie: what have I done?'

Callie rolled right round, in order to press her forehead closely under the window, into the curtains, against the wall. Her weeping continued to be soundless: now and then, unable to reach her handkerchief, she staunched her eyes with a curtain, disturbing slivers of moon. Pepita gave up marvelling, and soon slept: at least there is something in being dog-tired.

A clock struck four as Callie woke up again – but something else had made her open her swollen eyelids. Arthur, stumbling about on his padded feet, could be heard next door attempting to make no noise. Inevitably, he bumped the edge of the table. Callie sat up: by her side Pepita lay like a mummy rolled half over, in forbidding, tenacious sleep. Arthur groaned. Callie caught a breath, climbed lightly over Pepita, felt for her torch on the mantelpiece, stopped to listen again. Arthur groaned again: Callie, with movements soundless as they were certain, opened the door and slipped through to the living-room. 'What's the matter?' she whispered. 'Are you ill?'

'No; I just got a cigarette. Did I wake you up?'

'But you groaned.'

'I'm sorry; I'd no idea.'

'But do you often?'

'I've no idea, really, I tell you,' Arthur repeated. The air of the room was dense with his presence, overhung by tobacco. He must be sitting on the edge of his bed, wrapped up in his overcoat – she could smell the coat, and each time he pulled on the cigarette his features appeared down there, in the fleeting, dull reddish glow. 'Where are you?' he said. 'Show a light.'

Her nervous touch on her torch, like a reflex to what he said, made it flicker up for a second. 'I am just by the door; Pepita's asleep; I'd better go back to bed.'

'Listen. Do you two get on each other's nerves?'

'Not till tonight,' said Callie, watching the uncertain swoops of the cigarette as he reached across to the ashtray on the edge of the table. Shifting her bare feet patiently, she added: 'You don't see us as we usually are.'

'She's a girl who shows things in funny ways – I expect she feels bad at our putting you out like this – I know I do. But then we'd got no choice, had we?'

'It is really I who am putting you out,' said Callie.

'Well, that can't be helped either, can it? You had the right to stay in your own place. If there'd been more time, we might have gone to the country, though I still don't see where we'd have gone there. It's one harder when you're not married, unless you've got the money. Smoke?'

'No, thank you. Well, if you're all right, I'll go back to bed.'

'I'm glad she's asleep – funny the way she sleeps, isn't it? You can't help wondering where she is. You haven't got a boy, have you, just at present?'

'No. I've never had one.'

'I'm not sure in one way that you're not better off. I can see there's not so much in it for a girl these days. It makes me feel cruel the way I unsettle her: I don't know how much it's me myself or how much it's something the matter that I can't help. How are any of us to know how things could have been? They forget war's not just only war; it's years out of people's lives that they've never had before and won't have again. Do you think she's fanciful?'

'Who, Pepita?'

'It's enough to make her – tonight was the pay-off. We couldn't get near any movie or any place for sitting; you had to fight into the bars, and she hates the staring in bars, and with all that milling about, every street we went, they kept on knocking her even off my arm. So then we took the tube to that park down there, but the place was as bad as daylight, let alone it was cold. We hadn't the nerve – well, that's nothing to do with you.'

'I don't mind.'

'Or else you don't understand. So we began to play – we were off in Kôr.'

'Core of what?'

'Mysterious Kôr – ghost city.'

'Where?'

'You may ask. But I could have sworn she saw it, and from the way she saw it I saw it, too. A game's a game, but what's a hallucination? You begin by laughing, then it gets in you and you can't laugh it off. I tell you, I woke up just now not knowing where I'd been; and I had to get up and feel round this table before I even knew where I was. It wasn't till then that I thought of a cigarette. Now I see why she sleeps like that, if that's where she goes.'

'But she is just as often restless; I often hear her.'

'Then she doesn't always make it. Perhaps it takes me, in some way — Well, I can't see any harm: when two people have got no place, why not want Kôr, as a start? There are no restrictions on wanting, at any rate.'

'But, oh, Arthur, can't wanting want what's human?'

He yawned. 'To be human's to be at a dead loss.' Stopping yawning, he ground out his cigarette: the china tray skidded at the edge of the table. 'Bring that light here a moment – that is, will you? I think I've messed ash all over these sheets of hers.'

Callie advanced with the torch alight, but at arm's length: now and then her thumb made the beam wobble. She watched the lit-up inside of Arthur's hand as he brushed the sheet; and once he looked up to see her white-nightgowned figure curving above and away from him, behind the arc of light. 'What's that swinging?'

'One of my plaits of hair. Shall I open the window wider?'

'What, to let the smoke out? Go on. And how's your moon?'

'Mine?' Marvelling over this, as the first sign that Arthur remembered that she was Callie, she uncovered the window, pushed up the sash, then after a minute said: 'Not so strong.'

Indeed, the moon's power over London and the imagination had now declined. The siege of light had relaxed; the search was over; the street had a look of survival and no more. Whatever had glittered there, coin or ring, was now invisible or had gone. To Callie it seemed likely that there would never be such a moon again; and on the whole she felt this was for the best. Feeling air reach in like a tired arm round her body, she dropped the curtains against it and returned to her own room.

Back by her bed, she listened: Pepita's breathing still had the regular sound of sleep. At the other side of the wall the divan creaked as Arthur stretched himself out again. Having felt ahead of her lightly, to make sure her half was empty, Callie climbed over Pepita and got in. A certain amount of warmth had travelled between the sheets from Pepita's flank, and in this Callie extended her sword-cold body: she tried to compose her limbs; even they quivered after Arthur's words in the dark, words *to* the dark. The loss of her own mysterious expectation, of her love for love, was a small thing beside the war's total of unlived lives. Suddenly Pepita flung out one hand: its back knocked Callie lightly across the face.

Pepita had now turned over and lay with her face up. The hand that had struck Callie must have lain over the other, which grasped the pyjama collar. Her eyes, in the dark, might have been either shut or open, but nothing made her frown more or less steadily: it became certain, after another moment, that Pepita's act of justice had been unconscious. She still lay, as she had lain, in an avid dream, of which Arthur had been the source, of which Arthur was not the end. With him she looked this way, that way, down the wide, void, pure streets, between statues, pillars and shadows, through archways and colonnades. With him she went up the stairs down which nothing but moon came; with him trod the ermine dust of the endless halls, stood on terraces, mounted the extreme tower, looked down on the statued squares, the wide, void, pure streets. He was the password, but not the answer: it was to Kôr's finality that she turned.

The Dolt's Tale

I THINK often one thing leads to another. Man I knew slightly happened to take me round and stand me a couple of drinks at a small club existing for that purpose. Place seemed friendly and it was on my beat; so I filled in the form, he O.K.-ed me and I became a member. Thus I formed the habit of dropping in. The original chap left London; but my principal object is to relax. In order to relax you must be somewhere. However, I can get cracking if that is wanted; and in due course I found myself getting to know the crowd. Place was a double room; it had probably been a shop. It was nicely done up antique, as Margery pointed out – whoever put money in saw his money back: supplies were good, but naturally at a price. The back where the bar was was the cheery end: the front was more where you could relax.

I am talking of around June '44, which was the time I first got to know the Timpsons. Bloody great long heavy convoys used to shake the place up, it being on a through road in and out of London. On account of that it was quite a port of call; a number of chaps in this crowd being on essential, they in most cases had their cars on the road. In this club I should say you saw the better side of the war. Ken Timpson proved to be in timber. Most evenings he dropped in for one or two for the road, and to pick up Margery. Margery and the rest of the pack of wives used to roll in somewhat earlier on, having I take it come to the end of whatever girls do with themselves all day.

All these girls' backviews looked to me much the same. In the first place I noticed Margery's dog, thinking one that size must eat a great deal of meat. The dog's leash was always yanked to the same stool, that being the one on which she sat. I know for some time I did not specially join her up with Ken, as they were both of them of the life-and-soul type, cracking away with all who came along. Not that I ever take much notice. I came to put two and two together from seeing them piling into the same car, preparatory to heading out of London. At the beginning one thing that put me wrong had been also seeing Margery in and out with a type called Denis; which could have been taken to mean that they were a couple. He looked somewhat sissy to me, but you never know. It proved however he was Margery's brother and was in one of the art rackets, having a duodenal: it was thus in order for him to dress the part.

It seems true how brain can run in a family. The first occasion I got into talk with Margery, owing to stepping on her dog, she got on to the subject of my character. The lurch the dog made me give lost me the better part of the drink I was carrying and had just bought, and I mentioned it seemed the hell of a big dog. She said, 'Well, you're no lightweight yourself.' In fact I tip the scales around fifteen stone. She said she had often wondered about me, and expected I really noticed more than I seemed to do. She said she instinctively felt that I just sat in order to think a lot. She said was I not somewhat a lone wolf? She had the kind of large eyes there seems not much room between. Going would have been better if I could have heard what she afterwards said, but they then had the wireless on full blast: the invasion around that time was making rather a splash. Finally Ken came up and said they should buzz along.

Then on a subsequent evening Ken moved in on me, the lady wife having not so far shown up. He and I got together, proving to have this and that in common and ultimately getting around to contracts: I having let drop one or two things, he said how if I came along back sometime to their place in order to continue the conversation? For my part I saw nothing against that. It was put to her when she showed up, whereupon she said, 'Oh, fine.' She was, I should say, blonde; quite a little thing, round the thirty mark, very taking ways, always tailor-made, lots of style. Ken was about of my build, full-blooded sort of chap. On the evening fixed we accordingly pushed off in their Alvis. I recall the weather seemed pretty stinking, though doodles were not as yet showing up. I ought to say that Denis was of the party; he and I piled in behind Ken and Margery. Dog got on top of Denis and settled down; I also formed the idea that he had passed out, as he made no observation during the run. Run was I should say around ten miles. At one point Margery turned round and said she supposed I knew I should have to pig it?

Their place however struck me as pretty nice. The right size. Any number of gadgets; also solarium and so on. Countrified without being out of the world. Built up over a cutting of the by-pass, of which you got rather a fine view. Garden was terraced up and must itself have cost quite a pot of money; looked on the steep side for my tastes; however, you did not have to go out of doors. She was telling me, place had quite a history: Ken got it off some chap who had come a cropper for what was practically a song. It turned out they had a kid, but it was in bed. Ken took me off to view the drink situation; and she melted, saying something about the ice. Denis steered for a settee and put his feet up: I should say he knew where he was well off.

As a rule it is much the same to me where I am: apart from getting around in the way of business, I am in favour of staying put. I am not, that is to say, one for visits, as they seem bound to involve chat. At the Timpsons', however, they both did you well and just let you sit. You would not have known they had a dog or a kid. Margery did the necessary with no fuss, so that you would not have noticed there was a war on. Where she got it all was of course nobody's business; and I must say she was a wonderful girl. When I say she sat on the arm of my chair I do not mean she made any sort of pass: apart from the fact that it ought to stick out a mile that I should not care at all for that sort of thing, the Timpsons were absolutely above board. But she said I felt to her like the rock of ages. She said how Ken was struck by my grasp of things, and how if there were more like me in the business world the country would not be in the state it was. Ken referred to the one or two things I had let drop, saying they opened up various possibilities. It would not be too much to say that he and I then talked turkey. I had really had no idea I had half such a grasp of things. She used to be there listening all in a sort of dream, with her quite large eyes fixed upon my face. Denis meanwhile played patience or some other variety of a sissy game, Ken's and my talk being somewhat above his level.

Therefore that first trip out was the first of many enjoyable evenings at the Timpsons'. Joining up at the club, we would then trool out to their place, Ken running me back into town again next morning. At the club itself the Timpsons now seemed far from keen I should get mixed up with the rest of the other chaps. I know she said once, 'Are Ken and I too awful? I suppose we want you all to ourselves.' However deep they were into it with the gang, she or Ken always kept one eye out for me. I saw no real objection to being sought after, the Timpsons being as cheery as they come. A woman as fascinating as Margery could, I should say, have been quite a honeypot; but for reasons known to herself she preferred me. Also Ken set store by our rather interesting talks and by my opinion, which I will give when asked. We came to have various irons in the fire. As he said, there is a way round everything when you come to look. I do not say there was anything not above board. But as he said, chaps must look out for themselves, or where as a whole would the nation be?

I ought to say that around this time the doodles had opened up and were coming thick. During the daytime that rather put one out; and the chaps' wives stopped showing up at the club. I was frequently glad enough to be bedding down at the Timpsons', as not so much stuff was dropping out their way. Denis also took the odd quiet night, being apparently somewhat highly strung. This where I was concerned was a slight snag – it was not so much what he said as what he did not say. I somehow got the feeling we had not much in common. However, live and let live. And also most of the time he usually played some parlour game or read some book.

On occasions around the dance band hour he and Margery switched on the radio and used to dance. This was a work-out for Margery, for whom the doodles doubtless made life a bit dull. Neither Ken nor I had the twinkling toe.

However, up to that last evening I cannot say I remember looking at Denis twice. This is where I come to the rather odder part of my story. To begin with, it was one of those stuffy evenings on which everyone seems a bit off. Even out at the Timpsons' you could hear the doodles popping about the metropolis. And personally I had arrived out there feeling pretty much all in, due to a spot of bother during the day. If you asked me if there was any difference between our Income Tax johnnies and the Gestapo, I should reply, no. One could in fact wonder what one is fighting for. I had looked forward to getting things off my chest; but no sooner had I opened the matter up than Ken started to give me decidedly narrow looks. You would have got the impression that he was shying off me. I have heard him say about what he feels about anyone he is in with putting a foot wrong. At the time I simply took it he too was under the weather. Therefore after the meal he and I got down to two or three doubles each, otherwise keeping our traps shut. The fire was as usual brightly lit: owing to the fire and general fug I do not mind saying I then dropped off.

What next I became aware, there seemed to be nobody. The Timpsons as a family must have turned in, also turning out the better part of the lights. Bottles of any interest were now missing, though there were empties and glasses all over the place ad lib; the fire was defunct and the lounge I must say looked like the end of the world. I squinted through the arch at the electric clock in the solarium, and saw we were now into the small hours. Everywhere seemed to be beastly quiet. I felt myself in a sort of a way stranded, and though I was willing to turn in did not feel somehow able to make the start. Therefore I sought the nightcap Ken would want me to have. The doings I knew were put to bye-byes inside a device representing antique books. The snappy device was however, I found, locked.

At the same time Denis said, 'Mean as hell!'

This gave me rather a start – as did the way he shot up his head at me over the settee back. It was like seeing something. I felt so far from fit as to have to sit down in the chair again.

I then said, 'Oh, hullo; I did not know you were there.'

He said, 'I speak as one of the family. If you ask me, you've had the last you'll get. I should say they have now finished work on you.' I resented this.

He said, 'Cold, rather, isn't it?' and began to scruffle around himself in the settee cushions. He always kept spare parts of his wardrobe tucked around like nuts in any place where he was: he now therefore pulled out another pullover and pulled it on over the one he already wore. Having folded his arms across the ensemble, he said, 'However, Margery's nice, isn't she? Or at any rate wasn't she?'

I replied I always thought highly of her and Ken.

'Of course to me,' he said, 'they are not in the same class. True he is smart enough for you; but I am afraid that would not carry a man far. He imagines he's smart: Margery really is. I have loved and studied the little thing from a child. She has got more than the brains; she's got inspiration; she ought really to have been Lady Macbeth. The world is open to Margery if she pulls out in time; and I shall hope to see to it that she does.'

I must have looked at him pretty hard: I soon saw this have some effect on him.

'Tell me,' he said, 'do fish suffer? Or would you only know about stuffed fish?'

I said I did not like his manner more than I ever had.

'There may be much ahead that you may not like,' said he. 'At the best, you had better take it this party's over; and be thankful if you get out without anything worse than that. You have served one purpose – you've come across. It seems far from impossible that you may serve another. If this ploy you boys are so busy with *should* slip up, who do you suppose is going to cop it? Ken?'

I said I had no idea what he meant, as everything was completely above board.

He rolled his head on one side and said, 'It's simply this frightful war: it does seem to make everyone so suspicious. Of course in this lovely house we are all friends – all the same, supposing somebody spilled the beans?'

I thanked him, but pointed out that all this was considerably above his head. I advised him to stick to art.

'Oh, I do,' he said. 'Haven't you seen me playing about the floor?'

At this point we both heard a suspicious sound: I should call it a sort of cloppeting on the stairs. It was proved to be the heels of Margery's mules by the fact that she afterwards came in. She came in through the hall arch, at the Timpsons' there being few doors. Owing to her manner, I should say 'entered'. Even in slumberwear she was tailor-made: zipped up the front with her monogram on her chest. She said she supposed we knew we should wake the kid?

Denis said, 'Of course, you have got a kid.' And he said to me, 'The now famous sleep-walking scene.' On which, she gave Denis what I should call a look. She did not appear to see that I was there, though she referred to me by later saying to Denis, 'Anyway, what the hell are you two doing?' He said, 'So to speak, taking down our hair.' That led her to give me the once over: her manner was not so intimate as formerly. She said to him, about me, 'There's not much hair there.' He said, 'What there is, I have taken down for him. If you want to know, I've attempted to tip him off.'

Margery then surprised me by standing on one leg in order to take the mule off her other foot. Dot-and-carry-one, but at quite a speed, she then proceeded across the parquet to the settee on which Denis lay, and started laying into him with the mule. She attacked him, chiefly about the head. When he got the mule away from her, they had no breath left. They had to look at each other.

I rose and said I thought on the whole I'd be turning in. As no other move was made, I sat down again.

She sat down on the end of the settee and put her mule on; and he started rearranging his hair. He reached for Ken's box and they both lit up cigarettes. He then said to her, 'You don't have to be so conventional with me. You know I know you won't be wanting him any more. The thing is, you. You must see you've got to think about pulling out. And there isn't so much time as you might think. You won't want to be encircled along with Ken? – Lamb,' he said, with his thumb on one bruise she gave him, 'you belong with the bigger and better crooks.'

'Who are they?' she said.

He said, 'Me and my friends. Only give us a few more years and we'll have closed the ring. Unbeknownst we are all the time moving in. Ken keeps too busy making a ring round *that*' – at this point they looked towards my chair – 'to notice we are making a ring round him. That goes for all Ken's outfit and all his lot. You must see, we've got the solidarity.' He said, 'By the time we're through, there won't be a thing to choose between Ken and *that*!' They both of them now seemed to be considering me. I again said that I thought on the whole I'd be turning in. She took a sort of dreamy pluck at his hair and said, 'You know what you are: you're a saboteur.' She went on, in for her an uncertain way, 'Besides, I don't know the first thing about art.'

He said, 'You've got the first thing it takes!'

This could have been a dream. I ought, however, to say I am practically certain it was not. I had not eaten anything; and unless I have I have never known myself troubled in that way. It was like the sort of dream that you are told about, which I have I am glad to say never had. Not, I mean, like any form of real life – in that I think I may say I always know where I am. Having never paid any call on a nuthouse, I am unused to conversation with no sense. Another thing: had she and he not been of the same family, I could well have felt the atmosphere was immoral, and should have felt it up to me to inform Ken. As it was, there was a silence over the Timpsons' place like there is overhead when a doodlebug has cut out: that or something or other gave me gooseflesh. Things did not seem to me altogether right. Much may have been due to the late hour.

I do not recollect how I got to bed.

I had previously understood I was to be at the Timpsons' over the week-end. However next morning Denis said my taxi was at the door. Not being yet altogether conscious I entered the taxi and was trooled away. Subsequently I found myself back in London. I took it there had been some explanation I had not at that hour quite taken in: in addition, I expected a buzz from Ken. Having received no buzz throughout the Sunday, I passed Monday at the end of my business line. I even reviewed the notion that they had copped a doodle. Somewhat baffled, I rolled around to the club, but however failed to contact the Timpsons there. At this I do not mind saying that I began to think. Much that had looked all right was not looking so good now.

To cut a long story short, I decided to breeze out; which I did. None too soon, as events proved. People who get me taped get me taped wrong. Somebody did Ken Timpson a dirty turn: the inquiry made pretty thoughtful reading. However, all things blow over in due time. It was, I remember, the week that we crossed the Rhine that I once more ran across Margery, quite her cheery self. She said when she had found some place I ought to drop in. She said she was now on a magazine. She had had to put down the dog on account of the meat it ate. What became of the kid I would not know.

Post-War Stories

I Hear You Say So

A WEEK after V.E. Day, the nightingale came to London – unnoticed until it began to sing. It pitched itself in a tree in a northwest park. Until the first notes were heard, the warm night had been remarkably still; the air was full of lassitude after the holiday and of emanations of the peace – which, like any new experience, kept people puzzled and infantile. It was now about half past ten; the rose garden in the centre of the park had been closed and locked, leaving the first roses to smoulder out unseen as dark fell. The whistle had sounded from the boathouse and the last oars had stopped splashing upon the lake; the waterbirds one by one were drawing in to settle among the dock leaves round the islands. The water, which had dulled as the sky faded, now began to shed, as though it were phosphorescent, ghostly light of its own. From all round it came the smell of trodden exhausted grass. After sunset, the sky held for so long an intense liquid and glasslike whiteness that people begn to wonder if, after all, this might be going to be a Polar night: just now no miracle seemed impossible. The air did darken, but it remained transparent: couples walking together or standing on the bridges never quite ceased to discern one another's features, or the white reflections from the north in one another's eyes. Those lying down, however, became blotted into the monotone of the grass.

In streets outside the park and here and there along the terraces round it there still hung victory flags. Householders were unwilling to take them in, and passers-by were unwilling to see them go. This tense and aimless, tired and tender evening loved the directive of the remaining flags, whose colours one gradually could not see. Stripes, crosses, stars, and swags of bunting showed with lymphatic softness against the evening-hardened faces of the buildings; but the flags that were stretched on lines or hung out on poles stirred now and then, over the windless perspectives of the streets, as though their own existences gave out breath. Best of all, outside a gate of the park, one flag was dipped back at a corner into its own colours by being caught in the ray from a lighted window.

High up, low down, the fearlessly lit-up windows were like

exclamations. Many stood wide open. Inside their tawny squares the rooms, to be seen into, were sublimated: not an object inside them appeared gimcrack or trivial, standing up with stereoscopic sharpness in this intensified element of life. The knobbed or fluted stem of a standard lamp, the bustlike curves of a settee, the couples of photographs hung level, the fidgeting of a cockatoo up and down its perch, the balance of vases on brackets and pyramids of mock fruit in bowls all seemed miraculous after all that had happened. In few of the rooms, oddly, were any inhabitants to be seen; possibly they were standing out in the street looking in wonderstruck at their own windows. Rooms in their mood tonight seemed to have been illuminated in their own honour. Each of these theatres was its own drama – a moment perpetuated, an integration of all these living-unliving objects in surviving and shining and being seen. Through the windows, standing lamps and hanging bowls overflowed, spilling hot light into the warm dark.

The hulks of buildings, of terraces that were still nailed up, blind, uninhabitable and hollow, were nugatory. The unconscious people could have stumbled against them: they seemed to belong to another time. Just inside the park three poplars, blasted the summer before by a flying bomb, stretched the uncertain leaves they had put out this year towards those of the showering unhurt trees; and away down the lake lay one ruined island. These few scars begging to be forgotten had no part in the night.

The only wireless that had been turned on had been turned off, inside an open window, a minute or two before the nightingale began singing. One was not to know this – Violet, hearing the first notes, naturally said: 'Listen, they got a nightingale on the wireless!' On the grass slope some way up from the lake she was lying beside her friend, one arm stretched out and the back of her hand reposing against his forehead. He rolled round his head to listen: she raised her hand but then let it drop back.

'That's not the wireless,' he said. 'That comes out of the trees. There's nothing only the park all the way up there.' After a minute he said: 'That must be a thrush.'

The back of her hand was the only sensitive part left: in it she could feel the now cooler stickiness of his forehead. They now lay a little apart, completely relaxed, knit into a double crucified pattern by her arm. His khaki and from her crushed dress the last drop of the scent he had sent from France mingled with the exhalations out of the grass and syringa in flower the other side of the path. A cigarette carton was stuck in a tuft of grass between their two bodies. She stared up into the particles, neither light nor dark, that made up the air that made up the sky and said: 'Why must it be a thrush?'

'Well, think, how could it be a nightingale really?'

They listened. On paths that crossed the different planes of the night were footsteps – Army boots, summer shoes – and the dry grass back from their ears creaked as people came treading near them. Up through the pores of the ground came the vibrations of London, and muffled pulse-drumming ringed the horizons round. Long whispers, exclamations and laughter ran like waves towards them then sifted back. 'It's flown away, anyway,' he said. 'Never mind.'

She said: 'Funny if you and me heard a nightingale.'

'You and me don't look for that sort of thing. It may have been all very well for them in the past.'

'Still, there must still *be* nightingales, or they couldn't have put one on to the wireless.'

'I didn't say they'd died out; I said they don't come round. Why should they? They can't sell us anything.'

She clenched her hand, making her knuckles dig into his forehead bone, and said: 'Oh well, leave it.'

'Well, can you wonder?'

'All right – but look what's happened now. The war's over.'

'They say.'

'Well, it's over – look at last week.'

'Half.'

'Well, that's half the difference again. You begin to wonder. I don't say I know how I feel, but I seem to know how I could. I can't help thinking – suppose the world was made for happiness, after all?'

' – Hark!' he said. 'Hush – there it goes again!'

Unseen rays of night pin-pointed the nightingale, in the concentrated and somehow burning blackness of its unknown tree. It sang into incredulity like the first nightingale in Eden. Note after note from its throat stripped everything else to silence: there was nothing but the absolute of its song. It sang from a planet, beyond experience, drawing out longings, sending them back again frozen, piercing, not again to be borne.

Violet withdrew her hand from Fred's forehead and for consolation laid it against her own. He was right, she thought, we're not made for this, we can't take it. He felt for the carton against her thigh, pulled a cigarette out, lit it, rolled over on to his elbows, pressing his midriff against the ground. Staring haggardly, he saw syringa blossoms printed on the trails of the bush.

In the lake a cigarette sputtered. It had been cast on the water, as though at a given signal, by a man who had been standing on the kerb of the lake, glancing this way, that way, over his shoulders. This obsessed-looking, aimless man always seemed to be putting in time, on tenterhooks, waiting for a clock to strike. Habitually he patrolled the park like a keeper, once dark fell: his movements gave rise to the idea that there was something or somebody hidden there. Head down, he now started towards the bridge in a dodging hurry. He could not outdistance the throbs of the nightingale.

From the bridge a family party, unequal skyline of figures, was staring down the lake. Three elbows rested on the high studded bridge rail, above two heads of children, out late, clambering on the trellis. Night loosely welded the party, whose inclination towards the singing end of the lake sent their behinds sticking out some way. The boy, gripping the trellis, swinging out like a monkey, stared at the man dodging past the row of behinds and observed the light from a window flickering stealthily in his glasses.

'Hi, Mum,' he said, jogging her elbow, 'I seen a burglar.'

She was pushing her pompadour back with her other hand, saying to her sister: 'Who would have thought it, really.'

'Really, you'd think it knew.'

The sister's husband said: 'They don't know the difference. Ever so many of them we had out in France in the last war. Sang the guns down. One we had in a copse, it kept us awake three nights. Great fat bird, by the sound. Were we fed up.'

'Where was the corpse then, Oswald?'

'Copse, Kathleen. Out there in No Man's Land.'

'Ah, well.'

'Hi, Mum – '

' – Stop pulling. Don't be so awkward. Listen.'

'Why?'

'Uncle Os's been telling you: that's a nightingale.'

The boy began to whimper: 'But I thought the war was over.'

The mother, with jocular fondness like a she-bear's, pushed the boy's cap forward over his face, explaining meantime to her sister Kathleen: 'He's disappointed he didn't see the floodlights.' She attended to a few more notes, then said: 'How it keeps it up. Funny in London, when you come to think.'

'Nothing,' Kathleen said, 'seems funny to me now. Not after everything we've been through. It's all one to me what I hear now, I tell you frankly, provided it isn't a siren.'

'I've heard lions roar off of this bridge,' said Uncle Oswald.

'I'd soonest a siren,' said the little girl, pertly ducking and weaving under their elbows. She started imitating the nightingale, and the party, somewhat relieved, laughed, and laughing trooped off the bridge towards the gateless gate of the park.

The boy's burglar-man had not, after all, left the range of song. He stood staring about him, trying to calculate its effect on other people. At this side benches were spaced out, facing the lake across a wide asphalt walk: each bench was extinguished into darkness by having the canopy of a tree. It could here and there be seen, and always sensed, that not a bench was empty; and the physical intensity of each silence was disturbing to the neurotic man. Ever since railings had been taken away, he had not ceased to brood on what must be the consequences, nor had he ceased frequenting the night parks. Now a big dog, like a bad spirit, ran past him and all along the seats, head down in silhouette against the grey of the lake. All the time, the nightingale paused and sang.

Now a car, a plough of powerful light, swept round the road that swept round the park. The headlamps floodlit the seats. On the first, two middle-aged women in whitish coats sat rigid, innocent. Leaves flamed for the instant above their heads: they instinctively put up their hands to their hollowed faces until the car had gone.

'That was too much, I'm afraid,' said one to the other. 'Yes, that's all. It has certainly flown away.'

'Wait, it has stopped before. To listen. They say they listen.'

'Listen – a nightingale listen? How curious. Is it known what they expect to hear?'

'I have no idea, Naomi.'

'Disappointing for them to listen, perhaps,' said Naomi. 'But why not? Why should a nightingale get off scot free, after everything it is able to do to us?'

'Poor bird. It's our fault; it's ourselves we hear.'

'Why – Mary?'

'Naomi?'

'Nothing. Only you spoke in such a curious voice. – Has there been anything you have never told me?'

'No, why? Is there anything you've never told me?'

'Nothing – I'm glad to say.'

'Yes,' said Mary doubtfully. 'Apparently we have nothing to regret – unless we begin to regret that we have nothing. Is that what you mean by what nightingales do to us?'

The nightingale, sounding nearer, trickled note by note up into song again: now the fountain was balancing – jug jug jug jug jug. 'It's getting cold,' said Naomi, leaning forward, rewrapping her pale coat across her knees. 'How about turning home?'

'Yes, how about going in?'

As they got up, Naomi observed in her firmest voice: 'Apart from anything, it's too soon. Much too soon, after a war like this. Even Victory's nearly been too much. There ought not to have been a nightingale in the same week. The important thing is that people should go carefully. They'd much better not feel at all till they feel normal. The first thing must be, to get everything organized.'

'How I agree,' said Mary, looking back at the lake. 'But can people live without something they cannot have?'

Not all the lighted windows were now empty: figures of listeners darkened them. Possibly they could not all hear; some had been merely drawn to the windows by the sensation of something going on. At intervals, late-night traffic in and out of London changing gear at the traffic lights drowned everything. A counter-movement of people who did not know anything about the nightingale, making their way home northwards round the park from the pubs and cinemas, with linked arms, whistling and laughing, occurred in gushes. These annoyed those who had come out, to listen, on to the balconies of the ornate houses farther up the park, most of which were still shut up. Cars passing swung light over the chipped stucco columns, and made slow lightning in the mirrors of the long-forsaken drawing-rooms behind the balconies. Tormenting memories of blue velvet nights or ideas of Vienna began to crowd back. From one balcony, an old gentleman, keenly verifying the nightingale after a few notes, bolted indoors to write the letter that should be first with *The Times*.

In a top front room of one of these grander houses, a young woman woke to find herself standing in the middle of a carpet. She often woke like this, and was not surprised; but she asked herself to what room the carpet belonged *this* time. Here were two windows, outside which the sky was not quite dark. She failed to establish the position of the bed she had left while she was asleep: it might be anywhere. She was afraid to move until she was quite awake – and, as it always did, the hope flashed through her mind that the whole year might be a dream, and that someone else lay breathing here in this room, having come back or else never gone away. But in that case she would not have left their bed.

The telegram had sent her back again to walking in her sleep. She was called Ursula, so when she was five or six someone gave her the picture of St Ursula's Dream, which set up the trouble of having to be the angel at the foot of her own bed; until she outgrew that and forgot that and that was no longer even a funny story. Then, the night after she got the telegram, she found herself being the angel rather than be St Ursula. Her fear was, that they would come in and find her before she woke up, and lead her back to St Ursula's narrow form. So this made her fugitive, never staying long under any kind of roof, always wanting to be in an hotel or apartment house where she was no one's business.

Lights travelled across the ceiling and through her brain: tonight she was in Roland's grandmother's house. A young widow staying with an old widow. An evening of trying to comfort the old woman who had come back to London and was brokenhearted at everything outside the reopened windows of her house. The beautiful spearheaded railings of the park were gone; every place was invaded and desecrated; Roland had left no child in Ursula's body. 'I shall be glad to go,' said the old woman. 'Look at the shameless people rolling on the grass. Is it for this we have given Roland?'

Tomorrow, Ursula would be able to say, 'Grandmother, you never told me you had a nightingale in your park!' It must have been singing always. Roland slept in this room when he was boy: nothing in this room is impossible. As a very young man he stayed here to go to dances; he tied his white tie in front of the mirror *I* am now seeing between two windows. Those were May nights.

Ursula felt in the presence of someone she had not met yet. You have not known me, he said, in the old days. Their short marriage was part, for him, of savage, tiring war. Strain, noisiness, hurry, passion, wondering where he was going to be next. It seemed to be all nights and no days. All they had hoped of the future had been, really, a magic recapturing of the past – the magic dilatory past they had not had; their, really, irreparable loss. It was in this young room, probably, that he had been himself.

Standing in the middle of Roland's room, she listened to the nightingale with profound happiness. It had woken her. Soon its last note dropped: to her disappointment it sang – or she heard it singing – no more that night. Disjected lines of poetry, invocations, came flooding into her mind. *I cannot see what flowers are at my feet.* She looked down at the carpet, wondering if a secret were in its pattern. Naturally, it was too dark to see.

Gone Away

'I'm afraid,' said Mr Van Winkle, hurrying up the Vicarage garden path, 'I'm a little late?'

'Don't think of it twice, dear fellow,' replied the Vicar, stepping genially out of a french window.

'Still, I hope I have not kept you waiting about. What year is it?'

'Ten past five.'

'But what year is it?'

'Oh, I beg your pardon!' the Vicar told him. As the two old friends entered the house together, the concern in Van Winkle's expression deepened, not to be charmed away by the cheerful scene — tea, an abundant spread, was set on the study table, and the housekeeper soon bustled in with another cup. 'You know,' said Van Winkle as they sat down, 'I shall have to do something about my habit of dropping off. I relaxed today (or today as it seems to me) for what felt like two or three minutes after lunch, and — well, look where we are! Or should I say, *when* we are? It could get quite serious: I've got a bad heredity. Five or ten years more each time!'

'There's something or other, you know, in most old families,' said the Vicar, passing the buttered toast. 'I shouldn't let this prey on you. What are a few decades?'

'Little enough, apparently, in *your* case,' said Van Winkle, glancing appreciatively at the Vicar, then round the room. Dogs' hairs still covered the mellowed cushions of the 'Varsity chairs; photographs of classic ruins, Alpine glaciers and peaks and hirsute college rowing groups patterned the study walls; a half-shut roll-top disgorged papers. Tracks, trodden down to the nap, in the turkey carpet recorded the Vicar's pacings as he composed sermons. On the table, the glaze of the squat brown teapot reflected the afternoon. Van Winkle was now replete, but his eye continued to travel sentimentally over the muffin dish, rock cakes, seed cake, gentleman's relish and strawberry jam, and over the gold-rimmed china's landscape of blue and white. Though the window stood open, the room smelled slightly of carpet, pipes and old golf balls chewed by dogs. '*You* have not changed.'

'I am under contract not to,' replied the Vicar. 'I should, by now, be difficult to replace; and preserving me, apparently, is a costly business. It is up to me to make myself last – more tea?'

'No – thanks.' Van Winkle, frowning over his empty cup, still had the puzzled senses of the awakened sleeper: he was sounding the hush that surrounded the Vicarage. This *could*, of course, have been due to nothing more than the hot and hazy intensity of the afternoon – outside the window, June standard roses, outsize, lolled from their leaves. Above the garden trees rose the church tower: from where Van Winkle sat there was nothing more to be seen. The outlying silence, however, had not that rich boundless laxity that suggests the country: it was at once closed and dead. And indeed, Van Winkle, during his hurried transit by taxi to the Vicarage gate, had received, he was sure, a long unbroken impression of squares and streets, of soap-clean arcades and polished perspectives, of glass, of dizzying architecture soaring rigid into the mauve-blue sky. But the impression had been of the vaguest kind: still dulled by the fumes of his recent doze, he had thought, most, of not keeping the Vicar waiting for tea.

It seemed simplest to talk of their college days. The Vicar had to confess he had not kept in touch with any of their contemporaries: he did not seem to see, on the other hand, that anything else was to be expected. Filling his pipe from a crested jar, he looked like a Vicar in an advertisement. He then said: 'Well, care to come for a turn?'

Van Winkle was struck, as they stepped through the garden gate, by the almost hallucinatory old-worldness of the scene. He might have been stepping into a picture postcard. A pub with a Lion sign, a row of creeper-draped cottages, two plum-red late Victorian villas, a stucco gentleman's residence, a smithy, a gabled post office showing bottles of sweets, a once new-art village hall and a general shop all stared at him with the two-dimensional brightness of a cinema set-up. Blades of grass in the green, which contained a pond, stood apart as though they had been freshly combed. As Van Winkle, conducted by the Vicar, shifted his line of vision by walking on, he perceived that much of all this *was* in fact a set-up, the greater part of the buildings being façades only, supported by struts behind. The pump, and other village accessories, bore informative labels. And a second, dubious look at the pond showed him that its flotilla of very clean white ducks had been stuffed and neatly attached to floats. The Vicar said: 'You must glance at our church, I think. We have had additions since you were last here.'

It was only as the couple passed through the lychgate that the Vicar himself could be seen to cast at the churchyard a, for the first time, decidedly harassed look. Striking, to any eye, was the hyper-congestion of antique gravestones. These, so closely set edge to edge that you could not have slipped the blade of a knife between them, flocked up in serrated ranks, each rank being not more than inches behind another. Yellowstone cherubs and swags of the seventeenth century gave place to Augustan eulogies, weeping willows, scrolls, clasped hands and green-streaked white marble angels of succeeding periods. Here lay, according to the restored lettering, Nathaniel Highbottom, Joshua Nuggins and Sarah Pye, and a host more; who had, by this showing, dwelled, then passed into bliss, in every conceivable part of England. Van Winkle, his brain reeling, peered over rank after rank and mused on name after name. 'But they can't *all* lie here? There is not room.'

'They *lie*,' the Vicar said, ' – if you speak of their mortal dust – somewhere under the mileage of levelled concrete necessary for airports, speedways, "clover" crossings and helicopter parks. But, as the Board of Art says, one cannot go into that. As the Board young man who controls our Reserve puts it, no *recherché* tombstone must go west. All I have had to say to the Board of Arts is, that really our capacity is not infinite: they must not keep on and on sending lorry loads. Our young man has the faults of his qualities; he is an enthusiast. "I cannot help it," I said; "if you go on dumping any more pew ends, crusaders, pitchpine panels or neo-gothic radiators inside my church, Miss Chough, Mrs Ramsay and Lady Issenbist, not to speak of myself, will no longer be able to get in." Then, he wanted to stack showcases in the porch. "If you do that," I said, "you'll be covering up the Ten Commandments, and *then* you or I will soon be getting complaints!"'

'From Miss Chough, Mrs Ramsay or Lady Issenbist?'

'Oh dear no: from the Brighterville visitors. The Ten Commandments have proved our first attraction. In their leisure hours – and Brighterville living having been so arranged, its young people aged quickly under the stress of many – the young people queued up, right across the Reserve, in pairs, in order to study the Ten Commandments. "Dear me," I used to say, till I grew used to this. One young fellow one day, rounded on me quite sharply. "What *do* you expect?" he said. "Out there," and he jerked his thumb over the Reserve paling, "we've got no prohibitions, no inhibitions, no anything!" At that point, the press of the queue behind pushed him on. But he had had time, I fancy, to drink his fill; for he left the Reserve, I noticed, looking a good deal brighter. Ah, here comes Lady Issenbist!'

Across the speckless roadway of the Reserve, a lady emerged from what looked like a real door in the stucco house, wearing a toque and bearing a bunch of lupins. She signalled with an air of vivacious authority to the Vicar. He murmured: 'So dependable – coming to do our flowers. But I think perhaps we'll defer our chat till another day . . . ' So speaking, he guided Van Winkle to an escape outlet behind the east end of the church. Fortunately, Lady Issenbist's attention was diverted in the direction of another, thinner lady, who with an air of purpose and resolution, was now bicycling up and down between the façades, dismounting at intervals to drop leaflets into letterboxes. The bicycle bell seemed to drown Lady Issenbist's cheerful cry. 'Miss Chough is getting very deaf,' said the Vicar, casting a glance backwards, 'but the Board do not seem to object to that. She is durable. The only thing that bothers them is, replacements.'

The backway from the churchyard brought them head-on into the Reserve boundaries, which were demarcated by high wire fencing, Whipsnade type. The Reserve, Van Winkle was able to judge from here, must be situated at the centre of Brighterville – model avenues rayed out from it in spoke formation. Only the summer shimmering of the distance blurred Brighterville's perspectives, sun-flashing glassy heights and cheese-pale cubular opaqueness. Calculatedly steep, mathematically playful, the skyline of this en-lightened town rippled round the Reserve, closing every horizon. The civic lawns and parterres, the shadow cast by lines of exactly similar trees were of such faultless brightness that Van Winkle almost thought they must be in paint. Numerous fountains not so much played as functioned with a precision that made them look like Lalique glass. All round, Brighterville stretched, soared, stood, with the tame blamelessness of a realized ideal.

'Could one go out?' asked Van Winkle, poking in the direction of one of the avenues with his walking stick.

'But certainly – how stupid I am! I had forgotten this might be of interest to you. That way? – the other? All is much the same.' They passed through a Reserve gateway, gay with the lettering of the Board of Arts, and set off at their slow amble, for they were not young men, down a perspective never likely to stop. They were hailed, about four blocks down the avenue, by another bicycling lady, laden with bags and parcels: 'It's really quite creepy!' she cried, as she pedalled past. 'Mrs Ramsay, I fear, has been looting,' observed the Vicar. 'But, on the other hand, what, really, are we to do? Not a word from the Board since all this occurred.'

'Since all what occurred?'

'Of course,' said the Vicar, immersed in his own anxieties, 'they may have decided to discontinue us. We are an amenity, after all, and one cannot use an amenity with no public.'

No public. Creepy. Mrs Ramsay's flying remark seemed an understatement. For in Brighterville, exposed to the daylight like a cut-open fruit, no life, not so much as an insect, stirred. Briefly, it was a ghost town. Traffic had, as though by some irresistible suction, been altogether drained from the streets and squares. From inside buildings, an almost bursting silence escaped through doorways, pressed against staring panes. Every door stood open: uninterrupted spokes of sunshine pierced the classless dwellings. Gleaming lift shafts in vestibules, silhouettes of sky-high machinery were to be glimpsed. With the propriety of mutes the Vicar, too thoughtful to speak, and his for some time quite speechless companion, entered where they would: pressing button after button in building after building, they whizzed from floor to floor. Unnervingly, all machinery remained animate: in factories nothing abated the soundless whir, in the lofty cinemas, culture centres and galleries with their reproductions of almost every one of the world's masterpieces, plants did not cease to condition the unbreathed air. In the cafeterias, conveyors laden with plastic plates laden with frozen salad kept up their river-like motion past rows of stools; while in the gymnasia riding machines, clattering their steel stirrups, jogged away briskly. Van Winkle gave thanks that his most gripping sleep had not yet been attended by such a dream. Cased in glass and whiteness, whose effect was the same whether one stood nominally indoors or out, stupefied by the now turgid beams of the latening sun, or belted across the eyes by hard, toneless shadow, he began, he thought, to feel his own senses stop. Here and there – but here and there only – as on the *Marie Celeste*, there were to be found traces of interruption, of the startled abandonment of some meal or task.

In face of the monstrous enigma of this evacuation, Van Winkle did not know what question to ask first. Reciprocal shyness, even, crept up between himself and his old friend – Van Winkle growing more morbidly conscious of disqualifications due to his dozing habit; and the Vicar, with that sensitive diffidence that was his greatest charm, uncertain, palpably, at which point it would be least hurting to begin to enlighten him. The queasy silence between them, augmented by the voicelessness everywhere, was broken when the Vicar at last said: 'On the whole, they left everything very tidy.'

'Yes . . . I suppose what happened was in the papers?'

'I could not say,' said the Vicar, 'if there have been papers since. Shall we sit down? I see no reason, do you, why we should not sit down almost anywhere?'

Indecision added the last touch to their nervosity: wandering round and petering out in circles, the two at length collapsed on a couchlike bench in what was entitled The Lovers' Grove. All round, quotations from the more amorous poets were staked, like keep-off notices, into green dells, grots and sinuous beds of flowers selected, it could be told, for their swooning smell. The groups of statuary, now not unsuitable pink in the setting sun, had been chosen, Van Winkle could only think, to revive in the young people of Brighterville a flagging interest in one another. The Vicar was shortsighted: he had leaned back, snuffing the heliotrope, enjoying the cool of a spray that, revolving nearby, mistily hosed the lawns. After a minute, pulling himself together, he volunteered in a firm voice: 'You'd like to know that happened?'

'That is to put it mildly,' said Van Winkle.

'It all happened rather suddenly, in a moment. At the peak of a day – unfortunately, I cannot remember which. – No, looking back I see there *had* been symptoms; but who is to know the symptoms of a malady unknown and on such a scale? The increasing congestion of our Reserve, the unwillingness to leave it at closing time . . . The painful dawn of something like an expression on our visitors' closely similar faces . . . In their behaviour, a jittery variation hitherto unknown . . . It was their part, however, to study us: we were under no contract to study them. When it happened – '

' – But *what* happened?'

'The day dawned as usual – in point of fact, it could hardly do otherwise. You may not know that since weather control was perfected the sun has not ceased shining for five years, and that any moody variation between the seasons has been corrected. The day, as I say, dawned: the night 'planes came down, the day 'planes went up, making the heavens throb like an aching head, a headache to which one becomes resigned. On the ground, the Brighterville traffic, flashing, proceeded along its grooves; and the pedestrians proceeded along theirs. At the avenue corners the amplifiers switched themselves on and emitted their diurnal quota of pep talks alternating with music. These had been introduced to fill any awkward silence when it was found that the Brightervillians had ceased to talk, being able to think of nothing further to say. The young children were, as on every other morning, released by the civic nurses on to the lawns surrounding the Reserve: all aggressive or competitive play having been condemned, they went round and round in rings, chanting ditties they had learned from the amplifiers. Their parents, garbed for sport or in snowy factory overalls, moved in ribbons, like old-world toothpaste pressed from a tube, in and out of the factories, sportsdromes, cafeterias and culture centres. The automatic clocking-in machine sounded its bell as each individual entered or left a building; and bells recorded the entrances, two by two, of the adolescents to the de-fixation clinics. The noises of Brighterville were, in fact, as ever. We noticed nothing until it stopped.'

'Stopped?'

'Stopped. It was as though an inaudible siren had sounded a note always dreaded but never heard before. The reaction, instantaneous, was appalling.'

'What happened?'

'Everyone was appalled. Stopping dead in their tracks they stared in each other's faces. The communication of the idea of doom must have happened before one could say knife. The psychic blast travelled through the Reserve, knocking Miss Chough off her bicycle. Lady Issenbist rushed to the paling, and I followed. Outside, the poor infants, breaking off at the high note of a chanty, had collapsed in their rings like little pricked white balloons; their nurses, covering their eyes with their hands, fled shrieking down the avenues in the direction of the horizon. In the distance we perceived people, too impatient to await the descent by lift, leaping from upper windows: owing to the pneumatic nature of the streets, they bounced. Having picked themselves up, pellmell, they began to run. Some paused to hurl unbreakable plastic objects, it appeared angrily, into the amplifiers. "Something must have happened," said Lady Issenbist. I went back to the Vicarage for my stronger spectacles, then returned to the paling. The stampede was by now, I am sorry to say, wholesale. People were swarming on to trams, cars and trolleys, which, immobilized by the undue weight, stopped. Those who had been pushed off began to push behind. At the same time, an uncanny silence emanated from the sky: the 'planes, like a swarm of midges into the heart of which one has puffed smoke, dispersed in horror, making for the horizons. This completed the panic. Mothers, heroically returning, swept up their offsprings from the lawns. Lady Issenbist said, "Their eyes are starting out of their heads." I said, "Ladies, can I be of any assistance?" But they were gone. Running.'

'Running where?'

'Like everyone else, out of Brighterville.'

'Every soul, in a minute?'

'Not a soul could bear it a minute longer.'

'Why?'

'One must leave it,' the Vicar said, 'that they could not bear it a minute longer.'

'You can't be suggesting, surely, that they were simply bored?'

'You and I,' said the Vicar, 'have done hardly more, in our lives, than glimpse the verges of boredom. As to its cumulative pressure, its extreme, its dire frenzied last breaking-point – what do you and I know?' He looked round again, sighed, and said: 'It *may* not have been that, of course.'

'They fled.'

'As you see . . .'

'So, where to? Some other town?'

The worried, regretful expression on the Vicar's face deepened. '*All* our cities,' he said, 'are now other Brightervilles. Would they receive gladly that disaffected inrush; would they welcome infection carriers? I fear, no. All our countryside, with the exception of the twenty-five Beauty Spots, has been levelled over. No, I fear the assumption is that our Brightervillians ran till they reached the coast: those who could not take ship swam out to sea.'

Van Winkle, speechless, opened his cigarette case: the cigarettes, however, sent out a musty smell. 'Dear me . . . ' Snakes of twilight wound through The Lovers' Grove; a crow, black and cumbrous, winged its way across the space between the skyscraper tops. The silence that supervened on the Vicar's voice was no longer merely null; it was shocking. The silence, however, was cut in on by a sharp, imperious, peevish human cry. Electrified, the Vicar and his companion faced on each other. '*Somebody's left behind!*'

The cry, repeated, gave a line for their search: it drew them, finally, in through the portals of the Euthanasia Centre, which, by some whim of town planning, faced on The Lovers' Grove. The reception hall of the Centre was gay and tasteful; magazines, littered on glass-topped tables, offered to while waiting minutes away. In the middle, angrily upright in a wheeled chair, sat the old lady who had been making the noise. She glared at the gentlemen as they came in. 'Ho, so *there* you are! And about time – *I* heard you out there, gabbling away all night.'

'Had we thought for a moment – ' the Vicar said.

'Well, you didn't. Forgotten how to. They all have. A pretty pack! How much longer am I to sit waiting round for? I *told* them, I've changed my mind. "Oh dear, oh dear," the young lady assistant says, "that's not often done." "Well, it's what I'm doing," I told her, "and why not? When a lady can't change her mind, things have come to a pretty pass!" She seemed quite put out. "Well," I said, "what *is* the matter with life?" Ho, that started something! You'd think a mouse had run up her back. My lady goes flouncing out of the room, and for all I know goes flouncing out of the town. All I do know, there's nobody been back since. – Well, come on, what are you staring at? You'd better run me home now: I want my tea.'

'The position is – ' said the Vicar, cocking an eye despairingly at Van Winkle.

'They won't half not laugh,' she said zestfully, 'when Granny comes rolling home!'

There was clearly only one course to pursue. Manoeuvring the wheeled chair, which trickled ahead of them with a faultless lightness, they propelled the recusant from euthanasia clear of the portals and off round The Lovers' Grove. 'Hi,' she yelled sharply, 'not *that* way!' The Vicar, inclining towards her ear, said: 'For a little time, you are coming to stay with me.' The ancient emitted a flighty cackle. She looked ahead of her down the void, darkening streets, and now and then up the buildings, but without comment: they dared not ask what she saw. Trotting to keep up with the chair, the Vicar and Van Winkle headed steadily down the last of the avenues in the direction of the Reserve.

Overhead, in the colourless crystal sky, there appeared a cloud the size of a man's hand.

Hand in Glove

JASMINE LODGE was favourably set on a residential, prettily-wooded hillside in the south of Ireland, overlooking a river and, still better, the roofs of a lively garrison town. Around 1904, which was the flowering period of the Miss Trevors, girls could not have had a more auspicious home – the neighbourhood spun merrily round the military. Ethel and Elsie, a spirited pair, garnered the full advantage – no ball, hop, picnic, lawn tennis, croquet or boating party was complete without them; in winter, though they could not afford to hunt, they trimly bicycled to all meets, and on frosty evenings, with their guitars, set off to *soirées*, snug inside their cab in their fur-tipped capes.

They possessed an aunt, a Mrs Varley de Grey, *née* Elysia Trevor, a formerly notable local belle, who, drawn back again in her widowhood to what had been the scene of her early triumphs, occupied a back bedroom in Jasmine Lodge. Mrs Varley de Grey had had no luck: her splashing match, in its time the talk of two kingdoms, had ended up in disaster – the well-born captain in a cavalry regiment having gone so far as to blow out his brains in India, leaving behind him nothing but her and debts. Mrs Varley de Grey had returned from India with nothing but seven large trunks crammed with recent finery; and she also had been impaired by shock. This had taken place while Ethel and Elsie, whose father had married late, were still unborn – so it was that, for as long as the girls recalled, their aunt had been the sole drawback to Jasmine Lodge. Their parents had orphaned them, somewhat thoughtlessly, by simultaneously dying of scarlet fever when Ethel was just out and Elsie soon to be – they were therefore left lacking a chaperone and, with their gift for putting everything to some use, propped the aunt up in order that she might play that role. Only when her peculiarities became too marked did they feel it necessary to withdraw her: by that time, however, all the surrounding ladies could be said to compete for the honour of taking into society the sought-after Miss Trevors. From then on, no more was seen or heard of Mrs Varley de Grey. ('Oh, just a trifle unwell, but nothing much!') She remained upstairs, at the back: when the girls were giving one of their little parties, or a couple of officers came to call, the key of her room would be turned in the outer lock.

The girls hung Chinese lanterns from the creepered veranda, and would sit lightly strumming on their guitars. Not less fascinating was their badinage, accompanied by a daring flash of the eyes. They were known as the clever Miss Trevors, not because of any taint of dogmatism or book-learning – no, when a gentleman cried, 'Those girls have brains!' he meant it wholly in admiration – but because of their accomplishments, ingenuity and agility. They took leading parts in theatricals, lent spirit to numbers of drawing-room games, were naughty mimics, and sang duets. Nor did their fingers lag behind their wits – they constructed lampshades, crêpe paper flowers and picturesque hats; and, above all, varied their dresses marvellously – no one could beat them for ideas, nipping, slashing or fitting. Once more allowing nothing to go to waste, they had remodelled the trousseau out of their aunt's trunks, causing sad old tulles and tarlatans, satins and *moiré* taffetas, to appear to have come from Paris only today. They re-stitched spangles, pressed ruffles crisp, and revived many a corsage of squashed silk roses. They went somewhat softly about that task, for the trunks were all stored in the attic immediately over the back room.

They wore their clothes well. 'A pin on either of those two would look smart!' declared other girls. All that they were short of was evening gloves – they had two pairs each, which they had been compelled to buy. *What* could have become of Mrs Varley de Grey's presumably sumptuous numbers of this item, they were unable to fathom, and it was too bad. Had gloves been overlooked in her rush from India? – or, were they here, in that *one* trunk the Trevors could not get at? All other locks had yielded to pulls or pickings, or the sisters found keys to fit them, or they had used the tool-box; but this last stronghold defied them. In that sad little soiled silk sack, always on her person, Mrs Varley de Grey, they became convinced, hoarded the operative keys, along with some frippery rings and brooches – all true emeralds, pearls and diamonds having been long ago, as they knew, sold. Such contrariety on their aunt's part irked them – meanwhile, gaieties bore hard on their existing gloves. Last thing at nights when they came in, last thing in the evenings before they went out, they would manfully dab away at the fingertips. So, it must be admitted that a long whiff of benzine pursued them as they whirled round the ballroom floor.

They were tall and handsome – nothing so soft as pretty, but in those days it was a vocation to be a handsome girl; many of the best marriages had been made by such. They carried themselves imposingly, had good busts and shoulders, waists firm under the whalebone, and straight backs. Their features were striking, their colouring high; low on their foreheads bounced dark mops of curls. Ethel was, perhaps, the dominant one, but both girls were pronounced to be full of character.

Whom, and still more when, did they mean to marry? They had already seen regiments out and in; for quite a number of years, it began to seem, bets in the neighbourhood had been running high. Sympathetic spy-glasses were trained on the conspicuous gateway to Jasmine Lodge; each new cavalier was noted. The only trouble might be, their promoters claimed, that the clever Trevors were always so surrounded that they had not a moment in which to turn or choose. Or otherwise, could it possibly be that the admiration aroused by Ethel and Elsie, and their now institutional place in the local scene, scared out more tender feeling from the masculine breast? It came to be felt, and perhaps by the girls themselves, that, having lingered so long and so puzzlingly, it was up to them to bring off (like their aunt) a *coup*. Society around this garrison town had long plumed itself upon its romantic record; summer and winter, Cupid shot his darts. Lush scenery, the oblivion of all things else bred by the steamy climate, and perpetual gallivanting – all were conducive. Ethel's and Elsie's names, it could be presumed, were by now murmured wherever the Union Jack flew. Nevertheless, it was time they should decide.

Ethel's decision took place late one evening. She set her cap at the second son of an English marquess. Lord Fred had come on a visit, for the fishing, to a mansion some miles down the river from Jasmine Lodge. He first made his appearance, with the rest of the house party, at one of the more resplendent military balls, and was understood to be a man-about-town. The civilian glint of his pince-nez, at once serene and superb, instantaneously wrought, with his great name, on Ethel's heart. She beheld him, and the assembled audience, with approbation, looked on at the moment so big with fate. The truth, it appeared in a flash, was that Ethel, though so condescending with her charms, had not from the first been destined to love a soldier; and that here, after long attrition, her answer was. Lord Fred was, by all, at once signed over to her. For his part, he responded to her attentions quite gladly, though in a somewhat dazed way. If he did not so often dance with her – indeed, how could he, for she was much besought? – he could at least be perceived to gaze. At a swiftly organized river picnic, the next evening, he by consent fell to Ethel's lot – she had spent the foregoing morning snipping and tacking at a remaining muslin of Mrs Varley de Grey's, a very fresh forget-me-not-dotted pattern. The muslin did not survive the evening out, for when the moon should have risen, rain poured into the boats. Ethel's good-humoured drollery carried all before it, and Lord Fred wrapped his blazer around her form.

Next day, more rain; and all felt flat. At Jasmine Lodge, the expectant deck chairs had to be hurried in from the garden, and the small close rooms, with their greeneried windows and plentiful bric-à-brac, gave out a stuffy, resentful, indoor smell. The maid was out; Elsie was lying down with a migraine; so it devolved on Ethel to carry up Mrs Varley de Grey's tea – the invalid set very great store by tea, and her manifestations by door rattlings, sobs and mutters were apt to become disturbing if it did not appear. Ethel, with the not particularly dainty tray, accordingly entered the back room, this afternoon rendered dark by its outlook into a dripping uphill wood. The aunt, her visage draped in a cobweb shawl, was as usual sitting up in bed. '*Aha*,' she at once cried, screwing one eye up and glittering round at Ethel with the other, 'so what's all this in the wind today?'

Ethel, as she lodged the meal on the bed, shrugged her shoulders, saying: 'I'm in a hurry.'

'No doubt you are. The question is, will you get him?'

'Oh, drink your tea!' snapped Ethel, her colour rising.

The old wretch responded by popping a lump of sugar into her cheek, and sucking at it while she fixed her wink on her niece. She then observed: '*I* could tell you a thing or two!'

'We've had enough of *your* fabrications, Auntie!'

'Fabrications!' croaked Mrs Varley de Grey. 'And who's been the fabricator, I'd like to ask? Who's so nifty with the scissors and needle? Who's been going a-hunting in my clothes?'

'Oh, what a fib!' exclaimed Ethel, turning her eyes up. 'Those old musty miserable bundles of things of yours – would Elsie or I consider laying a finger on them?'

Mrs Varley de Grey replied, as she sometimes did, by heaving up and throwing the tray at Ethel. Nought, therefore, but cast-off kitchen china nowadays was ever exposed to risk; and the young woman, not trying to gather the debris up, statuesquely, thoughtfully stood with her arms folded, watching tea steam rise from the carpet. Today, the effort required seemed to have been too much for Aunt Elysia, who collapsed on her pillows, faintly blue in the face. 'Rats in the attic,' she muttered. '*I've* heard them, rats in the attic! Now where's my tea?'

'You've had it,' said Ethel, turning to leave the room. However, she paused to study a photograph in a tarnished, elaborate silver frame. 'Really quite an Adonis, poor Uncle Harry. – From the first glance, you say, he never looked back?'

'My lovely tea,' said her aunt, beginning to sob.

As Ethel slowly put down the photograph, her eyes could be

seen to calculate, her mouth hardened and a reflective cast came over her brow. Step by step, once more she approached the bed, and, as she did so, altered her tune. She suggested, in a beguiling tone: 'You said you could tell me a thing or two . . . ?'

Time went on; Lord Fred, though forever promising, still failed to come quite within Ethel's grasp. Ground gained one hour seemed to be lost the next – it seemed, for example, that things went better for Ethel in the afternoons, in the open air, than at the dressier evening functions. It was when she swept down on him in full plumage that Lord Fred seemed to contract. Could it be that he feared his passions? – she hardly thought so. Or, did her complexion not light up well? When there was a question of dancing, he came so late that her programme already was black with other names, whereupon he would heave a gallant sigh. When they did take the floor together, he held her so far at arm's length, and with his face turned so far away, that when she wished to address him she had to shout – she told herself this must be the London style, but it piqued her, naturally. Next morning, all would be as it was before, with nobody so completely assiduous as Lord Fred – but, through it all, he still never came to the point. And worse, the days of his visit were running out; he would soon be back in the heart of the London Season. 'Will you ever get him, Ethel, now, do you think?' Elsie asked, with trying solicitude, and no doubt the neighbourhood wondered also.

She conjured up all her fascinations. But was something further needed, to do the trick?

It was now that she began to frequent her aunt.

In that dank little back room looking into the hill, proud Ethel humbled herself, to prise out the secret. Sessions were close and long. Elsie, in mystification outside the door, heard the dotty voice of their relative rising, falling, with, now and then, bloodcurdling little knowing laughs. Mrs Varley de Grey was back in the golden days. Always, though, of a sudden it would break off, drop back into pleas, whimpers and jagged breathing. No doctor, though she constantly asked for one, had for years been allowed to visit Mrs Varley de Grey – the girls saw no reason for that expense, or for the interference which might follow. Aunt's affliction, they swore, was confined to the head; all she required was quiet, and that she got. Knowing, however, how gossip spreads, they would let no servant near her for more than a minute or two, and then with one of themselves on watch at the door. They had much to bear from the foetid state of her room.

'You don't think you'll kill her, Ethel?' the out-of-it Elsie asked. 'Forever sitting on top of her, as you now do. Can it be healthy, egging her on to talk? What's this attraction, all of a sudden? – whatever's this which has sprung up between you two? She and you are becoming quite hand-in-glove.'

Elsie merely remarked this, and soon forgot: she had her own fish to fry. It was Ethel who had cause to recall the words – for, the afternoon of the very day they were spoken, Aunt Elysia whizzed off on another track, screamed for what was impossible and, upon being thwarted, went into a seizure unknown before. The worst of it was, at the outset her mind cleared – she pushed her shawl back, reared up her unkempt grey head and looked at Ethel, unblinkingly studied Ethel, with a lucid accumulation of years of hate. 'You fool of a gawk,' she said, and with such contempt! 'Coming running to me to know how to trap a man. Could *you* learn, if it was from Venus herself? Wait till I show you beauty. – Bring down those trunks!'

'Oh, Auntie.'

'Bring them down, I say. I'm about to dress myself up.'

'Oh, but I cannot; they're heavy; I'm single-handed.'

'Heavy? – they came here heavy. But there've been rats in the attic. – *I* saw you, swishing downstairs in my *eau-de-nil!*'

'Oh, you dreamed that!'

'Through the crack of the door. – Let me up, then. Let us go where they are, and look – we shall soon see!' Aunt Elysia threw back the bedclothes and began to get up. 'Let's take a look,' she said, 'at the rats' work.' She set out to totter towards the door.

'Oh, but you're not fit!' Ethel protested.

'And when did a doctor say so?' There was a swaying: Ethel caught her in time and, not gently, lugged her back to the bed – and Ethel's mind the whole of this time was whirling, for tonight was the night upon which all hung. Lord Fred's last local appearance was to be, like his first, at a ball: tomorrow he left for London. So it must be tonight, at this ball, or never! How was it that Ethel felt so strangely, wildly confident of the outcome? It was time to begin on her coiffure, lay out her dress. Oh, tonight she would shine as never before! She flung back the bedclothes over the helpless form, heard a clock strike, and hastily turned to go.

'I will be quits with you,' said the voice behind her.

Ethel, in a kimono, hair half done, was in her own room, in front of the open glove drawer, when Elsie came in – home from a tennis party. Elsie acted oddly; she went at once to the drawer and buried her nose in it. 'Oh, my goodness,' she cried, 'it's all too true, and it's awful!'

'What is?' Ethel carelessly asked.

'Ethel dear, would you ever face it out if I were to tell you a certain rumour I heard today at the party as to Lord Fred?'

Ethel turned from her sister, took up the heated tongs and applied more crimps to her natural curliness. She said: 'Certainly; spit it out.'

'Since childhood, he's recoiled from the breath of benzine. He wilts away when it enters the very room!'

'Who says that's so?'

'He confided it to his hostess, who is now spitefully putting it around the country.'

Ethel bit her lip and put down the tongs, while Elsie sorrowfully concluded: 'And your gloves stink, Ethel, as I'm sure do mine.' Elsie then thought it wiser to slip away.

In a minute more, however, she was back, and this time with a still more peculiar air. She demanded: 'In what state did you leave Auntie? She was sounding so very quiet that I peeped in, and *I* don't care for the looks of her now at all!' Ethel swore, but consented to take a look. She stayed in there in the back room, with Elsie biting her thumb-nail outside the door, for what seemed an ominous length of time – when she did emerge, she looked greenish, but held her head high. The sisters' eyes met. Ethel said, stonily: 'Dozing.'

'You're certain she's *not* . . . ? She *couldn't* ever be – you know?'

'Dozing, I tell you,' Ethel stared Elsie out.

'If she *was* gone,' quavered the frailer sister, 'just think of it – why, we'd never get to the ball! – And a ball that everything hangs on,' she ended up, with a sacred but conspiratorial glance at Ethel.

'Reassure yourself. Didn't you hear me say?'

As she spoke Ethel, chiefly from habit, locked her late aunt's door on the outside. The act caused a sort of secret jingle to be heard from inside her fist, and Elsie asked: 'What's that you've got hold of, now?' 'Just a few little keys and trinkets she made me keep,' replied Ethel, disclosing the small bag she had found where she'd looked for it, under the dead one's pillow. 'Scurry on now, Elsie, or you'll never be dressed. Care to make use of my tongs, while they're so splendidly hot?'

Alone at last, Ethel drew in a breath, and, with a gesture of resolution, retied her kimono sash tightly over her corset. She shook the key from the bag and regarded it, murmuring, 'Providential!', then gave a glance upward, towards where the attics were. The late spring sun had set, but an apricot afterglow, not unlike the light cast by a Chinese lantern, crept through the upper storey of Jasmine Lodge. The cessation of all those rustlings, tappings, whimpers and moans from inside Mrs Varley de Grey's room had set up an unfamiliar, somewhat unnerving hush. Not till

a whiff of singeing hair announced that Elsie was well employed
did Ethel set out on the quest which held all her hopes. Success was
imperative – she *must* have gloves. Gloves, gloves . . .

Soundlessly, she set foot on the attic stairs.

Under the skylight, she had to suppress a shriek, for a rat – yes,
of all things! – leaped at her out of an empty hatbox; and the rodent
gave her a wink before it darted away. Now Ethel and Elsie knew
for a certain fact that there never *had* been rats in Jasmine Lodge.
However, she continued to steel her nerves, and to push her way to
the one inviolate trunk.

All Mrs Varley de Grey's other Indian luggage gaped and
yawned at Ethel, void, showing its linings, on end or toppling,
forming a barricade around the object of her search – she pushed,
pitched and pulled, scowling as the dust flew into her hair. But the
last trunk, when it came into view and reach, still had something
select and bridal about it: on top, the initials E. V. de G. stared out,
quite luminous in a frightening way – for indeed how dusky the
attic was! Shadows not only multiplied in the corners but seemed to
finger their way up the sloping roof. Silence pierced up through the
floor from that room below – and, worst, Ethel had the sensation
of being watched by that pair of fixed eyes she had not stayed to
close. She glanced this way, that way, backward over her shoulder.
But, Lord Fred was at stake! – she knelt down and got to work
with the key.

This trunk had two neat brass locks, one left, one right, along the
front of the lid. Ethel, after fumbling, opened the first – then, so
great was her hurry to know what might be within that she could
not wait but slipped her hand in under the lifted corner. She pulled
out one pricelessly lacy top of what must be a bride-veil, and gave
a quick laugh – must not this be an omen? She pulled again, but the
stuff resisted, almost as though it were being grasped from inside
the trunk – she let go, and either her eyes deceived her or the lace
began to be drawn back slowly, in again, inch by inch. What was
odder was, that the spotless finger-tip of a white kid glove appeared for a moment, as though exploring its way out, then withdrew.

Ethel's heart stood still – but she turned to the other lock. Was a
giddy attack overcoming her? – for, as she gazed, the entire lid of
the trunk seemed to bulge upward, heave and strain, so that the
E. V. de G. upon it rippled.

Untouched by the key in her trembling hand, the second lock tore
itself open.

She recoiled, while the lid slowly rose – of its own accord.

She should have fled. But oh, how she craved what lay there
exposed! – layer upon layer, wrapped in transparent paper, of

elbow-length, magnolia-pure white gloves, bedded on the inert folds of the veil. 'Lord Fred,' thought Ethel, 'now you're within my grasp!'

That was her last thought, nor was the grasp to be hers. Down on her knees again, breathless with lust and joy, Ethel flung herself forward on to that sea of kid, scrabbling and seizing. The glove she had seen before was now, however, readier for its purpose. At first it merely pounced after Ethel's fingers, as though making mock of their greedy course; but the hand within it was all the time filling out . . . With one snowy flash through the dusk, the glove clutched Ethel's front hair, tangled itself in her black curls and dragged her head down. She began to choke among the sachets and tissue – then the glove let go, hurled her back, and made its leap at her throat.

It was a marvel that anything so dainty should be so strong. So great, so convulsive was the swell of the force that, during the strangling of Ethel, the seams of the glove split.

In any case, the glove would have been too small for her.

The shrieks of Elsie, upon the attic threshold, began only when all other sounds had died down . . . The ultimate spark of the once-famous cleverness of the Miss Trevors appeared in Elsie's extrication of herself from this awkward mess – for, who was to credit how Ethel came by her end? The sisters' reputation for warmth of heart was to stand the survivor in good stead – for, could those affections nursed in Jasmine Lodge, extending so freely even to the unwell aunt, have culminated in Elsie's setting on Ethel? No. In the end, the matter was hushed up – which is to say, is still talked about even now. Ethel Trevor and Mrs Varley de Grey were interred in the same grave, as everyone understood that they would have wished. What conversation took place under the earth, one does not know.

A Day in the Dark

COMING into Moher over the bridge, you may see a terrace of houses by the river. They are to the left of the bridge, below it. Their narrow height and faded air of importance make them seem to mark the approach to some larger town. The six dwellings unite into one frontage, colour-washed apricot years ago. They face north. Their lower sash windows, front steps and fanlit front doors are screened by lime trees, making for privacy. There are area railings. Between them and the water runs a road with a parapet, which comes to its end opposite the last house.

On the other side of the bridge picturesquely rises a ruined castle – more likely to catch the tourist's eye. Woods, from which the river emerges, go back deeply behind the ruin: on clear days there is a backdrop of Irish-blue mountains. Otherwise Moher has little to show. The little place prospers – a market town with a square, on a main road. The hotel is ample, cheerful, and does business. Moreover Moher is, and has been for ages, a milling town. Obsolete stone buildings follow you some way along the river valley as, having passed through Moher, you pursue your road. The flour-white modern mills, elsewhere, hum.

Round the square, shops and pubs are of many colours – in the main Moher looks like a chalk drawing. Not so the valley with its elusive lights.

You *could*, I can see, overlook my terrace of houses – because of the castle, indifference or haste. I only do not because I am looking out for them. For in No. 4 lived Miss Banderry.

She was the last of a former milling family – last, that is, but for the widowed niece, her pensioner. She owned the terrace, drew rents also from property in another part of the town, and had acquired, some miles out of Moher, a profitable farm which she'd put to management. Had control of the family mills been hers, they would not have been parted with – as it was, she had had to contend with a hopeless brother: he it was who had ended by selling out. Her demand for her share of the money left him unable to meet personal debts: he was found hanged from one of the old mill crossbeams. Miss Banderry lived in retirement, the more

thought of for being seldom seen – now and then she would
summon a Ford hackney and drive to her farm in it, without
warning. My uncle, whose land adjoined on hers, had dealings
with her, in the main friendly – which was how they first fell into
talk. She, a formidable reader, took to sending him serious magazines, reviews, pamphlets and so on, with marked passages on
which she would be dying to hear his views. This was her way of
harrying him. For my uncle, a winning, versatile and when
necessary inventive talker, fundamentally hated to tax his brain. He
took to evading meetings with her as far as possible.

So much I knew when I rang her doorbell.

It was July, a sunless warm afternoon, dead still. The terrace was
heavy with limes in flower. Above, through the branches, appeared
the bridge with idlers who leaned on the balustrade spying down
upon me, or so I thought. I felt marked by visiting this place – I was
fifteen, and my every sensation was acute in a way I recall, yet cannot recall. All six houses were locked in childless silence. From under
the parapet came languidly the mesmeric sound of the weir, and,
from a window over my head, the wiry hopping of a bird in a cage.
From the shabby other doors of the terrace, No. 4's stood out,
handsomely though sombrely painted red. It opened.

I came to return a copy of *Blackwoods*. Also I carried a bunch of
ungainly roses from my uncle's garden, and a request that he might
borrow the thistle cutter from Miss Banderry's farm for use on his
land. One rose moulted petals on to her doorstep, then on to the
linoleum in the hall. 'Goodness!' complained the niece, who had let
me in. 'Those didn't travel well. Overblown, aren't they!' (I
thought that applied to her.) 'And I'll bet,' she said, '*he* never sent
those!' She was not in her aunt's confidence, being treated more or
less like a slave. Timed (they said) when she went errands into the
town – she dare not stay talking, dare not so much as look into the
hotel bar while the fun was on. For a woman said to be forty, this
sounded mortifying. Widowed Nan, ready to be handsome,
wore a cheated ravenous look. It was understood she would come
into the money when the aunt died: she must contain herself till
then. As for me – how dared she speak of my uncle with her bad
breath?

Naturally he *had* never thought of the roses. He had com-
missioned me to be gallant for him any way I chose, and I would
not do too badly with these, I'd thought, as I unstrangled them
from the convolvulus in the flowerbed. They would need not only
to flatter but to propitiate, for this copy of *Blackwoods* I brought
back had buttery thumbmarks on its margins and on its cover a
blistered circle where my uncle must have stood down his glass.
'She'll be mad,' he prophesied. 'Better say it was you.' So I

sacrificed a hair ribbon to tie the roses. It rejoiced me to stand between him and trouble.

'Auntie's resting,' the niece warned me, and put me to wait. The narrow parlour looked out through thick lace on to the terrace, which was reflected in a looking-glass at the far end. Ugly though I could see honourable furniture, mahogany, had been crowded in. In the middle, a circular table wore a chenille cloth. This room felt respected though seldom entered – however, it was peopled in one way: generations of oil-painted portraits hung round the walls, photographs overflowed from bracket and ledge even on to the centre table. I was faced, wherever I turned, by one or another member of the family which could only be the vanished Banderrys. There was a marble clock, but it had stopped.

Footsteps halted heavily over the ceiling, but that was all for I don't know how long. I began to wonder what those Banderrys saw – lodging the magazine and roses on the table, I went to inspect myself in the glass. A tall girl in a sketchy cotton dress. Arms thin, no sign yet of a figure. Hair forward over the shoulders in two plaits, like, said my uncle, a Red Indian maiden's. Barbie was my name.

In memory, the moment before often outlives the awaited moment. I recollect waiting for Miss Banderry – then, nothing till she was with me in the room. I got over our handshake without feeling. On to the massiveness of her bust was pinned a diamond-studded enamelled watch, depending from an enamelled bow: there was a tiny glitter as she drew breath. – 'So he sent *you*, did he?' She sat down, the better to look at me. Her apart knees stretched the skirt of her dress. Her choleric colouring and eyeballs made her appear angry, as against which she favoured me with a racy indulgent smile, to counteract the impression she knew she gave.

'I hear wonders of you,' said she, dealing the lie to me like a card.

She sat in reach of the table. 'My bouquet, eh?' She grasped the bundle of roses, thorns and all, and took a long voluptuous sniff at them, as though deceiving herself as to their origin – showing me she knew how to play the game, if I didn't – then shoved back the roses among the photographs and turned her eyes on the magazine, sharply. 'I'm sorry, I – ' I began. In vain. All she gave was a rumbling chuckle – she held up to me the copy of *Blackwoods* open at the page with the most thumbmarks. 'I'd know *those* anywhere!' She scrutinized the print for, a line or two. 'Did he make head or tail of it?'

'He told me to tell you, he enjoyed it.' (I saw my uncle dallying, stuffing himself with buttered toast.) 'With his best thanks.'

'You're a little echo,' she said, not discontentedly.

I stared her out.

'Never mind,' she said. 'He's a handsome fellow.'

I shifted my feet. She gave me a look.

She observed: 'It's a pity to read at table.'

'He hasn't much other time, Miss Banderry.'

'Still, it's a poor compliment to you!'

She stung me into remarking: 'He doesn't often.'

'Oh, I'm sure you're a great companion for him!'

It was as though she saw me casting myself down by my uncle's chair when he'd left the room, or watching the lassitude of his hand hanging caressing a dog's ear. With him I felt the tender bond of sex. Seven, eight weeks with him under his roof, among the copper beeches from spring to summer turning from pink to purple, and I was in love with him. Such things happen, I suppose. He was my mother's brother, but I had not known him when I was a child. Of his manhood I had had no warning. Naturally growing into love I was, like the grass growing into hay on his uncut lawns. There was not a danger till she spoke.

'He's glad of company now and then,' I said as stupidly as I could.

She plucked a petal from her black serge skirt.

'Well,' she said, 'thank him for the thanks. And you for the nice little pleasure of this visit. – Then, there's nothing else?'

'My uncle wants – ' I began.

'You don't surprise me,' said Miss Banderry. 'Well, come on out with it. What this time?'

'If he could once more borrow the thistle cutter . . . ?'

'"Once more"! And what will he be looking to do next year? Get his own mended? I suppose he'd hardly go to that length.'

His own, I knew, had been sold for scrap. He was sometimes looking for ready money. I said nothing.

'Looking to me to keep him out of jail?' (Law forbids one to suffer the growth of thistles.) 'Time after time, it's the same story. It so happens, I haven't mine cut yet!'

'He'd be glad to lend you his jennet back, he says, to draw the cutter for you.'

'*That* brute! There'd be nothing for me to cut if it wasn't for what blows in off his dirty land.' With the flat of her fingers she pressed one eyeball, then the other, back into her head. She confessed, all at once almost plaintively: 'I don't care to have machinery leave my farm.'

'Very well,' I said haughtily, 'I'll tell him.'

She leaned back, rubbed her palms on her thighs. 'No, wait – this you may tell my lord. Tell him I'm not sure, but I'll think it over. There might be a favourable answer, there might not. If my lord would like to know which, let him come himself. – That's a sweet little dress of yours,' she went on, examining me inside it, 'but it's skimpy. He should do better than hide behind *those* skirts!'

'I don't know what you mean, Miss Banderry.'

'He'd know.'

'Today, my uncle *was* busy.'

'I'm sure he was. Busy day after day. In my life, I've known only one other man anything like so busy as your uncle. And shall I tell you who that was? My poor brother.'

After all these years, that terrace focuses dread. I mislike any terrace facing a river. I suppose I would rather look upon it itself (as I must, whenever I cross that bridge) than be reminded of it by harmless others. True, only one house in it was Miss Banderry's, but the rest belong to her by complicity. An indelible stain is on that monotony – the extinct pink frontage, the road leading to nothing but those six doors which the lime trees, flower as they may, exist for nothing but to shelter. The monotony of the weir and the hopping bird. Within that terrace I was in one room only, and only once.

My conversation with Miss Banderry did not end where I leave off recording it. But at that point memory is torn across, as might be an intolerable page. The other half is missing. For that reason my portrait of her would be incomplete if it *were* a portrait. She could be novelist's material, I daresay – indeed novels, particularly the French and Irish (for Ireland in some ways resembles France) are full of prototypes of her: oversized women insulated in little provincial towns. Literature, once one knows it, drains away some of the shockingness out of life. But when I met her I was unread, my susceptibilities were virgin. I refuse to fill in her outline retrospectively: I show you only what I saw at the time. Not what she was, but what she did to me.

Her amorous hostility to my uncle – or was it hostility making use of a farce? – unsheathed itself when she likened him to the brother she drove to death.

When I speak of dread I mean dread, not guilt. That afternoon, I went to Miss Banderry's for my uncle's sake, in his place. It could be said, my gathering of foreboding had to do with my relation with him – yet in that there was no guilt anywhere, I could swear! I swear we did each other no harm. I think he was held that summer, as I was, by the sense that this was a summer like no other and which could never again be. Soon I must grow up, he must grow old. Meanwhile we played house together on the margin of a passion which was impossible. My longing was for him, not for an embrace – as for him, he was glad of companionship, as I'd truly told her. He was a man tired by a lonely house till I joined him – a schoolgirl between schools. All thought well of his hospitality to me. Convention was our safeguard: could one have stronger?

I left No. 4 with ceremony. I was offered raspberry cordial. Nan bore in the tray with the thimble glasses – educated by going visiting with my uncle, I knew refusal would mark a breach. When the glasses were emptied, Nan conducted me out of the presence, to the hall door – she and I stopped aimlessly on the steps. Across the river throve the vast new mills, unabashed, and cars swished across the tree-hidden bridge. The niece showed a reluctance to go in again – I think the bird above must have been hers. She glanced behind her, then, conspiratorially at me. 'So now you'll be going to the hotel?'

'No. Why?'

'"Why?"' she jibed. 'Isn't he waiting for you? Anyway, that's where he is: in there. The car's outside.'

I said: 'But I'm taking the bus home.'

'Now, why ever?'

'I said I would take the bus. I came in that way.'

'You're mad. What, with his car in the square?'

All I could say was: 'When?'

'I slipped out just now,' said the niece, 'since you want to know. To a shop, only. While you were chatting with Auntie.' She laughed, perhaps at her life, and impatiently gave me a push away. 'Get on – wherever you're going to! Anybody would think you'd had bad news!'

Not till I was almost on the bridge did I hear No. 4's door shut.

I leaned on the balustrade, at the castle side. The river, coming towards me out of the distances of woods, washed the bastions and carried a paper boat – this, travelling at uncertain speed on the current, listed as it vanished under the bridge. I had not the heart to wonder how it would fare. Weeks ago, when first I came to my uncle's, here we had lingered, elbow to elbow, looking up-river through the green-hazed spring hush at the far off swan's nest, now deserted. Next I raised my eyes to the splendid battlements, kissed by the sky where they were broken.

From the bridge to the town rises a slow hill – shops and places of business come down to meet you, converting the road into a street. There are lamp posts, signboards, yard gates pasted with layers of bills, and you tread pavement. That day the approach to Moher, even the crimson valerian on stone walls, was filmed by imponderable white dust as though the flourbags had been shaken. To me, this was the pallor of suspense. An all but empty theatre was the square, which, when I entered it at a corner, paused between afternoon and evening. In the middle were parked cars, looking forgotten – my uncle's was nearest the hotel.

The hotel, glossy with green creeper, accounted for one end of the square. A cream porch, figuring the name in gold, framed the doorway – though I kept my back to that I expected at any moment to hear a shout as I searched for the independence of my bus. But where *that* should have waited, I found nothing. Nothing, at this bus end of the square, but a drip of grease on dust and a torn ticket. 'She's gone out, if that's what you're looking for,' said a bystander. So there it went, carrying passengers I was not among to the scenes of safety, and away from me every hope of solitude. Out of reach was the savingness of a house empty. Out of reach, the windows down to the ground open upon the purple beeches and lazy hay, the dear weather of those rooms in and out of which flew butterflies, my cushions on the floor, my blue striped tea mug. Out of reach, the whole of the lenient meaning of my uncle's house, which most filled it when he was not there . . . I did not want to be bothered with him, I think.

'She went out on time today, more's the pity.'

Down hung my hair in two weighted ropes as I turned away.

Moher square is oblong. Down its length, on the two sides, people started to come to the shop doors in order to look at me in amazement. They knew who I was and where he was: what should *I* be wanting to catch the bus for? They speculated. As though a sandal chafed me I bent down, spent some time loosening the strap. Then, as though I had never had any other thought, I started in the direction of the hotel.

At the same time, my uncle appeared in the porch. He tossed a cigarette away, put the hand in a pocket and stood there under the gold lettering. He was not a lord, only a landowner. Facing Moher, he was all carriage and colouring: he wore his life like he wore his coat – though, now he was finished with the hotel, a light hint of melancholy settled down on him. He was not looking for me until he saw me.

We met at his car. He asked: 'How was she, the old terror?'

'I don't know.'

'She didn't eat you?'

'No,' I said, shaking my head.

'Or send me another magazine?'

'No. Not this time.'

'Thank God.'

He opened the car door and touched my elbow, reminding me to get in.

Bibliographical Note

'First Stories' were first published as *Encounters*, Sidgwick & Jackson, 1923; 'Ann Lee's' appeared in the *Spectator*, July 1924, 'The Contessina' in the *Queen*, Nov. 1924, 'The Parrot' in the *London Mercury*, July 1925, and 'Making Arrangements' in *Eve*, Nov. 1925; 'The Visitor', 'Human Habitation', 'The Secession', 'The Storm', 'Charity', 'The Back Drawing-Room', and 'Recent Photographs' were first published in the volume *Ann Lee's*, Sidgwick & Jackson, 1926; 'Joining Charles', 'The Jungle', 'Shoes: An International Episode', 'The Dancing-Mistress', 'Aunt Tatty', 'Dead Mabelle', 'The Working Party', 'Foothold', 'The Cassowary', 'Telling' and 'Mrs Moysey' appeared in the volume *Joining Charles and other stories*, Cape, 1929; 'Her Table Spread' first appeared as 'A Conversation Piece' in *The Broadsheet Press*, May 1930; 'The Tommy Crans', 'The Good Girl', 'The Cat Jumps', 'The Last Night in the Old Home', 'The Disinherited', 'Maria', 'The Little Girl's Room', 'Firelight in the Flat', 'The Man of the Family', 'The Needlecase' and 'The Apple Tree' were first published in the volume *The Cat Jumps*, Cape, 1934; 'Reduced', 'No. 16' and 'Love' first appeared in the *Listener*, June 1935, Jan. 1939 and Oct. 1939 respectively; 'Tears, Idle Tears', 'A Walk in the Woods', 'A Love Story', 'Look at All Those Roses', 'Attractive Modern Homes', 'The Easter Egg Party', 'A Queer Heart', 'The Girl with the Stoop', 'Unwelcome Idea', 'Oh, Madam . . . ' and 'Summer Night' appeared in the volume *Look at All Those Roses*, Cape, 1941; 'In the Square' and 'Ivy Gripped the Steps' first appeared in *Horizon*, Sept. 1941 and Sept. 1945 respectively; 'Careless Talk', as 'Everything's Frightfully Interesting', in the *New Yorker*, 1941; 'Sunday Afternoon' in *Life and Letters of To-day*, July 1941; 'The Demon Lover', 'The Cheery Soul', 'Green Holly' and 'Gone Away' in the *Listener*, Nov. 1941, Dec. 1942, Dec. 1944 and Jan. 1946 respectively; 'The Inherited Clock' and 'Happy Autumn Fields' in the *Cornhill*, Jan. and Nov. 1944 respectively; 'Songs My Father Sang Me' and 'Pink May' in *English Story*;

'Mysterious Kôr' appeared in *The Penguin New Writing*, no. 20, 1944; 'I Hear You Say So' in *New Writing and Daylight*, Sept. 1945; 'The Dolt's Tale' (1944) in *A Day in the Dark*, Cape, 1965; 'Hand in Glove' in *Second Ghost Book* by Cynthia Asquith, Barrie & Rockliff, 1952; and 'A Day in the Dark' in *Botteghe Oscure*, 1956.